CW01551616

THE LAND WITHOUT DEATH

THE LAND WITHOUT DEATH

(The Amazonas Trilogy)

by

ALFRED DÖBLIN

Translated

by

C.D. Godwin

Galileo Publishers, Cambridge

First published by Querido in Amsterdam in 1937 - 1938.
This translation follows the text of the 5th edition
(Walter-Verlag 1988 / dtv 1991), which has been used in all
subsequent editions including Volume 14 of the current
Collected Works series published by S Fischer Verlag,
Frankfurt am Main in 2014.
Published under licence from the copyright holder.

The first few pages of Volume One were published on the Brooklyn Rail's
In Translation website in August 2018.

Published by Galileo Publishers
16 Woodlands Road
Great Shelford
Cambridge CB22 5LW
www.galileopublishing.co.uk

Distributed in the USA by SCB Distributors &
in Australia by Peribo Pty Ltd

First Edition

p 482-3 Sophocles: *Oedipus at Colonus*, lines 762ff. Tr. Robert Fagles.
p 708 Tr. G. Barrie 1885 in *Goethe's Works Vol 1 Poems*. PD.

ISBN: 9781912916825

Printed in the EU

Alfred Döblin is the most versatile writer of our time. –
J. L. Borges

CONTENTS

INTRODUCTION

by Chris Godwin

From the first page the reader is plunged directly into a world of The Other – vivid, real, three-dimensional, peopled by human beings who behave … not quite like us. What are they up to, the women creeping at dawn down to the river? Their menfolk on the warpath … sympathetic magic … ghosts in the night … Before any clue as to where or when this is happening, we are already deep in the cultural world of Amazonian indigenes.

In his earliest epic novels, written before and during the first Great War, Döblin revealed a rare capacity to conjure up other worlds in convincing colourful detail: 18th century China with no trace of chinoiserie, 17th century Europe with no trace of antiquarianism. In *The Land without Death* (a.k.a. *The Amazonas Trilogy*), his imagination fired first by colourful atlases of South America and its 'river-ocean' the Amazon, then by reports of explorers, anthropologists, historians[1], and not least by his own lifelong quest for answers to the riddle of existence, he weaves a vigorous, multi-layered, thought-provoking fictional tapestry from the mid-16th century Conquest to the late 18th century end of the Jesuit Republic on the Paraná River, where Paraguay, Argentina and Brazil meet. (Note that Döblin provides not a single date: his epic is no dry chronicle, but an imaginative excursion into "deep history" of cultures and mentalities.) His overarching concern – drawn into sharp focus when the narrative returns to Europe in Volume 3 – is to question the trajectory of 'Progress' from the Renaissance to the Nazis.

This, the first English translation of *The Land without Death*, comes unheralded by prior reviews or analyses in English that might help the reader navigate its rich complexity[2]. The Introduction must therefore shoulder several tasks:

1. Summarise the **themes** that form the warp of the novel, as the weft of events is woven in;
2. Outline the **shaping** of the narrative;
3. Sketch the biographical and political **background;**
4. Trace the novel's fractured **publication history;**

5. Examine its **critical reception**, noting misreadings and misconceptions that current scholarship is decisively correcting.

(1) Thematic summary[3]

NATURE AS AN AUTONOMOUS POWER

In 1948, looking back on his writing career, Döblin recalled the genesis of his South American epic:

> Maps of South America with its mighty Amazon river: what a joy. ... I immersed myself in its character, this marvellous river, river-ocean, age-old thing. Its banks, its animals and people belonged to it[4].

His depiction of exuberant Nature runs as a static counterpoint to the course of the plot – a hymnic celebration, joyfully unfolding Nature's boundless power. Immense fecundity is one constitutive element: decay and death are also ever-present. Amid numerous depictions of delight, tones of suffering emerge, e.g. a dawn chorus of monkeys changes at once to a lament. Images of suffering and death pile up: a spider sucks a beetle to an empty shell; dead crocodiles float downstream. Nature's essence lies in the interchange between becoming and decay. At the centre is the mighty Amazon, primal river, descending from the mountains as a 'monster with billowing mane' to claim the plains that are its estate. It is the source of proliferating life; but its floods bring dissolution and death.

HUMANS WITHIN AMAZONIAN NATURE

The minds and actions of Amazonian Indians are shaped by the overwhelming power of this life-giving, death-dealing Nature – it is by no means an Indian paradise. A connection among all beings – humans included – is of central significance. Numerous myths of human origin centre on the bond to earthly spirits of Nature. 'This murichi palm is the ancestor of mankind,' a chieftain explains to the conquistador Federmann in Part Two. 'Animals and humans are of one blood, else how could the tapir be our ancestor?' an Indian tells Bishop Las Casas in Part Three. Such bonds encompass every layer – rocks, plants, animals; they cross time (ancestors are reborn in new children) and space (women refrain from shivering so their absent menfolk won't show fear).

The Indians exercise caution in every enterprise, and seek constantly to propitiate the dominant power. Naming overcomes the anonymity of a perilous environment: in the first few pages we have a rock called 'grass', a village called Toadhole, a watercourse named Yari-yari. (Later on, Spanish horses present a dire threat: not knowing the beast's name, the Indians have no way to engage safely with it.) But the culture is no mere instrumental technique; the Indians are not antagonists of Nature; they dwell in and with her, in the many phenomena that have relevance to them, that they must try to interpret. Only from a European perspective, where Nature is an object to be known and acted upon, does the Indian stance seem superstitious.

TWO MYTHS: THE LAND WITHOUT DEATH, AND THE BLUE JAGUAR

The jungle drums that announce the arrival of Europeans bestow on death a new and extraordinary quality: 'Take care! Great danger... We shall all die... mountains shake. Wild beasts fall upon people... The Dog Star has moved closer to the Moon, and will eat it.' Now there is no polar balance between life and death: instead, death is inevitable. Hence the imperative need for a Land without Death, a paradise free of ageing, sickness and toil. This entails not just freedom from death's power, but the dissolution of the Indian life-world. Their one world splits into a Beyond of absolute life, and a Here-and-Now of absolute death. Repeated failures to find this land only bind the Indians more tightly to a hostile world of death.

The motif appears four times in the narrative: in the Conquest era of Volume 1 (Parts One and Three), and in the present day at the end of Volume 3. It is cited by the wretched soldier Puerto, who recognises that the European invaders suffer from the same hopeless yearning – in their case, for the gold they mistakenly believe will remedy their alienation and despair. And the Indians who confront Las Casas' arguments discover that

Heaven is not the fabled Land without Death – for one must die to get there.

Jaguars appear in the narrative with great frequency as (literal) wild animals; as (by analogy) the ravening invaders; as the ancestors of certain tribes; and as a quasi-magical beast (Walyarina). The Blue Jaguar, given prominence in the title of Volume 2 and two chapter headings in Volume 3, is the mythical symbol of total destruction, employed by Döblin as a warning that baleful tendencies in modern civilisation can turn the Indian myth of destruction into a reality.

The Women People

The story of the Women People that frames Volume 1 skilfully foreshadows the central motifs, and provides an interpretive framework for the whole trilogy.

The grim news transmitted by the drums has caused the menfolk of many tribes to abandon their villages and their women. The tribal community, in which the individual is subordinate, is dissolved; the women, who were not even told why the men had to leave, repudiate their inferior status, and in the process become conscious of individuality. This before any direct contact: the culture-destroying myth precedes the Europeans like a curse.

So the women's uprising is no autonomous development of feminism; it is infected by European masculine structures. The women no longer accept suffering as a given, but grow disgusted with men, and treat them as bargaining chips. The ensuing slaughter of men is inevitable.

At first the women seek an identity fundamentally different from that shaped by a (masculine) culture: they themselves will become one with Nature, even to the extent of taking an animal lover. They self-consciously identify with the great river: 'Amazonas! It was their river.' But the Amazon means both life and death; hence the women understand that since 'all living things come from the woman, then we must kill as well.' Descending into a murderous cruelty (thrown into relief by the tale of a girl and boy discovering their humanity), they forfeit the protection of nature-spirits.

The first direct contact with Europeans, depicted in a brief, offhand, ghostly manner, indicates the structure of European action. The three Spaniards with their fixed prejudices are incapable of understanding the Other. The Indians are cautiously helpful, but the strangers, who expect only violence and cannibalism, react with deadly violence and disappear as eerily as they arrived. Their lack of relationship to their surroundings reveals a nihilism that is elaborated in Part Two.

The tale told by the refugee Inca prince Cuzumarra at first presents the Inca realm as the innocent victim of sheer murderous plunder. Penetrating enquiry by the women uncovers a new aspect of the novel's central theme: the Incas claim to have evolved a Land without Death, where, unlike the jungle Indians, Nature was subdued to their service. But did they subdue death as well? The Inca realm is revealed as a totalitarian welfare state, its people reduced to 'monkeys and parrots', the anonymous dominion of death is replaced by totalitarian overlords. The realm was rotten even before the Europeans arrived.

The lesser-known realm of Cundinamarca, the focus of Part Two, has also freed itself of Nature's dominion. The Muisca people are prosperous, their culture highly developed, with no sign of totalitarianism. But even they can offer no resistance to European objectification. Why?

The Muisca built their culture on consciousness of the overwhelming power of death. Their ruler's pilgrimage 'through the web' is a balancing act over the menacing abyss of death: the Zipa's hopeless self-sacrifice shows that Muisca culture, like the Inca, was simply not equipped to save itself from destruction.

THE MODERN WORLD

Scattered through the first two volumes are snippets and extended scenes from a rapidly changing Europe. Before returning to the South American jungle in Part Ten, Volume 3 homes in on the Europe of the 1920s and 30s, where four centuries of scientific and technological progress have brought not only wonders, but wars and despair too. As the glory of the Middle Ages faded, a blooming culture grew rotten. The reciprocal vassal-lord relationship dissolved; now vassals suffer from the anonymous whims of bureaucracies and bankers. The urbanised individual is adrift from both nature and society; millions of disorderly colliding wills lead to unrest and war. Religion, once the centre of the mediaeval world, gains a life of its own outside any social context in a secularising world. The only consolation for the isolated individual is the promised Afterlife. Instrumental action provides a perverted sense of meaning, in public life and in the private life of the emotions: Weber's 'soulless professional, heartless hedonist'.

(2) Shaping the narrative

Döblin's epic fictions are symphonic constructions[5]. The content (descriptions, events, conversations) is modulated by form (tempo, tone, mood, recapitulation) through the medium of a language of extraordinary deftness and precision. Meaning lies not – as a cursory or shallow reading might suggest – in a motley collection of individual scenes, but in the interplay of motifs and signifiers across different – sometimes widely separated – locations in the text.

Volume 1: On the Amazon

The three 'movements' of Volume 1 are tautly structured; the momentum never slackens. Cinematic shifts take us from wide-angle scenes to close-ups, from everyday life to epic action to vast landscapes. Realism and 'magical realism' are blended.

PART ONE

Two interlocking strands depict the rise and fall of the Women People, and the fate of refugees from the shattered Inca realm. South American landscapes are hymned. Mythical spirits, personified, insert themselves. The first depiction of Europeans – desperados in an unfamiliar climate and landscape – presages what will come in Part Two. Why do they suffer so horribly? 'The Whites wore their rags and felt powerful.' They pray: 'Armed with my virtue I find rest in battle ...' Why inflict such calamities on the native cultures? To note that 'they grow drunk and unruly, and look for gold' is no explanation. At the very end we see Orellana, the first European to travel to the mouths of the Amazon: 'All trace of [him] was lost somewhere along the river … forests and plains closed behind the Whites … The mighty river … called out to the ocean: you strangers were never here!'

Part Two

The unflattering view of European landscapes and people that opens Part Two digs deeper into the 'why' motif: 'Here people … grew strong, savage, immoderate. They were born of the struggle against death. They roamed around in great armies. They broke out of their twilight lands.' A great ruler retires exhausted from the struggle against unmanageable change: 'The people were in constant ferment, concerning nations and imaginary things in the sky.' The king had to raise armies; for this he needed money; the Welsers (financiers from Augsburg) advanced loans, and were given the right to enrich themselves in the New World (saving one-fifth for the king) by conquest, pillage and slavery.

The narrative follows four Welser-financed mercenary bands, three of which converge on the highland capital of Cundanimarca (today's Bogotá): a name unknown to most readers, who will therefore bring fewer preconceptions gleaned from familiar accounts of Mexico and Peru.

Cruel Alfinger is so alienated from his humanity that he can sear poisoned flesh from his own leg, and wonder if his head might be transplanted onto a horse. He dies an accidental death; his lieutenants plot to steal the king's fifth.

With Quesada's band we come again to the 'why?' 'They did not know how to explain it. They said: we must conquer a new empire for the Spanish crown, we must find gold, we must spread the word of our ghostly god.' But they were driven to 'find oblivion and lose themselves'. And who was Quesada? 'A White man, church and king his backbone, fame and glory his heart and blood. He was no better or worse than anyone else. What it was that drove him, he knew as little as the others.' We follow the enthralling narrative of the expedition until it reaches 'a land of dreams … a land of gold … truly a heavenly land. Mine, all mine!' They bellow out the rancour they feel for the Spain they left behind: 'Hey dear Mother! … Hey dear Father! … Hey dear Sister … Hey dear Bride …!' Quesada tries to hold them back: 'The Crown appointed me governor of a province, not a wasteland.' But intent on slaughter and rape, his men ravage the place.

Urbane Belalcazar has already helped to conquer Peru; his arrival threatens to dilute the spoils of Quesada's band. Armed standoff ensues. Meanwhile traumatised natives wonder how to survive when all has been polluted by the strangers, and the Zipa, their ruler, is bewildered and incapable.

The band of Nicolaus Federmann from Ulm has made its way across the savannah, where grass 'closes over the head of a man on horseback'. They are enchanted by tales of a South Sea. Gradually, to the displeasure of its priests, the band begins to go native: 'no more thought of the King of Spain and home and being a wealthy man … On, on, on to the South Sea.' Now they view landscape, vegetation and creatures through native eyes. But when the band turns to the mountains 'the trek … degenerates to a savage hunt.' Hearing of Cundanimarca they give up on 'natives, turtles, jaguars, lakes … they scrambled for gold … gold and pillage! Women and war!'

The three commanders agree to head back to Spain to report on their achievements (but first the invading rabble inflicts total devastation on the town). Before they part, they envisage longer term conquest and colonial settlement, and formally found the town of Santa Fé (today's Bogotá): 'We need terrain such as this. Maybe they'll even send food over to Spain sometimes.'

On it goes, as the invaders 'fulfill their frothing, puling destiny': a ghastly Dürer-like procession of Belligerence, Misanthropy, Avarice. All three commanders eventually meet ignominious deaths.

Meanwhile the bewildered Zipa makes a forlorn pilgrimage to a sacred lake; but descent to the Underworld brings no hopeful auguries. The Zipa sacrifices himself.

Part Two ends back in the Amazonian jungle, where another group of Inca exiles looks for aid from the god Viracocha, who has failed their land. 'Far to the east … the remnants of the destroyed empires lodged ... The ground, the fiery sky, the gushing waters were stronger than anything.'

PART THREE

The figure of Father Las Casas, whose complaints of atrocities for decades annoyed the Spanish Court and Church, provides the focus for a provocative querying of religion in Europe and the Americas. The repellent soldier del Puerto, who kills a dozen heathen every day to give thanks to God for deliverance in battle, explains conquistador motives: 'Not to save souls, certainly ... Over there they have no use for us. Whoever doesn't go for a monk is lost ... The Crown can't provide all the offices we need, and I am no peasant.' The natives are sub-human Others: 'Just because someone guzzles and makes babies doesn't make him human ... We should exterminate the heathen.'

Theological debates between Las Casas and fugitive baptised Indians again question the 'why' of the Conquest: spreading the Word of God cannot be a motive, for the invaders' actions run squarely counter to the Bible. The Indian flock try to help their shepherd, who dreams ecstatically of sailing back to bring the true Gospel to godless Spain. Sensing he has lost the argument, Las Casas blames Satan, 'the satanic forest ... Which is stronger, Christ or the forest?' – a motif reprised at the beginning of Volume 2.

The (fictional) death of Las Casas – in a paragraph amended by Döblin between the first and second editions – occurs during a tussle with the river spirit Sukuruja. The original wording suggested that Las Casas surrendered to the river spirit. Having converted to Catholicism in the meantime, Döblin has the priest cling to his crucifix.

Volume 2: The Blue Jaguar

The narrative of the longer and more expansive Volume 2 covers almost two and a half centuries, from the founding of the Jesuit Order to its suppression (roughly 1540–1767). The location shifts southward to Sao Paolo, the Paraná, and the River Plate; the theme is the rise and destruction of the Jesuit Republic and its protected Indian population. Meanwhile momentous changes in Europe also come to the fore.

Parts Four to Six track the first Jesuits as they encounter the raw slaver culture in Brazil, and form their plan to set up protective 'reductions'. The first attempt ends with destruction at the hands of an army from Sao Paolo.

In Parts Seven and Eight, the Jesuit Republic on the Paraná develops a distinctive culture and an adapted form of Christianity, against a backdrop of constant hostility from colonial settlers and royal functionaries. Eventually high politics in Spain and Portugal, and growing hostility to Jesuit influence from the Church and monarchies, dissolves the experiment and almost destroys the Order.

Part Four

Sailing for the New World, the young priest Mariana wonders if a European religion can thrive in the heat of a different land. His superior Emanuel rebuffs the thought: the Church is universal. On landing they at once encounter comically passive-aggressive defiance from the founders of the settlement that will become Sao Paolo, and struggle to understand the interplay between colonisers and natives. Their discovery of a ghastly concentration camp arouses horror in the younger priests, but Emanuel, stern commissar, forbids them to prejudice the mission by making trouble, and even sends some to accompany a slaving expedition. Finally the Jesuits realise they are in mortal danger if they remain.

Part Five

As the Jesuits trek into the wilderness, natives cautiously track them; some join the train. Mariana becomes ever more attached to Indian ways, and ends as an apparent sacrifice to Sukuruja, the river-spirit. Slavers from Sao Paolo form fake Jesuit trains to trap more victims. We learn the backgrounds of the men who have become Jesuits.

PART SIX

Dour King Philipp of Spain (the current 'I the King') sees the Jesuits as 'a ray of hope' amid all the discouraging reports from his colonial officials; he relishes their plan to settle on the Paraná. Two itinerant Jesuits arrive at the camp, bearing an order from the provincial governor permitting the Jesuits to create protective settlements for Indians. The governor's mismanagement provokes a native rebellion; refugees flock to the Jesuits, a town arises, and the idea is formed of a 'Christian republic'. But they are still too close to Sao Paolo. When a swashbuckler takes power there and sends out an invasion force, the Jesuits and their Indian protégés suffer devastating slaughter.

PART SEVEN

In a burlesque narrative, the victorious swashbuckler in Sao Paolo is defeated by rivals from Sacramento, a Spanish colony on the River Plate. The surviving Jesuits and their flock float down the Paraná; Indians select a site, and new reductions arise – this time not in joy, but in grim determination. The Indians develop a new mode of life and religion, supervised by just two priests per reduction. A delegation heads for Rome, where neither Jesuit leaders nor the Pope know anything of events on the Paraná. But the Pope is flattered to be asked his advice on defence, and writes to nuncios and bishops in support of the Jesuit enterprise. Montoya, the new Superior, sees the enterprise as a crucial bulwark against rotten Europe. When the Spanish king acknowledges the Indians as 'most loyal vassals', Montoya is spurred to create armed defences; and obtains royal consent for this after marauders from Sao Paolo seize royal gold mines in Peru.

The reductions blossom, to the annoyance of other colonists. Bishop Felix appears – humanist with his books and Greek statues and mistress and daughter – on a 'state visit' to the reductions with a royal Visitor: a marvellously evocative chapter. Back in Asuncion, Whites angered by royal interference in matters of forced labour offer fake evidence of Indian love for their servitude. Eventually Felix sails back to Rome; but his household falls victim to riots in Asuncion, leaving him bereft. In Rome there is suspicion of Jesuit power.

Part Eight

Heightened prose depicting the accelerating changes in Enlightenment Europe presages the change of focus in Volume 3. The reductions have grown prosperous, with sumptuous churches, productive farms – and well-drilled militias. Yet the Jesuits patronise their flocks as childlike innocents. Broad-brush prose depicts the transformation of South American landscapes into commercial plantations and farms. 'I the King' is faced with Portuguese rivalry in trade; the old aristocracy loses ground to parvenu merchants. The great kings of previous centuries are succeeded by nincompoops. The Portuguese and Spanish courts plot to divide up Jesuit territory. War erupts; the reductions are doomed. A reforming Spanish king cracks down on the bloated clergy – and sets eyes on the Jesuits next. All Jesuits on the Paraná are rounded up for deportation to Europe. In Portugal, ruthless Marquis Pombal eliminates all Jesuit influence.

Volume 3: The New Jungle

The narrative comes full circle, ending in Part Ten back in the jungles of South America in the present day (i.e. the 1930s). But it begins (after a brief Preamble) with the Polish Faust-figure Twardowski summoning from their graves the Enlightenment luminaries Copernicus, Galileo, and Giordano Bruno, to account for the ills attendant on the scientific and technical revolutions they helped to unleash. Between the powerful beginning and the powerful (and moving) end, Döblin depicts the alienation and despair of some exemplary mid-European characters, in whom exploitation and manipulation have replaced love and humanity.

Part Nine

When Bruno fails to recant his views, Twardowski presents three examples to show the evil side of modernity: the pretty but alienated Extra, hoping to attract a sugar-daddy but ending with a baby and a hopeless marriage; Jagna, the heartless Don Juan with his cold delight in seduction; and the two young Germans with their thoroughly instrumentalist view of human action. (One of them settles in nicely with the new German regime; the other hopes to survive by keeping mum.) The snake-like seductress Theresa, as heartless as Jagna, at last can't bear to live. Bruno agrees that these scenes are not nice; but asks for more time to allow humanity to adapt to their post-Renaissance mental world.

Part Ten

Jagna, having fled in self-disgust from his nihilistic hedonism, is found in Paris about to head for South America, where a friend, a murderer, has been condemned to Devil's Island. His friend escapes; and Jagna leads a small group of fugitives upriver into the jungle. Their conversations with native Indians develop into a stark reckoning between European and 'primitive' modes of life, in which Europe cannot prevail.

With all the fugitives dead, the last chapters revert to the Amazon, where spirits summon the souls of all the fallen since the time of the Conquest. Sukuruja appears. New bands of pilgrims seek the Land without Death.

(3) Biographical and political background

Döblin was in his third year of exile when he began to formulate ideas for his new novel. He had been deprived of his medical practice, most of his target audience, his German citizenship, and his daily immersion in the language of Berlin. Yet since fleeing Nazi Germany in February 1933 he had already written one large epic and one realistic novel[6], as well as numerous contributions to journals, and to debates about possible futures for the Jews.

The Land without Death is one of several historical novels produced by German émigrés in the 1930s. Indignant voices asked why Germany's intellectuals could not focus on the current crisis: were they escapists? Döblin vigorously defended the historical novel as an apt medium for exploring a "deep history" of personal and social life and relationships, of a kind not found in the "shallow history" of academic works and the daily press. He insisted that "the historical novel is firstly a novel, and secondly no history[7]". In fact, this novel holds a mirror to the destructive forces (social, economic, political, psychological) that characterise Europe's rise to global dominance, culminating, at the time of writing, in the Nazi menace. Döblin's stance was clear: "The nature of this celebrated civilisation has long been obvious: its cold imperialism, churches squeezed to the sidelines, warmongering nations... Countless people bewail the emptiness of their existence[8]."

(4) Publication history

Döblin began composing the seventh of his great epic fictions[9] in the Paris Bibliothèque nationale in 1935, and completed it by September 1937. The **first edition** from the émigré publishing house Querido in Amsterdam comprised two books in non-uniform bindings appearing just over a year apart, *Journey to the Land without Death. A novel* in April 1937; and *The Blue Jaguar. A novel* in May 1938.[10] The latter included the two Parts later separated as a third volume, and belatedly identified both titles as components of a single work under the covering title *The Land without Death.*

Banned already in the Reich, the novel lost other potential readers with the Austrian Anschluss in March 1938, leaving only German-Swiss and émigré Germans as potential readers. The few reviews were generally positive, but shallow.

When Döblin returned to Germany in late 1945, attached to the French Occupation Authority as a cultural officer, he explored opportunities to publish his several works written in exile, as well as new material. The **second edition** comprised three titles from the Keppler-Verlag in non-uniform bindings appearing over a nine-month period: *The Land without Death* in October 1947; *The Blue Jaguar* a month later; and *The New Jungle* in July 1948. It is not known who decided to separate the final two Parts of *The Blue Jaguar* into a separate title; possibly paper shortages made it necessary. This edition also attracted few reviews, mostly of single volumes rather than the entire work.

Neither of the first two editions included introductory material. Neither achieved significant sales.

Some years after Döblin's death, the Swiss publisher Walter-Verlag launched a Selected Works series, edited by Swiss literature professor Walter Muschg in association with Döblin's surviving sons (who had vetoed Döblin's close friend and confidant, the

French Germanist scholar Robert Minder, for the task.[11]) The **third edition** of 1963 was a single book titled *Amazonas*; it included an editorial Afterword. Muschg, however, decided to omit the third volume (*The New Jungle*) entirely as "artistically not up to standard", and made other questionable interventions in the text. He claimed Döblin as the source for his choice of overall title, although evidence has not been forthcoming. His editorial overreach stimulated controversy, which both perpetuated and challenged the prevailing misjudgements.

The **fourth edition** in 1973 from the East German firm Rütten & Loening was a single-volume reissue of the second edition, now titled *Amazonas: a Trilogy of Novels* and for the first time provided a scholarly introduction.

In 1988, at last, a reliable **fifth edition** appeared based on careful archival work on Döblin's manuscripts, an investigation of his sources, and a judicious appraisal of the work. It was published by the Walter-Verlag, who thereby repudiated their third edition. The editor, Werner Stauffacher, retained the overall title *Amazonas. Trilogy of novels* which he thought had become generally accepted since the third edition, even while noting that much of the narrative is located outside the Amazon region: "So the theme … is not simply 'South America' but at least just as much 'Europe', the Europe of the great expansion between the 16th and 20th centuries."[12]

In 1991 the Büchergilde Gutenberg, in its series of works by exiled writers, published the **sixth edition** which followed the Stauffacher text but reverted to the two-volume format (with the two final Parts re-incorporated into *The Blue Jaguar*), and restored the overall title *The Land without Death*. It included a valuable book-length study of Döblin's use of sources, as well as his essay 'Prometheus and the Primitive'[13] written at the same time as *The Blue Jaguar*.

Subsequent editions have followed the fifth edition text, with new Afterwords capturing some of the scholarship that has proliferated in recent decades.

(5) Misreadings and faulty interpretations

Some examples of faulty judgements can help illuminate the strengths of the novel.[14]

Döblin's depiction of South American Indians was misread[15] as an idealised image of childlike innocence in harmony with Nature: a view hard to reconcile with his far from dewy-eyed narrative of the Women People and the totalitarian Inca state.

One critic, claiming anachronisms, inaccuracies, and an absence of dates, was apparently unaware of Döblin's stance in the debate about historical novels outlined above. The same critic castigated Döblin's "unsound, trivial, sloppy, tangled, scandalising" prose. In fact, Döblin's vivid narrative is presented in a language of exemplary precision, clarity and nuanced impact. The very first sentence provides a case in point. It depicts the Amazonian village woman waking *wie* (like; in the same way as) a bird that is calling in the jungle, instead of the expected *als* (as, at the same time as). The act of waking and the bird's call may well be linked by more than simultaneity: many later passages show Indians constantly alert to uncertain signals from the fecund death-dealing Nature that surrounds them.

Döblin was said to be "running at an open door"[16] in depicting evil Whites and innocent Natives. Yet the author's aim is not to cast blame, but rather to pin down the fundamental causes of European rapacity, greed and belligerence, as well as the inability of Native cultures to mount effective resistance. Condemning the perpetrators is not enough: what has made them so? What drives them? Döblin identifies humanity's ambiguous position both in and above Nature; the problem of individuation vs. embedding in a social order; and weighty missteps of Western culture all the way from Genesis ("dominion over all the earth") to the Promethean rationality that launched the modern world and cast humanity adrift from its favoured place in Creation.

W. G. Sebald's 1973 doctoral dissertation[17] was founded on a dreadful misconception of Döblin's attitude to violence. Far from glorying in the many depictions of horrors in his fiction, ever since his experiences in the Great War Döblin had used his writer's art to work through an extended process of grieving about the human lust for destruction prevalent in the history of European civilisation even up to our own day.

The verdict of a Germanist scholar may help to counterbalance these shallow misreadings:

Döblin's epic oeuvre stems from an extraordinary imaginative power of the highest precision and densest plenitude, of unassailable certainty... That [his epic writing] seems so real to us is due to the abundance of reality in the vision, the surging, inexhaustibly inventive wealth of detail and the vivid force of its representation in language. Every aspect of this reality, the large and the small, the delightful and the terrible, are grasped with equal intensity. Everything is placed in the same very hard light that makes the façade transparent, penetrates through the surface and illuminates every nook and cranny where Romanticism likes to lurk. The intensity of imagination is transformed into the dense busy rhythms of the language ...[18]

Other Germanist scholars have produced an ever-growing body of analyses and critiques since the 1980s, which reveal this Trilogy to be an accomplished, multi-layered work in which virtually every sentence and paragraph contributes to a significant whole, composed and structured by a consciousness intent on confronting issues of existential concern to modern Europeans.[19] Describing the creative process that worked in him, Döblin spoke of a "surging psychic process"[20] a "soul-condition of peculiar brightness ... of an abnormal spiritual clarity in which all riddles are solved" and "letting oneself go, playing, for example having the courage to undergo inward bewitching."[21] A later passage explores the process more fully:

I see myself placed in front of a picture, shoved into landscapes and situations that emerged in me – I can't say I thought them up or invented them. I could neither summon these phantasies nor protect myself from them.
... I was always surrounded by a great company: by words, by language. Words ... served for constructing, playing, shaping. They wore a kind of spirit-clothing.
... I never started until the ideas had reached a certain

ripeness, and that occurred when they began to clothe themselves in language. Once I had this image, I dared to set out with it, in my pilot boat, out of the harbour, and soon I spotted a ship, a huge ocean steamer, and I stepped aboard and off I went. I was in my element, I voyaged, made discoveries, and only months later came home from such a great journey, sated, and could tread dry land again. My voyages behind the closed door took me to China, India, Greenland, to other ages, and out beyond Time. What a life.[22]

*

In the eight years between embarking on this translation and submitting the faired manuscript for publication, I have benefited greatly from the advice and support of Professor David Midgley of St John's College, Cambridge. In 2017 David invited me to give readings at a symposium he organised on 'Legacies of Conquest', where some of the assembled Latin American scholars became aware of *The Land without Death* for the first time.

C. D. Godwin
Stroud, UK
June 2022

NOTES:

1. The main sources in French and German available to Döblin in the Bibliothèque nationale in Paris were:

Koch-Grünberg, Theodor: *Zwei Jahre unter den Indianern Nord-westbrasiliens 1903/1905*. [*Two years among the Indians of NW Brazil*] 2 vols, Berlin 1909; and *Indianermärchen aus Südamerika* [*South American Indian Fables*], Jena 1927.

Krause, Fritz: *In den Wildnissen Brasiliens. Bericht und Ergebnisse der Leipziger Araguaya-Expedition 1908* [*In the Brazilian Wilderness. Report and findings of the 1908 Leipzig Araguaya expedition*]. Leipzig 1911.

Métraux, Alfred: *La religion des Tupinamba et ses rapports avec celles des autres tribus Tupi-Guarani* [*The religion of the Tupinamba and its relation to those of the other Tupi-Guarani tribes*]. Paris 1928.

de Charlevoix, R P P, SJ: *Histoire du Paraguay* [*History of Paraguay*]. 3 vols, Paris 1756.

von Murr, Christoph Gottlieb: *Geschichte der Jesuiten in Portugal unter der Staatsverwaltung des Marquis von Pombal* [*History of the Jesuits in Portugal under the regime of the Marquis of Pombal*]. Nuremberg 1788.

Anon. *Histoire de Nicolas 1er Roi du Paraguai et Empereur des Mamelus. [History of Nicolas I King of Paraguay and Emperor of the Mamelus]*. Sao Paolo 1756.

2. Despite a growing stream of research and commentary in German, almost nothing has been published on this novel in English. The one easily accessible essay is Helmut Pfanner's chapter in the *Companion to the Works of Alfred Döblin,* Dollinger, Koepke & Tewarson (eds), Camden House 2003. Even the English Wikipedia page on Döblin, which has greatly expanded in recent years, merely mentions the title in one brief sentence.

3. This section draws heavily on a valuable monograph by Hubert Brüggen: *Land ohne Tod: Eine Untersuchung zur inneren Struktur der 'Amazonas-Trilogie' Alfred Döblins* (Land without death: an investigation of the inner structure of the trilogy). Peter Lang 1987.

4. 'Epilogue', translated in *German Masquerade: writings on politics, life and literature in chaotic times*, p.258, at https://beyond-alexanderplatz. com/german-masquerade .

5. Döblin outlined this in a public lecture in 1928: 'The Construction

of the Epic Work', translated in *German Masquerade*, p. 206 (see note 4 above).

6. *The Babylonian Exile* (1934), tr. C D Godwin at https://beyond-alexanderplatz.com ; *Men without Mercy* (1935), tr. T & P Blewitt, Gollancz 1937.

7. 'The historical novel and us' (1936), translated in *German Masquerade*, p. 224 (see note 4 above).

8. *Flucht und Sammlung des Judenvolkes* (Flight and Gathering of the Jewish people), November 1935.

9. Döblin's nine great epic fictions are:

* *The Three Leaps of Wang Lun* (written 1912, pub. 1916, in English 2015 at ISBN 9789629965648);

* *Wallenstein* (written 1917-19, pub. 1920; in English 2021 at https://beyond-alexanderplatz.com);

* *Mountains Oceans Giants* (1924; in English 2021 at ISBN 9781912916245);

* *Manas* (1927; in English 2021 at ISBN 9781912916214):

* *Berlin Alexanderplatz* (1929; in English 2018 at ISBN 9780141191614);

* *The Babylonian Exile* (1934; in English 2021 at https://beyond-alexanderplatz.com);

* *Amazonas/Land without Death* (1937-38);

* *November 1918* (1938-1949; in English, incomplete, at ISBN 0880640081 and 0880640111; the missing Vol. 1 and deleted passages can be found at https://beyond-alexanderplatz.com);

* *Tales of a Long Night* (written 1944-46, first pub. 1956 in E. Germany. In English at ISBN 0880640170).

10. *Fahrt ins Land ohne Tod. Roman*; and *Der blaue Tiger. Roman.*

11. The sons probably resented Minder's detailed knowledge of Döblin's decades-long affair with his muse/lover Yolla Niclas. See https://beyond-alexanderplatz.com/yolla-and-alfred-part-2 .

12. Stauffacher: 'Afterword', p.221.

13. In English at https://intranslation.brooklynrail.org/german/prometheus-and-the-primitive .

14. The reviews cited are included in Schuster & Bode (eds): *Alfred Döblin im Spiegel der zeitgenössischen Kritik* (AD as reflected in contemporary criticism), Bern/Munich 1973.

15. Ferdinand Lion (1937), reprinted in Schuster/Bode p. 345.

16. Kurt Kersten (1938), reprinted in Schuster/Bode p. 349. Notably, in 1920 Döblin had criticised Gerhart Hauptmann's play *The White*

Saviour by praising (with apparent perversity) the 'reality' of the Spaniards against 'the dream' of Montezuma, castigating the impotence of idealistic dreams in the face of brute reality. He had also, around the same time, denounced the 'incapacity' of leaders of the 1919 working class rebellion in Berlin, violently suppressed by the nominally Republican government at the cost of many lives, including that of Döblin's own sister.

17. W G Sebald: *The Revival of Myth: a study of Alfred Döblin's novels.* University of East Anglia, 1973. (Published in German as *Der Mythus der Zerstörung* (The Myth of Destruction), Stuttgart 1980.

18. Professor W. Rasch: 'Döblin's *Wallenstein* and History', in a 1948 Festschrift for Döblin's 70th birthday. His verdict on the earlier novel can apply equally well to *The Land without Death*.

19. Significant works include:

> H. Kiesel: *Literarsiche Trauerarbeit* (Grieving through Literature), 1986;

> H. Brüggen: see Note iii above;

> W. Stauffacher: *Afterword* to the 1988 edition;

> F. Pohle: *Döblins Kolumbusfahrt in der Pariser Nationalbibliothek: Versuch einer Annäherung* (AD's Columbus voyage in the Parisian library: a tentative approach), annexed to the 1991 edition;

> V. Hildenbrandt: *Europa in Alfred Döblins* Amazonas-*Trilogie: Diagnose eines kranken Kontinents.* (Europe in the *Amazonas* Trilogy: diagnosis of a sick continent), 2011.

20. 'The epicist, his material and the critics' (1921).

21. 'Construction of the Epic Work' (1929).

22. *Schicksalsreise* (Destiny's Journey) (1948), p.113.

VOLUME 1

JOURNEY TO THE LAND WITHOUT DEATH

CONTENTS
Volume 1
Journey to the Land without Death

Part One

ON THE AMAZON

~

Departure of the Women People

THE OLD WOMAN woke up to the udu's calling in the forest: *tru tru, udu udu*. She went from hut to hut. Women came out, thirty women and grown girls. The old woman stayed by the clan house. They went down from the mound into the forest in single file, one behind the other, leaving plenty of space between them. The forest began to lighten, an early mist was rising. From its tree the udu kept calling: *tru tru, udu udu*. The path made a bend, a rock was called grass. Then they came to the little watercourse. They had eaten nothing, drunk nothing, were unpainted, unadorned. They wore only hipstring and loincloth. It was damp underfoot, dew lay. But on their shoulders they wore no matting, so as not to burden their menfolk away on the warpath. They tried not to shiver, so that their men would not tremble. Vegetation along the trickling water separated them, nobody spoke. They had walked slowly, so as not to tire their men. They stood in dark water among reeds.

Why did they not speak, why did they not call, why creep so furtively from the village? Each held in her hand a strip of silvery bast. None looked at the others, they crouched low in the reeds. And each whispered into her little strip of bast, some closed their eyes, some smiled, each spoke a name, the name of a man she'd had something with apart from husband or favourite. She tied a knot around her infidelity, locked it up inside. She crumpled the bast in her hand, parted the reeds in front of her. Knots flew from thirty hands into the little river. Now it was done, they had made their men easier. Silently they walked back through the reeds, around the rock, one behind the other.

The village was called Toadhole. As the sun rose higher, women roasted manioc outside the huts and the clan house, others toiled in the gardens, some climbed down to the river with nets. When the old woman at the great fireplace in front of the maloca, the clan house, looked around for a young woman who had been grating meal into a pot with water, she was gone, and the children said she'd run into the house. The old woman found her behind the house, where the forest began. She vomited there and ran away. The old woman caught her: "Why are you hiding?" Because the young woman was sick, a medicine man who had stayed behind in the village was summoned. She was taken to a little hut, somewhat secluded. They all talked about the sick woman: she was newly married. Next day she was hot. The sorcerer took his rattle and strutted around her. In the village they talked about the sick woman, dared not say what they thought. When another woman and a child fell ill before evening, there was great fear. Next morning the medicine man fetched an even older sorcerer from the nearest village. They told everyone to rub ochre on their bodies for protection, then they began to investigate who in the village had done something bad. They pointed to two old women, but no one in the village believed it. Still none dared say what they feared.

During the third night, loud wailing arose. Shrieks came from the clan house, they came running from the huts with blazing torches. A woman in the clan house had dreamed her man had returned, a spear was in his chest, it wasn't in deep, he couldn't pull it out, he asked for a drink. As the woman whimpered, another woke up in her hammock. They heard knocking on the wall. Now they knew their men lay out there unburied, and had come to fetch their things. They had been gone five time ten suns. Wailing spread through the village. Parrots flew up from roofs and squawked. In the grey dawn a boat with four women came from nearby, at once turned back in fear; their men too were away at war, five times ten suns, and had sent no sign. They drummed the news into the surrounding country.

≈≈≈

The river by the village was called Yari-yari. Its waters emptied into the Rio Negro, which carried them past hills, sandy plains, forests to the mighty Amazon. Mists swathed hill, forest and plain.

Women squatted beneath mat awnings. The seeds of the urucu bush were red and yellow, they grated them with palm oil, colour dissolved from the seeds, they scraped it from their hands into the bowl. They fetched cooking pots from the fireplace, scraped soot into the bowl. All the while they talked. A woman suckled her child, an older woman spurted milk from her breast into the mouth of a protesting baby monkey, another oiled her baby's hair. The women said: "Why don't the men come back. We've done nothing to drive them away. We must dance to bring them back." The nursing mother let tears trickle down her little face. They slapped her: "Why are you crying? Didn't we wail enough in the night? We'll upset the men." So the woman laughed.

Beside the water lay a boat that the men had left half finished. It rested on two wooden runners. They fetched palm leaves, in the afternoon burnt it away from the inside, fetched palm leaves, burnt it from the outside. They did this so their men could travel. In the evening a thunderstorm broke. The old women kept the manioc mash until everyone was back from fishing, grilled the fish. Then there was loud laughter, children stayed by the fire in front of the clan house, young women and grown girls disappeared into the huts. They painted themselves a beautiful black with soot and red with urucu, they oiled their hair, the almond eyes of the young ones glinted with pleasure, they hung necklaces of black seeds around their necks, tied threads of red cotton on arm and calf. Then one of them leapt from her hut, she was the first, she swung the dance-rattle and whooped, she wore a net shawl over her shoulders, a little red parrot sat on her head. The others ran out, they looked beautiful and happy. They formed a line one behind the other, arms crossed at the breast, swayed left, swayed right, they sang a dancing song, filed past the clan house. The children and old women stood up.

Two lines in the dirt – it was a river, the young women leapt along the bank, they wanted to cross, they were the men. One rowed on the river, his back covered in palm leaves – the River

Spirit. They bowed down to him, he let them cross. They greeted the old women and the others. Then they faced each other, two by two, heads lowered, hands covering their eyes, man and wife, and wept greetings.

The dance ended, darkness fell. They laughed and ate, radiant in the firelight.

≈≈≈

Gallinules gargled in the forest, cicadas chirped, monkey-cries fell silent, toads set up their croaking. It was night, starlight hung over forest, plain, rivers.

In the dark an arrow flew close to the fire. It planted itself quivering in the dirt. Nothing moved in the village. Two longboats lay in the reeds, people crept crouching up the slope, they croaked like toads, waited for daybreak. Now the stars went out one by one. They ran, uttered warcries like the raging of howler monkeys. As women and children screamed and tried to flee, the raiders set fire to the clan house. By the light of the flames they separated old women from the younger and the children. They threw spears after the old women. The young women and children were herded together.

The village burned, drums sounded from the next village, the fire had been seen. The raiders, Maku, painted black with red stripes from ear to ear, armed with clubs, spears, bows and arrows, beat their prizes, drove them down to the boats. Into the boats climbed all the young women and girls, still in yesterday's festive markings. The boat they had burned out for their men came with them. Up above, the village smoked. They were carried away into the dripping forest.

≈≈≈

Among the Duck people, not far off on Vaupes river, the headman's wife was Toeza. It was a large village close by the water. In this village, women were strong. They had no yearning for their men. Some women could throw spears and shoot arrows. But women were excluded from counsel and were never taken on campaign. The men left them just one old boat for fishing. But the women knew how to make dugouts, they paddled across the water to islands and lakes. Toeza wore many threads at her throat, on arms and legs. Her husband had two other wives, she was dominant. She went hunting in the forest. By the fire she dismembered the deer she had killed, skewered pieces to grill, and said: "We catch what we can. We eat what we like. The work is hard, but easier than when the men are here. We can rest whenever we want. And the children thrive too." An older woman came, took her child from the hip-sling and placed it near the fire, saying: "We bend our backs in the gardens. No man ever helps. When we're young it's easy. But us old ones." The children at the fire giggled and pointed. Everyone ate. The old woman told a story:

"A young girl married a rich man. Everyone wished her joy and brought presents. Her parents pretended to weep. After the feast she followed him across the little lake. He set her to work in the fields, cutting and weeding. When she finished she had to prepare mash, bake flatbread. There was no firewood. He sent her into the forest. It was the rainy season, she didn't find much, the river had carried it all away. The day was ending, she didn't have enough. Back home her husband scolded her.

"Next morning she rose, had to go deep into the forest, the howlers pitied her, broke kindling. She went home, her husband was still not satisfied, she'd taken so long. Next day she went even earlier into the forest, the monkeys sat among cocoa-pods, threw some down to her, she refreshed herself, gathered firewood, the monkeys helped. Then she went home, her husband was still angry, she was out of breath, it displeased him. And when the firewood was used up and she had to go back into the forest she wept: 'Oh why did I marry a rich man, when all he does is set me to work? When I rest I'm pretty, but then I must go into the forest. When I bring firewood I'm ugly, he doesn't look at me.'

"She ran around the lake to her mother. 'Why did you marry me to a rich man, when all he ever does is force me to work? Better you'd given me to a howler monkey. They threw cocoa-pods down and broke twigs for me.' The mother was afraid her daughter would go to the howler monkeys.

"The girl had a brother. The mother summoned him. He

broke one of the Sun's legs. So the Sun moved slower. The day lasted longer. The young woman was able to gather enough wood, her husband was satisfied."

The women ate, glanced at the sun, looked at one another, said nothing. One told the old woman: "Eat now. What's all this about your mother? You're no longer young yourself."

Where the rapids flow between rocky banks, there the black jaguar has his cave. Walyarina is his name. He, they say, is the source of the water's dull roaring. Nearby was the women's bathing place. Toeza cried out: "The men are away. Why did they leave with bow and arrow, shield and blowpipe and with the best canoes? They told nobody. They think our little sons are cleverer than us. What will they do? Catch men and women to slave for them. They attack men in the forest and steal their women and children. They will grow richer and we shall toil harder than ever. Better for us to take up spears and confront them when they come home." The women splashed around in the water. Toeza uprooted a lily and threw it towards the waterfall: "The black jaguar, my bridegroom, lives there."

With ten young women she made herself up, took weapons, went hunting again. She led them from the north to the waterfall where the forest growth was stunted. They stood before the jaguar's cave above the rapids, the others ran into the trees when the black jaguar came strolling out. He blew yellow foam. Toeza laid her weapons on the rock and crouched beside the beast; it slavered and stroked its whiskers and purred. Slowly she settled beside him. Then he stretched and looked straight ahead. Later Toeza returned with her weapons. The women swore to keep the secret. Toeza confided to them: "Walyarina, the black jaguar, is my lover. Walyarina is our watchword." Every day they went to the waterfall, the women ate, hunted in the forest, and waited for Toeza to emerge from the jaguar's cave.

The men returned from war, not all of them, they were unhappy. They brought no spoils. For three days they kept to the men's lodge. They ordered the women to fish, tend the gardens and prepare meals for them. But Toeza continued to hunt, she had secreted spears, bows and arrows in the forest. When the chief appeared in his hut the other two wives said: "Toeza's in the forest." The chief said nothing. He sent a young man out. He reported: "They're sitting by the waterfall, guzzling." Next day the youth said: "They summon the black jaguar, Walyarina."

The chief waited for dusk, when all the women were back in the village. He watched Toeza to see if she ate, and when she ate nothing asked her why not. She said she'd eaten in the forest. "And cooked as well?" She said: "Yes." And as he lay in his hammock in the gloom he called her, but she would not come, he dragged her by the hair and was stronger than her, she pressed hands to her face and wept.

But very early, while everyone slept, the chief slipped into the forest with ten men, upriver to the falls. He had told Toeza he would go hunting, she was to gather cassava roots for bread. At the waterfall the men dropped to the ground, the youth called out "Walyarina" just as he had heard. The black jaguar was sleeping, it took many calls before he came out of the cave, looked around, and when the youth again called "Walyarina" he raised his head and exposed his chest. The chief's spear caught him in the throat, the jaguar tumbled into the falls, they shot arrows after him and hauled him from the water. They loaded him onto branches and dragged him to the village, his head dangled and dripped blood and foam.

At noon the women filed back and saw him lying there. The chief said: "We'll have a hunting feast, bake lots of bread and prepare strong beer." Toeza ate with him, she could not speak for grief. The women followed her into the forest. "The men have dealt us a cruel injury. They have killed Walyarina. We must have revenge, today, before they can attack us in the night." The men hunted all afternoon, brought back game and fowl, the women baked and roasted. Then the men demanded pavari beer to drink. Humbly each wife presented a gourd to her man. They had put cassava poison in the beer. The men drank. And with the poison in their bellies they grew pale and anxious, they looked at one another, looked at the mat, looked up at the sky, looked at the women. The women asked: "Do you need something?" They groaned: "What did you put in the beer?" They called for the medicine man. His head too was slumped on his chest. The women hastened to empty the gourds behind the house. The men turned over on their mats, twitched and died.

Toeza danced with her women before the clan house. "The men are gone. Don't grieve. No one shall ever beat us again." They ran into the huts and brought out weapons. They loaded up with mats, cooking gear, food and trekked into the forest, children alongside and at the hip. "Walyarina" was their war-cry. They called themselves the Women People. When they came to a village they fought the men and called the women to their side. They let them follow with their children.

When the neighbouring village drummed and received no reply from the village of the dead, boats came across. Vultures were feasting on corpses. After funeral ceremonies they set off in pursuit of the women. These concealed themselves in a dense thicket. The men outnumbered the women. They surrounded the thicket and threw spears. The women responded. Some women fell, some men fell. The men discussed firing the thicket.

But they had seen so many corpses in the village, their friends who had returned with them from the warpath. Now more men were lying here, and women over there. They said: "What good to us are women who kill their men? If they want to go into the forest, let them."

So the Women People withdrew. They wandered through the forest, kept this side of the Yapura, came to the mighty river of the Amazons. They were subject to no man. And men feared them. From the men they stole even the black monkey pelt of the great spirit Yurupari and his voice, the trumpet.

They took men as consorts, tolerated their presence only as outsiders and slaves.

≈≈≈

Thus, in two places, ended that campaign conducted so stealthily along the trails, which had lasted five times ten suns.

And it was in truth a stealthy campaign, and the men who

came together to pursue it had every reason to keep at a distance any of whom they were unsure.

For it was the first attempt, later so often undertaken, to find the Land without Death.

In the forests, drums pounded endlessly.

There was a big drum called the Man, deep-toned, and a smaller called the Woman. They throbbed with beats short and long, deep- and high-toned, across lakes small and large, over swamps, rivers and streams, through forest and savannah. The drums lamented: "Take care! Great danger. None shall survive. Towards sunset the Great Spirit who holds up the earth made the mountains tremble. Wild beasts have attacked people. Whole tribes are perishing. Look at the sky: the Dog Star is approaching the moon. He will devour it."

Thus the two drums lamented through the endless dark forest. And the dusky people ran out, paddled out onto lakes. There in the sky stood the evil star Yaouare, Jaguar, already close to the moon. And in the villages they gathered, waved sticks, yelled, beat on pots, drummed and cried to heaven: "O great father, o my great father, are you well? Are you well? O great father, o my great father, are you well? Are you well?"

Envoys came to chiefs, they were to assemble their warriors swiftly and in secret. And one day, without naming their goal, the men slipped away from the villages, men of the Tariana, Opaina, Carijona, Incuna, from Vaupes river, Yapura and Caqueta. The call to arms ran thus: "Towards sunrise lies the Land without Death. There is a tree that provides all kinds of fruit, it is the father of all beasts and people. If you climb the tree it draws its branches together and lifts them up and anyone sitting there is borne higher and higher, above the mountain peaks, up into the sky. And there the ancestors dwell, the great spirits." The men were away a long time on their quest for the Land without Death, five times ten suns.

Calm settled again over the people of the forests. The mound of Toadhole with its burned huts remained deserted. No one visited the mound where Toeza and the women had killed the men. Everyone avoided looking at the sky, so that the stars would not notice them. Sometimes in the forest, hunting for honey, a man would peer between branches to see if perhaps a strange bird would show itself, from that distant land that they had sought in vain. And women sang to their children: "Far away towards the sunrise is a huge water. In it there's a land where people live forever and never grow old. No one does bad things. In this land a tree grows that bears fruit of all kinds, the father of beasts and people. No one has to work."

Three weird strangers

THE SUN BURNS hot on the mountains to the west. Their mass is riven by gorges. Rivers gouge their way through the gorges.

Such colossal mountains. Their peaks are skittles, spearpoints. They are ice-clad, some open up and from their craters fire spills from the Earth's insides.

Waters tumble from the peaks down the mountain flanks. The waters know their way. They fall from the sky to the icy peaks down into gorges. They fill the gorges and gnaw them away. They invade side valleys. From springs and streams, rivers grow. Lauricocha, Quiquiacocha are the names of source lakes.

The Marañon plunges from its lake headlong into an abyss. Its waters strike like a chisel. The valley walls are bare, heights glow like a furnace. It follows the valley from south to north. Towards the east high passes lead out of this land, beyond the river's reach. Furious winds howl from the east over the passes. They snatch birds that fly up from below, snipe, ibis, heron, the wind whirls them up, dashes them to the ground, drives them with hail and snow against cliffs down into the lakes. The river must break through the mountains. It finds the gate. Pongo de Mansariche is the gate, here it will go through, leave the mountains behind. It shoots narrowed through the gate and ahead lies open land. The land sinks from the craggy west where ice-crowns glow and volcanoes flaunt their plumes, eastward to the one immense plain. The river's own plain.

And like a monster with flowing mane the Amazon leaps from the mountains down into its plain. From left and right, as if they had awaited its coming, waters are drawn to merge with its stream. Its coming affects vast tracts. These tributaries turn, follow entranced and sink themselves into its waters, where they disappear.

The Amazon has broken through the mountains and carries them along. What once hemmed it in, what it seized and ground to fragments, now it hoards before it and below as spoil, mud and silt, spreads it over the plain as it surges on. Once the plain was a broad gulf, the sea filled it, the river drives back the sea and with the waters brought by a hundred streams from left and right becomes a flowing freshwater sea.

Those rivers are white and black. Amazon itself is white.

A hundred meters deep it flows; twice that at start and end.

When at last it leaves the plain behind it is strong enough to drive ships back, miles out to sea. It carries away tree trunks. It colours the sea white.

The hot sun hangs over this land. Primeval forest spreads across the plain, animals teem. Palms, bamboo, rubber trees, ferns, vines, eucalyptus shoot up. Swamps, forest canopies along the river, floating mangroves.

Bright hummingbirds flash across the water. Crocodiles drift lazily with the current. The sloth complains from the trees. The anaconda goes hunting for monkeys.

And in the pulsing waters a thousand kinds of fish are born and die.

≈≈≈

To the northwest, on clustered hills and mountain ranges deep in the forest, and lower down around the Yapura and the Vaupes, lived tribes of the Duck people, Jaguar people, higher towards the source there were the Armadillo people. They had fixed settlements. Their dwellings on the hills were of timber, stood on tall piles, were roofed with palm leaves, they had communal houses where several families lived, and smaller huts. The chief's house was sheathed in bark and decorated with pictures. Outside the mask house stood the tribal spirit carved from wood, coloured black, yellow and red and covered with secret lines that kenned the good and evil spirits of swamp and forest. It was the rainy season.

The old net was torn, they had woven a new net, the family was at peace, they were at peace with their neighbours, it was a good net, it would see lots of fish, they would approach and not be afraid. The days were hot, nothing of note was happening in forest or village, they could try out the net. The man, his brother, a friend and his wife determined the day. Then the rains came earlier than usual, they waited with the new net. They went down to fish in the lake beyond the fence. As they reached the shore a swarm of wild bees came and settled in a tree on the wooded bank. Two took up paddles and beat the still water, the third stood tall on the seat and steered. Hills glided past, the banks rose high, they travelled a long way, turned into a narrow channel, then came to a lake, they could hear monkeys, these lived on an island in the lake, they had swum across on driftwood. The people glided into a little cove, the water was muddy from rain, they could see no fish. At the forest edge piles had been rammed into the lake and covered with bamboo leaves, they guided the boat through. Then they ran into the forest and bent down, timbo grew here, they broke off long stems, made a big heap and beat the stems with branches until they were soft. Thick dark juice oozed out, they waded into the lake and swirled the stems around. And as they swirled, one man stood in the boat and stirred the water with a paddle. The water grew blacker and blacker, the poisonous sap spread, the fish were paralysed.

No sound came from the forest. Then one of the men in the lake grabbed the other by the arm and held him fast. He stared into the trees. The man in the boat stared into the trees. A distant crackle, something was moving. In an instant the two men were hidden in the reeds, the man in the boat dipped his paddle twice and with one bound vanished.

The crackling, rustling came nearer, stopped, silence reigned, the crackling and rustling came out of the forest towards the lake. A call, a human voice, another.

And as the three men in the dense reeds, feet in water, stood side by side unmoving, they saw, stepping from the forest into the clearing, figures that froze them to the spot. They had the appearance of men, but the bodies, legs and arms were draped in colourful cloth, the faces and hands were white as fish scales, and dark hair hung from the cheeks and chin of the biggest. Each wore a belt from which hung a slender stick, each had a club peeping over his shoulder. What the three ghastly figures who emerged from the forest were saying, the men in the reeds could not understand. These were unknown spirits. The strangers threw themselves down, laid their thin sticks aside, rasped, growled, snarled, acted like humans who were tired out. Then the one with the black beard stood up, another followed, they stepped down through scrub to the lakeside, the water drew them. They stood side by side, knelt, lay on their bellies and – the fishermen in the reeds still transfixed with fear – they began to drink the lake water, slurping as if dying of thirst. They dare to drink poisoned water, they can drink poisoned water, maybe they're looking out for the fish, want to render the sap harmless.

Now the two at the lakeside jumped back, spat in the water, stood up, groaned, retched, stumbled, tried to run away. But they were caught fast. Before they reached the nearest bushes they twisted around, writhed on the ground. There they lay, motionless in their coloured clothing, the one with the beard face down, the other on his side. As the third stranger ran down, the fishermen rose as silently as they could from the reeds. One after another they hurtled into the boat. The stranger on the bank saw phantoms: dark people paddling just offshore, through the palisade and away.

In the village was alarm, the chief came, they described the place. Thirty warriors seized weapons and climbed into boats, the medicine man had to come along. At the lake, below the bushes, Alonzo sat on sand between the two lifeless bodies and cried so loud they could hear him from the channel. His knee breeches were split, he had loosened his breastplate, his arms were bleeding, his right cheek was a flaming sore, he cried and laughed, implored Our Lady of Guadalupe, drew his sword. Then he sobbed into the cavity of his breastplate and called to his mother in Biscay. Boats with armed natives approached. He stood, shook himself, buckled his armour, swore at them. Though unsteady on his feet he dragged himself to the edge of the dark water, waved his arms, brandished his sword, his eyes rolled. The boats halted at the palisade, the chief's boat pushed through, on the black surface a mass of paralysed fish floated with red and white bellies, the boat ploughed through them, the men in the boat stood and readied spears for throwing. The creature on the shore was brightly clothed, white like a fish, the shape of a man, they were all much afraid, the medicine man trembling.

Then Alonzo grew quiet, sat on the sand and rested his head. The men climbed ashore. The medicine man nudged the big bearded one, yes, he was flesh and bones, water dribbled from his mouth, poisonous sap. The chief and the medicine man conferred. They hauled them all into one boat, the young fellow offered no resistance.

Women and children thronged the village mound, they were forbidden to look at the strangers and were driven into the huts. They carried the three past the village to an old mask-hut. There the medicine man treated them so that they yielded up the poison, and by next day were better. Then food was brought. They ate, drank, and slept a long time.

When they were restored to their senses they looked around for their weapons, found them on the floor and were puzzled. When they stepped from the hut, there among the trees was the village. Close by stood young painted warriors with shields, bows and arrows and spears. The Whites wore their rags and felt powerful. The bearded one nodded: "Here's the end of our song. We swore: to Hell with a green grave, a green grave! We'll soon find out if a Carib's belly makes a better grave."

Alonzo stared straight ahead: "How they watch us. They won't let us escape. First the brutes poison us, now they fatten us for a feast."

"And what say you, Pedro?"

"We won't be the first these animals have tried it on. They do it not out of hunger, but just because they're animals."

Young Alonzo began to cry, he had a fever, he spoke of Odysseus of old who came to a witch, she turned his companions into swine. Pedro the bearded one stroked Alonzo's swollen cheek: "You must chew grass and press it to your wound, then the fever will abate. Buck up, Alonzo. Better we'd never come down from Peru and were still in Spain. We'll find no gold here. These brutes, look at them, how they paint themselves. For each one we kill we earn a grace. Look at them. They knew we were coming from the west. What do they do? Poison the water."

Alonzo: "Why did they save us?"

The bearded man glowered: "They want to eat us, you heard. By the Virgin's grace we'll escape their clutches. I'd like to return to our people and lead them back here. They'll pay for that water. I command you: pray to St Michael and St James."

They did so. Then they sang, the guards heard the words without understanding: "Armed with my virtue I find rest in battle, rocks are my bed, waking is my sleep."

Neighbouring chiefs arrived. They inspected the strangers, their nature was unclear, they might be ghosts, perhaps departed ones since their skin was colourless, perhaps strange great sea fish. The warriors on guard must keep them away from the village. Unnoticed by the weird strangers, magical lines of raffia were laid outside their hut to prevent them from walking across to the village. To improve their mood and encourage them to leave, gifts were brought of bananas, manioc, dried fish, beer in gourds. The chief and the medicine man sought to explain through gestures that the dance was in honour of their departure, and that more presents would be brought.

The three bided their time for one night.

The villagers decided to hold the feast next day, no one knew what misfortune the three weird visitors might bring. They would take them to the water, put them in a boat and row them far away. Then they would see what direction they took, and who they were.

That evening when the fire was lit and the guards were

drinking, the three Whites raised their fire-tubes and took aim from the darkness of the hut. They had already bundled up and shouldered the food. They shot to right and left of the camp fire, the noise was tremendous, two guards fell, the rest ran like the wind. A few breaths later a wild exodus began, away from the village downhill into the forest, with loud screams. Quite soon the village lay deadly quiet. The fire burned down.

The three Whites fired another round as a frightener. Then in the dark they climbed down to the river. The sky was clear, at first they had the light of the camp fire, then the moon, and always there were flies flickering above the path, gold-yellow and green, sunflies and moonflies. They marched through the night as far as they could. They even passed the lake where the fishermen had surprised them, by moonlight they overturned the rammed piles of the palisade, scattered the leaves. Big toads croaked. They kicked at them.

When the villagers sent scouts up the mound next morning they found it empty, the strangers gone. Two guards lay in pools of blood by the cold fire beyond the houses. The villagers trudged back. No one dared move the two corpses. There was discussion of what to do. They were placed on branches, and as the families cowered indoors were carried down to the forest, buried side by side; stones were heaped on the graves as a warning. Up on the mound the medicine man struggled with ghosts for two hot midday hours. He leapt, whispered, swung his rattle.

≈≈≈

The trio, led by unflagging Pedro, came upon their captain north of the Yapura in the company of thirty Whites and as many native warriors. Young Alonzo died. They tried to persuade the little band to undertake retribution against the savage tribes of the region. The captain mocked them: had they thought to find the Land of Gold all by themselves? They turned towards the mountains. They meant to skirt the cursed flood plain with its swamps and snakes and crocodiles, and march north through mountain defiles.

So the troop marched and paddled its way back. They waded through rivers, no crocodile could be seen, but suddenly a swimmer would shriek horribly, heartrendingly, and was already under, and when they rowed to his aid and pulled him out, instead of a man they had a skeleton in their hands, little fishes clung to it, thousands more roiling the water snapping at meat. Blood stained the water red. What they pulled out, with its gaping grin and hands clutching an excavated breast, was a corpse.

They saw giant beetles like cockroaches fly past, occasionally one had a fat spider riding on its back, the frightened beetle flew to a plant, sat there, the spider kept hold, swelled, and now the beetle was an empty shell. No covering protected from swarms of mosquitoes. When they could they climbed ashore, buried themselves to the neck in sand and mud leaving only the head free. Fifty strong men had come down from the mountains, now just twenty limped back from the green hell.

When they came to the first hills along the Putumayo they rested. Each had a pack of cards and a relic at his breast. They took out the holy relic and kissed it. Then they lay up in the ruins of a post station of the former Inca empire until their wounds healed. They wandered with many others north to the coast. There a great army was being assembled, and ships built for the conquering of new lands.

St Michael and St James! Weapons my ornament. In battle I find repose. The rocks my bed. I know not sleep, only wakefulness.

Refugees from the western mountains

RIVERS SHRANK in the middle of the year and then rose again for a short while, there came a time of cold rain and south winds, later there were thunderstorms that swelled the rivers anew, at year's end they were at their lowest and began slowly to rise again. Almost every day brought rain and thunder, and by the middle of the year the rivers were at their highest.

There were days too of scorching sunshine, nights cool and clear. Often the sky was veiled in haze all day long, distant thunder could be heard but no rain fell. Now and again a tempest roared in from the east, the sky darkened, it became night, a terrible storm broke. It was as if enemies had taken up position on all four sides of the world and were throwing heavy balls of stone, they exploded with a crash, and every throw was preceded by a fiery flash bright enough to ignite the treetops. Everything cowered silent and afraid. The croaking from the swamps ceased. The mirror of the waters was lashed by rain. Then the heavens closed again, rain hissed in darkness, toads tried out their voices, children stopped trembling and went to sleep.

Next morning the forest was filled with the tremendous shrieks of monkeys. They sat high in dense foliage in families, the black guariba, tails wrapped around a branch. The father laid his bushy body atop a strong branch. He clung to it with all fours, his body hung down at an angle. In this position he sang out rhythmically, females and young males responded, he trumpeted mightily: "Oh oh, ow, ah." Females and young males answered in chorus: "Oh oh, ah, ha, ah."

≈≈≈

Across the hills the drums, big and little, spoke: "Men are on the move from the direction of the sunset, they look like us, come from the cold mountains and wear cloaks and shirts, they are needy, let them be welcomed, they'll soon leave."

Drums asked: "Are they many?" Drums answered: "Three, five, eight, they have no weapons, some have died."

A boat came up the narrow river, women in the garden screamed, young men had already heard the splash of paddles and came running downhill with spears. In the boat sat men of a dark olive complexion. The boat halted across the river from the village, the villagers waited for the chief, then paddled across to them. With the strangers was a local man who understood their language. He said: These are refugees from the mountains, they bring a message. And so they brought the boat across and led the strangers to the chief's house.

They squatted on mats, drank, spoke little. The strangers were stocky, seemed troubled, each wore a short sleeveless shirt, over it a colourful cotton cloak, their faces were unpainted. Mussel shells ornamented the cloak of one of the strangers, and golden discs hung in his ears.

The strangers were allowed to snooze in hammocks through the midday heat. Then there was a meal of roasted fish and bananas. In the evening the strangers spoke. Their leader made himself understood.

"Beyond the rivers and hills and forests come big hills and mountains, and then the great mountain range. We live on the other side of those mountains, where the sun sinks into the sea, and we gaze towards the mountains to see the sun rise."

The chief: "Have you watched the sun sink into the sea? You are not burned!"

The leader of the strangers: "It sinks far away, the sea is immensely big."

The chief wanted to be sure: "So over there in the west is the sea, and you come from the mountains between the great forest and the sea?"

"That is so. There is our home." He lowered his head, the others lowered their heads. "There *was* our home. We are Quechua, which in our language means: people of knowledge. Our land is Tahuanti-suya. We were driven out. Our people are vanquished."

No one spoke. The chief whispered to the man beside him, who nodded, and the others who overheard also nodded. But they kept silent and their expressions were not friendly.

The chief asked: "Your people are vanquished. How is it you are alive?"

Cuzumarra said: "We seek revenge."

The fierce expressions of the villagers relaxed, but they remained thoughtful.

When Cuzumarra said that their enemies were men from a distant kingdom across the sea and that they were white like fish, the villagers were seized with great excitement. They recalled the three strangers who had appeared in the area some months ago, who had drunk sap-water and killed two guards with thunderbolts. They told of this and looked anxiously at Cuzumarra.

"The very same, they came to our coast by ship in their hundreds, they have big animals with them, four-legged, they sit on them taller than a man, they run very fast, much faster than the fastest runner, and tireless. To protect their chests the Whiteskins wear armour of iron, many also have shirts of chain mail that no spear can penetrate, and under their shirts they carry little bones and pictures of their spirits that protect them."

The chief was beside himself: "And they can summon thunder!"

"No, they cannot. They have tubes that they fill with sand and a ball. They can make the sand burn, then the ball kills. But they cannot summon thunder from the clouds."

"But they put some in their tubes."

"That is our ruin."

The villagers whispered in horror. The chief asked again: "And where are your people?"

"They are vanquished. We are enslaved. They have killed countless of us with their tubes."

The chief: "And your ancestors tolerate them on your land?"

Cuzumarra: "They frighten even our ancestors."

The chief was uncomprehending. "And you have fled, you forsake your ancestors and your people, how can you live?"

But they did not want to talk more that day.

≈≈≈

The moon rose. Older villagers recalled terrible tales of the world's destruction, they dared not look up at the Dog Star. In the huts women laughed, parrots settled on rooftops, a cool breeze blew.

Next morning when the strangers came to the oldest chief, he regarded them with apprehension. "You wander about, alien spirits can attack you, you don't know them and don't know how to handle them." He summoned the medicine man, who gave them red pigment, feathers and little nuts for protection.

They continued their conversation that afternoon in the chief's hut. Cuzumarra told his story again. Then he spoke of his people whom the Whites had defeated and were now exterminating. As he spoke, his expression stern and fixed, the chief regarded him attentively, leaned forward and placed a hand on his knee: "Cuzumarra, you will die soon."

He was unmoved. "That is happy news to me. It tells me many of my enemies shall die too."

The chief nodded gravely, almost shocked. "Do not delay, Cuzumarra. You do wrong to leave your kin to their fate."

"I shall receive their forgiveness when they know why I have waited so long. For we cannot take revenge all by ourselves. We must make preparations to ensure that it happens." Again the chief nodded gravely.

"I want to tell you about our land behind the great mountains from which the rivers flow. Our land, Tahuanti-suya, is large and fertile, it extends across mountains and high valleys and along the sea coast. So many people live there they cannot be counted. They live on their land and do not wander about. There are no large rivers to drive them from their homes. The heat is not so great."

The chief was astonished and whispered to the others: "We have never heard of this! We have heard of a Land without Death where nothing evil happens. It is said to lie towards the sunrise."

"We live on the plains, in the mountains, along the coast and in cities across the great mountains, towards the sunset. Our greatest city is called Cuzco. It has many streets. The streets are paved with small stones that we carried there and tamped smooth. The houses are low. Families live in them. Everyone wears the same costume, you see it on my companions, men a brown woollen cape over their white shirt, women a long underskirt that they cover with a green wrap crossed at the breast and fixed with a pin. Many tribes live in our land, they all wear the same, but those called Canari wear a coronet of wood on their head so that people know they are Canari. Those called Colla wear a linen cap, the Yunca come to town with flutes and clappers and drums. Some of our tribes live along the fish-teeming coasts, on Lake Titicaca, on the high plains where fiery mountains smoke. Their leaders wear some mark of distinction, a silver plate at the breast, discs in the ears, sandals on the feet. And there are guardians at the ancient places who carry a great condor on their back or the skin of a puma on their head. All have their prescribed place in our city of

Cuzco, when they attend to bring news or receive instructions and take part in ceremonies of worship."

Now at the chief's request the leader's companions had to stand up, he asked permission to inspect them. One by one they showed the chief their clothes; they had thick long hair, deep black, their eyes were small and black, their expression did not change during the inspection, their faces were smooth. They sat. There was a long expectant silence.

Cuzumarra of the big ear discs spoke: "Our great city is Cuzco, which means Navel of the World. We had a great chief, the last emperor, his name was Huayna Capac. He sat in Cuzco in the Temple of the Sun, in the great hall on his throne of pure gold. His body was clad in a broad cloak of vicuña wool, his feet were protected by sandals, two gold plates hung in his ears, a broad red band circled his head five times and hung over his brow, at his belt hung a leather bag filled with coca leaves. But none of us ever saw Huayna Capac, he was our last chief, he left us before our lives began."

Here the leader of the strangers had to break off, for the chief was staring at them and made uneasy gestures but said nothing. He wanted to ask what this meant. As the first chief kept silent, after a while another said: "You spoke the name of your first chief. He is dead." Cuzumarra nodded.

"Are you not afraid to speak the name of your dead first chief?"

Cuzumarra: "We are not afraid. We did everything we could to placate him, at all times he feels content to be with us." They looked at him with big eyes, he should continue. "You shall see who he is. In the hall where he sits, a stone wall faces him. On it hangs a golden shield, this is the urei from which humans came, as we have been taught. Below it to the left hangs the silver disc of the moon, to the right the sun. That one I have seen myself, the golden sun with its mouth, eyes, nose and the rays which it casts. Above the golden shield the stars of the sky stretch away up to the roof, beneath the shield the great constellation of the Cross gleams. The Llama Train is there too, with its two guardians. Seven round eyes in the wall designate the highest deity. And along the wall in front of the king stand golden chairs where his mummified ancestors sit swaddled, adorned with costly jewels. All this did our last great chief see and understand. He was an Inca.

"Now I have said who our Inca was. Tumbez is a city on the coast, would that it had never been built! From there the murderers of our kinfolk came into our land. Pachacamac is a holy city, and Nazca, Paramunca. Roads were built all across the land, the roadbed firm so that people could walk and run and no rain could loosen it. Bridges crossed streams and rivers. In our land no man or woman or child had to worry about food or clothing or shelter. Everyone had two sets of clothes: one for work and one for festivals, everyone ate twice a day, and we prescribed what the people should eat and it was always there. Working times and rest times were regulated, the same for all, and when anyone came of age he received a house, a pair of llamas, a strip of good land. When he grew old or sick, he would be cared for. In return everyone had to work on certain days for a certain time in the Inca's fields. We ensured that all were married, and tolerated no single adults. We detailed people to work in the weaving sheds or in the mines, and at the proper times changed them about. To preserve good order and supervision we had leaders and overseers for ten families, five times ten families, ten times ten families. They distributed feed for livestock, manure for the soil, seeds for sowing, took charge of the harvest and distributed it. The greatest chief took bread baked by virgins who had never set eyes on a man, and offered it to the highest spirits."

The chiefs received this report with the greatest attentiveness and pleasure, they cast friendly looks at their guests and wanted them to see their benevolence, but although the report was so pleasing the guests kept their heads lowered, even Cuzumarra, whose voice as he spoke had grown ever softer.

"Well," said the chief, "if your land was really so well organised and ordered, you did well. Peace must surely have prevailed."

Cuzumarra whispered: "You see us here."

"Then you must have become divided, Cuzumarra."

"It is true. After the great emperor there were no more. He had two sons."

"Ah!" the chief raised his hands, the others shook their heads. "You should have killed one."

"Then the Whiteskins arrived in their great ships and came ashore at our city of Tumbez. They killed the two sons, who were fighting one another."

"Ah!" repeated the chief, "you became divided, and so evil spirits were able to meddle. How would the beasts of the forest let themselves be caught, if they knew we were divided? We would find no honey in the trees. We would die." All the chiefs nodded gravely.

Cuzumarra let his arms droop slack on his knees. Back bent, he sank into himself. "We always kept good order. That was much. And when our great emperor left our land for his other home, we lost our balance. Evil spirits came. Beware of them! Never talk with them, never come close to them, never placate them, bring them no gifts. All that is in vain. They want to live in your land, they want to possess your huts, make you their slaves, they want everything that you gather and hunt and fish."

The chief smiled in disbelief. "As long as we are peaceable and our ancestors help us, it will not happen."

"Tomorrow, learn how it went with us."

≈≈≈

The strangers, whose skin was a dark yellow-green, had wooden flutes, they blew on them when they sat in the village and people left them alone. One sang a sad song:

"My mother bore me in rain, in mist, so that I would cry like the rain and vanish like the clouds. You grow in a cradle of grief, said my mother as she fed me. The rain, the storm have let me grow. When I seek friends I wander through the world and find misery. Oh cursed the day of my birth. Oh cursed the night when my mother conceived me. Cursed, forever cursed."

That afternoon Cuzumarra described the last days. The chiefs all blamed him and his people for the calamity. Cuzumarra said:

"I know you place all the blame on us. Now hear me to the end. The White devils who burst upon our land at Tumbez are long since dead."

"Ah!" cried the chiefs in satisfaction.

"The White leaders, whom we trusted, murdered our princes, then murdered each other."

"Ah!"

"Others came after them, always more. The lands beyond the great sea towards the sunset must have an inexhaustible supply of wicked, violent men. Their ships are bigger than any we had ever seen. They carry not just blowpipes that make thunder, they sit on big beasts, fast as the wind, that allow themselves to be steered and have an iron bit placed in their mouth."

"And this beast, what is it called?" asked the chief, deeply impressed.

"They call it 'horse'."

The chief: "Who knows what its real name is? They would not betray its real name to you. Is this animal fierce?"

"It is gentle and lets itself be led. It goes to its stall like a llama."

The chief nodded doubtfully. "We would like to know its name."

Cuzumarra: "From the ships they bring big carts with wheels, these are gigantic thunder tubes. When they shoot from these, the walls of our houses collapse. They come to us to take the gold that grows in our mountains, and silver, that also grows in the mountains. We don't know what they do with the gold. At first we thought they give it to their horses to eat, because a horse is always chewing on the bit in its mouth. Then we learned that the horses don't even eat meat. And they send the gold on their ships back to their own land, where their emperor gathers it all up. We gave them all we had. In their search for gold and silver they plundered and ruined our palaces, and the temples where we worshipped the highest spirits, and the buildings of our leaders. Whole villages fled from them, then they ransacked and burnt the whole village, but the people were starving, so they hunted them and drove them into the mines to fetch gold and silver from the rocks. Most died. For in the mines there is no light and the air is noxious. They allow them no rest but force them to toil until they drop. The people fall ill and have bad food.

"White leaders with warriors and horses and thunder tubes came from the ships. They went into the land, burned cities, killed people who resisted and carried the rest off into slavery. They lack a human soul, but they desire everything that glints and beautifies. So our people on the coast had to slave for them and fish for pearls. Oh, how long ago was it that our parents lamented thus? We stayed quiet. We obeyed. For our empire was destroyed, our cities and villages in ruins, the people scattered, the Whiteskins took the daughters from our houses and made them their wives. This was already so in our parents' day, we have never known otherwise. But the shame they heaped on us, the burdens they laid on us, became unbearable. Honourable chiefs, you judge that we are guilty, that if we had remained peaceable the Whiteskins would never have come and placed us under their yoke. And even if we bear much guilt for what happened before – for what happened next and what we have lived through, none of us can be blamed, for it is an outrage, you cannot imagine."

The chiefs grew restless at this speech, they whispered back and forth and objected: "Were you bewitched by a powerful enemy?" Only courtesy prevented them from leaving, but some were minded to keep a distance from these strangers who stood under such baleful influences. They exchanged troubled glances, they would have to part from these guests before long.

Cuzumarra: "They prayed to their terrible god. They wanted us to pray to him too."

The chief, puzzled and solemn: "And you? He heard your prayers?"

"No. It was a lie. They meant to mock us. False creatures tempt us on all sides. Many of our people prayed to their terrible god, in the houses the Whiteskins built for him. They prostrated themselves, he did not free them from their bondage. Their misery grew worse, now shame was added to it. No, we made no pact with the evil spirit who seeks to exterminate us. Our land was happy and well ordered. If we want to survive we must vanquish this powerful spirit.

"Hear what they do now. They send their recruiting agents through all the provinces, and every able-bodied person must assemble in that place and draw lots. And whoever is chosen must go to the mines under the earth. But most die there. So for us this event is treated as a funeral. The chosen one puts his house in order, his relatives come and follow him part of the way in mourning. And one of the Whites comes and holds up a cross. That is the sign of their spirit who is our enemy. The man splashes them with water and they must pledge faithful service to the king who lives beyond the sea. This they do.

"Listen, so that you do not say: when someone has been cast down and has let himself be cast down, of course he must suffer greatly. I speak that you may hear what befell us there over the mountains. You see me and my companions, already Whiteskins have been here with you, you shall know what they are.

"When their leaders want to travel about our land, they sit on their horses. But they do not have many horses. So they have themselves carried by our wretched people. And because these grow weary on long journeys they have six or eight others following, to change around. All carry heavy loads. They are chained together. The load is often very heavy and it is very hot and the mountains are steep. So our people often collapse and die. And because they are fixed to the chain by a neck-iron they hang there and the line cannot move. But the White overseer does not want to open the chain. So they just cut the head off the corpse or the dying man and throw the torso and head onto the road. They come to our villages and find the people placid. They ask about gold, and if our people have none, they beat them. But sometimes the people have already fled, because they saw them coming. Then the Whites set fire to the houses, destroy provisions, lay waste to the fields, and our people die of hunger with their families. Our fields and trees yield good fruit, the sea provides fish, our soil and water are fertile. But the Whites have no desire to breath our air, eat our fruit and fish. They grow drunk and unruly and look for gold. Nothing else matters to them. They only ever pray to their great god that he enable them to find more gold. So, as ever more of them came to our land to extort gold, the Tumbo gathered together at the Nieve river, in the mountains, a cliff hangs over an abyss, and one day all the families of the Tumbo threw themselves into the abyss. There's a place called Aconcaha, the people there had no more gold, and almost all the inhabitants were doing forced labour on the coast or in the mines. But the Whites sent an official and wanted more gold. So the women ran to a neighbouring place, the people gave them a few pieces, they heated it and seized the official and poured the molten gold down his throat and left him there. Then the people of Aconcaha fled into the mountains. We don't know what happened to them after that."

The chiefs fidgeted again, but did not speak. Cuzumarra was oblivious now to their unease. He thought only of his people and their cruel suffering.

"Our faces are smooth, and when hairs grow on our skin we pluck them out. Although our faces are smooth and we do not grow beards, they forced our men to take sharp knives and salves for shaving, they had to do labour service to pay for them. The Whites cover their feet and legs, they brought hose made of fine fabric, we had to take them, we protested and showed them our costumes that we inherited from our fathers, they would not relent, they made marks on their tablets and made us do labour service for hose we do not wear. The Whites go in their great ships across the sea and know many lands and seas and rivers and mountains. And because they wander and seek and never find rest or peace, they have made big leaves on which they have painted all the lands and seas and rivers and mountains that they know about and have wandered through, and have certainly subjugated and destroyed. That is what they do, it suits their nature and makes them proud. They showed us these pictures and forced us to take them. We told them we have no need of the pictures, they would not relent, they made marks on their tablets and for the pictures we had to do labour service in their fields, build their houses, while our own houses fell into ruin and the sea broke through our dykes. ·

"I have spoken at length, esteemed chiefs, leaders of your tribes. You have been good enough to grant our request and guide our boat here, receive us, protect us and hear us. We are not strong. What is strong in us is only memory, which says: we must remain strong and everywhere tell of the Whites, who are starting to come down from the mountains."

Cuzumarra lifted his gaze. The oldest chief stood, the others too. The strangers stood. The chiefs' eyes flashed. They left the hut. Young people crowded around. The oldest chief called to one of the men, at which all the young men ran off, while the women and children stood about. They cried: There'll be a dance! The chiefs left the strangers alone in the chief's hut, with a message that they would be summoned soon. There was great excitement and much animated chatter.

The dancers wore ancestor masks. After the dance they drank together deep into the night. The warriors sang and laughed by the fire. Then they slept far into the day. In the morning the chief said: "We shall prepare a parting feast for you and make presents of anything you desire. But we ask you please to tell us how you escaped from the Whiteskins, and what paths lead from there to here."

≈≈≈

In the afternoon Cuzumarra spoke to the chiefs, his friends, in the chief's hut, his seven companions sat to his right and left.

"We often doubted that the Whites are human. We begged to be allowed to feel their swords, they let us feel their arms and legs. They only objected if we tugged at their ugly beards, then they hit us. When they came into our land we were fairly sure they were human, and our leaders advised the Inca, our chief leader, the emperor, to lay by sufficient rope to bind men and beasts, for when they saw our greater numbers they would run away. But then we learned by their cruelty that they are possessed, and we made to defend ourselves."

The strangers sat upright on the mat, and it was clear that they were warriors.

"Our lord of Tangasuku," Cuzumarra continued in a low voice, "cacique of Condorcanqui, did not wait for the envoy of the Whites to flog him in order to extort his gold. As the White man approached from Tinta with his entourage, our cacique waylaid him and by his own hand hanged him from a tree. He was of the line of the Inca, the one who was beheaded. He took the name of his ancestor and started to make war. The people called to him. He became strong. They all came to him. He had no thunder tubes, no horses, our people flocked to him. Our land wanted to be free of these evil spirits. He was victorious even though he lacked weapons. Like a fire that kills wild beasts even though it has no teeth, he surrounded and killed the Whites. Then someone close to him betrayed him." The strangers uttered a cry of rage, and twice more, their faces grew tighter, their little eyes glinted. The chiefs likewise sat erect, the words seethed within them.

"They set upon our lord of Tangasuku in his sleep, carried him to the Whites, we know the name of their leader, Jose Antonio Areche. He condemned our lord of Tangasuku, fallen into his hands through treachery. The wife of our lord, his two sons and his brother in law were beheaded in front of him. Our lord himself was brought to stand before the Whiteskin, who spat on him, then the executioner cut the tongue from his mouth, tied ropes to his limbs, attached the ropes to four strong horses, they were whipped and tore apart our still living lord. Then they burned his torso, the head and limbs they sent in baskets to all the places that had stood with our lord because they yielded up no gold and refused to take the beard salve and the coloured pictures. Our lord's house was torn down, his possessions given to Whites, his brother was taken from his homeland, put on a ship and carried across the sea, we don't know where to.

"When the villages saw the arms and legs and head of our lord Tangasuku, they wailed, and then beat those who carried the baskets, seized the baskets and buried our lord's limbs in a safe place. Anyone who had seen the limbs spread the news. No one remained calm. We were on the point of death. We suffered this. A man came from the house of our lord, Andres, and beside him was

Catari, they showed themselves. We all wanted to die, but not by leaping into an abyss. Andrés and Catari spoke words that warmed us: they demanded five hundred White heads for each of those murdered along with our lord. Then the Whites were seized with fear. They saw that they were found out. Sorora is a town in our mountains. Many Whites fled there and with them many of the wicked of our land who had let themselves become corrupted. They had thunder tubes in the town, big ones carried on carts pulled by horses and llamas. When the thunder flashed, the balls ripped through ten and ten. They relied on these and on the walls of Sorora. They had food. But it was our land, and our ancestors were there, and we had signs that they stood with us. We dug ditches above the town to collect water, and when the snowmelt came we guided the water and the mountain torrents against the walls of Sorora. The water tore a breach, we followed the water and were in the town. I was there, and these. We cannot tell you how many Whites and how many of the wicked of our land fell to our spears and swords. The whole town was surrounded and was already burning when we entered it. Not one of the countless wicked who hid there survived. Anyone who escaped the sword was burned in the fire or drowned in a mountain torrent."

Again they uttered their cry. The chiefs raised their right arms as if to throw a spear, and yelled their war cry.

Cuzumarra concluded in a rasping voice: "Our chiefs Andrés and Catari were captured at last. The Whites prevented us from gathering. They sent men after us into the mountains to catch everyone who fought against them. We escaped. We are going back. We shall tell you the paths that lead to and from the mountains."

Following the strangers' report, the chiefs consulted the elders and witch doctors who were present: "Once we received a message: 'Take care! Great danger. None shall survive. Towards sunset the Great Spirit that holds up the earth made the mountains tremble. Wild beasts have attacked people. Whole tribes are perishing. Look at the sky: the Dog Star approaches the moon. He will devour it.' Then the chiefs of that time gathered their warriors and went with them across the rivers to defend themselves. They learned that the Land without Death lies towards the sunrise. They tried to find it. When they returned they said they had not found it. The cacique Cuzumarra, a stranger, has come to us across the mountains and we have taken him in and heard him. Whiteskinned men are in his land, they are destroying his people, they have fire tubes and big animals that we have never seen. Go to the mask-hut and ask the ancestors and animals that protect us. Will the White men come to us? Will the great spirit who carries the mountains destroy us?"

The elders and witch doctors consulted Cuzumarra, who described for them the terrible power of the White men, their animals and firearms. Their priests pray to an evil power beyond the sun, who supports them. They are murderers, robbers, liars, drunkards, cheats. Then the old men and witch doctors fasted and danced.

The ancestors did not speak, dreams were unclear, birds they consulted gave differing answers. So the chiefs postponed their decision. Cuzumarra observed this with sorrow.

They departed. As they left the village in two canoes, drumming could be heard. They reported the journey of eight strangers from the mountains, they are unarmed and friendly, they have important news, listen to them. The chiefs who had come from other villages returned home and spread the message.

Southward

THE EIGHT EMISSARIES from the Land of the Four World Regions travelled for many days on rivers and lakes towards the south and the sunrise. Their homeland receded farther and farther behind. They passed from tribe to tribe, and always they had company, people welcomed them, heard them, relayed their news, guided them onward. Those who died had died in the first days of the great journey. The eight survivors were quiet, and grew quieter.

It was a time of low water. Rivers, channels and lakes they traversed were all black. They left the hill country behind.

Sometimes a few fell sick with fever, but always they found a medicine man to scratch their skin and blow smoke over them.

To the east rose the blue Cupati range, the great Yapura river opened up before them, they felt a new wind. They skirted wild cataracts, sometimes they hauled the boat through. The boat they travelled in had an awning against the sun, always they were preceded by a boatful of young warriors who watched the forest and hunted and fished. There were clearings and grassy stretches, then tall trunks soared again, storey overtopping storey as if every species sought to clamber over all the others, trunk jostling trunk. The river was lined with grasses and tangled scrub, trees soared up out of the clinging scrub, and when it let go the trunks were enmeshed in a new confusion of leaves, dark green and yellow and worm-eaten, then the trunks broke free and spread their fans and umbrellas. But even taller trees towered over them, and from the very tops ropes and lines dangled from plants with gaudy great flowers that had found no space below and so dropped roots from treetops down through the air.

Sometimes a scent of violets wafted from the forest. They glided over wide dark water, the riverbanks were bare, trees stood leafless, their branches crippled and dying. Long black-brown and green-brown shapes protruded from the shallows, little humps, the eye hardly notices, but then, look, a stir in the hazy river, above them flies swarm like fogbanks, they stand on thick short legs sticking out at the sides, a black bony tail sweeps the surface of the water, they are long creatures, caiman, mouths gape wide, they appear to be asleep, one swims behind the boat, then the eddy vanishes.

When they crossed the Yapura they had already visited many tribes, all were hospitable, listened to them in horror and astonishment. Chiefs and elders conferred, the people showed fear and would not let them stay. Everywhere they described their country, their people, the old and new rulers, described the Whites, their malice, their weapons and animals, how they disregard all laws and customs and pour up from the coast into the mountains. Villages, towns and provinces where they appear all die. The strangers who spoke these things, and always spoke them anew, disturbed and agitated the tribes, they left unease in their wake but gained nothing. The companions asked Cuzumarra how much further they would wander, ever further from their homeland. He said, his voice barely obeying him: they should think of their kinfolk at home, and what had happened to them.

But when once again the hour came to leave a village and climb back into the boats, the seven companions saw their leader seized by an attack of despair. Cuzumarra knelt at dawn by the hut where they had slept and called to the Sun, the all-powerful father god. He cried in the language of their country: "Father, show yourself to us! Father, do not forsake us! However great our sins, do not punish us too severely. Do not destroy us utterly. Or will you yield your dominion?" He raised himself from the ground, glared into the fiery clouds and trembled: "Oh to suffer this. Let us know what you intend. Do not keep it from us, mighty father." His friends crouched sullen beside him.

People asked when they would turn around, and were afraid to guide them farther south. If you keep south you come to the mighty river, its forests are too thick to penetrate, along its banks are mounds where wild warlike people dwell. And when the strangers asked who these tribes were, they learned what had already been whispered secretly in the north: a cold tempest blows across the great river, it buffets the water so that it becomes whirlpools and spray, destroys boats, so the river is called Boat Destroyer, Amazon, on it dwell the Women People who came from the north. The women clear strips in the forest and along small rivers. They name themselves after the river. They make war and steal men. Men of the Passa tribe said: the Women People have gone away to the south, they are turtles and armadillos, you must beware of them.

At the strangers' request they were guided through the maze of waterways around the Iça river, which flows into the Amazon. They passed through swamp forests. After a hunt young warriors painted themselves, danced around the fire with their spears, worked themselves into a frenzy and menaced one another. They drummed and sang. They invoked their father, the Anaconda. Suddenly they threw themselves down. Two huge serpents emerged from the bush. They swept into the clearing, reared up and flicked their tongues. The warriors dropped their spears, averted their faces and covered their eyes. Suddenly one of them sprang to the fire, threw bloody lumps of venison, at once hid his eyes again. The two snakes emitted a hiss, lowered themselves to the ground and swallowed the meat. They stood stiffly side by side in the clearing away from the fire. Then with a crackling and rustling they vanished.

The warriors danced again, chanted greetings and thanks to the snakes.

They were now far to the south, lakes were more numerous, the wilderness was behind them, the silence was immense. Bats swarmed through the forest like ghosts in the dusk, occasionally a butterfly came by, parrots screeched from trees, crickets chirruped. Cuzumarra grew ever more silent. The sweltering heat overcame him and his companions, their skin was always wet. They were tired even without moving, and yet alert and full of expectation. They walked for hours through the forest, their guides knew little paths to the next watercourse, wild pigs splashed in swamps, fat opossums darted by. Then Cuzumarra said to himself: "I no longer know what to say. I am losing my words, I can no longer think of Vilcas Huaman where I was born, I still know the name of the Empire of the Four Suns, but a sorcerer has stolen from me all that I knew of it."

Thorns and jagged undergrowth had long since torn their clothing to shreds. Cuzumarra still wore the rags, golden discs still hung in his ears, but his companions spoke as little as he and had made themselves girdles of raffia. Otherwise they were as naked as the forest people. In fact, they had even painted arms and legs and torsos black and red like the forest people.

During the first months of their journey they grieved and could not sleep, now they enjoyed long sleeps, laughed, and were amused when the forest people wrestled with each other. The forest people would suddenly grab each other by the throat, squeeze until the faces swelled and they must surely choke, then let go. They would smile and say: that was good. Cuzumarra wanted to pose a question to his companions: did they wish to leave him and return north. But they looked so placid with their moist gleaming eyes. So he said nothing.

One day they came to a village mound. It was overgrown with crippled trees, there were trees with blue flowers and yellow flowers amid fallen trunks. When the forest people saw these trunks they were afraid and said: "We must go back." The trees were charcoal. Even the grassy terrace they were walking over was charcoal.

Hard by the steep slope of a new mound, without any warning the forest people suddenly ran away. When the strangers looked around for them, they had vanished into the bush under buriti palms.

All at once arrows flew down from the mound. There was nothing to see. At Cuzumarra's command his shocked companions stood up from the grass and extended empty open hands.

He broke a branch from a bush and waved it towards the mound. Nothing happened. They heard nothing. After standing a while they squatted uneasily in the grass, afraid to move.

Then voices came from the forest behind them, and they thought their friends were returning. But it was dark people running in file, garishly painted. They held up little round shields. At the same moment voices grew loud, and dark people with spears came running down the slope. Cuzumarra and the others stood. Only close up could they see that the dark people with the shields were women. The spear carriers too were women, with little pointed breasts. They ran crouching, feet turned inwards, they ran on tiptoe, leaning forward, you couldn't see their sex as they ran.

The strangers could not understand their speech. Soon Cuzumarra noticed that their words were curiously drawled and similar to some languages in the north. The female warriors surrounded them, the women were smaller than the forest people who had guided them. When a warrior woman came forward, decked in bright feathers around her body and forehead, Cuzumarra pointed to the forest and gave to understand that they had been led here by people. The woman spoke to the others, who brandished their spears and shouted threats into the forest.

They started moving around the hill, the path was long and muddy, silence all about them, the women's feet made no sound. And when at one point Cuzumarra closed his eyes and heard only parrots squawking overhead, he thought he was on one of the many forest paths he had trodden these past months. But he opened his eyes, here were the silent warriors of the Women People, their backs and stocky thighs painted with blue and yellow snaking lines, heads shaved all around leaving a black knot of hair on top, red ribbons on wrists and above the knee. Sometime later the path became treeless. They approached an even higher mound, planted to the rear with maize and manioc, great palms swayed overhead and blue smoke rose between them. They heard shouts and dogs barking. And having ascended a broad, stone-paved path up the side of the mound they came to a spacious village, bigger and more populous than any they had seen since coming down from the mountains.

They walked past sturdy wide houses of wood. There were dry-season houses with mighty gable roofs almost to the ground, the side walls were low, the roof thatched with layers of palm leaves. Throngs of warlike painted women and women with infants in hip-slings moved to and fro among the houses. They saw darkskinned males carrying baskets, who avoided the strangers' gaze and went with downcast eyes. Farther on, facing a patch of grass, stood a scattering of low round huts walled with leaves, vultures tied to doorposts hopped about. They had built shade-roofs and walls on piles. The whole village, its houses stretching away in long rows, was filled with loud voices, but at their approach silence fell and the women drew back. No one looked at them.

When the strangers from the land beyond the mountains came down the northern rivers and stopped at villages, they were received as guests, welcomed and cared for, given presents when they left. The village of women was richer than any of those they had seen in the north since their escape over the passes, but here they were escorted like prisoners.

Below lay a wide, smooth lake, they had a good view of it, boats carried people to and fro, tall grass and clumps of reeds loomed over its mirror, the water gleamed very pale. The view opened up even wider as they were led around a bend in the hill, the lake lay behind them, in front the hill fell away gently, covered to its foot and beyond into the plain with fields and meadows, dotted with little huts and toiling people. Farther on there was scrub, then thick black forest like a frontier wall. But here and there breaches had been nicked in this wall, and pale water, endless water glimmered through. Their hearts leapt into their mouths, they forgot where they were, they thought it was the ocean. They conferred and traded questions.

And now one of the spearwomen grinned, pointed to the pale endless water and said proudly: "Amazon!" This was their river. The strangers stared at one another, incredulous.

Caught

THEN, WITHOUT A word, they were led one by one into a longhouse. It was a big empty structure, seemed to serve as a guesthouse. On the floor were sleeping mats with pretty patterns, several chairs lined the back wall, doubtless for chiefs, decorated with coloured strips of raffia. The chairs were shaped like animals, made of wood, you could see a black head with big ears, and eyes made of little mussel shells. Fat tufts of gaudy parrot feathers hung motionless from beams. Stout wooden rollers decorated with snaking lines lay in front of the chairs. These were neck rests.

By the time the strangers were all brought inside this big empty house, the last light of evening was shining through the door. They walked in, no women followed, they looked about them, observed everything, and waited. They knocked on walls, picked up chairs, beside the door they found empty arrow stands. Outside, a big fire had been started to combat the swarms of mosquitoes that invaded the dusk. Smoke drifted through the door, red flames lit up the room where the strangers stood and moved about. A few women warriors crouched around the fire, chattering and laughing.

Two men entered the house. They looked like men of the last tribe the strangers had come to. They brought gourds with a pale strong-smelling concoction. Then they brought flatbread, bananas and roasted ants. Cuzumarra asked what tribe they were from. They made no reply. When he held up a gourd and asked them what the brew was called, they glanced fearfully at the lighted doorway, gurgled and pointed to their mouth. The tongues were stumps. The shocked strangers squatted on the mats, tried to eat and drink. They feared poison, but they were dying of thirst. They slept only for the first part of the night, were then wakeful, fearing attack. A thunderstorm rolled briefly past. The fire outside burned low. When Cuzumarra strode angrily to the door a woman stood up, then others, twenty women. They barred the way with spears. Cuzumarra stood still, said not a word. It was quite chilly. They poked up the fire. He went back into the house. The men wrapped themselves in mats.

The companions spoke to Cuzumarra: "We have come far to the south. Who will listen to you here? These are Amazons, enemies of men. We are afraid."

Another: "They cut out the men's tongues. Why did you lead us here? Do you know what they will do to us? They won't spare you."

Cuzumarra could give no answer. Like them he complained: "We have come too far south. People did not listen to us. We should have turned back. Don't scold me. We must gather our courage. Perhaps we can sleep again."

"It's too cold, Cuzumarra. We'd rather sit and talk. We've been meaning to talk with you."

"Then talk."

"We had no courage, because you are the leader and we the led. Cuzumarra, we beg you, let us go. We are bewitched and cannot follow you."

He sighed: "What is your plan?" Now they would say what he did not trust himself to say.

"We fled from the Whites over the passes with our clothes and weapons. Our weapons we lost long ago. The forests stripped our clothing from us. Our skin is covered in sores. We have been too long away from our country, we have come too far south through this steaming forest, to this terrible river. It lies just over there, we feel it even in the night. It sends up a cold mist. We have no thoughts of home any more. We have lost everything, and everything has been taken from us by witchcraft. Sometimes we speak about the Whiteskins and what they have done to us and our families, then we forget it again, laugh, and are different men. We follow you, Cuzumarra, but we no longer know why we follow. Help us."

Another said quickly: "We are bewitched. We speak of the Whiteskins but without anger, as if they were just agoutis that dogs hunt in hollow trees, or dolphins. The Whites don't hurt us. Why do we no longer hate them, Cuzumarra? It was because of them we made this terrible journey, and now we laugh and drink and sleep."

Cuzumarra hid his face in the mat so they would not see by the light of the fire how he rubbed his forehead. "We shall turn back. We shall go back."

One said: "But I – I am not going back. Never."

Another said loudly: "I – I am not going back. I shall never go back."

A third: "I shall never, never go back. Never again shall we go back up into the mountains."

Cuzumarra listened in horror from under the mat, not showing his face, they spoke his thoughts. "And you would betray your kinfolk?"

They made no reply, it grew chillier, one smiled, one yawned, they stretched out. They snuggled into the mats. They slept.

Next morning two elderly women came behind the two captive men, stood outside the door and called to them: They would soon be brought before the queen.

They entered a big finely decorated house. On the mats many women sat with legs tucked under them, fists anchored at their hips. Some were young, some older. Along the wall three sturdy older women sat on the wide animal chairs and gazed sternly back at them. Nobody spoke. No one indicated that they should sit.

The woman in the middle had yellow circles on her cheeks. She asked Cuzumarra who they were. He replied. She asked want they wanted. He replied. When he spoke of the Whites she whispered to her neighbours. She bade Cuzumarra approach, stared at his ragged clothing, stroked the skin of his face, touched his golden ear discs. Then she turned to the companions. One by one they stood before her. She whispered about the strangers' hairstyle and skin colour. Cuzumarra was invited to speak to her in his own language. After he had done so the women engaged in rapid conversation. Finally the queen invited the men to take their place on the mats. Then everyone ate hot mash.

Following this interview they were allowed to wander as they liked through the village, alone or together. They were assigned an escort so they would know where they were welcome and where not. They saw the extensive village and its gardens, and not far off on a neighbouring mound was one even larger, and across the river there were supposedly many more villages of women. They were allowed to talk to men, only a few had been rendered dumb, most were crippled by mutilation of a leg, an arm or an eye. There were many children and nursing mothers. The men who were these women's lovers were nowhere to be seen. The women demanded of Cuzumarra and his companions more stories of their homeland and the Whites than any of the northern tribes had wanted. And after Cuzumarra's first comprehensive account of the Whites' cruelty, and the women, like the men of the north, had danced their spear dance and the women of the next village had answered their war cries, Cuzumarra beamed at his companions: "Are you content? Are you still afraid? They will lead us back. We have done what we had to do. The Whites will come down into this land and die in a trap."

They were not content. He realised with a shock that they really had no desire to go back. In the guesthouse where they lodged they turned on Cuzumarra: "What did you say to the queen? Again and again about the Tumbo and how they leaped into the abyss and about the defeat of our lord Tangasuku. We beg you, stop telling these stories. We believed them once. Now we don't believe them."

Cuzumarra thought they were mad: "All right, so we tell the queens and the women that the Tumbo are still alive and we live in peace with the Whites and we deserved what came." Cuzumarra grasped their hands and regarded them one by one.

"It won't do any good," they said, "to gaze at us one by one and hold our hands. We told you we no longer want to go back. We shall never wear the white shirt and coloured cloak again. You go to Cuzco, if you yearn for the Son of the Sun on his golden chair. We thank you for leading us over the passes. Otherwise we would have stayed the same as our parents."

"You are bewitched, my dear companions, can you not sense it?"

"Thank you. Once we were bewitched and now we are no longer. Cuzumarra, recall what they told us in the north and along the dark river? They said we must have been divided for the Whites to cast us down like that. They saw things more clearly than we did. For there is more to the story than what you tell, Cuzumarra: that the last great lord with his fivefold red headband had two sons and they allowed the country to fall into the hands of the Whites. Division was among us long before that, during the time when our parents and grandparents toiled and order reigned and leaders of five families and ten families were set over us."

Cuzumarra could not bear to listen, and wept. But when they tried to leave he held them back and asked: how had he injured them? For they were his good companions at home and in war and they had faced so many deadly perils together and who knew what more lay ahead, he had always understood them and did not want to misunderstand now and leave them abandoned to the wilderness.

So they continued, and said words that broke his heart: "We do not blame you, Cuzumarra. If we are to speak, please let us speak without causing you pain. We all toiled in the salt pans, as long as we had gold we made golden vessels, fetched red cinnabar from the earth for pigment, tended coca bushes and brought home the harvest three times a year. We never disobeyed. You say we were happy. We were neither happy nor unhappy. We hate the Whites, those wild jaguars, just as much as you, but they only destroyed what we too had no wish to keep."

Cuzumarra groaned in horror: "You summoned them! Your spirits invited them to our country!"

"Understand, Cuzumarra, we do not mean to wound you, don't hurt us, we don't hate you."

"You hate your country."

That roused them, they surrounded Cuzumarra and shouted: "Not true! We blame the princes, and if you number yourself among them, then you too. It is your fault that the Whites have conquered our land and murder us and burn our villages. What you did with the land was not good. No, Cuzumarra, all those roads and granaries, welfare for the old and sick and the apportioning of seed and harvest, all those things you speak of, none of it was good. Were we ever allowed to say a word that was not already approved by the Inca and the princes and the leaders he set over us? We never donned a garment that you had not accounted for. You tallied every mouthful that we ate. Are we bewitched when we say: that was not good? We suspected it already back in our homeland. You curse us as traitors. But Cuzumarra, you princes knew how to raise traitors among us so that we could never prevail. For there was nothing that bound the traitors to you. They could find nothing to honour. So they became wretches, criminals and traitors. You led them along this path, because you trained them to be parrots and monkeys."

"Were you not happy, were your parents not happy, was the empire not happy?" Tears coursed down Cuzumarra's face, and he sobbed aloud: "Why did you not say this earlier? Why did you come with me over the mountains? Why let me wander this way and that through the forest, and most of those who came with me perished in the swamps, why, for what? Oh, if only you had taken pity on me at the right time. Now I am here, alone, and curse my life."

So they all sat around him on the mats and tried to console him. They said he had asked them to speak out, they would stay with him and bring him as far as he wanted to go. He lay on the ground and would not be comforted. They feared that the women would become suspicious and accuse them. So they sat for long hours with Cuzumarra in the house. Then Cuzumarra roused himself again and for the first time heard and saw his companions speak and act with him as friends. They combed him. They made him cast aside his filthy rags and put on a skirt of raffia and a belt like them. They took him down to the lake to bathe. They danced around him in the water. He allowed himself to be led back up, where they painted him yellow and red. They drew snake lines over his arms, they said the women liked it.

That evening as they sat drinking with the warrior women around the big fire, there was peace among them. Cuzumarra desired to sleep. And as he slept he dreamed he was ill again, and was being lifted from a healing spring in the old country. Men manipulated and massaged his limbs. But when they stopped the limbs grew stiff again, finally the attendants walked one by one out of the room with their cloths and salves. But as soon as they left the room, he felt himself lifted off the ground, he flew and bowed down to the sun that rose over the mountain peaks. And because he was still bound around with bandages like a corpse, he flew on ever higher. The sun began to burn terribly. The heat was beyond measure. In fear he tried to stop. But the impetus of his flight did not abate. Smoke poured from his body, the bandages loosened and smouldered. Now he knew he was an offering and would be sacrificed. He was enveloped in hideous pain, suffocating.

He awoke. He stood up. It was dark. Ah, they were with the Women People. Oh woe, what the companions said to me. He lay down again, pulled the mat over him and fell asleep at once.

Dreaming, he landed on a big jagged leaf, next to it grew a huge flower, he flew into the flower, he was a hummingbird, he stuck his long beak in, the flower wouldn't let him, he stabbed and stabbed and then it held him fast, and he sucked honey, sweet cool honey, sweet honey flowed without cease into his beak, the beak was glued to the flower, he sucked and sucked, it was heavenly.

When he awoke the fires were out, dawn was breaking. He lay still. His companions slept on.

Inti Cussi the queen

CUZUMARRA HAD SPOKEN with Inti Cussi, queen of this place. Through two of his companions he informed her that he wished to travel on. She requested that he and his party stay. He consulted his men, they were afraid to refuse, but the sight of the men in this place discomfited them. Two of these men, toiling in a field of maize, had explained they were prisoners of war, and had to serve as slaves, each had had a foot broken to hinder escape. Women often stole secretly to some of the companions in their hut and lay with them in their hammocks, afterwards the women gave them some gift, but otherwise everyone kept away. They led a dull life.

The captives asked the strangers where they came from, whether their tribes still lived in the old places. And when the olive-skinned strangers said they would soon travel back, the slaves were astonished. They did not say it in so many words, but they emphasised their doubts: whoever comes here, stays here.

Cuzumarra grew insistent. He sent word to Inti Cussi that he would leave soon: would she tell him along which paths and how far towards sunset she could supply guides for him and his companions. Two days later, instead of a reply from the queen he received an invitation to come to her. He went with two men. They found her in the chief's house with a few women, seated like her on mats. Inti Cussi was a stocky woman of mature years, with round cheeks and full breasts, the women around her were young warriors. When they finished eating their mash and roasted fish, they talked.

The queen wanted to know more about the lay of their land. Cuzumarra spoke of the high wide plateaus with their fiery mountains that shake the earth, there are many towns, llama herds graze in the meadows, maize needs long periods of cold in order to ripen. He thought he should talk about the Whites as he had done before. He said: "On these high plateaus no mountain and no valley is without its sad memories. Once the towns of Pancerolla and Chuquita bloomed here, now the strangers have emptied them. Whoever follows in the war train of the Whites finds mountains and valleys full of the corpses of our people. They froze to death there."

But the queen was not interested in this. She asked attentively about weapons and the spirits that the Whites invoked to their aid when they set off to war.

Cuzumarra remarked: their strongest god is a man who was tied to a cross, they bewail his fate and demand that everyone join with them to weep for this god. They can bewitch you with just some wood from this cross, and everyone makes sure to have his picture always on their person.

Queen: Could you not have stolen such a picture?

Guest: They gladly gave them out, they forced them on us.

The queen was ecstatic: "And you? You have one?"

"And they sprinkle us with magic water when they hand out the pictures, and we must repeat magic words. Many of my own relatives tried this. But the god does not help us out of our servitude. Men who followed the Whites into war accepted the pictures and allowed themselves to be splashed with the water. They thought they could return to their fields and their families. And those who rose against the Whites took the pictures and let themselves be splashed with magic water. It did no good. The former froze and starved on the high plateaus, the latter enjoyed no support from the god in battle, even though they were brave and went into the fight with favourable auguries. None of our priests or medicine men has enough experience or power to win the god to our side."

"Then you will all be defeated for sure. So, Cuzumarra, how do you plan to resist the Whites?"

"We must try to win over one of their magic priests, and draw him to our side. We must take away their thunder tubes and horses."

She interrupted: In his country, did women fight?

Cuzumarra praised the women of his country: they were

brave helpers and always shared the fate of the men.

"You have spoken of your prince in former times, the Inca. Did he have a wife?"

"He had several. From only one did he have true heirs."

The women's faces darkened. For a long while they said nothing, so that Cuzumarra had the impression the conversation was over. But the queen stood up from her mat while the others stayed as they were, and seated herself on her chair. From there she bade the men, without looking at them, to tell more about the women of their country.

Again Cuzumarra praised them. If they guarded their purity well they were considered holy. Maidens who wished to consecrate themselves to the Sun God were placed in convents. Only they might prepare the bread that the Inca offered to the Sun God in his Temple of the Sun.

A long silence ensued.

"Did the Inca's wives also bring gifts for the god?"

"They did not enter the temple. The Inca with his fivefold purple headband sat there alone."

The queen inhaled with a hiss, breathed it out. She railed loudly: "I know your Inca! I know what he looks like. I asked about your women. The Inca's wife is not allowed in the temple. The maidens are in the convent and bake bread for the Inca when he makes an offering. And what do they do in the convent, these maidens? What do they do?"

Cuzumarra had not attended the queen in order to be assailed with questions about the women of his country. He could not rise. He said angrily: "Our convents are destroyed. I do not know what the consecrated maidens did in the convents. I am a warrior. I know they were closely guarded and were never allowed to look on a man. If, when coming to a place, you wanted to find the convent it was easy: on the walls hung the bones of young girls who had broken the commandments."

"For example, who had seen a man?"

"Certainly."

Cuzumarra caught a fearsome look from the queen. The

women rose from the mats. The audience really was over. Anger twisted the queen's face. She spoke no parting words. And Cuzumarra was so agitated he forgot to repeat that they were going to leave and how far would they be escorted.

It was only in the guesthouse, where he sat with the companions and conveyed to them what had been said, that the danger in which they lay became clear.

They were still in discussion when a shout from the doorway ordered him to return to Inti Cussi's presence. In the chief's house he found the queen on her chair and the women on the mats, just as he had left them. In her fury the queen had ordered that the eight men be taken before nightfall into the forest and killed. The women had calmed her. Then Inti Cussi wanted to speak with the men right away. Like an uncanny serpent that feigns sleep, her face showed anger and friendliness intermingled. Again they drank in silence. The queen thanked him for the report of his homeland, as if nothing had happened. She wanted to tell him about her people, of whom they had so far learned little.

She squeezed shut her eyes, which had been painted in the interval with black circles, there were circles on her cheeks and black lines led towards the corners of her mouth. She looked fearsome and alien, the women on the mats had black circles on their backs.

The queen said: "In the trees lives a big lizard, she has a round head and a strong tail. You would not think the tail is strong, but the lizard kills snakes with it. A woman planted maize, manioc and sugarcane, worms came and ate it all up. She planted again. Ants discovered it, an army of ants came, went all over the field and cut through the stalks. She had a pig. It died. A fox lived in the forest. She had a hen. The fox jumped up and killed the hen. So she sought help. Tayu Assu, the great lizard with the round head, came down from the trees to the woman's hut. She said: Tayu Good-for-nothing. Tayu walked with her in the fields, the worms dared not come out. Tayu waited at night outside the henhouse, the fox ran away. Tayu ran around the field and frightened the king of the ants. The woman saw her and thought Tayu Assu was the devil who brought her all this bad luck. She ran up and threw a big pot over the lizard. Tayu cast off the pot and hit the woman between the eyes so that she fell down. The worms and ants came and left nothing standing."

When she had finished her story the queen opened her eyes wide and stared hard at the strangers. Cuzumarra scorned the farmer woman as a fool. He was alarmed to see how ill-disposed Inti Cussi was towards him.

She strutted before her people: "We are descendants of queen Toeza. Men treated us like slaves, stole us from our parents, our parents sold us. Thus it was before the time of queen Toeza. Men took spears and bows and went to war. We women and children were left alone. We had to plant and cook and bear children. If a man grew rich he bought another wife, and the old wife was put aside. Toeza took a spear and her husband could not restrain her. She chose the black jaguar, Walyarina, who was stronger than a man. He became her lover. But the men played a cunning trick and killed him. So Toeza killed them with cassava poison. We came from the north. You know, Cuzumarra, since you came through the north, how the tribes fear us."

Cleverly he said: "They fear you greatly, and warned us about you, and dared not escort us here." The women laughed with pride, and whispered. Gourds were filled and drained.

Serene and proud, Inti Cussi spoke of her people and the Women People along the river: "We live along the whole Amazon river, on mounds, and to the south we are pushing into the forest. Men retreat before us. We make war on them, they always fall back. Look around, you can see Women People, settled and peaceable. Our villages are richer and bigger than the villages of men, where they lord it over women and children. We have houses, huts, weapons, farms, fields, gardens. From morning till night we toil in the fields and gardens, at fishing, hunting, looking after children. The heavy time of carrying and giving birth we suffer alone. We must care for the children, clean them, see that they learn. We build houses for them. So much work we must do because of them, and the houses and fields. So we have no desire to let wild animals destroy our work. When the men go off for months on their warpath, they can't expect us to sit calmly here, waiting to see who will be the victors and fearful all the while that we shall be stolen away and our children made into slaves. We are not as weak and stupid as our men think. We don't have to sit waiting for the men to win a war for us. We never sent them off to their stupid war. But since they are such forest creatures, skulking around and biting, we showed them that we too can defend what we have made. We are not hostile to men. We just don't let them live among us. Otherwise they would again conspire against us and tell fables to the women about how strong they are and how they must protect us and how we must sit quietly in our huts and care for the children. We give them no opportunity to come out with such fables. That happened in a few villages. We had to rescue the women. The moon, animals, plants are kind to us. They delight in us."

The queen said this with great pride. She asked about the fabric Cuzumarra was wearing when he arrived, how it was woven and dyed. The women were astonished. In his mountains they dyed with cochineal. "Thorny plants grow in our mountains, and little beetles live on them, the male beetle can fly, the females pierce the leaves and lay eggs. Our people set fires around the plants so that the smoke blows over them. The female beetles die after laying their eggs, they exude wax and cover the brood with their bodies."

Inti Cussi, deeply moved, made him repeat this. The women whispered together, seemed oblivious to Cuzumarra's presence. The queen gazed sadly before her. Cuzumarra had to repeat the name of the little creature and the plant. In a friendly tone, absently, she thanked her guest. He left. Later they brought him a painted gourd as a gift from the queen.

That evening was painful for the guests, for five of them were missing, and the queen would give no information when they enquired.

And when Cuzumarra lay that night with his two remaining companions, who feigned sleep, he learned that the five had not been taken prisoner or killed, but were sleeping in the slave huts.

Women had come to them and whispered with them.

Cuzumarra could not control his anger. He denounced the traitors, hurled imprecations at the two for not restraining their friends. The shame! Shame in front of the women! How they would laugh! And then: it is a crime, they have transgressed the law of this place. They will never let the five go, they will remain here as slaves.

One of the companions said: "That's what they want. And why should they not stay here, since they no longer have a homeland? In their own country they would be killed."

To this Cuzumarra could make no reply. Despair overwhelmed him. All night long he wished for death. He thought about the Whites, he was filled with disgust, they occupied his country, his people wandered about helpless and died, the Whiteskins sat in their houses, where was the Sun God, why had he forsaken them?

In the hut

AS THE QUEEN did not send for him next morning, he went to her. She was away hunting. He had stayed long enough. The old women he found in the chief's hut advised patience. The queen would let him go soon. That day several young warrior women came to them in the guest hut, led them without a word to little huts standing in the fields behind the great rows of village houses. They said the queen was away hunting, visitors had come from other villages of women, the men would be treated hospitably even in the huts. Cuzumarra and the two companions saw preparations for a feast and the brewing of beer from sugarcane juice, like the sora of their homeland. But the huts were slave huts.

The strong tireless warrior, who for many months had carried no weapons, stepped from his hut into the rippling field of maize, knelt down with his face towards the veiled sun, reproached himself and uttered the ancient prayer: "Mountains and plains all around, circling condors, owls and nightbirds, hear this avowal of my guilt."

He went down to the pond where his companions had bathed him when they removed the last of his clothes from home, and uttered the prayer again. He pressed his forehead to the ground, and washed himself. He cursed himself for giving in and allowing the companions to throw away his rags. When he saw himself naked but for skirt and belt he wept, dizzy with anger. This was a long dying. He asked after the companions. Answers were evasive.

Helpless he squatted by the slave hut on a mat. To the sun, now sinking low amid enormous yellow and red clouds, he sang words from home: "Cunac Nusta, lovely young daughter, here is thy brother who shatters thy vessel and hurls thunder and lightning. Queen, thou makest bright water to fall as rain. Water borne up to thee by Pachacamac, who set thee in thy place and gave thy soul to sing."

≈≈≈

Before evening two young warrior women came to the hut, sat with him and said they came from the queen. It was beyond their skill to weave fabrics as fine as those he had worn from his homeland. But they wanted to untangle and oil his hair and, as far as they could, to decorate his body.

He became hoarse with fury, swore: they were deceivers, they had already deceived his companions, they would attack the guests for breaking the laws of this tribe. They left, and returned with older women. They assured him no laws had been broken, and the young warrior women only wanted to make him up as best they could in their own style, since the queen had no means to provide fine fabrics. He mulled this over for a long time. All at once he felt limp and defenceless. He succumbed, glowering. They set to at once.

And again the old feeling overcame him from that long trek through the forest, where the sweltering heat never let up and dampness fell constantly on their skin, as they trudged for hours each day along narrow forest paths and fat opossums darted by, the homeland falling ever farther behind: I no longer know what I should say, I am losing my words, where is my home, we are bewitched, a sorcerer has stolen everything from me. The companions had said the same; they had foundered sooner than him.

The young warrior women plucked hairs from his body, even

removed his eyelashes. They had sharpened sticks of bamboo and wanted to trim his hair. He was reluctant. They scolded, called him monkey, forest-man. He yielded enough for them to start cutting. And as they proceeded, one on the left and one on the right, they followed their fancy. They shaved his head in front and at the sides, and left a long tail to dangle down his back. They had no pigments with them, it was already dark. They shook the mat. Each gathered some clippings and tucked them into her belt. When they left they said they would return in the morning.

He lay alone in the hut. A fire burned not far away. Even here he was watched. In disbelief he fingered his scalp. He was no longer Cuzumarra. They did with him as they wanted. Flocks of little bats flew like dry leaves, he could see them in the firelight. His hand kept touching his bare skull. "Circling condors, owls and nightbirds, hear this avowal of my guilt."

It was deathly quiet. Voices from the village above. Piping frogs.

He slept. No dreams brought relief.

≈≈≈

Next morning as he trudged across fields towards the village, he was witness to a dreadful scene. Four women were dragging a corpse on branches. And as they slowly passed, unaware that he was concealed among the stalks of maize, he recognised through the foliage the body of one of his companions. The face was smooth and peaceful, torso and arms likewise, one leg lay awkwardly and was swollen. They had broken his bones, he had died. The women screamed when Cuzumarra blocked the path. Soon warrior women came running, they seized him and dragged him aside. He demanded to follow the corpse. He wanted to sink into the earth with it. They grasped his arms and held him fast. When he struck out they flung him to the ground, trussed him and left him in the field.

Before noon women came and freed his legs and led him up to the village, arms tied behind his back, a rope around his shoulders. Inti Cussi came out of the chief's house and laughed when she saw him coming. Many women had gathered, they wanted to kill him. The queen burst out laughing when she saw his shaved head and the long dangling pigtail. On the side where they had thrown him down, his face was clotted with wet mud. His body and limbs too were smeared with dirt. She had him untied. He stood quietly, listening to the women's hostile screams. She waited to see what he would ask. But he would not look at her. When she asked if he would disturb the peace of the village again, he cast a cold glance and shrugged. So she had him brought into the hut and repeated the question. He said: "You killed my companion. Is that what you call peace? I came as a stranger, to warn you about the Whites."

She looked sympathetic: "Your hair has been nicely done. The mountains are far away. You will never see them again."

"I!" he cried.

"Cuzumarra, your empire is gone. Your companions told us more. Your empire no longer exists. Don't be angry. No one ordered your friend's death. They only meant to deter him from escaping and harming us. He died. We shall throw spears at the woman. You can watch, and see what is our justice, so that you'll do nothing bad to us."

"Where have you taken him?"

"To the foot of the mound. He has been buried. We'll dance for his spirit. Do nothing bad to us."

New moon

THEY CLIMBED TREES a little way from the mound, hacked branches, took honey from wild bees, brought some to him in the hut. He ate and was happy. It was honey to make you laugh out loud. The queen had said: "Your friends like it here. Our spirits are powerful and friendly." He wanted to know these spirits. As soon as the wish formed, there they were with him. He had stood before her pleading: "Kill me, Inti Cussi." She gave him some drink, then had him taken back to his hut. He did not go into the village for the trial by spears and the dance for his friend. Inti Cussi sent a message: "Your friend's spirit is appeased. Do you hate us?" He sighed: "No." It was the truth.

The two warrior women who had cut his hair in the doorway

of the hut tried to steal his soul. They had taken clippings, they glued them together with wax, spoke words over the figure, wrapped it in raffia, buried it in a maize field as they made their way once more to his hut at evening. He sat there happily and greeted them with a laugh. They painted him, admired his strength and waited to see what the next days would bring.

Ten days before new moon there was a stirring in the village. From neighbouring villages drums pounded constantly. Violent crashing from the great river rent the night. Birds and turtles were on the move, the first flood surges were lifting the waters.

Sukuruja, great Mother of Waters, entered the river. The river swelled and spread itself in happy pride.

And this was the time when young Amazons went raiding. The queen kept in seclusion, warriors fasted and danced for the ancestors. The noise of the river's rushing filled the valley. Preparations were completed. The warrior women were swallowed by the forest. The village grew quiet.

They returned three days before new moon. The first day was spent lamenting the dead and appeasing the spirits of the fallen. The warrior women purified themselves. Meanwhile, slaves and older women had erected huts in the fields and forest edge for the warrior brides. The captured men were accommodated in the guesthouse and nearby huts. In the afternoon of the feast day the strongest and most noble of these were fetched, bathed, oiled and painted, they were given cachembo, a cordial made of honey, and led to the festival ground behind the chief's house. The whole village was waiting there in a circle.

There was the dance of the recent ancestors, Toeza's exodus from the village of men. Sorceresses strutted in masks. The hobbled prisoners, those selected as strongest and most noble, were led out to the dance circle as an offering to the great spirits. They were felled one after the other by a thrown spear. The witchdoctors crouched and smeared themselves with sacred blood, sprinkled blood on the jubilant crowd that thronged forward, crouched, rubbed the precious life-sap over their own hearts and throats.

Now came the day of the new moon. For half the day a

thunderstorm rumbled, horrendous torrents of rain fell. Tumult and excitement still gripped the village. The young captives, having been bathed and oiled and painted and made to fast all day, were led by old women out of the guesthouses down the hill and across fields to the huts where their brides waited. During the procession and for the whole evening, deep drumbeats sounded without cease. They besought blessings from the ancestors and the spirits of soil and field.

The couples in the huts lived in isolation, kept from contact with others. Food was brought by older women with covered faces, who never spoke. When three weeks were up, the warrior brides fasted for a day and bathed. Then old women came to them with pigments and feathers, made up the young woman and the captive both. Now they could show themselves. On the day of the new moon the young women were welcomed joyfully back in the village. The celebrations were high spirited and noisy, with feasting and dances of thanksgiving.

But one group refrained from rejoicing and dancing this day: the young couples decked out with feathers on their heads and around their bodies, sitting near the great fire. The young women knew what was coming, but the captives were deceived. Although every tribe of men knew how the Amazons behaved, the young men still believed what they had been told by the old women and by the young ones they had embraced: they were chosen, they would be released. But at evening the young women, forbidden to cry or scream, were led amid loud cheering to the clan house. The men were killed before sunrise behind the chief's house.

Painted with their blood, queen and sorceresses and old women danced in terrifying masks under the new moon, danced through the whole village, went singing to the clan house and any house where a young woman sat, and smeared blood on the doorposts.

≈≈≈

Floodwaters had reached the mighty river. It roiled swollen and yellow-white. Waters stormed over the confining banks. It overwhelmed long winding lagoons, nearby watercourses, leaving devastation in its wake. It ripped chunks from the bank and bore them bobbing away. Great green tangles of grass rode the muddy surface. The river drove its waters on, spread them out to each side, drowned swamps and filled the broad flat valley with its silty mass until it came up against the hard-tamped flanks of the village mounds.

Cuzumarra was a guest at the feast. He looked around for his former companions, could see none in the village or at the feast. Cuzumarra importuned for his release. Unknown to him, following the return of the warrior women the queen had planned to have him killed before the feast: she blamed her guest for all the many losses they had suffered in battle. This intention receded amid the general mourning.

Inti Cussi entertained a neighbouring queen in the chief's house.

After the feast she had Cuzumarra brought in and said: "You told me about a little creature in your country that lives on a flower. It lays eggs, then covers them with its body and dies. Your report made us sad. Now you have seen something different."

He lowered his gaze. She was mocking him. He shook himself: "If you hate men so, why not just release them?"

"All life comes from the female. For that reason we must kill as well. You live by our great river. She is mother of the earth. She is hungry. Every year she comes seeking prey and must eat her fill. The forest too is hungry. The earth and the spirits need blood, or else they will not provide maize, manioc and sugarcane."

"Will you let me go, Inti Cussi?"

"Cuzumarra, where can you go, all alone. We are not cruel."

"I don't want to stay with you."

The queen's laugh rang out: "That's how women used to beg. I don't want, I don't want, leave me alone."

"Men have never treated women the way you treat us."

She shouted: "Never, you wretch? Never? And do you not still do so today? Buy them, sell them, force them, beat them? Never? Listen to you, coming here to make us cry with tales of your Inca, you, who made slaves even of your friends?"

Cuzumarra was happy that they conversed so frankly, and he gave a frank reply: "I have seen many things here with you women, and you have told me many things. I see how good it was that we met."

Hear, circling condors, this avowal of my guilt

WHEN CUZUMARRA AWOKE from the blow inflicted by a spear to his head, he was lying in a boat. It was gliding very fast. He saw trees but no riverbank. Women were sat in front and behind him. They were paddling. One stood tall at the stern, gazing across the water. He felt his forehead, touched blood, groaned. Then he slept again.

He recognised the strong young woman crouching beside him on the mat, watching him. She was the queen of the neighbouring village who had visited Inti Cussi. She nodded at him. He saw her lips move but could hear nothing. He sat up, his head lolled, he was in a little hut. She grabbed his head, pulled pith from his ears, now he could hear. "Where did your spirit go for so long, Cuzumarra? You were dead." An old woman holding a little basket knelt by Cuzumarra, felt his head. He noticed his forehead was wrapped in a soggy mass. "Inti Cussi gave you to me," the queen explained. "She thought you were dead, and was about to order you buried."

"You should have left me."

"I don't want you as a prisoner, I shall let you go wherever you want."

These were a different, a flourishing Women People that he now lived among. He no longer desired to strum his old tune of Incas and Whites. Not any more. Not ever.

On these mounds, a day's journey from Inti Cussi, they kept men as slaves and lovers. They ruled over the men, went on the warpath with other tribes, but were not hard and grim like those other women. They made their men look nice, groomed them, left them in the huts to care for the children.

The village children were all girls, well loved, they chased cormorants across cold fireplaces, they toddled and probed, mothers and older women carried infants, the infants carried kittens, bigger children ran down the hill to sit by a watercourse. There the big arcanhas, fish otters, whistled and slurped, they were fearless, otters and children regarded each other with little black eyes and whispered secrets, the otters had lovely shiny pelts and a long moustache. The big girls told about a dolphin:

"In the dry season, women moved their huts down to the fields to be closer to their boats. A shadow stole by night to a woman. Several saw it. It came out of the reeds and vanished. It had its eye on the drying rack with its maize and manioc, it was scared off. They couldn't see what it was because it kept close to the ground. The other women gave the woman a club, because she was afraid. Nothing happened, and this woman went farther into the fields, gathered firewood in the forest, dug roots and went out on the river to fish. Now and then she was visited by a man, she couldn't see his face clearly in the dusk. The woman kept these visits secret. The man sat with her behind the hut, she gave him mash, he asked her not to mention he'd been there, and she too was afraid to talk. She accepted presents from him. Later at night he came and loved her. She was nervous when he loved her, he smelled funny, and the overseer women when they came down to the fields asked what that smell was in the hut, had she been caching fish. But she denied going on the river. Once when he came she didn't recognise him and shrank back into a corner, asked if he was the ghost of a dead person or a sacrifice, or from the forest. He smiled and said no. Then she said they were going to hold the first harvest festival, and if she put all his presents around her neck and on her arms he should come too and protect her, otherwise they would beat her. The stranger became sad, said he wasn't strong, he couldn't protect her, he would ask his friends back home to come with him. And when it grew dark and he went away down the hill, she was frightened. His feet faced backwards. He was a dolphin. She didn't say anything to the others. She waited for him to return. He didn't. She wept, down by the river."

≈≈≈

These were rich villages, with their fields and houses.

The queen kept several men. Some built the fire. One knew how to cut her hair, and comb and oil it. One knew how to paint her. One had found out what songs she liked best. One played the flute.

She let Cuzumarra recuperate. When he was well again he left the hut and became her husband.

Cuzumarra no longer wanted to think of his homeland. But thoughts of the Whiteskins and their cruelties tore constantly at his vitals. The queen asked many questions, he had to tell stories, these were followed by endless female chatter.

In these rich villages they knew how to weave, though not as finely as in his country. He was given a handsome piece of cloth, and sat with other men on mats when the queen received visitors and wanted to display her wealth. They marvelled at his golden ear discs.

While the great river became sated and began to shrink and islands appeared, Cuzumarra grew fat and idle. Every morning like a cockerel he woke the queen with a favourite song from her childhood. He was given little to do. He avoided looking to the setting sun, anyway could descry no mountains or snowy peaks, no smoke from volcanoes. The land lay peaceful, green, endless green, a sea of green, and over there the great milky-white river flowed on, devouring field and forest; and sky, steaming air, heat of the day, cool nights. He stood as people ran around him and children laughed, women and slaves ground meal, wove raffia, carved spears, stood under buriti palms. His mouth, which every morning had to crow, now breathed: "Hills and plains all around, circling condors, owls and nightbirds, hear this avowal of my guilt."

On each shoulder sat a red parrot, the queen's favourites. They squawked in his ears, he rubbed his bare neck on their plumage. He smelled the queen's pungent oil with which he massaged her. His companions now lay mouldered in the damp earth.

And when the first Whites came downstream in heavily manned boats, and alarm drums pounded and people recalled his tales and his companions, he too had long since mouldered.

He lived long enough to see the next slaving raid. In the three weeks before the next new moon all laws were cast aside. The warrior women and their captives took every liberty, no one kept them apart. Since the captives were unhobbled and only loosely guarded, some managed to escape, but most stayed, these were days of delight for young men and women. They were fed with everything there was to be had. Guards were few, because the older women who had no children to tend were busy fishing, hunting, working in the fields. Day after festive day they had to roast, serve, prepare beer. The young men and women adorned themselves anew every day, played, slept, ran around in the forest.

Queen and overseers had heavy duties during these weeks. They were not allowed to be strict because, according to custom, the young warrior women ruled. There were legends that long ago the queen and overseers had to quit the village entirely for these weeks, to live in huts in the forest, and only at the new moon, just before the great feast of the warrior brides, were they welcomed back with much pomp and restored to their normal status. But the quarrels both major and minor that broke out among the young people in these weeks demanded the presence of the older women. For the young did not form fixed couples, the warrior women were allowed every freedom, and this was the cause of many quarrels. And because passions were already high the quarrel was sometimes bloody, and sometimes whole mobs of warrior women clashed. So now queen and overseers stayed in the village.

During the last days before the new moon, the one who once was Cuzumarra saw terrible deeds among these women. The time of parting for most grew near. Women danced themselves to a frenzy of rage and cruelty. They were like ships in a storm, rushing with full sail headlong onto rocks. They went down to the river to bathe, and as if they had flushed out a swamp creature and let it climb onto them and into them they cleansed themselves and were transformed into birds, turtles, bats, leapt shrieking at each other and attacked men, who were no less frenzied.

On the day of the new moon they built themselves huts in

the fields. Their cries rang out all night long, it was tumult, lust, savagery, pain, rage, it was considered holy, no one came near the huts that night, the children had to be calmed, many children were taken for safety well away from the village.

At daybreak masked priestesses led couples from the huts. Several of the young women had not cut their hair during these three weeks, they wore their animal stripes and pelts. Now they had stiff raffia woven into their hair. And as big drums pounded, young warrior women stepped out, each leading a man who had allowed himself to be tied up in play. Other women dragged a man, already throttled by winding his hair about his neck, laboriously across the fields and up the hill behind them.

That evening they performed the great armadillo dance. There before the great fire the armadillo leapt. The hero was called Rairu, he danced close to the powerful beast, it grabbed him, he had to throw away his spear, the beast struck his shoulder, he had to throw away his bow and quiver of arrows, the beast butted him in the chest, he had to throw away his shield, he fled from the strong armadillo and crawled around in the dirt, circling and again circling, the armadillo danced around Rairu, first on one leg and whooped, then on the other leg and whooped. It drove him towards the pit trap, he tried to escape, it grabbed his head and pulled him into the pit, and the pit collapsed on both of them, the big armadillo and Rairu.

The armadillo has disappeared!

The great armadillo has defeated Rairu!

The great armadillo has pulled Rairu into the pit!

And people clambered out of the pit, greeted forest, river, sky, greeted the moon. The great armadillo had vanished into the moon.

The young warrior women and their captives danced when the people sprang out of the pit. The women held spears, the men held shields, but they had to die.

Cuzumarra the fat warrior squatted with the queen on a mat. It happened that, unremarked by others, the spirit of the great armadillo came down from the new moon to him who was once

Cuzumarra and spoke to him: "And you, Cuzumarra? Stand up! Or is even that beyond you now? Stand up. Dance with them."

The great armadillo in the new moon, unseen and unheard by others, encouraged Cuzumarra to stand and dance. The queen squealed when he rose from the mat and pushed into the circle of dancers.

The spirit told him not to heed what they shouted at him, and to take a shield from a dead man. He did so, and stood with the men.

A monstrous howling greeted the new moon that showed itself in the blue between palm fronds. One by one, men fell, Cuzumarra among them.

Women thronged drunkenly towards the blood that sorceresses sprayed, the older women to regain their strength, the young women for their lives and children.

Frogs boomed from the swamps, a thunderstorm rumbled. The river flowed silent under pale moonlight. Through the nightdark fields, masked dancers paraded with clappers, feeding the ground with blood from gourds.

≈≈≈

Not long after Cuzumarra's spirit joined the armadillo in the moon, the Whites he had heralded came via the Napo river down the mighty Amazon. They were Francisco Orellana and a handful of armed men. With axe and knife they hacked their way through primeval jungle on the eastern flanks of the mountains. His band were starving, they came to the Coca river, they had no boats. They attacked villages, took boats. They captured young men, forced them into the boats, they had to row, weave rope from lianas and haul the boats over cataracts.

Orellana could not return up the Napo river, the current was too strong, so he pushed on, came to the Amazon. On the forested banks they saw women. Arrows showered down on them. The women took fright when the men in boats drew near to the bank. What monsters were these men, faces and hands yellow-white, their eyes flashed, they were hung about with a tremendous number of puzzling artefacts. The women hid in dense reeds and threw spears. They heard the giants yell, saw them fall down. Then thunder and lightning erupted from their tubes, the warrior women fell back and fled horror-struck into the bush. After the Whites disappeared and the warrior women hastened back they found wounded trees, shiny stones lodged deep down in the wounds. Some trunks had been torn apart. They were sorely afraid of the thunder from the tubes.

As Orellana proceeded along the river the current took him, and he did not want to stop until they came to the end. He gazed up at villages in amazement, the wide houses, carefully tended fields. No women came near his boats. The river was wide, the boats sped along. The Whites feared the night, when they had to make fires on a sandy bar or on a forested bank to keep away cold and mosquitoes.

The Mother of Rivers, Sukuruja, withdrew again. It was low water. Spirits that the Whites had disturbed stormed away from the valley. Witchdoctors had their work cut out to calm things, the spirits removed themselves from the river, from the forests, game animals fled, they were defenceless, lost, had to invoke every spirit, bring them gifts, implore them to stay.

All trace of Orellana was lost somewhere along the river. He passed through wilderness, always hemmed in by the huge walls of forest. At last no more land, no more trees. He floated between hummocks of grass and driftwood. Infinite horizon. Huge waves. The boats on the milk-white waters were driven backwards. The current released them. It was the eastern ocean.

And just as savannah grass closes behind fleeing game, so the forests and plains closed behind the Whites.

A sea wind from the east blew across the watery expanse and swept away all trace of the boats, blew, foamed: It was nothing! The wind eradicated their very breath.

As the mighty river rolled east it called out to the ocean: you strangers were never here!

≈≈≈

Part Two

THE KINGDOM OF CUNDINAMARCA

~

Charles, the Emperor

ACROSS THE OCEAN lay the continent of Europe, with its high mountains and lowlying plains. Its forests were mostly long since uprooted, its rivers neither large nor raging, you could travel along them for miles. They rarely burst their banks. They emptied into the ocean and a small sea. The land was not hot, hardly ever suffered storms and tempests. On this continent, in the south, grew trees similar to those engendered by the hot lands: palms, mimosa, figs, eucalyptus. In sandy regions there were even cacti that bore flowers and succulent fruit. But trees and flowers were all small and puny, most fruited only once a year.

Here and there hares, harts, wild swine ran, and wolf, fox, beaver, badger. But no bright jaguar crept through the grass, no turtles crawled on riverbanks. No crocodile, caiman, alligator thrived here. Birds nested in the trees, their plumage was dull, no parrots, no hummingbirds, vultures seldom seen, all were demure, their song pretty and heartfelt as if lamenting their lack of colour. And once a year, when this landmass grew cold, when the only defence of the trees against the frost was to shed their leaves and withdraw their life into the dark earth, when water fell white and solid from the sky and the earth creaked, then even the birds wearied of these lands. And restlessness stirred in them, they rose from plain and mountain, gathered in great flocks and headed south. They flew cloud-high back to their old hot homeland, to lovely wide rivers, plateaus and swamps, and returned only when they had recouped their strength.

≈≈≈

Men, too, lived in these lands. They had lost their colour, you could see blood coursing under pale skin. Heaven granted them less than its full light, even the stars that came out at night, hanging far back in the sky, sparkled less lustily than those of the south. Here people could only grow wan like ghosts. But they resisted Death. They grew strong, savage, immoderate. They were born of the struggle against Death. They roamed around in great armies. They broke out of their twilight lands.

In Brussels, the man they called the Emperor Charles the Fifth gathered about him in his palace all his counsellors, knights and nobility. He had to lean on a staff, rest his arm on another powerful man's shoulder. On his white head he wore a round cap of ermine, his frail body was warmed by a long sable cloak, the crowned pommel of a sword jutted at his waist. He spoke, standing before the raised throne, beside him his black-eyed son who neither could nor would live otherwise than he. His voice was barely audible:

"In this hall, forty years ago, my reign began. Soon my grandfather died, and I was elected emperor. I have made numerous journeys by land and water, and many wars have been forced on me. All this has cost me much toil, and is to blame for the wretched condition in which I now find myself. A too heavy burden lies upon me. I can no longer sustain it. I have done all that was in my power to do. If it has not been more, and has not brought good fortune, then I regret it. Now my son sits at my side. He is grown to manhood. Let him take up the burden that my shoulders can no longer bear."

He drank from a wine glass and spoke even more softly: "Be loyal to my son. Some among you I have wronged, I beg your forgiveness. I now quit this land of my birth."

There were tears in his eyes, and in those of the counsellors, knights and nobility, it made them feel better.

After he arrived back in Spain there welled up in Charles, that pale old man, a yearning for solitude and atonement. The monastery of Yuste lay nestled among well-tended trees, sheltered from the north wind. There he dwelled, once emperor, now merely an old man, listened to music, walked beneath chestnut trees. When he heard that some people he knew, not far off in Seville, held deviant ideas, he uttered a wish that they might be burned, and rued deeply that he had not burned a man who introduced many bad thoughts among his people: a monk called Luther. He felt himself nothing, a nullity. He arranged a requiem for himself which he attended, gazed ardently and with love into the open coffin that would receive his corpse. Other news reached the monastery, of dangers threatening Holland, so he wrote letters. But a dry wind blew over the land. The old pale man turned on his side, and expired.

≈≈≈

In those days the pale people were in constant ferment, concerning nations and imaginary things in the sky. Charles had had to raise armies to take part in these conflicts. For their arming and provisioning, and to ensure that they fought and died for him, he needed money.

In the German town of Augsburg lived rich people, of various families. They sent a man called Seyler to the court in Madrid, and advanced funds to the emperor. They had already lent him five tons of gold. He needed more. So he conferred on Seyler and, through him, on the Welsers in Augsburg the right to voyage to the new found lands they called the Indies, to make conquests there on their own account, and earn what profit they could. One fifth of all they might find there of gold, silver, pearls and precious stones would accrue to the emperor, and four-fifths to themselves, the Welsers, along with a certain strip of territory and its dusky inhabitants, whom they might enslave.

Ambrosius Alfinger

WHERE THE RANGE that the Amazon breaks through veers away from the west coast and sets its last peaks down by the lagoon of Maracaibo, there sits the town of Coro, by the sea.

Ambrosius Alfinger, a battle-hardened captain, was sought out by the Welsers and appointed governor of Maracaibo. He was to gather gold, and procure darkskins for sale in Coro's markets.

Accompanied by two hundred Whites, halberds, muskets, arquebuses and a number of horses and bloodhounds, Ambrosius Alfinger struck out from Coro. The men had flocked together for war and adventure, rapine and murder. In the lands of the

Whites, in Spain, Portugal, Italy and Germany they had nothing to lose. They were not bad men, they were what they were and could not be otherwise.

Alfinger came to the Perijá range. He had to cross it. His band began to go hungry.

As they climbed higher, the sun burned terribly. They had no time to make themselves understood to the darkskins. When they found the first village they stormed into huts, shoved the occupants aside. Once sated, they looked for gold. They chained the people and heaped loads on their backs. On they went.

Ambrosius Alfinger was a wiry man, already over fifty. He wanted gold and slaves. But he saw only desolate mountains. He descended into the valley of Upar. He sent envoys to the dark men and women in the villages, he wanted to trade. He was afraid they would run away. And so it was that unsuspecting chieftains welcomed him, led him into their houses, he squatted there with some of his companions. Meanwhile others of his men looted the place. Screams penetrated to the chieftain's lodge, they stood up to investigate. Then Alfinger rejoined the others and together they cut down the chieftains and the rest.

Entering the valley of Upar was easy, leaving was hard. The Sierra de Tairona was their next goal. The path into the mountains seethed with refugees. A poisoned arrow from an ambush in the rocks above hit grey Alfinger, who always had a friendly smile and organised everything without fuss.

The poison was known as twenty-four hour poison, because it killed within twenty-four hours.

Alfinger had himself lifted from his horse, all men are mortal, they ate of the Tree of Knowledge and so are cursed. They waited for him to name his successor. But they had to lay him beneath a tree, erect a shade for him, then the dark man who was his interpreter sucked at the wound below the knee. Blood flowed, the knee swelled and turned blue. The leg grew heavy, and three hours later the lieutenant came to Alfinger and said: "If you don't name a successor, General, there'll be fighting among us and we'll all die tonight." The governor demanded hot water, threw in some herbs and drank a large jugful. He had them remove the shade, covered his head with cloths, lay out in the sun. The band's chaplain appeared, admonished him, pointed to the swollen leg. Alfinger received the last rites. He had twelve hours left.

Then he sent three envoys out to find among the darkskins a witchdoctor skilled in healing. One of the three returned to report that the country for miles around was empty of people, the other two had gone higher into the mountains. These two were pursued for a while by Alfinger's men, and killed. So for an hour he waited in vain. In these long hours Ambrosius Alfinger suffered agonies. He grew despondent, and did not speak. When his lieutenant told him that the two envoys who'd failed to return must have deserted or been seized by the natives, he regained his smile. He understood. Now he could sit up, drink another jug of hot bitter tea. His head was still unaffected. Alfinger stroked his long beard:

"We were ill prepared. I had no idea they use poison in these parts. Otherwise I'd have brought along a proper witchdoctor, he'd have cut off my head and set it upon a horse."

The lieutenant, a brave man, joked along: "But would they obey you, with horse-legs?"

"What about horse-legs? It's not my legs you obey. It's not my boots you watch."

He summoned the dark-haired interpreter and asked if he had ever heard, among his people or elsewhere, that someone could be cured of the poison by cutting off his head and quickly placing it on a horse's neck. The interpreter stared uncomprehending at the lieutenant, but Alfinger spoke in earnest.

Then he asked the interpreter if he was prepared to hack off the leg with a sharp sword and an axe. When the interpreter made no reply, Alfinger asked if the lieutenant would perform this service. The lieutenant summoned the chaplain, and the chaplain admonished Alfinger not to cling to this life. Whoever dies here is surer of Heaven than someone dying back home, for he dies as a warrior for the Holy Church. Alfinger breathed easier: this was his view too, but he owed the Spanish Crown large debts, and maintained that a warrior shouldn't be allowed to die without a struggle, and once again desired the lieutenant to hack off his leg. The lieutenant was accompanied by two soldiers with arquebuses, Alfinger knew they would shoot him unless he died soon. The lieutenant waved dismissively towards the poisoned leg that lay exposed and swollen green-blue all the way to the hip, and said: it's too late anyway. The chaplain agreed, and set up a loud rapid praying. Now Alfinger named the lieutenant his successor, in order to be rid of him. So the lieutenant, content, withdrew with his arquebusiers. Alfinger smiled his old smile, told the interpreter to lay an arquebus by his side, and whispered with him.

The interpreter soon reappeared at the place where the general lay and the chaplain prayed, accompanied by a mercenary skilled in ironworking. This man brought a crucible, a long stout iron bar, and tongs. He heated the bar in the crucible until it glowed red. Then he handed Alfinger the tongs. The chaplain followed all this nervously, peering over his book. Now he held the book close to his eyes, stopped praying, and his breath hissed. Smith and interpreter clenched their fists, eyes started from their sockets. Scorched flesh sizzled and smoked. Alfinger sat up straight and burned the flesh away from hip to knee. When he was done and threw down the tongs and iron bar, his face was rigid, and both thought him dead. But he pressed his back against the tree, remained upright, and his eyes blinked. An hour later he had tea brought, and looked for the sun. It was about to set. His hand felt for the arquebus.

As dusk fell the lieutenant came with torches and a litter made of branches. But Alfinger was sitting upright staring straight ahead. The chaplain crouched at one side, the interpreter at the other. Alfinger ordered that two mercenaries should make a fire nearby and keep armed watch all night. The lieutenant obeyed. In the night Alfinger, set like a stone under the tree, had hot oil poured onto the wounds. The chaplain slept by the fire, it was morning before he took up his book again and stared in horror at Alfinger sitting there rigid, then made haste to resume his prayers.

Early that morning the twenty-four hours were up. The governor had himself carried on a litter into a closed tent, chewed coca leaves that the interpreter had slipped to him in the night. They helped him sleep. At noon the lieutenant stepped warily into the tent. The chaplain was asleep by the bed. In the gloom, Alfinger beckoned to the lieutenant and in his old mild voice asked for a report.

Two weeks later they broke out of the eastern valley of the Sierra de Tairona.

They led the general's horse behind his litter. His leg was stiff and withered, he shuffled awkwardly on two crutches. They had to help him mount the horse. Though they took men, young women and children with them and butchered the old, although they left behind nothing but deserted and burnt-out villages, news of their coming spread into the mountains and down into the western valley. But they made abrupt detours and came upon plenty of unsuspecting places. On the western slopes of the Sierra de Tairona they had several hundred captives. These they drove before them, roped together. Alfinger ordered his second lieutenant to take them on to Coro. He detailed twenty arquebusiers to go with them. One third of the captives reached the Catotumbo river, which flows down to the lagoon of Maracaibo. Ships from Coro met them there. Hundreds lay where they fell in the mountains.

≈≈≈

Alfinger camped in the hot wide valley of the Magdalena river. He calculated according to his experience: for every consignment of captives you have to catch five or ten times as many. Better to search for gold.

He sent captains with small detachments across the river. They came to hilly districts along the Porce. They were told of people who lived in swamps and in trees, there were the Nutubes and Tuhames, they were rich, tilled fields, wove cloth and had a bit of gold too. But little came back with them. So Alfinger had himself set upon his horse, chewed coca leaves and ordered a march eastward, up the valley of the Lebrija.

They came to a populated place. Alfinger had all the inhabitants seized and detained in a stockade that he ordered built. He explained to the people that anyone who wanted to be released should pay gold for himself, his wife and his children. To encourage them to prompt action he withheld food until they brought the ransom. Some of the people sent to their houses to fetch gold, and were freed. But once they were back in their houses, Alfinger sent Spanish and Italian mercenaries to seize them again, and again they had to buy their freedom. A few suffered this three times. Those who had nothing to bring were left in the stockade, where they starved.

He imposed method on the hunting of fugitives. Any captured in the mountains were thrown from a cliff. Those cornered in scrub were driven thirty or forty strong into a straw house, where he had them burned. He unleashed bloodhounds. These knocked dark people to the ground, mauled and gnawed them.

Dogs chased a sick woman who was carrying an infant. They caught up with her in a village, she couldn't flee. She hid in an open-walled hut and hanged herself from a beam. She hanged the infant from her feet. Dogs pulled it down. Men of the cloth accompanying the band happened upon them. They found the dogs with the child, prised it from their jaws and baptised it before it died.

Alfinger's reputation as the cruellest of the cruel preceded him. His soldiers thought it unnecessary to provide food for their dogs. They drove along, like calves or pigs, several savages that they traded among themselves to throw to the dogs. Once Alfinger came to a place that seemed prosperous. Without further ado he seized seventy people, had both hands amputated, and strung the seventy pairs of hands on a pole in the marketplace so that all could see what to expect if they kept gold from him.

With fire and sword they swept onward. He crossed the mountains of Velez. At last a more copious stream of gold came flowing to him. A massive slave transport set off for Coro, over a thousand strong, the people were of different skin colours, on the heights and in the valleys the tribes were like species of parrot. His band worked at full capacity.

Who was Ambrosius Alfinger? White, a man, a hunter, no

worse than others. Belligerence was his backbone, whenever he managed to defeat someone he felt good. Fame, power and gold were his heart and blood. The dark people were sand beneath his feet.

On the way down from the cold Velez mountains he said to the chaplain: "We must return to Maracaibo. Every day they pour oil onto my wounds. But the leg grows worse."

And as they marched in the mountains between Pamplona and Cucuta – Alfinger dry as a stick, armed men before and behind, bearers laden with looted gold as far as the eye could see – he had to be lifted from the horse. The bone had been scorched. He was carried at night into a cave. He ordered the looted gold to be piled at the entrance to the cave. His captains cursed one another, swords drawn. One captain, feeling disadvantaged, wanted to attack the treasurer and take the king's fifth for himself. When they heard Alfinger calling for the loot to be brought nearer, they closed ranks and explained that the entrance was too narrow. The general demanded to be brought outside.

He could no longer stand, he was holding the loaded arquebus under his arm. As they carried his litter out of the cave by the light of torches, the bearers stumbled. The arquebus under his arm fired, the ball buried itself in rock. A chunk of stone came loose, and crushed him and the two bearers.

Next morning they pushed on in a forced march. Monks and chaplain positioned themselves around the king's fifth and Alfinger's share, carried by darkskins under the eye of the treasurer. The captains foamed like jaguars, and hoped for a defile where they could tip the transport over the edge after first looting it.

But the mountains fell away. The land became flatter and flatter, they sat on their horses and played guard over the transport.

The place where the tyrant Alfinger died was given the name Miser Ambrosio.

On the Magdalena river

THE WHITES, THOSE savage warlike tribes of men, had even more people.

Rodrigo Bastidas was granted the region from Cape Velez to the mouth of the Magdalena river. The town of Santa Marta owes its existence to him. His companions speeded him to the next world.

Garcia de Lerma was drawn into a fight with the Tairona. These were a flourishing people. After a while there was no more trace of them. Or of Garcia.

Fernandes de Lugo. As his deputy he appointed a lawyer from Granada, a man in his late thirties, Gonzalo Ximenes Quesada. Lugo died at the start of an expedition. Meanwhile Quesada had landed up in an enterprise that would draw him deep into this country.

≈≈≈

Quesada had a thousand foot soldiers and a hundred mounted men. They were Europe-born and couldn't survive back there. The northern lands were overrun by ruthless kings, princes and mercenary warlords. Many, young and old, were dead and mouldering. So they thought it best to go to war in some lord's service. Spain was half covered in fields of weed. Noblemen tramped with begging bowls, while monks sat a hundred thousand strong in splendid monasteries. For the pale people knew nothing of sky or earth or animals or plants, only of a god in farthest heaven; but priests in their millions could not bring them to follow his commandments.

For some time a profound restlessness had stirred in them. They could not but swarm out across the whole world. They had to set sail and seek adventure. Everywhere they found new lands. On and on they were driven. They couldn't explain it; they said: we must conquer a new empire for the Spanish crown, we must find gold, we must spread word of our ghostly god. But they were driven only to discover more lands, seas, rivers, tribes, to find oblivion and lose themselves.

Ximenes de Quesada had a thousand foot soldiers, a hundred mounted men. He ordered one of his officers to sail up the Magdalena river and rendezvous with him in the mountains.

Captain Alcobazo climbed aboard. He had five ships and two

hundred men. The chaplain blessed the ships, the men sank to their knees, prayed to the Virgin. For days from the river's mouth they saw only marshland, in the middle of the river were large tree-covered islands. They had brought darkskins from Coro, who showed them what fish could be eaten. When the river narrowed, huts of palm thatch stood near the banks. The people were copper-coloured, had never seen Whites, were poor and gave them everything they wanted. They prostrated themselves before the Whites, said they were Coygaba, humans, come down from the mountains to fish.

They were asked about gold. They said: in the mountains are many people and much gold. The people are all born from rocks. The Whites could only laugh.

They made their leisurely way upriver, no need to hurry, Ximenes de Quesada would surely make slower progress through the mountains. Snowy peaks on their left glowed evening red, the moon's disc rippled yellow in the mirror of the water, gloomy shadows fell across the horizon, green forests became blue, black, became a great dark cavern. They sailed over a wide lake, and people they came across on an island next morning said: a river called Cauca comes from the south, it makes the wide lake, the Cauca has a long valley, many people live there. But the ships continued up the Magdalena. Sandbanks became more frequent, crocodiles lay in packs, stared at the brigantines, the strange tall ships with yellow sails.

The primeval forest around them grew taller, islands were overgrown, some were a single mat of green and grey, here and there little monkeys hung on coconut palms and fled into the treetops. The flotilla carried the White mercenaries upriver, five ships one behind the other, on the first and biggest Quesada's captain Alcobazo, the ensign of the Spanish Crown flapping overhead. The sky was wide and open, the river broad, no voices challenged them, they pressed on unhindered. Land, river, air, nothing offered resistance; land, river, men all drew together, feeling, touching, they knew nothing of one another, all was unfamiliar. But the Whites were cheerful, the going was good.

Who would raise a hand and claim: you were never here? For sure we shall leave traces behind us.

Mountains rose higher on all sides. It grew hotter. The level plains were behind them. They were besieged by forest. But they were a flotilla, five ships, two hundred mercenaries with muskets. They sang, shouted, played cards. Alcobazo was no martinet, the men liked him, he won't cause trouble when it comes to parcelling out the loot.

Trees stepped into the water, gnarled roots rose out of water. Banana trees with enormous leaves, you wade ashore, clamber up to them, pluck fruit, break leaves to use as sunshades, throw them down on the water. Trees loomed everywhere, they stood in the way of the ships. The river was unsure whether to flow or become forest. At night the sky opened above them, displayed the dreadful glitter of its stars. Forest pressed in on all sides like a fortress.

The river lost its water. They began to take soundings, had to sound the bottom constantly. The wind had long since dropped. They rowed and struck bottom, dared not row too hard, too strong a pull could land them on a sandbank. Mud and sand swirled from the riverbed. Dead crocodiles floated belly-up. Whoever was not rowing or steering stood around the leadsman. But no need for a plumbline now, you can touch bottom with a pole.

Fear gripped the officers. Captain Alcobazo was a poor dissembler. He ordered a service of rogation, the chaplain stood beside Alcobazo at the sternpost of the leading ship and held a cross over the shimmering water. The sun sucked up mists, which a breeze wafted away to the mountains. They made the ships fast to a grassy islet and waited for water. Bad days came. Alcobazo lay in a fever, the officers climbed ashore and tried to shoot game in the forest. Before they had gone far they were unnerved by the profusion of snakes.

Alcobazo ordered: wait. Then Heaven took pity. Clouds gathered one morning, the thunderstorm that broke lasted all day, it withdrew into the mountains and then raged again in the valley. They had never heard such thunder, never stood in such roaring torrents of rain. Twice in succession lightning struck, first close by, then on the captain's ship, a mast was shattered, the flotilla's chaplain was killed along with three darkskins he was leading at prayer. Immense torrents fell from the sky, along with cool winds. By evening they wanted to move on despite the rain, they were not bothered by the chaplain's death, all their thoughts were of danger and rescue. But the captain and all available men went ashore next morning, and buried the chaplain at the forest edge.

Then they hauled in the anchor lines, and the ships, now riding high, glided on once more. Profoundly content they watched the forest recede and sink back. The wind that rose was strong enough to fill a sail, their ears rejoiced at the chink of cleats and the hum of rigging. They sailed through the day. Next day, the wind having dropped, they rested. Then when they set off on the third day, the two lightest vessels in the lead became stuck. The others came to the rescue. They had ventured into a side channel. They toiled for days to drag them off, to no avail. Impatience and fear mounted again, they lacked fresh manpower. Amiable Alcobazo became angry and peevish.

There were five ships, two had to be abandoned in the mud of the side channel. The remaining three were now heavier and more cramped. There was nowhere to lay the sick. There was talk of setting them ashore for collection later, but they protested loudly: no able-bodied man will want to stay with us, and anyway the fit cannot be spared. When deaths were reported Alcobazo made no enquiries, the cloth-wrapped bodies were swiftly buried.

At last the current came faster, the banks grew higher, the river flowed through rocky terrain, there was foam ahead. Then men from all three ships confronted tetchy Alcobazo, who now never removed his breastplate, and demanded to know how much farther they were to go. He who had always calmed them now screamed: anyone who wants can quit the ship! There are the mountains, anyone who wants can climb them!

This enraged the men, and several were of a mind to use the opportunity thus offered. They wanted to leave the river and the hot valley and make straight across the mountains towards Quesada. When the captain heard of this, he too wanted to come along. He was oppressed by arguments with the sick, disgusted with the stinking pestilential ships. He set himself at the head of the men. They were pleased. He appointed a deputy to oversee the ships. They would make a foray into the mountains, be back in a week or two. Meanwhile the sick should be tended, the able-bodied can recoup their strength.

A week later they were back, the march through jungle had exhausted them, they had met no one, there were no springs of water, they were near starving, and when Alcobazo asked along the way if it would not be better to go on by ship, they turned back without a murmur.

≈≈≈

But back on the river in its rocky course, they suffered shipwreck. They attacked some rapids and overcame the first. Again and again they tried to defeat the second, which was higher and wider. The lofty banks were fringed with meadows and majestic forests of palm. They worked sails and oars and levered the boats along the rocky riverbed. Oars gained no purchase, there was no holding the vessels, the current swept them back. Some crewmen sat at the oars, others stood on deck and shoved and coaxed the sturdy vessel with poles, naked to their loincloths. Most of the people went ashore, coiled ropes around shoulders and chest, and hauled from the banks. These were covered in sharp stones, it was hard to keep a footing. A line broke, flinging the men on that side like berries on a twig down into scrub. The ship lurched. It swung sideways. For a moment the haulers on the other side were relieved of the strain, then all at once the rope was torn from their hands and any who did not let go flew in an arc out over the river. The ship was caught by the current, swept like a toy back over the lower rapids hurtling headlong downstream with its masts and flapping sails. Above the constant roar of the rapids there was only a feeble sound when the unlucky vessel, Spanish ensign at the masthead, crashed against the rocky bank. Prow in the air, broad stern leaning awkwardly, it groaned and split apart.

Now debris swirled, screams rose unheard from the sick. Below deck, green thick water swirled up. Men could be seen clinging to masts and sails. They tried to swim, but were seized and dragged under by the current. Downriver they collected bodies and the injured.

Next day they tried again with the second ship. This time they were lucky. To demonstrate his resolve, Captain Alcobazo himself stood on deck and directed operations. And above the rapids they floated in a calm basin between meadows and palms, and rested and readied themselves to haul the other ship up next day. To give courage to those in the lower ship, Alcobazo spent the night with them.

They were startled awake when the endless roar of rapids was overlain by a terrific crash. Men screaming close by. And when torches were lit, the ship they had hauled up yesterday was listing helplessly not far off, beam-on across the current, its rigging sprawled like dead limbs. At the sight of this and the helpless men spinning in the water, and amid the din all around him, Alcobazo wept and beat his breast. They rescued what they could in the dark. They laboured by torchlight until the triumphant sun returned. The rapids roared on.

Slowly they realised that this place was evil. This is what it will look like, the place where we meet our fate, we who came together from Spain, Portugal, Switzerland, Italy. This is how the sky will show its face, how purple clouds will build, how water will gush when we all shall perish. Sky and water were not for a moment different from anywhere else. Fear penetrated their bones.

The river foamed and played around low cliffs, trees thrust mighty crowns into brightness. The men clutched their amulets. They pressed around Alcobazo.

The day after the burials the decision was taken: whoever can walk will follow Alcobazo up into the mountains. The sick will remain on board with a handful of men, who must swear to the captain that they will not abandon their post. The captain will march slowly and leave trail marks in case those left behind want to follow. They were instructed that, unless the situation changed, they should sail as quickly as possible back downstream to the coast.

Alcobazo marched off with fifty fit men. From the nearest high point they looked down on two ships, one broken and one whole. They knelt and prayed: forgiveness for themselves, deliverance for those below.

≈≈≈

Endless rain and storms lashed the valley of the Magdalena, the men allowed the flood to drive the ship, their meagre provisions became a soggy mess. They railed against Alcobazo and Quesada and this whole expedition that had brought them here from Mexico, from the islands and security of their homelands. Under the vigilant eyes of the sick they steered out of the mainstream to the bank, climbed ashore with muskets. Earlier they had asked the sick: who wants to be shot? and administered a good number of coups de grace. The terrified cries of the last survivors rang out behind them as they climbed the bank. They took no notice. They knew that what lay ahead of them was just as bad.

And in truth: two weeks after Alcobazo's departure not a single man survived of those he had left behind, whether able-bodied or sick.

In the thorny scrub where they lay motionless and no longer hungered, those who once were fit provided feasts for beetles and worms and birds. Above the silent ship flocks of vultures wheeled, rose on heavy wings, and scattered the bones of men driven here out of their dreary homelands.

In rushing water, in treetops, in dank thickets they met their end.

Trek over the mountains

BUT QUESADA AND his people marched on, those brawny intemperate men. Europe sent them across. They knew nothing of the others' demise, and even if they had known they would have said: "Why talk of that?" and marched on.

Quesada, deputy to Lugo, governor of Santa Marta, who had meanwhile died – for here life and death are swift, things are born and destroyed, rivers fling their waters about and grow dry, heat embraces the mountains and shatters their stone, forests grow tall and tree-ferns slowly decay into bog – Quesada climbed into the mountains of Santa Marta. He passed with his army through the southern part of the valley of Upar, traversed not long before by the tyrant Ambrosius Alfinger.

Who was Ximenes de Quesada? A White man, church and king his backbone, fame and glory his heart and blood, he was no better or worse than anyone else. What it was that drove him, he knew as little as the others.

The country became hilly. Two rivers flowing from the south discharged into a big lake, Lago Zapatosa. The ground quaked as they marched, horsemen, carriages with small cannon, and infantry. This was a swampy region. The two rivers drained vast amounts of water and carried it seawards, but the ground still oozed wetness. The army granted itself no rest, they were drawn on by the blue line of mountains, the snowy peaks, they wanted solid ground for their feet, for the horses' hooves and the wheels of carriages. Here and there wide mirrors of water lay on the earth. It stank.

They had come together for adventure and violent deeds. In the lands of the Whites, in Spain, Portugal, Italy, Germany, they had nothing to lose. Come, you new found land, hand over all your riches.

The blue mountains drew nearer, very slowly the ground rose. The troop was glad to enter the forest, leave behind stinking water and fleshy plants with their poisonous sap. They camped above the swampy plain, which pursued them still with feelers of mist. They dried out, men, horses, blankets, vehicles, cannon and muskets. They found springs of sweet water.

They camped around a fire. They had food and drink, darkskins brought unfamiliar roots from the forest, one was called cracha, it was celery, it calms your hunger and keeps you alert. Butterflies filled the air, and all around rose palm trees taller than they had ever seen. Slender as reeds are the curas palms that clump together like a bush, then stretch insatiably higher and higher into the boundless light to unfurl their fans. The darkskins knew every tree, every species, clambered up trunks, scraped them, brought down handfuls of yellow wax.

Mercenaries chatted with a monk by the fire. "You, monk, you think to fool us. You can fill your belly in Spain, what do you look for here? You want to grab the best morsels for yourself."

Another: "Truly, priestling, there's no pope or king here to protect you."

"Monk, you're here to steal souls. What did you ever do in your monastery but sleep and guzzle and drink? A belly like yours doesn't grow from nothing. How many girls have you dandled on your knee? Wish my dad wanted me to be a monk. But I had to cart dung."

Another: "I tried it with my axe, the carpenter's trade, cut posts and doors and rafters for them. By the time you're journeyman you're bandy and timid. And by the time you make master you've already sold your blood to your master, you're just an empty shell. I'd like to burn their rafters, knock down their doors. A soldier's life is fine. You can lord it over people."

They bawled songs. The celery they ate, the wine they drank had their effect. They wanted women. Governor and captains were pleased: such men would not be ground down.

Patrols sent by Quesada into the mountains brought bad news. The darkskins knew only narrow paths for single file, the forest was locked tight, the patrols in rags, their hands scratched to pieces. So Quesada conferred in his tent with his deputy and the monk. Amid jaunty music of drum and flute from the campfire, Quesada advised – retreat.

"I have experience of these forests. We must catch savages, but they know how to hide. They rely on thorns and undergrowth. I have staked much on this venture. If I go back with nothing gained and everything lost, I shall never leave the debtor's prison. The Crown will look favourably on my caution and avoidance of rash acts."

The monk nodded: "The Crown has little love for bald mice. If you have doubts, governor, turn back and preserve your money and the Christians that we already have."

"And you?" the governor asked Barreda, his senior captain, of whom he was afraid.

"I am obliged to you for making me your deputy. I wouldn't want to deputise on a retreat. Do for me what you did for Alcobazo: two hundred men and weapons. Wait around while I give it a try."

"Do you have nothing to lose, no bride, no wife at home, no father, no mother?"

"All of those, sir governor. Still I want to try."

"But why, captain?"

"I want to, want to."

"That is no answer."

Then there was silence in the tent. In the clearing, drums and flutes played without pause, horsemen charged by, gunners fired test rounds, the Whites knew what was coming, were ready for it.

The captain: "Give me two hundred men."

The governor screamed: "You heard what I said! You understand nothing. I'll send you off to find Alcobazo." When he stood up he ordered them to keep the discussion to themselves.

Two days later Barreda noticed preparations were being made to break camp without informing him. He went around and by evening had gathered two hundred men. Next morning, while drums and pipes sounded for decampment and tents were being struck, he set off eastwards at a fast pace with his foot soldiers.

The governor summoned the notary royal to his tent. "My deputy Barreda is a scoundrel. He has mutinied."

"Where do you intend to aim for across the mountains, sir governor?"

He had to admit, as the notary gaped in astonishment, that he planned to retreat. The conversation ended with advice from the royal clerk to assume misunderstanding on the captain's part, and to request his prompt reappearance at the camp together with his men. This happened, and Barreda found himself back in place. No quarrel occurred between Quesada and his deputy.

On the morning when they finally struck camp, Quesada, under duress and filled with loathing, had the whole army assembled for Mass, and spoke after the priest: "These forests and mountains are a wall, separating us from an empire of gold. You want to press through, and you shall press through. Let no one say I failed to do my utmost to bring you to the goal."

At this point he could speak no more for rage. Barreda saluted with his sword and took over: "Some may already have asked yourselves: why did we have to leave home, why is gold so rare back home while here the heathen pick it from the sand? Heaven was mindful of us poor people when it hid gold in faraway sands. The rich are born rich, they inherit, they're kings and princes, dukes or merchants. While the soldier who puts his life on the line must stay forever poor. For him there's only the Kingdom of Heaven once he's dead. But it's not so. Soldiers have fists and courage and horses and muskets. We can shoot, and take what comes to hand. That's justice. You all know what lies ahead. You would not be soldiers if you thought that all you have to do is sit at table. It can't be done without war. The war starts now. Holy Mary be our guide!"

Then they set off.

They faced forest, thorns, insects, worms, scorpions, heat, damp, hunger, thirst, exhaustion. They had brought blood-hounds along, to hunt savages. The quartermaster set trusted men around the hounds so they would not be slaughtered and eaten. When something edible was found it was given first to the riders, so they would not butcher the horses. The darkskins, who knew the paths and understood the forest, were treated with respect. The Whites learned like them to pluck fruit from tall trees and grub for roots with sticks. During the first two weeks there were losses to desertion. After that everyone realised they had to make it through, or else they were lost.

Away from the swamps and quaking ground and into jungle, thorn bushes and liana-hung scrub. If any were not soldiers before, they were now. They were Whites, born from the struggle against Death, they saw neither forest nor thorns, no worms or scorpions, they felt no heat, hunger, cold. The forest kept silent while blades and murder raged within. They struck and stabbed, hacked and throttled, killed and died. Quesada and his captain Barreda drove the army out of the valleys onto high mountains. They chose the high road so they could look down into the valleys. It wound up and down, from steaming heat to frost. Once the jungle had torn their clothes to shreds, leather became superfluous. They put straps, sheaths, cuirasses, armbands to good use, sliced them up to cook and eat. Sometimes Quesada had to halt for days in high places, the bleeding sickness was on them, they were too weak to continue. Wandering darkskins like charming butterflies approached, some big and strong, some of the Coygaba tribe that Alcobazo had encountered, who indicated: our people are far away, they have gold and much to eat. They were tied up, and made to lead the way.

Vultures followed their progress. Jaguars stalked the forest, took weak men from their hammocks. Many stumbled and were not in their senses, but they marched and obeyed. The soldiers had to be restrained from cannibalism. On rocky cliffs cacti grew with flowers of yellow and white. They implored the Virgin of Pilar. They boiled tree-bark and tried to eat dirt. Sometimes they ascended so quickly from a valley to the icy cold of a pass that they spat blood. Not many complained. Quesada, now won over to the expedition, and his commander both set an example. But the men needed none. Their rage dragged them through. On the steepest paths they corkscrewed their way higher. Like a wounded man losing blood and no one knows how much more he has to lose, the troop lost men and lost men and left them lying in its wake.

When they approached the highest peaks they were still three hundred strong. And as they lurched half naked through the passes of the icy Paramos, another hundred or more froze to death. Some who had become blind along the way were strapped onto horses.

All around, endless forests wept and howled. The men heard none of it. Trees that die and fall. Hurtling winds screaming their pain as they melt snow and ice to feed the becks. Suffering, all of it. And the deer and the ponderous birds. Trunks groaning, boughs cracking, water wearing away. Terrible speechless world.

Through it marched the murderers and desecrators.

Up, down, week after week.

When they came to a narrow river, they turned to follow it up the valley. They set to with axe and knife. Each man received daily eighteen grains of maize counted out into his hand. The desperation brooding in them was ready to burst. Then one horribly wet morning, as they roused themselves after a stormy night to face yet another day of struggle, there on the river, the Opon, came two slender boats, rowed by darkskins. The boats stopped. They were laden with salt and bright cottons. The rowers were not to proceed, must serve as guides for a while, they accepted an axe for the whole load.

Then scouts up ahead spied fields and flower gardens. The savannah.

It was a broad landscape with lakes. Mountain streams poured down from side valleys. A slow muddy river wound across the plain.

≈≈≈

Barreda went down with a few armed men and native guides while the band waited at the edge of the forest. And as they stumbled down the gentle incline with their monstrous beards and long tangled hair, faces yellow and haggard, sunken doleful eyes, thin white arms bare, shoeless, clad in rags and leaves – a shrill wailing rose to meet them from the valley floor, endless wailing. The forest, speechless, suffering, began to ululate.

A hundred dark people, men, women, children, stood there below with arms raised, crying and wailing. Weird spirits have come down from the sky, in broad daylight, into our valley.

Barreda's people, aided by natives, hauled bananas, maize meal, pigeons, hares back up the slope, all handed over for nothing in return. The faces of the dark locals showed amazement, disbelief, horror. Again and again bearers trudged up and down, brought cloth, exotic jackets and skirts. The soldiers smartened themselves up, and when they saw themselves in the outlandish clothes they twisted their gnarled faces into the semblance of a smile, like corpses.

The governor held them back, made them rest up for two days. The camp was a field hospital. They held a service to thank the distant mighty god who had given them knives and axes and guns and guided them through the gloomy forest. They were a hundred and sixty six strong. Sixty two horsemen, a dozen arquebusiers, sixteen crossbowmen. The rest had only sword and shield.

Cundinamarca

A HORDE OF Whiteskins, debris of an army, feverish, emaciated, their baggage a few chests, having escaped annihilation descended into the little valley with some horses and dogs and a few weapons. They were only half in their senses. And as they trudged down the gentle slope, limping even worse than in the forest, again they heard shrill wailing from the valley. Again a hundred villagers stood there with arms raised, wailed and cried as the uncanny spirits with their weird animals approached. They prostrated themselves in horror.

The limping soldiers picked up speed. They could see a big town down on the savannah. Quesada, disordered in his senses like the others, had enough presence of mind to hold back the men who still remained to him. What could they do in their wretched condition? But they pressed on, deaf to advice. Quesada himself was dazed by reports from the interpreters: this was a realm heaped with gold. Villagers said the same.

The next days brought continuous thunderstorms. They were on their last legs. A few days more and they would be done for. They lay there for a week, no more died. Then they roused themselves, moved out of the valley they dubbed the Valley of Wailing, and to the tap of the only drum they still had, belaboured with two sticks by a weary drummer, they stumbled, rode into the blooming savannah. People from the village ran ahead to raise the alarm.

The river below was called Funza, as was the extensive town that lay beside it. Quesada quartered his troops at the town's edge.

It was a happy place, you could hear singing and lively

commotion. Maize fields and flower gardens stretched far into the plain, all carefully watered. Crowds of darkskinned people with placid faces came streaming from the town. Men, women and children stared at the strangers. Their colour was a deep dark olive-brown. The men wore hats of animal skin, of wool with feathers, long tunics, some wore long white gowns. They walked sedately and had a decorous, even dignified demeanour, some were solemn. The Whites were astonished to see how marvellously alike they all looked. In the throng were persons with nose rings and huge ear discs of gold, and golden half-moons at their brow.

When the Whites extended a hand to the people, they shrank back exclaiming. A peaceful convoy wound endlessly back and forth between town and camp, dark natives and Whites carried timber, cotton cloth, game, fruit, maize, yams, potatoes, and huge jugs of maize beer. The warriors in camp began to guzzle and swill, drank and drank. There was no holding them back. They groomed the horses, made a horrible din sharpening swords, cleaned muskets and the mighty skull-smashers, wooden macanas they had fashioned on the native model. They patched up the remarkable breastplates they had cobbled together in the forest after their cuirasses were gone and they had to throw their armour away because they could no longer carry it. They had trimmed thin slats of wood, tied them together and hung them between scraps of cloth; these ugly cages were meant to stop arrows.

The men, stuffed full and brains on fire, played cards and tried to calm down. With one bound, avarice had seized them. The expedition was over.

When these men close to death first spied the savannah, they saw it as a bed, it was blissful not to have to drag themselves on any farther. Now they were themselves again. Meat, maize, beer, fruit had done the job. They were once again the Whites that Quesada gathered around him on the coast. Blood surged in them. And now it had come true.

They were in the land of dreams. They were in the land of gold. Truly in a heavenly land.

Mine, all mine!

They danced in the camp.

Hey dear Mother, you bore me, and I grew to a rogue and ran away, hey, dear Mother, thanks for my life. Huzza huzza, I'm rich!

Hey dear Father, you sired me, let me grow to robber, churl, rogue. I damned and despised you. Hey dear Father, thanks for my life. Huzza huzza, I'm rich!

Hey dear Sister, you grew to serving girl, milkmaid, fat and dirty, never found a husband, threw yourself away on good-for-nothings, no makeup or baubles, no shoes or ribbons, and I, I had nothing to give you. Hey, dear Sister, you can have anything you want. Huzza huzza, I'm rich!

Hey dear Bride, hey dear little bride, Lucinda Dorinda Teresa Camilla, with your ruddy cheeks and your pale arms, you sit at your window and scorn me, waiting for a fine man, a knight. Now I'm a fine man with money and gold, all of us have ten thousand in gold, you'll all lick our boots. A whole town fell to us, a golden land fell to us, I'm a nobleman, a count, a marquis. Hey dear Bride, I'm coming to fetch you, today and tomorrow and next day, wait for me just a little day. We're dancing for you, my new little bride, the golden bridegroom is coming to you. Huzza huzza, ten thousand huzzas.

≈≈≈

Small groups already sworn to plunder roamed the camp singing insolent songs.

They waited for the signal to attack.

When the governor's tent was up, the flag of Castile hoisted, he summoned his commander, the elder of the two Dominicans (the more cheerful man of the cloth had been left lying on a high pass), the notary royal and some officers. He shook their hands laughing, something he never did, babbled, thanked, complimented them on the coming victory. He was intoxicated like the rest, tried to gather his wits. He was even giddier than the officers, the ground swayed beneath him. A tremor rippled across his smiling haggard fever-yellow face that ended in an untidy goatee, as if his avarice sought to break through. Heedless of his status in their company, he treated them to one of his hypocritical speeches:

"I intend to set an example of peaceful conquest. The Crown appointed me governor of a province, not a wasteland. We shall place a prosperous new region at the disposal of the Empire. I would hear your opinion."

All concurred. The commander with reservations. The governor saw how none dared gainsay him.

"This is no conquered land. The defenceless natives will surely offer no resistance. By proceeding with prudence, all will fall into our hands: gold, slaves, precious stones."

The order was given to confine all troops rigorously to camp. The governor would initiate the necessary negotiations. Outside the tent, commander and officers eyed one another, notary and priest hurried away. The officers lifted their hands in a gesture of helplessness, the commander looked grim: "We're led by a shopkeeper. The men sweated blood for a glorious venture. They're denied what they were promised." The officers: "The governor summoned us in secret, he wants accomplices. He daren't set foot outside his tent. Why doesn't he address his fancy words to everyone? He dare not."

An hour later they found that the governor had strengthened his bodyguard to ten men. The soldiers were glad: it'll start soon. Officers whispered together. Soon officers and functionaries were summoned again to Quesada's presence. Quesada begged their pardon, but something had come up, of importance for him and the whole band. He paced furiously about the tent, kept his voice low, they saw how he struggled with his agitation. He unrolled for the officers and functionaries to see – how fortunate that it was preserved! – the deed appointing him deputy to Fernandes de Lugo, governor of Santa Marta. He showed them the baton, long familiar to them, emblem of his rank: "What lies ahead goes, of course, beyond the agreed objects of this expedition. I have no authority for the relevant measures. Appointments from home are not possible. The troop must now choose its own leader."

They were taken aback. He concluded by urging officers and functionaries to confer and nominate a chief for the coming activities. Would they make their choice known to him within the hour. They huddled together in a daze, Quesada had placed his tent at their disposal. "Of course we must choose him," said the notary. "Surely he won't abandon us, just at this moment." They asked one another: "Has someone annoyed him, upset him?" The notary suggested: "He is terribly aware of his responsibilities. For this place will become nothing less than a Viceroyalty." A shudder ran through them, and quite involuntarily their faces, those wizened wrinkled folds of skin, twisted beneath their tangled beards into smiles: flames licking beneath a sheet of ice.

Barreda, stocky little commander, daredevil and man of iron, would have liked nothing better just then than to shoot the governor down. He saw through the manoeuvre. The fox just wanted to make himself independent, unconstrained by any governor in Santa Marta. Barreda marvelled at the governor's greed and effrontery. But Quesada had the wind at his back. Barreda swallowed his opinions. Ximenes de Quesada tugged his little beard as Barreda, on behalf of all, conveyed to him the request that he retain command. He embraced the notary, embraced the commander – his comrade in arms and companion in adversity – and clapped him on the back. Quesada had lost all measure.

≈≈≈

Late in the afternoon, the air still hot, gawkers at the camp gate drew back. Out of the seething encampment poured the whiteskinned bearded host, many barefoot, some in native pantaloons, some with feet and legs bandaged to the knee and higher with rags. The damnable enchanted forest had ripped their flesh, hundreds and hundreds lay dead back there, never forget. They walked and rode in caps and shirtlike garments that came from the natives, over them the clumsy wooden chest-cages. Many still spat blood from scurvy and mouthrot. They spat too at the dark people who ran past them towards the town. They dragged their bones along. They were on their way to shake gold and women out of the natives. Near the town a crowd of dark people joined up with the Whiteskins' train. They imitated every movement, strove to comprehend the strangers. In the van, surrounded by armed men, the governor. An envoy had gone ahead to announce him.

The town had paved streets and wooden houses, wide roofs shaped like shallow cones, small low windows and doors, only a few had doors of wood, most had curtains of long bamboo slats tied with string. Narrow streets. Everywhere olive-green men stood around, drew silently back into the walls and dappled shadows. Some wore big gold discs at the chest, glittering armbands, some wore nose rings. Young women stood outside the larger houses, wearing dainty caps seemingly of spun gold, and girdles of similar stuff. Hooves clattered on stone, bloodhounds bayed.

They came to a round sunscorched marketplace, where a large house of stone stood between others of wood. The place was hemmed in by a dense silent mass of people, dark heads above bright clothing. Quesada's troops entered the plaza. They found themselves at the wide low house of stone, its roof made of slates, facing almost a hundred men and women, kneeling or prostrate, elderly and very old, hands bound behind their backs. Horsemen formed a semicircle around the governor, who wore a tunic over his shirt of mail, and a heavy gold chain. Several men flanked by spear-bearers stepped from the stone house, their garments dazzling, colourful designs embellished their cloaks, their tall round headgear was of gold, plaques on their brow flashed rays of light.

The governor's dark interpreters came to him. The Indian leaders bowed low and stood in silence, kept a distance. From his horse Quesada asked if these men had something to say to him. Let them approach. After a lengthy conversation between interpreters and leaders, they reported: The cacique of this place presents these trussed people to the emissaries of heaven, and prays for mercy.

Quesada asked what he was meant to do with them. If they were hostages, and what sort of people were they.

The interpreters returned: The Whites are gods, or like gods, these men and women are given to the Whites as sacrifices to be killed and eaten. The interpreters spoke quite openly and, only moments after the soldiers heard this, the plaza echoed to a gale of ribald laughter. Sober Quesada kept a straight face. He bent down to the priest at his side. "They think us cannibals."

Then he dismounted, took from one soldier a sword and from another a flag with a likeness of the Holy Virgin. Then the notary royal read from a scroll:

"Long live the illustrious King of Castile! We make known to you that there is one God, one Pope and one King of Castile. In the name of the King of Castile we take possession of this land. And if any ruler, whether Christian or heathen, should assert any claim to this land, then we are resolved and prepared to contest such claim and defend the rights of the King of Castile."

The interpreters translated. The banner was planted firmly in the middle of the open space. As the discussion proceeded, the drum sounded and Quesada ordered that the plaza and surrounding streets, and also the route back to the camp, be secured. He himself sat with his bodyguard, some officers, the notary and the priest in the shady portico of the stone house.

The Indian chieftains, who called themselves usacs, informed him that their overlord was the great Zipa, they were his servants and must await his instructions. The Zipa's kingdom was called Cundinamarca. Everything to the east between the two mountain ranges, from the mighty Magdalena river to the mountains of Merida, belonged to the Zipa. The town was called Funza, a long way off lay the town of Muqueta and the town of Sogamoso. They were called Muisca, People.

They reported, as the notary began to write: This is the seat of the King of Tunja, whom the Zipa has just now subjugated. The Zipa pursued the vassal king with a huge army. Now the High Priest of the kingdom has brokered a ceasefire, for twenty moons.

Quesada asked uneasily: where at present is the army of the great Zipa? With satisfaction he learned that on the High Priest's advice both the great Zipa and the unruly vassal had disbanded their armies. For politeness' sake Quesada uttered a few more remarks. Then, with an eye to what was to follow, he asked how the Muisca counted and reckoned. The reply was curious, but unlike the notary, who lent half an ear to the conversation, he did not smile. They counted on their fingers, then their toes, that made twenty, and so on, quite reliably as Quesada discovered, even though they named their numbers strangely: one was frog, two a nose with its two nostrils, three was two eyes open, four, two eyes closed, five, two faces joined, nine, two frogs embracing.

During this conversation the delighted notary memorialised as never before in his life. As he wrote he glanced enraptured across at the governor. Who should we thank for this. He rejoiced for all the Indians who had gathered in this place and built this town. Wonderful how they allowed themselves to be discovered by our band. Governor, notary, commander and priest set their names at the end of the memorial. It was superfluous to exact a signature from a plenipotentiary representative of the late government, since the natives had no writing. Anxiously they followed the mysterious movements of the notary over his scroll. What magical signs is he making there. With growing dread the people glanced back and forth between Quesada and the little notary. One of the uncanny beings spends a long time making marks on the flat sheet, now other men make strokes on it, now the first man stands and forms the sheet into a tube. The usacs on the portico could no longer stand upright for horror, they sank to the ground and stretched out their arms, begged for mercy. Quesada turned aside in disgust.

In order not to be caught in the town at nightfall, Quesada ordered the leaders on the portico to bring to the plaza, without delay, all items of gold or of the value of gold, whether public or private. He wanted a first glimpse of the riches of this place.

The order was obeyed without demur. Riders formed a circle around the enormous heap that rose under the banner of the Virgin. The clamour and excitement of the soldiers at this sight was brutal. Quesada's own agitation mounted. The sight exceeded all expectation. The circle around the heap had to keep widening as shields, head plates, neck rings, arm rings, ear pendants, figures large and small of people, lizards, frogs, suns, moons were piled onto it. The heap grew, people ran like ants hither and thither. The heap overtopped the horses, so that riders on one side could no longer see those on the other. And all of gold! They sampled some pieces: heavy gold. Sometimes silvered, a lot set with emeralds and rubies. For these people, it seemed, gold was what copper or steel were elsewhere.

Quesada could not take his eyes from the heap. He spoke with those around him, it was mere jabbering, he didn't even know himself what he said. Governor, officers, even the two Dominicans, all were stunned. This truly was the land of gold, Eldorado. Soldiers on horseback in their chest-cages, those untamed greedy beast-men, victims of misfortune, robbers, vagabonds, pardoned gallows-birds, all giggled, nudged one another, laughed in derision and delight. If only we could set to. Blood, sturdy women, strapping women, a waist to grab.

Before sunset, in the seething plaza – dark people still ran whispering hither and thither, urging each other on – Quesada gave the signal to move out with the goods. Neighbouring streets were already in uproar as soldiers slipped away on their own initiative, invaded houses. Protected by his bodyguard, Quesada supervised the transport. Cart after cart moved off, darkskins hauled them and shouldered sacks. Quesada was glad to have given the signal in good time, it seemed the massive heap would never shrink. The horde of darkskins laboured in silence, an endless caravan stretched along the road out to the camp. Soldiers looked on, yelling and laughing their heads off. They were in a madhouse, the whole world was crazy. As darkness fell, Quesada moved out of the plaza.

They were stupefied. It was almost beyond bearing. They arrived here naked. Now kingdoms, dukedoms!

A raucous mob of soldiers came on behind. They were offended by the withdrawal. Quesada heard them shout: "Give us some savages to eat, at least!"

Having set a strong guard around the camp and undertaken by torchlight an initial division of the spoils, after first subtracting the king's fifth, Quesada thought the camp would calm down. But the tumult grew louder by the minute. This was the moment of crisis.

Barreda conferred with some officers, spat: "We are subject to the orders, not of a governor but of a shopkeeper." With any of them at his back, he would murder Quesada. He saw that the others, the whole camp, were ripe for anything.

Quesada, profoundly uneasy, tasted the air, summoned the officers: "I will not acquire the reputation of a butcher. Castile, indeed all Christianity, is watching us." At this fancy prating the officers lost all control, they shouted across each other: "Our men waded through swamps, hacked through forests, died. People and town belong to us, it's the rules of war."

Quesada (what will become of us, we must hold back) nagged: "This is not war! Until now no one has given us so much as a hostile look. We have no grounds to attack. Our task is to take possession of the land, secure it for the Crown." Commander Barreda, hands and knees trembling, gazed wild-eyed at the others. All had the same thought: shall we strike him down?

Barreda sneered: he has ascertained that a number of muske-teers remained behind in the town on their own account. Quesada bristled: "And are still there? And you knew it only now?"

The governor could not restrain himself, he saw the danger, he feigned desperation, flung back the tent flap: "Listen to the tumult! Is this an orderly camp? It is not my doing. No one can demand the impossible. If you persist in your plan, I can vouch for nothing. How is your authority over the men?"

"Governor, we give no guarantee that us officers and you yourself will survive this night."

Quesada closed the flap. He drew the commander aside. "But for you, this whole dreadful excursion that has cost so many lives would not have succeeded. You know that."

"Others would have come."

Quesada nattered away to this subordinate who wanted to murder him, said anything that came into his head, he sought to flatter Barreda, make him accomplice to his shabby intentions, Barreda won't come away too badly. Barreda was sickened. Since he did not yield, Quesada put on airs: "You officers lack sense, you'll ruin everything." He almost wept. "In any case you share responsibility for all this, and for the state of the men, which is not seemly for an army." Barreda waited for the conclusion. "I wash my hands of all that's coming. You have deserted me. It is a disgrace, but I am powerless."

"We must find the musketeers."

Quesada's smile was full of loathing: "Find, commander? In the middle of the night?"

Uproar surrounded the tent. The men demanded town, plunder, women. Quesada cocked an ear. He clapped the commander on the shoulder and beckoned to the priest: "Just listen to that! They want to eat people after all." The commander concealed his disgust at this duplicity.

≈≈≈

Black night. A drum sounded the alarm. The mob assembled by torchlight. They made a riotous departure. They took along all the hounds. A small detail guarded the camp.

All mine! Gold! Women!

They ran. Could not be held to a marching pace. Officers swore. Only when they reached the houses did they close ranks and quieten down. The hounds in their midst bayed furiously.

The town stirred. Streets filled with confused anxious people, who followed the procession. You lot'll pay, every farthing, every penny, if there's a door I'll break it down, my belly, my guts are rotted, I keep vomiting and you must pay. They brought wood to the marketplace, it gave warmth and light. No natives were there. In some streets they drove old men and women from the houses to witness the sacrifice and feast that was to come, people ran and knocked on doors to fetch them. An officer at Quesada's side in the plaza raised a banner, the drum rat-tatted briefly, a soldier shouted towards the silent houses illuminated by the flames:

"Know there is one God, one Pope, one King of Castile, and the Pope has given you all to the king to be his slaves. We order you to obey. If not, we shall make war on you with fire and sword."

They camped in the marketplace. The hounds kept up their beastly furious baying. The Zipa's palace and a temple were placed under guard. A search was made for the soldiers who had remained in town. A rumour spread that they had been murdered. The troops, raging, were beyond restraint. Quesada stumbled on his lanky legs from one group to another, he could not believe they wanted plunder, they could have all the women they wanted, but to squander and fritter away such riches. He wandered here and there, at his side the merciless villain Barreda, the spoiler. There they lurked by the fire, ready to leap, panting, a pack straining at the leash. He tried to implore this one, that one, but they just stared or ignored him, he could not speak.

During the third night watch, a trumpet sounded.

A tremendous roar erupted. A salvo was fired off. They ran with torches in hunting packs through the streets, bellowing wordlessly. Doors were burst open with shoulder or axe or halberd. Rapine began. Hey, dear mother who bore me.

Men overpowered women. The town was a single blur of shooting, bellowing, crackling, screaming, wailing, panting. Old people in the street suffered what they expected: they were knocked down and trampled by horses. Hey, dear father who sired me, you let me grow to robber, churl, rogue.

All mine!

Horror throughout the town. Panic on a sinking ship at sea, terror amid the tumult of war. Overpowering all thought, all feeling. Demons have alighted on our roofs, they run about our streets, the weird strangers are tearing us apart, hear how they strike and scream, there they are, hey! dear bride, little bride, Lucinda Dorinda Teresa, who sat at your window and scorned me.

Patrols tried to stop fights among the plunderers. Fires were started. Men looted, grew sated, slept far into the day. From sunset to sunset the town belonged to the soldiers. The natives offered no resistance. It was all the same to the soldiers: resistance or no resistance, they slew or spared at whim.

The town was large, home to some ten thousand dark people. The Whites could not possess it all in a night. Drawn now to left, now to right, giddy, ecstatic over the loot, they rampaged from house to house, stacked piles of gold in the lanes, left them, ran off, drank, forgot everything, stayed indoors with women. I'm coming to fetch you today, tomorrow, next day, the golden bridegroom's on his way.

That night packs of jaguars appeared in the streets, roamed the town, busied themselves with corpses, leapt into houses. The bloodhounds of the Whites confronted them. Hideous baying. Their drunken masters joined in, suffered wounds. By daylight dozens of jaguars lay in the streets, torn to pieces by the giant hounds. These were jaguars that had been tethered by order of the magistrate at the doors of recalcitrant debtors, they had torn free, dragged chains and sometimes half a door.

Next morning the Cistercian monks came into town, summoned by haggard defeated Quesada, who had stayed all the while in the plaza. Sometimes he was alone, cursing at flames and shadows, even the notary had deserted him. When the monks arrived they invited him to pray. He mumbled bitterly with them, hollowed out by his impotence. The monks dared only a brief look around, it would not take much to trigger an assault, the men thought they'd come to steal. They tried to baptise the dying. In the streets they found jaguars busy with human corpses, mauled beasts, bloodhounds running loose, outside many houses were household implements, sacks of food, heaps of gold, no one guarding them, the owner snoring somewhere. Alleys slippery with blood. The town lifeless. Officers were courteous to the priests and guided them around. On advice from the priests, crowds of darkskinned men – trembling slaves now, unadorned, clad in rags – were driven from houses and assigned their first task: collect the dead of their people and throw them into graves east of the town.

The Zipa

THE ZIPA'S PALACE lay at the edge of town in an extensive park, his wives' houses behind.

It was a round building. The roofbeams were of precious wood inlaid with gold. In the big open space in front of the house stood the Pillar of the Sun, by means of which priests measured shadows and determined the time, and the calendar for feast days and harvests.

Late that afternoon Quesada, abjectly shuffling, exhausted, liverish, was led to the palace. The huge round building amazed him, its centre rising in a slender pyramid high as a palm tree. Before the gate they saw a gigantic carved pillar which aroused their revulsion: on a square plinth of stone stood a rectilinear carving of a wide-mouthed idol with retracted head and tiny body. The idol's cheeks were garishly painted, heavy gold chains hung from the chest, the girdle was sprinkled with precious stones. Then they were led in by men with nose rings and a half moon on their forehead.

Their amazement never let up. The corridors they were led along were endless, they went through empty rooms, came to more and yet more corridors. Corridors zigzagged, some led in a semicircle, they traversed bare lofty halls. Quesada looked around for his commander. They were in a labyrinth. It was a trap. But they had swords. All the Whites had been transformed by that night. It was as if they all went about with a dagger clenched between their teeth.

Suddenly they stood at a little door, in no way distinguished from others they had passed. But now the guides halted and turned their backs to the door, knocked on the floor with their tall staves until a signal came from within. Then, without turning, they opened the door.

In a low wide room, the fat old king sat against a bright wall and kept his eyes closed. A row of low gold-chased chairs had been placed some distance from the throne.

The dark courtiers who accompanied Quesada and his retinue walked backwards into the middle of the room. Then one crawled right up to the king's feet and spoke without lifting his head. The conversation lasted a long time. The servants of the Zipa too, all in sumptuous garments and at their breast golden shields of varying sizes – on the heads of some, above their long black locks, swayed great gaudy feathers alongside a golden half-moon, others were adorned with little caps of spun gold, everywhere big emeralds sparkled – all of them, olive-green noblemen, vassals, courtiers, stood with eyes downcast. Quesada was asked to repeat what he had told the cacique regarding the purpose of his mission. As Quesada spoke – along with his retinue he had meanwhile sat down, sword in front of him, apathetic, and here in the deep calm slowly felt his way back to the role of governor that had deserted him – the old man above regarded one by one governor, priest, commander. His eyes were small and bloodshot, a little white beard sprouted from his chin, he wore a red headband, his strong face showed no expression. His head was set low between his shoulders, with his short arms and legs he was the very picture of a giant turtle.

He asked about the country and the gods of the Whites. The priest stood, advanced closer, held up the cross. He challenged the Zipa to renounce the shameful idolatry indulged in by him and his people, and accept baptism. After some crawling to and fro and translating, the old man murmured something. The Whites learned that the highest god is called Bochica. He bestows protection on the Chibcha people. He carries the world on his shoulders.

The priest, when he heard the translation, smacked an indignant hand on his book. Then the Zipa murmured something more. They learned that he wished to be carried to the market place, to see the band of White men and also the big animals that they sit on, not to mention the tame jaguars and thunder tubes. Quesada, impatient already, nodded, and they stood up.

Outside, a handful of soldiers were swiftly drummed into line. This was no easy task, but there was no hurry. Hours went by before the Zipa was properly attired and borne forth. Officials with little drums and trumpets ran ahead through the devastated streets and, as if nothing had happened, ordered everyone to stay indoors, for the Zipa was venturing out of his palace. Accompanied by several dozen lancers and archers, preceded by a little orchestra blowing on conches, horns and flutes, ever so slowly the old king's purple-curtained litter moved through the wide open palace gates. It lingered a while by the huge stone idol, at whose feet the Zipa laid a string with stones.

In the plaza soldiers had again piled up firewood, for evening was approaching. A small group of riders sat on their mounts, which were still mere skin and bone after the terrible privations and exertions in forest and mountains; the riders only reluctantly and with some nervousness imposed any load on them. Nearby, under a mat awning, menaced the five small cannon, only two of them serviceable, rust had ruined the other three. Behind them, feet apart, presenting musket, halberd, arquebus, stood the few foot soldiers rounded up at such short notice. Most were still snoring indoors, and many were drunk. Even of those available for this honour guard, the majority were drunk.

And so it was that, as the Zipa and his curious solemn train proceeded into the plaza to the endlessly slow tempo of the orchestra, and the governor and officers sat on their horses, the Zipa was greeted by roars of laughter. Some of the riders stationed at the entrance to the marketplace fell off in their excitement that the king himself had come to visit, and their efforts to remount drew ribald comments from the foot soldiers. The musketeers were dirty and bloodstained. They looked like a troupe of mummers, for they had grabbed whatever garments and fabrics came to hand in the houses; to celebrate their victory most wore the colourful woollen shawls of women, splendid necklaces, on their heads the fine spun-gold caps of women. Even the big hounds they were feeding with pigeons had enormous bright ribbons around their necks.

The Zipa's train proceeded with unchanged slowness and solemnity. Excited mercenaries yelled: "Tcha, tcha, giddy up! On you go!" Governor, officers and priests made not the slightest effort to dampen the noise and high spirits, they too were infected.

At the stone house, residence of the town's cacique, the orchestra stood away to one side, still playing. The Zipa's chair was carried towards the horsemen. The chair halted, and as the whole plaza looked on in mounting suspense, the old man with the purple headband climbed out with the aid of his entourage, and stood in front of an emaciated nag. He inspected the piebald beast from the front, thrust his head close to the beast's nose and eyes. He stepped sideways a couple of paces, looked at long bony legs, ribs, tail. The rider grasped the bridle, laughing and jesting as he tried to set foot in the stirrup, it kept eluding him. Then the Zipa, to jeers and raucous laughter, bowed awkwardly to the animal, which stood there following his movements with big dark eyes.

Now the Zipa stepped across to the musketeers. Since the governor feared mischief from this unruly band, an officer took an arquebus and blocked the way. The old man dared not move. He murmured something. A translation: The Zipa would know what one says to the thunder tube when one wishes to do magic with it. At Quesada's word the officer took aim and fired into the air over roofs. The bang caused the old man to fall to his knees, the entourage threw themselves to the ground. The mercenaries hopped and squealed in delight.

After some minutes the Zipa stood up, looked about him in a daze, the drunkard on his horse gestured at him with both hands. The entourage led the old man back to his litter. Before climbing in he bowed deeply to governor, mercenaries, horses. The governor raised his sword in salutation, seething with rage. The behaviour of his troops was beyond all bounds. Amid halloos and mocking shouts from the mercenaries, who were already dispersing back into town, the Zipa withdrew, preceded by the gentle tootling of the orchestra, at the same slow stately pace. A guard of mounted officers protected the train.

On his way back through the devastated town – his possessions now so great he forgave the soldiers, they were his companions in fortune – Governor Quesada encountered scenes that he accepted and gathered like a bouquet for a reconciliation.

Here and there one of his soldiers ran along a row of houses, behind him another carried a sack, from the bamboo screens that served as doors they ripped away the little gold plates that jingled to announce visitors.

In one street he comes upon a disturbance. Riding up he sees that a patrol has detained three people. The guards, like all the rest, are not sober, the weakened bodies of the men are unused to native liquor, they laugh and babble: These are suspicious, they wear women's clothing but are men. And it's true: the three dark people wear long female skirts and girdles, but their hair is cut short, and they have deep voices. These are men, the drunkards want to show the governor right now. The governor summons his interpreter. One quick glance at the prisoners and they report: Yes, they are men, bad people, they ran away during the recent war, they had their heads shaved and were sentenced to wear women's clothing. "Let them go," Quesada orders, and rides on. They have the customs of humans, these heathen.

He arrives at the edge of town, where big houses are set amid palms and mimosas. Outside a burned-down house a captains has halted and gathers objects passed to him from the debris. Quesada with his retinue greets and questions the captain, who shows him figurines of gold, big as a hand, and several puzzling small golden whips inset with emeralds. He hands one to Quesada. "What's this? Do they ride animals?" Only one interpreter knows what it is, and he is reticent. "This house belongs to a prince. Even a prince can offend. Somebody has to punish him. It must be one of his wives. That's what the whip is for." Quesada keeps the dainty little thing, the story pleases him, he'll put it in his report, his mood improves.

And when they are out on open ground in sight of camp and Quesada spurs his horse to a gallop, he hears a commotion from a grove of bamboo. They push their way into the grove, Quesada waits outside. Then the commander beckons him. Quesada dismounts and follows. A crowd of women is gathered around a fat man who has been tied to a laurel tree, the women have beaten him severely with sticks, torn his clothes. But the man seems not to care, he's elderly, he trills and sings. The commander points at him: there's a merry fellow. The women prostrate themselves. Quesada: "What are they doing with him?" The interpreter bends down, whispers to a woman, she makes no reply. He turns to the man, who lets fly at once, jabbers, laughs, spits and threatens. The interpreter's face is impassive. "White men came into his house, he gave them everything they wanted, then he became drunk and behaved indecently to his wives." Quesada shakes his head

in astonishment. "Indecently! Let them beat him some more."
He rides off. Barreda at his side is agitated: "Those are rebellious
women, we should make them pay." Quesada yawns, exhausted:
"Whatever you like, my son."

It was all so wonderful, overpowering, he would become
marquis.

The Zipa's treasure

AT NIGHTFALL THE soldiers left town and moved back to
camp. Patrols guarded routes out from the town.

And at the very moment when the last soldier with the last
ruddy torchglow had disappeared and the drumming and roaring
had faded away, in every street and on the marketplace people
emerged from their houses. They knew the streets, dared not
make lights. Great Heaven to whose stars they prayed took pity
on them and drove away the thick clouds, a half-moon sent bright
rays down, the enormous canopy of stars pressed over them,
heavy and near. They were still alive. They went outside to wail,
and to mingle their wailing.

This was once a town of priests and warriors, tax gatherers,
merchants, artisans and farmers, creditors and debtors, of the
wealthy and the downtrodden. Now they slipped by one another
as equals. They recognised each other, man or woman, by voice.
Most were naked. Although they shivered from cold, they went
out into the streets, sobbed, joined their tears, clutched one
another.

From some houses, men and women who had become mad
ran screaming. They were led back indoors and made secure.

Young men had sent bolts of cloth to the parents of the bride,
the father had accepted the cloth, the young men sent a second
batch together with half a deer and some of the hayo they chewed
like coca leaves. That was yesterday. This morning the suitor was
meant to sit at the door of the bride's father's house and make just
enough noise to be noticed. The father calls through the door:
"Who sits there? Who are you? A robber? I owe no debts. Go
away! I haven't invited anyone." The daughter comes out with a

jug of sweet drink, offers him some, tastes it first. Where was the door? What had become of the one he was to wait for?

There were some who had awaited the coming day with dread. Adulterers, who on this day would be made to eat pepper and allowed no drink. They had no need to fear the pepper.

In many houses young women had cowered in corners, hidden under dark rugs, they were pubescent, the ceremony was already planned where they would be led through an avenue of relatives and friends down to the river for their first bathe. No relatives, no ceremony. Young Ipakes wandered through the streets. Assassins and rapists had come through the forest, trees had submitted to the blades of the alien murderers, human flesh was weak, and lamented.

Everyone thronged to the edges of town and saw that there was no escape, watchfires were burning, weird strangers sat around them. They pressed back to the marketplace. Debris and rubbish. They averted their steps from hazardous ruins, milled around outside the Zipa's silent palace. Bats flitted overhead. From the Zipa's garden came sweet delicate music, his wives were singing, they still had no idea. The crowd, several hundred strong, silently seething, thronged through from the street, sank to the ground by the stone pillar, and waited. A cacique came out from the palace, gaunt priests beside him in black robes, black caps. The cacique knelt at the pillar, the priests burned a strong balm in censers, one paced around the pillar, sang in a low voice. The crowd responded.

The cacique, protected by men with spears, said: "Uncanny spirits have attacked us. They were sent by Heaven. They are evil beasts, shameless spiteful devils. We have no magic to counter them. You must try to flee. The demons with white faces will fade away."

Already that night a few managed to slip past the watchfires, escape into the mountains.

≈≈≈

Next day when the governor came with a small escort into town, his beloved town, his hometown, he pointed his horse at once towards the Zipa's palace and demanded entrance. He required the handover of all gold and silver. No more theatre. The Zipa, in the same room as yesterday, glowered. He said, according to the report of his servants as they crawled back and forth, that in a few hours they would find all the palace gold and silver in this room.

At a hint from the notary, the governor also demanded all gold and silver and precious stones in the Zipa's houses and gardens, even that belonging to his women and servants. The Zipa nodded. He explained that some items were for religious use, no one could touch those. The priest's face expressed outrage, the governor raised his hand angrily: "Precisely those items will be removed."

After a long pause the Zipa asked the alien chief to inform him again what mission had been assigned to him by his country and his god. Reluctantly Quesada asked the priest to do so. Then the Zipa insisted more vigorously on knowing more about the country they came from, and how they had reached here. Impatient and irritable, Quesada let priest and notary report on their country, church, pope and king, and their voyage by sea.

Meanwhile the first golden vessels, engraved discs large and small, countless moulded figurines of gold and silver were brought in and heaped on the floor near the Whites. The old Zipa, motionless, regarded the gloating faces of the Whites. Once he asked: "Do you or your horses or hounds eat gold and silver?" The Whites laughed, they weren't here for conversation. The governor ordered two musketeers who stood behind him to take down from the wall on either side of the throne the great round golden discs showing the Sun and loathsome visages. But when the two mercenaries reached for the discs, the people behind prostrated themselves, pressed faces to the floor. And the ponderous old man too opened eyes and mouth wide, fell from the throne onto his knees. And it so happened that, tangled in his flowing robes, he lost his balance and toppled. He fell to the floor in front of the throne, thrashed about like a fish in a net, tried to raise himself on one arm. Failing in this he lay there snuffling. To the amazement of the Whites not one of the servants sprang to help the groaning man. Some lay there not looking round, others ran out from side doors. Then at a sign from the governor, two musketeers set to. They had to invite him by signs to put his arms around their shoulders, since when they just tried to lift him he fell back again, tripping on his great long red cloak embroidered all over with heavy gold brocade. They plumped him down roughly, like a doll.

Then the same courtiers hastened back in through side doors with two old men. These did not proceed backwards like the others, but to protect themselves from the Zipa's gaze held the left arm across the eyes. The Zipa sat timidly, mumbled and nodded, they approached him, he murmured to the priests. The interpreter explained: the Zipa must retire. The Whites made no objection, this audience was meaningless, they didn't like the Zipa, the rascal seemed to be sizing them up.

The governor went off, left the commander with the notary and two musketeers in charge.

In the palace, priests initiated rituals to purify the Zipa. The weird strangers, those wicked demons, had lain hands on him. To remove the influences they made him vomit and fast. He spent the day in a dark chamber, the priests wanted to keep him there the following day, but he was distraught and declared that all this was not enough.

Next morning he concluded the interview with Quesada. The interpreters extracted two sentences from his mumbling. First: whether the Whites had no land and no towns in their own country, and therefore came here. "Why do you not stay at home, sowing and reaping? Why do you destroy our country?" Barreda whispered to the governor: "The Zipa spouts empty words. He misprises the situation, or pretends to." The governor shook his head and replied: "The Zipa has never seen Spain." He does not know the might of the Castilian king, in whose service they have come here. The great king accounts to no one for his actions.

Then the Zipa: "Your pope and king live across the sea. Nobody here has seen them. They know nothing of us and our country. How can the pope give the king a country that he does not know and does not belong to him, and how can the king accept such a present?" The interpreter did not translate the Zipa's next scornful remark: "Pope and king must both be idiots." The governor borrowed the commander's words: "The Zipa prates empty words. If all he wants is to make conversation with us he is welcome, but this is not the moment. We have work to do. Furthermore I have some advice for him: if he wants an answer to his question, he should fit out some people as the King of Spain fitted us out, and should order them to journey across the sea. They'll find the answer."

The Whites burst out laughing. The governor also made clear to the Zipa that he was under suspicion of withholding property of the Spanish Crown. He was granted until evening to deliver the remainder of the required goods, after which forceful measures would be taken. The Zipa, his face quivering, murmured that he planned to leave town next morning and travel north to the holy place Irica on the Sogamosa river.

Before the governor could express a view on this astonishing remark from his prisoner, loud voices and footsteps could be heard from outside, Spanish voices and others. Of course no one was allowed in. Barreda stood up, flung open the door, shouted into the maze of corridors. The footsteps came nearer. Captain Manzanarez came up to Barreda, he was agitated, asked for Quesada, entered the hall. The governor was already on his feet, the captain reported: there's a gang of savages outside the palace who claim that a huge glittering procession of Whites is on the march, they have the same animals and thunder tubes as us.

The Whites in the hall stood perplexed, exchanged glances, the governor adjourned the conclusion of the conversation and with a curt nod left the Zipa sitting there, still awaiting an answer. Outside he questioned the native messengers. Their testimony was explicit. Quesada rode uneasily back to camp with his retinue.

The second conquistador

A FEW HOURS later all doubts dissolved. Into the camp, which they had begun reinforcing with tree trunks, familiar sounds drifted across the plain: drumbeats and trumpet blasts.

And it was true, an army of White men was on the march, more magnificent and better disciplined than they, a most improbable sight, with many sturdy horses and a great train of Indians, up from the south past maize fields along the high road. At the head they could see one of Quesada's sentry details: two riders, and musketeers wearing native caps.

Governor Quesada was an educated man. He trotted slowly with a few officers towards the glittering procession. Ever since their luck had changed, everything was different between Quesada and his officers, even his shadow Barreda: now all were well-disposed. So immersed were they in fact in their rapture and bliss that none was in condition to feel alarmed by the new arrivals. What did these *knapsacks* want? First come, first served. Quesada twisted in his saddle and offered reflections: "Captain, you've no doubt read some of those absurd romances that enthral people these days, the Knight of the Sun, or Bernardo del Carpio who killed Roland at Roncesvalles, the Knight of the Flaming Sword who with one sweep of his blade sundered two enormous giants? Well, it really seems to me we are now in such a romance, and here is a frightful travail we must overcome. If I didn't look around and call to mind that foolish impudent Zipa and observe our people erecting earthworks back there, I could believe these are armed knights riding towards us to conquer the King of Trebizond."

Barreda, his arrogance ever growing: "Do you recall our conversation before we climbed into the mountains? You wanted reinforcements, I warned you we had no time, I was ready to move without you."

Quesada smiled amiably at his subordinate: "I vetoed your march."

"I was right about the danger. See, there they come. That's them."

"But too late," crowed Quesada. "Anyway, they are just a rabble. What do they look like! Who have they been plundering? What do they want here?"

Barreda: "The villains will tell us soon enough."

The great procession came to a halt. Drums and trumpets

fell silent. Five men rode towards them on strong sleek horses. Quesada whispered: "Holy virgin, just look at them. Where did they acquire such horses? They'll ride us into the ground."The five riders halted, saluted courteously with their swords. Both sides waited to see who would speak first. The governor, who had but a feeble voice, signalled to his commander: "Speak to them. Don't let them take the upper hand. We are here."

The commander stood in the stirrups and called across: "Who are you?" At once came the expected reply: "Who are you?"

"On my right is the governor of Santa Marta, Gonzalo Ximenes de Quesada. I am Barreda, his commander and captain-general. We hold the king of this country, the Zipa, captive in his palace. The governor has taken possession of the town and this country for the King of Spain, and secured one fifth for the King."

"Then we are surplus to requirements."

"Who are you?"

A powerful full-faced man dressed in scarlet stood laughing in the saddle, he wore a tall pointed hat with feathers, his arms and legs were splendidly armoured: "I am Sebastian de Belalcazar. And these with me and behind me are my people. We came upon a savage in Quito who told us about his king and his homeland and that the king, before he bathes, sprinkles gold dust on his body. This impressed us deeply, for we deem it a misuse of gold. We thought, the king can change his bathtime habits. So we set off, Whites, many Indians, bearers, strong horses, and came here through the Magdalena valley to make changes."

"Mister Sebastian de Belalcazar, we rejoice at your visit. We shall place a number of houses in town at your disposal, where you can recuperate from your journey."

Belalcazar thanked him cheerfully: "Don't put yourselves to any trouble. Thank you, captain, but we have brought tents and axes and spades. We have ample manpower. By the grace of God we shall be a burden to no one. I notice you have a camp, and are erecting defences. Ergo, the country is not secured. Just as I thought. So you will understand if we prefer to camp outside the town, hereabouts or a bit farther down. I'll give the order right away to set up defences, so that we may be secure before nightfall and have no need of your protection. Tomorrow we shall show the savages our brand new arquebuses and five powerful cannon and investigate this story we were told which dismayed us so."

The commander screamed red-faced: "You come too late, Mister Belalcazar. You heard me."

"Why so exercised, commander?" Whereupon the big jovial man saluted, his retinue doffed their hats. They rode away slowly.

Quesada and his men stayed rooted to the spot. "Are you bold enough, commander, to attack these villains before they dig themselves in?" The commander stared in astonishment: "They have five cannon, better than ours. Only two of ours are usable. Of our forty muskets and arquebuses, barely twenty-five still fire."

"Well well. Not half an hour ago you were boasting to me how this expedition was your handiwork, and if you hadn't pressed on then others would have got here first."

But the commander wanted to return to camp and speed up defensive works in case of an attack by night. They galloped off.

The newcomers settled themselves two arquebus shots lower down, and without asking sent armed men into town to fetch provisions. Quesada's sentries, alarmed, came seeking instructions. The commander ordered that all gold, silver and precious stones that had been gathered be brought away from the town; otherwise the newcomers were to be left alone. The guard at the Zipa's palace was reinforced and provided with serviceable weapons. He agreed a signal with them in case any newcomer should venture near the palace. Quesada's camp was greatly relieved when nothing happened that evening or night.

≈≈≈

But next morning as they conferred in his tent with Quesada, who could not conceal his dismay, news came from the entrance to the camp that envoys of the newcomers had arrived. During the night the commander had caused decoy cannon to be fashioned from logs, and covered by mats. Quesada had the envoys taken past these menacing artefacts, and awaited them full of wrath. He had thrown his hat, taken from a native, to the ground, his sword lay on the rough table in front of him, he sat on a splendid chair from the Zipa's palace. He assumed his cold severe official's face, only the warhorse, his commander, was in there with him. In addition they had concealed ten men behind the tent, who were to burst in at a signal from the commander and take the envoys captive. They were ready to stake everything, the soldiers were with them to a man.

The tent flap was thrown back. Six White men in gaudy feathered cloaks and with gleaming weapons stepped in. Quesada stared ahead frowning, and waited to be greeted and addressed. But how astonished he was, he and the commander both, when the leader of the Whites sank to his knees at the entrance, buried his face in his hands and wept openly. The other five stood in silence, heads bowed. Quesada and his commander exchanged glances. They suspected a trap. The governor leaned forward: "What message do you bring?"

The leader opened his hands, raised his damp face, a memory jolted Quesada. The commander jumped to his feet, ran to the man who slowly stood up, the commander and the man in the feathered cloak stared at one another, then fell into each other's arms, and Quesada even heard a gentle sob escape the commander. Quesada slowly approached the two men, sunlight through the tent flap dazzled him. The commander released the stranger; Quesada recognised Alcobazo, leader of his river flotilla. He stood there transfixed. He extended a hand towards the man with the bushy drooping moustache, speechless seated himself again on the Zipa's golden chair. Everything was clear.

The other five men in feathered cloaks came forward behind Alcobazo, the commander shook hands with them and had them wait outside. Alcobazo was back in their power. He must make his report. But when he began to report that those five men in feathered cloaks from Peru were all that he had saved from the five ships and two hundred men who had set out with him, yes, from five ships and two hundred men, his voice failed.

And for several minutes, for the first time during all those terrible events, the other two men lost composure at the thought of what had happened here, and the memory of the cruel months they themselves had endured. For the first time a subtle tremor ran through them, profound darkness in which one lives and strives.

They gathered their wits. They were once more governor, commander, captain. Alcobazo told of the initial fair voyage, the grounding of the first ship, the silty side channel, the struggle against rapids. He reported how they had lost the first ship in the rapids. He wept in hopeless outraged fury: they had encountered no enemy, had not even fought forest and mountain as the others had done and they themselves did later on, they had merely fallen ill and starved. In the end they had no way out but to make an assault on the mountains from the rapids where the last vessels lay. He reported at length on their desperate struggle with forests, mountains and hunger. When only ten remained some natives took pity on them, tended them for a few days, finally the same Indians mentioned a great band of White men marching through the mountains. They thought it must be their governor. It was Belalcazar. He took them in, he had plentiful provisions and enough equipment for an army. When Belalcazar heard they belonged to the governor's band, he speeded up the pace. And now they were glad to see that the governor had reached here first. But again Alcobazo's voice broke.

The governor soothed him: Did Alcobazo now regard himself as Belalcazar's man? The captain shook his head vigorously: Why, because Belalcazar rescued me? No. He asked the governor only that he treat graciously with Belalcazar, who had been sent here to stay.

Then Alcobazo and the others were taken to lodgings in the camp. Quesada and the commander sat facing each other in the tent, baffled.

They were in the New Indies.

To the south the Amazon surged across its plain and drew rivers to it.

They had heard the voice of Sukuruja, jubilant river spirit.

The Sun is silent

DARK PEOPLE MOVED through the streets of Funza. The few children running around were naked, men and women clad in rags. They were hungry, needed to go to the fields. The White tolerated this, they too needed fresh produce. The fields in which the dark people toiled were their fields, they had been assigned to them, tools lay undisturbed where they had left them, the sun shone as harsh and big as every day, but the Sun, the great Father in the Sun, kept silent about his decisions. The Sun had sent the Whites, fearsome as jaguars. So the Father wanted to destroy his people. In the plantations they climbed trees to pick fruit, but they were afraid of the tree, why should it hold still, perhaps it would shake and break and throw them to the ground? The Father in the Sun had sent the White jaguars, who knew what lay concealed in the fruit, could you eat it, was it poisonous? O great Father.

They toiled in the fields, those who survived that night and day, fed grain to doves. They were allowed down to the river to fish. But the paralysis never left them, the Father had sent these White jaguars to destroy them. They feared they might pollute fish or fowl and suffer some new calamity. There was no one to give advice. Doves in their big coops fluttered and eyed them, pecked as usual, their droppings looked normal, their cooing was unchanged. But what would happen to these lovely creatures if they were to peck grain from their hands? And after all that had happened, how could they cast net or line, the fish would sicken.

Looms in the houses lay smashed, rags of the Whites beside them. Having no priests they had no idea what to do with these malignant items. Covering their faces, groaning and praying, they used sticks to drag the Whites' refuse into the street, burned it, buried the ashes.

In the houses were women and girls who had been assaulted by Whites. Their husbands and parents avoided them, fasted and cowered in corners, called fearfully for priest and sorceress. The Whites out there disputing Belalcazar's arrival had no idea what was happening in the houses. They were surprised how many savages starved to death over the next few days, and were carried out of town. These were all women and girls who had endured molestation by the alien demons. Many were killed out of fear, and could be moved only by using sticks in the same way the Whites' rubbish had been cleared. This was really a job for priests, now they had to fend for themselves. Even more awful were cases where a girl or woman lay down in front of brother or husband or father and begged: "Kill me," and where fear, desperation, horror, love wrestled together. Sometimes Spanish soldiers surprised dark people at such deeds, which they labelled beastly, and sometimes the woman, once a nobleman's spouse or daughter, survived, and was abducted away to the camp.

Town and surrounding countryside were disturbed by the throb of alien drums, sending mysterious instructions into the air so that no one knew how to go on living in the town. The governor's sentries outside the Zipa's palace saw ever more people gather around the idol pillar with flowers and fruit, the only offerings left to them. Darkskins came out of the palace and spoke to the throng. On the second evening following Belalcazar's arrival a big discussion took place outside the palace. The soldiers, who found the cowardly stupid savages ridiculous and repulsive, paid no attention to the nonsense and endless chatter going on at the pillar.

Just then the people received happy news from the palace. The Zipa would depart from the town in a few days and make his way to the holy place Sogamoso. He was even now making preparations for the journey. Those who wished to purify themselves must leave town.

≈≈≈

At the first blush of dawn the imperious commander appeared with a contingent of troops, marched across the marketplace and along the main streets, sent patrols into side streets and had more than a thousand able-bodied men herded into the plaza. There they were loaded up with provisions. A few hours later he marched with them back to camp, where they were set to work digging defences. There was still no direct contact between Belalcazar and Quesada, but quarrels and provocations between the two bands of soldiers were becoming frequent. It was clear that Belalcazar would not delay much longer his preparations for a showdown, for ever since the initial division of spoils the governor's soldiers had flaunted their gold rings, chains, discs too openly, and gave themselves lordly airs.

But there came no attack by the governor on Belalcazar, nor by the latter on the governor, and no local disagreement led to an outbreak of hostilities. Instead something happened that neither Quesada nor Belalcazar nor anyone else in their camps had expected.

The volcano called Europe had begun spewing out its people. They fell to earth on every coast. They were on the hunt for gold, discoveries, they wanted war, dominion, fame. They stormed across the earth, like autumn birds surplus to requirements in their native lands, flying in inexorable masses to their tropical home, cloud-high, thousand upon thousand. Their desire: death, or transformation.

Across the savannah that Quesada and his half-dead troops had been the first to glimpse from the terrible mountains, and over which magnificent Belalcazar had ridden with his glittering train clad in gaudy feather cloaks of Peru, together with a great quantity of coloured people, cannon and muskets – across this abandoned landscape of maize fields and flower gardens, on the same day as the first mustering of slaves, dark people came loping, they had been hunting game in the eastern forests, and at the gate of Belalcazar's camp conveyed news which spread to his soldiers and from there to Quesada's soldiers: White men are hastening down from the mountains to the southeast, a great train, many wild animals, two who went close to look have already been shot.

And soon they came storming up, White men, a considerable horde, following their darkskinned scouts but lacking other auxiliaries. They must have assessed the lay of the two camps from the heights above the savannah, for without hesitation the new arrivals came to rest beside Belalcazar's camp at the south-eastern exit from town. At once a small detachment separated from the horde, half came swarming out across the fields, the rest marched with arquebuses into town.

They had the shape of men, the corpse colour of the sickly northern lands. But they looked like animals in their skins of jaguar, lion, deer. Like animals they hurled themselves on field and town, seeking food. Whites and darkskins kept out of the way. The newcomers croaked: "Move!" and devoured whatever food and drink they found, many at once vomited. Then they gathered sacks and baskets and jugs and began to carry provisions to their camp, and returned to fetch more. Clearly most of the horde was too weak to seek its own food.

What befell Nicolaus Federmann and his band

THIS HORDE WAS led by Nicolaus Federmann from Ulm – the Feather Man. At first they were a merry crew, eager to stake all. They wanted the same as the others: a journey into blessed doom.

Federmann sailed from the port of Sanlucar de Barrameda in Andalucia. He had a wonderful voyage. They came upon an island of birds, no humans lived there, only birds. They lived so densely packed you could kill them with a stick and carry them off. The noise was deafening, and when the boat sailed into a bay the birds flew up in such clouds the men were frightened. On another island they found dark people, but there were already Whites there, with side arms and small cannon.

When Federmann and his people went ashore, a soldier fell in love with the daughter of a White trader. And as the ships prepared to hoist sail again, the soldier went with ten accomplices to the girl's house and stole her away along with her old nurse and a quantity of possessions, and brought her on board. A few hours after they set sail a violent storm arose, the ships struggled against the tempest and had to return to port during the night. But many of the island's inhabitants, Whites and natives together, torches flaring, thronged the beach. They made a great noise and sent a boat to Federmann: he was to deliver the girl and the nurse and the possessions and hand the soldier over for punishment, or else they would all be helped into the next world. Federmann refused.

Now the Whites of the island brought up their cannon and

fired. The first ball brought down a mast, the second hit the stern, the third wounded a number of people and destroyed some rigging. At this the flotilla's crew demanded that the lovesick soldier and the girl be handed over. They had not ventured here to gamble away their lives on account of a romantic attachment by one of their number, and since he had not asked their opinion he should carry his own skin to market.

Next morning, the storm having abated, Federmann invited some of the Whites to come aboard the flagship for talks. He at once conceded to the negotiators that they had been wronged, and declared himself ready, as an upright man, to deliver the girl and all the rest. But when he had the girl and her companions brought before him and the others, an insuperable difficulty revealed itself. In the interim the flotilla's chaplain had formally married her to the soldier. What on earth was to be done? Federmann asserted that he was powerless. The girl's father tried to force her to go with him. She refused. He wept, had to give in. The aggrieved islanders disembarked. Federmann magnanimously declared that he would forego punishing the island or demanding compensation for the damage, there was no time. But when they arrived at the town of Coro, he dismissed the soldier, his bride and the servant because of all the trouble they had caused the flotilla.

Coro, on the gulf of Maracaibo, was once ruled by cruel Alfinger. The town swarmed with White adventurers, bandits, deserters and slaves, Alfinger had bequeathed his brood. General von Speyer and Federmann his captain-general augmented their forces from this resource, and ventured inland with them. They agreed to march separately, Speyer to the east, Federmann to the west. They would rendezvous on the coast of Barquisimeto. They marched together for a while along the line of mountains. Then Federmann left the mountains and made his way into the savannah.

Dark jungle clung to slopes. They came upon a huge deposit of salt in a river bed, it was a high bank covered with earth.

Federmann was a big broad-shouldered man with a flowing red beard and bright blue eyes. He would bawl out a song when in the mood. He had found the voyage irksome, because of the need for strict discipline. On the march he sighed with relief and laughed. They fell upon the country like a flock of blithe young birds.

The plain of the llanos stretches away uniform, endless. Grass stands tall and dense, a green and yellow sea, the hottest of suns burns overhead, grass stands unmoving, now and then cloud shadows flit across. The grass stands so tall it closes over the head of a man on horseback. Slowly clearings begin to open up, little watercourses trickle, muddy lagoons appear, red ibis pace in the water, garzas are snow-white, complaints rise from blue waterfowl with long-toed feet. Down through glowing air, shimmering in the heat, huge white storks descend. They wear purple throat rings, and jab their strong dangerous bills in the mire.

The band wanders, wanders. A marvellous journey begins.

They trip over tree roots. There are no hills or mountains to afford an overview. But they encounter forests of chaparro trees, which they climb to look for smoke. The chaparro groves are shady and refreshing, the horses graze, soldiers remove their doublets and stretch out, trousers rolled, they don't mind the scratchy grass, but insects bite. They are thirsty and must be stopped from throwing themselves at muddy puddles. As they march off they break big leaves from the chaparro trees to cover head and shoulders, some make a complete cloak, but let it fall, the leaves are too heavy.

At last they find smoke, a village. These are poor dark people, they have a banana plantation, offer fruit and fowl and game as well, but cannot be persuaded to serve as bearers. They are nervous. The horses in particular frighten them. When the general has the horses led out of sight the chief relaxes, and the gift of some red bonnets and iron fish hooks secures forty bearers and some guides. Their docility does not last long, half the guides vanish in the long grass, and the general has no option but to rope the rest together. For the grass is so overwhelmingly dense and the people so nimble that they vanish within a moment of leaving the train. The remaining natives tremble and are scared out of their wits. Native interpreters, tasked to find what is bothering them, report that it is the horses, just the horses that walk along beside them and sometimes whinny. "Why don't they like the horses? They are tame, eat grass, drink water."

"You sit on them. They carry you wherever you want. You are in league with the horses, but later all the people, or the best of them, will be given to the horses as a sacrifice."

"Tell them that is stupid, they are our horses, our beasts of burden."

"They won't change their minds."

"The devil with them!"

The plain of grass is endless, it rises and falls gently like waves. One night all the bearers are gone and only three guides remain, who act like lunatics, weep and implore. The general watches the drama, he sympathises and at first, irritated by their unhelpfulness, is prepared to release them, but he needs them. He has them whipped, threatens them. They move on south.

He addresses his people: "We promised Georg von Speyer we would march west. Here's an enormous plain of grass. It extends to the coast. The chief and the more sensible people from the village we passed through have told us: it goes on and on but then reaches the South Sea. So what should we do: march west and meet Georg von Speyer at the coast? Or head for the South Sea? I think we should head south and discover new islands. In the west people all run around like dogs chasing the same bone. Let them crack each other's skulls, for all we care."

He laughs and sings the evening through while the men confer, and not one wants to desert him. And what would Georg von Speyer think and would he punish them and should they leave him there waiting on the coast. That, boomed Federmann, is my business. Men who discover the South Sea cannot be bully-ragged like little girls.

There are two bold captains in the troop, Sandoval and Lopez, both of noble blood, impoverished warhorses from families whose pride they are. Sandoval is a short man, powerful, has bandy legs, grizzled beard and hair, chestnut brown. He has lost his front teeth, and lisps. Lopez is pockmarked, blond, broad-chested, he killed a man in a duel, is a wanted man. These two, bosom friends who huddle together in endless palaver, are fervid backers of the South Sea plan. The darkskins annoy them with their stupidity and cowardice. The monk execrates the idolatry of these heathen. When they come to a new place all he does is look for water so he can consecrate it and baptise the heathen. He can't do much by way of instruction, there's no time, and he finds their painted faces so abhorrent that he merely utters a few pious words and pours a bucket of water over their heads. Then he has a good wash, and curses this profession that has driven him to strange lands and beasts like these, while others sit cosily in their cloisters and gorge themselves. Gonzalo and Roman, the two noble captains, want to head for the South Sea, the captain-general has named the goal, they will indeed reach the South Sea and these mules, these donkeys the darkskins impede their progress.

If these obstinate donkeys wanted, they could just let themselves be baptised without further ado, and then gratis and for nothing would become good Christians, just because they've been discovered, while all around thousands of their fellow savages still run about like beasts of the forest. And what do we ask in return? Not even gold, for these forest creatures have none, or conceal it. Only food and bearers and guides, and an interpreter for the neighbouring tribes. For these brown forest beasts lack even the wits to speak the same language, but after a day's march speak a different one, and there's another good reason not to fall in too deep with them. If not for the food that can be had from them, best would be simply to kill them. They should make an honest decision to clamber in the treetops like monkeys, and stop pretending to be human.

Little lisping bandy-legged Gonzalo would prefer to fling them all over a cliff. He is coarse and direct, always has the best horse in the troop. He importunes the captain-general: "Isn't it enough that we drown here in this sea of grass, shrivel in the sun – not to speak of hunger, snakes, pests – but we must also suffer the company of these heathen?"

"Then what will you live on, Gonzalo?"

Gonzalo advocates surprise attacks. Alas these are not always practicable, drums transmit reports from village to village, there are refugees who spread rumours. This enrages Gonzalo: "We baptise them, let them share in God's mercy, and they run off to spread rumours. Wipe them out, general, wipe them out, it's the only way." The general utters soothing words.

As they pull south the sun is always overhead, but on every side there is tall grass and the ground underfoot is hot. If you wear a cuirass you cannot remove it on the march, under the cuirass everything dissolves and becomes a sponge. Horses find food, but not the men. They pray: if the South Sea's going to come, let it come soon. Who can go on like this. Oh for a breeze, a breeze. There are not many villages, who would want to live here, and when you do stumble on a village it is unaccountably empty, the people have left their rubbish lying about. So you do what you want, and out of aggravation burn down huts and houses. Federmann warns: the enchanting South Sea surely lies not far off, but if we have no guides we might walk round in circles and find ourselves one day in the mountains with Georg von Speyer. The soldiers see the sense in this, but what good are empty huts. The general replies: "We must show the heathen we are men of peace who treat them kindly, then they won't run away." But he has to listen as a monk explains: "It is not because of us they run away, but because of the horses." The general joins in the soldiers' bellowed laughter.

At last they come upon a settlement on a riverbank behind a lagoon, and the red-brown people who live there are – dwarves! The tallest reach only to the chest, the women are even smaller. Three brown guides are still with them, a certain understanding is achieved. They know nothing of a South Sea. But when gold and silver are mentioned, they point to the south and mention a very wealthy people. "Ah," sighs Federmann, "how often have we heard that. And when we tell them to guide us, they run away." Food is brought, and they are astonished to see what can be made from just one tree. This murichi palm, the chief explains, is the ancestor of mankind, and when a great flood, a deluge, covered the whole world, only this was saved of all living things, and people came from it.

At discussions of this sort with the little people, who showed the usual fear of horses, the two captains were in their element. Truly, they said, you eat the fruit of the murichi tree, which is sour-sweet, you drink beer made from its juice, which makes you merry, timber from the trunk makes huts and houses, and its fibre serves for hammocks to sleep in. But for God's sake, when all's said and done you must drive out of the skulls of these dwarves the ludicrous fancy that this tree is their ancestor. You simply cannot let such nonsense loose in the world. During their rest days in this village of dwarves the two captains keep two educated men at their side. They gnaw away at the topic. They recruit soldiers to help reveal the surfeit of idiocy, stupidity and ignorance of these people. Once they go so far as to ask the chief of the dwarves to show them their burial sites, to prove that the skulls of the heathen contain not brains but flesh or some kind of weed. The chief told them a funeral would take place next day. So now they experience a remarkable thing, and the world grows even madder.

Next morning a number of dwarves have assembled behind a house, from which an ostentatious singing and wailing had come all the previous night. The soldiers think someone is sick. Then in the morning people line up outside the house and more line up at the back, and after lots of speeches and shilly-shallying some take up spades and begin to dig. The whole village is now in great commotion, the little people have smeared themselves in gaudy colours, lounging soldiers see fantastical figures emerge from an outlying house. They carry huge trumpets and blow into them, they leap about in the most comical fashion until they reach the small open space where many people, including women and children, have gathered. The Whites near this house – Federmann is there with one of the captains – observe a grisly scene. At first they don't understand the purpose of the natives' digging, and are puzzled that they're allowed to watch the unearthing of a treasure, or they think someone has died and soon they'll bring the corpse along.

But two men with feathers waving about head and chest

climb into the hole and lift out a tall painted pot. They place it on a mat of palm leaves. Loud cries erupt from the bystanders. They prostrate themselves in reverence. And now the two men with feathers remove the lid from the pot and tip out something dry and black. It is a corpse. It is quite naked. Its head is pressed onto its chest and the legs are tucked up to the chin. They lay the bundle, which does not seem heavy, on the mat beside the pot. They are surrounded by cries and lamenting. And now the masked figures and trumpeters dance away from the open place. The people behind the house have lit a big fire, and the Whites see how the corpse that has lain so long in the pot is being burned on a stack of logs. The masked figures leap endlessly towards each other with curious movements, and all the while the trumpeters blow long hollow notes. They drone and bleat, sometimes just one instrument, sometimes several together, sometimes all at once in their different registers. The nervous general asks the interpreter what it all means.

"It is a funeral."

"But the man has been dead for ages."

"He died fifteen years ago. He was a chief."

"And why do they not leave him there?"

The interpreter, a darkskin, answers: "They keep the custom. The dead demand it." He gives no more information, Federmann already knows that he keeps many things to himself.

The corpse burns on the pyre, they bring a fresh pot, throw the charred bones into it and now, after filling in the hole behind the house, all traipse back to the open space. And only there do they witness the biggest horror, which had escaped their notice at the pyre: the corpse was not completely burnt, one of the masks carries the little shrivelled black skull in his hands, a ball on a short stick. Surrounded by the ghastly trumpeting, he proceeds solemnly at the head of the other masks, they leap, stamp, slide away to the outlying house. At this point the open space grows merry, cooking fires are lit, the people who were gathered behind the house squat around, they have the pot with the charred bones. You see them pound the bones, heat the pot over a fire, keep pounding and grinding, and now huge gourds of cashiri are brought, the festive drink, they add it to the bonemeal in the pot, strain it, the chief drinks first, then the others in the centre and then it goes around.

The White general sees this, he says to the captain: "If we're not careful they'll offer us some of that."

The monk speaks to the captain: "You're right, these are not people, they're beasts, they eat their dead. Those over there in the middle, I know them, both are his sons, they quaff beer containing the ashes of their father."

Pockmarked Lopez, big and blond, mocks: "Padre, you baptised the whole lot yesterday, all your mercy has gone for nothing."

Federmann quits the festive scene in disgust, but the two captains wait until the happy noise abates somewhat and the people start to mill about, then they draw the chief and a few others to one side. Coarse Gonzalo, through the interpreter, asks the chief: "Do you know, wretch, that you are baptised?"

"Yes."

"What have you just done, dog? Guzzling on a corpse."

"He was a great man. He has lain there for fifteen rainy seasons and dry seasons, now he is our great ancestor and will help us."

Exasperated, Gonzalo asks his friend: "Can you understand this, Lopez? Should we not break their heads right now for such shameless nonsense?" He roars at the priest: "And you saw it all, padre, you baptised these people."

The priest frowns and lifts his arms: "Better ask the general."

"Break their heads," Lopez roars at the chief, who shrinks back, "translate that, interpreter."

The interpreter too is frightened, but Lopez draws his sword, the cacique understands this. He and the others run away, Lopez can barely restrain the rabid bandy-legged captain, who froths at the mouth, it must come from the sun's terrible glare. For it burns relentlessly from an immense bright blue sky directly onto their heads, the sky a single blue crystal, sea of blue fire, the sun a ray streaming from it.

The village is in a panic, the feast has dispersed in haste. Federmann rushes from his tent, what's happening, hurries to the open space, it's empty, he questions the captains who come up to him, they shrug, but the general at once suspects the bandy-legged cavalier, Gonzalo, whose face is still red with anger and who reports on his encounter with the chief.

Then Federmann, downcast, returns with them to his tent and swallows his rage. Wearily he urges moderation on Gonzalo: "We'll never reach the South Sea. Look at the sky: an abyss. Look at the plain: an abyss. We thresh around between them. And you concern yourselves with what these heathen eat. Let them rot, as long as they provide bearers and guides."

"They are Christians, believe me, general, they are false lying wretches. General, if we don't show these donkeys that they must abandon their idolatry and we do not relish their games...."

The general interrupts: "You're a good captain. Now let me warn you in earnest. Look at my face, Captain Gonzalo, so you don't misprise me. Remember the soldier who caused that scandal on the island: I brought him along as far as Coro. If he had been more than a mere soldier I'd have executed him at sea. The only one who gives orders here is me. The natives are to be well treated. Do you understand this order, captain, yes or no."

"General, I treat them well."

"Yes or no."

"Yes, general."

So he shakes the little bulldog by the hand. Next morning they break camp, luckily they have caught a good two dozen people for bearers and guides.

In the land of turtles

THEY ARE WELL laden with provisions, they have dried maize in quantity, they come upon bananas, the sky is veiled, the plain a burnt yellow, breezes loft clouds of yellow dust.

One day the clouds are strangely thick and hot, and now they see and smell that it is not dust but smoke. They have long feared this, the plain is burning. The horizon above the clouds glows red. Flames leap and fall. But it is remarkable how calm the bearers remain, they nod at the sight and keep on. The wind drives smoke towards them, they evade it, the black fire-filled world moves away to the north, a crackling roaring heat-emitting force, at its edge birds of prey swoop down on fleeing creatures: hares, lizards, snakes.

Now the sky is changeable, sudden gouts of rain pour down. Then cicadas start singing, the shrill song emerges from trees and bushes, by evening it is like a seething cauldron.

The march heads southeast, they are glad of the rain, it refreshes and then stops. Life with the dwarves indeed proves tolerable if they are left unmolested, they are harmless and gentle, horses and bloodhounds are kept out of sight as far as possible, they hand over what they have and sigh with relief when the strangers leave. The country becomes swampier, lagoons are as big as lakes.

Plants with shiny green leaves grow in dense bushy groves. Horses nibble at them. Then the troop must halt, to the consternation of the riders the horses sink to their knees one after another, their heads droop, they can't move. Finally some fall over. For many hours they remain motionless. They sleep. No amount of prodding puts them on their feet. Then one after the other they become lively, prick up their ears, swish their tails, their skin twitches in the thorny scrub, and at last they stand up. They are thirsty, drink what they can, and plod sluggishly on. That was the guacamacha bush.

The region becomes more enchanting. There are no mountains or forests. Much is stirring on the plain, in swamps, which rain has turned to actual rivers. They cross rivers in dugouts, horses are driven across, hounds wade and swim. Enticing green-fringed water. The soldiers would like to march in water all day long, they can proceed slowly beneath foliage, it's shady. And then a sleek snakelike creature shows itself, breaks the surface, on its belly a finny fringe undulates, it is yellow-brown like the mud it wallows in, long as an arm. Woken from the mud it approaches a man's legs, or his belly and back if he's swimming, he screams and jerks, has to be helped up, he's had a shock. It takes time to calm him down.

It's the electric eel. When they wade through deep water they hear blood-curdling screams from horses, and if they're not quick enough the beast is dragged under and swept away.

This world of swamps, plain and grass comes to an end. Wild swine run grunting over burnt ground, the earth shakes under the short legs, they run in herds a hundred strong, leader at the fore, big and small together. They charge along, black and bristly, close to the ground, best keep out of the way.

And here at last are rivers that wend their way to the South Sea. Water builds in the sky and on the earth. Weeks ago the sky was a single glowing blue crystal, they were enveloped in drought, trudged along between the abyss of sky and the plain. Now, in the cool damp night, flocks of big bats dart overhead. They make camp on little hills. And as they gaze out at night, there over the swamps and nearby stretches of water a blue fire appears. The flames die, flare up somewhere else. When later they ask dark people about this they are evasive, they make a secret of countless things in their land. The soldiers are nervous, and press on.

Such rain. Rivers swell. If only they could divert to higher ground. But they are the band of Nicolaus Federmann from Ulm. They are aiming for the South Sea.

Progress slows. They fall hostage to raging torrents of rain that force them to seek shelter wherever they stand, under trees, tents. Sometimes half the band sits in trees to wait out the storm, so as not to be swept away by the rain. But afterwards all their provisions are wet, and disgusting vermin have penetrated everywhere. They stand on the banks of rivers grown wide as lakes. Always there are villages of coloured people. But even these are migrating north, away from the rain. You could believe they are fleeing the llanos and leaving it to the Whites, who mean to drown here. When shall we see the South Sea and its new isles of gold? It won't be easy to find. For if it was, others would already have scrambled there from every side and plundered it. But we shall come through under our Captain-general Federmann.

And there is no more thought of the King of Spain and home

and being a wealthy man at home, whether in Castile, Andalucia or Italy or Germany. On, on to the South Sea.

And now they awake at dawn, which lasts no time at all, and the red fireball erupts straight from night into the sky and hurls grey shreds of night away behind it. The sun sits in the sky and calls out: It is time, see there the paths, rivers, mudholes, I grant you a handful of new hours for the South Sea.

So they go on. Water surges across lagoons, small fowl strut on the shore, they puff themselves up, bob and whoop in front of their females. They are messengers and pathfinders for the South Sea.

And when you climb into boats with the dark people and they shoot fish, you are grateful for the fish and the dark men, fish nourish you for the journey. And you look around tranquilly, and go to sleep under the vault of night sky decked out in all its medals for a magical ceremony. You know you are nearly at your goal.

And so they come to the Otomaco people. The wide river is called Apure. Apparently this flows only a short distance before joining a huge stream that empties into the sea. This is called Orinoco.

Along with the rivers, forests appear. Spreading mimosas stand at the water's edge, and when you touch them their leaves snap together like living creatures, it runs along the branches, a marvellous sight. The Otomaco live here, they have no murichi palm but some other tree. They peel its bark, so soft they use it for clothing. The Whites seize on this, happy to throw away their disintegrating rags. On the general's orders a load of bark is gathered and packed securely for the march. Fine hopeful days follow. You must protect yourself from leeches that cling to the legs and suck your blood. The natives live among a thousand species of animal that they distinguish and have a special name for, some they do not name, and you know this is because they're guarding a secret. Hummingbirds fly, you've never seen so many, and how they flit swift as lightning through the air no bigger than a butterfly and, hovering, stick their beak into a flower. Parrots, fiery orange troupials, crowing loros.

The brown people show the Whites their enemies – but they do not call them enemies, they speak cautiously, respectfully: termites that live in field and forest in little mounds that look like clumps of soil, they keep guests in their cells, beetles and spiders. They are so numerous, explain the brown people in wonder, that no human tribe can compare with termites. They themselves have taken to the river to avoid them, their houses stand on piles in the water and so are safe.

But termites are strong beings, even though small and blind. The natives point to old huts they have preserved, they knock on a plank, a finger goes right through, it is like sponge, the tiny termites have devoured everything.

Now they are surrounded by jaguars. The big cats slink around the band. No one knows what they want. They come in packs, never attack anyone. But the band of Whites attracts and unsettles them for some reason. As always the darkskins say nothing.

But one night the Whites are wakened by their sentries. They seize weapons, wonder why no alarm is sounding, but the darkskins make signs to keep quiet and follow, weapon or no weapon.

The broad rushing Apure lies below in the gentle light of the moon. Nothing breaks its rippling surface. Reflecting stars and moonlight, the river runs swift, the Apure, heading for the Orinoco. A cool breeze blows from the forested banks. No birds call. But as they step cautiously down from the forest to the river they hear a strange persistent noise, a rubbing, scraping, scrabbling. Sometimes a clacking and creaking. Sometimes a dull heavy crash, followed by the same general scrabbling. They realise it is not in the water but on the bank. A broad smooth high beach of white sand and mud extends along the southern bank to the east. In the moonlight a low dark mass is moving and shoving, it is many yards long, sometimes it seems to rest, but keeps coming at a steady slow pace. It is a huge dark blanket being drawn across the beach. They whisper to one another and marvel: these are turtles. They come to a halt. It's a whole army. Hiding by day, at night they go wandering, and now you can pick out individuals on the edge, brown-black chequerboard shells, a little sharp point like a sign, the triangular head stretched upward, hemmed in. They proceed, shell hard against shell, a huge movement of giant dark moonlit shells marching in their myriads. They halt in a clump, some are forced over the backs of others, the ones on top keep moving, the double-decker keeps on until a gap opens and those on top clunk down again. And behind them slink big wild cats, jaguars that encircle the moving mass, lunge at the scrabbling edges and try to pick something off. The turtles toil in the moonlight, the whole mass stops, loses itself in sand and mud, they bury themselves, this is their breeding season.

The Whites ask about the nightly procession of turtles, the brown people know all about it, they pay grave attention to the lengthy discussion. One indicates that he wishes to tell the Whites something of the turtles. The interpreter translates:

"The turtle has no malice. It is a good person. Once a turtle settled under a tree to rest. The tapir came, stretched its snout and said, 'Go away turtle'. The turtle closed his ears. The tapir nudged his head with its snout, huffing and puffing: 'Turtle, go away.' He poked out his head, scratched with his legs, said: 'You snuffled at me, that's rude.' 'Turtle, go away.' He pulled his head back into the shell. 'This is my tree. You are rude, tapir.' The tapir has horny feet, it steps on the turtle's legs, the turtle goes away saying: 'I'll see you when the rains come.'

"Rain fell, the turtle set off. He came upon a spoor, the turtle bowed and said, 'I have come a long way. Here's some grass for you.' The spoor said thanks. The turtle asked: 'How long is it since your master was here?' The spoor said, 'A long time.' The turtle set off again. There was another spoor, the turtle bowed: 'I come from afar. I met one of your sisters here, I brought her reeds and bamboo.' The spoor: 'It's lonely out here. What is my sister up to?' The turtle replied: 'These are leaves from the forest where your sister lives. How long is it since your master came this way?' The spoor looked up at the sky: 'Stay till sunset, tell me about my sister, you'll meet my master in two days.' The third spoor:

'I have heard about you, turtle. The ants reported it.' 'Here's a flower from the forest. When did your master come by?' 'Today. Stay with me tonight, I'll make myself pretty for you.' The river surged angrily. The turtle dared not speak. At noon he crawled down. 'Where is your father?' 'I don't know.' 'Why not?' 'You are angry with my father.' 'He kicked me.' 'Leave me alone.' The turtle dug himself in. The tapir came out of the water, the turtle confronted it: 'I have found you. You huffed and puffed and trod on me. Now we shall see if I am a man.' The tapir turned its back, the turtle bit its testicles and would not let go. The tapir turned round and round and cried for mercy. The turtle would not let go. The tapir jumped in the river, the river foamed to protect its father. The turtle would not let go. The tapir climbed onto the bank and died. Then the turtle let go. He called to the ants: 'Tell the spoors I have killed their master, because he behaved rudely to me.' To the tapir he said: 'Your son the river shall mourn you. I killed you. My relatives await me in the hollow, I shall summon them, we shall eat you.'

When the soldiers heard this tale they laughed. The brown people took this as a sign of gratitude and laughed in turn. Later they often believed it best to laugh loudly when the Whites said something to them. But the Whites misunderstood this sign of great courtesy, and behaved coarsely to the bewildered natives.

And in truth the deluge of rain makes progress impossible, days become weeks and weeks months, during which for better or worse the Whites are at the mercy of the brown people. On you trudge on for a few hours, have to turn back. If the brownskins who happen to be around were braver and more warlike, they could destroy you. But they see how the Whites want to move on, the rain prevents them, the rain is more powerful than the Whites, so they help and give.

And so as days become weeks and weeks months and the Whites come no nearer to the South Sea, a yearning grows among Federmann's troops to march and discover the South Sea and sail on great corvettes and sloops and brigantines to marvellous islands where they will become viceroys or gather gold and return home as knight or marquis – but others lose all such desire. Rain falls, thunderstorms rumble, you sit or lie in the damp heat in huts of palm, in the native rain-huts, you exercise the horses so they won't go lame, polish your guns. As you clean the little cannon you've dragged along you hear from one or another the tale of a seafarer and his crew who set out from Spain to find the mighty Amazon and sail up it. He had cannon on board, two or three. And when he came to the mouth of the river there were many islands and side channels and they got lost, and then a terrible storm rose, the anchors dragged. Then the people regarded their lovely cannon and said: "Before these ever fire a shot we shall drown and float in the water. Why carry them along." And they lashed anchor trees to the cannon and threw them overboard into water and mud. And there they stuck.

You watch the brown people, how they fish and do nothing, hunt and do nothing, sleep, eat, dance, love. You see how they prepare for the hunt, you are puzzled, you go with them and then do as they do. You learn to use a blowpipe, observe the trees, listen to the waterfowl. The Dominican and Captain Lopez are concerned and vexed to see this, they curse the endless rainy season, sent by the Devil to be their ruin.

"If we stay here much longer we'll see a pretty state of affairs. We were sent to win the heathen over for the Holy Church. But perhaps – I cannot say it."

The Dominican, coldly: "Our soldiers are becoming heathen. They are so already. We must urge him to move on. None should be led into temptation. We shall find ways to deal with sinners."

The Captain-general is in a cheerful mood and lends no ear to their complaints. At last the storms abate, waters recede, the time of waiting is over.

How hard most of the soldiers find it to part from the brown people. How they load up the bearers and themselves and mount the horses. Some sick men ask to be left with the natives, they're not afraid, and if Federmann's or some other troop come by they will tag along. The priest opens his mouth: "It has come to this already." Federmann orders the sick to be placed in boats, he presents gifts of fine glass to the brown people, and bids a sincere farewell. He wants to head south. You march off, say goodbye, give and receive presents.

Many of the Whites have actually painted themselves in festive colours.

To Cundinamarca

NOW THE TWO captains Gonzalo and Lopez, one bowlegged, one pockmarked, urged on by their spirituality, can no longer refrain from settling one last score with the brown people.

With a handful of men they turn back, ostensibly to fetch a forgotten item of provisions. Indeed they do demand provisions, assault the astonished people and at last give vent to their heart's desire with curses, threatening that they have a dozen bloodhounds with them. The brown people are gentle but not cowardly. The captains sport with them as the stupid brown creatures deserve. Now they have to fetch something. As the clerics advised, they go to the mask hut and bachelor house, overturn the stupid wide-mouthed wooden idols, hack them to pieces, the masks worn for idol worship are shredded with a few dagger thrusts. They take possession of the disgusting black skulls that hang there, painted black and yellow and hung with feathers. One shot from a crossbow brings them down, a blow from a club smashes them, the fragments are trodden into the earth. They have a little wooden cross that they fix to the wall as a replacement. Then it is the turn of the villagers. No brownskins are to be seen, a few are caught fleeing and tied up. As they approach the village a hail of arrows greets them. The dark people flee from the gunshot blasts of their enemy. The captains set fire to the huts, but the fires only smoulder and are soon extinguished by the rain.

From this sortie, Federmann realises that the cunning brown people suddenly show themselves hostile when they find themselves facing just a small number of Whites. He is mistrustful. But mistrust is useless. There are swollen rivers to cross. Now villages they come across, which ought to promise boats, are empty, the old dreadful scene. Federmann berates the captains, the men of God hold their tongues and dare not intervene, at last the general asks: "Do you mean to bring disorder to our band?"

Now the priests accuse him openly of provoking the excessive actions of the captains: "We are subjects of the Catholic king, destruction of idols is one object of the expedition. Instead the soldiers have become savages, many wear secret amulets given them by the heathen." Federmann declines to laugh, he foresees complaints in Spain. He thanks the priests for their information, the soldiers probably wear the amulets only as keepsakes, a joke, he'll confiscate them. He needs the priests' help. But he cannot tolerate sedition or division within his small troop.

What a rampant landscape they now find themselves in, bursting with steam and heat. Swamps filled with tall luxuriant vegetation. Dense towering groves of bamboo climb the hills. Then forests, now with broad yellow clearings full of fallen and rotting trunks, now shady and overgrown. Creepers climb high up the trunks of palms, drop from aloft like snakes and then twine back up. Deathly silence.

The wind wafts fragrances, the soldiers think: if only we had stayed with the brownskins. They wear their amulets concealed. Curious beards hang down from trees, long and grey. Once these forests seemed bewitched, now you listen out for bird calls to know how the day will be, check branches and the ground, and your thoughts and desires are those of an Indian. Hanging grasses make whole swathes festive, they twist in garlands between crown and trunk and dangle to the ground – what do the natives see in them? You see roots, snakes, kill a few and roast them. When a kind of typhus breaks out in the band and they come to a large, recently abandoned village, they make a halt. Everyone senses a decision is near.

You feel torpid. You want a sacrifice. Federmann the captain-general is here. You saw him throw spears with the brown people and shoot arrows, the brownskins liked him. But when the capricious captains, friends of the priests, are sent out here and there with a small detachment, they never fail in their rage to set fire to any village they find empty. Yes, they even fetched masks and skulls from one hastily evacuated village and pursued the people, and those they caught were forced into masks and made to hack the idolatrous skulls to pieces themselves. This is told later among the troops, who hate the officers. As the band rests in the empty village and rumours of this heroic deed circulate, the captain-general shuts himself away in his hut and ponders. Next morning when he summons officers, notary and priests to council, and orders Gonzalo and Lopez to appear before him, they are absent. Soldiers report that they rode out in the night and are not back yet. Federmann condemns their behaviour. Then the stern commander explodes: when the captains return they are to be brought to him, he will clap them in irons and hand them over to the governor in Coro for sentencing.

The horses of the two captains turn up that afternoon close by, but no bodies are found. It is never clear whether they were murdered and quickly buried by Indians, or by their own men.

The camp is silent. The sacrifice is made. Homeward march.

From the huts of quiet gentle tribes into whose secrets you have forced yourself, the way leads back to the familiar desolate sea of grass. They are in the region between the Apure and Meta rivers. To the east flow the Cunaviche, Capanaparo, Arichuna, Caicara. You pass through the territories of the Otomaco, Guamo, Quiva. The troop is no longer a troop, although it has a captain-general on whom it depends, and a field-captain, quartermaster, notary royal, priests and a monk. The priests again seek a way to reach the men. But they find to their horror that they are greeted with bored faces. The men avoid them, frowning. Nothing is said out loud against them. They complain to Federmann: we drag depraved semi-heretics back with us.

They reach the first foothills again. And though Federmann says nothing he knows that loyalty lies with the brown people the soldiers live among, a life with animals and on the water, and the priests are right, the men seem enchanted by the natives. Mountains, separation, will do them good.

But these forests, mountains, valleys, gigantic peaks that tower up ahead of them green and sombre, they are filled with brown tribes. And this time the captain-general agrees with his comrades: we must do battle! The men still sing songs from the llanos whose words they do not understand, you mock them but they won't be dragged from their way of seeing and questioning. They believe they must preserve themselves from danger with pigments and signs, they paint chest and arms and hips. Faces they dare not paint. Such strange huddled conversations they engage in. When a priest or officer approaches they fall silent.

You trudge through mountain forests. The air quivers with butterflies, fish in the rivers crowd so thickly that the water ripples over them as if over rocks.

Horses have done good service everywhere, now in the mountains they become a burden, stumble, must be unloaded. So you revert to the old search for native bearers. Federmann is glad to take the offensive, captains and priests are on his side. A captain sets off with fifty men, returns to camp with a hundred and fifty dwarves, soldiers look on encouraged, they know there's nothing for it but to fight these people, many dwarves were left lying and some soldiers were wounded, as you march off again the train is attacked by furious midgets trying to free the captives.

When you surprise a big village of dwarves, the chief, to whom you speak in friendly tones, offers himself as guide. He honours Federmann with some bows and arrows, and the biggest surprise comes three days later as you march off: the chief brings to the red-bearded captain-general a lovely young brown girl, she reaches to Federmann's armpit. The girl weeps, like all the others she takes the Whites for evil spirits, but Federmann delights in her, and the whole camp rejoices as the general, ignoring the headshakes of the priests, hugs the girl and keeps her at his side. She becomes the troop's mascot.

The trek over the mountains degenerates into a savage hunt. The men's mood is of unfocused resentment. They are belligerent, disappointed, enmeshed in their rage. The priests note with satisfaction that now they behave like proper soldiers. The troop refreshes itself in an appalling way. Among the Cagantuo they find lovely valleys, the people plant, dig, trade, they are proud and warlike. They do not deign to go with the Whites, the soldiers make violent assaults on some villages, then Federmann reins them in, they meet him halfway, a hundred and fifty Whites, four thousand natives, they hand out fishhooks, knives, axes and stay for weeks in the villages, the troop still cannot leave well alone. The villages are regular fortresses with palisades of wood. But living there you are already lord and master, the scornful White who stays aloof from the games of the savages. It happens that a fever afflicts the Whites, and when more than half the troop fall sick Federmann sees it as a sign and decides to break camp, for no White must be allowed to die here. The sick are strapped onto horses in pairs and led away, the rest are carried on litters bedecked with feathers, for these are great lords, you tell the natives, they don't go on foot.

There are surprising finds of gold in houses. You prick up your ears. Where was it, who was there, what, what?

Now every last shred of weakness disappears. You are ravished by the old lust for booty, glowering avarice is back, you're your old self again with your craving. Brown, red, turtles, jaguars, forget it all.

They came upon a large village, men with spears and arrows were standing on the heights beside it. Federmann walked down to the place. In the empty square they had put two stools with gold. When no natives appeared and Federmann entered the chief's house, it was barricaded from within. The general made it known to those inside that nothing would happen to them, he wanted to reciprocate the gifts, and was placing them on the ground. Then a hundred armed men came out with the chief. And when without preamble Federmann asked about gold, the anxious natives relaxed and brought a great quantity. The soldiers erupted in cheers. The general too was happy, and soothed the natives. They complained that he had treated neighbouring tribes badly. He stroked their hands: That was not his fault, just the anger of the horses after one of them was wounded.

The natives told of Cundinamarca in the mountains, a city called Funza and the great Zipa.

Now the final stage of the march. The soldiers had given up on natives, turtles, jaguars, lakes, had lost them all, scarcely a tremor left in them of all that. They scrambled for gold. They must grab it all. This stage of the journey turned them into savages. They went over icy passes. No bearers with them. They ate horses and hounds that froze to death. They hunted bear and jaguar. They were clad in animal skins.

And there, down below, lay the savannah.

Horsetrading among the victors

WHEN QUESADA HEARD how the new arrivals conducted themselves and that they were almost naked and clad in jaguar pelts and deerskin, once the first shock had passed he felt – he did not know why – a warm glow. He would help these have-nots. Clearly, they had endured many hardships. It reminded him of the lamentable condition in which he himself had arrived here. Yes, these poor devils turn up thinking to inherit something, and there were no more seats at the table. Sad, but alas that's how it is. The newcomers released Quesada from the incubus laid on him by Belalcazar the Magnificent.

And as the commander and all his troops laboured at the camp defences and considered a surprise attack on one of the other two groups, Quesada's thoughts ran on quite other lines: namely, that he now had lots of gold and could do something with it, and how to keep poor Johnny-come-lately in his poverty. For the poverty of the newcomers pleased him more and more. He observed the miserable sick rabble from afar, that's how we looked once, we were like that, and he thought with the equanimity of a marquis and a viceroy: what a dismal condition men can fall into. And he confided to Barreda his intention to preserve his men from the folly of joining forces with Belalcazar.

"For me it will be a mere bagatelle," he explained to Barreda, "to reach an understanding with Belalcazar on my own account. You don't believe me? I tell you, Belalcazar fears that the newcomers will take away what's left, or that I will ally myself with the newcomers against him. But I shall not do so. Why? I think that despite all the torments the newcomers have undergone, they are still merely in training, and we should not spoil them. In the end

Fortune can bless only one man." And with a sangfroid that won the hard savage commander's respect, the former functionary Quesada despatched two officers to Belalcazar to invite him for a meeting. Quesada, already wearing viceroy's boots, proceeded with all the assurance of a sleepwalker. How he blossomed under Fortune.

And Belalcazar came. The discussion took place in the open between the camps. Belalcazar exuded cordiality. They shook hands, and had mutual acquaintances in Toledo. Belalcazar's brother in law had almost married a niece of Quesada's, they were engaged but the girl preferred the convent. These were happy tidings.

They arrived at a general regulation of relations. Neither side would bring the natives joy by undertaking military action against the other. Quesada urged fervently: "With what these savages have, two such as us can live well." A large party of natives, escorted by numerous soldiers and surrounded by blood-hounds, came by heading for Quesada's camp, they made way for it. As they rode on a little, another train of people, a double chain tethered together, all dumb. Then the governor began to explain his plan to the other White man, in view of his solidarity. He offered enraptured Belalcazar an enormous amount of gold, to be weighed on the spot. A further quantity would follow. Belalcazar was moved: "I expected no less of you. The times when men kill for gold are over, thank God." They shook hands.

Awkwardly suppressing the urge to embrace, since this could cause them to fall from their mounts, they rode into Quesada's camp. "Peace, peace!" Belalcazar called to the suspicious soldiers. The men did not understand. When it was explained to them they said: "His gold comes out of the King's fifth."

At the weighing, it occurred to Quesada that he might have reached this agreement at the first and without the newcomers, since the magnificent man with his feathered cloak and sleek horses and well nourished men at his back seemed disgustingly lazy and out for easy pickings, and if you give them some they'll be content and go off to find new hunting grounds. Who

Belalcazar was showed itself in the ugliest manner shortly after this brief smooth encounter. The magnificent man, once masks were allowed to fall, initiated a lively commerce between his camp and Quesada's. He sold a number of his horses to the astonished governor, at a stupendous price. As for his weapons, which Quesada showed particular interest in relieving him of, he proved reticent. The Peruvian was exceedingly happy when the governor made an astonishing offer for the cannon and some arquebuses, and afterwards the governor himself laughed with the Peruvian in his tent. For it was obvious: if the Peruvian sold his armaments, the governor would have him cornered and could retrieve everything at his leisure. Belalcazar laughed tears: "What an affair that would be, governor! You are a clever chap. If I were King of Spain and had to decide whom to appoint to this new province, I would say: you and you alone!" This was one of the few moments during the expedition when the governor laughed aloud with others.

At this meeting, where everything went so happily and they put all travails and troubles behind them, mountains, poisoned arrows, swollen rivers, quagmires and hunger, Belalcazar began to prate and recount something of himself, especially how he had seized the city of Quito in the south by means of a surprise attack, and indulged himself extensively on the topic of his brilliant lieutenant, Ampudia by name: "Those colourful people will not forget my bold lieutenant. His chaplain has told me how Ampudia proceeded: like lightning and quicksilver. Like quicksilver he extracted all the metal from the houses, and like lightning he reduced the houses to ashes." The Peruvian's laughter rang out again.

Quesada coolly uttered a few compliments: "As long as this lieutenant makes no difficulties for you with the Spanish Crown."

"Oho, my good man. We bring gold. What problems will the Crown raise?"

Later that evening, over Indian beer, the wily Peruvian again spoiled the pleasure by broaching the matter of weapons. Quesada must provide something more before he can hand them over. He has not received enough for them. The governor lost his composure.

But why? He feared a trap, perhaps the Peruvian had heard about his decoy cannon and was indulging in blackmail. And indeed his opening gambit is: he knows Quesada's arquebuses and cannon are unusable. Quite different from his own case. Then he paused, and his tremendous laugh rang out at the dismayed governor: in point of fact his own cannon are really just for show. Yes! The barrels have long since rusted away inside. But on the outside they are cleaned and polished, he insists on that. Quesada is an innocent. All these savages need is a bang and a flash. The guns can manage that at least.

With heavy heart Quesada (oh the shame) asked: "And in what condition are your arquebuses?" Now he was furious, felt like a gullible wretch, and intended as soon as he could to wring his contractual partner's neck. Observing this, the latter said: "The arquebuses, thank God, are all in good order and skilled hands." And if Quesada doubts it, they can fire a demonstration volley at fleeing prisoners.

Quesada smiled sourly and sipped his beer. You can't believe a word the rascal says, he's a scoundrel, a blowhard, how to be avenged, you'll taste my vengeance. Truly, phlegmatic Quesada has learned to hate.

After this Belalcazar remained affable, and engaged on a grand scale in his horse-trade business on the savannah, which at least for him had turned out to be no battleground. His horses proved to be like his guns: they looked good on the outside, but were rotted away inside. When confronted over some horses, Belalcazar made no denial. Why should horses carry loads here, where there are so many heathen! The only thing a horse has to do in this country, he explained, is to live, show signs of life, really just keep standing on its four legs. It is enough that it breathe and keep its eyes open. Once – and this was attested by his men – he had a sick horse carried on a sort of wooden litter by several dozen natives. The savages had sooner or later shown reluctance to carry every other kind of load, but this they took up without a word, they made no attempt at all to escape. And when the horse died they flung themselves down before the bier, and were ready to follow it into death.

≈≈≈

Meanwhile Quesada attended to the leader of the savage newcomers, whom he referred to as his dear beggar. He sent him soft clothing and food, but it was no easy matter dealing with the newcomer, who to his astonishment revealed himself to be captain-general Nicolaus Federmann of Ulm, deputy to Georg von Speyer. For the newcomers were not after gold, but gold and pillage! Women and war! Just like him!

Quesada was flabbergasted. This place produced no end of surprises. A blind man scrambles up here and explains that he can't accept charitable gifts, he wants pillage. A starving robber captain makes demands, as if anyone were in a position to make demands here. But Federmann explained in complete guilelessness as they rode together on an outing: a payoff will not serve my turn. There was no meeting of minds. Let's think about it further tomorrow. But then it poured the next day, and the next. And then Quesada rode up to Federmann's camp, the general came out, they rode off side by side in conversation, and Quesada requested permission for his commander to ride into the stockade with a small detachment, to see Federmann's people. Federmann saw nothing amiss in this. He said: "He wants information about our strength. Let him. My soldiers are good, they have hair on their teeth. I'd advise no one to trifle with them." Quesada's commander had the same impression. Barreda met his leader an hour later and quietly made his report.

"Whatever shall I do with you!" confided Quesada – the chess player, merry cozener – to Federmann with a laugh, "do we really want to slaughter each other, and then perhaps my friend Belalcazar will wade in for the kill once one of us is lying there? Hand over your soldiers, give them to me! I like them. I shall pay them, and you, handsomely. And afterwards your soldiers can pillage to their heart's content."

Federmann was astonished, and growled in disgust: "A monstrously simple solution." And after he had thought over at length what it meant for him and his troop, he acceded. For though Federmann saw all the gold round about them, the journey had drained him, he had no stomach for fighting, he was a German and homesick. He admitted his suffering to the governor: "Say a good word. Say how we can manage this without loss of honour." There was nothing Quesada wanted more.

So they reached an accord. All three of them, Quesada, Belalcazar, Federmann, today, tomorrow or the next day, would set off for the Spanish court to report on their deeds and receive honours and distinctions. Meanwhile Quesada, given that Federmann felt himself too wearied, would lead the troops commanded by Federmann on a first reconnaissance march to the south. The rest should be decided back home.

Federmann insisted on the same share for himself and his soldiers as the Peruvian had received. The jubilation among his men was tremendous. They considered it a down payment.

And that night the town belonged to them.

And the remaining natives – there were still some thousands there – suffered another round of death, violation, horror.

And this time it was thorough, with no frenzy or drunkenness. Rage and destruction were the watchwords of Federmann's men.

That night the town was annihilated.

And now fire gained the upper hand, spread through carelessness, started out of spite by Barreda's men who disagreed with Quesada's orders. A night of peril. Whites fought one another in the flickering streets. Federmann and Quesada made an appearance to calm things.

In the morning over two hundred Whites – shot, many of them charred – were hauled from the rubble.

≈≈≈

On the high plateau the governor ordered slaves and his soldiers to erect a dozen big straw houses and a straw-roofed church. It was August, long months since they had set out, he from the mountains of Santa Marta, Federmann from Coro, Belalcazar from Peru. The three leaders rode past the low houses, Quesada pointed them out, the other two gentlemen congratulated him. The magnificent Peruvian said: "Surely the place is big enough already, the Indians have run away into the mountains and to the south, what do you plan to do with these houses?"

"They're for the soldiers."

"What soldiers?"

"Ours."

The gentlemen were greatly puzzled, and Federmann tugged his chin and said: "You must not think, governor, that our men came from Spain, Portugal, Holland, and Germany to dwell in a barn and keep guard over your church of straw in case the heathen try to burn it down."

"And what is your view, general? What? What will our soldiers do here?"

The two generals regarded each other. The Peruvian, on Quesada's other side: "You can't be serious, governor. Our soldiers squatting in these huts! Look at me. My father was a wood-cutter in Andalucia, I ran away, now see my weapons, my gold trim, the hat on my head, and me riding at your side and now we're off to the King of Castile where we can secure our rights. Holy Virgin, I'd like to see the fellow who could make me or my men sit in such a house."

They trotted over the silent savannah, behind them the town lay dead, the river wound muddy and slow.

Quesada: "In my native land there's a book they read about a knight with the same name as me, but they say it Quixote. I was telling my commander Barreda about it not long ago. This Quixote is a serious fellow, he rides out with lance, targe, shield and squire, engages in all kinds of silliness. Back home they laugh over this book. We consider Don Quixote mad. Can you believe that any man who rides around the open roads of Spain bearing arms and doing heroic deeds has his wits about him?"

The others asked him to continue. "Our heroes of the hour will quieten down. A few will have gold and return to Spain. Not many. And the gold will soon be gone. They won't want to be peasants over there. The only solution: let them live in my houses."

"To be peasants here?"

"If they want. If not, there is much more to conquer. But in the end every general must have troops he can trust to hold a place, so that no one can attack his rear." Now they saw the light. Quesada went on: "They can live in comfort here. They can catch savages whenever they want and put them to work tilling the soil. Martial ardour fades with the years." The other two liked this as well.

Belalcazar confided: "We need terrain such as this. Maybe they'll even send food over to Spain sometimes. For if there's no change, it is possible that people over there really will starve. Monks are good, but so many monks! If only they would fast, at least."

Federmann relished the joke: "No, they don't fast, those monks, they don't fast."

Quesada fixed them with a hard eye: "They pray. In the better monasteries they fast. Never forget, gentlemen, that we have two tasks to fulfil here: to conquer provinces for the Spanish crown, and to spread Christian doctrine."

Federmann sighed. Belalcazar whistled. The governor stared sternly ahead. Federmann stood in the stirrups and plucked bananas from a tree for himself and the others.

≈≈≈

Next day the generals came together with their staff on the open ground in front of the new church, and formed a circle in the thick grass. The Castilian flag was hoisted in the centre. Riders dismounted.

The governor bent down, plucked some grass, and augmented the previous provisional declaration by taking the country definitively into Spanish possession.

The country, wrote the notary royal, shall be called New Granada, the town Holy Faith, Santa Fe. Then, hats in hand, they entered the new church. Las Casas, Fra Bartholomew, said the first Mass.

Victors' spoils

THEY DID LITTLE more up there on the plateau. It was enough to have arrived. And their soldiers were of the same mind. They came into the land like a sickness into a body. They were there and observed the decay.

They learned of the exodus from the town of Funza. Riders from south and west brought reports of new wonders. Then Belalcazar and Federmann, accompanied at first by the governor, set off for the coast, and Spanish honours.

They proceeded sleek and happy, the vultures, fifty armed men as escort. The route led westward.

The savannah persists a while, then the mountains close in, the Funza forms a small lake, and here the god Bochica took up his magic staff and hurled it through the mountains. The Funza dashes wildly against cliffs, the little river thunders as it nears the sacred fissure, bursts through, drops a short distance over a ledge, and only now sees what lies before it after the tiresome savannah: nothing, a broad endless emptiness, sky and abyss. This is what the god decreed. And it does not hesitate. It hurls its swelling waters over the ledge and surges open-eyed into the deep empty vastness. Sky and abyss and death and life. A broad sweep ahead. A drop that is sheer joy. Then sizzle and hiss and over we go. And it surfaces again in a cloud of mist and celebrates the leap with a multitude of rainbows, acclaimed by birds and lianas.

They rode to the Magdalena river. Cold fog rose over rocky passes. They descended at a trot, it grew warmer, the chest felt constricted, the sun reappeared from its foggy concealment. And below you could see the river, languid after its breakthrough. A fertile landscape all about. Round peaks visible across the valley, blue lines of mountains. The valley floor was hot. They came to the wide plain of the Magdalena and made halt. They began at once to build boats to carry them downstream. Quesada gazed about with his companions and realised: this valley with its coconut trees is a good base for despatching the riches they have collected. A small detachment of Whites was summoned from Funza, and across the river, on its left bank, they built the settlement of Honda, designated a transhipment depot.

Here the Guali flowed foaming into the mighty river, formed seething rapids, and thundered downward. And this river was the

Magdalena, upon which Quesada had embarked with five stout ships at the start of his expedition. The plan was a good one, and if only they had reached this spot and climbed into the mountains from here, then everything would have gone without a hitch. This is clear. At Quesada's side is Alcobazo, his ship's officer. They look at one another. Fortune smiles now. They continue downstream a short way. The rapids are no obstacle. Here are the narrow banks, cliffs, the loathsome forest. They stop, look around. Here the ships with the sick moored, over there was where they climbed up one morning only to become lost, nearly die, and then encounter flamboyant Belalcazar and his doughty train. High above they see condors and vultures, ahead the rushing waters. No men, no spars. Heat drops from the sky. They search along the banks, forest edge for traces of men. Rattlesnakes coil down from trees, rustle through the undergrowth. An army of ants marches from forest to river, a marvellous tribe, each carries a leaf bigger than itself like a green wing, and pulls it into their nest in the riverside gravel.

Quesada took leave of the two generals.

≈≈≈

He set off to take possession of southern Cundinamarca for the first time.

The conquistador horde had grown strong. The first frenzy of pillage was over. They had what they had, wanted more. It was the chance of a lifetime. Plunge everything in blood. Their throats still growled: hey dear bride, Lucinda Dorinda, Theresa with your rosy cheeks, white arms, you wanted a knight, a fine man. Their eyes were bloodshot, their rage never left them. Many had gambled away their loot, some lay in chains after robbing their fellows, it was all the same to them, dozens had set about each other with dagger and war club, inflicting blows and serious wounds.

On it went. They intended to fulfill their frothing, puling destiny.

At their head, behind the tambour, sat *Belligerence* with helmet, cuirass and real human legbones, its weight borne by a horse, it swung its sword and made not a sound when it hit true.

You couldn't see who it was behind the closed visor. If you were to pull it from the horse and strip away the cuirass, then oozing mould and stinking puffballs would spill out, it would implode and smear itself over the ground as thick sticky slime.

Behind marched *Misanthropy*, halberd in hand, a little round shield at the left breast. Gay feathers drooped from hat to forehead and shaded the hard white-grey face. But it had no flesh or skin or blood, it was a skeleton. It could not stay put in its myriad graves, it had heard that men still lived and breathed, and as long as that was the case it would wield its halberd and thrust them into the next world.

In wide peasant costume with an enormous skirt, someone waddled alongside and crouched down and stretched both arms out over the ground. The coarse woman walked crooked in her heavy garments, she sweated and couldn't move, a kick to the bottom and she fell down, filled her apron, gathered and wheezed. *Avarice.*

And behind these three the soldiers, howling to the crashing music of the band that marched among them, drums, trumpets, conches and flutes.

They blared and pounded, they were the fathers who sired them, the mothers who bore them, the sisters, brides who awaited them.

≈≈≈

They aimed for the southern capital Muqueta, or Bogota. They came to empty villages, their approach still engendered horror. In the villages they found whole storehouses stuffed with food, cloth, even gifts of gold. Trying to buy them off. But such gold! Such gold! They wanted more. They wanted death, for themselves and others.

The Funza affair repeated itself. They found old people tied up in open spaces, piles of wood beside them: sacrificial offerings. During the trek through the mountains events occurred which they had not understood before, but now regarded with equanimity: frightened people hastened from villages towards them, and hurled their living children over cliffs. The people sought to soften their rage. And truly it did, it calmed them.

In villages south of Sorocota other rumours had spread. They met resistance. Behind Sorocota there was a gorge to cross. As they approached they were attacked by natives from the opposite side, using slings. It was evening, they were jittery when they made camp. But in the night a lovelorn pair of horses broke loose from the trees, and fought. The stallion escaped the maddened mare and in the dark galloped down the slope, the mare at his heels. Neighing they leapt across the whole breadth of the gorge and raced up to the Indian camp. Panic ensued. The horses spread terror. The natives fled, panicked by the wrath of these demons. The Whites hardly noticed what had happened. When they assembled next morning and prepared for an assault by the natives, the gorge was already clear. The two horses grazed calmly on the other side.

An act of judgement by Quesada helped to enlighten the natives. He was no Alfinger. He wanted no murder or burning. He meant to rule a civilised country, and furthermore wanted all property for himself. So when a soldier called Juan Gordon stole valuable goods in Suzuka, he had him hanged. Let that be an example. But there was an unexpected effect. For the first time the natives saw a dead White. These uncanny beings can die. Shortly thereafter, the White rearguard behind Suzuka was set upon by a horde of Indians. The southern prince, carrying the embalmed bodies of his ancestors with him, had come forward for the decisive battle, blocking the road to Muqueta, the capital, to any Whites from wherever they might come. The darkskins were despatched by firearms, horseback assaults and swordthrusts. The battle was horrifying in its desperate savagery even for the Whites, who for the first time suffered many dead and wounded. The capital could not hold. The empire of the natives was doomed. Cundinamarca was gone, gone, could not but be gone.

Everything fell into Quesada's hands. Even in Funza, during the first horrors, some hundreds of native warriors had placed themselves at his disposal. After the breakthrough at Suzuka thousands came over to him, and he had a tidy army. He came to Bogota. The Whites having now been thoroughly unmasked, the capital was abandoned, the fleeing populace evacuated along with all foodstuffs and every trace of gold, silver and precious stones.

Then Quesada turned back. For the duration of his absence his captain-general had charge.

≈≈≈

Quesada was fortunate. He reached Spain. He was honoured like the old conquistadors Pizarro and Cortez.

He returned to his realm of Cundinamarca, land of the Muisca.

Fighting had reached a desperate level. The ballad of Zaque-zazipa circulated for a long time, about the general who fought and when he could fight no longer threw himself from a cliff. Barreda, Quesada's merciless field commander, had pounced all over him, hemmed him in. The native prince promised gold, his servants brought gold in the morning and Barreda's men stole it at noon out of mockery and greed. And when the field commander returned after fourteen days there was none left. The prince knew: they are our ruin. The Whites had the prince flogged. Barreda screamed: "Where's your gold?" The prince said not a word, and died.

The cacique of Tandama defied Barreda, he concealed himself with his people in a swamp. Horses could not reach him, fire-tubes lacked the range, they sat behind tall palisades, the Whites searched for the paths by which natives carried maize and water through the swamp. Then someone betrayed the path. Horses rode across, riders stabbed with steel swords, guns roared. But by the time they secured the fort the Whites were almost annihilated. The usac sued for peace. The Whites made a treaty. The usac brought gold. Barreda picked up a hammer and said: "You have not given enough gold, so I cannot keep the peace. I take this hammer and smash your gold." The usac begged for time. Then Barreda swung the hammer and smashed his skull.

Quesada undertook the repression with pride and joy.

On the coast leprosy raged, soldiers from the Moorish wars had brought it in.

Leprosy took to the governor in Santa Fe, and carried him off.

≈≈≈

When magnificent Belalcazar had traipsed around the realm of Cundinamarca for long enough and appeared on the coast at almost the same time as Quesada, to his shock and indignation he found officers of the court awaiting him. He was accused of brigandage, outrages, disobedience, the usual, from his earlier days in Peru. No doubt he had Quesada to thank for the investigation, he'd brought it on him out of spite to avoid the inevitable falling out. He was right, this was revenge. The haughty man lay humbled in Cartagena gaol. The great ocean stretched before him, Spain on the other side. He worked on his defence. How could they play this trick after all his successes. He took a fever. He grew thin. Before an answer came from Madrid he was dead.

≈≈≈

Nicolaus Federmann, captain-general, wanted fame and honour back home. He also wanted to defend himself against the greedy rich men of Augsburg who had placed him at the head of his troops and now, like the hucksters they were, accused him of excesses. He embarked as proud and cheerful as ever. At his side was the dwarf woman presented to him in the grassy plains of Venezuela. He had decked her out like a Spanish noblewoman, a princess. On board she strutted beside him in purple satin brocade, under it a bulky satin dress with a train, at her belt hung a cedarwood rosary, a bushel of green and blue feathers drooped from her wide hat. During the voyage she sat beside him at table on a raised gold-chased stool that he'd had made for her in Coro. Oh, she cried, she was afraid of the water and the spirits of the storm. He had to let her paint herself under her clothes with protective pigments she had brought with her, every day she smeared new circles, lines, spots on her skin and even on her little brave face, each mark protecting her from some particular danger. And perhaps they did. But against one danger they were powerless: the ship's wine store.

Federmann was still in celebration mood. He advised all his companions, captains, quartermasters who had starved and suffered with him in the llanos and on the high passes to behave likewise, for soon the moneybags of Augsburg will clap open their books, Herr Seyler and Herr Pegner, they'll perch eyeglasses on their noses and start lecturing, and you'll stand there like a little boy and suck your thumb. Keep up your courage! With toast after toast they wished the sly scribblers in Hell, and ran competitions in cursing and execration. The little woman had to repeat the ripest curses, and was drilled like a parrot until she learned them, so that as soon as they reached Spain she could fling them in the faces of those Knights of the Iron Backsides. The thought of this caused the company delirious amusement every day. She was their queen.

But the little woman had an enemy on the ship: the chaplain. He had tried to prevent her coming aboard. When this failed, he harassed her by making her sit still every day among hawsers and chains while he prayed at her, and to her grief wiped the coloured marks from her face with a sponge that he carried in his cowl for this purpose. Now one day she came promenading amidships after a hearty luncheon, painted as always, and for fun had taken up her rosary and was swinging it merrily through the air, all the while trilling curses the company had taught her that day. The black Dominican encountered her, heard her thin little voice and her folderol and was scandalised to see that the tawny creature was painted again and larking with her rosary. He waited until she was close by, she failed to notice him behind the mast, and he gave her a couple of resounding slaps that knocked her down. As she lay there he snatched the lovely rosary from her hands. Hearing her screams, some came running from the messroom, heated, full of Dutch courage, lips unwiped, hats flopping at the neck. They pulled the bawling little thing to her feet, she screamed for her rosary, the wild men demanded it from the monk, he stuffed it in his girdle and retreated.

Finally Federman himself arrived, tipsy. When he had surveyed the scene and learned what had happened, he set the princess at his hip and ran after the monk. He would, he should be punished at once, the stupid blackrobe, he would, he should carry the Indian princess on his hip just like this, five times around the ship as punishment. The monk, seeing the state of Federmann and his company, ran to find the captain, the helmsman. He climbed to the quarterdeck. It was a stormy day, all the sailors were busy. Federmann, the dwarf clinging to his neck, climbed up behind him, hard on his heels came his mob of table companions, conquerors of the savannah and high passes, his men. He would and should catch the wretched monk.

But he did not catch him. For what the savannah and the high passes of terra firma could not accomplish, the sea did all of a sudden. A wave, not especially big or strong, broke over the deck. Federmann and his bride slipped in the wet and lay against the rail. Were he not drunk he could simply have regained his feet and moved away. But he threshed around to escape the water, still gripping his lady's legs, but in the wrong direction, slid across the sloping deck and overboard. They saw him come up, the little creature on his shoulders clinging to his hair. She hampered his swimming, in her fright clamped hands over his eyes so he couldn't see the lines they threw to him. The men stood there, sobered, filled with horror, waited, eyes starting from their heads to see what their lusty captain-general would do. They lowered a dinghy. But he was already a good way astern tossed up and down by the waves, the heavy red-bearded man. The little dwarf had let go and bobbed behind him like a pretty ball over green-white crests. Both were dead. Nothing more could befall them.

The chaplain, no longer hunted, knelt with some people at the ship's rail. He raised his wooden cross over the water in the direction of the floating bodies.

≈≈≈

This was their end, the generals and governors who had rampaged so.

They had no father, no mother, no children.

They had no ancestors or descendants.

They were stones spewed into the air from a volcano, that fell to earth, and shattered.

The path through the web

WHITE SOLDIERS SWARMED across the land.

From Coro, Cartagena, Quito, the lure of new Eldorados brought fresh supplies of Whites. They were the same species as the earlier ones.

To the south, by the source of the Cauca and Patia rivers, on the high plateaus of Tuquerres and Pasto lay wealthy villages, often a hundred families to a house, the most pacific of the dark people. Spaniards came from the north with horse, arquebus and bloodhound. As a branding iron burns the skin and causes blood to flow, so they came into this happy land, a few hundred men, outcasts from savage Europe. The natives saw their ruin draw near. They could not name it, but when it arrived they had to flee or die. Ahead of the White horde, thousands of dark men, women and children fled in a mile-wide stream leaving behind homes, fields and animals. When they left a village where the graves of their ancestors lay, they dropped pebbles behind them and swept the ground with branches so that the ancestors would know the way and follow them. Those who could not escape barricaded their houses and hanged themselves from the rafters in their hundreds. In the forests they had no food. White demons were on the march. Again and again children were thrown from cliffs so that the Sun would accept their blood and show mercy.

And as Whites came along the Popayan road in the high valley of the Cauca, they faced the menacing volcanoes where the earthquake god dwells. But the long road as far as the terrace of Tuquerres was sown, as with blossom falling from a tree, with people who had been abandoned by their god and from whom life had drained away. It was not war or plague that murdered them.

Now the Whites could take all they wanted of gold, silver, emeralds and cloth.

≈≈≈

In the valley of the Iraca, near the Sogamosa river, stood a temple. The high priest of the country lived there. He was known as "He who makes himself invisible".

The Zipa made a pilgrimage to him. White spies followed at a distance.

The dark people divided their days, these for the service of deities, these for labour, these for repose. Three days were for the service of deities. Now the procession did not move. Three days for labour. Then it crept forward along the road. Three days for rest. Then it did not move.

With the Zipa came a host of priests, gaunt men in black skirts with black caps who spoke little, fasted a lot and kept awake so as not to miss at any hour a call from their Heaven.

More than a hundred of the Zipa's wives were carried in curtained litters. His sickly young son was surrounded by priests. They had taken him from the temple, and protected him from the awful sight of the Sun. His litter was closed tight. When they brought him food, the priests placed thick blindfolds over his eyes. He wore heavy ear discs and a big nose ring.

When the three travelling days came, the road ahead of the Zipa was swept clear with brooms and covered with cloth upon which flowers were strewn, so that when he left his litter he should not disturb the earth.

There were large and small settlements along the way. Fortifications had been erected against enemy attack. They were ringed by a double palisade, the poles lashed securely together, stout awnings stretched between them to protect the defenders against arrows. So as to be remiss in nothing when they built the settlement, into the holes dug for the kingposts they threw pious young maidens of noble family, who had begged for this honour. The sharpened ends of the kingposts pierced the pious bodies, to the glory of Heaven. From every place people came out to join the pilgrimage. People even came from the lowlands, to which terrible rumours of the White demons had penetrated. They carried dried food in baskets on their backs, and small gold and silver figurines in their hands.

The sacred way began at Chalcha. The lake of Guatavita is called "Fire of the mountains". It lies on a height, surrounded by thick forests. The summit of the mountain flattens itself to a little plain, and a cone rises from it, its base a circle, the summit encloses the clear lake, which is as round as the mountain that embraces it. The wife of a great king threw herself into this lake, the spirit of the lake took her to wife, in times of need they call to her as well. Extensive temples, dwellings for priests and laity sprawled around the foot of the tree-covered holy mountain. To the east, the sunrise, the plain had been cleared, and a broad avenue lined left and right with stones led to the sacrificial circle.

Sugamuxi, the high priest, cacique of Irica province, received the guest in his dwelling.

Sugamuxi, black markings on his face, in a loose black cloak, grey hair over his ears and down to his shoulders, a low golden mitre on his head, as old as the Zipa but lean and sharp, with black expressive eyes, sat across from the Zipa. The bamboo screen at the window was hitched up, a cool mountain breeze wafted in. The Zipa sat with heavy rugs across his knees. No one else was there.

The Zipa glanced at his host. "Sugamuxi, I have no gifts to bring for your temple."

"Thysquesuska, you are welcome here."

Zipa: "Whiteskinned bearded men have fallen upon Cundinamarca. They have fire tubes and strange beasts. Funza, the town, is destroyed. Many people are dead."

Sugamuxi kept quite still.

Zipa: "You advised me, Sugamuxi, to make peace with the king of Tunja. Peace came. I meant to thank you at the festival of Huan."

Stern Sugamuxi closed his bright eyes for a moment. "It is a good day for the Zipa to journey here, at Huan, the festival of kings. In ancient times Ramiriki rose to Heaven at Huan and entered the Sun."

"The bearded White men are criminals. Their king is a creature of no understanding. He makes a gift of Cundinamarca, which does not belong to him and which he has never seen."

Sugamuxi fixed the Zipa with his big eyes. "We learned of a bearded man from long ago, who taught the people of our country many good things. They called him 'the Man who Disappears'. He wandered through the mountains and his cloak hung from one shoulder, his beard reached to his waist, an animal with two humps went with him. He died in Boza. Do the bearded White men look like the Man who Disappears? What do they teach?"

"They kill and take gold from all the houses. They have beards. There is a black man with them, he carries a black box with a cross and says this is their highest spirit."

"Have you spoken with this man, Thysquesuska?"

The old man shook his head: "I spoke with the leader of the criminals, to find out what they are. They forced their way in to me."

Sugamuxi: "Cundinamarca is well appointed with priests, warriors, craftsmen, peasants. Priests perform their office, craftsmen toil in the settlements, peasants in the fields. What do the warriors do?"

"My general Zaquezazipa advised me not to go into battle. When the fire tube bangs, people fall down with holes in their bodies."

"Does blood flow?"

"Yes."

They were silent. Garishly painted vases stood along the walls of the low square room.

The Zipa leaned forward: "Sugamuxi, has Bochica forsaken us? Has the pillar of the people left us? The White criminals make slaves of his children. Many died and cannot be buried."

"Thysquesuska, I shall enquire."

≈≈≈

Two days later, early in the morning, a ceremony of supplication took place.

Once the world was shrouded in darkness. Bochica contained light in himself, he created great birds, black in colour, he tasked them to fly all through the universe and carry light everywhere, the birds were filled with light. And every place that they pecked at with their beaks became light. People appeared on the earth, from a mother who came out of the sea.

Next day the Zipa allowed himself to be massaged with the juice of a plant called trejelon. They puffed gold dust all over his body. The procession wound from the little plain up the flank of the sacred cone, along a narrow path. At its head were priests in black, they blew on conches and trumpets. The mountains responded with tremendous echoes.

Behind them leapt figures in pelts of jaguar, lion, bear, conveying the homage of powerful beasts. Behind these a crowd of people who wept and cried and filled the air with their laments, sought to move Heaven. Behind them others who rejoiced, laughed, danced, wanted to thank Heaven.

And then the Zipa's entourage, with sumptuous fabrics they swept the path clear for the Zipa's chair. It was carried by six noblemen.

They arrived at the summit, before them the dark blue lake Guatavita, above and around it and them the dome of great purple-flaming Heaven, light, emptiness, cool wind.

The lake was ringed by people. Their blowing, wailing, singing, crying, laughing, the echoes from the mountains, all rose up to Heaven.

Two naked crones squatted at the entrance. They wore nothing, for Death robs a person of everything. One, eyes downcast, blew gently on a flute. The other held some webbing. A person goes into Death on threads as slender as spider's silk.

A wide raft was moored to the lakeshore. The priests and the Zipa, that ponderous gold-glittering man, together with his entourage climbed onto it. The raft floated to the middle of the lake. Endless wailing, trumpet sounds, rumbling echoes.

In the middle of the lake, nobles poured water over the Zipa, the gold washed off. Priests, prostrate on the ground, eyes closed, packed shoulder to shoulder, sang to Bochica who climbs with his rays into the depths of the lake and rejoices in the gifts. Robes were draped around the Zipa, he dropped his golden discs and vessels into the water.

≈≈≈

Sugamuxi, the high priest, lay for hours alone in the temple on the black prayer mat. Above him stood the huge Sun-disc, image of Bochica. Sacred pottery vessels, painted, of many different shapes, stood along the walls, in them sacrificial offerings, golden suppli-cants with rays around the head and a staff in each hand on which a little bird perched, worshippers and supplicants from the animal kingdom, insects, lizards, snakes. This was the priests' chamber.

The high priest's soul left his body. It came out of his mouth and wandered to the middle of the earth. It came to a river. There were spiders. They span him a web and led him across.

The priest's soul saw some who had just recently arrived, they still looked proud, they wore ragged clothes, and many were naked. The priest questioned them. They said: we died at our own hand, there is no one to care for us and clothe us.

"And why did you lay hands on yourself?"

"White demons came."

The high priest asked, asked ten, asked ten, asked ten. The same reply. He pretended not to understand. He was seized with great fear. I want to go back, I must leave, too many have come. The flood of souls continued unabated. A swarming heaving tumult surrounded him. He asked: "Are many more coming?"

"Many more, so many, look around you, oh look around you."

The throng was endless. And there came a long line, with men in the lead wailing and women behind weeping. It was the litter of Thysquesuska the Zipa.

The soul returned to its body, felt its way over the chest and into the mouth. When Sugamuxi opened his eyes it was night. He was lying on the black prayer-mat, priests crowded around.

In the morning the Zipa spoke to him: "Sugamuxi, did you enquire?"

Sugamuxi: "I passed through the spider's web into the Underworld. Many spoke of the Whiteskinned men. A litter was borne along, surrounded by wailing men and weeping women. Wailing men and weeping women followed it. The odour of Mocoba was around the litter. He had emeralds in his eyes, emeralds in his ears, nostrils, navel."

The Zipa was frightened: "Where did this dream find you?"

Sugamuxi: "In front of Bochica's image."

After a long silence the Zipa looked across at the implacable priest: "Summon your assistants. Let me prepare."

≈≈≈

For five days they prepared the Zipa in the temple. He prayed, fasted, and did not sleep. The people learned that he would go personally to Bochica.

Before sunrise priests led the Zipa along the dark stone-edged path to the sacrificial circle. The dense forest was black, the sky blue-grey, the air was icy.

The priests, faces to the east, knelt. The old Zipa, painted black and red, in the regalia of a king, stood on the stones at the foot of the huge column of Bochica.

As the vault of Heaven began to lighten and the first weak rays of sun struck the column, Sugamuxi thrust the sacrificial spear into the Zipa. The priests laid him on the stones, opened his breast, cut out the bleeding heart. The high priest showed it to the Sun. Flutes and conches sounded, the priests sang.

≈≈≈

When the band of Whites came up from the south, along the Suarez river from the region of Velez, the host of desperate refugees was surging westward into the Cocuy mountains. The mass of corpses they found in their path horrified the Whites.

Temples and all other buildings at Iraca were in flames.

Return to the wilderness

THE WAY TO the north and west was blocked. From the south new bands of Whites moved up with bloodhounds. Ships came from Europe, anchored off Coro, gathered coloured people, sailed up the Magdalena to Honda, climbed into the mountains.

The broad Amazon plain was free.

Mountains stretched in chains, two or three side by side, fell sharply to the west, in the east merged with the lowlands. So many volcanoes in the south, Minchinmarido, Corcovado, Tronador, in the north Llaina, Callaqui, Antuco. Maipo was the highest. In the region of Aconcagua two chains parted, one led to the coast, on the other rose hot-mouthed volcanoes, Copiapo, Antofalla, Llullaillaco. Huallago and Marañon flowed through longitudinal valleys. These, the Cordillera, were ancient mountains, sandstone and shale rested on basal crystalline rocks, volcanoes spewed lava on top.

Palms, cacti, reeds stand erect, all they can do is cast their seed and turn away.

But people don't have to endure heat, floods, annihilation where they stand. Though they can't rise into the air like birds on happy wings, they can use their legs to move, mountains offer gorges, the world spreads out, no eyes can see so far, no horse or hound can track so far.

Across the mountains and the ancient wide plateaus, the human throng descends into the lowlands. They follow the northern rivers and those that merge with the Marañon.

The pampas were there, near the Pastaza river lay the big lake Rimachuima. Tribes from north and east sought safety here. They paddled along unknown rivers, each day and each night brought them farther from home. They no longer bothered to leave stones and branches on the ground or let branches be carried by the current so the ancestors would find the way, the ancestors must stay behind, it's not possible for them to follow, and if they follow they will only be angry because we cannot worship them. The refugees had no help, no succour from the fields, no succour from the animals, no succour from the trees. Mountains and animals and trees were unknown to them, and did not know them. Many refused to go on.

Just as hundreds lay in the valley of the Cauca river on the Popoyan road, so hundreds – dispirited empty husks – sank down here in the eastern mountains, in the valleys of the Napo, Iça, Pa, Pastaza. They waded through swamps that swallowed them, paths led through primeval jungle, along clifftops, on bridges across gaping abysses. For as long as they could they drove their llamas with them.

Terrible mountains. Clouds billowed up from the valleys and lay like white caps on the peaks. It thundered all around the people, rocks hurtled down. Then torrents of rain. Their own country had dried up, the dead in their graves desiccated into mummies. Here water formed pillars joining heaven and earth. It burrowed and churned the ground.

≈≈≈

Groups of survivors gathered in the south, on the Marañon. Dark people lived there, who gave them support.

On Lake Rimachuima groups from the lofty Inca realm squatted in wretched palm huts in hot steaming air, groups whose blood still pulsed, men, women and children of the race of long dead Cuzumarra who had tried to rouse the dark tribes, even the Women People, to make war against the White barbarians. They no longer wore feathered cloaks, no distinction was made between princes, overseers and subjects. Elders preached revenge, the young inherited the hatred, and everyone had to hunt and fish with neighbouring tribes. Epidemics of murder broke out, for a belief spread among the young that the Sun God had turned away from them because of the crimes of their elders. Already on the trek here there had been murders. In the lowlands the young men, and women too, little by little did away with all elders, princes, officials and overseers.

To the west of Lake Rimachuima there settled groups who were of the dying race of Cuzumarra, who had journeyed here to find help, the Amazon queen Inti Cussi beat him and gave him away, his companions died among the Women People, at the feast of the New Moon the great armadillo invited him to dance and he was felled by spears and sacrificed.

The men built a village. At evening, flutes accompanied the lament that Cuzumarra's companions had sung:

My mother bore me in rain, in mist, so that I weep like the rain and vanish like mist. You grow in a cradle of sorrow, my mother sang as she nursed me. Rain and storm kept me awake. When I seek friends I wander through the world and find misery. Cursed, the day of my birth. Cursed, the night when my mother conceived me. Cursed, forever cursed.

In the meeting house a mid-sized statue stood on a plinth by a wall, a male figure of wood with short angular legs pressed tight together, the body dumpy and square, broad face, square mouth, long nose, right angles painted on the cheeks. There was a pointed cap on its head and it held its hands in front of its body. People from the sacred high valley of Tiahuanaco and Ac Capana had carved the statue of Virococha from the hard wood of these forests.

"See Virococha," said the very dark strong man of the Inca race, still young, who had been baptised up there with the name Cristobal Paillou, to those sitting with him in a tight semicircle, "we have kept faith with Virococha. He is protector of our mountains. Our fathers hesitated to worship him, they were willing to bow down only to the great Sun. They prostrated themselves at his feet too late. Now they destroy his house. He waits for us to gather and for those up there to grow weak, then he will lead us back."

The young men shouted out the mighty name.

Paillou told them: "Cuzco is a throne over the land. A blue lake lies there. A royal road led past it towards Potosí. Our great Inca Huayna Capac was born there in Tiahuanaco, in a side valley. Oh, that hardly any of you have seen the house, the house of Ollontai, above the valley of Vilcamayo. Thousands of our men toiled more than ten years to build it, carried stones from the mountains across wild rivers, threw bridges across chasms, cut blocks and polished them, laid pantiles of granite under the ground. It was an enormous building with circling walls and a courtyard, broad pillars. Within stood statues of our people, women sat there with children at the hip, men drank from a beaker, some people crossed the river. These were our people, our poor people, who protected Virococha. Whites destroyed his house. Woe to them.

"Know this: Virococha dwelt in Tiahuanaco from time immemorial. The terrible god of heat betrayed us. Before new adepts arise among us, we must devote ourselves to him who is more. Virococha is the one who lifted us from the ground, he made the muscles of our men strong, took them by the shoulder and led them when the path grew perilous. He stood behind them and showed them how to plough and weave and build."

"Why did the White men come to us?"

"We do not know. When the time comes, Virococha will again send to us a man to destroy the Whites. Who are these Whites? It is our greatest torment and desperation to think who these are who fell upon our country and spread murder and devastation. We found out too late. We took them for spirits, for gods even. Some prostrated themselves before their horses. Our parents believed that Whites cannot die. Oh that we were so befuddled! What sins did our parents and grandparents commit that no one stood by them and opened their eyes? What they saw was so far beyond normal that they believed in superhumans. The crimes, the lies were without precedent. A particular country was created for these ravening beasts on the other side of the ocean, a wide sea was placed around it to protect peaceful beings from them. Their demonic spirit gave them strength enough to break through the barrier, they found their way to us and will find yet other peoples. They are evil demons, yes indeed, no one has weapons to oppose them. We have no weapons against them, but we shall make some. And we know: they will destroy themselves. It will be fashioned, the spear that fells them. Who was the captain who murdered our kings and princes? A swineherd, a wicked soldier, Pizarro, in his own country he was nobody. What kind of warriors did the swineherd have at his back? A mob of savages, half as many as this little village on the Huallaga, and thirty horses. And so he came ashore at Tumbez and lied and murdered, and our fathers were stupefied and took the ravening jaguar for a god."

Another: "This is what I heard them say among themselves: their greatest care is for weapons that they can use to rob and kill. In their country everything is in disorder. No spirit looks out for them. They have fallen under the spell of great magic, wicked sorcerers have gained the upper hand. They will destroy each other. Good people keep silent and no longer know what's what, they dare not denounce the others. The wicked do their deeds in broad daylight, make laws, rule kingdoms."

A low moaning came from the crowd. "Tell us, Cristobal, ask Virococha if he too no longer wants us. Must we perish? Pray to Virococha in his mercy to tell us if we are to perish. We toiled underground for the ravening White jaguars. Was it not told that jaguars and dragons would one day be set over us and that all that lives would be destroyed? Once Virococha rained fire, now he rains

White jaguars. We can slay their horses and hounds, we can even wipe out an army, but they are so much stronger than us, like a jaguar against a turtledove. They will penetrate to every inhabited region. We are finished. Pray, Cristobal, and ask Virococha if we are to perish."

Others called from the crowd: "Yes, ask, Cristobal. Why wait. You see how we sicken away. How damp it is here. Our fathers and mothers, as they lay down in the road and took leave of us, they knew everything. They understood the commandment. The earth will be laid waste, the Whites are the ravening beings who take away life so that a new world may be born. We are of no account: ask Virococha. We shall submit."

A long pause before Cristobal's response. "A murderer is not destined to enjoy a long life. He is a fruit hollowed by worms. He will kill himself. I shall ask Virococha. I shall pray for an answer. Oh brothers, how lovely was our land! Oh brothers! We were struck blind and could not see one another."

Someone struck up a muffled drumming, softly they crooned a lament. Many clutched small figurines, images of Virococha of pumice, green slate, some of gold. Darkness fell quickly, big fires were lit outside. Smoke drifted in. Whispering started. They exchanged news from home: who had evaded the Whites' latest manhunts and might perhaps make it to here. A postal service up into the mountains was suggested, and everyone agreed that leaders should be despatched with provisions for refugees. It was told how roads were crumbling, all the bridges collapsing, channels drying up. Grief lay on every brow. Our country is finished. When can we go home? Virococha, hear, and Virococha, see us here, stay with us. There was talk of slave hunts and how the Whites auctioned off whole villages. How they hated the Whites. Oh, they were not immortal, they could die under torture like anyone else.

The red glow from the fires played over the angular image of Virococha. His hands were in front of his breast, in the right a short wide sword, in the left a beaker into which a man had fallen, you could see only his legs, bent at the knee.

As they left the house and Paillou closed the door, flutesong wafted from the village into the darkness. Little specks of stars up above, down below swirling hosts of fireflies.

≈≈≈

In the north out of Cundinamarca, where the Zipa's people were journeying down the Pastaza and Morona rivers, the same laments could be heard. They were joined by groups from the regions around Antioquia, slaves from the gold and silver mines, who reported what the White beasts were up to.

"Everywhere we burned down the temples and the houses where we used to pray. We left no one behind in the settlements, so no one could betray us. But they created suspicion and eavesdropped on our conversations. They are cunning, they have many who speak our language. They tortured people to say where gold and silver can be found. None of us knows what they do with gold and silver. They have carried away whole shiploads, but we took care that it will not be to their advantage: we deployed all the priests we could find to curse the gold and silver, the pearls and precious stones, all the treasure they haul away from our land and dig from our earth, it will bring disaster, it will inflict sickness and infertility and war on them, it will rend their souls and confuse their spirits. We have dug in the mines and diverted water from the rivers. They took us to Irica, to the burned holy city, we had to dig channels in the ground of Guatavita, we had to scrabble in the lake-bed for gold. When we found some we brought it to them and shook it out in front of them, the overseer sat on a chair, his stewards stood there with spears and thunder tubes. They picked up the yellow poison and weighed it and were happy. As they did so, every one of us repeated the curses under our breath and called on the stones to activate the curse and be of help to us. None of us ever handled gold and precious stones with such drunkard's greed. We consecrated it. As anyone dies who looks into the face of the consecrated, so they will die when they hold up a mirror. We know that the stones heard us.

"But they laid our people out on benches and placed a brazier beside the bench and lit a fire in it. Then they questioned our people. They asked the people on the torture benches where gold and silver and precious stones can be found. And if they did not answer, the priests warned them to obey their superiors. And if they kept silent, the fire was brought closer and they were burned on the soles of their feet. Then many of them spoke."

There was weeping at what people had endured.

"They found poor people among us who were paralysed by fear and did not know how to flee. They forced these to lead them to graveyards in the burned settlements."

At this, there was shouting.

"They opened the graves, dug up the dead, removed their ornaments, marks of honour and gifts. They boast that they recovered more gold from the graves than from our houses. Oh, this is true. We had gold for our ancestors and those we revered."

≈≈≈

Dreadful was the cleansing initiated by the masses pouring from Cundinamarca. The Zipa's death, the burning of the temple at Guatavita, were not a signal for an uprising.

When the building with all its shrines and treasures, all its cloisters burned, the White soldiers were alarmed and braced themselves for an attack by desperate natives. But the dumb masses flowed away like a deep current, particle by particle, some particles rose higher and others sank lower, and the farther they moved from the mountains, across the Upia river – which of them knew the destination – more and more people sank down. At last the only ones left were those who would not die. And now there came to the fore, with their weapons and strong bodies, men of the warrior caste, who had so rarely received a command from their rulers to attack the Whites.

They felt their time had come. Alongside them trudged peasants, artisans, priests. The warriors came together and murdered priests who raised their voices in the crowd, whose words were still received fervently, with yearning, they still conducted services of invocation, while warriors were despised as having no right to flee. Now they showed their prowess with the spear. And so they became leaders. The refugee mass became a bellicose swarm.

Small bands came to the watery region where the last hills sank down to the swampy plain, along a broad waterway.

And as they lay on the bank, they discovered shards of jars and bowls under the bushy cliff.

When they dug into the cliff, water flooded down. It led deep into the rock and was an ancient urn-field. Huge salamanders darted in the gloom. They handled a few skulls and pots and retreated.

There were dead people here.

Far and wide there were no tribes here now.

At the entrance stood a tall, brown-black pot, like a sentry. Its body bore an image: a monkey with one arm around a tree trunk, beside him crouched a naked man, head down, hands on his knees.

They quickly moved away from this place. They came to the region of black rivers that flow into the Amazon. Their numbers fluctuated, sometimes they were tens of thousands strong, separate streams that communicated with one another, then they were challenged by tribes and whole bands were wiped out. They suffered thunderstorms and floods, rise and fall of the rivers. They had to adapt to new foods. Once they dwelled in orderly towns and villages, and now they travelled homeless in dugout canoes through forests of rubber trees, and speared fish, collected wild honey and roots. Given their strength they could have settled in the territory of other tribes. But the past would not let them go. New hordes poured down from the mountains, here and there whole bevies were caught and kept prisoner. Straggling feral hordes came to the river forests of the Marañon, and mixed with other refugees. This exodus ended only after many decades.

≈≈≈

Drums pounded their message from one bank to the other, reported what was happening. Once upon a time Cuzumarra's companions began to dream and laugh in the forest, the oppressive heat overcame them, dampness fell on their skin – they said: "We are weary even when we stop moving. We no longer know what to say. Apart from the name we know nothing of the Empire of the

Four World Regions, some magic has stolen all that we knew of it;" – thorns and undergrowth ripped their clothing, they painted themselves red and black like the forest tribes. Likewise the bands that came down to the Amazon plain from the heights of Cundinamarca. Already you could hear: "But I, I shall never go back. Never." Another: "I shall never go back." A third, fourth, many: "I shall never ever go back. Never again shall we climb into the mountains." Even those who once had lived in Cundinamarca under a Zipa learned to pound the drum.

All were renewed, all became peaceable, grave and strong. They lost their names. They learned about the sorcerers of the local tribes. Far to the east, down from the mountains into the great plain, the remnants of the destroyed empires lodged, settled on the edge of that wide plain suffused with the breath of the great river.

The great basin dipped towards the east, across it flowed sweet waters, gentle and immense. Trees, grasses and plants grew endlessly, plants shot up quickly. The ground, the fiery sky, the gushing waters were stronger than anything.

≈≈≈

Part Three

Las Casas and Sukuruja

~

Puerto's Vow

WHEN HE FOLLOWED Governor Quesada out of Coro, and in the presence of Quesada, Belalcazar and Federmann consecrated the first straw-thatched church in Santa Fe, Las Casas was a young man. Death had seized and sundered the three generals and warlords. The white-haired Dominican still went among the darkskinned people, was bishop of the state of Chiapas and tried to preach Christianity.

New ships came constantly from Europe with officers, mercenaries, weapons. The human volcano kept spewing. Long and terrible the path the Whites must tread in order to annihilate and lose themselves.

Merchants landed at the ports, brought wine, oil, vinegar, salt pork, clothing, horses, hounds. Soldiers herded dark people together and sold them to the ships in exchange for these goods. One horse was worth a hundred people. If a captain fancied a keg of wine, he would trade for it the prettiest girl of the village that he owned.

Once a captain came from an island where he had engaged in heavy fighting with natives. In a moment of great peril he vowed to honour the Twelve Apostles by butchering twelve heathen every day. He was young and amiable, suffered from glands like many soldiers. Las Casas, indefatigable, had rejoined the army as it crossed Darien and was in the service of this captain, Juan del Puerto. One day, when several young Indians wept and would not attend to their lessons, Las Casas came in to inspect the class and the young priest who taught it, and learned from the children that their parents had died the day before. Las Casas could obtain no further information. But he heard from soldiers that this was Juan del Puerto's daily sacrifice. Either he takes bloodhounds into the bush, or else he seizes some slave labourers. He's already had alter-cations with the bailiffs about this. But he's an honest man and always provides replacements.

Las Casas invited the young captain to his tent. Juan looked wretched, dragged his feet. He sat down at once, complained of his burdens and cursed this land of poisons and snakes where he had acquired his infection. Las Casas noted the feverish eyes and strong trembling hands. He forbade the captain to curse and asked if he attended Mass regularly. Juan said yes. Then Las Casas spoke of the lesson and what the children had said. The captain was surprised. What has this to do with him.

"It seems they are children of natives whom you have killed."

"Heathens. It's possible."

"Were they really heathen? These are children under our instruction."

"The ones I kill are heathen."

"They say you have even killed some labourers."

"Heathen. Anyway, lord bishop, if you want to lay a complaint against me, don't bring me to your tent. We're at war. Anything I do in war, I answer for to my general."

"Do not strut so, Juan del Puerto. It is not my place to complain. I am an old servant of the Church. You know that, my dear man, it's why you came, and you were right to do so. You are sick, and none of us knows when we shall stand before God's mercy." The young captain kept silent. "Every day you kill twelve people."

"I made a vow when we stood in mortal peril and only eight of my twenty men were alive: if we are saved, I shall offer a daily sacrifice of twelve heathen, the number of the Apostles."

"And you have maintained this for weeks, twelve people a day."

"Yes."

White-haired Las Casas planted himself before the captain's stool: "People!"

The captain: "It is a vow."

"You shall go to confession and pray to be relieved of this vow."

The captain looked dubious: "You'll take on the responsibility, lord bishop? Will you?" Las Casas' big black eyes flashed with anger, then became small and dull, softly he said "Yes," and sat down.

The soldier wanted to leave, but the priest bade him stay. He asked the soldier to approach, his eyesight was no longer good. Then Las Casas sat beside Juan del Puerto, held the rosary in his fingers and murmured and tried to feel what it was that sat beside him. "When you made the vow, captain, and struck down the first twelve people, what were your thoughts?"

At Las Casas' gentle tone the face of the young captain, averted and glowering, became even more tense, menacing folds appeared above his nose: "You have no say in this, Father Las Casas. You always travel in the baggage train, let yourself be carried or ride a horse. You don't see what it costs us to be here."

In the same gentle tone the priest asked: "And why did you come all this way?"

"Not to save souls, certainly not! If I wanted to save souls, my own would be first, cursed as it is. And my companions are no better, be they Spaniards or Portuguese or Hollanders or Germans. Whoever catches the bug over there and can't help but cross the ocean, he is cursed. It's our fate, all of us. It's a glorious voyage of discovery. You only have to look around here for a month, a week, to see it. Gold drives you over here, and you must pay. If only the world knew nothing of gold. But maybe they'd find something else. There's nothing wrong with us, bishop, believe me, I may be young still, but I understand people."

"Please go on."

"Over there they have no use for us. You know that. Whoever doesn't go for a monk is lost. The Spanish Crown cannot provide all the positions we need. And I am no peasant. It's good that the King himself wages war. Otherwise truly we would have to band together and incite him to make war on us. And if the King should have no wars with White men, he must set us up with lands where we can put our swords to use. As the plough is to the peasant, so the sword is to us. We sow and harvest with it, for the King and for ourselves. It's a matter of blood, we know that. But we pay dearly, sometimes with our own blood."

"You have been in the wars a great deal, for a young man. I believe you no longer know what a human being is, captain."

"Stop. What humans, here? They're weeds. I pollute my sword with them. Just because someone can guzzle and make babies, it doesn't make him human. Even my horse is better than a man, I can rely on him, he's loyal. But the Indians are deceitful, they're like dry grasses and weeds, there's no blood or it's poisonous, growing so thick you can't push through, it tears at your arms and legs, you cut it down and it springs right back up."

"Tell me again, what does it do for you when you kill them?"

The young captain was silent. He sat with head bowed, as if pondering. He broke out in boyish laughter: "I'm sorry. Something occurred to me when you said 'kill'."

"Well?"

"Since you are of such a tender disposition, I'd rather not say."

"Please speak, captain."

"Once we were somewhere, I had a good friend who was sick a long while, and he's under the ground now, somewhere. We had orders to march, and among my friend's servants was a lad he treated well, like everyone else. So one morning as they're all preparing to march he says to the lad, Jose or Ignaz or whatever his name is, Jose, fetch my targe, we're off. The lad says nothing, fetches the targe, my friend mounts up, me beside him, and we ride off towards the mustering ground, maybe a quarter of an hour away. The lad stays at the edge of the place like an old donkey, doesn't move from the spot. My friend shouts: Well, are you coming? The boy says nothing. My friend is not at all an impatient man, he's just puzzled and says to me: what shall I do with the idiot? He dismounts, hands me the reins, drags the lad across: you will pick up the targe and come with me. – I stay here. – You're coming, I tell you. So he doesn't reply. So my friend draws his dagger and says: here, see this dagger? You have two ears. If you don't come, I shall slice off your ears, one by one. The lad says nothing. My friend grabs his head, and calm as you like, swish swosh, cuts off his ears one after the other."

Las Casas covered his eyes with a hand: "Impossible."

"But I was there. As I said, your nature is too gentle. The lad stood quite still, his face didn't change, he knew what to expect, just blood trickling down to his shoulders, he knew: that's how it should be."

"How it should be?"

"Of course. My friend said: see, that's for your disobedience. Will you come along now? But he shook his head. Think again, lad, I don't want to hurt you. You're not a pretty picture just now. The girls won't admire you. You'll come along now. He doesn't answer and puts the targe down on the ground. So my friend grabs his nose and slices off his nose and top lip all in one go. The lad says not a word. My friend gets back on his horse, he's annoyed, curses: you can't do anything with these donkeys, they're all the same. When I look round the stupid lad is lying on the ground, and people are running from the village towards him. He must have lost a lot of blood."

After a pause the captain said: "The tale just came into my head. My friend was a good man, for sure. He was a dear comrade. He's long dead now."

Las Casas struggled with himself. No thoughts would come. The ghastly repellent presence of this man. He passed a hand over his eyes. "Forget your friend, speak of yourself. Why did you make such a vow? Think."

The captain's gaunt face turned to him with a smile: "But you must know! I hope for grace."

"By killing the defenceless?"

"Father Las Casas, I have never killed a Christian, unless maybe in the fighting in Italy. I strike down these heathen and set them a task: go before the throne of grace and say: I am a damned heathen soul sent here by captain Don Juan del Puerto. And that will astonish."

"And you never feel pity?"

"Never. This land is cursed. We should exterminate the heathen. They have poisoned me. From me they can expect no mercy."

Then the young captain stood up and excused himself, he had duties. The old bishop grasped his hand: "This is the hand that holds the dagger. I shall not let go until you swear to me that today you will strike nobody down, and will go straight to confession and pray to be released from your vow."

The captain stood dubious and sombre: "You have not persuaded me, Father. My friends will laugh."

"I am the bishop. Your father confessor will tell you, the good of your soul depends on this."

"Well, if you say so."

Las Casas remained for hours in his tent. When next he sat at his desk he had before him all the letters and memorials he had written to clergy and the Spanish Crown. He laid his head on them.

Sermon in the Forest

IT WAS STILL early, he wandered through the camp, everyone was busy and greeted him with respect. Five riders trotted past on their steeds, one jumped down when he saw the priest, it was the commander, he declared his pleasure at the priest's presence in the camp and mentioned that they would conduct a hunt today for fugitives from some nearby villages. "We shall gather the heathen again, and your school will once more be full, bishop."

Las Casas said sadly: "Let them flee."

"You have doubts? You could never be a warrior in a land with a rabble like these. Take courage, we shall have them back with you. And they shall become good Christians, even if I must send a detachment of soldiers with whips to sit beside them in the school."

"You are most amiable, captain. Would you allow me to approach the fugitives, speak with them and invite them to return before you start your hunt?"

"Gladly. It'll spare us work. But how will you find them?"

"Thank you, may the Lord bless you. Give me a couple of days."

Three times Las Casas sent envoys to the Motilones with

presents. The envoys brought the presents back. When the last one returned, Las Casas wept. He tipped the envoy and shut himself away. But this envoy went back to the Motilones and reported what he had seen. Then they debated for a long while. The White priest's distress unsettled them. They arranged a meeting with him.

Near Mahates, Las Casas climbed from the boat and up towards a plane tree where he could see a cluster of dark people wearing ceremonial plumes, one group was armed. As he approached across the grass the spear-bearers made a signal. Those escorting Las Casas explained: he was to take himself to the spot assigned to him, within earshot of the group. When the priest heard this and saw the spearmen, he stood still. He sent one of his escort ahead to announce that he came as a friend, unarmed, they could search the boat. They answered at once that he was welcome, it was their custom to arrange things so.

Slowly and sorrowfully, almost fifty paces from the natives, Las Casas lowered himself onto the grass at the spot they had marked with a broken branch. As he sat there he prayed and asked help from God. Then he began to speak boldly. He asked if they were his enemies, had he harmed them or any of their tribe. – They denied it. – Then he asked: why had they abandoned their old villages. – Because of the animals that they hunt, these have moved away from the old places. – And why they no longer come to the lovely little church and let themselves and their children receive instruction. They are baptised, after all. – They replied: also because of the animals. When they and their children go to church, the hunting is bad.

It pained Las Casas to hear this, he knew their dreadful superstitions. His eyesight was no longer keen, he strove to make out their faces. He named the two chiefs and their eldest sons, whom he recognised: "Have you been busy again with reeds and leaves, making mask costumes? Have you built another hut for your masks?"

They shook their heads, but he could not see their faces at that distance. He turned to one of his dark escorts and whispered: "What are they doing? Are they signing to one another?"

The man said: "They look calmly across to us, Father."

"They do not wrinkle their brows?" – "No, Father."

Now Las Casas tried again: "You know I am well disposed towards you. You have guided me for great distances and have spoken for me to your friends. I have often sat by your fires."

"You are still our friend. So we have come to greet you and sit across from you. We rely on your friendship."

"Tell me in accordance with the truth, why you who have been baptised avoid my instruction and keep your children away."

"It is hard for us, Father Las Casas. We are poor people and have much to do, and we cannot send our children by themselves. It is our poverty, Father Casas."

"You were not nearly so poor before. Now you live in a bad area."

"We are not as clever as White people. We like to sit with you when you talk to us. We are not clever. Do not scold us for that."

"You have made no masks?"

"No, Father Las Casas."

He prayed quietly that it might be true.

"Listen to me, my friends. You are Christians like me. There is no barrier between you and me. We are brothers. I beseech you, do not go into the forests. The Devil dwells there. You are my brothers, but your faith is a tender plant, and weak. You risk its destruction. You must strengthen it. I will keep you from temptation. Here I have several rosaries for you, they bestow great strength when you take them in the hand and speak the words I have taught you."

Las Casas stretched his hand with the bundle of rosaries out towards them. They started whispering. Then two young people came slowly over with spears, stopped a good way from him and one of them held out a spear: "Give."

Las Casas, red with anger, berated them: "What? Are you not ashamed?" They stood there uncertain and glanced back at their people. The elder of the chiefs said:

"We have experienced many bad things from the Whites, and we are afraid."

In anger Las Casas flourished the bundle: "These are holy chains."

"We know them, Father Las Casas. Be our friend still. Several of us and our children have them. When the rains come we shall sit in our huts and carve some more."

"You will carve idols."

"We beg you, Father Las Casas, do not be angry. Do not be aggrieved. Be our friend still. Accept presents from us."

The two young warriors ran back and fetched a live graceful deer, a dwarf deer, pulled it along by a string, and one held a pretty parrot.

The young men at once ran back to their people. Las Casas stroked both creatures, his escorts held them: "I am greatly pleased. I see that you love me still. But will you accord me one more gladness? Will you listen to me?"

"What would our friend Father Las Casas say to us?"

"Oh, but see how I must talk to you, you placed leaves here where I must sit and you sit over there, it is my misfortune. But I will admonish you and beseech you to the best of my ability. My dear friends, for whose salvation I would give my life, do not forget what you have learned from us."

"The White man should not weep. He knows we have learned much from him."

"When tribes first meet, they are ignorant of the other's language and their customs, and if they come from different parts of the world, discord easily arises. But the hour also comes when they understand one another. For we are of different skin colour but are all the same humanity, created by the one and only God, and the one and only Saviour appeared to us all."

"You speak clearly, Father Las Casas, and your words are honey to our ears. But why do you speak to us and not to your own people? We never encountered your people, because we never sought them. Our ancestors and fathers lived here in peace."

"In Heaven dwells eternal God, who created Earth and Heaven and everything above and below, in six days. He has ordained all that shall pass. He separated light and darkness, set sun and moon in their place. He formed the grasses and herbs, trees and plants that bring nourishment, and fishes in the waters, and everything that creeps upon the earth, and the fowl of the air. He ordained that the sun shall revolve and there shall be day and then night when the stars and the moon shall shine. He directed the rivers to rise and fall, and drought and rain to follow one another, so that every plant and animal finds sustenance. On the last day He delved in the earth and from the clay in His hand fashioned the figure of Man, in the likeness of Himself the great Creator, and when He saw the likeness He blew His own breath into him. Then He placed the man down among the trees and plants, birds and creeping things, and gave to humans dominion over all that lives, even all plants and herbs. And this was the creation of the world.

"And then men grew wicked and heedless of His word. And then – He sent a great flood over the whole Earth, and all the seas and rivers rose and the floodgates of Heaven were opened. The waters rose over every valley and hill, all flesh that moved on the earth was drowned, birds found no tree where they could perch, and found no nourishment and starved and fell into the mighty waters. And the waters rose and rose. Men fled. But the waters that poured down from the heavens and swelled up from the earth were too fast for them, and even though they climbed to the highest mountains and clung to the tops of the tallest trees, they were drowned. And even those who took to boats could not withstand the tempest and were thrown into the water. And if they withstood the storm for day after day, they became weak from hunger. Great whales emerged from the water, Leviathan, and rammed their ships, none were left on the water.

"And in this way, my dear friends, all the people and beasts and plants of the earth would have been destroyed by the deluge, sent by almighty God in His wrath at the wickedness and depravity of mankind, were it not for one who was good and who took pity on living things. And He set this man the task of going into a ship with all his family. He was to build this ship, a large one, with doors and windows and decks, lower, middle and upper. And into this ship the good man led his wife, his sons and their wives and a pair of every kind of animal and every kind of bird. And when seven days had passed the man, whose name was Noah, closed up the windows and doors, for the great flood broke over the earth, as had been ordained so that all flesh would be destroyed because of the terrible, unfathomable, incorrigible wickedness of mankind. The judgement lasted forty days and forty nights, the waters overran the highest peaks. Everything that lived on dry land died because of man's guilt. And when the waters receded, Noah and his family left the boat, and animals and birds spread across the earth again."

Las Casas paused. He stroked the delicate deer, which nuzzled against him. Las Casas thought of the unfathomable ineradicable depravity of humankind and how he was now sitting among his friends.

The chief praised the White priest: "Truly you are a man of great knowledge. We rejoice that you remain our friend, for we would learn from you more things that we do not yet understand."

The other chief: "All people are descended from the great father Noah, who travelled in a ship over the mountains?"

"Yes."

"Do the White people know this? Have you told this to them?"

"You ask something, but leave something unsaid."

"They do bad things to us, and you say to them that great father Noah is the common father of them and of us."

"I have not told you the end of my story, what happened on the earth after they rode on the waters that drowned the wicked people. Once the waters receded people spread again across the earth, and many tribes and peoples arose. They dwelt under other skies, they were of different colours, they began to speak different tongues. They forgot their common father and almighty God, the one and only, who created them out of clay according to His own image and blew His breath into their nostrils. They no longer knew one another. And afflictions again grew great."

The chief: "You will tell us of this also." The little deer had settled calmly at Las Casas' feet, the brown people were pleased.

Las Casas raised his arms in their flowing Dominican sleeves: "I have still not reached the end. If this were the end, I would have to sit here before you and lament: see, my friends, it has come to this, the great destruction of the earth was to no avail, humanity did not pass the test, it again fell into iniquity. War, murder and hatred ruled. I would have to sit here before you, embrace this placid creature and beseech great God in Heaven: Lord, do with us as Thou wilt, we deserve nothing else! But it is not so. Now I shall bring my report to a conclusion. Great God in Heaven saw what we see. His ears were assailed by lamenting over the crimes of humanity, over their iniquity and wickedness. The poor also gained a voice from Him, He hears poor and rich, ruler and servant. And as the lamenting grew beyond all bounds, this time He did not send a punishment upon man. For it was He Himself who created him from clay. Instead, in His goodness He sent succour. He came down to a human virgin, whose name was Mary, and she conceived a son by Him. The son of God was called Jesus. He appeared on the Earth. God sent him to humans because He pitied them. Jesus lived among people, in a distant land, a long time ago, in the form of a man. We know the words he spoke. He became the saviour and redeemer of people, of all people, of every tongue and every colour. The Whites and many dark peoples know of him. They rejoice in him. Now all can attain in Heaven the state of happiness and peace that they cannot attain on earth. God has opened His own Heaven to those who believe in Him and his son."

For a long time no one spoke. Then the chiefs whispered among themselves, the elder thanked Las Casas for his report: "You are our friend, and we shall ask you later about those things we do not understand. But tell us, Father Las Casas, if it is no trouble to you: we would like to go to this heaven where peace and happiness are. Our old men speak of this place but do not agree on where it is. Tell us, where is this heaven of peace and happiness, and what paths must we follow or cut to reach there. Some of our tribes have sought in vain."

"Heaven lies above the clouds, beyond sun, moon and stars.

There sits the Creator of us all, the one mighty God. His son sits at His right hand, Mary and many angels are there with Him. No road leads from earth to there. God alone calls those to Him who die believing in Him, who love His son and obey His commandments. To these He shows the way, these only."

This seemed not to satisfy the dark men. The chief asked: "What are these commandments?"

"Not to kill, to be peaceable, to worship God, Jesus and the saints. Come to me as you were before. I shall tell you everything again."

But the dissatisfied expression remained on the faces of the people. The chief sat up straight, his voice was very firm: "With these words, Father Las Casas, you yourself betray that God wants to know nothing of the Whites. We have discussed your words that you have repeated to us and came a long way to say to us. If you had travelled alone across the wide ocean, Father Las Casas, we would have welcomed you as a friend. You would have become our brother. We would have made you our leader and teacher. But you came with warriors. You know the bad things they do to us. They chase us from our huts and drive us into the mines. Preach to them, hinder their actions. But we have seen that you are powerless among them. They just take you along when they attack us. Father Las Casa, either you are playing a false game, or you are seeking help from us."

Las Casas pushed aside the little deer, which at once stood and ran around him. He was shocked: "You are my enemies?"

"We know you are honest. What help do you seek from us?"

"I want to advise you to be peaceable, to leave the forest and attend the church and school that you built."

"They will force us to do work that we do not want to do. Will they release our brothers from the gold mines?"

"Everyone must work, and obey their superiors."

"We are not prisoners."

Las Casas sat slumped, he held a hand over his eyes and they saw that he was weeping. The elder chief spoke more gently: "Tell your Whites that they must release our people from the mines.

Then come back." Las Casas nodded and remained sitting. The chief screwed up his eyes and spoke more softly, as if he were alone with Las Casas: "Perhaps our friend does not dare to speak out in front of these men. Perhaps he fears betrayal. None of our people will betray him. If you are afraid of your escorts, who are known to us, we shall seize them."

Las Casas: "I have no secrets."

≈≈≈

When the priest and his escorts had travelled a little while along the river, deer and parrot at his side, the men shouted that a boat was pursuing them. It was paddling fast, with a dozen dark men on board. They called across that the priest should step alone onto the low bank, the chiefs have one more request. Without hesitation, Las Casas gave the order to land. The chief climbed from the other boat. They walked a hundred yards from the beached vessels. The chief once more assured him of their friendship and affection. He wanted to know if Las Casas was looking for help from them. They were ready to give it.

Las Casas, bewildered, asked: "What help?"

"You are a good man, a wise man. You live among wicked people. They ignore your words. You did not finish your story of the son who was sent by the creator of the world, but I have heard it from your mouth on another occasion. He came to the Whites and they murdered him. You carry the awful cross with you, in his memory. But we do not understand why the Whites still speak of their shame. You come to us, you have no success with them, they remain wicked. Accept our welcome. We shall heed you. We shall destroy the wicked."

"Is this why you came after me?"

"You can speak here. If you want to keep your thoughts hidden from the Whites, we can pretend to kidnap you. We shall take your escorts prisoner. All is prepared."

At this point, when Las Casas looked around at the boats lying peacefully side by side on the bank, something happened that he never forgot.

He was overcome suddenly by a terrible, quite alien fear, and was filled with an eerie sense of dread. His sank to his knees, closed his eyes.

And at once he was gliding between two rows of dark houses down an alley that led straight to the water, the sea, and he was standing on a ship, a huge heavily armed battle frigate under full sail, and when he looked around there were many others following in its wake, and he was their leader. They sailed soughing over the sea. The wind allowed no doubt as to where they were heading. A line could already be seen on the horizon. And when he walked the deck it was most sweet to see how friends surrounded him, many dark friendly people with open faces, his dear children, and it was given to him to carry them to Spain. They all prayed to the Lord on the great crucifix, sought forgiveness for his sufferings, and it was certain that the Saviour in his suffering smiled down upon them. Gangplanks were run out, from a hundred ships they went ashore, it was Spain, flags flew, every bell rang. Hostile towns fell like dry thistles at their approach, armies took up position, he destroyed them with a wave of his hand, you saw horses run away, the battlefield was littered with weaponry. Then there was a castle where the King sat with his counsellors. He gathered his courage and said: "We set out, Spanish majesty, to conquer foreign lands for you. We bring back no gold. For what do you want with gold, in a short while we are all dead and must stand before God. But we bring you heavenly messengers. And so that you and your counsellors may believe this, I have brought proofs. We found peaceful people, huge numbers of them, on islands and the mainland, on mountains and in plains, on rivers and in the savannah and in forests. We found them everywhere in the wretched lands that you commanded us to discover, and they covered the earth like autumn leaves. Goodness and peace exist on the earth. Then some of your generals believed it necessary to make war on them because they are still rude and Christianity has not yet penetrated to them. But I put a stop to it and am here with them."

Thus he spoke to the King, who sat on a raised throne amid his counsellors, and Las Casas knelt. But now Las Casas stood upright before him, dressed in his black Dominican habit, and held the crucifix in both hands, his myriad friends were with him and that gave him strength: "And now I say to you, King of Spain, and to you, the King's counsellors, now I say to you, the great nation over which the King reigns: here I stand with my people, they have become Christians and are dark-skinned. Our Saviour loved all people of whatever colour equally. Go down from your throne, King of Spain, make way, counsellors. You have done what you could. But it was bad and must stop. You sent out robbers and murderers and incendiaries, you have disgraced the name of the Whites and have not introduced Christianity but rather eradicated it. You have allowed yourselves to be deceived by churches and monasteries in your own land. But I have seen your people in the New Indies, and they were guided not by Jesus Christ but by Avarice, Belligerence and Misanthropy. They breathed wickedness and cruelty. Therefore be not tardy, King of Spain, in coming down from your throne, if you are truly a Christian. Admit that you are powerless. Look across to the New Indies and see how millions of people lie dismembered, flayed, starved. This was the work of your people."

And now he raised his voice and cried: "Down from your throne, King of Spain, it no longer belongs to you. And if you want me to spare you, then take yourself to a monastery and atone!"

And the throne fell over without a sound, and the King and counsellors and the entire palace were blown away like paper. From the cathedral the archbishop emerged with a great retinue. The archbishop climbed from his chair, the old gouty man embraced Las Casas, they wept together for joy. Receive our thanks, Las Casas. Our sins cried out to Heaven. None of us knew what to do. God's kingdom will come. Blessed, that I see this day.

Las Casas twitched. He opened his eyes. The chief stood a few paces away, his face showed awe. When Las Casas glanced across at him the chief moved his lips, but controlled himself and said nothing. Now Las Casas stood, looked behind and saw the two boats on the bank. He forced a smile and said: "Your friend is old, he dozed off in the afternoon."

"What did your dream tell you?"

"It told me good things about you."

The chief beamed: "What answer do you grant me?"

"I am sorry, I forget what your question was. Please excuse this old man."

"You are wise, and a dream visited you by day. I offered you our help. If you are our friend, come to us whenever you want, send us a sign, a feather from the parrot you accepted from us as a gift of honour. Answer in your own good time."

On the way back neither spoke. The natives departed in awe. The Dominican's lips remained sealed all day.

A major roundup of fugitive tribes was undertaken in the hinterland of Mahates as far as the Dique river. The campaign was a failure. Only a handful of prisoners were brought back. Las Casas approached them, they sat in a wooden cage. He was shocked to see one of the chiefs among them. The monk spoke to him. He turned his head away. The monk saw only hostile faces. The commander of the camp stood behind him with some officers.

"You observe our captives. Because of you we missed many others."

"Your spoils are meagre. Even without me they would have been no greater. You would have caught a few more people, that is all. I can only tell you again, commander: this is not the right way. We were not sent here by the Crown, and the Holy Father in Rome did not promise these lands to the Spanish Crown, so that we could play the Deluge and exterminate every living thing."

"I know, and so does everyone else, that that is how you see it, bishop. If only we knew how to arrive at your better methods. We gave you time to try. It failed, no?"

"We must try harder."

"Then what, then what? Shall I tell you what? We'd better quit this land and leave it to the heathen! Then they'll be happy." The officers laughed their agreement. The commander pointed to the young gentlemen: there you have it.

"We must adopt slow, peaceful methods."

"I know, bishop. You are the great friend of man and friend

of the heathen. But believe me: it's best if each sticks to his own profession, you to your preaching and us to our soldiering." The gentleman squealed: "Quite right!" One said: "A soldier gains Heaven more easily through fighting than through prayer." The commander smacked the young warrior's laughing mouth. They walked on.

The heart pounded within the old man Las Casas. He left the camp and wandered slowly towards the plain. A young monk came up from there, joined the bishop, they did not speak. Las Casas was tired and could not walk far, the day was growing hotter. They halted in a stand of eucalyptus, huge trunks side by side made a palisade, it was shady. A yellow-brown owl was watching the entrance to an armadillo's hole. They both stared at the large bird as it sat unmoving in the shade.

Then Las Casas thought of the captain Juan del Puerto. Had he murdered again today and yesterday? What does the Church seek here? It would be better to have no hand in this. Las Casas turned to the young priest, who was waiting to be addressed:

"Do you consider the officers in our camp to be good Christians?"

The priest: "They are."

So that was it. They were good Christians, they appeared so, this is the result of our labours after a thousand saints and martyrs, the sufferings of the Saviour, Mary's intercession with God. The earth must be destroyed once more. Las Casas groaned. He laid an arm on the young priest's shoulder, and slowly they strolled back from the forest. The owl had not moved.

Next day the bishop asked that the captured chief be sent to him. He came into Las Casas' tent, escorted by a soldier and shackled with chains, and stood there with downcast eyes. The bishop ordered the soldier to wait outside. He invited the chief to sit. He refused: "You betrayed us."

"No one has asked me where to find you and I have said nothing. You did not tell me the name of the place."

"You are no longer our friend. We gave you presents."

"What do you want?"

"Give back the araras and the deer. We trusted you, but you work magic with them against us."

"Chief, I shall free all of you who have been captured, you shall not go to the mines, you shall work in the plantations and I shall speak with you every day and instruct you."

"Will you give the creatures back to me?"

"Won't you leave them with me?"

"Give them back."

Las Casas nodded: "And you will obey me and not run away?"

The chief smiled: "I know why you want to free us. Because the Whites do not listen to you. But you think we will."

"And will you?"

"Speak to the commander, set us free, take away these chains and give back the creatures. Then I shall answer you."

≈≈≈

After a long discussion with Las Casas, the commander released the captives. Whether they would be allowed to leave camp and remain unguarded would depend on their behaviour.

In his tent Las Casas handed the two creatures back to the chief: "I kept my word. Sit down." The chief squatted on the mat.

After lengthy pondering he said: "You told us how the world was created. But you said something untrue, and so my people do not want to listen to you. You said: On the last day God delved in the moist soil and from the clay in his hand he made the figure of man in his own image and blew his own breath into him. Then he set the man on his feet among trees and plants and gave the man dominion over all that lives."

"Yes. He said: man shall have dominion over the fish of the sea, the fowl of the air, over the cattle, and over all the earth, and over everything that creeps upon the earth. And when God had made the man and the woman he blessed them and said to them: Be fruitful and multiply and replenish the earth and subdue it and have dominion over the fish of the sea and the fowl of the air, and over all the creatures that walk on the earth."

The chief squatted there on his mat, not moving, he wore only a scanty loincloth, black stringy hair fell in a tangle over his face. The dwarf deer stood just as motionless at his side, and the red parrot on his left fist that rested on his knee.

"Why do you not speak, chief?"

"I asked the parrot if you used him to make magic against us. He said no. I asked the deer too."

"You thought ill of me."

"You told the truth, Las Casas, you did not use the deer and the parrot for magic against us. But you did not tell truly what God said. For animals and humans are of one blood. Otherwise how could the tapir be our ancestor."

"We received breath from God, He created us in His image."

The chief laughed: "Then after we die we must become God."

"After we die we go to Him in Heaven, if we are baptised and faithful and keep His commandments."

The dark man was still smiling: "We know the tapir is our ancestor. And if we were to rule over every animal, bird and fish…" He laughed out loud. Then he struck himself on the mouth, wiped away the smile and looked nervously at the two creatures, which did not move.

"I do not know why you laughed."

"Because you are a wise man, but have never been on a hunt. We have a lot to do to catch a fish, find honey, hunt game. We must not frighten them. We are good to them and they to us. We propitiate them all the time. Then they let us catch them and we can live. But if we are bad and have not made them friendly towards us, they avoid us and we and our families go hungry. That is how we hunt, wise bishop, and catch fish and find honey."

"You are right. I have never been on a hunt. But people have told me about your hunts, and I know how it is done in my country. There the hunters have spears and crossbows, some have fire tubes, and throw spears and stab and shoot the game."

"And what do they do when it does not come?"

"They seek it out."

"But they can't find it."

"They find it."

"Then your forests are very small. We cannot find it and we have better eyes than Whites."

The old bishop was exhausted. "We have big forests too."

The dark man shrugged. "The game does not come when we have offended it. Father Las Casas, we do not rule over the animals. The tapir is our ancestor, other tribes are descended from the howler monkey."

"No, no," Las Casas roused himself. "What are you saying again, I forbade you to speak so, they are not of your blood, you are not animals, you are human, Jesus Christ is our blood, I would like to take away those creatures that sit beside you. You must pick up the rosary and look at the crucifix."

The dark man said calmly: "Many of us did so and worked in the mines and are dead."

"It's war, the men are agitated, know not what they do. Pious people do not act like this."

"Send us pious people, Father Las Casas. We shall live in peace with them."

Las Casas was weary and sent the chief away. He tried to calm himself before the crucifix, but failed. The natives were recalcitrant, Satan was up to his tricks, kept enticing them into the forest where he dwelt with his demons. The satanic forest.

≈≈≈

He wandered through the empty settlement with the young priest. His heart contracted when he saw his church, the door open, early Mass already said, no child and no adult at the door for instruction, little birds flitting through the building, parrots squabbling on the altar table. The priest ran to shoo them away. Las Casas looked dumbly on. When they came out, a horde of little monkeys was leaping around on the roof. The young man laughed: "Stones are the only thing to chase them away."

"Let them be, let them be." Then Las Casas said he realised that Satan must be fought on the ground, in every nook and cranny. We build towns here, but the people flee.

"We must hold onto them," was the pious young man's view, "we must make things more pleasant for them."

"We cannot engage in a contest with the forest. I see that one day the forest will grow over our heads. It has already started. Which is stronger: Christ, or the forest? We must go to them ourselves. We must take the struggle against forest and animals to that very ground."

"Perhaps you are too gloomy, lord bishop."

"One cannot be too gloomy. In ten years, if I am still alive, you will fall at my feet and say: lord bishop, take me away from here, let me return to my monastery, I can't go on, I want to remain a good Christian. For we have no help, we are alone, we carry in us an evil force from Europe that hinders us."

"What do you mean, lord bishop?"

"Our people. You've seen it already and will see more. If I could and if I were still young, I would leave this land and go back to the savage countries, to Europe, and try to preach Christianity. But I am old and without hope."

"Lord bishop."

"What 'lord bishop'? Whose bishop am I? Tell me! Of the state of Chiapas, yes. Is it the task of a bishop to play doorman to the kingdom of Heaven for people who do not belong there? Do we have any task other than to deceive them as they lie dying? They should roast in Hell if they are wicked, from king down to beggar, every knight and warrior and peasant, if they want nothing else. Christ appeared, his teachings are there, you pray, but if you saw the horrors they inflict with a cold heart every day and every night, you would stand at our church with hammer and nails and nail every door shut. And no sacrament for any of them, no absolution. If you want to be dogs, so be it."

"Lord bishop."

"Stop calling me that, child. We are not bishops here, but despairing Christians. What has happened here, on this beautiful earth, stinks to Heaven and deserves no mercy."

"Oh Almighty, oh Mary, oh Jesus."

"Yes, let us kneel, child."

As they returned through the village Las Casas repeated: "We cannot hide out here, and they lurk in the forest. I have no more interest in the Whites, I cannot bring Christ to them, stronger men than I must come."

In the tent, the priest saw him prostrate himself before the crucifix.

≈≈≈

Las Casas sent to Cartagena and from there forwarded a letter to the governor of Chiapas, stating that he would go with a few priests on a mission to the interior.

The governor knew the obstinacy of his bishop, he wanted to alert him by letter to the dangers of the expedition, but he said to his clerk as he signed and sealed it: "Las Casas continues his old fight with us, he is a spirit that does not understand the world. No doubt he has again denounced us in Spain and been rebuffed. Now he goes to sulk in the corner. Perhaps he hankers for a martyr's fame."

The clerk: "Not hard to acquire in these parts."

"He's an old joker. What hasn't he put us through! We're supposed to achieve the impossible. We, mark you, who answer to the Crown with our honour and our purses and have wife and children to boot. He doesn't. He always answers to 'God' and makes speeches. Wish I could do that. When I think how many years I've had to work with this hobgoblin of a bishop, I count it scarcely possible that I'm still alive and haven't lost my wits. My head spins when I think about it."

"My lord governor has persevered bravely."

"The man has cost me years of my life. And he has no shame. What he really wants is to disqualify us all from being Christians because we won't go along with his harebrained schemes. When the heathens shoot poisoned arrows at us, we're supposed to respond with honey-cakes. Anyway, thank goodness I don't have to speak to him this time. I always end up with a fever after he's been here. Last time I put him on the spot, I said to him: 'If one properly comprehends your whole approach and considers your views about us and the heathen in the right light, then the correct course of action would be to vacate this place and just leave it to the heathen.' The fellow answers quite seriously, 'Yes.' I ask: 'And how is it going with the conversions?' He replies with his usual frankness: 'You stand in our way.' So I ask: 'And why did God allow us to come over and let Cortez and Pizarro and the others overthrow whole empires of heathen.' Are you listening, clerk?"

"Of course, lord governor. I was just wondering how a clerical gentleman, a bishop no less, could allow himself to adopt such a tone with you."

The governor: "Las Casas! Who does not know him. They told me at the time of my appointment, 'Down there you'll have old bishop Las Casas, he loves the heathen.' I knew what they meant. So I ask, why did God allow Cortez and Pizarro to overthrow the heathen empires so convincingly with just their little finger. And he answers – "

"How then, lord governor?"

"What answer would you have given? Because there's no denying they were overthrown."

"He'll have talked his way out of it by – the question is really so framed that one cannot duck and weave, he is scuppered."

"You see. So how does bishop Las Casas answer, our good brother Bartholomew? As calm as you like, as if he had the answer already prepared, he declares: 'It is not God who gave us these lands. Not God, but Satan. The curse of our depravity should ripen fully. And God is waiting for this. So he lets it happen.'"

"What!"

"Classic Las Casas!"

"One can only shrug one's shoulders. Really, he is too old."

"Now he goes into the forest. Let him. He cannot hinder our descent into depravity. We won't stand in his way if he hankers for the honour of martyrdom."

Las Casas spoke secretly with the young chief in the camp. He gave the man two parrot feathers and advised him to make sure that they reached the elder chief, and say they could expect him for a discussion at a place to be determined by the chief. He would be accompanied by young priests, unarmed.

When he handed over the feathers, the captive smiled in disbelief, looked at them in the hollow of his hand, and his face showed great joy. Long days later Las Casas received a response. He said to the two young priests: "The shepherd follows his sheep. When the sheep run into the forest, the shepherd must go into the forest. Will you come too?"

They rejoiced in his trust, and agreed.

≈≈≈

During the long time of waiting – the tribe had moved far to the south, the young chief's envoys were searching for them – Las Casas encountered young captain Puerto again.

The bishop enquired after his health, the officer cast his eyes down. Since a noisy firing practice was taking place, they walked through the camp, the sprightly bishop as usual wanted to stroll outside, but the officer, hollow-cheeked and jaundiced, excused himself and lay down on one of the many treetrunks that were lying about. Las Casas sat by him: "Things are not well with you."

The young man bit his lip. "I am hurting. No one helps me. I'll be dead before I go home."

Las Casas patted his hand: "Are your bandages fresh? Did they give you sarsaparilla? I have people who know where good sarsaparilla grows in the forest."

"I've been there myself. My glands keep thickening, my belly swells, there's purulence too, and then my mouth. Don't come too close."

"Lie down."

The young man smiled: "Let's not talk of my sickness. What you want to know is, how do things stand with the twelve heathen each day."

"Will you lie down?"

"No, lord bishop, don't talk of it, I don't want to, please don't. I've given up the business with the twelve heathen. That must make you feel better."

"How can you speak to me so, what have I done to you."

"Nothing. You've never done anything to me. You trouble yourself with the heathen and are surely content now. I can't give you back those that are dead."

"Puerto, I do not understand why you are so bitter."

"Now, lord bishop, you'll enquire just like my father confessor as to whether I feel good after giving up on the twelve savages. To spare your questions I shall tell you right away: thank you, it goes well with me."

Las Casas sat a while, hands in his lap. Then he suggested: "Maybe I should take my leave of you." The officer shrugged: "As you like. When you find yourself in a crowd it's always best to go away."

"For Heaven's sake, captain, what has happened to you?"

"I'm dying and many of my friends are dead and many others are going to die. And that's why we are merry and make sport of the people here. You are quite the victor now. You took away my twelve savages, you're proud of that, oh yes, and come here and keep working away at it, rescuing ever more savages, the darker and stupider the better. Meanwhile – we who are merely White, who came to you from over there – "

"What are you saying?"

"— we die as a punishment. That is justice. God keeps a strict court, we suffer fevers and glands. It's direct evidence for the existence of God."

"Do not jest, captain."

"We die for the glory of God and so you can show your savages: see, that's what happens to those who do evil. Once I suggested we go to the cookhouse and fetch pots, paint ourselves with soot. Maybe if we're black, the high clergy will notice us, see that we too are here."

Las Casas was beside himself: "I don't understand, I don't understand."

"We know that. You think, lord bishop, that we came over from Spain just like you, to do good to the savages. We learned from sailors and from your writings how many savages and heathen there are here, and so we set off from Spain and Portugal and Italy and other places, and said: we don't see it like that, we must go over there and put an end to the misery. That's what you think too. Look at me, lord bishop, and at my friends and the soldiers and everything that's happening today, and speak. Please clarify what you think of me, what you expect of us, how you see us. We'd like to hear it."

"You fling accusations at me, young soldier – forgive an old man if he should speak so – I beg you, tell me at last what you mean."

"I talk and talk, what more can I do. I would really like to know what you think of me and how you see us. Have you the faintest notion what a man is, who does not sit in a monastery and pray and guzzle pious offerings – apart from the fact that he's a sinner and comes to you for confession. For surely he has a life above and beyond his sins. Otherwise you'd have no clue as to why he exists. Did it ever occur to you that even the Whites, and even those who have come here across the ocean, lead a life and are human."

"Yes, of course, for God's sake, how you torment me."

"At least you will concede that I have been courageous and – that I must die here."

"Puerto, my friend, you will regain your health."

"No sympathy. Anyway it's something that you pity me, notice me despite my white skin."

"Puerto, how have I failed you?"

"So insistent, lord bishop. When I sit here and talk with you, it is not so much for my sake as for others. I was with you before and know it first hand, you advised me to give up the business with the twelve savages."

"My advice was good."

"Oh, but you had no more advice after the business with the savages! All it did was show me and my comrades how little we mean to you. Let a single hair fall from the head of a savage, and see how you cry. Farewell, lord bishop. I want to make use of the time I have left."

Las Casas stood over him, pressed him gently back down onto the log: "You shall not vent your spleen against me. How have I failed?"

As if he were making any random observation, the young man said softly into the air: "We are despicable... We come by ship from Europe, shout and sing, the sea is lovely, life is lovely, and then we fall into the grave, hunger, poison, swamp fever, glands. Whoever fails to escape in time is done for. You can't live back there, so men come in hordes, armies, they all huzza and hope and then – gone. What's happening here, lord bishop? You know it, I would so much like to know."

Las Casas sat bowed, white head in his hands, dumb.

"We are despicable. We want happiness. We are betrayed."

Hey dear Mother, you bore me and I grew to a rogue and ran away, hey, dear Mother, thanks for my life. Hey dear Father, you sired me, let me grow to robber, churl, I damned and despised you. Thank you, dear Father, I thank you.

Las Casas, without moving: "There is no happiness for mankind on earth. The dark people speak of a land without death, they yearn for it, a marvellous tree grows there and nourishes them. We know the world. It is a vale of tears. Were it not so, God would not have needed to send His son. Only with Him is there happiness."

"We could buy that cheaper back home. We never found it. They must take us as they find us. What the savages say of a land without death, a marvellous tree, we too thought that."

"And you too failed to find it."

"Right. And yet. And yet." He hunted for words. "It is not like that, lord bishop."

"What do you mean?"

"Think what you like. You can't bring us any farther. And if only you had just left us alone with the savages, when we came over here. It wouldn't have been so bad."

"What would you have done if we were not here? Murders would never cease."

The young man snorted: "You think so? Were you ever a hindrance to murder? No. But if you weren't here, maybe we wouldn't have done any murdering."

"What!"

"I believe so. It's what I think. Anyway, killing is not the worst. You don't see that. The worst thing – is us and the wicked way we live with the savages and the whole world here. It's your doing! Yours! I hate you! You force us to murder, you, you. We want none of it."

Horrified, Las Casas covered his ears. Puerto continued stubbornly: "That's how it is. We want none of it. You make us do it, you are our ruin."

"Come, captain," said Las Casas, standing suddenly. "I shall take you home to your cabin, I shall care for you, you must regain your health. Then we can think it all through together."

The captain stood awkwardly, they walked back, shots cracked nearer. Las Casas supported the man, who staggered, swayed, mumbled, was delirious.

Puerto: "A blessing that those arquebuses are not in your hands, Father. I'm done for. I'm done for. If I had any say, I'd just as soon turn them on you."

Next evening he lay in his room, expiring, his face inscrutable. Las Casas administered the last rites. Puerto's head lay motionless on the pillow, his eyes did not move: "What did you tell me, about the land without death?"

Las Casas spoke of the Heaven of the blessed.

Puerto: "We didn't want it this way. How good it would be to have it here already."

"God will receive you. You have repented your sins."

Puerto breathed: "Yes." A long pause: "I was so glad to come here. I've been at home in two places."

When Las Casas glanced up from his book a while later, Puerto was smiling so tenderly at him, eyes wide open. Las Casas felt his heart fill with joy. He seized the hand that dangled from the bed. The man smiled on, gaze directed at the door. Then Las Casas saw he was dead.

≈≈≈

Before he went down to the boat Las Casas wrote a long letter to Spain, to his friend and brother Dominican, Garcia de Loaysa, who was also confessor to the King:

"God permitted that the counsellors and appointees of our
King plundered and murdered so great and rich a world,

to the inexpressible shame of our faith. And they had no excuse for this devastation and reduction of the human population. For this occurred not on a single day or in a single year and not in ten and four years, but over sixty and more years, and the counsellors daily received reports from many monks and trustworthy officials on these occurrences and yet made no intervention. And so God permitted that the King, who could have become richer and more happy, has become the poorest. For although the generals and officials have extracted millions in gold and silver, pearls and precious stones from these Indies, all is even now vanishing like smoke. These sums have not aided Spain in delivering itself from eternal wars and crises. They have forced the pawning and selling of kingdoms. So splendidly has the government of the New Indies served you. And for all these injuries and losses, this poverty and these crises and other even greater retributions that loom over Spain, the guilt lies with the wicked counsellors and their murderous servants."

In a postscript he wrote: how he suffers under the infamy with which the Christian religion is regarded in the new lands because of the depredations of the Whites. He gives all his letters, submissions and writings into the hand of brother Garcia, and they are to remain his property when he, now grown so old, is called away. A second postscript reads: "I am assailed by inexpressible thoughts. Remember me in your prayers, my brother Garcia. The soul of your brother Bartholomew Las Casas belongs to the Holy Church."

The Inquisition

ON EUROPEAN SOIL, hard by the city of Seville, not far from the gulf of Cadiz where many galleons laden with gold arrived from the Indies and armed men with horses and hounds embarked for the Indies, the cathedral lay at the foot of green hills. A river, the Guadalquivir, led its glittering waters past the hills. Lemon trees beckoned from the heights, bitter-orange groves bloomed in gardens.

In the extensive monastery buildings overlooking the river, in the abbot's panelled room, a heavy square stone table heaped with folios and scrolls stood before two old men. These old men, enveloped in loose black silks, were supported and flanked by huge red armchairs in which they lay as if in bed.

The hands of one old man extended as balled fists from the ends of his arms, gout had fixed them thus. His eyes were bloodshot, they sensed the grey and yellow of the trees outside, but could not make out trees, oranges or river. This was Garcia de Loaysa.

The one sprawled beside him in a chair, lanky and desiccated, noble nose jutting from a yellow-white bony face, was the abbot of the Carthusians. His mouth, once scornful and severe, gaped now with its feebly sagging lower jaw. What in others would be called eyes had crawled deep into their sockets, guarded by yellowish lids. A bushy wreath of white hair fringed his little cap.

They shuffled the letter from the bishop of Chiapas this way and that. Garcia felt like smiling, there was a time when he could make any kind of gesture, now his face would not obey, it was as if it lay already in the coffin. In a high soft voice that still obeyed his wishes he said: "Our old brother Bartholomew! As he lives and breathes. It seems he's still good on his pins. Same age as us and he goes into the forest, to the Indians! Our letters have crossed, I wrote to him that the day of my demise lies not far off."

"Brother Bartholomew enjoys the rudest health, he was always the kind of man well suited to an army life."

"You mean more for the army than for the Church?" Both attempted smiles.

Garcia moved his hand: "Give me the letter. How do you understand this sentence from our friend: 'My soul is assailed by inexpressible thoughts.' What kind of thoughts can be inexpressible?"

"I have heard such phrases before."

"Where, brother abbot?"

"Spare me from saying."

"He writes: 'Remember me in your prayers, Brother Garcia.'"

"Do so. I think it is necessary."

They sat at the stone table and left lying on it the letter despatched by Las Casas from a distant land. One had aching knees and wondered how he could recover, he felt his legs would break. The other succumbed to somnolence.

The door opened behind them. A vigorous man in black silk strode loudly in. He had a large youthful face, white hair fell in thick locks to his neck. As he sat down facing the two old men, his back to the window, a monk placed a glass and a jug of wine in front of him and, greetings over, he at once downed long slow draughts of the heavy red wine. The he reached for Las Casas' letter. And as he read, he laughed out loud. Towards the end he grew quiet. Then he read it again without laughing and poured another glass.

Father Garcia suppressed his aches: "You have read it, Brother Juan?"

"Yes."

"And what do you think?"

"Revenge is always on the mind of the small man. A small man does not know how to rule. He cannot get along with people. He always thinks he must help. His feelings spur him on."

"True," croaked the abbot. "Such rebellious nagging. What a picture Brother Bartholomew has of the world. Goes to war and thinks the cannon are there just for play."

Garcia grasped the letter. "And what do you say to the conclusion?"

"Why?"

"The conclusion: 'I am assailed by inexpressible thoughts. Remember me in your prayers, Brother Garcia. The soul of your brother Bartholomew Las Casas belongs to the Holy Church'."

"Where does it say that? Show me." And he read it again, banged on the table and regarded the two old men, his broad chest heaved.

"We waited for you, this is why we requested your presence."

Juan Alvarez, Inquisitor of Toledo, pulled himself erect in his chair: "Well well well. I didn't read the postscripts. I know this blowhard, this zealot, dogmatist. He goes to the Indians in the forest to proselytize. He wants to go his own way. It's the Las Casas method of proselytizing. But it seems to go farther! Well now! We had better find out who taught him."

"Ah. That one is long dead."

"We might have lit upon a fine discovery here. Heretics beset us on all sides in France and Germany, we have our hands full keeping order even here. And then we receive letters from a bishop who wants to proselytize! 'Inexpressible thoughts'. Let us help him express them."

The desiccated abbot opened his eyes and brought his voice to utterance: "The bishop of Chiapas has simply grown childish, Alvarez. What could you expect from all his blathering about atrocities and exterminations."

Alvarez rested his arms on the table. "See how it begins. Always with the heart, the precious heart. But at the end of the path there blooms insolence, and then rebellion. How we have been plagued by these mountebanks ever since the days of that shameless heretic of Ferrara, Fra Girolamo Savonarola, those offspring of sin who unsettle and incite the populace with vain promises and who must be put to the torture until they acknowledge their own casuistry. Right to the end they cry: my crimes were committed for the glory of God. Pain, the pitiable tug of ropes on the limbs, is necessary to arouse doubt in such weak heads."

And he became enraged and his chair crashed back: "I hate such sentimental twaddle! Agitators are fools. I stand with the generals and captains who are the victims of Las Casas' complaints. Yes indeed! I stand on any side where I find myself opposing such mollycoddles and bleeding hearts. Trumpeting and crowing about abuses such as happen everywhere – 'Oh, criminals! You too are criminals!'— It neither safeguards the state nor serves the Church. A few false strokes do no lasting harm. What does this Las Casas want? That we lay down our arms? Is the world already one with the Church? No! Or should we say to his miserable savages: run away now! No! We shall not let them run! *We are the Church*, and the world belongs to us, piece by piece, every nook and cranny. And we tolerate no nonsense."

The two old men now sat bolt upright, and one after the other said: "God grant it be so."

Garcia tried to soften the tone: "The object of Las Casas' concern is not so much Christianity as the welfare of the Indians. He has nagged us for years, and we have given in to him. Despite opposition from every sensible governor and general, not to mention numerous men of the cloth, we have decreed that slaves should be set free. We have thereby harmed the revenues of the Spanish Crown and incurred the risk that its wars may not proceed to the best advantage of the Holy Church. But this was not enough for him, and still he writes and complains. We did at least add that it is permissible for Indians to be allocated to Christians, that in serving them they may forget their sins."

Again Alvarez shouted out in fury: "Do we possess the key to Heaven or not? That is the question that will trip him, as it does every heretic."

Garcia raised his arms in alarm: "Brother Juan."

"I say again: this is the question which must trip every bleeding heart, every philanthropist, free thinker. He is no different. Even a doctor when he falls sick suffers the usual ailments."

Garcia sniffed the glass that the big furious man had refilled: "Do not drink such strong wine, Brother Juan. It always makes you so turbulent."

"Do not fear for your friend Bartholomew."

"We shall urge him to withdraw from politics."

"Would that have sufficed in the case of Doctor Martin Luther, Brother Garcia?"

"For Jesus' sake!"

"Why so shocked? Las Casas is a heretic. He condemns himself. He goes into the forest 'beset by inexpressible thoughts'. He shall come here and express them to the court."

Garcia pressed a fist to his heart: "Is that how I must see my friend again?"

The lanky abbot averted his face: "You exercise the duty of a friend to him. We, the duty of a Christian."

At once two Dominicans, their orders already prepared,

were despatched with a letter to the bishop of Chiapas. He was summoned back to Spain.

Flight into the forest

LAS CASAS HAD never seemed so happy and alert as on that day when he climbed into a boat with his two companions and the young chief who had been placed in his care, and rowed away. The two young monks went with him, but as the houses and the squat tower of the church disappeared around a bend in the river, their eyes were moist. Las Casas sat under the awning and gazed at the water. After a while they left the boats and were accompanied south by White patrols, riding for days, then they were alone, the young chief led the way, near a village they came upon a river, the Sinù that flows into the Gulf of Morrosquillo.

Wonderful burning sun, thought Las Casas, it is a monster the way it hangs over the land, a monster. I can imagine it has jaws and is devouring us.

Towards midday rain roared down, the boat went on, the brown people paddled, one stood high in the prow on a bench.

Lovely smooth water. How everything fits together: sun and water, and plants growing. How God has shaped the world.

Tall mimosa trees followed the river, he exchanged glances with them. As evening approached, the rowers showed unease, the food was all gone. Suddenly another boat was there, emerging from a side branch. They led Las Casas' boat up the branch. Under a huge banana tree they had made huts for him and themselves, roofed with banana leaves. Las Casas slept in a hammock. He dreamed forwards and backwards, no walls anywhere.

They travelled two more days, their companions had some dried manioc, gathered roots. They came upon the tribe not far from the coast. They had come so far from their former homes. Las Casas warned the two young monks not to venture anything by themselves, and to stay with him at all times. He warned: just listen, and observe.

Then they went among the people, were greeted with respect, engaged in everyday conversations. All three wore the black

Dominican habit and conducted their daily prayers. During these months they saw no evil among the people.

Las Casas, seeing what good people they were, strove fervently to lead them away from their abominable customs. They allowed him to baptise some of their newborns, but then ceremonies took place where sorcerers used all manner of means to find out who these newborns were. Las Casas knew about it, he restrained himself from interfering, but spoke with the oldest chief and the sorcerer. Both said: "It is certain that the infants are our ancestors whose names you have heard. The mothers received them. We are happy that the ancestors have withstood the long journey and found us here."

"Your ancestors are long dead."

"They are dead, but we have honoured and cared for them. The great spirit of our tribe has sent us these spirits."

"And how do you think it is with the Whites? They do not care for their ancestors as you do, and yet you see how many they are."

"You have your great spirit, each of your tribes."

"Our great spirit is Jesus Christ. But he is the great spirit of all people who are baptised and believe in him."

"No," they smiled, "stay with us longer, you will see that every tribe has its own great spirit."

And at a naming ceremony, to his great sorrow Las Casas again saw masks and gaudy wooden poles, and the dancing around them.

"They must return to the town, to our settlements," said Las Casas to his two companions. "In the forest they are falling into their old ways." He began preaching earnestly to them. The people were eager to hear him. For many it was a great novelty, and they often discussed it among themselves. They thought they could use the knowledge of the Whites to gain possession of their great powers. They came to Las Casas and his pupils and asked them to impart the knowledge, declared themselves ready for instruction. Las Casas discussed this with his pupils, who congratulated themselves. "You think we have made such progress?

Perhaps. Every means must be employed. But you both know that what they want from us is better weapons for their struggle."

They agreed to provide instruction. Stretch a little finger to the Devil and he has you by the whole hand. Offer God a single hair and you are His entirely. Thus began Father Las Casas' mission in the forest. They were all three infused with marvellous joy. They found that the dark people sucked up instruction like parched roots in water. Convincing such gentle and sweet-natured pupils took no effort at all. Meanwhile their old forest thoughts flourished untouched.

The end

FOR LONG HAPPY months Las Casas and his companions heard nothing of the world. Twice they sent envoys to Cartagena to confirm that they were still alive and well. At the start of the rainy season they were dwelling by a fish-teeming river near where it flowed into the sea. Then dark people came, who told of a great sailing ship out on the sea, it had sent dinghies ashore at many places to ask about Las Casas, they had a message for him. The tribe debated how to react. Las Casas soothed them, it is only one ship, we can meet it nearby, you can observe the encounter from a distance and see if they are armed. Then they sent away the people who had espied the ship, and a few days later a great galleon anchored in the mouth of the river, and Las Casas and his companions allowed themselves to be rowed out to it. The two Dominicans on board explained their mission to the bishop of Chiapas, and showed him a friendly letter from Garcia. Las Casas bowed his head. "I had thought to end my days here. Now they summon me back."

But he was obedient. He went ashore with his pupils and the two emissaries, the ship's captain and helmsman came too. They stayed a few days, exchanged presents, gathered provisions.

Then the captain invited the oldest chief and his wife, as well as several other respected men of the tribe who had shown curiosity, to come aboard the ship, he would give them a farewell feast. Seventeen people from the tribe, together with the oldest chief and his wife, agreed to be conveyed on board.

As soon as they were aboard the captain hoisted sail, hauled in the anchor, and sailed away.

Las Casas and the others on shore at first thought it a prank. Then they thought it was just a little excursion. Then evening came, and night fell, and the oldest chief and the others had still not returned. They left the beach. The tribe was overcome with a terrible disquiet. Las Casas and his pupils sat in their huts and prayed. The Dominicans from the ship came to Las Casas in the morning, they were afraid.

"What has happened?" they asked the old bishop. They said they feared that the captain had kidnapped the people to sell as slaves on Hispaniola.

Las Casas concurred. "Who is the captain?"

"We don't know him. He brought us along for a hefty payment. He tried the same trick along the coast with other dark people, but they refused to be enticed.

"Why did you not tell me?"

"Forgive us, lord bishop, we did not believe a man could be so wicked here. For he is supposed to carry all of us, you too, back with him."

Las Casas breathed: "What are we to him. But what it is to us. The shame. The shame." And he threw himself down on the mat and sobbed aloud. "Now you have an example of what they do. And they come and preach Christianity." Las Casas gestured like one inconsolable. He asked that no one be admitted to him, he dared look no one in the face.

But when people came at midday he had to see them. They glowered, the young chief was among them, they saw Las Casas' great distress and paused. The bishop placated them, he pulled himself together and wrote two letters, one to Cartagena, the other to priests on the island of Hispaniola. He related what had happened, expressed his revulsion at the captain's action, and desired the priests to secure the immediate release of the abductees. At evening he went with his pupils and the Dominicans to the young chief's hut. He implored the people, who sat glowering with stony faces, not to cast blame on him. He hoped it was a mistake, or the prank of one man who would be punished for it. Their chief and their brothers would return. He staked his life and that of his companions on it. He kept imploring them not to grieve. He would vouch for a good outcome to the affair.

The people were not all of one mind, Las Casas thought some wanted to attack him without delay, setting aside all his teachings; they even suspected in a sudden overwhelming rush of fury that he was in on the plot. The chief, Las Casas' old friend, although conducting himself with great reserve, managed to persuade the people to wait and see what the efforts of Las Casas, who was after all a great man among the Whites, would bring. In the following weeks the chief spoke to Las Casas only once in passing, to remind him of a conversation they had once had in camp: "I said you are not a great man, they let you preach to us, you are powerless among them."

Las Casas begged: let him not think that, he should be patient, he would receive proof. The chief walked away calmly, he knew Las Casas was concerned entirely with the affair and not with himself.

Long weary weeks went by. The tribe kept to the same place, it was the middle of the rainy season. Now there were no discussions, no instruction. Las Casa and his people were shunned like an infection. They were given food and drink, but forbidden to walk where they might encounter natives.

More than three months were already past. Then at last a messenger appeared with a letter for Las Casas. The messenger complained: it was no easy task to deliver the letter, he had started out with a companion, a jaguar attacked them and tore the companion to bits, he himself lost the way. The chief was present as the messenger said this and handed the letter to Las Casas. The bishop trembled inwardly as he accepted it. He knew how important this report was in the eyes of the dark people, and he too was not immune from fear.

The priest in Hispaniola wrote: As soon as he received the letter he made enquiries about the seventeen abductees, indeed long before the letter arrived a ship bearing these seventeen had called at Hispaniola, but at once sailed away again as there is little demand for slaves here and the captain did not wish to dispose of his people at a poor price. This is alas all that he can report. They pray for Las Casas' health and hope he will soon leave the gloomy forests and come to them.

When Las Casas let fall the hand that held the letter, the oldest chief asked what it was he had read. Las Casas, the white-haired bishop, knelt before him and said: "I am guilty. I alone. I trusted them. I beg you, do not think otherwise." The chief had him read the letter out loud. The chief raised Las Casas to his feet. He was unconscious.

An hour later he came to himself, the young pupils and the Dominicans were at his side. Las Casas performed the last rites, the elder of the two Dominicans administered extreme unction. The bishop said: "The people know we did not permit this abduction, but we are guilty of it and they believe they cannot allow us to go unpunished." They prayed silently. One of the young monks at one point burst into tears, they interrupted their prayers to comfort him. Once they all succumbed to despair when Las Casas stood staring ahead with strangely contorted features and murmured: "The shame." The two monks hid their faces in their hands. But Las Casas regained his senses: "Do not complain, I have done too much of that in my life. The world is not yet ripe for redemption. We are dragged down in the undertow of its ruin."

Towards evening he admonished them to direct their thoughts only to God. He knew that the dark people would come before sunset. And so it was.

Loud voices arose in the settlement, people gathered around their tent, the shouting grew shrill and near. They knelt in prayer, their faces close to the ground. As the spears and clubs hit home, it was no great stretch for them to embrace the whole world.

≈≈≈

Search parties were despatched. The tribe that Las Casas had gone to was nowhere to be found. When no news came of Las Casas, the two young priests and the monks, it was considered probable that they had been massacred. But some months later rumours were laid to rest through a communication from Garcia and Alvarez, the inquisitors of Toledo: "The bishop of Chiapas, Father Bartholomew, most assuredly did not die a miserable death in the New Indies at the hands of savage tribes. He returned to Spain at the conclusion of his mission, re-entered the monastery of his Order, and there died a peaceful death."

The officers of the Inquisition hoped to prevent the suspected heretic brother Bartholomew from gaining the reputation of a martyr.

≈≈≈

The water spirit Sukuruja, Mother of Waters, glided from tree to tree in the gloomy forest in the guise of a snake. Sometimes she stood in human form beneath green boughs. She stood there with a heavy club, bow and arrow, gay parrot feathers adorned her long black hair, her dark skin glistened in the dark, her cheeks and forehead were painted red. She slid into reeds.

The tribe had gone. When they pulled out, the corpses lay piled over and beside each other in the little tent. Noon and evening came. In the dark a snake rustled from tree to tree, Sukuruja. She stood at the forest edge in the form of a man with bow and arrow, wearing a big feather headdress.

Sukuruja clucked like a hen, the tapir ran up from the river. "See my club, tapir. Fetch your brothers to chase away vultures." A crowd of tapirs came, chased the vultures from the huts. Sukuruja glided out of the forest in the dark. Stars twinkled merrily overhead. Sukuruja danced a savage dance through the deserted village, took ashes from the cooking places, painted herself, the night wind scattered ashes around her feet.

Sukuruja crouched at the hut of the White men, peered in, took Las Casas' corpse in her arms, laid him across her lap. "White man, are you there?"

Las Casas did not want to answer.

"White man, why did you fight me? For you did not want to." Las Casas lay still.

Then Sukuruja saw the chain with the crucifix at his belt and the rosary in his folded hands: "These are stopping your mouth." She laid them aside.

Las Casas opened his eyes: "Am I with you, Sukuruja?"

"You know me?"

"Where are my companions?"

"Let them be."

"Where is my crucifix?" He sat up. There was the sky, the merry stars, Sukuruja crouched on the floor, adorned with feathers.

Las Casas swayed to his feet. He picked up crucifix and rosary, they slid from his hands. He bent down. Again they fell. Sukuruja stood up: "White man, into the forest! Come!" The old man in the black cloak followed hesitating; twice, thrice he circled the objects on the floor. Sukuruja took him in her arms and carried him. Las Casas wept a short while.

They went down to the river. Vultures squawked insults. Weaver birds flew. Down there water snakes, alligators, fish broke the surface. As Sukuruja prepared to jump, Las Casas tore free with a cry, stood, raised his arms, fell and lay there, his face covered crucifix and rosary.

Sukuruja

WHEN THE AMAZON rose, water overflowed its banks for great distances, devastation encroached on the land, animals fled. Waterfowl left their islands and migrated away. Floodwaters surged in tumult. Here and there a bank collapsed, tall forests along the river swayed, water dug away the ground, freed the roots of giant trees, undermined them, trees tumbled into the murky spate.

Often the living waters forced their way in single-minded fury into loose soil, and then the river, a seething sea, carried away whole floating islands with trees and plants and monkeys and birds, even people; down the river they sailed. The raging grey-white water dammed tributaries, absorbed broad lakes and channels back into itself. Slowly the flood extended across the whole basin. Big lakes slowed its progress, and the trunks of giant palms were washed by a murky muddy tide. Animals took refuge in treetops. Dark people glided in boats over the crowns of sunken trees, settled in hollow trunks. Monkeys leapt around them. Ants left the ground and stuck nests together in branches. But the treetops bloomed in colourful profusion, brimmed over with foliage. Above the mud stretched a swaying garden, farther than the eye could see.

It lasted weeks. Slowly the current released back hill after hill, sandbank after sandbank. And as the wet earth emerged again and the sun glowed, turtles began to return to sandbanks, dig down and lay their eggs. Bushes and reeds rose out of the flood. The river had removed a forest from here, set it down there. Now came the time of the riverbanks, the great ebb, tapirs appeared, jaguars showed themselves and dangled their tails in the water. Tree-corpses, driftwood became stranded, began to rot, fungi set in, from outside it was a tree trunk, inside a putrescent mush. Garish parasitic plants settled on rotting logs, pushed up mighty stalks.

≈≈≈

In the savannahs and forests of the great river, on the Yapura and the Vaupes lived many people, tribes of the Tariana, Duck people, Jaguar people.

The maize was half ripe. Cobs were washed, people stood in a big circle as the medicine man sang and bit into them. May the spirit of the maize be merciful, provide a rich harvest. The weather was fine, firstborns came, they were given to the dead to whom the ground belonged, these took nourishment from them, now the people could eat.

Little dark people, Maku, wandered through the forest, they were captured. They said everyone should flee. Many brown people are fleeing from the Whites, dying. They waited. There were many lightning storms. They took children, collected parrots from roofs, gathered pots, jugs, utensils down from walls, built huts in the forest. The ancestors received much deer meat. After four suns men set out with spear and shield, crept up to the village in the dark. One gave a sign, they uttered warcries and ran through the village, beat on the ground, banged on roofs, burst through doorways. They ran back into the forest. Next morning they gathered children, animals, pots, jugs, utensils, returned to the village. The medicine man made a new fire. He gave each family an ember. They took it to their own hut.

The rains came. From a fruit tree the udu called: *tru udu, udu, udu.*

There is a big drum called the Man, deep-toned, and a smaller called the Woman. With beats short and long, deep and high toned, they throbbed across lakes big and small, wide rivers and narrow streams, across hill and forest and savannah: "Everyone must flee. Many people are fleeing. They come from the sunset and die."

Elders said: "Our parents told us: the drums lamented, look out for yourselves, everyone must flee, there is great danger. Towards sunset the Great Spirit that holds up the earth made the mountains tremble. There is a tree, it is the father of all beasts and people, you can gather all kinds of fruit from it. If you climb the tree it draws its branches together and lifts you up, the tree carries you into the sky where the ancestors dwell. That is the Land without Death. Our parents sought it in vain. Where should we flee to? In those days many women committed murders and moved away to the south."

Maku slipped through the forest, some were caught, they said: "Ever more dark people flee the Whites who came up out of the sea, ever more dark people are coming down from the mountains."

Chiefs went through the villages, fetched away old cripples who bring bad luck. They sent warriors with them towards the sunset, close to the great mountains. There they broke the legs of the cripples and left them, placed dead cats beside them. They would bring calamity on the Whites.

The warriors returned. They lived in peace, nothing happened.

Tiye and Guaricoto

AND FROM EUROPE there came more ships, more people. The human volcano kept spewing.

And as ever more White men, iron warriors, sinners, looters, and plaintive priests appeared – long and weary, the path to annihilation and self-destruction – dark people clustered in the forests and on the grassy plains. The silent forest adjusted and tidied itself around them.

Towards the east, beneath huge trees of the plain, the Women People flourished on the mighty Amazon, from the Yapura river to the Jamunda.

Tiye, the junior, said to Kudurra the elder: "Our queen Truvanare has sent a message that every woman, but not the old ones, must trim arrows. And we must build many boats."

"There are already many boats."

"She said so."

"How sad our life is, Tiye. Have you heard how women live in the villages of men?"

"No man has ever come near me. First they have to take me to the hut."

"A woman has her man, and they live in their hut all year round. And when the woman wants loving he comes to her. And when the man wants loving they are together. They are together in the rain time and the dry time."

So said Kudurra the elder to Tiye the junior. She already had two children. Tiye pulled the plough, Kudurra pushed it into the soil. Tiye asked: "If you have children, do you still need loving? The queen says: 'We women are the people. When the priestesses summon the moon, all our ancestors gather together. Then we must go on the warpath and catch men, so the ancestors can increase.'"

Kudurra replied: "I have already killed three men. I don't want to kill any more. I would like to keep them in my hut, and feed them like my parrot."

Tiye laughed and clapped her hands.

"Many of us think the same, Tiye. Our queen and our priestesses are hard. Many women have fled across the swamps to the other women. They don't kill men. When their priestesses summon the moon they go into the forest, and drink cashiri. They are friends with the men, the men are friends with them. Many women follow the men to their villages, many men follow the women."

≈≈≈

Truvanare was the mightiest queen between the great lake of Manacapuru and the Urubu river. She herself went to war, when the boats were ready.

She spoke to her commanders before they set off: "Protect yourselves, paint the marks clearly. Men are descended from vultures. Many years ago we were in their power. They disguised themselves and deceived us. Now they dwell out there and steal women, because they cannot reproduce themselves. They must all die. Then our Great Spirit will send us signs to tell us which fruit to eat so we may bring children into the world. Fall on their villages, burn their houses down, kill as many as you can. Bring back young men, we shall kill them later."

From the place where their boats lay, Truvanare sent emissaries to the men: "Make peace with us, and as a sign of your submission send us your young men. Their lives will be spared. If you do not send us your young men, we shall destroy you all."

The enemy chief sent a pot containing red pigment, the emblem of blood. The women surrounded the first village and uttered warcries. They seized some prisoners. They moved on. When they had enough they ate and drank in the forest. No one was allowed to talk to the men. When they were back in their village on the river, they built huts in the fields. Truvanare the queen and her sorceresses inspected the men front and back, and allocated them. The young women had to stay in the big houses with the priestesses, for a whole month they were relieved of work. They were given little fishes and manioc to eat, nothing else. But the men were given pirurucu fish, honey, andiroba nuts, and monkey flesh. In the evenings as the sun was sinking, the sorceresses led the young women into the fields, they danced and clapped. Only when the sun disappeared did the young women enter the huts.

≈≈≈

Guaricoto, a young man, saw Tiye by the light of the fire outside his hut. Tiye had signs on her breasts and thighs for protection. Guaricoto asked: "Why have you painted yourself? We're not going to dance." Tiye gave no answer. The man said: "Why have you come? I know you will kill us." Tiye said nothing.

They sat by the fire. He looked at her: "You brought your spear. Are you going to kill me?"

Tiye said: "No." Guaricoto laughed: "Not yet." She was silent. He said: "Why didn't you bring something to drink? People with spears and shields are moving around everywhere. Why don't we drink together? I can play the flute." He pulled her arm. She hit his hand. He laughed. He put an arm on her shoulder: "Come to me, look at me." She looked into his face and quickly away at the fire. When he grabbed her knee she jumped up and went for her spear.

Then he drew up his knees, gazed into the fire and sang to himself. She sat down and clutched her arms to her breast: "You're trying to enchant me, stop that singing."

He said: "You sing!"

"I don't know any songs, only what we sing when we're ploughing."

"Sing."

"Aren't you afraid I might enchant you?"

"You said you don't know any enchantment songs."

She saw his wounded leg: "What bit you?"

"When you speak it is like the chirping of cicadas. You speak like the rushes."

"Does it hurt?"

"The woman with the feathers around her waist stabbed me."

"That's our queen, Truvanare."

"That's why I couldn't run and so I'm here."

"You're sad to be here. I shall ask your friend what your name is."

"And I would like to know your name, but there's nobody I can ask."

"Call me Colibri. Are all men like you?"

"Now you look at me, Colibri, but you promised to sing to me."

"Come into the lodge so that no one can hear."

In the lodge he lay down in the hammock, her enormous shadow fell on him as she stood in the doorway. "Colibri, why don't you come in, you were going to sing."

"I forgot my spear, I left it by the fire."

"I'll fetch it."

"No." She raised both arms and crouched down at the threshold.

"Where are you?" She was resting her head on her knees. He crouched in front of her. He touched her shoulder. She brushed his hand away, he lost his balance. They crouched in silence. Then she started to sing softly. He said: "I shall sing too.

You have hardened your heart against me
You have hardened your heart against me
My love, he, he, oha.
You have hardened your heart cruelly against me
You have hardened your heart cruelly against me
My love, he, he, oha.
I waited for you and grew weary,
I waited for you and grew weary,
My love, he, he, oha.
For you I wandered wearily and came here,
For you I wandered wearily and came here,
My love, he, he, oha.
Now I will call to you with a different tune,
Now I will call to you with a different tune,
My love, he, he, oha.
Oh, I shall call with a different tune
So that you hear me,
My love, he, he, oha.
I shall go to the world below, to the world of spirits,
From there I shall call to you, from there I shall call to you,
My love, he, he, oha."

She held her head high, her face was in shadow, his face shone red from the fire. She whispered: "Sing it again."

He sang. Then she sang with him.

He stood up: "I shall fetch your spear. She whispered: "Yes."

And when he brought it she was on her feet and looking at him with big eyes: "Show me how you hold it."

He held the spear out to her. She pulled it to her: "It is my spear." She hugged it and rubbed her hair on the wood. She pushed it at him: "Here, you hold it." He took it. She said: "You have my spear." He nodded. Tiye said: "Raise it." He stepped back, turned towards the fire and swung the spear to and fro. She rushed up behind him and pulled it from his hand: "Stop, they'll see us." She laid it on the ground, stroked it. Guaricoto stepped close, slowly lowered his head beside hers where it lay pressed to the spear, and pressed his face to hers there over the spear. She tolerated this without moving.

Tiye whispered: "Do you belong to the vultures?"

"Yes."

"All of you that we caught?"

"I don't know."

"You must be destroyed. All men must be destroyed. We shall wipe you out. Soon there will be no more men." He shook his head. "Our great spirit will give us fruit so that we can bring children into the world and our ancestors will increase. The queen said. I want to ask you something."

They sat in the hammock. Tije held out her spear: "I pull the plough with Kudurra. Kudurra says, 'Some women live in the forest with men and drink cashiri, they are friends.' Is it true?"

"It is true."

Then she smiled at him: "Today I shall lie with you in the hammock. And for many nights."

"You work hard every day?"

"Not just now. Only the old women. Now we live in the big houses with the priestesses. We eat only little fishes and dried manioc."

He sighed. "Ah, you are fasting."

"So the spirits will hear us when we ask them for children." He sighed again. She nodded at him: "Don't be sad."

She checked around the hut, everything was quiet, placed the spear against the wall, stretched out in the hammock. She crossed her arms over her breast and lay on her side. He lay down beside her and crossed his arms.

She said: "So many empty hammocks up there." She closed her eyes and laughed softly.

Soon she slept, he too.

≈≈≈

In the morning she was gone. There were patrols in the fields. They brought the men food and drink. They were not permitted to gather, but communicated by signs from hut to hut.

Kudurra whispered in the big house of women, where they squatted on the floor: "Are you alive, Tiye?" Tiye looked at her in surprise. Kudurra studied her: "Yes you are."

"Why shouldn't I be alive?"

"When a man takes you, you die."

"Is it true?"

"Every woman taken by a man dies. That why we are here, so that we don't die."

"But Kudurra, what should I do when a man takes me? I shall kill him right away."

"Be quiet. He hasn't taken you yet. I was just testing you. Don't be afraid of him. The queen and the priestesses want you to be afraid. It is wonderful to die with a man."

"No!"

"It is, Tiye. He dies too. Then both of us, woman and man, receive new names."

"You're scaring me, Kudurra."

"Be quiet. The priestess is watching."

When they led Tiye to the fire that evening, Guaricoto was waiting at the doorway of the hut. Not waiting for her to speak, not waiting to see her face, right away he said:

"Make me a present, Colibri, I'm so poor. Bring me pigment so I can paint myself. Bring me a drink."

Then he saw her angry face. They stood there silent a long while, she by the fire, he at the hut. Little birds glided through the smoke. Midges buzzed. She walked past him and sat on the hammock with her spear, stared at the fire. He stepped towards

her. She brandished the spear: "Go to the side, stay in the shadows."
He stood motionless in the shadows.

After a while she stood up angrily: "Who are you? Your name
is Guaricoto. Show yourself. Why do you want to kill me?"

"I don't, Colibri."

"They send me here, send all of us here, to be killed by you.
So that we share our names with you. I don't want to. You keep on
being Guaricoto, I am what I am called."

"I don't want to kill you, Colibri."

"Don't lie. Woe to those who send us to you. If only we had
struck you down at once. Why do they do this to us?"

As he remained standing in the shadows, she called: "Come
here, Guaricoto." He did not come. She turned to face him:
"Guaricoto, I want to look at you."

"But I don't want to look at you."

She jumped up: "Come here, Guaricoto, I want to look at
your face."

He came quickly out of the shadows, knocked the spear from
her hand and trod on it. She whispered: "I can strike you down
without a spear."

He: "Go on." They stared at each other. He stepped off the
spear, took Tiye in his arms. She said: "Give me the spear." He did
not.

Then she pushed him away, made fists, crossed her arms:
"Now I can look at your face, Guari."

"And I yours."

"Let's sit by the fire. But first give me back my spear."

"So you can strike me down!"

"They mustn't see you holding my spear. Let's sit close so they
can't see you hold the spear."

It was night, the fire burned down, from time to time they
threw a branch on. When they grew cold they went into the hut,
lay in the hammock. They shivered, and warmed one another.
They fell fast asleep. When they awoke it was broad daylight.
Guari was crouching on the floor looking sad. She started up.
The women guards were at the entrance, calling her. Tiye jumped

down, grabbed her spear and scurried away.

"I don't want to kill you," said Guari that evening – she had brought a pot of honey from the urucu bee, the healing kind; "Bring me pigment and oil for my hair, so I can make myself beautiful for you. And bring cashiri so we can drink."

"Now I shall let you take me, Guari, because yesterday you didn't harm me when you held my spear. Do you promise not to tell?"

"Who should I tell, Colibri?"

He put his arms around her hips, there were tears in her eyes: "They'll laugh at me if they hear." She put her arms on his arms, her eyes flashed: "You are my friend if you don't boast about it. I talked to Kudurra about you. Don't be afraid. If you were my enemy you would have killed me. You are not my enemy."

"Why did you think I'm your enemy, Colibri?"

"The queen and the priestesses said so. But I'm not afraid of you. Show me your hands, open them. No, you have no enchantments against me. Stand up, I want to see your back."

"You won't see anything. But I want to paint and oil myself for you."

"You really want to, Guari? Why do you want to?"

"Because you should be my wife and I want to be beautiful for you. We must dance together. Why don't you send for drink so we can celebrate?"

"Our priestesses are strict. They mustn't find out what we're talking about."

"None of our priests are like that. And our chief is not allowed to treat us badly. When we marry we hold a great feast."

"What is marry, Guari?"

"When a man sees a girl who pleases him, the chief gives permission to marry, and the girl and he live together and they celebrate with a great feast."

"Is that what you do?" Tiye was lost in imagination. "Here we only know hunting and field labour and fishing, and the old women carry the children around and the priestesses leap about. Oh, it's no good without men. It's better with a man." She put both arms around his neck. "Now, I think, you have enchanted me. And it's true that I shall lose my name."

As they lay in the hammock Tiye said: "Why do you lie so far away, Guari? It's cold."

"If you bring me pigment and oil and something to drink, I'll be happy."

"I'll bring it tomorrow."

"Will you come tomorrow? How many more days will you come?"

She rubbed his cold hands and sighed: "Guari, you let me live. I won't kill you. And I don't want anything to happen to you. I want you to live."

"Really, Colibri?"

"Yes, Guari. And you?"

"I want to keep you."

"I'm very frightened, Guari. Kudurra whispers to me every day. She wants to go into the forest. But they'll come after us."

Guaricoto turned to her: "You talk about this, Colibri?"

"Often." He embraced her, they whispered half the night. When the footsteps of the guards came near, they kept quiet.

Big Kudurra squeezed Tiye's face. "You are still Tiye."

"Get hold of pigment and oil for Guari, Kudurra, he wants to make himself beautiful for me and wants to drink with me."

"I've been waiting for you to ask, Tiye. We've already prepared everything for the men. Some of us will go across the fields before dark, they'll put pots under a tree, in a pit in the earth, with a big leaf on top, I'll show you the tree. When they take you to the hut, keep an eye on the guards and take note of the way."

Guari painted and oiled himself by the light of the fire. She had brought cachembo, honey liquor, she too took a little sip.

In the dark he leapt a couple of dance steps in front of her.

≈≈≈

Next day when big Kudurra checked Tiye's face in the house of women, it was thoughtful and the mouth was tight. Kudurra said: "Did you drink?" Tiye nodded. Kudurra took a necklace of dried seeds from her throat and hung it on Tiye. "What did he call you?"

"Colibri."

"Shall I tell him your name now?"

"Yes."

That evening he called her Tiye. She was not friendly to him. She railed against her friend Kudurra, complained half the night that Kudurra had betrayed her name to him. For many days she was the same, but every evening she brought a gourd to drink. She rejected his comforting. Kudurra became frightened when Tiye would not talk to her and refused the fish and ate only manioc. Already the women were loudly discussing the new moon feast. There were more whispered conversations in the bride huts. Tiye asked what they should do.

≈≈≈

Cruel Truvanare the queen could not wait for the new moon, and four days early, as a sign of her loathing for men, she brought the man who pleased her out for sacrifice. Priestesses surrounded her, night just fallen, young women not yet taken to the huts, all of those who would soon embrace their man attended the terrible mask dance, the summoning of the moon and the wild beasts that slink through the forest and tear the living to pieces. With claws of the panther whose pelt they wore, with the saw of the sawfish, the priestesses hacked apart the sacrifice whom their queen had embraced. His blood sprayed in a circle. Two young women danced around the fire and received the blood. In a frenzy they went to their men, and these too were set upon and torn apart by the masked creatures.

But great mother Toeza came there all black, stood among the trees and watched them dance. She was hung with strings at throat, arms and thighs, palm leaves lay on her shoulders, her hair fell loose and white as mould down her back. She stood unmoving, leaning on her spear. Sometimes the fire shone on her ancient wrinkled face. Watching the women she was filled with revulsion and grief. She sat in stunted bushes by the mask hut, called into the forest with a bird call. Walyarina, the black jaguar, glided to her covered in twigs and leaf mould, he lay down at Toeza's side. She said: "They are dancing for us. It gives me

259

no joy. I sent signs to the queens, they ignored them. They are frenzied. They insult us."

"What are they doing?"

"They kill men, murder and murder. We never did that, I never taught them that. We were oppressed by men, so we freed ourselves. We had no choice but to move away. They even killed you, by a trick."

"I had my revenge."

"Now they murder at any time, this is not the day of sacrifice, they are criminals, they have become as bad as the men." Old Toeza wept, the jaguar shook himself and growled menacingly, they heard him in the village.

When Truvanare demanded that other warrior brides who seemed to her too bright and happy should deliver their men before the feast day, Toeza in the gloom of the mask hut removed her feathers and loincloth and rubbed herself with musk.

She growled: "The queens have grown hard and evil as crocodiles. They defy us, challenge us." She spoke with the moon.

Then she painted herself anew, put feathers and loincloth back on, took shield and spear, bow, quiver and arrows from the wall, and said: "They must be wiped out. Come, Walyarina, we shall no longer protect these realms, they are the ruin of our daughters. We shall destroy these realms."

Kudurra stole the great jaguar pelt from the mask house. That was the signal. There were whisperings with guards. That night spears, bows and arrows were carried to the men. Some men were freed, they hastened back to their tribe.

On the day before new moon, with the first rays of the sun, Kudurra in the jaguar pelt leapt through the maize, women and men came from the huts, the sacred jaguar leapt, they ran behind with spears in their hands and fell on the village and struck down queen and priestesses.

Then Kudurra became queen, they ate and drank and celebrated.

In the afternoon warriors came out of the forest and landed their boats. They joined the dancing and continued on.

The war spread to many Women People. Men and women fought side by side, to the horror of queens and priestesses.

Return of the Amazons

IN THE EAST of the great river basin, beyond the lake of Manacapuru and beyond the mouth of the Rio Negro, Women People dwelled in the savannah of Jamunda. The moon that rules over fertility stood serene in the sky, they could see no threat. But as the war spread the queens sensed unease, and they decided to quit Jamunda.

They moved north. That was where their foremothers came from.

They were numerous and strong. They wandered slowly through the savannah. They wandered for many months. They wandered for years. They never forgot their festivals. Grass in the savannah stood yellow and tall, it was crisscrossed by huge gloomy forests of palm. Island landscapes opened up. They wandered along the Rio Negro and crossed the Rio Blanco to the west.

For many years they wandered. Their songs lamented: "The moon is rising, mother, mother, the stars are weeping, mother, mother."

Tribes avoided them. They celebrated the annual sacrifice with men that they captured. Rivers rose and fell. Turtles crawled across sand.

The women carried with them the black monkey pelt of Yurupari that Toeza had stolen. Yurupari emerged from the river and was the wisest of all men. He knew the strongest magic. He went down to the river to wash himself. The Mother of Rivers had not seen him for a long time, she appeared before him and he fell down dead. She recognised him and wept. People found the corpse and burnt it on the bank. The Mother of Rivers mourned on a rock. And when the fire died down she crawled into the ashes. Out of the ashes grew a paxiuba tree. Yurupari's spirit climbed into it. He wore a monkey pelt. When he went to the great ancestors, he bequeathed it to the men of the Tariana. This was Toeza's tribe, the first Women People.

The women wandered through the forest, they had Yurupari's pelt with them, their trumpet was of paxiuba wood, no tribe of men could withstand them. Men were afraid of them. And when the women had gone through the forest and crossed the Vaupes river, savage Maku came running to them and told them that the Tariana held the town of Iauarete over the river, men would make a stand there against them. The women had no rest, the priestesses said this was the place where our foremothers were defiled and so went away, where Toeza had lived and made "Walyarina" their warcry.

Here we were conceived and born. Here we shall settle.

Old mother Toeza followed them, but she would not protect them.

So it came to a great battle. The queen of the women put on the macaracan, the black monkey pelt, into which she had woven hairs of men to give her power over men, and blew on the paxiuba. And as the battle raged Yurupari appeared, saw who had summoned him and said: "It is enough," and chased away the queen who had summoned him.

She ran from one watercourse to another. Once she stopped, crouched down to drink and wash herself. Yurupari seized her from behind, overpowered and ravished her. She screamed for her companions. There were some nearby. They made no move because they recognised Yurupari and were horrified. He took the pelt from her and killed her.

Then he climbed into a tree and dropped the pelt. Warriors picked it up, pulled out the hairs of men. They hurled themselves at the women crying "Yurupari, Yurupari." The women saw they were lost.

They prayed for help to their first queen, prayed to great Toeza, prayed to the jaguar Walyarina, prayed to the ancestors. These gave them colourful pelts of jaguar and snake, they slipped them on. They ran into the dark forest, into the savannah, the swamps, and lay low.

Toeza ran with them, the great mother, bent, without rings, threads, feathers. One by one bow and arrows, shield and spear fell from her hands. She pulled grass and moss and foliage over herself as she ran, as she sank down. Loud her weeping, savage her cries.

≈≈≈

Thunderstorms raged, thunder and lightning greeted those who came to the forest and the waters. Ancient trees splintered.

The water spirit Sukuruja glided as a snake from tree to tree. He stood in human form beneath green boughs, tugged on a hanging vine. With his heavy club he leapt onto a floating log, the parrot feathers in his long black hair swayed. He sat on a dolphin and huzza'd. People in the huts saw him.

He swam on his back. He dived. The river surged.

≈≈≈

END OF VOLUME 1

VOLUME 2

THE BLUE JAGUAR

CONTENTS

Part Four: Sao Paolo 269

≈ *Voyage*
≈ *Surprises on arrival*
≈ *The town of Piratininga becomes Sao Paolo, but remains what it is*
≈ *Starting with the women*
≈ *Slave camp*
≈ *Invitation to a share of the business*
≈ *Warpath, slave drive*
≈ *Aftermath*

Part Five: Trek through the wilderness 308

≈ *Exodus from Piratininga*
≈ *Doubts and laments of a Father*
≈ *Pilgrimage to heavenly grace*
≈ *Emanuel de Nobrega*
≈ *Indian diplomats*
≈ *Contacts with Sao Paolo*
≈ *The first assault*
≈ *Mariana is bewitched*
≈ *Requiem and lament*

Part Six: The Indian Canaan 351

≈ *I the King*
≈ *Paolista Theology*
≈ *Arrival in Guayra*
≈ *The document*
≈ *The plan*
≈ *Custom does not permit it*
≈ *Forced into exile*
≈ *On the road again*
≈ *Distant thunder*

Part Eight: Turning Point 527

PART FOUR

SAO PAOLO

Voyage

THE AMERICAS, THE New Indies, had been discovered.

The empires of the Indians collapsed.

Their peoples melted away.

Some Whites tried to help.

Among the Indian tribes the memory of just one old white man was preserved: Las Casas. In the Venezuelan savannah, on the Gulf of Maracaibo, in the hot valley of the Magdalena river he had protected them.

They told of a great and good sorcerer among the Whites, the Whites themselves betrayed him and brought about his death.

Some said: the great sorcerer Las Casas fled to the native tribes to save himself, but the hounds of the Whites chased him up a tree. And there he lives still. The dark people bring him food and drink. When the Whites are gone from the lands of the Indians, he will come down.

Such tales annoyed White soldiers and traders along the coasts of the New Indies. But some of those who came there grieved.

For in the northern lands across the great ocean, in Spain, Italy, Germany, fraternities had grown up which grieved for mankind. There were many wars. No joy was found among the White people. They were driven by their great inner turmoil, and every goal eluded them. New wars forever tore them apart. A home had been built for them above the world, and in a thousand churches it was drummed into them: after death you will find redemption, obey the commandments we teach you, which come from God. They were not comforted.

This was the great hunger that gnawed the Whites, who flooded the world with their conquests and discoveries.

Where were peace, friendship, love to be found?

Seeing the White people in such misery, the fraternities took counsel among themselves. Salvation cannot come from man, so the only hope is to bind people ever more securely to eternal God in His vast distant Heaven. This requires a major diversion- but it is required.

And they embarked on difficult work, lived at first apart from others in monasteries, then went among the people.

One pious fraternity was called Warriors for Jesus. They were many young men who wanted something new. They mingled with the people. Some boarded ship in Cadiz. They journeyed to the coloured people.

≈≈≈

The voyage was long. It grew hot, and hotter.

"Do you feel the heat, Brother Emanuel?" asked callow Mariana. "Feel how strong Nature grows here! It's good that we left our mild homeland. You see how powerful our adversary is."

Emanuel was Superior of the mission. He mused aloud: "A great deal is demanded of us. How short is the span of man. I see many, many ships sailing south before our task is done."

"And when you feel this heat, this peculiarly dark torrid heat, Brother Emanuel, tell me: what do you think of Brother Las Casas?"

"Las Casas? What connection has Las Casas with the heat?"

"The heat exists. But you pay it no attention, Brother Emanuel. You merely perspire. I beg you, pay attention to the heat."

"Come, dear boy, what is the heat to me? It's nothing good."

"It is a force, Brother, that we must resist."

"The heat?" The older man laughed heartily and clapped the other on the shoulder: "That's a good plan. If you can manage it, I have no objection. You'll earn yourself great merit. But this is a side of you I haven't seen before."

"I think you misunderstand me. It is not a matter for me alone."

"No, you don't need me for this. Don't be cross with me, Mariana. I can't fight against the heat. You must take up that struggle on your own."

"You see the funny side, Brother Emanuel. But it's no laughing matter. If we do not combat the heat, we might as well abandon our mission right away."

Father Emanuel regarded him shrewdly: "So, in that case we'd better turn back."

"No, no, certainly not."

"Such a jester. But amusing all the same."

"Brother, listen to me. Tell me: how do you think to do it without combating the heat? You see, this was Las Casas' error. Las Casas proceeded just like you. He came sailing on a ship and noticed: it's hot. And sweated. And thought nothing more of it. So he landed. Then he saw the savages and found that they're human and should be brought to the Church. He was better and cleverer than others; he said: I must seek them out in the forests. But once there, he left the natives to the heat! Heat really is a force. If you think to make your peace with it just by sweating and saying 'It's nature' and the sun shines as hot as ever, you make the same error as if you were to ignore a sin of pride or insolence. That too is nature."

At this point the older Father invited the other to join him under the shade of a sail, and there they sat, it was cooler. The Superior had watered wine brought for him and his friend: "It seems we've landed ourselves in a miserable soup, and never knew it."

"So what is your response?"

"Such a miserable soup. Explain to me again. Why did Las Casas fail, what was the cause?"

"He regarded everything as Nature, and condoned it all."

"Insofar as he included the instincts, then he was wrong."

"I've read his letters and notes, Brother Emanuel. I have excerpts from several letters in my luggage. He wrote to the Spanish authorities, and to Garcia. He saw the natives as people, and that was his achievement. But his only one. Non-humans can be treated like animals, as things to use or exploit. That's what the soldiers and slavers did. He showed that for all their darker colour they are people, created by the same eternal God who created us, inspired by the same divine breath, and priests must bring the light of Revelation to them."

"Now, why do you pause?"

"Millions died. He presented himself to them. But he didn't tear them away from Nature. He spoke to them as he'd learned to do, as a priest. They learned to pray, hold a rosary, they were baptized, he brought them everything, followed them into the forest to save them from traders and soldiers. He saw Nature, and failed! He didn't take an axe and split them away from Nature."

The older man took the younger by the arm, they went below deck. They sat in the narrow cabin. "Do you feel better here?"

"Why?" The younger man was deathly pale.

"Lie down. Why will you not lie down?"

But Mariana's eyes were sunk deep in their sockets, the skin around his white lips was flushed. "I'm quite well, thank you for your concern."

"Just lie down. I still don't know what you're trying to say, my dear Mariana."

"He heaped on them every gift of the Church, and right behind were brigands who took it all away, devoured or trampled it. Nature. It's a terrible, diabolic force. Feel it. Imagine being born under such a sun."

"Christianity does not depend on the climate."

"The breast of the savage is free of evil, I read that in Las Casas. We'll bring them enlightenment, but there will be no light. The darkness, I feel it, pressing in from all sides against our light. We shall never succeed. I don't know who could. They're speeding to us already across the water. So far ahead do they send their envoys."

The young man sat in his black robe, back bent, his head twitched strangely. The older man became alarmed, he held his companion's moist cold restless hands: "You're feverish."

"I looked forward too much to this voyage. I came gladly. We shall go through the forests, we shall cut a path through, they will come to us, we shall live with them."

The other shook him. The young man slumped like a lolling corpse.

"Grass, fields, churches, bells. That's where we shall live, look." His breathing was heavy, laboured. "It's lovely, bells, the singing, they sing like children. There's a plant with many leaves, so fresh and green, we water it. The creature sits in the shade, stretches out a hand, stuffs leaves in its mouth, we wait, the creature sits in the shade, its arm is long and hairy."

Emanuel seized him by the shoulder:

"Mariana, wake up! In the name of Jesus Christ, wake up!" The young man's eyes remained closed. He laid himself down. He lay askew. The older man ran to fetch vinegar water.

That evening they joked together, the older man was cordial to his companion. As stars appeared and they sailed soughing through the darkness, Emanuel pointed to the clear sky: "Look! Clear unyielding Heaven above us. That is the eternal law, it's written just as clearly as this, and our task is likewise clear. That is the whole world. No riddles, no danger, no abyss."

The younger man embraced him: "We shall always praise Loyola."

"Before the will of the pious man, Mariana, all the powers of this world prostrate themselves like tamed beasts."

Then they knelt, and both were happy. They prayed together beneath the wide clear sky, faces to the dark rushing ocean.

In the morning, after they said their prayers and the older Father had gone to the sailors, Mariana knelt again in his cabin and read: *"Therefore being justified by faith, we have peace with God through our Lord Jesus Christ: knowing that tribulation worketh patience; and patience, experience; and experience, hope: And hope maketh not ashamed."*

And as his eyes read, his thoughts drifted and he shivered with a chill: They wander about, already they're coming to meet us, why did the Holy One not remove the beast entirely, why did he place the burden of salvation on us poor humans, where should we find hope, who'll give me strength to endure?

"Therefore as by the offence of one judgment came upon all men to condemnation; even so by the righteousness of one the free gift came upon all men unto justification of life."

I love you, Redeemer, grant me steadfastness, grant me patience. If you cannot bring me peace just yet, give me patience to await you. I love you. Redeemer, let me not fall into despair. Let me not perish. I am afraid, I'm afraid. You gave strength to the knight George so that he could kill the dragon. Think of us. I am afraid, I've never been in battle. O Lord, O dear Saviour, you know that all those around me are happy and feel nothing – why do you make me feel it? Shall I fall? Must I fall? Oh do not test me too severely! I am not strong. O my Redeemer! I love you. *"For if by one man's offence death reigned by one; much more they which receive abundance of grace and of the gift of righteousness shall reign in life by one, Jesus Christ."*

Eternal judge, help me not to die.

≈≈≈

Emanuel the Superior along with others who wore the black robe strolled among the sailors, rigging, masts and piles of luggage and provisions. They sat with sailors, chatted and laughed. Some were young, some older. They observed the operations of the crew with great interest.

On the quarterdeck a warrior for Jesus stood beside the ship's captain, and was initiated into the mysteries of the helm.

On the foredeck, two other priests had removed their venerable robes. These fluttered overhead on a line. The priests sat in a semicircle like the sailors and copied them, twisted rope, compared results left and right. After a while one of them studied his palm. The sailor beside him grinned and spat into the man's hand: "A bit o' dirt more or less won't do no harm."

≈≈≈

The ships sailed in a wide arc past the lands that Pizarro, Quesada, Belalcazar, Federmann had invaded. Slowly, propelled by a gentle breeze, they sailed south along the east coast. White water surged from the silent continent, uprooted trees floated by. It was the river that Orellana had travelled. The Amazon. The clerical gentlemen marvelled.

The sailors said: "It's hard to go into the river. Some have been content just to make their way out again, for there are numerous channels left and right, you sail up one and suddenly there's no river, you sit in a lake, a channel, can't go no farther and must turn back. And sometimes savages lurk there and it's a trap, and they're on you as try to push the boat around."

This led to talk of cannibalism. It amused the sailors to tease the Jesuits. They encouraged them to tuck in while still on board, they wouldn't make much of a meal for savages in their present condition, and that would be a shame, for what impression would it give of Whites. "No," countered some of the clerics, "they will certainly gain a good impression." They showed off their strong biceps, and one grabbed a sailor and swung him aloft in fun. This was a surprise to the sailors. True, they had noticed it before, but they were more and more impressed: these are a new kind of clergy, these Jesuits!

A sailor asked: "And can you shoot?" And there was no little astonishment as several priests gathered knowledgeably around a crossbow, and it was settled that to mark the end of the voyage – black coastal hills had accompanied them for many days already – a seabird-shoot would take place, in which contest the clerics acquitted themselves commendably. They ended the voyage in the best of spirits.

≈≈≈

Where were they headed, these warriors for Jesus? From a distance the land looked the same in every direction, the only certainty was that sooner or later they would stumble on savages and heathen. But they avoided the region where some time before a certain Cabral had landed, his forenames Pedro Alvarez, near the hill of Pascoal, he was Portuguese. He voyaged and discovered, and if there was anything to take he took it. The land appeared in front of him, with a single bound he attained the shore, in a harbour he had a cross erected in the sand, on which he engraved the coat of arms of his king. The crew of his ship assembled around him, Senhor Cabral opened his mouth and declared the land discovered, by him no less, and he took possession of it for the Kingdom of Portugal.

On board were two convicts, he no longer wished to haul them along. When he returned to the ship after the ceremony, he had the two lice-ridden wretches brought before him in chains and asked which do they prefer: be thrown into the sea, or let loose on the beach. Since they had differing opinions and he wanted the same answer from both, he gave them an hour to think it over. For, he explained, it would mean nothing, either by sea or by land, if he were to rid himself of them one by one. On land they could defend each other, and in the sea one wouldn't make a meal for a shark, the sharks deserved a double portion of their kind.

For an hour the two wretches discussed which was preferable: to be eaten by savages, or by sharks. The argument dragged on. And just before the hour was up, the one who wanted to go ashore struck the other on the head with his fetters so violently that when they were hauled before Cabral he was able to announce their unanimous decision that they preferred the land. Which was at once put into effect.

On the beach sailors removed their chains, placed arquebuses and ammunition some distance away, together with knives, sabres and shears, a firkin of wine and some dried fish, and then left them there. They had to hurry because, although the two wretches had never learned to shoot, the first thing the one who had now regained consciousness did was rush to the pile of goods, manhandle the arquebus, and set up target practice on the sailors. The other also succeeded in bringing a shot close to the boat, to the surprise of the sailors, who predicted a great future for the wretch. For fun they returned a few shots, and this salute completed the parting, which was also the first settlement of this region, named by Senhor Cabral as Vera Cruz. What's more, this was not the mainland but an offshore island, which in their haste they had failed to notice. For that very day Cabral sailed on. At this time voyages of discovery were in progress everywhere, and someone might come ahead of him. Apart from which Senhor Cabral had not been aiming for this place at all. He meant to reach India, sailing from Lisbon around the whole of Africa, it hadn't worked out, he'd come too far west and now must make haste to recover ground lost to others.

More trustworthy than Cabral's harbour, in the view of the

Fathers in their stout sailing ship, was a region somewhat to the south, on which a certain de Souza, Martin Alfonso, had recently taken pity. They were sure to find traces of him, and he couldn't have unleashed too much mischief in such a short time. Souza had written home that he'd come upon a region where some earlier explorer had landed who had not brought it to anything, while he, Souza, had already founded two colonies comprising Whites and Indians: one colony was called San Vicente, the other Piratininga. The clerics, who didn't know de Souza personally, had no wish to dwell on his memory, but they had a gloomy foreboding about these colonies he'd left behind, comprising Whites and Indians. But once these gentlemen arrived after such a smooth and pleasant voyage, they would chase away all cares and face whatever came.

Surprises on arrival

THE CAPTAIN DECLARED, on accepting a gift from his passengers – it consisted not of a crucifix or a rosary, or even merely a pious blessing, but a firkin of good wine – that this was the smoothest, most pleasant passage he'd ever experienced. And the crew, after loading the copious baggage of the clerical gentlemen into boats, was of one mind: it's a shame such people have to take themselves off into the wilderness, they must have got wind of something there for the taking, such people don't cross the seas for nothing and again nothing.

First of all there was a bay, lovely and wide, a good anchorage, favourable for the pursuit of every peaceful trade. Then they traversed a hot, wide sandy beach; to the left it was evidently swampy, they could see a patch of water, the whole place smelled bad, and to the right another broad arm of water stretched away, doubtless an indentation of the sea. Beyond stood a few huts, called Santos after Santo Andres de Pira, but it was no great hamlet. They eyed the huts gloomily, and learned that some people fished from here. All this stemmed from the time of that blessed man who had failed to bring it to anything.

When they had trudged across the sand for a considerable

time they came towards hills, and on these, overlooking the sea, Piratininga was said to lie. The pious Fathers had been ferried from the ship in boats, bombarded along the way with lively chatter in Spanish and Portuguese about the beauties of the landscape and the splendid opportunities for trade, as the locals tried to find out who they were and what they intended. The padres were pleased to find such helpful people, and declared that such a tumultuous welcome was quite unexpected. The huge quantities of baggage, all carefully packed, were shifted cheerfully. The settlers, as chatty and curious as children, wanted to know what was in it all. The Fathers smiled: "Playthings, and food." They would overcome the world through play. This made the settlers even more lively. They strode ahead of the patriarchs. The Jesuit invasion rolled along in a great column from the ship across the beach to the hills rising on the right. Others too had come from the ship, they peered around inquisitively and were regarded less amiably by the settlers. No one carried *their* luggage. The settlers, clearly a most pious community, all gathered about the gentle Fathers.

And now, after much wiping of brows, here is Piratininga, consisting of a great many miserable huts, little houses and lanes, as well as hints of a church on a wide empty area that might one day grow to a plaza. The sturdy ragged crew guiding the Fathers smile: "We've left space for everything." They won't take them right away around the whole settlement, it's very extensive, there are many branchings and buddings, it stretches a long way, it'll be a new Cadiz. This the Fathers were able to confirm that day and the next.

Despite all the jollity, the walk had been strenuous. They rested and enjoyed the rather damp floor underfoot and the hut roof that leaked rain.

The first notable news that reached them during these days concerned their baggage. Quite understandably given their goal, this was very considerable and had made up almost the entire contents of the ship's hold. Some part of the baggage had, regrettably, disappeared. Two Fathers had been entrusted with supervision of the transport, its unloading, loading and storage. The

Fathers reported anxiously: according to their inventory, more than half the cargo was missing. Half must still be on the ship. At this the Fathers rushed down the sweat-inducing path from the hill to the huts that the blessed Ramalho and Senhor de Souza had built, threw themselves, accompanied by several settlers, into boats and rowed across to the ship still anchored there. The captain, along with the entire crew, welcomed them with reverence and joy, the wonderful voyage still in their thoughts. He was not a little astonished to learn the reason for the unexpected visit. The ship had been emptied completely, the captain declared, like a cork it floated a yard higher in the water after the unloading, and to convince the gentlemen he led them down into the hold, where it was very dark and many tarpaulins and sails and spare masts lay. Lights were shone here, shone there, showed up this corner, that corner, there were rats, but the Fathers had no use for those.

Back on deck they discussed what could have happened.

The captain said: the first thing that comes to mind is that the inventory is wrong. Who drew up the inventory? But it had been done by the two Fathers in person. Had they seen everything themselves, marked it all with a cross, been on the spot when it was loaded aboard the ship? He showed them in his ledger how he did it. The padres said yes, they did it just the same way, but more legibly. Nevertheless they did admit that they had stood some distance from the ship as it lay in harbour while they checked off the goods, which had been loaded without delay onto the ship. The captain treated the matter from a humorous angle: he placed the entire ship at their disposal for another search, they could turn it upside down if they had levers and winches with them, and knock on the bottom to see if anything fell out. Well, what was going on? It was one of those mysteries of the sea, the padres were men of the world, but clearly not so much men of the world as they ought to be in a seaport, dealing with sailors and stevedores. At this the padres looked moodily down at their black robes. The captain advised them to take refuge in prayer. They thanked the pious man. There was nothing they could do but leave this ship that had grown so dear to them, this witness to so many pleasures, and erase the bad impression their enquiries must have made.

Outside they noticed that the ship was even now being reloaded, numerous boats were moving twixt ship and shore, the Fathers now realized what other purpose was served by the supposed fishing place of Santos: big canvas marquees had been erected and a kind of giant shack improvised, they looked across with interest, the rowers explained that this always happened when a ship was about to depart, sometimes people even stored goods here pending the arrival of a ship. Although they noticed the Fathers' great interest in this mighty commerce, they rowed vigorously around to the other side of the ship, for they must not become entangled with all the boats, also a man stood on the beach quite openly signalling with a white cloth, pointing to the west.

Empty-handed, their prayers unanswered, the Fathers climbed back up. They rode on mules. Along the way they passed an unending stream of merchandise heading down. A merry life. What a shame, thought the Fathers, that such an aggravating circumstance prevents us from joining in the general merriment. Suddenly they noticed that several chests closely resembled those that had gone missing. They commented to one another, pointed, one of the mule-drivers let fly a contemptuous remark: "There's lots of stealing here! You can nail something down and it'll be stolen away, nails and all!" Another driver shouted: "Don't tell tales! That stuff going down comes from the big store sheds, it belongs to Senhor Johann Conquisto, a very rich man." The padres repeated uneasily that the chests did indeed greatly resemble theirs, they really should stop. The mule-drivers all laughed: "Chests are chests." The padres wanted to dismount but were embarrassed, you had to be careful among new people.

Before they came to a decision, thanks to the fleet-footed beasts and unusually vigorous yells from the two drivers, they were already at the top. And at once they took their dark suspicions to the Superior. They debated back and forth. The Superior praised them for guarding their thoughts and not making the terrain, already tricky on its own account, even more hazardous for them.

During this conversation one of the two Fathers was seized by an unruly notion, he excused himself and slipped away without explanation. After a considerable time he came back, his face flushed, inventory in hand, and under the Superior's gaze he compared the list of goods still there with the earlier list. More chests were missing.

"What a climate," smiled the imperturbable Superior, "disappearances on a tropical scale." Without betraying any hint to those around, they quickly checked all the items. It was indisputable that other goods than those of the Fathers had been stored in the sheds, it was not entirely to be ruled out that theirs might have been carried away in error. The Superior voiced this conjecture, with all circumspection, to the chief supervisor of the storeshed, whose presence they requested. He declared himself ready to check the whole of the consignment for the ship. Father Emanuel sighed with relief and thanked him. He asked that this be effected without delay, for clearly mistakes had already been made, and since huge quantities were involved, more than half a ship's hold, it should not be too difficult to ascertain the truth.

The chief supervisor hoped they would not form a bad impression of Piratininga right away. That lot down in Santos are a useless bunch, but Piratininga is a real place, here you must dare to tackle things head on, he'd already had a dagger at his throat. And he would have regaled them at greater length with cases older and more recent, but Father Emanuel assured him that they believed him, that it was precisely Piratininga's reality that had led the pious troop of Jesuits to this place, and once again would he go with them down to the shore and check the loading of the ship. But as was inevitable with such a phlegmatic temperament as the chief supervisor's, upon hearing these words from the padres he burst out at once in a stream of delighted exclamations touching on their trust in him, and could not praise enough the Fathers' understanding of people and the world, so different from those other men of the Church he had encountered along the coast, who could be persuaded so easily that U was O.

Father Emanuel grew insistent, his two companions exchanged anxious glances. And then at last the inspector, a very slow comfortable man, immersed deep in his memories, gathered himself to leave the store shed and go to his room nearby to fetch a leather jerkin and leather boots for the journey. He had so much in his heart, the Jesuits had such an effect on him, they deserved such trust, he was so happy to have someone in whom he could confide his view that the only thing lacking in Piratininga up to now was the Fathers, the Jesuit fathers, only them.

And while the Fathers listened to all this, looking now towards the sea and now back into the room, they noticed that their ship, their dear ship, was moving. Their dear ship had hoisted all sail and was leaving harbour under a stiff breeze!

And now the chief supervisor appeared, booted and spurred, came over to the visitors and bellowed a frightful roar: "The robbers, they're evading our inspection! They seek the open sea. Hah, just let them come back." And gazing blankly ahead he sat on a basket, sucked at his pipe, seemed to become annoyed with his heavy boots, flung them aside, took off his jerkin. The clerics were frightened, his anger seemed directed at them, they were happy to make it with skin intact past the fellow sitting there with a huge straw hat jammed on his head, feet bare, swinging a stick. Slowly, as Indian children ran around them whooping and the wind sang, they made their way to the little house.

As they sat together that evening, the Superior moved hesitantly from one to the other, gazed at them, his black-robed brethren, gave each his hand:

"I am glad that you at least are still here. It's not impossible that one of us might disappear in just such a puzzling fashion."

The town of Piratininga becomes Sao Paolo, but remains what it is

THE TOWN WAS called Piratininga, the Whites there had not yet had time to re-christen it with a name all could agree on. The pious Fathers called together the town priest, mayor, judge and town notary. And because their wretched ship had arrived on the eve of the festival of the conversion of Saint Paul, Brother Emanuel the Superior bestowed on the town – so that it too might be transformed, like Paul, from impenitent to proselyte – the name Sao Paolo.

The place seemed to be developing well. To their sorrow, even after the christening it remained Piratininga.

It was situated high on a plateau, not easily accessible. It gave an impression of desolation, a scene of demolition rather than construction. It was a clearing in primeval forest, in which a couple of thousand people had set their huts as the fancy took them, everything seemed improvised and thrown together. Mighty palm trees stood singly or in little groves, parrots and monkeys sat in them. Then there were deep holes where people had torn out trees, the roots lay there still. Felled and sawn-up trees, sad stumps everywhere. Then came – though you were hard pressed to say where – huts and little houses thatched in straw or palm in the Indian style, they blended in well with the forest floor. In grassy clearings native women sat with infants beneath improvised awnings; bigger children, quite naked, rocked screaming babes in hammocks slung between trees; some small children rode in a sling at their mother's hip. Here a fire smoked: it was the hearth. Then without any warning a street took off beside a series of holes, groups of little houses and sheds that seemed frightened of the desolate scene out there and so huddled tightly together. Between them you could see the ubiquitous lovely forest floor, here and there abysmal chasms over which planks had been laid. A number of these untidy straggling lanes encompassed an area designated as the marketplace.

But something held together this demolition site and field of debris: some distance away stood a double line of ditches and walls. Starting at a point in the west completely cleared of trees, it extended in a huge semicircle around the whole place. Behind it, beyond the town, palisades of tree trunks had been erected, and in four places wooden towers loomed.

And this in fact was the solution to the riddle: they were in an armed camp. Outside the town they came upon sentry posts with muskets and halberds, huts and big dogs were nearby. Several new heavy bronze cannon pointed west and south. Towards the sea, and towards the forest as well, among the confusion of huts and little buildings, stout blockhouses had been constructed of logs, with an added protection of palisades. These houses, it transpired, were the original Piratininga when men first climbed up from the shore; for some time these fortifications and a few men were all there was.

Newly-christened Sao Paolo contained several thousand people; around a third were White, and these all male. A small group seemed to have arrived earlier than the others; they possessed power and respect, strutted not in the civilian straw hat but in broad plumed headgear with an arquebus and in several cases a sword, they were elderly scarred fellows, some lame, one-eyed, one-armed, all wore mustachios, many sported extravagant sideburns. They were thoroughly sinister and brusque, and ruled the roost in this huge encampment. The town commander, who styled himself governor, was one of them. This coarse man, like many others, was assailed by the Indian glandular sickness, it had eaten away his nose leaving only the two nostril holes, his forehead was covered in large boils, and when he spoke it was more like barking; to top it all, the man carried a broken arrowhead in his lung. The disease from which he suffered reaped a terrible harvest in this place, they tried to save themselves with sarsaparilla, many died, but the old man stayed alive and ruled the place. He swore freely, a government office building had been started but was left unfinished because he detested Europe, he lodged outside the town in one of the blockhouses with the others. His secretary, a former monk, sat in the ruins of the unfinished government house, treated the man's sickness, and conducted correspondence with the King of Portugal on his own initiative.

The Jesuit Fathers chatted a great deal, not with the martial but with the more amenable elements. People had found their way here – so they explained to the clerics, the young world-improvers – in all sorts of complicated ways. None of the lullabies sung to them in the cradle ever predicted they would find themselves stranded in this forsaken corner of the world. For back in the old world – so they told the credulous visitors – they had held high office and rank, came from noble and wealthy families, fell into difficulties through no fault of their own, or else withdrew from the wicked world to make a completely fresh start over here. The Jesuit Fathers, armed with Christianity and courage, could not have found a better field for their activity. Only a few admitted that, through unlucky chance, they had fallen into a particular situation they did not wish to speak of. All in all, it sometimes seemed to the Fathers that in Sao Paolo they were close to a royal court, among grandees, innocent exiles.

They were quite strange, the sketchy narratives told by this collection of distinguished men. It took the Fathers many days to become attuned. A man might tell how he set out one morning with two others, they had ample provisions, it grew very hot, they slept, had a meal, everything was going well, then the provisions ran out, the others grew tired and returned home. This was a jaguar hunt. Or a hunt for something. There were violent adventures aboard ship or boat, crucial details of which were veiled in a fog of mystery. Since many native people could be found in the new Sao Paolo – all the females were Indians – the pious Fathers thought: they have picked up this laconic style from the Indians, we must grow used to it. Then it became clear: the distinguished gentlemen wished to spare them, they thought they were tender priests on a mission to the heathen like many tender priests before them, and were unwilling to burden such admirable characters with profane matters.

When the Jesuit Fathers – one group had already departed on a mission farther inland – when they confided in some Whites their intention to promote Christianity here on the coast among both Whites and Indians, and this most earnestly and steadfastly so as to bring honour to the name of the Whites, they met with the greatest understanding. Their plan was hailed as wonderful and timely. The Fathers were congratulated on their magnificent idea; for sure, Europe was still the fount of the finest thoughts. And to think they had selected Piratininga as their field of operation! Their approbation was soon replaced by strange behaviour.

For example, they pressed on the Fathers all the printed

material they could lay hands on far and wide, and showed themselves enormously eager and ready for instruction, so that large gaps, long unfilled, could at last be made good. During the lessons the gaps only grew. The natural consequence was that the Fathers were besieged at every hour by settlers demanding quite importunately to be made into true Christians. A regular timetable evolved, the settlers grabbed at any free hour, and the result was that the clerics, oppressed by such eagerness for learning, complained that they were never able to leave the house.

Fortunately this zeal abated after a while. The Fathers staggered out from house and church to take the air. And see, again they are surrounded by neo-Paulinian zeal, this time in another shape. The Fathers had already noticed that they were never allowed to wander around Sao Paolo by themselves. As soon as any of them stepped outside, several scruffy gentlemen loitering in the neighbourhood would attach themselves and walk with them in order to chat. So the Fathers were never able to explore the environs of the town, or even to establish good relations with individuals in the town. Misgivings slowly germinated in them. Those who accompanied the Fathers advised that the native people were not dependable, there were assaults, the savages were full of hate because they had been taken from their forests, only in small numbers of course, to be settled here and acquainted with the blessings of a peaceful way of life. This accorded with the Fathers' understanding. As they left, the people would say: "What we have here is a healthy development, which the world will one day marvel at. We are not soldiers, rampaging all over. We live in harmony with the savages. We speak to one another on familiar terms. We take them as they are. Their women we took right from the start." The Fathers found all this good, in general, but why were they never left alone? On one occasion the Fathers were taken farther out, past the blockhouses. There were fields and huts. And there dwelled Indian families – all of them, as could not be concealed, under guard. The landscape was wonderful. But the sight of the fields, the guards and the miserable Indian hovels dismayed the Fathers. The settlers tried to mollify them. Those families are in danger, they separated from their tribes and the tribes will never forgive them. "The tribes often come here to kidnap them. We have to protect them."

Slowly the soldiers of Jesus realised how dangerous was the environment they now lived in. The savages must be protected, and they themselves must be protected, and everyone lent the Paolistas their strongest arm. It was clear that the Paolistas were the offspring of great knights.

≈≈≈

The truth will out.

Once the Fathers were relieved of the burdensome lessons and allowed to wander freely around the town and the lush yet enclosed outskirts of Sao Paolo – oh, this plateau of Sierra do Mar would lead them onto sorrowful paths, and before the year was out they would traverse the plateau for the last time, reviling this cruel depraved Sao Paolo that they hoped never to see again – they came once more upon settlements and fields and gardens and the native families that lived there. The Fathers tried to converse with the dark men. But even though no Paolistas accompanied them, the natives fled in droves at their approach, and hid. They caught one: "Why are you here, are you baptized, what is your name?" No answer. "Do you not understand?" The Fathers had their questions repeated by a native interpreter, he spoke at length with them until the Fathers grew impatient and then the interpreter, who had not come willingly, fell silent too. Later, as they prepared to turn back to Sao Paolo, still having gained no enlightenment, the native interpreter knelt at their feet in the forest, where he felt safer, and begged the Fathers to forgive him, they must not betray him. The Fathers quickly hauled him to his feet, calmed him, promised they would not tell. Then he flung himself down again. And he revealed what they were seeing here but had not yet understood:

Sao Paolo, in its blooming infancy, was only from the outside a shiny apple; inwardly it was devoured by a sickness no less severe than the Indian disease from which so many suffered. Here, they were informed openly for the first time, was instituted the *mita*, of which the Fathers had already heard in Spain. The Whites fetched whole villages from the forests and savannah, and forced them to settle close by their permanent quarters and do labour duty. Were they fetched away through armed force? The interpreter denied it. But they can never repay their debts. New debts are constantly piled onto them, they are continually forced to accept new things, at last they are in the trap! They try to run away, are caught, compelled, yes, finally they are compelled and have to do labour service here. Their villages stand empty.

This was the plague that the Fathers stumbled across in the outskirts of Sao Paolo. Without delay Emanuel sought out the governor's secretary and the town priest. Both admitted everything. The acclimatized priest gave his opinion: "How would you do otherwise? The people wander around in the forest. You have to make them settle down. You must start somewhere." The secretary to the noseless man who never allowed himself to speak said he would bring their observations to the attention of the commander. Emanuel was astonished at such impudence; the man acted as if the commander knew nothing of it. He heard not a word more about the affair.

There the Fathers stood, come from Europe with their high principles, and were now a little wiser. How surprised the Paolistas were at the lack of sputtering from the Jesuit Fathers!

The new arrivals, who ever since they landed had had the wool pulled over their eyes by the cooperative efforts of the whole place, swallowed their observations and refrained from pieties. Gracious and sympathetic, they listened to everyone. Some youths worked with them to remove tree roots, fill swampy holes, it was friendly work, they learned something of the Indian tongue as well. "They're a sensible breed of Bible-thumper", said the Paolistas, "they know when to turn a blind eye." The governor, who had seen them around town, agreed: "I shan't need to arrange reprieves for these foolish newcomers."

≈≈≈

Once when a couple of Fathers went down to the beach at Santos, they fell into conversation with some Piratiningans loitering by their sailing boats. "They treated you badly up there when you arrived," said one, tipping his hat. The others showed interest. "That was a scandal. Weren't you furious?"

It seemed they were on well-tilled soil. "The way those people behaved makes a man ashamed of his town. The governor knew what was going on, but he didn't interfere because they bribed him."

One of the seven Paolistas, a silent man who played with his big black beard and had a wonderful way of letting flies settle peacefully on his arm or hand and then squashing them, this man said: "That wasn't the worst thing. The worst would have been something else. But it never came to that." Asked by the Fathers what he meant by this enigmatic remark, he looked around the circle of his people, and once he had their general assent he sighed. "If I hadn't been there, and two of my friends who also got wind of it, the dear Fathers would not be standing chatting with us today."

"What, what?" exclaimed the dear startled Fathers. A snigger ran along the line, the sun climbed higher, the terrible swampy stench grew worse, they retreated under a sail awning. Blackbeard spoke in a penitent tone:

"From the very start you were to have gone back on board, all and sundry, where you'd had such a good time anyway. And then," Blackbeard laughed, the others knew already, they all laughed, even the discomfited Fathers laughed, they knew not why, "and then, it would be a case of 'whatever the case may be'. That was the word we were supposed to bring to the captain. Either he should take you back to Spain, Cadiz or Malaga, wherever you came from, or he should set you down in some harbour or on some island along the coast. You were supposed to find out what it's like for thirty men to sit somewhere in the jungle, if you just pray all the time like you do here. Some told the captain he should just sell you."

"Not possible," countered the horrified Fathers.

"No, it was not possible," said Blackbeard with an amiable nod, "for who could he sell you to? To Whites? What good are priests to them? Who'd buy a priest? To savages? Maybe. Wouldn't have been a bad idea. But how to round up any who have gold to give."

The three priests stood in shock. One of the group added: "The captain was taking a consignment for Coro, and had no stomach for mixing up Whites and Indians."

"It'd be too hard here," confirmed a third. "In the Mediterranean, from Genoa across to Africa, it might be done. You can mix Whites and Blacks together there."

Blackbeard nodded sagely: "Yes, over there. But you have to be in the Med first."

In the grave silence that this wise commercial consideration demanded, the priests turned to go. The mariners one by one extended an honest hand to them: "Don't worry. We'd never meddle with clever people like you."

One of the three Fathers was able to pull himself together enough to ask Blackbeard, who was seated again on a barrel squashing flies in his malicious way: "Tell me, are we really making your lives difficult?"

This was acknowledged with not so much as a look.

Starting with the women

AT THIS TIME the Jesuits had begun to engage with the natives, particularly the women. The so-called governor once summoned Emanuel to meet him outside the blockhouse, and asked him whether the Fathers had settled in enough that he could now count on their support. For what, he did not say, it seemed to have something to do with general cultural tasks to put the native people more at ease.

Now the Whites were living together with Indian women, a rough and ready lot, some even unbaptised. The women were house-slaves, and the Fathers said: This is nature, this is how it starts. The worst thing was that there were good marriages, many good marriages! The Fathers often grumbled, without becoming any clearer on the matter: "On the one hand these fellows are rogues who regard the Indians as animals, inert things whose blood means nothing to them, they don't feel their pain, on the other hand they embrace their women and adopt their customs! Many allow themselves to be stroked and coddled, and guard them jealously!"

The mayor's house, the notary's house, everywhere swarmed with Indian women, little shy things, incompletely clad, clearly unaware that in addition to a loincloth they should at least cover their breasts. Before going out they would paint a stripe across the chest or around each breast and then a few dots around the navel, and this was their full attire. The town priest had already raised objections, but to no avail. Now the White men referred the Fathers to the women themselves, and when one of them cornered some women they proved to be the most acquiescent creatures, their obeisance was unbounded, they could deny nothing demanded of them by a White, and they promised everything, eager to avert mischief, would dress chastely. They trembled at the descriptions of the infernal punishments awaiting them for fornication. But then they went away, and days later looked just the same, and were unperturbed when a Father appeared and they again had a stripe across the chest and dots around the navel. They had forgotten it all. What you said to them was like the rain here, which fell in the mightiest torrents and ten minutes later everything was dry again.

And it was not only the women. The men, apparently well-disposed towards the Fathers, had refrained from making their lives difficult. When on one occasion the Fathers summoned a gathering of all the men, and barely twenty turned up so there were almost more Fathers than guests, one of them declared: they would cut timber for a church and build a school, but as for all this grumbling about women's clothing, the Fathers should provide some clothes themselves, they couldn't afford to pay, that's how it goes here and why not.

And when the Fathers spoke of decorum and modesty, the men declared: we're not nearly there yet, it'll take a while to settle in, you mustn't overturn everything, you can't bring decorum and custom up against the general situation here on the east coast.

One of the Fathers lost patience: "And then you'll say: the present situation in Sao Paolo does not allow for the building of a church."

"I wouldn't go as far as that," he replied calmly, "we plant a church down everywhere we go, so the savages see it's all over with that traipsing around in the forest."

The Fathers distributed fabrics and made the women happy, the women put them on but only when they were not busy, which was seldom. The Fathers were content and remarked: it's a start. The men either let the women go clothed to Mass and mistreated them, or let them go unclothed and told them to tell the priests they had lost the fabrics. Then they brought more fabrics, which the men sold.

The Fathers grew wise to this. What to do? They had a plan, they would advance into the forest with one settlement after another, Sao Paolo would be the springboard. And already they sighed: "Sao Paolo is a hard case, a hard case."

Slave camp

AND AS THE Fathers, who had come as missionaries, went about the town and its outskirts, one day, in order to be rid of them for a while, they were led eastward along a surprisingly wide and well-trodden path down into a valley, and there they came upon a sturdy enclosure. Sharpened tree trunks had been set up like a palisade, a broad deep ditch encircled an extensive camp that covered the entire valley floor. It lay in a wonderfully forested region, they had diverted a stream into the ditch, water stagnated there, it was full of stinking filthy matter. The Fathers were puzzled. They asked their White escorts, but received various answers. "So," breathed one Father, "it's a prison. A place like Sao Paolo naturally has its malefactors." The escorts gazed steadfastly ahead. Human voices came from the camp, and singing. The Fathers listened. "Those are Indians. Are there so many malefactors among them?" One of the escorts nodded. The Fathers were shocked, Mariana said: "It must be perplexing for you that you have to lock away so many. Could there be some error in your methods of instruction?" The Whites shrugged their shoulders: "It's been ordered." "By a proper court of law?" "We don't know."

They came halfway down one of the long sides of the camp. A little wooden bridge lay across the ditch, two men with pikes and arquebuses stood there on guard. But when the Fathers approached and asked if they might enter, the sentries looked at one of the escorts, who uttered what sounded like a password, they banged on the gate, which was locked from inside, armed men opened up, after a short exchange of words between the sentries inside and outside, the Fathers walked in.

They were horrified. It was heaving with people. A few huts and shed-like structures had been erected among the trees. Here and there a squad of armed Whites sat gambling. Otherwise all those standing or sitting were dark people, Indians, most completely naked, many were lying down and looked ill. They were all males. They all looked wretched, many were emaciated, and wherever the Fathers with their guards approached, several rushed forward mumbling, stretched out hands, pointed to their mouths. Those on the ground sat up, flung themselves at the visitors, tragic and frightful figures. They came upon men who stood stiffly upright and gazed away over the visitors. Mariana: "So, these are all prisoners? So many malefactors?" "Yes." And what are their crimes? This is horrible." "Resistance, rebellion, murder, theft." The Fathers exchanged glances, walked on.

Again there was an awful smell, they were among sick people, they lay packed together like cattle, the camp was too small. "There is not enough space, the people cannot move." "They're used to it, and it won't be long until they move on. There's more room in the other two camps." "You have other such camps?" "Yes. But there's more to see here."

A palisade had been erected across the middle of the camp, they banged on the gate. Before it opened they drove the Indians back. The Fathers and their escort passed through the gate. Their hearts stopped. Here were only women and children. But right at their feet a naked infant lay in the sand. A Father bent down and staggered back, said nothing. The others looked down. They saw that the child was dead, thrown onto the path. Among the men they had heard quiet pleading and the whimpering of the sick. Here there was an uproar of cries and screams and lamenting. It stank horribly of faeces and rotting fish. Women carried little wooden buckets of water, it was not at all clean, the women carried the buckets on poles across the shoulder, people came up holding bowls and gourds, slopped water into them, bigger children crawled like dogs behind the swaying buckets, took hold and stuck their faces in. As on the other side, here a squad of Whites sat gambling.

The Fathers' escorts observed the children grabbing at the buckets, laughed, looked for a smile on the Fathers' faces. But the Fathers pushed through the heaving mass of dark flesh, through the filth, their faces betrayed no emotion.

At a bend in the camp where it rose slightly, around thirty women were gathered uttering a monotonous wail, and when they finished lamenting, one sang. Mariana asked what was going on. One of the guards hurried across, pulled some women aside, came back shaking his head. "Because someone died. That's why."

They turned back keeping close to the palisade, came to the men's camp again. Mariana: "So you have more such camps?" "Yes, two. But there they work. These here will move on soon." "Where to? Where will they move on to?" "Don't know." He laughed. All the guards laughed: "One here, another there. It's all the same where they end up. If only they get something to eat. For if they wanted to work –." This was the longest speech the Fathers had heard during the whole tour. The guards' faces showed nothing but contempt and distaste.

The great gate opened again for them, the Fathers gazed straight ahead. At last they were out on the path.

The looming hill, the screaming parrots. My God, if only it could be as before. They walked, legs did their usual service, but head and heart were no longer the same, they had been dragged through ice and ice still clung to them. Once they had left the palisade behind, the gruesome silent row of stakes, Mariana turned to the escorts: "Thank you for your assistance. Now we shall walk for an hour across the hills."

The helpful leader explained: "The other two camps lie over

to the right and behind."

"We thank you all, and each one of you. We shall walk for a while." So the escorts went off, and they stood, the seven Fathers, together there, and not a word passed their lips. When at last Mariana spoke it was a relief: "We daren't look around." He stepped out of their circle and, with a smile on his lips approached his brothers one by one, taking both their hands: "In the name of Jesus Christ," and from each elicited a quiet: "For ever and ever, amen."

Then Mariana invited them to kneel and remember the passion of Christ, who had taken upon himself all mankind's sins and brought mercy. On the way back they spoke not a word.

In the town they went to the Superior's house. Soon the rest of the Fathers gathered there.

"I have attested," concluded Mariana, "to what we have seen."

Their Superior frowned. "It seems the others have nothing to say." The Superior himself, lounging in his chair, had no such shocked, thunderstruck and tormented expression. He looked scowling out of the window, lips pursed for whistling, shook his head left and right. He drummed his fingers on the table. "These people are slave-traders. It's nothing new. Perhaps they also engage in other business that is not pretty.... We suspected this. Now we know it."

Mariana: "We have read in Las Casas how they treated the savages. But this is a thousand times worse."

The Superior sat back in satisfaction: "True. We didn't come here for nothing and again nothing." He turned mock-threatening to the Fathers who had undertaken today's excursion. "Now it is of some importance to us all to hear what you think of this business, and if you have any suggestions." It was clear the Fathers had not yet recovered from their shock. The Superior was understanding, but at once came out with his opinion: "Under certain circumstances, the Whites have an explicit right to take as servants any natives who are recalcitrant or prisoners of war."

Mariana: "These are men and women and children."

"They don't want to separate families. They take whole families together. Not a bad stroke."

Another Father: "No words can describe what we saw. In what degradation they live, herded together like cattle. When we went in, there was an infant lying dead on the path. Someone threw it there. The people seemed starving."

The Superior raised a hand: "They won't be allowed to starve, it would be against the interests of – let us say, the owners. But the infant, did you pick it up? Had it been baptized?"

Mariana: "We didn't ask. We picked it up. It'll be buried."

Again the Superior frowned, pursed his lips. "We don't want to behave like delicate men. We have work to do here. You should have ascertained whether the infant was baptized."

The Fathers were silent. After a while the Superior continued more mildly: "This is a lesson for us. Why after all should an infant not die when a hundred are locked up together? They don't have enough to eat. It's always hard in wartime."

Suddenly he changed his tone, planted both hands on the table and sat bolt upright. "Just say plainly now what you think! You stand there like wet poodles. A child dies, people die, some are criminals – well then, how do you think the world goes? Are we in Heaven? We came over here precisely because it is as it is; and because it is as it is and would not improve, Loyola founded our company. Your horror, your disgust! You'll go away from here and make accusations. You can do that. Your stupid feelings. Feelings are not serious. When Paul IV was still Cardinal Caraffa of the Inquisition, he passed sentence mercilessly. Mercilessly. Do you understand?"

The Fathers sat in silence. "But please, do not inflict your hard-done-by expressions on others. Mariana, what have you to say?"

"Forgive us."

Later, when Mariana was alone with the Superior, Emanuel said: "My dear fellow, we are well on the way to falling into the same error as Las Casas. We can quarrel with these people and, so to speak, take our chances. Then the precious soul can be at peace, and feeling is salvaged. Nothing is achieved. We can take ourselves off by the next ship. I want no part in such an old-fashioned manoeuvre."

"The people thought to compromise us."

"They'll have a hard job. Think of the last Council of Trent. Who would once have thought such decisions possible? Every stickler for principle fainted away. They thought: Luther has allied himself with the German princes, his abortion of a church will not last the year, and now the old stern Church will show what it is made of, and will flee gloriously into the wilderness with banners flying! How now! Flee into the wilderness! The Holy Father reached an accommodation with the Emperor and the kings."

"I am afraid, Brother Emanuel. What plans do you have for us?"

Emanuel laughed: "I shall show them my teeth. They already see that we are not like other priests who have crossed their path. They shall see something else."

And he pulled the other to him and whispered in his ear: "We can play! Whoever is safely with God can play with the Devil."

≈≈≈

During the night, the seven who had been in the camp were tormented by the terrible scenes. In the morning, rain pelting down, some wanted to talk to the Superior and confess their weakness, the rain prevented them from leaving the house. And when the deluge stopped just before noon, they became players in an even more grisly drama.

A ship had anchored in the harbour the previous evening, boats lay off Santos. Now noises were heard in the streets of Sao Paolo, the clip-clop of horses, clink of weapons, murmuring of a crowd. And out of the trees came a host of dark men and women and children, horsemen escorted them, bailiffs with whips and big dogs ran about, the men were roped together in groups. The misery, the shame of the Whites was driven out of the green forest, waded through the morass of flooded lanes, wended without looking up past the little houses in front of which the

Fathers stood side by side in their black robes. The heart-stopping drama lasted a long, long time.

Several hundred people were driven past. They dragged this disgrace to humanity over the hill. After a while the snake wound its way down the path. In the little house the noon bell tinkled, the Superior gave instructions to delay the meal, they saw the first arrivals at the beach. They sat at table. And when they stood up, boats were still moving across to the ship. The last boat carried armed Whites and bailiffs. Riders started back up the hill. The boats returned empty from the ship. It was a while before the ship upped anchor. Now the great sails billowed, a gentle breeze blew, it sped away to the open sea, the masts were still visible, the skies were radiant, white blue.

Invitation to a share of the business

THE SUPERIOR PASSED a hand over his eyes: "A memorable scene." He parted from the Fathers. The governor's secretary and two other men sat in the dining room. The secretary had come to introduce the two men, whom the Fathers had already met, and to recommend them to the Superior, then he left. The two men smiled ingratiatingly, Emanuel had met them in the governor's fort, they belonged to the warrior class here, but despite their martial trappings, these two greyheads were more businessmen, ship-owners, importers, exporters.

Emanuel: "Well now, whatever are you gentlemen up to? We were sent to convert the natives, and you go shipping them off."

Laughter rang out: "We left you standing! It's not so bad. They're like sand in the sea."

"And how did you get hold of them? Where did they come from?"

"That's why we're here. My friend said: the Jesuit fathers are not the same as other clerics we've known. But why do they stay around in town, always in the town? They can read their books just as well out there. They don't understand the situation. We must try to help them. That's what we said."

His neighbour banged the table with his fist. "Exactly!"

"And now my friend says: you need a guide, because you can't find your way. Whenever we go into the forest we need a guide. We want what's best for you. Here in the jungle we're even more stalwart for the Holy Church. That's all. That's why we sought you out. We're not yet far enough on to welcome our guests with music and theatricals. But we have practical gifts for you. Come into the forest! See lovely nature, rivers, animals, trees, what you will. We'll make an excursion. Your voyage should not be in vain. And then the savages."

"You will gather some?"

"They won't come by themselves." Both laughed uproariously: "That's a good one, come by themselves. Maybe later, when we've made the town pretty. Then they'll come in droves, to plunder us. For the time being we have to go to them."

His neighbour, who was not so free with his words, made a run-up and delivered a complete sentence: "And so the pious Fathers will come with us, there's so many of you," banged on the table, the speaker clapped him approvingly on the shoulder: "Done and dusted."

Emanuel thanked them for the invitation, it was a surprise, he was pleased make such useful acquaintances. The neighbour swung his arm vigorously in order to seize and shake the padre's hand as if to rip it off, but said not a word. The speaker came to his aid: "A great pleasure for us. We shall let you know when it will take place."

"I shall discuss it with the other priests."

"To be sure, no formalities." And the tapirs stomped out.

The Fathers whom Emanuel found outside the dining room and ushered in were still angry. He asked: "Has something happened?" Jovially he invited them to sit, walked around the long wooden table, mentioned the invitation the gentlemen had extended, you couldn't hope for better, we'll be right at the sharp end, it'll become interesting, of course only a small number will take part in the excursion. When the Fathers made no comment, he expressed puzzlement: "Dear Lord, what in this world carries no risk?"

One raised his head: "What did the gentlemen say about the camp and the transport?"

"Naturally we didn't discuss that. I'm glad of it. What good would it do? They run their business, and we are of a different opinion."

No one spoke. Mariana said, hesitantly: "And the camp?"

"I told you, the camp didn't come into the conversation."

"For God's sake, Brother Superior, what then was discussed?"

"You're not listening. We shall join an expedition."

"And the camp?"

"We shall leave the camp be."

"My God."

"If you could let it rest, Mariana, please." And after a pause for thought, Emanuel laughed: "They think to mock us. The cheek of these fellows! It would be amusing if they weren't such scum, such a disgrace to humanity. Their king should put them on trial, but he doesn't, and I leave it up in the air whether he ever will. You'd have to put them to the sword, gallows all along the coast, one for every White. But – we brought no gallows with us."

A Father: "And this expedition: have you decided, Brother Superior, that we shall join in?"

"You mean because it will be a slaving party, Brother Faber? I know nothing of this. It will be a campaign, one of many campaigns the Whites must undertake in order to pacify the Indians. Of course priests are needed, for conversions and so on. The entire campaign is after all at the service of conversion."

Silence. Another Father: "You have decided, Brother Superior?"

"Unless you have some other suggestion, Brother Faber –?"

Mariana looked at him dispiritedly, made to leave with the others, at the threshold turned back and appeared, from his flushed face, ready to revert to Emanuel with a question, stood indecisive, left.

≈≈≈

Five days later, when the gentlemen came to the Superior to say that a small exploratory party had been formed, just as they'd mentioned, and would set off in the morning, and would the Fathers be ready please, the Superior had in fact received no other suggestions. Clearly the gentlemen wanted to conduct their wicked business on a legal basis, the Fathers would provide legitimacy. One of the gentlemen grew blue in the face with enthusiasm at the Fathers' acquiescence: "Such men of the world!" he exclaimed. "How the Church has developed. When we were at school the clerical gentlemen knew only the torments of Hell. If we weren't Christians already, you'd have converted us." The other hung back from gushing on account of his speech impediment, in the end they almost fell into each other's arms. A league seemed to be forming, the Council of Trent celebrating its revival on the Atlantic coast.

Warpath, slave drive

THUS BEGAN THE trek which in so many ways launched the career of the Warriors of Jesus in this new continent. The Superior ordered, and they went.

On the morning of their departure, the Superior spoke to Mariana as they left the settlement's wretched little church: "Now, my friend, what will you say when you hear that you're to go with them?"

"This is decided?"

"Yes."

"You give me joy."

"What!?" Mariana preceded the Superior out of the building, they strolled together around the sunny church square. "I wouldn't want the others to hear me, Brother Emanuel, they think me an enthusiast, they think I should have kept to the monastery. Brother Superior, I have waited for you, night after night I have been thinking over what you're doing."

"I knew it. You fear for my soul."

"Don't laugh."

"Did I not say to you: whoever is safely with God can play with the Devil?"

"That's the point. You dare to do it. We must have courage.

301

You dare a great, a tremendous venture."

"I shall let them lead me by the nose. These heroes! They invite us and we accept. I accept every move they make. We'll see who comes out on top."

Evidently Mariana was attending only to the tone, his expression was dreamy and blissful: "Now I know. We should not be afraid of crime. It is a demonic inscription on the world. Our pious wear the halo, the wicked wear the mark of Hell. I see him, as do you."

Emanuel stood and grasped him by the shoulders: "Surely you are not in a reverie again."

"Why?"

"I thought you were. Look at me. Good. What then would you do about these crimes?"

"I would know that I'm engaging with the world. It's my own rotten flesh that I cauterize. Oh what a great thing is the Seat of Judgment. But I would lack your courage. I'd be afraid."

They walked on. Emanuel: "You were once an angry little fanatic."

"Not any more, here I learn everything a thousand times faster. What a world is here, Emanuel."

"Well then, you shall join the expedition."

"Thank you."

"Really?"

"Emanuel the tempter."

Emanuel took his arm and stroked it: "You really want to go?"

"I fly under full sail. Like you. I shall not be lost."

Emanuel hesitated, he embraced the young man, looked him in the eye: "Full sail? Meaning what? Where are you headed?"

"Wherever you want."

"You have dedicated everything that you are to the Church and the Order. You know this."

"And you are my guide."

"Yes."

Emanuel felt a faint stabbing in his heart. As they separated the Superior held the younger man's hand in an iron grip. The latter thanked him in a faltering voice.

When Emanuel crossed the threshold of his house with a heavy tread, a thought whispered to him: perhaps he will not return from this expedition? But the thought vanished as soon as he entered his room, and he couldn't locate it again.

≈≈≈

The expedition lasted more than six months. It was conducted by a strong contingent of White soldiers with native auxiliaries, seventy Whites, a hundred natives, a few horses, they had ample guns and dogs. They advanced over the plateau of Sierra do Mar, reached the upper Rio Tiete and pulled on into the Sierra Mantiquera, parallel to the coast, into the hills by whose feet the Parahyba flows. This was the territory of the Tomoga, Itatin and Caryo. The Fathers saw everything they wanted to see. In future they would be able to expatiate more fully than others on such expeditions. They saw the Paolistas' contempt for death and their unsuspected courage. The same people who at home lounged about and eyed one another in mistrust now moved freely, spoke and looked around differently. In the little town they were swaggering oafs who wore their criminal past on their sleeves, here they conducted themselves as prudently as a cat, a tree, a cloud. The priests worked as hard as the Whites and natives, wanted only to press on. They hacked through the bush: priests, laity, Whites, natives.

As they descended to the coast towards Ubatuba they were observed by a coastal tribe. The White camp on the cliffs suffered a surprise attack by Indians with a huge superiority of numbers, the crack of firearms made no impression on them, the native auxiliaries fought with frenzied bravery. The battle raged for three hours down from the forested hills. The Fathers lived through moments they would never forget. They had orders only to provide support, but several raged at their inability to handle the arquebus. Possessed, all of them, with such a lurid thirst for battle, so austere, swift, cool. Among the Indians swarming everywhere was the same cold directness, they leaped and screamed, eyes flew left and right. The Whites made every movement count. When they and the natives above them, their enemies, saw each other, they were like friends.

In the last hour of the battle, a Father who had ventured too far forward was hit by an arrow shot from below through the bottom of his mouth, it pinned his tongue to his gums. He fainted from pain. Two Fathers dragged him aside into a hollow. Above stood one of the auxiliaries, who knew something of medicine. As the two Fathers stared helplessly at the long arrow that poked from the wounded man's chin and wobbled horribly across his chest, the coloured auxiliary slid down, knelt over the wounded man, inspected him, grasped his chin and pulled down on the arrow. A stream of blood gushed from his mouth, he seemed to choke. Then the brown man gripped his mouth, stuck a finger in and hooked out the broken arrowhead. Then he made signs to the Fathers which they failed to understand. So he pulled the rest of the broken arrow out himself. They turned the wounded man onto his stomach to keep him from choking. The Fathers plugged the wound under the chin with fabric torn from their clothing. The brown man ran back up and left them alone. The Paolistas lost three Whites and twelve natives in this battle.

They pursued the Indians as they began to run away. Everything on legs joined the hunt. The Indians ran across the hills like dogs, stumbled over one another. There was shooting only at the start, now the hunters surrounded them and had them, several hundred, and herded them together.

Then they continued on, sustaining themselves on fish, deer, wild pig. The Whites stood marveling before the tree they dubbed St John's bread, and ate its fruit. They loved this land they were in, they all loved this life, they loved each other and were all good friends. Natives approached, offered provisions, they traded in the usual way, fishhooks, knives, glass. But when they came near a village they found strong defences, the natives had surrounded it with ditches and hedges, the attackers stumbled into traps. The campaign proceeded westward, away from the coast into hills and mountainous terrain, they planned to circle around and head for home, but came to an arid region where the heat was unbearable.

They were fortunate to catch some wandering Indians who told them where to find water. And then these nomads showed them another way to quench thirst: they shot a deer, slit its throat and drank its blood.

In the seventh month, when the rainy season returned, they headed home from the south over the Sierra Paranapiacaba. They had two thousand captives and were in the highest of spirits. Black rags hung flapping on the Fathers, their sunburnt faces sported long beards.

Aftermath

IN THE TOWN everything was oppressive, grim, ready to explode. The Fathers were still there, but had made no progress. They were mocked for not all joining in the expedition; they feared for the Fathers who had gone, it seemed they had fallen into a trap and would be slaughtered out there. What weeks did Emanuel endure, the Superior who had given the order. He swore a hundred times to himself that he would leave this land and return home, if only the Fathers would return safely, he had taken things too far; but in front of others he pulled himself together and was a model of cold assurance. They had suffered a shipwreck, all felt this. Even the so-called town priest, a drunkard who belonged squarely to the Paolistas, was against them. "Nobody knows what you want," he mocked.

The worst thing was that they themselves did not know. Impossible to talk to Indians engaged in road building, tree clearance, hunting, they were always busy, overseers drove the Jesuits away. They were allowed to walk around in the slave camps, treat the sick, but a man with a halberd was always at their side. In addition, the dark people were as mistrustful of them as of all other Whites. There were still the many women and children in the town, but a barrier was imposed by the mistrust of the men, who wanted their women to stay as they were without instruction; the men, as they freely admitted, liked them better without Christianity. Nevertheless some women were enticed with presents to come to instruction. An evil, even repellent trade grew up in which the Fathers almost had to buy off the husband hour by hour; but on one occasion someone struck dead his Indian wife (they lived together like savages) because she had gone to instruction against his wishes. Anger was directed at the Fathers, Brother Faber was dragged from the house and severely mishandled.

Into this situation the expedition returned home. The warriors embraced their weeping friends. They found weary, desperate and frightened people. Emanuel could not let go of his friend Mariana. "What do you bring, what do you bring?" he asked. Mariana had to tell everything. Emanuel tried to save himself from the labyrinth of his dejection. "Now all our hopes are on you," the warriors heard from every side. And in this dismal situation, salvation did indeed come from them.

The Fathers who had joined the expedition and made friends with several of their comrades brought back an important deal. The new captives were to be settled in the neighbourhood and not sold, and the Jesuits were to have rights of supervision and instruction over them. Now this was a powerful win. But once back in town, it was all forgotten. The Fathers saw themselves meanly deceived. To Fathers who insisted on the deal, their former friends responded with mocking laughter and then with threats. Finally they were given a handful of people as an "experiment".

The Jesuits remained silent. They saw all the others, a thousand, taken within the palisades of the slave camp. During the transport of one group down to the ships, outside the dwellings of the Jesuits it came to altercations and blows, which developed from a minor skirmish to an open battle. Two of the young Fathers recognized among the line of captives several Tomoga Indians to whom they had become attached along the way. They tried to pull these people from the line, although they were bound around the waist with the same stout rope that linked all of them. The entire train had to halt. The Fathers embraced the natives and would not let go. They protested against the transport with loud voices. Mounted men appeared from up ahead. They tried to separate the Fathers from the people. They were struck. Other Fathers came out to help. From the Indians' point of view it was a perilous situation. But the outcome was never in doubt.

Emanuel put an end to the dreadful scene when he came onto the street with some others; they carried the wounded Fathers into the house. The train swiftly moved on. The lane where the Jesuits lived was patrolled after this by a guard detail. They could see that their days here were numbered. That night, those people whom the Jesuits had brought together in a little model camp were stolen away.

They considered taking the next ship and heading farther south. But if they came across Whites there, who could guarantee they would be any different? All were beset with gloomy thoughts. They must, they could, be glad that the Paolistas did not insist on their immediate departure from the town. They waited. Nothing happened. They were locked in. They were not allowed out of the lane. It was a blessing that Emanuel was now fully awake again. His second word: "Criminals. Gallows along the whole coast."

After two weeks of dull waiting, when some mission brothers returned from the interior with good news, the long-deferred decision was taken. They determined to break out and put an end to this ignominious and shameful prelude to a rescue of poor persecuted Indians.

At last the Fathers were in deadly peril. When the Paolistas noticed which way the wind was blowing with the Fathers, they planned to organise an attack on the town by Indians, whereby several houses including those of the Fathers would be burned down; any Fathers who escaped would be carried off. The project, similar to the one they were to have been subjected to on their arrival, was revealed to them by well-disposed Whites. So they cut short their preparations.

Sao Paolo had shown itself their enemy, and would remain so.

≈≈≈

Part Five

TREK THROUGH THE WILDERNESS

~

Exodus from Piratininga

SUPPLIED WITH PROVISIONS and fresh matériel from a Spanish ship, accompanied by two hundred redeemed Indian slaves and two dozen White camp followers, they set off into the interior. And during their departure from Sao Paolo one radiant morning, baggage carts piled high, native bearers, White followers with their weapons, and they themselves, men of the Society of Jesus – for the first stretch of the way the Paolistas gave them a send-off. The Fathers had to endure this further mockery. The few lanes of the settlement were draped in bunting. At the exit from the town a marching band placed itself at the head of the convoy, blared laments, and carried a big gaudy banner showing a tree with a burning nest and the inscription 'Sao Paolo'; from it rose a creature that was no doubt meant to be a phoenix. On its leg was a shield with the words 'Society of Jesus'.

When they made camp at noon on the first day of the trek, on the heights of the Sierra do Mar – the ocean no longer visible, they would not see it again – the Fathers were only twenty-four strong – the wounded man was dead and buried in Sao Paolo, they had tidied the grave the day before and entrusted it to the keeping of the town priest, three were to be invalided home. This noontime the Fathers kept silent, concealed their distress. But as they gathered in a tent around their Superior, another feeling grew dominant. They looked at one another out of their demoralized silence, and embraced one by one. They were already brothers of the Order, now they renewed their fraternity. They were still shattered, but now they could laugh.

Emanuel praised their good luck – his too: "We escaped death in that town. Staying would have been the greater misery. God is guiding us along an arduous path, and has put us to the hardest test at the start. What will happen now? They'll attack us. It will enrage them to be seen as villains in our eyes. But I swear, we shall not meet them with their weapons."

The sun shone, parrots screamed in the trees, inquisitive black monkeys scampered along branches, uttered short sharp cries. For the first time this virgin forest resounded to pious song. It praised an eternal God, who sits enthroned over the world and from his hand has let loose humans, animals and plants.

This was the same plateau on which Sao Paolo lay. Huge ferns, mighty trees loomed everywhere, palms, rosewood. As they trekked, the land rose, palms became rarer, ferns, they pushed through ever denser bamboo.

Doubts and laments of a Father

THEY ADVANCED VERY slowly. No people, no animals attacked them. One morning, as they broke camp and the Superior watched the little band go by, carts, baggage, a few armed men and the Fathers, he had to laugh: "There they go with lance and gun," he called to Mariana, "take a good look, do you know them? That's us, a nag under us, old shield on our arm, bonnet on our head, a visor of cardboard, squire Don Quixote de la Mancha, our nag is called Rosinante and she's stronger than Alexander's Boucephalos and Cid's Babieca. Now we are proud Spaniards and don't deny it. We belong to the Order of Knights Errant. There's the forest, the vast forest, we must go into it to put right all injustice among the brown and red people and among beasts, snakes and birds, and expose ourselves to every kind of peril, overcoming it will cover us in glory. Hail, noble Mariana, hail!"

Mariana kept by his side, the train had gone by, Emanuel smiled: "Well, mighty hero?"

Mariana looked down: "I –I haven't been able to speak with you for a while."

"We're both very busy. Now, what can you tell me at last about that expedition, Mariana, did you enjoy it, did you learn anything from it?"

"Why do you mock me, brother?"

"But I don't, not at all, you know we need lusty warriors. Are you sad?"

"Oh, the shame, that we must go into the wilderness. Such weakness, brother! A defeat, no doubt."

The Superior dropped his hand, and looked thoughtfully at the grassy ground as he walked beside the other, who fixed him with a hard stare. "A defeat. In war there are always defeats, dear friend, it signifies little for the outcome of the war. As you see, we go on."

"Where to, Brother Emanuel? And what can we expect in the wilderness, in the open field? You don't defeat an enemy by withdrawing from his territory. I am so reluctant to let Sao Paolo go."

"It's not our task to purify Sao Paolo."

"That's the point, Brother Emanuel. Now we are free, like someone who should carry a load and throws it off."

"Were we tasked to subdue the Paolistas? We came here for the heathen, the natives. We are doing what old Las Casas failed to do, Mariana."

"I hear you."

"We had to leave the town, for how can we combat savage Nature, heathendom, when we meet such resistance in our own camp."

"Yes, Emanuel."

"Yes, dear lapwing, but you mean no. We must free ourselves of such impediments, or they will crush us. We must go into the forest."

Mariana pressed hands to his ears: "Into the forest."

"You don't want to? Mariana?"

He stammered: "No, no, I do. I just meant: the town is still there in our rear. Whatever we do, they are there. What are we without them? Whatever we do, they are there and you merely postpone the reckoning."

"Dear lapwing! But it's no use."

"You impressed on us that we're not monks, said: Ignatius de

Loyola founded us to march out into the world as the Army of Christ. He didn't say monastery and didn't say wilderness."

"So what does my dear lapwing want, then?"

"What can I do except follow you. I have no will apart from that of the Order." They walked side by side, pushed and trampled through bamboo, the air on these heights was marvellously fresh. The Superior: "Now it's granted to us to enjoy such conversations, deep in the primal forest. I shall tell you a story, walk beside me. Back there in our old Sao Paolo, while you were on your expedition, I received news from Rome. It's a most instructive case.

"There was a man by the name of Accolti, excessively pious. He knew everything. He was relentless in his claims. He made predictions, said he saw visions, was going to walk unharmed through glowing coals. He predicted: the Greek and Roman Churches will reunite, the Churches will subdue all apostates, including the Turks. And then he stood and preached in the public marketplace. There will come a single universal monarchy, the Pope will stand at its head as a saint and bring true righteousness to the world. So far, as they wrote to me, all well and good, Accolti was merely an enthusiast. Unfortunately he was also a fanatic. It seemed to him that all was not proceeding as he imagined, the universal world-monarchy would not appear so soon, the German emperor, the Spanish king stood most aggravatingly in the way, and he also had a bone to pick with our Holy Father Pius IV, who was not holy enough for him. So what could Accolti do to speed things up? He decided to murder Pius IV."

"No!" – "But yes." – "Did anything happen?"

"Hear me out. Accolti decided to murder Pius IV. He conspired with another, by the name of Antonius Canossa, and they both stood at the wayside in Rome as a procession passed by, waiting for the Pope to appear. After a while the Pope comes by in his sedan chair, unguarded, just as we are here, anyone can shoot from above, the side, with arrows or arquebus, or hurl a lance. And as the Pope comes by in his sedan chair, Accolti and the other kneel in the road, each holding a sharp dagger. A trivial matter, two paces and plunge the dagger into the breast of the eighty year old."

"Nothing happened."

"He stands up, the Pope is two paces from him, the Pope's hand readies itself for a blessing, he looks around amiably, stretches his hand out in blessing – and Accolti abandons the plan."

"Praise God."

"He's confused, gazes about and sinks again to his knees. He prays silently. But he is discovered. They questioned him, he gave contradictory answers but did not betray himself. But then Antonius Canossa was there too, his tongue they were able to loosen. They wrote to me that both men were brought before the court in Rome and sentenced to death. Accolti will have an opportunity to prove if he can walk through fire unharmed."

Bamboo, ever more bamboo, those ahead have already hacked and trodden it down, it springs quickly back on both sides, you must swim through it, spread your arms wide in the billowing green.

"So that, Brother Emanuel, is the picture of an enthusiast. You are a realist and treat me kindly, as you would an idiot. I repeat: you do me wrong. You cannot bring things to a reckoning without Sao Paolo. That is the way of the world, as they taught us in college, and you, you in particular, have emphasized to us a hundred times: one cannot fly above it, one must press through, and it is this that Ignatius showed us. And that is why I went to him."

"Would you go to him again?"

"For God's sake, Brother Emanuel."

"Well then. Compose yourself. You understand nothing. You will learn here. Understand?" Mariana, shocked, pressed hands to chin. He bowed his head. Emanuel left him standing there.

≈≈≈

But next morning the young man came to Emanuel again, wept. He was contrite, distraught. Emanuel, who observed his approach with irritation – for Mariana was frighteningly in the right, though not entirely right – took him aside and saw that it was not a clever or a stupid man who spoke to him, but a poor tormented soul.

"Forgive my foolishness," Mariana begged, "it's hard for me to say what I want to say, and if I speak words I do not mean to utter, then I have to bite my tongue, and the other becomes annoyed. Don't hold it against me."

"What then did you want? It's not as if you were wrong, all things considered."

"Brother Superior, I want to say: you didn't scold me on the ship, didn't send me back. I don't know what you plan, but it's good and I love you. Sometimes I long for my monastery cell, there, all was clear, I often had visions, dreams, I confessed them, it was saints I saw. Now I can't find a way back. What am I to do, Lord help me, in the forest, what's to become of me?"

Suddenly Emanuel recalled his conversation with Mariana the morning before he left with the expedition. "I fly under full sail," Mariana had said, it had puzzled him.

Emanuel took the young man by the hand and shook it cordially. "We have the same tasks we had in the town, brother. Soon you won't need to ask."

"I love these dark people so intensely, Emanuel. I have to force myself not to abscond to them. And this is the forest. Where they live."

"It is good, brother, you will be their guide."

"I find everything so ineffably good. My judgement is all confused. I have no judgement any more. I don't know how to contain myself. I tell them our doctrines, I tell them who Jesus was and how his life is a model for us all – believe me, I feel proud and blessed that I am able to tell them this, how blessed we are already, who came earlier than others to this knowledge – and they sit there with their black hair, staring eyes, and words dissolve on my tongue. I am happy, I look at them, brother Emanuel, I am no longer a priest but have become their mirror."

"Have you taken an Indian as your lover? Do you desire one?"

"No. Neither woman nor man. I love them all, beautiful and ugly."

"Then you have no need to torment yourself, Mariana. Nothing will happen to you."

"Even if we press on?"

"Even then. We cannot make it through without love."

"It torments me. I am afraid."

"A brother will keep an eye on you. You will come to me often, even without my summons."

And when Mariana had gone, seemingly content, Emanuel frowned after him and grasped after a fugitive thought. Every time he leaves me, my head spins. I don't understand him. Too much love. You need just enough love to get to grips with the world, no more. And he recalled his life before he entered the Order, the time when he was a Spanish captain. There was a village in Italy, a woman lived there. To work, to work.

Pilgrimage to heavenly grace

THEY TREKKED THROUGH the forest, crossed the campos that stretched away to the coast. But they headed away from the coast. They trekked through wide spaces that were as good as empty, treeless, covered in brush, often only stumps. It was an enormous land, a continent for giants, Sao Paolo was far away, a nothing, a dot on the shore. A river glinted, they headed away from the sea, followed rivers inland. Billowing plains of grass.

It was not here that cruel Alfinger had roamed, the sinewy man sought out by the Welsers in Augsburg to fetch back the five tons of gold they had lent Emperor Charles for his wars – with his men, horses and hounds he acquitted himself of the task as best he could, he looted, murdered, burned and impaled, he sent gold home or kept it with him, slaves came to market, the business ran smoothly, he was crushed by a rock at the place called Miser Ambrosio. Then the earth received his flesh, his skin and bones, and they nourished its profusion.

From Santa Marta came tall learned Ximenes de Quesada with a thousand foot soldiers, a hundred horse and countless hounds, he was of the same stock, he sent five ships up the Magdalena captained by Alcobazo, they found neither gold nor slaves, they were carried off by flood, hunger and disease, and whatever did not drown in the waters and end in the maw of fishes was left to the vultures that sail above the trees. Quesada himself found what he was after: Cundinamarca, realm of the Muisca, an inexhaustible seam of gold and people, he shipped the gold, herded slaves into the mines, he appropriated the title of Marquis, then leprosy set to work, plucked him limb from limb. Nothing was left but a demolished realm, all its people either dead or fugitive. Masses of gold that fed new wars in which more people died and became fugitives, and he himself became a dungheap topped by a cross.

And it was no different with his two colleagues, who came together on the high plateau by the town of Funza and were astonished to find themselves up there.

One, Nicolaus Federmann with his unruly hat and purple scarf, he who was supposed to follow General Speyer but made himself independent, a man warm as a calf, eyes formed from the blue of the sky, frisky as a colt. How boldly he trekked with his men, his sturdy horses and his hounds through the savannah of Venezuela, and bright jaguars ran through the huge grass, and he felt good and the grass felt good and the jaguars felt good, they knew each other and were all linked together, and when they shot or attacked it didn't hurt. He too came to Funza, met Quesada, amassed huge quantities of gold, they ordered him home to answer for himself, he obeyed and boarded a ship, and after some merry sailing drowned in the sea with his Indian lover around his neck, the sea reflected the blue of his eyes back to the sky, it dealt with his belly in the usual way, blew trumpets on it.

Magnificent Belalcazar, third man on the heights of Funza: how he set up house and worked the land, produced children with brown, red, copper-coloured women so that after his death, which he foresaw early on, many more of his kind would still live. And to provide well for his children and ensure that the earth would yield something for them, he planted the length and breadth of the land, from the valley of the Magdalena up into the mountains and the high valleys, higgledy-piggledy with human corpses – with what louring clouds of sorrow did he fill the valleys. The piping of birds, squawking of parrots, howling of monkeys for months drowned out by the laments and wailing of the adults and children he tore away from life and trod into the ground.

Oh the ground, how it gnawed at them, how its breast swelled at their approach: the people had no recourse but to turn to it. Belalcazar sat in his cell in Cartagena, oppression lay now on him too, no longer did he wear his feathered cloak. After doing the one thing that befits a person – rejoice – he did the other – mourn. He didn't mourn for long, spiders wove webs in his cell, the cell became a spider that drank his blood, he was done for and his body collapsed, skin and bone and muscle, no more did he guzzle, beget, kill, he no longer desired another's status, he had done enough for thirty years. And the earth received him, laughed and rejoiced over him, he complained: I'm too young, there's much still to live for. The earth smacked him on the mouth: "What, live for!" And rolled him flat as a pastry.

The men now trekking from Piratininga – that fishpond which in vain they had christened Sao Paolo – traversing the Sierra do Mar in the company of a few hundred natives, were of a different kind. They had no use for gold. They went happily on their own two legs. They felt it when their bellies grumbled, so fed them, watered them. Otherwise took no notice.

They wore black robes, to show that they entertained no friendship with life. And yet they were not dead. They hoped to abolish human misery. They had cut themselves off from their natural parents, brothers, sisters, relations, from their townspeople, their own name, and no longer acknowledged them as parents, relations. They were merely conceived and born in flesh. God's own true son descended from Heaven to the land of Galilee and clothed himself in human flesh in the body of the Virgin Mary. He left his flesh behind and followed the path of sorrow back to God and showed the way to go.

These are twenty-four creatures in human form, with human head and hair, human eyes, human voices. Every day they lay themselves down on the earth. If they have doors and windows in their houses, they close them tight. They pray and follow the dictum: be mindful of your sins, that arise from your birth into flesh. Because of just one sin, many angels were cast down into Hell. Because these are men, Christ takes them by the hand and draws them to him and the saints pray for them. Heaven and firmament, animals and plants are at their service. They want to be freed from sin. They want to avoid falling victim to Death. They are human, want to follow the path of mankind and guide others along it.

Let us remember the crucified man. Let us gather around him. Let our thoughts cleave to him when they seek to stray, so they forever have their seat in him, his shoulders, arms, hands, the soles of his feet – so we may never die in our sleep, so when he walks we may feel him, when he moves his shoulders, when he clasps his hands beholding our imprisonment, when he lifts his feet to come towards us.

As they tramp beneath the hot southern sky through tracts of bamboo, thorn scrub, day and night coursing over them, they are what these tracts and this scrub have never seen: a flock of spirits. But these lurk in no pond or river, they still bear the burden of human bodies, draped in black.

Cut off from mankind, this flock of spirits enters the forest so full of trees, birds, animals, ants and snakes. Entranced, the forest receives them with bated breath.

How happy they are, these Jesuit fathers.

Everything has changed since they quit the hell of Sao Paolo. And the farther west they go, the dimmer grow their memories of Sao Paolo. The town is merely the narrow gate beset with snares through which they had to pass to enter this land, they left hair and hide hanging there but made it through. And they are as happy as dancers.

Loyola's teaching is now becoming real. With these spirits, as they pull away across the plateau of the Sierra do Mar, are several hundred Indians whose freedom they have purchased, and a handful of Whites. These are not merely companions, but dedicated followers. Each of the Fathers achieves a role among the people, he leads his group like a shepherd and is with them day and night. Just as sun and night time are their companions, just as hunger and thirst pursue them and demand relief, just as their bodies feel repose and weariness, so the Fathers, these spirits, are to their group and regulate their lives. They weave the net of their thoughts into their corporeal existence. Again today there is hunger, thirst, weariness, repose, this desire and that desire that dominates everything, tomorrow it will be something else. Today there is the temptation of a woman, a man, venison, wine, banana, tomorrow it will be the blood of Christ. Heavenly joy streams down stronger than the sun.

Now there are only twenty-four Jesuit fathers. As they go through the forest, across the savannah immersed in their group, their life in the Order ends. Ignatius de Loyola allows his instrument to fall, to shatter. From the pieces many new instruments are formed, this one trumpets, another drums, a third fiddles, a fourth sings from its own throat. The tune they play together is the song of seduction, song of wandering on the path to heavenly grace.

Emanuel de Nobrega

THE SUPERIOR IS called Emanuel de Nobrega. He is a man with long steel-grey hair and a full ruddy face. He is muscular, and impresses the natives with the strength of his spear-throw. In the mountains he competed at stone-throwing with the first natives who attached themselves to him, by this game they cleared rubble from the track. The Superior knows how to transform work into pleasure in the carrying of loads or conveyance of the sick. Under his guidance everything proceeds happily, sometimes franticly. They have their devotion times and lesson times, they all kneel, absorbed, and then – features severe and bleak, as if back from a long journey – they stand up.

The Superior was once a captain in the Italian wars, with the Spanish army under the Duke of Alba, camped in the Naples region to check the Pope in Rome, whom the Spaniards hated.

And when the Pope would not yield – he was Paul IV, Peter Caraffa – Alba took his army northwards to Rome. Then, during a tumultuous advance, fate led Captain Emanuel de Nobrega to a hilly countryside in Campagna, a place meaning no more and no less to him than any other, where his people granted themselves a day of rest which they employed in gathering provisions, and this, in the usual army fashion, with beatings and crimes. Here, north of Capua, near Teano, dwelt the family of his bride, a fact which escaped him in the heat of war. When the war broke out, his bride had returned to her parents, she wanted to be nearer to her future husband, but of course did not expect to encounter him in person. The father and brothers of the bride were stiff-necked peasants with a certain property. And when Captain Nobrega's mercenaries came for wine, corn and fowl, they had to tie up the men; the young woman they found in the house caught the sergeant's eye, and he raped her.

When they brought the three bound peasants to the captain as he sat quietly at lunch with his officers, and demanded exemplary punishment for them, he half-turned on the bench, asked what was going on, and shouted at the men: what's the idea, shall he string them up from the nearest tree. What were their names, how much money did they have, how much could they scrape together to buy their freedom. The old man kept quiet, one of the young lads gave his name. The name, the name – the captain: "What did you say?"

The lad repeated it. "And what is this village?"

They said: "Teano."

The captain's face cleared, he threw his hat down on the table, stood arms akimbo and laughed, laughed towards the peasants! He laughed to his companions: "This is a tale for the theatre, friends, a prank someone might have invented." And yells at the puzzled mercenaries: "Untie these people, untie them at once, all three." And to the table: "These are my relations! This is my bride's family! My Elvira! I never did ask where we are, and I'm stomping around in my own relations' parlour." Delight and exclamations around the table.

They insist that the peasants sit at the table, the captain embraces the old man, his eyes are damp with emotion, he apologizes, war is a rough trade, it's the work of Satan, but what can a man do, kings and emperors at each other's throats, the Pope won't yield. But the peasants sit silent there on the bench to left and right of the captain, he pours wine for them, has bread placed in front of them, they take sips and stare straight ahead.

And suddenly the lad, the bold one who spoke out before, fixes the captain and his people with eyes blazing in a hard stubborn face, and asks: "How goes it with your bride, our sister, in Spain, sir brother-in-law?"

"I don't know, I've been away near half a year."

"She came to us, she wanted to visit us before the wedding."

The captain seized the father by his torn red blouse: "Elvira is with you?" He nodded. "Why didn't you say? What?"

And he sees their implacable faces. He yells: "Did they beat you, did they steal from you?"

The father nods, shrugs his shoulders: "That as well."

"You'll have it all back, every penny, and I'll match it in compensation. But the Devil take it! I must away to see my bride, I can't sit here any longer. Excuse me, comrades."

And he stands with a tumultuous bleak anxious feeling and prods the old man and the lads to their feet: "Come, we'll drink later. Elvira shall offer me a welcome cup. I want to hear forgiveness from her lips." And with that he leaves the company, who now have a sense of foreboding, the three peasants trot ahead. The officers at the table exchange glances, and three of them and some soldiers follow behind.

They don't have far to go, it's a little tidy village in a valley, hills climb away to the north, the peasants lead them past the church, as they pass a farmyard they turn and point to a sergeant just going in through the open gate. At once the captain among his companions shouts across the yard: "Well, where is she?" But the people still say nothing, now he knows something's up. He screams red-faced: "Where then? Damn it, where, stop playing the fool." The officers, his companions, are at his side, they clap him on the shoulder. They have entered the low cottage, and one of the peasant lads indicates the wooden chamber door right by where they stand. The captain ups with a bound, the door is locked, he rattles the latch, cries: "Elvira." The father adds his lament:

"Elvira, dear little daughter."

A man's voice answers from within: "Go to blazes, you clowns."

For a brief moment the captain stands frozen. Then he pounds the door with his fist, kicks it, an officer tries to restrain him, he hurls his shoulder against the door, it comes away at the hinges, splinters into the room. The sergeant who just now slipped through the gate is standing by the wall with drawn sword, the door at his feet. The captain is on him like a wild beast, unarmed. He leaps straight for the sergeant's throat – at the sight of the officers the man has dropped his sword, paralysed with fear – and wrestles and throttles the wriggling man and drops on him and bangs his head against the floor. Then he lets go, you can hear terrible rasping breath. The captain, who has looked neither right nor left, stands up, shouts to the soldiers: "Out with him!" They drag the body by its feet into the passage and fling it down.

In the room on the bed, beneath a picture of a saint, a human figure lies covered to the head. Father and brothers press forward, touch the linen cover at the foot end, low groans can be heard.

Nobrega turns aside, his face rigid, and says to the father: "Uncover her, hold her, I cannot."

The father sits on the edge of the bed and slowly, as if lifting skin from a wound, draws the cover down from the head. Thick black hair appears, then something blue-black that might be forehead or eyes or cheek. "My child, my child," the father begs. The son looks across, stares at the soldiers. The father uncovers the girl as far as her breast, she has a blue dress and her red shawl is over one arm, blood has trickled from her face, from her severely beaten cheek down her throat onto her breast. Her lips move. The father implores into her ear: "What is my little daughter doing? Elvira, we're here. Come. Your bridegroom the captain is here."

And at these words the girl moves, raises herself to a half-sitting position, hands at her back, the red shawl slides from her arm, her wide-open eyes look around the room, recognise Nobrega, her eyes rest on the stony face which betrays not a tremor, and his knees sag and tremble and then the captain pulls himself together. And she utters a scream, raises one arm and falls back, and cries, and cries.

At this alarm call the two sons turn as if at a signal and storm off down the passage, you hear them muttering, they are back right away, one holds a scythe, the other a flail, they roar: "Father, out!" And already they are at the officers. Two are down at once, the lads keep lashing out, the other officer is downed by the terrible threshing. Then soldiers are there, they seize the lads from behind, throw them down and drag them out. They go for the father, but the captain intervenes with his sword, says: "Leave him."

For a quarter of an hour, having stood the broken door back up, he stands motionless at the bedside. He sinks down beside the father. The person in the bed whimpers. The whimpering does not touch the captain, no thoughts stay in his head, no words leave his lips.

Some time passes. Then a tumult arises outside, loud distant cries. Trumpets sound the alarm, drums roll. The captain is swiftly on his feet, hat picked from the floor, belt adjusted, he grabs the door, sets it aside, and is out.

In the village a battle is raging. The village saw the seizing of the two lads in the farmyard and how they were dragged bleeding into the Spanish camp, a number of peasants came together. A raid, the brothers were freed, soldiers downed.

In the battle, church bells clanging wildly, the captain does no more than is necessary. Not until the next day do they dare enter the smouldering village. The farmhouse he is looking for has been burned so that only the walls stand. No trace of bride or father.

The captain saw this campaign honourably through to the end. He entered Rome along with the others. Then he returned with his regiment to Spain by ship and took himself off to Alcala, where ailing Villanova had gathered many men around him. Villanova – and this was the trick of fate – was a pupil of Loyola.

Although Nobrega had no great sins to atone for, he felt guilty and trapped. It was not enough to receive absolution. He was too distraught and heartbroken. Villanova helped.

≈≈≈

Father Faber was a poor farm boy, he resembled the Father Faber who lodged with Loyola in the dormitory of the College of Saint Barbara in Paris. Father Faber struggled a great deal with his senses, he was broad and tall, his body inclined to fat, they stuck him in a monastery when he was still young and he became a gloomy monk. There the voice of the Spaniard Salmeron reached him, he heard him speak in the monastery and gained his confidence. And hardly was Faber back in his cell when "Forget these exercises," said Salmeron, "cease your fasting, what demands you make of your poor body, you tire yourself, you are like a traveller with a long journey ahead, who instead of using his legs exhausts himself and before long cannot even stand. It is all much, much easier." And he led him to obedience, to service. This was a stroke of luck, a semi-redemption. It was even better when he came together with other brothers of the Society of Jesus. And look at him now, here on the Sierra do Mar, in the savannah, along the forested rivers. It was a rebirth. After Christ left the world, an inconsolable yearning for him remained among humanity, they constantly created men in his image. The reverence of the natives for big-bodied Faber bordered on worship. They hung on his words, tried to imitate his actions. This confused him, and his confessor had to calm him down.

≈≈≈

Son of a great warrior and himself pursuing a martial career since leaving home, Father Daniel was a young man, small, unusually strong, with a patrician nose. The same Salmeron taught him that every warlike deed must retreat before that which leads mankind to the throne of God. He, however, was not told: "It is all so easy, much easier than you think." He was guided to undertake the most strenuous days of fasting, his vanity was spurred to impose impossible demands on his body, and then he had to practise staying awake. Daniel entered the Order as a warrior, inclined to a dour implacability. And after they left Sao Paolo, where he shared all their humiliations, the man was in his element. How quickly others gave up and wanted to rest. Father Daniel resisted and drove himself on and on.

Then there were the theologians who thought to make a profession of scholarly bickering. They were brought into the circle of decisive men, several of them pupils of great Loyola. What a world, such earnestness. You willingly traded father and mother for it. They became Warriors for Jesus, tireless explorers, pitiless goads of mankind.

Indian diplomats

THEY MARCHED for weeks not stopping anywhere. They wanted distance between their band and Sao Paolo. North of Sierra do Mar, across the heights of Alto da Serro, they trudged through swampy valleys declining to the northwest. Forests covered the hills to the west and continued north to the source of the Mogy-Guaçu and the Rio Pardo. But to the south where the Fathers were headed, the campos began, trees and saplings only on the flanks of hills.

Two Fathers and a number of natives strode along at the head of the column with axe and machete, cleared the path where necessary, were relieved after a while. Then came natives and Fathers and straggling groups, carrying and hauling baggage, altars, books, crosses, quantities of goods for trade, cloth, dried meat, salt. The Whites among them were deployed to catch game and fowl, where they could they fished with the natives.

Immediately behind the pathfinders, dark men carried the great wooden cross they had carved just before their departure; Emanuel the Superior had consecrated it. At first they had painted a Christ on it, but the figure became too damaged and the priests had it removed. Those bearing the cross had to sing constantly. Apart from brief pauses, this pious singing never ceased during the whole trek, from time to time the entire train joined in.

The priests knew why they insisted on singing. They wanted to win over savage tribes. They had lost the Whites, had suffered defeat at the hands of Whites, their hopes were directed at the dark people. The Fathers knew that as they advanced through an apparently empty landscape, silent forest, they were under observation. Their natives told them so. These dark people, rescued at a price from the terrible camps of Sao Paolo, could have run away without difficulty. Some did so at the start, and later, mistrusting the Whites. But the Fathers reckoned correctly they would be back, they could always run away again, it was no bad thing to see a small number of vagrants roaming about, keeping an eye on them and telling others what they knew. The loyal followers then managed the rest of the propaganda. They belonged to various tribes, were allowed to go to their people, singly or more usually in groups of five or ten, they came back regularly bringing smaller and larger bands with them. Later whole tribes joined the trek.

It was with poignant attentiveness that the natives took part in leading the train, their train. They suggested where to stop, which path to take, and the Fathers never had cause to regret following their advice. The natives knew equally well the paths made by animals and those by men in the changing wilderness. Even in unfamiliar territory they found the way. No one before had trodden the wilderness of the new continent with no clear direction of march, unarmed and with no warlike intent.

And the Fathers, however joyfully they went, could not deny amid the fearsome silence surrounding them – to them all was silence, forest and savannah and watercourse, animals that ventured out of the bush, the sloth that lumbered away from them, vampire bats that whirred, the swarms of wild bees, the crocodiles, pumas, butterflies, the termites, monkeys in the treetops – amid all this profound silence replete with speech, the Jesuit Fathers could not deny that they were afraid. They were helpless here. If their dark friends abandoned them they would be lost from one day to the next. They would find no way forward or back, they lacked the skill to fashion boats quickly from material at hand so that they could cross water, they had too much baggage, an enticement to robbery by native tribes. When the terrible black night of the wilderness descended on them, the Fathers became frightened one after the other as they stood from their spiritual exercises and finally sank into the abyss of night, that cruel inertia. Intermittent storms and rain. Intermittent rustling and shrieks. Where had they come to? Did the mouth of Hell seem any different, to a demon? Then the eye sought out the camp fire, surrounded by dark men who encircled the train like a flock of angels.

As the trusty guides moved on ahead they maintained silence, their eyes flew right and left, they searched the ground, the trees, queried them, not forgetting the birds. They avoided the tracks of various animals, and of any tribe. The Fathers knew nothing of the frequent discussions of the natives among themselves – they spoke seldom to the Whites. At first they understood few of the Whites' questions, even those of the Fathers, and the Whites could make no headway with their replies. And it was not the way of the natives to mention what was self-explanatory, such as the reason why they avoided the clear straight paths of various animals and tribes. They respect such paths, bad things may happen if you go along them without the tribe's permission, you can ruin their hunting luck. So as far as possible they blazed new trails, and the alien tribes who understood what they were doing, and saw from footprints that dark people were among the party, took note and were pleased. This cautious wayfinding was of great value to the Jesuit Fathers, though they did not know it.

And now the difficult choice of camp site, and the necessary hunt. The Fathers never learned from their native adherents why this animal was avoided in this region, and another in that. The Whites who joined them on a hunt were simply held back, they learned that here you do not kill this or that creature. The Whites might laugh, but they obeyed, for Emanuel ordered them to accept without demur any signs relating to the lay of the land. With what circumspection did the dark companions ensure so often that camp was not made within sight or earshot of an unknown village. And when they broke camp, for more than an hour after their departure a cleansing detail remained behind, not to wipe away all evidence of their presence, but to cover up anything unseemly and deposit gifts at various places in the vicinity. At the first campsites the Fathers wanted to leave behind crucifixes and rosaries, and did so at some places, but the cleansing details always brought them back with the remark: it is not customary. The phrase "it is not customary" normally admitted no further questioning. If the Fathers asked: "Why should it not be customary to leave a cross here, Jesuits were never here before, let them know who we are", the natives, grave and unruffled, replied: "It is not customary." The reason was: the cross, the emblem of the White tribe, was alien magic, it disturbed the place, might harm the activities of the local tribes. If they were to insist on leaving a cross behind, they would inevitably draw the anger of the tribes down on their heads.

The Fathers despatched these dark solemn diplomats with gifts to tribes along the way. It was a much more serious business than the Fathers realised. The natives they approached debated for days among themselves before joining the march. This was not out of fear, but from concern that they might somehow, somewhere, transgress against propriety. They needed a lot of information, so you had to be completely frank with them and show why you were going along with the Whites. And so they painted themselves in various ways – the Fathers were unhappy to see this, but acquiesced. They also took scraps of cloth of different colours, tied them together with lianas or stalks of grass, strange costumes in which they stepped out with dignity. The Whites thought these costumes comical, and the long discussions among their brown friends remained obscure to them. They never understood that this was the only way the diplomats could enact their role. The clothes were in some sense their credentials to foreign princes. They represented specific animals, showed what tribe the wearer came from, what he thought of the Jesuit Father he served, and that he was a free man. An illiterate White would never understand the costume, but for the natives it was a careful literary construct that they laid out for exegesis by those capable of reading it. To accompany it, they worked in some songs and speeches of greeting. One made a speech with the character of a report, the others interjected a refrain.

The refrain was not always the same, it was carefully selected by the emissaries and formed the core of the mission. At the start they sang: "We go with the great Fathers and are all free." Around this they laid out their information, reported how gangs of White men had fallen upon their tribes, plundered them, dragged them off, locked them up in the notorious prison camps of Piratininga by the sea. They related how people had starved and died, and aroused sympathy and anger among their hosts. Then they told of their own fate. Some sorcerers came, the Whites' own great Fathers, and threatened the Whites. And when the Whites did not obey, the great Fathers came together in their black robes and secretly concocted powerful magic against the town of robbers. Then they freed the dark people from prison, the Whites were full of fear and gave the sorcerers even bigger presents, they carry these along, and the great Fathers in their black robes are coming now through the forest. The choir sang the refrain: "We go with the great Fathers, we are all free."

These reports aroused great attention along the whole route. Men were sent back with the emissaries to check the story out. And when the people returned and confirmed it all, villages and wandering bands sent out small groups to follow the train, support and protect it. Then the rumour spread: how the medicine men of the Whites had abandoned Piratininga, they are gathering dark people around them to punish the robbers. A wave of hope accompanied the trek of the Jesuit Fathers from the maritime hills through the forest to the great savannah.

Even more effective was another report that loyal Indians carried to neighbouring tribes, and the Fathers were able to learn from their native friends what kind of people they were dealing with. They discovered the importance of food. They observed the powerful impression made by the refrain: "We have plenty to eat."

Most of the followers came peaceably and gladly with them because they could obtain plentiful food with no effort. The Fathers did not at once see through this unbelievably simple circumstance, they believed that food supported instruction, to some extent you had to lure these simple folk with food, but that was not the point. Plentiful and secure food proved to the Indians the correctness of the proffered doctrine. How could the Jesuit Fathers not be mighty and benevolent sorcerers, when they came so easily and unfailingly into possession of the most important fowl, game, fish? So the Fathers realised before it was too late: it all depends on good hunting gear and skilled hunters. This is how Emanuel summed up the experiences of the past few weeks, after a silent thanksgiving prayer for their success so far: "God guide us and give us correct thoughts. For many, the way to instruction leads through eye and ear to the heart, but for many others, through mouth and belly. Why should one way be higher than the other? And even if one way is higher, why should it bother us?"

It was not hard to find people who knew all about hunting and catching fish, the natives were supremely adept once they overcame their superstitious fear of European tools. But it was not easy to provide a sufficient supply of firearms, crossbows, balls, powder. The numbers to be catered for rose alarmingly by the day. The Superior, for all his clever approving remarks about the way through the belly, had to concede that the trek was becoming remarkably carnal, almost a restaurant business, with the difference that, in a restaurant, one has to pay.

When a diplomatic mission returned one day in their fantastic costumes, beaming happily, and reported that several hundred newcomers were on their way and would join up with the train tomorrow or next day, there was serious concern. The catering problem was insoluble. And they had to accept this turn of events, unexpected as it was. For it was true: you showed your power by feeding people well. It was like the duel between the prophet Moses in Egypt and Pharaoh's sorcerers: they, like he, could do a lot, but finally Moses did more, all the firstborn in Egypt died and this proved the superiority of Moses' God. The Fathers could do what the sorcerers of the savages could not, but they had better not have to put it to the test.

Once there occurred the following incident, which had its comical side, like much that happened at this time. At the end of one of the typical hunts the hunters, who included a number of local Indians, came back looking terribly grave. The whole group conducted itself with great solemnity. The Whites explained when questioned that this solemn mood had overtaken their fellow hunters when some of the little ostriches of the campos were shot. The Fathers became uneasy, for they knew it was possible to make serious errors here. They asked if the dark friends had warned them, or held them back from shooting these creatures. Not at all. The three Whites, who had a good understanding of Indian ways, were certain that these were not among those animals that the people prayed to or feared. So what was up? Before they could reach the bottom of it, these Indians together with some others approached the Superior's hut where the Fathers were standing, and threw themselves to the ground at their feet, standing up only when earnestly ordered to do so. Then they withdrew in silence, still wearing expressions of the greatest reverence. "You see," said the White hunters, "that's how they behaved the whole time." Some hours later they found that the excitement among the people had not abated, that two had been deputed to return to their tribe and report on the hunt. It could be foreseen that a whole tribal crowd would descend on them. And so it happened. The explanation was that these birds were well-known to them, and not exactly rare in these parts. But for reasons to do with the cunning of the creatures and the capability of their own hunting equipment and the reach of their arrows, catching them was a highly complicated business requiring numerous ritual preparations. Thus the birds were powerful, and the subject of many current legends. So now, when the Jesuits came and their hunters killed several birds without preparations, they were perplexed. The guns had something to do with it, but not everything. That these swift, cunning birds allowed themselves to be shot by the hunters was due to Jesuit sorcery.

Contacts with Sao Paolo

THE NEW INCESSANT unstoppable stream of dark people, which gradually came to include entire groups with women, children and household belongings, filled the Fathers with joy and anxiety. When the Fathers assembled around their Superior they pressed each others' hands, embraced, not a day without prayers of thanksgiving and bafflement.

They must obtain more supplies. On reflection, they remembered notices from Spain which meant some new brothers of the Order must have landed in Sao Paolo by now. The thought bobbed up of sending some Fathers to Sao Paolo who, under cover of guiding the newcomers, would procure arms and equipment and perhaps persuade more Whites to join them. They were uneasy about making contact with Sao Paolo again, but it had to be done.

So the Superior, after several discussions that failed to quieten all anxieties, sent a delegation off to Sao Paolo with letters for the newcomers, and other letters to the Order in Spain and to the Superior-general. For the first time they wrote of the good fortune they had encountered. Only passing reference was made to the tensions apparent in Sao Paolo. The letters to headquarters were redrafted several times in order that not too much of the enthusiasm that suffused them should shine through.

When the delegation had traversed the familiar plateau of Sierra do Mar and now walked once again in the lanes of Sao Paolo with Peter Faber, tall as a tree trunk, in the lead, they met a true Paolist reception, not the malicious one they had steeled themselves for, but one accorded to friends who'd been warned against a perilous undertaking and now turn up safe and sound. The day after they arrived the governor's representative insisted on taking them personally to see the church building they had initiated. "Such a misunderstanding, your departure," was the topic of every conversation these days, "the town is blossoming, we need teachers, priests, you were exactly right for us." Faber, recalling the drubbing he had been subjected to, explained mildly that they would return, it was just a missionary expedition, a kind of study tour, he'd write at once to the Order's headquarters in Rome requesting them to send other Fathers across. "No," they cried, "you are the ones, only you, we want you, we're used to you, everything speaks for you." Father Faber and the Paolistas were of one mind: only after parting do you realise what you've lost. Despite his profound concern for the fortunes of the Fathers, the governor's syrupy secretary was unable to extract anything more from Faber than: "It's going well, it's not easy, we're in good health, God is with us."

The town's hoi-polloi spoke in other tones. Their irritation, mistrust and fear were evident. The song they sang as they sat together in their drinking dens was the old one: "We didn't quit old bad Europe just so that gang of religious can lead us by the nose again." And this was followed by a more serious complaint. Sao Paolo society had already heard something of the progress of the expedition; they had hoped the Whites would soon be massacred by a warlike or fugitive tribe. Instead they enjoyed free passage. Something seemed to be forming around these new Bible-thumpers, they were luring tribes away from the coast. Everywhere, from blockhouse to tavern, they cursed and drank: "Those dogs are ruining our business. Priests – spoilsports more like. The Devil with them."

"Shouldn't be surprised when the simple man says: church, a good thing, pope, all right, we need it, because you don't want to die without it and roast in Hell – but you have to draw a line and put a stop to their game."

"The black crows go into the forest, collect a few hundred savages and take them for a walk. What are they trying to prove? They had no luck with us, we showed them the door, now they want revenge and plan to jump us from behind."

That was it. They'd got it. The Jesuits are drawing away our very own heathen!

"We should never have let the black devils go."

"And who sold them two hundred savages?" Curses flew. Everywhere they roared: "Let's have at them! With hounds! Into the sea!"

On some days it seemed as if they really would decide to do it, for there could be no question of allowing such people to settle anywhere nearby. Then suddenly they drew back, as a new thought went through the Paolist head: "The black crows are collecting savages. Let them! When they have enough, we'll take 'em off their hands." And this was the clincher, and all argument was stilled. This was their answer to the Fathers' skulduggery and deceit.

The delegation encountered no resistance. They could buy

whatever they wanted, people were wonderfully helpful in the matter of organising a supply line that they promised to protect. Two Fathers remained in town to arrange everything and keep the Paolistas sweet.

The first assault

AS CERTAIN SLAVE hunters in Sao Paolo learned of the facility with which the Jesuits deep in the jungle hooked their precious red and brown fish, they said to one another: "We can do that." And they commissioned tailors to make a dozen black robes, and carpenters to bang together and paint a suitable number of crosses large and small, in appearance exactly like those the Jesuits carried with them. They had in their possession, too, a number of breviaries. They packed it all up, took a handful of reliable natives, hid fetters and guns in chests, they would have to do without hounds. Then this small group of Paolistas, no one in town any the wiser, set off in the footsteps of the pious train.

They did not stick entirely to the route. Some peeled off to left or right, always with pious singing from natives and Whites, crucifixes held aloft at the head of the procession. The leaders of the scoundrel band went in black robes. Rumours of the Jesuit train had spread far and wide, the Fathers had prepared the ground, the scoundrels reaped the harvest. Small groups of Indians appeared, the Whites gave them presents, spoke solemnly to them, divine words tripped more lightly from the scoundrels' tongues than from the Fathers, they enquired after the circumstances of the Indians, learned of sicknesses, the natives wanted medicines, they gave them some. The scoundrels invited the natives to stay with them and place themselves under the protection of the almighty God of the Christians. He knows no distinctions of skin colour, and bestows power specifically on the weak. Many of the savages only needed to hear this once, their hatred and fear of White marauders was universal. And so, after several weeks of slow advance, when the criminals had gathered sufficient natives together, one night they removed all bows, arrows, spears, shields that the natives had brought with them, opened the chests they had been carrying and brought out fetters and guns. They fell upon the Indians as they slept and chained them. Only a few had to be killed.

In the morning the whole herd, roped together and loaded with chains, was driven along at a forced march. There were ambushes along the way, some natives from the area had escaped and alerted their villages. But they made it. No one boasted of it, not out of fear, but so that the ruse could be repeated.

≈≈≈

The Warriors of Jesus have come singing, praying and teaching through primal forest, the thorn scrub. At first they followed the Rio Tiete, then turned south, crossed the Paranapanema. They heard of mobilisations and battles in infinitely distant Europe, of the amassing of gold and more gold to raise armies and suppress heresy. During the rainy season they had to stay in one place, press on in the good months, their progress slowed, the train ever bigger and less mobile. They do not forget their brothers at home in Spain and Italy. They learn that two Jesuit priests are stuck in Sao Paolo, that odious place, trying as best they can to organise a supply line. They try to keep intact the link between the Fathers and the motherland as they sink deeper and deeper towards the core of this new continent, as fearless and sure as the plumbline that seeks the centre of the earth. The camp of the Jesuits has several thousand inhabitants, it's a migrating village. The Fathers no longer proselytize. They are eager to arrive at the Paraná. What a mighty, solemn task awaits them there. The yearning, the impatience of the Fathers. How blessed they are, to have come across the sea and discovered such children, a whole continent of children to whom they can bring Heaven's salvation.

Then one morning, just after some men arrive, anxious whispering grows among groups of natives. When the Fathers investigate, they hear from the newcomers that other Fathers are in the forest. They come from the east, from the hills, and collect dark people. The Fathers report to the Superior, they don't understand, have the Dominicans or Franciscans sent a mission, but they had no news of this, they're unwilling to believe that rivalry among the Orders has reached even here. They despatch seasoned scouts, make camp and wait. There is unease and nervousness. The scouts, this has never happened before, fail to return after several days. They stay put for a week. Now they're afraid. The camp is drawn tighter. Some natives ask permission to go after their brothers. They quickly come back. Hard on their heels are tribesmen of the region, Ibiraya, small, very nimble strong people. And the scouts call out: the tribe is on the warpath. They beg the Fathers to distribute weapons. The whole camp is in uproar, men gang up together, the Fathers can't keep their weapons from them, they watch astonished as warlust transforms these peaceful people, in horror and revulsion they have to tolerate the war dance that rages through the camp.

The Jesuit Fathers are never afraid in time of peril. A brief prayer and they are invulnerable. They go in tens beyond the perimeter, through tall grass. No one accompanies them.

They notice rustling and movement in the majestic savannah grass. They make for it, singing. Suddenly they are surrounded by a crowd of small brown-red men. They force the priests to a halt. In a moment the grass parts, an old squat dark man stands attended by some warriors, he glares at them and he and the others lean on their spears. When he begins to speak – there are no greetings – it becomes apparent that the Fathers do not know his language, one goes back, escorted by warriors, to fetch interpreters.

"You do not have our people. Who has them?"

Emanuel explains that they have been marching inland from the coast for several months. If it was White men who seized your people, we do not know them. We are Fathers, we want to bring the brown people glad tidings from Heaven that are meant for everyone. The chief says: "The others who stole our relatives said the same. Some escaped and told us. They wear black robes like you, hold up the big log and sing. Then they tied up our relatives."

The priests stand puzzled. After a moment Peter Faber sees the hand of the Paolistas, this is one of their tricks. The chief observes him. A lively palaver sets up among the Whites. Walk while ye have the light, lest darkness come upon you: for he that walketh in darkness knoweth not whither he goeth.

"They have played a wicked trick on you. People who do such things are criminals."

"They wore black robes, carried the big log, and sang. They had white skins."

"They are deceivers."

While ye have light, believe in the light, that ye may be the children of light.

"Are there such deceivers among the Whites, they steal your magic logs? This cannot be, or else you would have killed them."

Emanuel, already angry, becomes hard at these words from the heathen chief: "Our strength is God in Heaven. We have no magic logs. The criminals will suffer the wrath of God." The natives, unconvinced, talk back and forth some way off. How is it possible for robbers to steal the magic logs and magic clothes of the priests? What does it mean that the white priests stand in silence? Maybe they are exercising their magic powers at this very moment. Emanuel realises with a jolt: here we stand, Christians accused, and must submit to their judgement. And for a moment the old soldier in him revives: *To arms, pursue the robbers, Sao Paolo, that pirates' nest, burn it down.*

The natives have been debating a long while. The chief has the Whites informed that they are to ensure the safe return of their brothers, fathers and friends. He threatens the Fathers: "You must bring them back." Suddenly they are gone. The Fathers return to camp, where people greet them and recoil from their bleak faces.

Some among the brothers break down in tears during the discussion. Emanuel is filled with bitterness. Late at night, as they go to their tents by the light of the camp fire, Mariana approaches the Superior. Emanuel strokes him like a loyal pet. Mariana grasps his hand: "You will come through. We shall defeat them, have no fear."

"They will massacre us. The Church is covered in shame."

"You will defeat them, Brother Nobrega, you will come through." Such bright eyes the young man has. A flicker of joy passes over Emanuel. He can lay himself down to sleep.

Difficult weeks ensue. The Fathers' camp empties alarmingly, panic does its work. Scouts report: the tribe is following at a distance, they wait for the Jesuits to bring back their brothers, fathers and friends, they are convinced the Fathers can do this, it's entirely our fault that they're still not back. The region they are passing through is thoroughly infected by the alarming news, it's like pushing into a vacuum. It upsets them to find deserted villages, they leave presents behind wherever they come, it's no use, treachery has done its terrible work, their own followers, whom they thought won over, melt away. Their failure to bring back the stolen people puts the trust of the natives to a severe test.

Then a miracle happens. Some stolen people return. They were able to flee from the big camp near Sao Paolo before being taken aboard ship. They tell their tribe: a thunderstorm swept over the valley, lightning hit the watch tower, flash after flash, the whole camp was swamped by a wall of water, the river raged down the valley, it was everyone for himself. The guards were struck down by lightning, and they ran away before anyone from Sao Paolo could reach the camp.

The Jesuits heard this first from envoys, for the escapees had gone straight to their tribe, then envoys came to the Fathers from the tribe that had been dogging their heels. This time there was a solemn greeting ceremony outside the camp, presents were exchanged, the taciturn natives expressed thanks. Now the natives show respect, the Fathers had sent the thunderstorm, a considerable feat given the great distance.

When they depart, the natives leave two of their apprentice sorcerers with the Jesuits to learn from them. They themselves will not be won over. They return to their own territory and make clear that they expect the return of all the others.

Mariana is bewitched

BEFORE THE JESUITS, coming from the north through the region of the Tayaoba and Ibiraya, reached the promised land on the Paraná, they suffered a serious loss.

Mariana, joy of every brother, the young man, died.

He dropped like a ripe fruit.

The trek had changed everyone. It was the unrelenting work on the natives. It was the day, the night that changed them, the great sun, white moon, the shocking force of the stars, of forest and savannah, birds and animals in the bush – they struggled with it all. It fell upon Whites who had passed their years in northern lands, mostly in towns, mostly poring over books, just as it once fell on the Conquistador warriors of old. Every plant and animal streamed its life out into this air. And then the immoderate rains that brought rivers to overflowing, mists that made forest and plain disappear.

Mariana twined around Emanuel. Emanuel was his Superior, friend and fate. Not a day went by when Nobrega failed in his duty to him, and the young man bared his soul without reserve. But Mariana did not reveal what he could not reveal. He led a life that darkened from month to month. One of his souls followed a path that the others would not allow themselves to follow. Like every Father, Mariana was entrusted with a group of Indians, always the same ones, now more, now fewer, usually around a hundred people. The Fathers had to manage the lives of their group down to the smallest detail. There were unmarried people and families. Designated Fathers selected from the groups those with special skills in pathfinding, setting up camp, finding food. Mariana knew his group, he loved them. He mourned when some children died. He implored Emanuel not to take any away from him. The Superior rejected his request, and one day exchanged a dozen of Mariana's people for others. Mariana accepted the blow and thanked him glumly. Emanuel laughed.

Mariana sat alone, a book of spiritual exercises on his knee, and thought. One of his souls prayed and moved his lips. The other soul: "We left a snake behind in Sao Paolo, it darts its tongue across our path, and that belongs to the world. Oh God, thou art my God, art thou also the god of these dark people? How they look at me, what they expect from me, I would like so much to say something to them. But I know nothing. I would like to listen to them. Jesus, Mary, forgive me, it is the truth: I want only to listen to them."

By now the Jesuits knew something of the natives' concepts, and Father Emanuel impressed on the brothers the importance of pinning down the reasoning patterns of these people. Like the other Fathers, he failed to reckon with the effect of refutations, but it was necessary to check on what they were thinking in order to ascertain how deeply the doctrines imparted to them were penetrating. Emanuel handed down this directive in connection with some troublesome accusations of sorcery that residents of the camp flung back and forth at one another, and which the Fathers did not understand. Mariana went even farther: he delved into the souls of his natives. He was not of the same nature as Emanuel, a survivor of war brought to the Order by a shattering experience. He had not yet come close to the world, and once he had the notion to do so, he was already enmeshed in a spider's web.

While the train rested up for a few days, he led a group of his wards into the forest, out on the savannah, where they stopped. Then he followed Emanuel's directive as passionately as he obeyed all his orders, but now with an added ecstatic fear, with swaying and giddiness. He knew he was there in the open, men on one side and women on the other, and they were telling him their fanciful stories, and he was able to report on this to Emanuel. But he did not know, and it quickly evaporated from him, that he himself had lain among them in the grass and begun to talk in the same way. He had been carried away.

It happened that natives were in the forest watching for birds. They made him stand with them in sight of a bird that hopped around in the grass, with his neck stretched out, hands on his knees, and observe with them what the bird did. Because birds know a lot. They are as clever as any animal, cleverer than people. They live in the forest, the swamp, in the savannah and along rivers, day and night. And so they know lots of secrets that people cannot find out. You can learn from them how to do this and do that, they can even conjure things up. Father Mariana kneels in the grass among the natives, they are glad he's such a clever man.

The little bird twitches its tail, turns its little head, makes a couple of jumps, utters a cry. A young Indian understands. And when the bird flies up to a branch and calls down, he makes a couple of jumps like the bird, jerks his head, succeeds with the birdcall. Mariana is entranced, his shoulders make little movements as if preparing to fly, his legs shoot out, it's a little leap, it works, another, it works, the others take no notice, they jump like him, it becomes a dance, it is a dance. The bird flies off. They stay in the grass, the Father shuts his eyes.

After a while they move on and sing. The brown people know his secret, they love him, say nothing.

When Mariana met the Superior he reported that his group were very attached to him, studied, sang. But when Emanuel reminded him of his task to look inside the heads of the people, Mariana was startled, and confessed he had forgotten, he would do so at once. "How clever you are," he said in awe, as if hearing it for the first time. "You are our leader, you. We must penetrate to them, our teachings must enter them like a seed that puts forth deep roots."

"I no longer have such high hopes," laughed Emanuel. And there he left his friend, who stumbled gravely daydreaming back to his people. And he exercised his oversight of them, strict, serious, unapproachable, he the Holy Church, tiptoeing on two light feet, looking into all their daily activities.

How the natives spied on him. What a deadly serious secret game they played with him. How they wanted to understand him. Something significant, they felt, was being made ready for them. The other Fathers shone down on their groups like dreadful stars, but this one descended from his star, his voice lost its thunder, took on the speech of their people. He would bring them power, lead them to the blissful wonderland of which their old great ancestors had told. Could he? Would the other White priests allow it?

When Mariana left the group every morning and evening to talk with the other Fathers, the natives became anxious. They studied him when he came back. His expression was always stern, he hid his face under a crust.

They made knots of grass and hung them on his robe when he went away, there was magic in the knots to ensure nothing happened to him. When he slept with them at night they watched over him and fixed little figures of grass and wood on the ground and from the roof of the tent, which showed the ancestors the way to him.

When Emanuel noticed the great attachment of the natives to Mariana, he was happy, but not overmuch. He had been unsure of himself ever since he allowed the hunting expedition out of Sao Paolo, that experiment, that temptation to which he exposed even Mariana; Mariana had agreed too readily. Emanuel knew one must be diplomatic with the natives, it wasn't easy dealing with them, they understood everything differently. So again he exchanged a large number from Mariana's group with people from another group. But some of those exchanged came to him and asked permission to return to Mariana. He dismissed them and formed a suspicion. Thereafter those who had been exchanged slipped away, a dozen remained in contact with their old group, they followed from a distance, showed themselves every couple of days, Mariana asked them to stay, but they would stay only with him.

It happened that one day they drew him aside and promised to go with him, they would follow him. Other groups would come too. Horrified, Mariana rejected the idea. He confessed to Father Emanuel, who praised him, gave new directives. It was Emanuel's style to tempt and let run until the situation played itself out – then he relied on his hard fist.

When the natives realised who it was there in front of them, under a spell, they would not yield. Mariana himself grew ever less able to stand firm. Like one riding a sled down a snowy mountainside, he was already hurtling away. They cast their bait in his direction. They brought him presents. From their behaviour he knew: these are offerings. He guarded himself, oh dreadful heathendom. But let him who is already bound hand and foot strike out. The company he led misunderstood what the Jesuits wanted from them, and Mariana understood ever more clearly, profoundly and without inhibitions what it was they understood. Everything played itself out in secret. The dark people who believed in Mariana closed around him like a league of conspirators.

For some time no one said it out loud, but then it came to his ears that they would follow only him. And when this was repudiated and censured a second, a third time, its tentacles were already wound around Mariana. He had been a tender youth when Father Emanuel called to him in Spain and took him to sea. He felt obliged to conceal from his brothers what was happening in his group. And so it all came to pass.

One noontime they were overtaken in the forest by torrential rain. They huddled helplessly together. Brown men and women persuaded Mariana to stretch out on the ground, they formed a roof over him with their bodies, through which the rain could not penetrate. And in this living house, with its smell of oiled bodies, Mariana heard a voice, Spanish, in a clear penetrating tone: "Now, Mariana, is it not enough? How much longer will you run at Emanuel's heels?" Thunder crashed, the bodies over him pressed together more tightly. "There is no point running after Emanuel any more. He could not defeat the Paolistas. He passes even these people by. Trust your eyes! Be brave!"

Tenderly the scrum pressed together over him. "See how they follow you. You know best who they are. You can lead them to the goal, Mariana."

They had made everything ready to flee with him. They would go by themselves into the forest, gather friendly tribes, Mariana would lead them, the White man, one of Those. Other voices quickly sounded: "He will free us from the Whites! Spread the news around!"

≈≈≈

By the first light of dawn young Mariana sank to his knees and read: *"Therefore being justified by faith, we have peace with God through our Lord Jesus Christ: Tribulation worketh patience; And patience, experience; and experience, hope: And hope maketh not ashamed."*

And as his eyes read, his thoughts strayed and he shivered: Why did the Holy not do away with the monster, why did it place salvation on our shoulders, where is hope to come from, who will give us strength to endure?

"Therefore as by the offence of one, judgment came upon all men to condemnation; even so by the righteousness of one the free gift came upon all men unto justification of life."

I love you, Saviour, bring me steadfastness, bring patience. If you cannot right away bring peace, then give me patience to await you. I love you, Saviour, let me not fall into despair. Do not suffer me to be ruined. I am afraid, I am afraid. You gave the knight George strength to slay the dragon. Think of us. I am afraid, I have never been in battle. Oh Lord, oh dear Saviour, you know that all who stand around me are happy and feel nothing – why do you make me feel it? Am I to fall? Must I fall? Oh do not test me too severely! I am not strong. Oh my Saviour, I love you."

"For if by one man's offence death reigned by one; much more they which receive abundance of grace and of the gift of righteousness shall reign in life by one, Jesus Christ."

Eternal judge, help me not to die.

≈≈≈

One evening Mariana's group, to which new bands of newcomers had attached themselves without this being reported to the Superior, failed to appear in camp. A heavy thunderstorm made it plausible that they had taken shelter and were waiting it out. After two days search parties went looking. Scouts reported that the group had moved on in the direction of the falls. A revealing move. Emanuel, with a gloomy foreboding that he might have erred, and feeling concern for Mariana, went out himself some days later.

The storm passed, the air cleared, it could not be because of the weather that they were encamped quietly at the falls. The journey was a long one. Emanuel was shocked how far the group had moved on already. Finally they heard trumpets and drums, then distant human voices, singing. But these were not spiritual tunes. The Indian scouts guiding Emanuel said: "Someone has

343

died there. They are holding a funeral."

"But why," Emanuel wondered, "why, if someone has died, do they mark a funeral with heathen songs? What is Mariana up to?" He swallowed his anger, he wanted to keep a clear head, he signed to his companions to approach the group's camp quietly, and find a place where he could observe the ceremony without being seen. This proved easy. The hilly terrain and the roar of the falls enabled Emanuel and two scouts to creep up like snakes. Soon the scouts who had moved forward came back to say they had found an empty tent close by the camp at the side of a hill, Emanuel could hide there unobserved. He followed them over rocks, crouching. The people at the falls – how could so many be gathered here – did not see him, all were looking towards the river.

In the empty tent to which he was led, carefully sited in the shelter of a cliff, Emanuel looked about him. What was that? There, lying in the hammock? A rosary! He picked it up, it was Mariana's! Mariana had left his rosary behind, had gone among his people without it! Emanuel weighed this piece of Mariana in the hollow of his hand. He peeped through the opening of the tent. I shall see what he is doing. What has come over you, brother Mariana?

They have spread branches with green leaves over the red-brown stony earth, something is lying under them, almost totally covered by leaves. And around it two people in crude giant masks are dancing in a circle, now and then uttering cries. Indian sorcerers. But this cannot be one of our groups. The people – there are many – squat in silence.

And now Emanuel's eyes find themselves focusing on the green foliage.

What is lying there.

There is a white face. It is the face of a White man. But the swollen features. He does not recognise him, the White man must have painted his face black and blue.

"Who is it?" Emanuel asks the two Indians through the tent opening. They have mixed with the crowd and are back with immobile faces, now they lie prone on the ground outside the tent.

Then both turn onto their stomachs and crawl into the tent to him. "Who is it?"

They stand at his side: "Do not go over there, great father Emanuel. They will kill you if you show yourself."

"Who is it? And where is − ?" And now Emanuel remembers that he is here to look for Mariana. And in a flash he sees it in the faces of the two natives standing at his side. "Dear Lord Jesus, Redeemer, Mother of God, saints," Emanuel's voice rings out, "it is Mariana. Tell me, is it he?" They say nothing. Emanuel rushes to the entrance, they expected this, they grab him by the shoulders, force him back, he tries to shout, a hand is over his mouth. Before he can make a move he is on the ground, the scout's hand stays over his mouth, they loom over him, whisper from either side: "Great Father, great Father, they will be your death. You will be your death. They say you're his murderer. They say you're the murderer. Lie still, keep silent."

Nobrega manages to push the hand away from his mouth. If he wanted, were he not so stunned, it would be a trifle for the big man to shove them aside. "What happened? What have they done to him?"

"He wanted to speak to the river spirit. He wanted to take them across the water to the other side. You said bad things about him to the river spirit. So the river spirit wouldn't let him cross. Do not show yourself. Their sorcerer has revealed all this to them."

Such nonsense, what nonsense is this, these men believe it too, oh hopeless confusion, oh God, into what abyss have you cast me!

"Release me," he whispers, "let us go back." They let him go, they ask forgiveness with contrite faces, whisper, "You are the most mighty, Father Emanuel, we shall stay with you." Emanuel's head spins.

The tent flap gapes, the noise down below grows louder, a third has joined the two dancers, and oh horror, he is carrying the black robe of a priest on a kind of fork, the robe of their Order, the Order of the Company of Jesus, it is Mariana's, wet, muddy, the man holds the fork high above his head, the robe billows over him, in the neck opening they have stuck a ball of wadding with bright feathers, it is painted, it is meant for a head. The people throw themselves to the ground, stand, call out to the puppet. Now they stand up, they all will dance. Emanuel looks on with his two companions, crushed.

As movement starts up within him and a hand rises to his forehead where mosquitoes sit, he sees – a rustic chamber, he is standing beside a bed. But who it is lying in the bed, who it once was, in another life, what draws him and stretches hands out to him, he no longer knows. "Into what abyss have I been cast, almighty God," his lips repeat. He creeps and crawls with the two natives, one in front, the other behind, back along the stony path.

Requiem and lament

WHEN TWO DAYS later they come within sight of the camp, Emanuel thinks of Mariana, his dear young friend. So beset with voices is he, so discomposed, that he moves only step by step, and shortly before reaching the camp has to lean against a palm tree. But standing there does no good, he parts from the tree and lets his legs lead him into camp. And Brother Faber and others come rushing up, they have heard the news. They gaze at their brother Superior and lead him, without enquiries, into their shared tent. They have learned from the native scouts what happened. When Emanuel begins his tale, they can fill in details and he learns more.

They really did intend to cross the river under Mariana's guidance. The priest must have lost his senses. Emanuel has the two scouts brought in, they think they are to be punished for their boldness and say nothing, Emanuel thanks them, praises them, asks them to tell everything one more time. Mariana was proclaimed Leader over there. He attended their preparations and the dancing. He often danced with them in the forest. When he summoned the river spirit to let them cross and climbed into a boat with two rowers, the river spirit took the one who obeyed great Father Emanuel. Emanuel sent them both away, their awestruck parting shot was: "You were stronger."

As the Fathers sat shocked on the edge of their hammocks, Emanuel's thoughts were already far ahead. "They say I killed him, Mariana, we cannot but thrust that accusation from us. But this affliction must be laid at our door. I curse these hands that touched him, these fingers that stroked him. I curse my heart that loved him."

And disgusted, tormented by the shame that had come upon him, he sobbed and struck himself in the face. (A rustic chamber, someone in the bed). I weep, I weep, I weep. Hush now, don't cry, you mustn't cry, I forbid you, mouth, close now, swallow it down! Don't want, don't let it start all over again.

And the thought sneaked through him: I failed to hold him back, it's my fault, I wanted to test him, sent him on the slaving expedition, it tore him away, he spoke of the hellish flames of crime. Oh what I must bear now all alone. What has crept away and left me.

"You must understand why I weep for Mariana, our Mariana whom Satan has torn from us, and we stood by and Satan deceived us. Brothers, I must accuse him. He was one of us, a soldier of our Company. In wartime, during battle he went over to the enemy. If one of the dark people keeps the sacraments and is baptised and repeats our words and then goes away, we do not break a staff over him. Light will slowly penetrate the darkness. But when one of our own, a votary of our Order, raised in the doctrine, leaves and throws all away, home, parents, church, our love, in order to cross a river and rule over them, when he casts everything to the winds before their beastly images and dancing – this is intolerable. It is intolerable. Clearly."

The train led by the Fathers has been unable to move for day after day. Mariana's death has cast Emanuel down. A terrible light has picked him out, once again a curtain has risen and he sees what he is and does not wish to be so and cannot gaze upon it. It was this that Mariana had tried to stammer out during the voyage, about the heat, the hot continent, and Emanuel had answered proudly: holy truth acknowledges no climate. Thus Emanuel came to feel: he too is Mariana.

He sank into depression. The brothers decide on a fast. When the hours of supervision and instruction are behind them, they withdraw one by one to scourge themselves.

≈≈≈

At last the Superior ordained a requiem for Brother Mariana. The spell was broken. Meanwhile, news came which proved that the dead brother had taken leave of his senses. People from his group, which had by now moved on with his body and the robed puppet, provided reports. He must have suffered hallucinations, visions, at the last had almost led a double life, prayed with the Fathers, confessed, and then at once gone into the forest to dance.

≈≈≈

The Fathers learned nothing of how Mariana really died.

As Mariana crossed the Paraná, just where it rushes towards the great falls, the river spirit spoke to him. An angry face with thick serpentine body reared up from a dirty brown wave, rattled, hissed, sprayed him. Mariana was frightened. The natives in the boat also noticed the serpent, and paddled furiously. The serpent pursued them. Then Mariana saved his companions from ruin. While the others screwed up their eyes, screamed and urged each other on, he spoke to the serpent. They were surprised he knew its language. He said he would bring presents as soon as they reached the other side.

Then the serpent flung spume in his face and licked at the water. "My sister Sukuruja has told me about men with white skins, such as you, evil spirits who steal life from plants and animals. This is probably because you have no life of your own. It's a good thing to kill you."

"Do not listen, great river spirit, to what others tell you. Many of us are bad, many are poor, I love you and will not steal your life. I do not want to live without you."

"You have no life, and must kill. What will you sacrifice to me?

"Whatever you ask, great river spirit."

The serpent reared up with a rattle and showered water onto them, the paddlers screamed, the steersman dropped his pole and tumbled head over heels into the boat.

"Then I would like to take you right away." And it fell on Mariana, twined itself around him and dragged him overboard. "Now I am sure of you."

He berated it on the rocky bottom, sobbed, wailed for his companions, then he looked around in the water, on the bottom, and much became clear, and he was no longer Mariana.

≈≈≈

As they read the requiem for their unfortunate brother, what groans, what fervent pleas in all their prayers – what wrestling for forgiveness in the prayers of the Superior: "Oh Jesus, saviour of the world, do not abandon us. Oh stay here with us."

They left this place of misery in great haste, heading south. The Fathers in a fever of impatience. The Superior drove them on, they must find a place for the first settlement. They had to put an end to many things. He felt he must build something around them to guard them from ruin.

The brothers heard the words of their Superior, who was irritable and dogmatically severe. His face was aflame, his lips and fingers trembled, his constant theme was: Jerusalem. Their settlement would bear this name. "God gave mankind a heavenly gift," said Emanuel, "the word of God. There was a people capable of receiving this gift, but they could not keep the Word. The bowl had to be broken. So God sent his Son. And now everything that is human partakes of the gift.

"Only since Jesus is the human gaze human. Only since Jesus are languages more than instruments of understanding. They are the voice of our soul, which seeks to know, to feel, to suffer and find redemption.

"Jesus is the content of thought. There is no consciousness without Jesus. Whatever rises in the morning, toils, speaks, lies down at night and does not have Jesus, it only appears to be conscious. But it is insensible. In our toil we run about and do not know who is running and what we want. The earth holds us and does with us and drives us like beasts of burden, and one day we fall down with all our baggage, like a beast of burden. We must turn a grindstone onto which no grain has been poured. Oh the sorrow of those without consciousness. In their fear they can only kill. It does not help them.

"Where the word Jesus is not heard, there can be no 'I'. Where it is heard, every 'I' receives its name. And there is victory and peace such as Nature can never provide. Every 'I' is named at once. Everything is summoned up with the one name alongside his own. No deeper consciousness is possible. Jesus is the profoundest consciousness.

"You have heard the phrase: 'I think, therefore I am.' There is false and true being, deceptive and genuine. The phrase should be: 'Jesus is, therefore I am.' This is the truth; it has the mark of genuine truth: it leads to a new existence. Now we know and cannot fall into ruin. How thankful we must be to almighty God that we know and cannot fall into ruin."

The Fathers stand with tear-dimmed eyes. The Superior draws his black robe tight about him.

He was a tall lean man, who like all of them had allowed a thick beard to grow, it was still as black as his eyebrows. When he drew his robe tight about him with both hands and pulled the collar up around his neck, the neck which he held severely, powerfully erect, he seemed to make a skin of the robe. His red burning face, from which the long narrow blistered nose thrust out, no longer twitched. The black of the robe climbed from behind over the grey hair and from the front over the wide straggling beard. Certainty gleamed from his eyes.

The Fathers complained to their Company and the Portuguese king about the Paolistas' deeds against them. One might expect heavy punishments to be imposed as a result, but they had become a dangerous growth, none dared stick his finger in. Spiritual weapons were useless against them, and the Paolistas would use all their advantages to foil an attack by the powers of the state. The position of the town on its plateau above the sea, the swamps fronting it along the coast, the jungle of Pernaboccaraba at the rear rendered it unassailable. Consider a blockade. How? With what troops? And did the authorities actually want this?

Part Six

THE INDIAN CANAAN

~

I the King

IN SPAIN, IN Buen Retiro, when I the King read what the Jesuit Fathers were planning he was certainly not pleased, for sourness was his nature, but when he stood up from the desk he could move his knee more easily. He was concerned with all that happened around him in the palace, for he felt duty bound to keep it under control, but what happened outside in his realm also concerned him, for the same reason. I the King was like a scullery maid in a hostelry, to whom at every hour from morn till midnight they bring dirty dishes, for the eating never stops, but all she ever sees of it is dirty plates.

The Fathers of the Society of Jesus out there in the New Indies were a ray of hope. There was no more pleasant reading for Philip than their letters, they were better, braver than those of old Las Casas. The scrolls found a place on his enormous desk, which was a kind of operations centre, close to the spot reserved for his right elbow, in a region that he secretly called the 'consolations of his heart'. Here were gathered a prayer book, his rosary, a locked box containing the daily report from his secret police about goings-on in the palace, in his immediate environment, especially among his family, for he almost never spoke to his family, preferred to be informed of their activities and opinions by spies. Beside this box a basket with food for his two massive hounds, trained man-hunters. And this is where the scrolls from the Jesuit Fathers in the New Indies ended up.

I the King, the dumb man – he had forgotten how to open his mouth to speak, speaking seemed such a servile activity, he would have preferred even to confess in writing, and his Father Confessor would not have minded, but there are rules – I the King had cares. He made no progress in the world. You could spy, decree, set up a ubiquitous network of police, troops, priests. Always something fell through the net. On some days I the King collapsed in his chancery under the burden of painful purgatives, reports of failings, complaints, and thought: it would take ten kings to put all this right. Then he had himself carried in his litter, sour and careworn, into the fresh air, and gazed through the curtains of the litter at figures who loomed close and vanished into the distance; meadows, woods, people, all looked so harmless, disgracefully harmless. But how they plague one with worries. However much one writes, decrees, punishes, orders, it all happens over again.

He and his Council of the Indies had issued particular instructions concerning the New Indies. But governors, generals, captains, eager adventurers brought it all to naught. It made one weep to compare the magnificent intentions formulated in the King's cabinet with the fate they suffered. For example, a certain governor Don Diego de Centeno died before he could take up office. Another was called Don Juan de Sanabrar. He was very rich, which was good, and taken into account. He was tasked to gather two hundred soldiers and a number of White families to accompany him. They considered in detail the country over there, which consisted only of forest and grassy savannah, inhabited by idolaters; in Buen Retiro they wanted only the best even for Indian forests, and instructed the governor to load his ship with wheat, barley, rye and seeds of other useful cereals and plants, and in addition to take ample supplies of iron, steel, provisions, they prescribed what kinds of artisans he should procure, and named him captain-general, governor, alguazil mayor of the province of Rio de la Plata, with extensive rights and authorities. These things the royal chancery, with utmost meticulousness, heaped upon Don Juan de Sanabrar. Who at once set off for Seville, and there at the last moment received a royal edict, forbidding him under any circumstances to engage in trade with the Portuguese. And Sanabrar, armed with these most sagacious instructions, stood gazing at his ships. And then died before they could sail.

They reported this to I the King at Buen Retiro. They wrote

that there was a son who mourned the hidalgo. The King decreed: offer the same commission to the son. He was just as wealthy, and still young. The son agreed. Ships, crew, cargo of passengers and merchandise were all in place, he climbed aboard, climbing aboard was all he had to do. For a long time no news came of the son and his squadron. At last he sailed into the great bay of Rio de la Plata and gazed upon his province. Then he suffered shipwreck and was drowned. Some sailors saved themselves with planks, and in the town of Asuncion told what had happened.

Hot on the heels of this, from the same troublesome region came a report of a remarkable novelty. Juan Romero, a brave captain of troops, had gone about the country with a hundred soldiers to pacify it, and in order to bring even the Indians of the riverlands to heel he made use of two brigantines. He travelled with these up a small river that flowed into La Plata. One noontime he went ashore with his soldiers and set up a tent on the riverbank for their dinner. And as they sat there eating, the whole broad bank suddenly collapsed and took them on an excursion downriver. When the people in the tent noticed that the bank was moving, and the ground under their feet loosened and gaped, they tried to swim to the brigantines still anchored nearby. Despite the strong swirling current they reached the ships. And as they stood dripping and breathless on deck, gazing at the suddenly swollen waters, the bank collapsed again, the ships themselves were overturned, and this time swimming was no use, it was as if a jaguar had been hunting a deer and now went for the kill. All the people and the brigantines sank and drowned in mud and debris.

Such incidents were reported all the time from the New Indies. And as for the authorities, who sat there having been selected and instructed with such care, their fascinating antics left nothing to be desired. Some conducted themselves like madmen, some scooped up gold with no attempt at concealment, as if the world were blind, and you had to arrest them, confiscate their gold and throw them in gaol. In one corner of this vast empire a man, an ordinary commoner holding no office, declared war on the King of Spain himself.

One day I the King limped as careworn as ever, his back hurting, into his study, placed his leather rug on the chair and sat down. His private secretary had already sorted the post from the Indies, and read out to his cantankerous sovereign a communication from the Marañon river, in the jungle: the people there had deposed I the King! A cadet officer called Fernando de Guzman had done this, and elevated himself to king. I the King despairs of the world this day, leaves his chancery and occupies himself only with his hounds. Later more of this letter is read to him: the crazed horde of this cadet Guzman has penetrated as far as the Orinoco, and has everywhere attacked those royal officials selected and instructed with such care by Madrid. In the end this band, so they heard, was led by a Basque hunchback, Lope de Aguirre, they murdered and raped among defenceless Indians. And His Catholic Majesty in Buen Retiro does not know what to think of this, where will it lead, when one day the text of a letter is placed on his lectern, from this very Aguirre, this hunchbacked nullity, this murderer, addressed to him in person from a town called Burburata:

"I, Lope de Aguirre, your vassal, a Christian, a poor man, born of poor but noble parents, I and those with me put an end to the cruel injustices exercised in your name by your governors and judges." And the man writes that he is lame and crooked from two arquebus shots sustained in fighting for the King, and curses: "From this hour forth all your royal mercy and pardons mean as little to me as the writings of the arch-heretic Martin Luther."

The King is long past astonishment, he would like to hear what his faithful secretary, who stands at his side reading and listening to everything, really thinks about it, about this madness, this chaos that ever and again trickles through one's fingers like sand, but his mouth is frozen, he cannot speak. Finally it comes to an end, at least this affair. The gang is captured. The mad Basque is not taken alive to be broken on the wheel. When all is lost, the tyrannical cripple strangles his own young daughter, and with this his comrades in arms have had enough of him, hoping to earn some merit they pierce him through with their spears. Thereupon the criminals all have to jump the sword. The soldiers suspend Aguirre's head in an iron cage and parade it through the scenes of his shameful deeds.

That distant land is truly a chamber of horrors. I the King is able, on one occasion, to smile as his secretary reads out among other curiosities: In the town of Asuncion, on the Paraná, the seat of a bishop, the royal lieutenant-general attends the cathedral to hear Mass, and the bishop has him arrested. "This cannot be true, the bishop, and my lieutenant-general?"

"The bishop holds the royal lieutenant-general prisoner in a dungeon. This is what the royal governor-general writes." All they can do is credit the report, and recall both men to Spain and never let them return.

In the place on his desk reserved for consolations of the heart lie letters from the Jesuit Fathers. The King has arranged it so that his right elbow nudges them as he writes. He immerses his thoughts in the Jesuits. They have had their fill of aggravations with stupid and useless events and people, and can no longer be bothered with them. They want to bring Christianity, people try to stop them, they leave San Paolo to its devices and go into the wilderness. If only he could do likewise. A clear plan, a settled system, every point thoroughly considered and put into effect without opposition, and in the face of all ridiculous events and people. Enviable men. They deserve every protection.

The secretary takes notes, he inscribes marks that attest to the King's pleasure in this matter. The marks are meant for various officials spiritual and temporal, who for their part keep a close eye on the King and his family.

Having settled this account, I the King is better placed to turn his attention to matters closer to home. The stagnating morass in the Netherlands can be set in motion, a duke is dispatched to the region with plenipotentiary powers and an army; the fools there want to become Protestants even though they are Spaniards, they are hanged and beheaded and then everything goes swimmingly.

The same method works also in Our own household in the case of Our son Don Carlos, against whom secret agents lay unfavourable reports.

Now, says I the King, lying abed one evening looking at his very pale thin arms and legs: this meagre flesh suffices to steer the affairs of the world. People have fat and heat. They are an utterly deranged, stupid and helpless breed. I believe that if they were not led, they would never take even one straight step. They would be at each other's throats out of sheer cluelessness, of course also out of caprice, lust for power. They have urges, and that is everything to the little creatures. I thank God that he made me. And placed me in this position, rather than one of those many princes who prance about the world. They make their nations unhappy. Perceptive people know to thank me. The masses of course do not. They scream because they cannot go where they want. I shall continue to shepherd them strictly and well. Thank you, Lord, for my office, for my wisdom. Finally thank you, great Creator, for me.

And he thanked his mother for being Isabella of Portugal, and not from the house of a mere marquis, hidalgo or, perish the thought, farmer. It was a major act of Providence that preserved me from such a fate and gave me this woman as my mother. And then he thanked Emperor Charles V for being Emperor of Rome, King of Spain, and his father. And thanked all their parents, grandparents and great-grandparents, lay on his bed and, after gazing once more at his yellow bony hands, fell asleep.

A remarkable scene occupied his dreams. He is strolling with his two hounds through the extensive gardens of Buen Retiro. A sentry stands at every crossing in the path, and as he approaches they thumb their noses at him. It's astonishing. He goes up to a sentry, tries to pull down his arm. But it's impossible. He goes to the next one. Same thing. He goes along the whole line, without success. Troubled, he seeks out a grove where he can't see the sentries. He thinks he should ask the sentries what they have against him.

Then he sleeps. In the morning he had no memory of it.

Paolista Theology

THERE WERE LIVELY discussions among the Paolistas about the Jesuit plan to settle on the banks of the Paraná. It went without saying that they would be left alone until the grapes were ripe for picking. But the situation required constant monitoring to ensure that things were not left too late. The Jesuits, for whom despite everything the Paolistas had some respect, because they had managed to slither away with their skin intact and follow through on their interesting project, might perhaps conceive the notion of linking up with a couple of warlike tribes for protection. So they sent friendly Indian spies, Tupis, to track them and provide timely intelligence. The Tupis, powerful free tribes to the west and south, took an interest in the business and showed an understanding of the Paolistas' plans, having joined with them occasionally in alliance against tribes they did not like, which then as a rule found themselves heading for the Paolistas' ships.

The affair, as it slowly ripened, also became somewhat clearer from a spiritual-religious perspective. The two brightest sparks in the young town as far as spiritual-religious matters were concerned, the ailing governor's clerk and the curate, blew on the same horn. Mello the clerk, a waspish elderly fellow who had cunningly wormed his way into the role of political secretary, and what is more never indulged in quarrels, but as a former monastery schoolboy had a feeling for paper and home comforts and lived in the best-furnished quarters in the whole town (he had prospects, once the governor was out of the way, of taking up the reins himself), composed these thoughts:

"Between Sao Paolo and the Paraná lie rugged mountains, grasslands, swamps, restless tribes. It is good to know this. Whoever in the world opens his mouth like these Jesuit Fathers, first presenting themselves as thoroughly sensible and then acting like Lenten preachers, should take himself off to a monastery. But when the monasteries are full, as unfortunately appears to be the case, then they have made a good choice in this land along the Paraná. It is said to be fertile; they can immure themselves there. But if they imagine they have thereby achieved something notable, and will be spared because they depict it as a blessing to us that they settle there and provide a base of support for savage Indian tribes, then they are mistaken. We shall not be prevented from monitoring them to see whether they remain sound in their religion and their prayers. We shall play the Pope off against them."

The foolish old town priest, who had been run off his feet by the demands of the Jesuits, seconded him as far as he could. Mello despised him but found his religious twaddle useful for documents of various kinds. True, the clumsy crooked man came out with all sorts of oddities that could be explained only by wine and climate. The worthy Hyacinthus uttered such pearls of wisdom as this: "We must be made ready for Heaven, and that's the job of the Church. But preparations for Heaven must be kept within bounds. It's not as if we can all be angels right away. That would make Heaven superfluous. And at the end of the day, God the Father must have known what he was doing when he incarnated the first man. He had the chance to create us as angels, and did not. So we should go peacefully about our human affairs and not make overblown efforts to escape this God-given condition. What the Jesuits want, as we ourselves saw here, comes from excessive haste. We have time. We should combat our flesh patiently and calmly. Why kill it off so soon? We've had original sin ever since Adam. Original sin oppresses us terribly, but in the end it's a necessity, we can't do without it. We have accepted God's decision and become accustomed to our flesh and original sin. If someone wants to turn us into angels, we shall point the finger at heresy. The flesh is weak, yes, we needn't be ashamed of that, it's confirmed by revelation."

Mello listened with satisfaction to the ramblings of the old drunkard. Mello's slack, pale, wrinkled face never changed expression. He poured not too many glasses for Hyacinth when he trailed mud into his quarters, lest he die too soon.

At Whitsun this meek creature mounted the pulpit and preached to the dignitaries. He proceeded from Scripture: "When they which were about him saw what would follow, they said unto him, Lord, shall we smite with the sword? And one of them smote the servant of the high priest, and cut off his right ear. And Jesus answered and said, Suffer ye thus far. And he touched his ear, and healed him." This reflected honour on none other than the Paolistas: "The Jesuits tried to cut off one of our ears. But it's still there."

During the sermon the governor, that old sick man with holes and boils all over his face, slumped in his seat of honour in the little church. Mello stood at his side shouting comments from time to time into his ear, for he was almost deaf. He just stared ahead, he was already demented and half-dead, but still they feared him.

Arrival in Guayrá

THE GREAT PROCESSION arrived in the province of Guayrá. This was an extensive region on the left bank of the Paraná, from the Iguaçu river up to the Tiete. The eastern bank was the border of Portuguese territory, to the north lay unknown stretches of forest and swamp. The dark people who lived here – Tayaoba and Ibiraya – dwelt in scattered hamlets and tilled the soil. Here grew cedar, pine, spruce, bitter dates, there was wax and honey and gembe corn.

By the end of the trek, not many natives were following in the Fathers' wake. They had left for various reasons and returned to their home territories. The Fathers let it happen: they'll come back in time. And they preferred to have a free hand in this new country. They were welcomed by natives at a village not far from the Paraná river. No Whites for many miles around, no Whites had pursued them. They entered the peaceful village. Emanuel de Nobrega gave the signal: our journey is ended.

And the journey had to end. They were crushed by sickness, exertions, fears. For the first time it became clear what Sao Paolo and the death of Mariana had done to them.

They had fled from that calamitous town in a forced march. But however fast they moved, they could never escape what had befallen them. The loss of Mariana, of just one young Father, had thrown their whole mission into disarray. A harsh glare emanated from the corpse they had all seen lying among savages on the riverbank, and this sulphurous glow pursued them through the forest. They sensed that the Paolistas were not their only enemy, there was also the desolate uncanny forest, the green surging sea that harboured not just insects, birds and monkeys, but dark people as well, it reached out for them, it had seized Mariana and dragged him into its terrible maw. Once they believed that Jesus would rise up against such a deed, and vanquish this primal world once and for all.

The Superior imposed a lengthy vow of silence, exempting only speech necessary for practical matters. In this way they came through the crisis after two weeks. And when they heard each other's voices again and gazed on one another, their next task was to understand: we have arrived. And now they could turn their attention calmly to the natives.

It was a joy.

Why was it so boundless and exalted, the joy they felt? They knew: because they did more than convert heathen and earn absolution. They themselves gained something. For the first time they were to become, were allowed to become, what they had so long and so readily believed themselves to be. They could emulate Jesus. Poor Mariana had enabled this.

And while they felt this, they felt something else too. What they would establish here would be unlike anything since the world began.

Jerusalem, o holy city, your name is peace. You who were built in Heaven from living stone, a thousand angels garland you like a woman, you have been chosen by blessings that none can name, adorned by the Father's grace. Jerusalem, you partake of the Beloved's treasure, you most beautiful of queens, the bride of Jesus, shining city of Heaven.

A few sowers of God's word had already penetrated into this fine populous region. They were but passing clouds, fructifying for a short while the fields onto which their goodness falls, but the fields soon revert to their former stony barrenness. Father Bolaños, long dead, had passed through here and preached, he was a pupil of the saintly Franciscus Solano who had taught in the hilly Chaco region to the northwest. After Bolaños came Fathers Ortega and Fields to continue his work as best they could.

And just when the persecuted Jesuits from Sao Paolo arrived, there appeared one morning two Fathers of their Order, come separately into the region from Tucuman where the Provincial of their Order, despatched by Rome for the new continent, had his residence. Alone in the village with just five Fathers – the others were swarming across the land, dividing up territories and exercising their spiritual profession down to the smallest detail – Emanuel was approached one morning by two sturdy sunburnt men in the habit of his Order, accompanied by some Guaraní. Axe handles protruded from their big knapsacks, they were armed with large cudgels, and called cheerful greetings to Emanuel from under black wide-brimmed hats. The cheats, tricksters, Paolistas who disguise themselves in our habit, here they are again, how far must we flee to avoid them – his heart faltered. He was sitting on a mat outside his little house, with two Guaraní. But they cheerfully shrugged off their knapsacks, and as he jumped up embraced him one after the other as if he were a thing, and spoke to him. He recognized them, brothers Cataldino and Maceta. "Look at you, you vagabonds!" The natives were happy to see the three Fathers standing together laughing. They crowded around.

The two stalwart Fathers had much to tell their Superior. Some was tricky to discuss, but they delivered it all in the kind of cheery tone that Emanuel and the others had lost along the way. Ah, breathed Emanuel, your faces and your voices are lovelier than cool shade.

They had been in Villarica and Ciudad Real, places south of the Paraná, along the road from the town of Asuncion on the Paraguay where the governor of the province had his seat. Words tumbled from the mouths of the two pious tramps with their huge beards.

Cataldino: "Asuncion. The bishop sits in Asuncion. But not a single priest far and wide. When we passed through the town we had to stay on for two weeks simply to hear confessions. The good bishop can't manage it all. And what they know of Christianity there..." They shook with laughter. "We would never have recognized it."

Maceta: "In Villarica there's a solitary monk, he looks like a vagabond. We asked him what's the matter, why do you roam around like a tramp, how can people respect you? He said: 'And what do you look like?' We said: 'We're on the road.' Then he says he's always on the road, all the time, back and forth, they need him out there. And it's true. He didn't have a scrap of monk's habit on him. They stole it along the way, he says, to do mischief with it. What did he wear? Thigh boots with spurs from a stray rider, hose that he tailored himself, a nobleman's waistcoat all in tatters, and a big plumed hat from which he hadn't even removed the feather. 'It's a pretty feather,' he says, 'why should I remove it, it's not a monk's habit.' He's a stout fellow. His Order's not bothered. He spreads his Christianity out there, Emanuel, baptism after baptism. Where we came, between Villarica and Ciudad Real, the whole world's been baptized by him and everyone bears a formal saint's name." And all three laughed and laughed from the bottom of their hearts. For the natives, who understood none of it, this was sumptuous entertainment, they followed the conversation intently, and laughed along.

Maceta: "What should we say. The people still haven't the slightest inkling of our faith, they're content with the mere name, and the same goes for our good monk."

Cataldino: "And the other one we met was a good-for-nothing ignoramus. He does baptisms too. But only in Villarica where he lives, he spares the region round about. He's an embittered old crank who esteems the native people not at all. He has varicose veins in his legs, and doesn't walk. Every day he said to us: 'Let it alone! Give it up! You are raw beginners. The Indians are a dead loss. We should use them as they are. Don't cast pearls before swine. They're happy enough just to guzzle and drink. Then all they need is a bit of fear and someone to put them to work.' We thanked him and left. The natives in the town, and Whites too, were well content with him."

Maceta: "But us they couldn't abide. They didn't like us at all. Oh this is a hard nut to crack, brother Emanuel. You haven't made your way around these parts yet, you had your little dance in Sao Paolo, but it's rife out here as well. The old monk in Villarica was right: the natives like to eat and drink; anything we tell them goes in one ear and out the other, they're children, children. And then the Whites, the Christians."

Emanuel frowns: "There are Whites here? Where?"

Maceta: "Not many, but too many. All over the place, a few here, a few there. In Villarica and Ciudad Real and Asuncion. When we came to Villarica, exhausted, they already knew we were coming and – they closed the gate, purely from a desire for order: robbers might come. We stood outside with our company of new converts, who had led us there. They were not a little astonished when we arrived after such a long and fatiguing journey at a town where Whites, our people, dwell, and they slam the gate in our faces. We spent the night outside and took comfort in the thought that it was all for the sake of good order. In the morning they were gracious enough to open up. They heard us out, they were respectable people, but they had something against us. They found us suspicious. Why? They feared we'd upset their business. I told them that was not our plan. We don't concern ourselves with business. They led us into their council chamber, we apologized for being so scruffy, but they aren't bothered by that, they're used to it, they look no better. We didn't even seem scruffy to them. It all hinged on the *encomienda*, the labour tribute, I'm sure you know about it, Brother Emanuel?"

Emanuel nodded gloomily: "Who does not?"

"They have authority to put defeated Indians to work. The governor has them mustered in brigades, then he allocates them to work for himself or others in fields, houses, mines, as needed. It's a lease system, the people have to pay." Emanuel was as unsmiling as they, the natives who stood around had also stopped laughing, as if they understood.

Maceta fidgeted with his staff, they had both laid theirs on the mat: "That is their main concern. We said you have the wrong idea about us, we certainly don't mean to take away your profits. We even explained that we fully share their opinion of the Indians' laziness and that they misuse their freedom and must be induced to work. It was no use. Their minds were made up. They must have noticed the snag in our argument. They insisted: they had their own priests already, they were happy with them, there wasn't enough work there for two more. The natives already had all the Christianity they need. Demand is supplied. We should set up shop somewhere else. They crowded around us with menacing looks. We asked them to let us stay in town for a week, so we could preach. We saw there was nothing doing. In the house they provided for us they guarded us like criminals."

Emanuel nodded: "That's Sao Paolo."

"We wanted to hasten our departure. We sent one of our natives into the area we planned to head for, to ask a cacique to come and be our guide." Then sturdy Maceta hammered on the floor with his staff, the natives looked shocked: "And then that gang seized him when he came to the gate, chained him and flung him in jail."

Emanuel: "In Villarica?"

"We lodged a complaint, of course. We threatened. When we explained that we needed him for our journey, otherwise we'd be forced to stay, they let him go. Oh, what we had to do along the way to pacify the good man!"

Emanuel: "Did they receive you well in the cacique's village?"

They both beamed: "Wonderfully! They could see who we are." Emanuel was pleased.

The Document

THAT EVENING HE asked how they saw their work here, in light of experience so far. And now they produced a surprise, and proud Emanuel was humbled when he took in his hand the sheet of paper that emerged from Maceta's knapsack, among scraps of food and knives.

Here they had nothing more and nothing less than an order elicited from the royal governor. The document declared that the governor grants to the two missionaries Joseph Cataldino and Simon Maceta of the Society of Jesus, or to such others as may join with them from the same or another society with the aim of promulgating Christianity in the province, licence and authority of the following kind: The missionaries of the Society of Jesus, whether named or others, may, wherever they consider it expedient or important or necessary, bring together and combine indigenous people in a given place for the purpose of instruction, and no town, fortress or settlement in the vicinity may interfere with said instruction. They may defend themselves and lodge an appeal against any attempted attack by others.

The two bold Fathers had carried this extraordinary document in the knapsack, and admitted that they had neither shown nor mentioned it to anyone other than the Provincial in Tucuman. They handed it over to Emanuel, their Superior. Emanuel's face was friendly: "There's a regular plan of campaign here." It turned out they had no particular strategy in mind. Maceta declared proudly: "As soon as we heard of your difficulties in Sao Paolo – Father Torrez in Tucuman told us of it – we at once said: this is not the way to go about things, they won't let us in, they're afraid we'll tie their hands and take away their labour force – and once anyone is caught in their *encomienda* they never come out again. So there's only one thing to do: preach, instruct, baptize, before they land up in the *encomienda*. Before! You see the point. Father Torrez discussed this with the governor as well."

"I do see," said Emanuel, astounded.

Maceta again laughed his good-humoured laugh: "One thing is clear: we suffered on that side of the Paraná in the same way you suffered on this side, and we have drawn the same lesson from it. Agreed? Or not?"

"Of course," nodded Emanuel.

≈≈≈

They retired early to their hammocks, and Emanuel could not master his thoughts. What had they brought to him! He lay half awake. He dreamed.

And Mariana, tender youth, his friend, approached. When he was close to Emanuel he turned his back. "Why do you show me your back, Mariana?"

Slowly Mariana turned to face him: "So, you'll gather them, go into the forest with them?"

"Yes."

"Then why did you scold me for doing so?"

"Is that what you wanted?"

"Yes, and even more than you." Mariana gave a smile, Emanuel's heart melted, he offered Mariana his hand. When Emanuel opened his eyes in the dark, dogs were barking, he could still hear Mariana's voice: "Even more than you." Mariana's smile unsettled his deepest being.

Emanuel sat up in his hammock. How long shall I keep you in my thoughts, Brother Mariana, and trade riddles with you. Now here you are again. Surely you won't tempt me to do what you have done? Do not demand overmuch, just because we've already forgiven you.

Emanuel lay back down. Mariana was stretched out among green leaves on red-brown earth. Shadows passed over his shining face, his face grew wider, brighter, it was a cloud-drift, Emanuel flew into it.

He fell into blissful sleep.

There was no choice.

≈≈≈

Some unpleasantness occurred in the village. The two new missionaries had allowed an elderly White man to accompany them from Ciudad Real. Emanuel kept this Spaniard, a carpenter, back for a few weeks, during which he ventured out from time to time into the surrounding country. He was a touching sight, apostolically pious. Whenever he returned there was something more missing from his garments; he had given it away, said: "You Fathers preach with words, like priests. A poor layman can't do that. I share the little that I have, and hope thereby to win some hearts." He proved proficient and knowledgeable in the language lessons he gave, and when he declared one day that he must leave, they were loath to let him go. But how great was their shock, after he disappeared, when angry faces appeared all around and they learned that the man had used his time there to buy children from poor families and send them off as slaves. The natives in the village where the Jesuits lived suspected them of having a hand in the matter. Gruff Maceta cried: "I'll run after him and break his legs." Although the Fathers protested their innocence, hostility towards them in the village persisted.

Other news, just as bad, came from the region of Asuncion, where brothers Maceta and Cataldino had toiled. Here forced-labour gangs had risen against the Whites, it came to open revolt, natives had killed Whites, the military were mobilised, the authorities in Asuncion trumpeted: the Jesuits have a hand in this.

Father Emanuel asked the two missionaries what was behind it, they looked at each other, worried at first, then smirked: "Did we instigate it, or did we not? No, we did not instigate it."

"Go on."

"You tell, Maceta." – "You, Cataldino." – "Why me?" – "You're the clever one."

"We told the natives, when they complained about the forced labour and wouldn't listen to us, yes, we told them: they are not slaves in the way they assumed, but were entrusted by the Spanish Crown to the good keeping of the Spaniards, for a certain time. And we have come to tell them this and teach Christianity. And so they learned that God in Heaven created all people and that we are all equal before Him. The Lord in Heaven – we couldn't conceal this from them, when they asked – stands over even the King of Castile. Of course we also encouraged them to meekness, moderation and obedience."

Maceta said: "That's exactly how it was."

"No one can use that against us, it's standard Christian doctrine. Anyone who objects commits a terrible sin."

Emanuel frowned: "You are good missionaries. But the people misunderstood you."

Cataldino: "And you, Brother Emanuel, when the Paolistas stole your robes and carried people off, what did you say to the tribes who wanted to attack you?"

"I did not shrink from explaining that rogues had donned our garments."

Cheerful Maceta: "Honesty is always the best policy!"

Then all three laughed heartily, and Cataldino clapped his friend on the shoulder:

"An angel led you to our Order, my child, to learn how to obey and hold your tongue."

Cataldino said that many refugees were already turning up from this rebellion in the south. Emanuel took a deep breath: "Many more will flee and come to us. Render unto God what is God's, and unto Caesar what is Caesar's. They flee from Caesar. We must make a decision." He drew the document from his robes and laid it out on his knee: "We share the same fate as the dark people. They are persecuted, and we are persecuted. If we were to decide merely to spout Christianity, we would have just as easy a time of it as the others. But because we are in earnest, matters have become deadly serious."

Cataldino: "I believe it, brother, and when I look at you I know that, as long as we only talked about it, we had a hard time. When we go all out, it'll be easier for us."

A tremor went through Emanuel: "You think so?"

"Don't you?"

Emanuel, leaning forward: "Why were we sent here?"

Cataldino: "And why did you and your people suffer Sao Paolo? It's intolerable merely to spout Christianity."

Emanuel stood up. Cataldino and Maceta too. Unable to control himself, Emanuel embraced them both: "You are the voice of Heaven. Stay with me."

The Plan

THEY WERE BOTH overjoyed when he quietly outlined to them his plan to evade every White attack, sever all connections, and find their own territory where they could live with the natives and teach them. The plan, as he unfolded it, now became clear to him for the first time. It became so astonishingly clear and was so complete that it seemed to him that it was not he who spoke: the plan was speaking through him.

"They can label us enthusiasts, they will do so. But only for a time. If I hold up a little seed and threaten a great mountain with it, the mountain will laugh and say: I only have to turn on my side and there will no longer be a seed. But let the mountain split apart, let the seed fall in a crack and sprout: the little plant shatters the rock. We shall not allow ourselves to be suppressed. How does the

Church fight, wherein lies its power? It's enough to make you weep. You know as well as I. It would never have come to heresy in Europe if the Church had not shown so clearly what it is, and if so many had not gone hither and thither making of Christianity a mere wordplay. It's a catastrophe for all of us. Our Saviour went about and gathered his flock. It never was a large one, and he died, but they were the apostles. We must follow him. We cannot reject the path of sorrows."

They swore to keep the secret until everything had been thought through. What they then decided was to found a small settlement not far from the place where they now dwelt. There they would gather new arrivals and pupils, they would learn there – and live like Christians! Singly, and in families. There was nothing for it: they would live there too.

When this had spoken through Emanuel – in fact it was already contained in the document the two monks had brought, although not in such good faith – they felt firm ground beneath their feet. The target was planted. Emanuel set to work without delay. He took the old cacique of the place, who had granted him hospitality, into his confidence.

≈≈≈

The cacique had allowed himself to be baptized by earlier missionaries, for obscure reasons (perhaps he thought to be rid of them more quickly). His baptismal name was Christopher, but he continued blithely to use the name Parayata. Old Parayata, a thickset loyal leader, had always thought that the powerful Whites who once honoured his village with a visit would approach him again on mission business. He waited long for a sign of recognition, and so was deeply satisfied when the White chief finally invited him to a confidential discussion; up to now the Whites had always been his guests, no official meeting had yet taken place. He painted himself formally for this diplomatic occasion, put on arm rings, took up his shield, his hefty spear, stuck feathers around his waist. Then that morning he sent two gourds of fresh beer to Emanuel's little house, together with two mats for himself and his escorts. As they made ready to set out, he loaded his three companions with fruit and mash.

When Emanuel saw them coming and vanished into the house in order to receive them properly, he was puzzled that the chief should bring an escort, he had already puzzled over the mats that had been sent. Then all became clear: the invitation was to an important discussion, he had delivered it in a particularly grave tone, the chief was therefore treating it as a major political event, and so everything was on the right track.

They sat down outside on the mats.

As he sat across from the stately silent people, Emanuel felt that a private and confidential session with Christopher, the cacique, pupil of those earlier missionaries, might have been a better way to broach his plan. But the ball was rolling. The dignified silence of the grave visitors lasted forever. Emanuel had his native assistant, young Mapiare, serve the mash and beer. They ate, drank. It took a long time. Meanwhile they exchanged courteous enquiries about their health. When Mapiare had cleared away the gourds and mash bowls, Emanuel and Parayata exchanged expectant looks. Each had to allow the other to open the proceedings.

The chief began by expressing gratitude for the invitation and the hospitality. He and his companions bowed where they sat. Now Emanuel heard with his own ears that, although it was of course Christopher, it was the cacique of the place who sat across from him. How to reveal the secret? He must begin with a formal account of his voyage from Europe across the mighty ocean, as if he had never met Christopher, for the cacique Parayata had heard none of the background. When Emanuel's account of his arrival in this place was completed, the old man took the floor to remark with pride that he had once greeted other great White men in this very house. Not a syllable about his baptism.

Emanuel picked up on the reference to the earlier missionaries – how rich in blessings their work had been, across great distances they had carried tidings of the great Father in Heaven, far away beyond the stars, and did the cacique not agree that these were great tidings. He agreed. And whether those who had received these tidings and accepted baptism should be protected. The cacique agreed, he discussed the question with his companions, who were laconic. Emanuel felt that he had touched on a sensitive point. After this last question the four native visitors looked at him expectantly, they realised this was the reason for the invitation.

"Will you, cacique Christopher, help us to protect all of you who have received the glad tidings? Almighty God and the spirits who are His helpers will be surer to stand by us and hold back the persecutors if we join together, direct our prayers together to Him in a church, and if we keep the feasts and commandments that He has ordained."

The cacique kept him waiting a long time for an answer. Reservations had emerged even during the whispered conversation with his companions, two of the people were not baptized. Now none of them understood exactly what Emanuel was proposing. The whole discussion was somehow not to the cacique's liking. Emanuel felt he should speak more simply.

"The great Lord in Heaven, Creator of all, requires us to worship Him in a beautiful house, sing and bring offerings. He requires us to teach our children to know Him and worship Him. And so we have decided to build Him a lovely house at a good location some miles from here."

The cacique approved of this, and his companions made no objection. They even declared themselves ready to help with the building. The place should not be too far away, they wanted the church to be within sight.

Emanuel said straight out that this would not do. The faithful and their dependants must live together near the church. The natives looked at each other in dismay. The cacique suggested: "Of course. We live here."

The answer came: "Any who attach themselves to us must live near our church." (Oh this is hard, thought Emanuel, I shall never succeed, help me, Eternal, grant me the right words.)

The visitors sat with downcast eyes on the mat and said nothing. Clearly they were silent out of courtesy. They did not understand what their host was asking of them.

Emanuel: "The great Lord in Heaven chose you, because

He sent us first to you. He requires those who are Christians and baptised not to oppose His commands. You are to build a church for Him in a good place not far from here, and live beside it with your families."

This was clear. Emanuel felt relieved. He had broken down the barrier between him and his guests, he was no longer a stranger receiving a cacique, but the propounder of a doctrine. They avoided eye contact and kept silent. Emanuel repeated his words phrase by phrase, he had the upper hand. And now, after a short low dialogue, one of the two unbaptised natives took over from the indecisive cacique: they would carry Emanuel's message to their people. Emanuel nodded. Let them talk it over.

His servant passed the gourd around, they spoke of a woman in the village who had long been sick, the cacique thanked Emanuel for his visits to her, one of the companions said thoughtlessly they already knew who was to blame for her illness, the cacique looked at him in dismay. Emanuel left them in their embarrassment, then warned against wicked practices that could attract the wrath of almighty God. The old man eagerly agreed. Soon they stood up.

As they left, the cacique stood solemnly before the priest and repeated: they would carry Emanuel's message to their people. The old man, in his ceremonial garb and conscious of his dignity, bowed to the Whites. He felt himself fully a cacique faced with a weighty decision, when he said: "I shall wait for a dream."

Emanuel did not know what to say. He remained courteous, grave.

Custom does not permit it

THE FOUR VISITORS were deeply unhappy, and for the whole day dared not say a word about the conversation. They were pressed hard, but would wait until next day to address the village. It was a serious matter. They hoped that in the meantime the chief would have a dream, or some other sign would appear. But the old man emerged troubled from his night, which was sleepless, and the other three remained silent. So he had to speak.

Old Parayata was the unhappiest of men. That morning,

before they went to parley with the oldest and most important people, he held an inconclusive conversation with his companions and asked to be excused. But the two unbaptised men took no part in the discussion. This saddened Parayata. He knew a storm would burst over him at the assembly.

In the chief's house ten young and old men sat in a circle, including the medicine man, the same age as the chief and his near relation. Parayata reported the white priest's invitation word for word, his three companions repeated it and added other bits from the conversation.

At once a sombre mood fell over the company. Even the pugnacious sorcerer sat in shocked silence. They waited for him to speak. He spoke: "Ever since the Whites came to our forests and rivers they have brought misfortune. Wherever they come they steal people and take them into slavery. Priests come with them, they too harm us and slander us. We can no longer worship our own ancestors."

Parayata: "You have heard: the great Lord in Heaven has spoken, and demands that the Christians and those who are baptised should build a church and live next to it."

The sorcerer at once answered: "The great Lord of the Whites will destroy us."

They waited for Parayata to speak. He kept silent, for he shared his relative's opinion. The medicine man took the floor: "The great Lord in Heaven to whom the Whites pray helps them. He helped them voyage here. He tells them they should come to our villages and take our people into slavery. His priests go unarmed, they think to lead us into slavery without force."

Then Parayata spoke: "All he asked was that Christians, and those who are baptised, should build a church and live next to it."

Now one of the others who had been at the meeting with Emanuel turned to the chief: "We could not speak in the stranger's house. He is our guest. We sat there in the house that we assigned to him as a dwelling. A stranger who dwells in the house that we assigned to him cannot issue instructions. If he has any instructions from a foreign people or a foreign god, he should send envoys and invite the people to hear him."

These words made a deep impression. Parayata nodded, the others too. They were all very relieved. The old cacique declared: "He went against custom. I did not want to annoy him at the house. He does not know our ways. We shall let him know."

Now they had the formula. They sat peaceably together and drank. They agreed to send presents to Father Emanuel one day soon, using trustworthy people who were not Christians and not merely envoys, tasked to explain that no reply could be made by the village to the communication conveyed by him to the cacique, as it was not permitted by custom.

Forced into Exile

THAT SAME MORNING, brothers Maceta and Cataldino felt uneasy in Emanuel's house. They disliked the way Emanuel had presented himself before Parayata as a priest of the White god, and in effect issued an order to the cacique. "Things are not yet ripe," they argued. But Emanuel was content and calm: "I didn't want to. But I was driven. It will ripen. We shall bring it to fruition." With memories still fresh of the way they had been hounded out of Spanish towns, they begged Emanuel to be cautious, to ask the Provincial first before taking the next step. At this he had to laugh: "Wait for months? Ask? But I have your document." Better they had not shown it to him.

They kept their ears open in the village. Emanuel waited the next morning, and the day after. No answer came. The two monks, who had lived among the tribes, knew what that meant. "Prepare yourself for a formal answer, an official answer." After the first few days they were no longer so anxious. It was certain what the missing answer would be, they were just curious to see in what form it would be clothed.

Then the little delegation appeared, accompanied by young warriors who stood sentry before the house. Presents, together with notice of the delegation, had reached Emanuel the evening before. The object of the rigmarole became clear after half an hour of silent courteous sitting, with the information: "A response by the village to the communication of the White Father, our guest, to the cacique of the village is not possible. Custom does not permit it."

Although Emanuel had braced himself for a rejection, his heart missed a beat. He pulled himself together. The elaborate composition of the delegation showed that this was an act of state-craft. He fulfilled his role with imperturbable dignity. Maceta and Cataldino helped.

After the natives left, Emanuel felt ashamed, and doubled up in vexation. "They are fools. They forced the comedy on me. Such nonsense."

Cataldino comforted him: "It all went well. It could have been worse. We thought they might give us our marching orders."

Emanuel grieved quietly: "Our Christians have left us in the lurch." He struggled for words: "So everything will remain as it is. You said you no longer want merely to spout Christianity. No arguing with that. You'll preach and go on. Dear brothers!"

Cataldino: "Not at all, Brother Emanuel. After all, we were the first to run to Brother Torrez, our Provincial, to complain of our mishaps. Torrez at once said: 'So, what you are planning is good.' And since fate, the document, was there, he gave it to us and said: 'You've shot their fox,' and embraced us."

Emanuel: "So he expects something from you."

Cataldino: "That's why we sought you out."

"You see how I'm fixed. They lured me into an ambush. I don't know how I got there. I didn't want to talk to the whole village."

Cataldino laughed: "You see, pact with the Devil."

Emanuel: "Enough! We'll say no more about it. I think of the apostle's words in the Epistle to the Thessalonians: 'Ye are witnesses, how holily and justly and unblamably we behaved ourselves among you that believe: As ye know how we exhorted and comforted and charged every one of you, as a father doth his children.'"

They were happy to hear these words.

≈≈≈

But the situation could not be retrieved. As the Fathers set more intensively about their missionary work of preaching and instruction in the village and outlying areas, people evaded them. Friendly conversations were broken off using various excuses, mistrust was evident. Through a chance encounter in the manioc plantation, clever Cataldino was able to engage the cacique in a dialogue; the old man declared frankly: "Everyone says you want to make slaves of us. You want to destroy our village, and we are supposed to serve the Whites in your village." With tears in his eyes, the old man explained that he must be careful not to be seen together with a Father. It had come to this. They would take away his title of cacique, which he inherited from his father. He left quickly.

Cataldino clenched his fists. What was this? Ever since that diabolical document came into their hands, they had lost all peace and everything went awry. Now they never spoke of it, the document lay buried, weighted down with stones in a chest. But the mischief continued.

The son of the cacique had a wife who was still young. Some years before, the wife had cruelly fallen into the clutches of Whites during a so-called punitive raid, and was taken to a forced-labour brigade in Villarica. There she toiled at first on the land, and then as a house servant. The missionary Fields, whose pupil she was, baptised her, and his intervention brought her release from the brigade. She came to this village. The chief's son took her to wife. When Emanuel asked why she no longer came to lessons with her little boy, and why she did not persuade her husband to attend, the woman proved recalcitrant. "You don't come to confession. Do you know what punishment may befall you?" She looked shyly up at the priest, but her expression remained obstinate. He enticed from her the statement: "My husband wants to become chief. But he'll throw me out."

"Because you are baptised?"

She nodded. He blazed: "I shall go to your husband."

They were standing outside the Father's house. She made him move to the side where no one would see them: "They say it is your fault that a woman fell sick."

"Who says this?" – "Everyone."

"Even the cacique?" – "He says nothing."

"And you?" – "I," she wept, "I wish I had never set eyes on a White man."

"In God's eyes there are no white people or brown people."

"Who brought you to this place? Who killed my father? Now my husband casts me out."

"I shall give him a warning."

"If he knows I have spoken to you, he will kill me and my child."

Emanuel could not detain her too long in this clandestine encounter: "Come to me this afternoon, before the lesson."

Two Fathers were sitting with Emanuel, he ushered her into the next room, screened off by a mat wall. The woman looked expectantly at Emanuel. He asked: "Well?" She gave no answer. "If I am not to speak to your husband, then I shall speak to his father, the cacique."

"My husband will throw me out. When you leave the village I shall come with you."

Emanuel could not believe his ears. He crossed his arms over his chest, almost burst out laughing in astonishment. "What are you saying, woman. We Fathers roam without women."

"The people talk among themselves. They keep it from the old cacique. He is afraid. When will you leave? I shall go with you when you leave."

Slowly Emanuel understood. Here lay danger. He considered. He said: "Come to us, to the house, day or night. Bring your child as well."

"Do not delay too long."

As the Fathers discussed this, they were calm. So they would move on. Anyone wanting to join them would be welcome. There was no more talk of the document.

The woman came to Emanuel and was insistent. All the Fathers wore big beards that they trimmed from time to time. Emanuel did not notice the woman spying when next he trimmed his beard. The young man serving him was baptised, but he knew what it meant for hair to fall into someone's hand, and always buried it carefully. The woman came unannounced into the room as Emanuel seated himself for a trim, he waved to her to wait, she dropped her net pouch and gathered a handful of clippings. The great Emanuel had an admirer.

On the road again

THE VILLAGE PROTECTING itself against the White intruders did not immediately set an auspicious date to expel the strangers. There were also differences as to the method: drive away only the Whites, or baptised Indians as well.

Before any decision was reached, the Fathers tied their bundles.

When they found themselves still unmolested some hours away from the village, they saw a small crowd of natives approaching from the rear. These, just as downcast as they but also happy, were converts and new pupils of the Fathers. The Fathers greeted each in turn, and when towards evening they came to a grove of palms they settled down and thanked God with prayers and singing. In wonderment the Fathers tallied their flock. They were not many, and more than half had never attended for instruction. Relatives of converts, fearing to stay put. The old cacique was not among them. They explained that he had renounced his faith in order to keep his position.

As they sat around the fire that evening, near seventy strong, some setting up hammocks, others lying on beds of branches or on bare ground, the Fathers kept watch together. By the fire Emanuel opened the chest, threw away the stones, took the cursed document, burned it.

Now they were not so downcast. Young Maceta had to recite from the Psalm of the Lord's Mercy: "*He hath not rewarded us according to our iniquities. For as the heaven is high above the earth, so great is his mercy toward them that fear him. As far as the east is from the west, so far hath he removed our transgressions from us. Like as a father pitieth his children, so the Lord pitieth them that fear him. For he knoweth our frame; he remembereth that we are dust.*"

While the natives slept, the Fathers watched the fire. They were despondent again.

≈≈≈

Next morning they wanted to move on south. But, barely an hour along the way, several men and women gave their opinion that after only one more little hill and a big forest of palms, they will have arrived at their goal. They said: "Goal." The Fathers were astonished. What goal? They had envisaged a long trek. They yielded to the people, who clearly did not like wandering and were not equipped for a long journey.

It was still only early afternoon when they reached the place. But now the Fathers were perplexed. Slowly they understood the meaning of "goal". The people set calmly about the building of huts, and a dozen men were already in the forest gathering roots, fruit and honey.

What could you say? They had taken their weapons and hunting gear with them.

"Lodging in the forest," joked the Fathers that evening, running fingers through their beards. They had no wish to discourage the good people who had latched onto them. The first thing some of the baptised had done soon after their arrival was to use branches to mark out a site for the church. Moved, the Fathers let them get on with it. Oh, the children! They would be driven on a great distance, and then on, and endure the first attack from the village they had abandoned, and perhaps from another direction too.

Thus passed the first days in this wild lonely place, where not many months later the first simple wooden church will indeed rise up, built by these and other dark people under the guidance of these selfsame missionaries. Now all is savannah and bush, jaguars prowl. Within half a year there will be streets with huts and houses of clay, they will celebrate the visit of the Provincial Torrez.

How far must we roam to find peaceful pastures for our flock, thought the Fathers in those first days. We found no such place in Sao Paolo, nor on the way here, nor in the little village. Is there any place on Earth so blessed with God's mercy that we can worship Him there in peace?

Distant thunder

WHEN FIELDS DRY up and shrivel, and peasants stand outside their cottages keeping anxious watch – the sky is grey tinged with blue, no clouds appear, no freshness in the breeze – they are filled with despair. And yet already, many miles away beyond the mountains, all is in train to relieve their troubles. The coolness they long for is there, clouds gather in slender streaks, and merge. No one is alone in this world, everything is intricately interlinked, much that appears young and fresh is threatened from afar, the ground opens up beneath it even as it laughs, and much that has believed itself doomed suddenly regains its sap and shoots skyward.

While the Jesuits were teaching in that little village and then fleeing from it, events were in train across the Paraná to the west, on the Paraguay river, that would touch even them. On this river, in Asuncion, a new governor for the Spanish Crown had established himself. From his writing desk, I the King had loaded him with many fine commissions; the governor enjoyed a better fate than the rich man Don Juan de Sanabrar, who died before he could leave harbour, and his son, who survived the voyage but suffered shipwreck in sight of land. It was with astonishment that the new governor upon his arrival took note of conditions prevailing in this country, it was enormously big, most regions still untrodden, and innumerable savages lived there, living on this Spanish soil as if they had descended from the moon, utterly ignorant of Spain, the King, Jesus Christ, the Church. They were cannibals with gruesome tribal customs, Guaraní, Toba, Lingua, Chamacoco. Some pierced their lips, others shaved their skulls, still others filed their teeth. He was told many things, and he saw them himself in Asuncion, his seat. Most of what he heard repelled him. He hoped to put it all in order as soon as possible.

The governor signed himself expansively Alvaro Nuñez da Vera Cabeza de Vaca. The Crown had again chosen a rich man, able personally to bear the cost of fitting out a fleet. He was nephew to the man who had conquered the Canary Isles, which was the source of his wealth; but the fortune was much diminished since those days, forcing the nephew to strike out again for the New World. "In truth," he said gloomily to his son during the voyage, "I have no idea if I shall bequeath to you anything more than our glorious name. The King bestows commissions, and allows me to pay. Such is the fate of the nobleman. We shall play our part, come what may. But I fear what will become of us one day, when it's all over with the New World. I hear that nowadays there are only modest takings."

"Father, it's an enormous country."

"So I hope. Given the circumstances I wouldn't advise you to accept a position such as mine. Ours is a desperate plight. Like an army going ashore and burning its boats, I've put almost everything I own into this venture. Unless we strike lucky, we are lost."

The son shook his head bravely: "No matter. I'll just go voyaging like Great-grandfather."

"But will there be anything left to conquer?"

"Papa, with a Spanish sword and Spanish courage, one can always go further."

"I'm glad to hear it. Bah, there are already too many squatting over there in the New Indies, trading, haggling. It's our grave. In Italy and Germany one already finds noblemen engaging in trade." The son almost burst his sides laughing.

Asuncion was encircled by a stout palisade. Six hundred Whites dwelled within, most had native wives. Native families and groups of forced labourers lived in and outside the town. As well as growing crops, they raised livestock. For the horses and cattle released by the first conquerors had multiplied dramatically in the immensity of the grasslands, as had the jaguars that fed on them, but the fecundity of the cattle and horses outdid jaguar appetites. Governor Don Alvaro sat glumly in this hole with his noble son.

The bishop was a certain Don Reginald de Lizarraga, of the Order of Saint Dominic. With his long nose, sad expression and stooped posture, he looked like a bedraggled hen. His conversations with the governor dwelled incessantly on his digestive difficulties. A dirty idle place, this Asuncion, not enough vegetables, they set a whole ox in front of you as if you are a lion, and the people are so lazy they don't even roast the meat properly, they'd really prefer you to chew the meat from the living animal. And then the shortage of spiritual workers. Understandable, for who would come gladly to such a place.

Don Alvaro consoled the bishop in the matter of roast beef, he had brought good cooks with him. "But so did I," wailed the bishop. "They are the laziest!"

Don Alvaro, taken aback, would wait and see. And how goes it with assistance in spiritual affairs? Don Reginald: "One should really deem it inconceivable that the majority of savages still run around in the forests unbaptised. But I can't chase after them. We need assistance. I have none." Such were the plaints of the episcopal chicken.

When Don Alvaro heard this, his royal instructions spread out before him, he made a decision all by himself. They should see that he was here. Holy Thursday was not far off. On that day he would invite as many Indians as possible into town, to see something of his inauguration and gain a true sense of royal power and the Christian religion. A colourful blend of troop review and religious procession hovered before his eyes. All neighbouring tribes should be invited, all who creep about in forest and savannah. The festival will be celebrated with the greatest pomp. In satisfaction the governor dictated all measures to his son. Later he would provide a confidential report to the Council of the Indies and the King.

He could already tell during the preparatory phase just how much interest the inhabitants took in this event: street decorations, festive garments for the choir, new banners and emblems, carts with saints, accommodation, a great public feast, they wanted the whole lot. Of course, when it emerged that they were to pay for it they backtracked, found the whole thing overdone. But the governor would not allow his fun to be spoiled. He said in that case he would deploy his troops to collect the money. At which they gave in.

The native tribes regarded Asuncion as a fortress. They needed no envoys from other tribes to know what the Whites were; it was a long while since anyone had mistaken them for ghosts; manhunts had revealed their all too corporeal form. To the north, bands from Sao Paolo had swept through the region of the Apitare. Ever since the day when the White pioneers Mendoza and Salazar had come down the Paraguay and selected the site of Asuncion for a settlement, a haven equidistant from Peru and Brazil, from that day on the dark tribes knew all about labour brigades, manhunts, punitive expeditions.

When a new governor appeared in town and invited them to a Christian festival, they accepted. But not for the reason the Whites assumed. The tribes had heard that all citizens would take part in the procession, unarmed. When Spaniards go through the decorated streets to celebrate their god, they bare the shoulders, and even carry whips to scourge themselves in honour of their god. So they had heard. They planned to turn this custom to their own purposes. They arrived the day before, eight thousand warriors, with the bows and arrows they always carried that should not without further evidence be regarded as weapons of war. They relied on the hands of the Whites being busy with their little whips and on the nakedness of their shoulders, so that at a given signal they could unleash a hail of arrows.

On the morning of Holy Thursday, most of the invited Indians were admitted into the town. Many thousands of dark people stood in the long streets and squares where, as they were told, the solemn procession would pass. They marvelled politely at it all. They saw their masters at doorways and windows, and clambered atop their middens. They were so many that a White was hardly to be seen, and the Whites hastening among the dark people towards the church felt unease. The governor too was shocked when he looked from his window that morning to see a heaving mass of native warriors below. He asked what it meant, where were his officers and men. The answer came: these are the tribes we invited. And apart from a small guard detail at his house, all the Whites are in church. Doubtfully he put on his dress uniform.

Just when he had made himself ready with the help of his servant, an old Indian woman who kept his house came weeping into his chamber and threw herself at the governor's feet. The governor summoned the interpreter. The woman on the floor explained haltingly what she knew. She did not want the master and his son to go unarmed to the procession, they must protect themselves.

Don Alvaro, already angry at the colossal stupidity he had brought on himself with the whole affair, made a decision. He had the woman bound and locked in a small room. He sent the interpreter to the church with orders that every soldier should discreetly make his way to his unit, and at the same time told his guards to confine all Indians to the main street and square, and clear them all without exception from side streets and especially from the square in front of the barracks. When he was informed that the soldiers had reported to barracks, and the commander appeared and they agreed on a plan for the coming action, Don Alvaro sent several Whites as heralds through the streets to announce with bugle calls that hostile Yapigans, a fearsome tribe, were moving against the town. Let all caciques in the town present themselves at once at the governor's house to discuss a common defence.

Twenty unsuspecting caciques appeared in the yard. They were pleasantly surprised by the heralds' announcement, for the Yapigans held exactly the same opinion of the Whites as they. Down in the yard they were relieved of all weapons. Then they were led one by one up the stairs, bound and thrown into the room with the old Indian woman who had denounced them. As they all lay there the governor appeared with his guards, regarded them as they lay lifting their heads in rage. He had them informed: "I know your plan. You'll receive your punishment."

The town gates were closed. Instead of a procession, troops swept through the town with arquebus, cannon and horse, and the bound caciques were led from the governor's house. In the main square the mass of natives stood like a wall facing the soldiers, unable to move. All at once the noise ceased, as cannon were rolled out. Their caciques appeared between armed men. One after another they were hanged from the decorated guns on display for Holy Thursday. The thousands watched in silence.

Once the executions were completed, the governor announced that this was the penalty for the treason they had planned. He held several dozen in the town as hostages. The others were brought forward group by group to swear loyalty to him, governor of the Castilian King. At evening the gates were opened and the dismayed masses were ejected. Bows and arrows had all been confiscated.

This experience was a surprise for the Indians. It was followed by an even bigger surprise for the governor. A serious rebellion erupted. It was later said of Don Alvaro: "How strange that a man of his worldly experience, cleverness and religious zeal should not have enjoyed more success in Paraguay." His actions, as his forebodings on the voyage had already presaged, were not blessed with luck. His soldiers were unable to gain the upper hand in the insurrection that his cunning had fomented. They were drawn deeper and deeper into the country, towards the east.

It was the usual slog of war, in truth no longer as easy as in the days of the earlier conquerors. It was like wading through a swamp. When a captain accepted surrenders, the next day these were forgotten. When the Whites sought an eye for an eye, and by intention or accident rained their retribution down on innocent tribes, these were the very tribes who had remained the longest time aloof from any troublemaking. It was a terrible time along the Paraná river, the outcome of that Holy Thursday so cunningly contrived.

People slipped away north and east ahead of the troops of Don Alvaro and his captains. Refugees appeared in the province of Guayrá.

And as group after group fled across the Paraná, the clouds that had been gathering in the distance reached the droughty fields, the miserable refuge of the persecuted Jesuit Fathers.

Rain falls on Emanuel's field

WHEN EMANUEL HEARD from itinerant Fathers that frightened groups of natives including women and children had paddled across the Paraná and were wandering through the savannah – starving, for to compound the disaster locusts had descended on this country and devoured everything – he sat with the Fathers. It was all a tragedy. War, with all its racial hatred, desperation, hunger and ruthlessness, was approaching. "Our late brother Mariana warned of this. 'What will you achieve,' he asked, 'you quit Sao Paolo, but nothing has changed.' Let us gather our little community together! Let us protect it as best we can. We shall pray to God for help. Nobody is to stray too far from camp."

For the Fathers it was still a 'camp', even though natives were still felling trees and forming logpiles with gay abandon. Even Cataldino and Maceta were shaken by the news. "Better to disperse before they fall upon us." Meanwhile their dark adherents swarmed about the country, and joyfully led bedraggled groups to the Fathers! Always there were natives standing before the Fathers, behind them their latest families and groups, rescued refugees, expecting praise! And the refugees themselves, how trustingly they gazed into the faces of the Fathers, their last hope. What could they do but take them in.

This they did, not happily. When one late evening large numbers arrived and crowded around with anxious importuning, Emanuel lost his strength. He had to turn aside to conceal the wracking sobs he was powerless to control. "I am not weak," he said to Cataldino, who came to find him, "but what can we do, we few men. If soldiers cross the river, they will not ask if we are here, they will not spare the people on our account. And so our people too will be lost. Oh believe me, Cataldino, we are on the wrong path. We should only wander and preach."

Their unease did not penetrate to the people. The little group from the village was imperturbable. They imposed their will on the Fathers. They were a chosen band. They clung like burrs. Among the most passionate was the rejected wife of the chief's son, who had been a slave of the Whites in Villarica and had already endured so much. Not a morning when she failed to appear after matins to regain her life through some words – any words – from Emanuel. She was fierce and different, but dependable, meek, and a huge influence on others. And when she appeared before him during these stormy days – he as if unravelled after a sleepless night – she was astonished, could not understand. She became uneasy and never left his side. When he set her a new task – every day new refugees came – she at once returned to him. She would not be dismissed. She had no idea what ailed him. There were new people here, strangers, many who hated the Whites, had one of them bewitched him, who was it, how?

When Emanuel noticed her unease he questioned her, she was glad, gave evasive answers. Then he complained, sickly as he was, how hard it all is, she mustn't slacken, he needs help. She beamed: "What shall I do?" And as he continued to speak and reveal himself, she realised he was a man in despair, who needed encouraging. The rush of joy. In the wildest protestations of loyalty she gushed: none from the village and no one else would surpass her, oh, no one would attack them here, they wouldn't dare, all the tribes have their weapons, just let them come. She's a kind of Fury, thought Emanuel as she stood there, how strange even the women are in this country. It is the Amazon strain.

Now that she knew how things stood with him, she took a great deal in hand. She became a kind of tugboat for the Fathers, who were big and clumsy. She cared for newcomers, gave orders, to men too. It was all well meant, sometimes it went awry, caused an Indian muddle but no serious confusion.

Reluctant colonists

SO THE FATHERS gradually stopped resisting. They began to think together, work together.

The first to decide was Cataldino, the builder and carpenter. The many logpiles were an enticement. The way the natives botched the construction of huts irritated him. And as their numbers rose into the hundreds and crowds surged around them, sullen, idle, awaiting instructions, and no soldiers appeared, he roused himself. He said: "Now it's my turn." He formed a team and set to work.

He had little time for idolatry, even less for huts of branches and mud. First he wanted to build big barnlike accommodation rooms, with a normal roof, walls and floor for the families, and then some individual roofed houses, little by little. And as he set to work, issued orders and curses, the other Fathers got moving. The life-spirit revived. Theology and despair are just not enough. Emanuel with Maceta and Cataldino still dreamed of their lovely New Jerusalem.

"It won't be a new Jerusalem," scoffed blunt Cataldino, "but they'll have a place to live, that's a start." Over his black robe he wore at his side a fat satchel from which poked an axe and a carpenter's rule. He was in his element and dreamed up something new every day. A hospital was already forming in his head. Meanwhile he erected sheds for fishermen and hunters. "Whoever gives more than he can is a charlatan. If you behave yourselves you'll have a church soon enough. But first things first."

And once they had dug the first turf and made holes for the first posts, news spread about the neighbourhood and the people no longer had to go out to implore refugees: "Come to us, you'll be safe." They came of their own accord. In what was once a camp, it was as if the work of construction moved a crank and a wheel. A whole great invisible engine was set in motion.

The Fathers were dumbfounded. They observed the living tumult, the many separate desires that meshed together, the incessant movement, and felt themselves seized with it. And people even looked reverently at them, regarded them as the instigators, which they weren't at all! They hadn't even planned these huts, which had been forced on them.

And they joined in with a will. Governor Don Alvaro and his captain Salazar inflicted injury; we'll do what we can to repair it.

The flood of refugees abated. Emanuel sent into the country and pulled in all the Fathers who could be reached. The young town, which they no longer saw as a camp, seethed with people, a thousand already, disciplined workers were sorely needed.

Every day, every hour brought new difficulties. The situation was reminiscent of the great exodus from Sao Paolo through the forest, when crowds attached themselves and had to be fed. Now everything was even harder, people thronged in from every side, but it was also in some ways easier, even exhilarating. Everything grew almost by itself, all you had to do was monitor and organise. The Fathers discussed it, more bewildered than joyful.

Cataldino the sly sceptic said straight out: "We've exchanged roles, our dark friends and us. They set us tasks. We wanted to proselytize. We never get around to it."

Maceta, who had learned smithing, praised his people enthusiastically: "How they study the tools, how inquisitive they are about fire-making, smelting, every hammer blow interests them, as if they want to pocket everything you've got!" The other Fathers sang a similar song.

"The mouth must now remain silent," was the view of big Father Faber, who turned to fat everything he ate and yet was the first to volunteer at any heavy work, wheezing with enthusiasm. "Now we're building Christianity. We're building it out of wood and clay, and in mats for sleeping, and in streets."

"You forget the church," Emanuel smiled. And at once corrected himself: "But no, that is also made of wood, straw and clay."

And they were all happy. Natives attached themselves particularly to fat Faber wherever he appeared. It was his mighty figure and booming voice. They could think of no animal with such a voice, and because he always kept strictly to practical work they understood him more readily. Here everything went according to his will. And young Father Daniel, bellicose son of a Spanish admiral, now had a chance at command; the time of mourning was over, it was as if they stormed a fortress, he leapt into the breach.

Cataldino the builder swooned and rolled his eyes. "I hope we find some stone at last, for our brother Arminio. Stone is heavy, but especially beautiful and interesting, even more than wood. Then Brother Armino can get cracking, he learned the stonemason's trade from his father, and longs to show us how sandstone and granite, maybe even marble, are preserved in this climate. Dear brothers, just imagine, a house of real stone on the Paraná!" For him this was the height of feeling. Others too cherished the thought of a proper stone house that they would erect here and you could live in it, the heart at peace.

≈≈≈

Stone buildings did not appear so soon. They were not yet done with wood and clay, needed shovels, axes, nails. In his knapsack Maceta had a few screws of various sizes, which made a tremendous impression. He landed himself, foolhardy fellow, with the construction of a cedar cupboard. Hour after hour he had to take out the screws and let the people practice screwing into spare bits of board. The positioning of grooves for the little auger, the insertion of the screw, all this took up a whole day and formed, so he felt, a true bond between him and the people. The people were thereby won over to the Fathers' cause. They converted. A faith community? Obviously. It was all a matter of faith. The Fathers had only to keep eyes and ears open to note how the natives mixed everything up into strange concoctions: screws with the wanderings of John the Baptist in the desert, nails and hammer with the Crucifixion. And the Fathers, who worked on buildings with axe, saw, chisel, and who learned the Indian language, sweated and taught, soon saw how necessity had led them along a good path which they would never have found by themselves. The dark people fused all together their place of residence, house, street, the many new objects and their lessons. They gave things funny names. This was no house, but a cave along the refugee trail, the heavy nail that penetrated the rough log was implored not to hurt and not to keep Jesus suffering on his cross, it was called "Have-no-fear".

The Fathers' thoughts strayed beyond the town.

Items of iron and steel were in short supply, they needed seeds and woven fabrics. Sao Paolo was over there, they could send to it, but the monstrous journey was now out of the question (will they forgive us if we buy elsewhere?). So they despatched a little expedition southward, along the left bank of the Paraná, to the town of Ciudad Real where it lay north of the Pequiry river, which flowed into the Paraná. They had to cross the Ivahy and Paquierica rivers. Friendly natives of the Ibiraya tribe guided them. It was Tayaobas who escorted them on the return journey to Villarica on the upper Ivahy. But their mission failed in both Ciudad Real and Villarica. The little settlements, forts rather, surrounded by a cluster of colonists, had nothing the Jesuits needed, certainly not in such quantities.

So there were more discussions in Guayrá, and since the only choice lay between Sao Paolo on the coast beyond the Sierra Espinazo, and Asuncion to the west and south, they chose Asuncion. And after only two days of rest the shopping expedition set off again, this time with more people – bearers, oarsmen, boat builders, and they travelled a good stretch down the glorious Paraná. They detoured around that unlucky place, the waterfalls of Salto de Guayra where Mariana had drowned, and paddled on until people from the Apitare tribe showed them the way through their region, and this they did gladly, for the Fathers had with them Apitare people who had come to them as refugees.

Salonio and Bombardo Arminio, called Brother John and Brother Leonard, led this expedition. They reached Asuncion, and after a brief courtesy call on the priest went about their business. They were watched suspiciously for incipient signs of agitation, but none such occurred. They shopped, loaded up with great boxes, with sledgehammers, knives, saws, smith's tools, nails, files, fabrics, and placed orders with dealers in iron and cloth. They held long conferences with these, for the dealers hoped to cheat them and go north to Guayrá to do business on their own account. But the Fathers dashed all their hopes.

In the course of this they heard by chance of a great fortified town in the south, near where the Paraná empties into the ocean, which was named "Our Lady of the Good Airs", Buenos Aires, because of its good air. The dealers, who obtained many of their supplies from there, told of the wonderfully protected position and astonishing growth of this town. Salonio and Arminio listened to these stories with satisfaction, and made careful note. On the return journey, among the Apitares, who were now pacified, they fell now and again into preaching. Then they were happy to take to the water once more and row north, to home.

≈≈≈

The noise of war across the Paraná receded. The storm left behind a remarkable gift for the Jesuits, who had been sent here to convert the heathen: a thousand dark people who clung to them. There would be no more wandering and proselytizing.

In the first weeks more than a hundred died or left. Those who died were men and women who had lost their homes, their tribe destroyed, ancestors abandoned, chiefs and witchdoctors all dead and who, fleeing from Whites, found themselves among Whites. But what could these give, what could they protect against, even if you overcame your hatred and mistrust? People sickened away, the Fathers saw it, they called it homesickness and thought they could provide comfort. But it was a peculiar kind of starvation, manioc mash gave no nourishment, the fish they roasted did not taste like fish, the people lived in a great fear that could be read in their black silent eyes. They left their hair tangled and unoiled, skin unpainted, they wanted to die. They would return to the friendly ancestors, eat, drink, and restore their strength.

A small number of dark refugees went away again, strong, mistrustful people. They observed how the village grew around them and how their dark companions in suffering toiled. "What are you doing?" they asked, "are you building a fort for the Whites?"

"We're building a village, the White priests are powerful, they will protect us."

They spoke to the chief of the Whites: "Great priest, what will you do with our people?"

"We provide them a place to live where they are protected, we tell them of the great Lord in Heaven who made the earth and everything in it."

"You cannot protect us against the fire-tubes of the governor in Asuncion. Do not deceive these people."

"Stay with us. You will see that it is different."

"We have seen Whites, priests, soldiers, traders. We will not stay. You seem good people, but you are leading everyone into danger. Send them back to their homes. Explain to us, great priest, because your heart is good and only your skin has the bad colour, why do you interfere with us? What do you want of us, with your god who does not listen to you? You see in Asuncion and Villarica who it is he listens to. He listens to the governor, the captain and his men, he has equipped them with weapons we do not have and with these he leads us into death or slavery. Have you come to deceive these poor refugees, take away their last weapons?"

Talk as Emanuel might, it all went over the heads of these natives. The obstinate edgy people spoke: "If your mouth speaks the truth and you wish us no ill, then teach us to make fire tubes. We have heard why you White priests travelled over the sea. You were fleeing to us."

These shattering remarks settled like mildew on the White priests, who knew how justified they were. It was good that they so seldom heard such words. The bitter accusers, who were not numerous, went away.

The flywheel spins

PEACE UPON THE grassy plains of Guayrá.

The Jesuits set to, taught, gave directions. The flywheel spun. The lines of a main street became visible, a square was marked out, a church rose out of the savannah soil. Grass, forever being dug up, grew again inexhaustible, lovable, innocently importunate, the slender green points entreated: please don't forget us. And the Whites did not forget; they directed the uprooting, for they were here to fulfill a new law, the law of Man the planner, master of Nature, no time for relaxation and play. Fences were built against wild beasts, which had to withdraw into the savannah to make way for a theatre human and divine. It was not long before they sent by boat to the nearest Spanish town to enquire about a bell, and altar furniture.

Furious toil devoured the brothers. Sometimes Emanuel was

seized by horror: this is not what we intended, for God's sake, we must turn about, flee, what have we let ourselves in for.

But then, after such nights, the dark people would appear for early Mass, and the hammering would start up in the smithy, their smithy, they were so happy to be blacksmiths, and the clattering and running in the streets, men calling, men singing, women carrying infants, the infants demanded a drink, boys played with monkeys, everything was as it should be, and we made it that way. Who could interfere, who had the right to disturb it? We intended it, did not intend it: now no one bothered with such questions.

≈≈≈

As the settlement grew around and over them, a visit by the reverend Provincial of their Order, Torrez, accompanied by the young padre Ruiz de Montoya, took them by surprise. They had not expected such a joy! And such happy words and blessings from the mouth of the old worldly-wise man. He stayed with them for two weeks. "Have no fear," he said, "keep hold of what you have, let no one drive you away. They won't dare. And should they dare, see to it that they burn their fingers. A goodly fight, in Christ's name! And all the better under the sign of Christ than under the coat of arms of some nobody."

He spouted fire and was glad to unburden himself. He saw the little place as a fortress against the monsters that would assail it: "Let them come. We would like to discuss what name to give this place. We won't be impetuous and jump the gun. But if not this place, then before long some other will be named Saint Michael, and anyone who wants can pit himself like a dragon against it. In old Europe they do to us as they like, those kings and lords. They'd like us to be the fig leaf for their sins. Our Ignatius de Loyola tore the mask from their faces and spurred his horse, rode away, lance on his arm, and down with them all in the name of Jesus Christ. To Hell with all governors and captains! There is no work more holy."

One morning the old man walked with Emanuel and young Montoya outside the settlement, for he loved two things apart from his faith: the dark people, and Nature. The wide fields had not yet recovered from the plague of locusts, and it was the dry season, forlorn islands of trees stood on the undulating plain. Leafless branches. If you looked east, the plain stretched away into the distance, vast and sombre. The yellow sun, although still low in the sky, breathed its mighty breath of fire down onto them, and the broad plain seemed to take a notion to start wildly up and race for the cool horizon.

Behind the three bearded Jesuits in their sandaled feet, black robes girded up, staff in hand, trotted a few dark people. And when the little group had wandered half an hour into the countryside, two lines of mighty trees rising green behind them along a water-course, the natives one after another uttered a little tremulous cry, everyone stopped, they peered tensely over the grass. All at once two of the people leaped on Torrez, Emanuel and Montoya, and without a word snatched their staves from them. At almost the same moment a huge bright jaguar stood before them, crouched as if ready to spring. The Fathers had already seen many jaguars from a distance and close to, but never had one approached so near to them.

It was a big, hungry, irritable beast. The two natives leaped forward with the staves, held them by the ends, and offered them to the angry cat.

The beast dropped to its belly and bit into a staff from below. It clenched its jaws, slavered and rolled its eyes. The man holding the staff began to work it, the beast tried to pull it from his hands, he followed the tug, pulled left, pulled right, up, down. The creature could have let go and sprung at the man, but it held on tight. It was annoyed by the movements, grew ever more savage, it was already chewing the man, already biting the man, even though the limb he extended was bone-hard. The man tried to retrieve this bony arm, the beast would not yield. It tugged left, right, down, up, its mouth bled. The beast pulled backwards. But the man set up a rhythm, and his two companions behind him growled and groaned with the rhythm. All three gazed intently at the creature as it danced along. Its body hurled right and left, the jaws would not let go, the tail whipped uselessly, sometimes it sank to the ground, now the body was rolling, the momentum was too great, the man turned it onto one flank, it tugged back, he threw it onto its other flank, it tugged back, with a twist he turned it right over onto its back, the mighty hindquarters threshed free in the air, the hot white body lay exposed. At once a man jumped forward, was over the beast, plunged his long sharp bone knife deep into the body and ripped backwards and out.

The jaguar slithered round and reared up. The game was over. The staff flew from its mouth. The men fled. It was over for the beast. A deep yawning cry pursued those who had abandoned it. Another. The pain was overpowering. It stuck head and tongue into the dreadful wound and they emerged covered in blood. It flung a gurgled curse after the fleeing men. Then it curled itself around the wound, collapsed and was dead.

"These men are good," said old Torrez, stepping proudly between Emanuel and Montoya, "we shall enjoy good times with these. All they need is discipline."

And then – here we are back on the plain – he began to explain how wonderfully things were progressing elsewhere. "It's the same ground old Las Casas trod, but all he ever did was condemn. These people are the grandchildren and great-grandchildren of those to whom he and his pupils preached. If only he could have seen the meaning of method. Our good bishop of Asuncion, gloomy Don Reginald, is also a Dominican. Recently he received happy news from the governor of Peru. Some tribes over there are ready to become subjects of the Spanish crown, and request missionaries. That's all right with the governor. Whichever way the fruit ripens it's all the same to him. He's pleasantly surprised, and asks our friend in Asuncion, the bishop, to see to it. This news scares the wits out of him, just like our jaguar. 'What,' cried Don Reginald, 'a priest among those cannibals? Am I a murderer, that I should allow this? Must I write a letter such as was given to Uriah?' He would not send anyone, said he was short of spiritual workers, his old complaint, and the few he had he was unwilling to tear themselves away from the pious and hand them over to barbarians. So the poor governor, hoping to spare his soldiers, lit upon the idea of consulting me. For our presence is already spoken of among the governors. So what do I think of the matter. I reveal to him my unshakeable love for the Dominicans and for Bishop Don Reginald in particular. I say the Dominicans are capable men, and it would be a blessing if Don Reginald were to soften. The governor took me by the hand and off we went to see the bishop. We implored him, and used honeyed words. The governor also spoke in military and official tones, he has the gift, this is an extraordinary opportunity, the savages offer themselves up, clearly they recognise their weakness and want to become the King's people and subjects. At first the bishop played deaf. I sang some more. Dominicans are over-sensitive when a Jesuit addresses them. He dismissed us, and as we left conceded: he might be inclined to send priests, but only if the governor would guarantee an armed escort. Outside, Don Alvaro complained: 'I can just as well send soldiers by themselves, without priests.' And then he asked me what to do. I asked for an hour to think it over. An hour later I appeared before him with some priests. The rector of our college in Asuncion threw himself at my feet and begged: here I am, send me. The governor was overjoyed."

Then Emanuel, slowly and with hesitation, made him privy to their own anxieties. Father Torrez gaped in astonishment. He could not believe what he was hearing. But when his protests made no impression on Emanuel he listened in silence, always ready to interject. Emanuel concluded: "There is no point talking more about the situation. It exists. But where will it lead us. Look at this vast land. It looks bare, but it is fertile. Before, whenever the people were attacked, they could flee. Now they place themselves under our protection. We confine them to one place. We tell them to trust us. And they do. And that is the dreadful cause of our anxiety. What if we are put to the test! Dear brother, we fear for them. We have undergone so much already." He felt as he spoke that this was not what he really meant to say; it was a pretext, but he had to present it thus. He felt compelled to say more, for could everything they had built and worked for really continue, was it the right course? The necessary course?

When Emanuel went on to speak of Sao Paolo, putting the best gloss on details of the journey, the assaults, the deceptions, and the sullen mistrust of the natives, which was all too justified, old Torrez grew thoughtful. Emanuel: "We must stay on the alert against both natives and white slave-gatherers. Should we seek military protection from the nearest governor? But who looks to the wolf for protection? Our Brother Cataldino recently remarked: to live as we wish to live, we must be as wise as a pope and instill the same fear a pope does."

He waited for Torrez' response. Jerusalem, holy city, thy name is peace.

Torrez: "If only you knew how they rejoice over our mission, back in Rome. A document was prepared concerning your settlements. Did Maceta not bring it?"

"We burned it."

The Provincial froze.

"Brother Provincial, you see how matters stand here. The document made us arrogant. We fell into danger as a result. We saw it as a temptation. When we were on the run yet again we burned it and swore to be nothing more than humble missionaries. And now this happens."

Torrez embraced Emanuel and held him for a long time. Emanuel still did not utter the thought that filled his being, his great fear: what kind of settlement is this, how did it come to us, how should we face up to it, oh this cunning headstrong force that is the native settlement, it has the character of the grass that we daily uproot and still it soars over our heads and over our roofs. He did not speak of this even as Torrez embraced him. He kept it to himself, would not expose it to the light, it was concealed within him, his secret, Torrez wouldn't understand.

The Provincial took Emanuel by the arm. "Ignatius Loyola has inserted our Order into this problem. Be prudent and cautious. Be more cunning than the serpent. Don't be seduced by any either-or. We bend things until they suit our purpose. Whatever we do, wherever we go, there are traps everywhere. But to live as a Christian is anyway a dangerous business." And after a pause he added quietly: "Our Saviour died on the cross, and yet he was God."

On the way back they passed in silence the arena where the jaguar lay in its blood. Vultures were already circling overhead. Torrez glanced coldly at the great dead creature. Like a lightning flash his expression changed, his face hardened: "Never has a company of Jesuits doubted that any difficulty can be overcome."

Maladonata, the red cat

IN THE SETTLEMENT, Maladonata appeared at Emanuel's side several times a day. She had acquired a long, red shirt-like garment. As she stood there he spoke to her in his head: You red cat, brown cat, I know you, you know what you want. You speak, and whatever I reply it's all the same to you, you do as you wish. You town-builder, you protector of refugees. I know you, sly wicked cat. Later you will kiss my hand, want to lick my hand, take strength from it and do with us what you will. What do you say of Mary, what do you know of Mary, Red Cat, is anything that your ears have heard kept hidden under that thick black hair?

He never uttered such words. She would report that she had prayed so and so many rosaries with the women. He did not say: Red Cat, how smooth your face, how firm your gait, it is your youth, and what youth, Mariana was right to warn about this country, he knew it already from the heat that fell on the sea, but he should not have died. Emanuel praised Maladonata: "You have become as diligent as an abbess."

"What is that?" He explained. Then she went off. She wanted to be his abbess.

Sometimes he hated her. She was a burden to him. He felt she was wresting his will from him and was always farther on than him. Inwardly he combated her: How you presume, creature, you shall go from my side, you shall not flash your bright cat eyes at me, I alone know what I want, I am a Christian and a soldier and will remain so.

And so as old Father Torrez' fanfare blared daily about him – it fired him up for battle, the banner of Christ fluttered – how the people of the place worked without stint, how Maladonata bowed over his hand, goaded his will and little by little carried his will away with her, and then one very hot afternoon, when everyone had retired to their tents and huts, it happened that as he lay in his hammock reading a spiritual exercise, a strange uncertain anxiety rolled over Emanuel. It came from the intestines. He lowered himself to the ground, sank to his knees, pressed his head to the floor. Fear rocked his arms and legs; he was no longer master of his body. It played around his throat and the back of his head.

Not this, Lord, not this. Lead me not into temptation. Why, after sending me so many trials and I am so often despondent and suffering, why send me here where everything begins to stir within me anew? I wanted to worship you, tell of your glory. Not beyond my goal, do not haul me away beyond my capacity! Leave me within my limits. Lord, have mercy on me, Lord, see how I suffer.

And there welled up in him every cold dark pain, buried sorrow, summoned horribly by the fear that congealed moment by moment. Abjectly he implored: Lord, see what they make of me, how they ruin everything for me, my life, consecrated to your glory. They leave nothing alone. They carry me away piece by piece. Lord, help me against them. Help me against these many people, this red cat.

On the floor he braced himself mightily, clenched his teeth: help me against them – when a blow fell on the back of his head and neck, expected, but not as this thudding violence, it squeezed a groan from his constricted throat and he heard his name: 'Emanuel' ring out with an immensity that filled every corner of his soul.

He lay slumped on his face. As he pushed himself up with his hands, again the all-engulfing call: 'Emanuel'. When he stood, sat dumbly on the edge of his hammock, his feeble hand reached for the crucifix and felt the back of his head. Then he sat there dully. Then he began to shiver. Then he flung himself back into the hammock and lay shivering and sobbing and shaking. Until it was better.

Later he went out. The heat was like an oven, everything dead in the harsh sunlight. People slept. He retreated. He sat for a long time shocked at himself.

When Montoya appeared, sent by the Provincial – he was a young man with hard features and ice-cold eyes – Emanuel was his old self again. Torrez accompanied them to the little church, which had just been completed. They inspected it quickly from outside, and then fled in from the glare and the heat.

Heart, rise up

CONSECRATION DAY for the church. It was a little straw-roofed building, similar to the one which many decades before, to the north across the Amazon, young Father Las Casas of the Dominican order consecrated near Funza in the Indian realm of Cundinamarca. Streams of blood flowed around the church at Funza, thick streams racing through all of Cundinamarca, that unhappy land. On the Paraná those who stood hat in hand were no bravos, no men of violence, White barbarians and tyrants, mad and desperate men who sought to annihilate and lose themselves – governor Quesada, the magnificent Peruvian Belalcazar, red-cheeked captain-general Nicolaus Federmann, all on the lookout for gold and slaves. Europe, cramped, unhappy, had other kinds of people. Some there were who looked inward, were not driven, who tried to atone and reveal the true face of the White people. This little church was surrounded by the faithful and by dark refugees swarming over the smoothed round plaza. It was the dark people themselves who had built the church, just as they had their own little houses and huts and the little houses for the White men who wanted to bring them true tidings, until now so long perverted, from across the sea. They had no fire-tubes, no artillery, no swords. Joyfully, tears streaming in heartfelt thanks-giving, old Torrez read the first Mass.

Emanuel baptised the place with its first name: Loreto.

Jerusalem, holy city, thy name is peace. Thou art built of souls, a myriad angels have watched over thee, on thy head rests the crown, thou lovely, thou wondrous city.

Chosen by grace without measure, by the father of all grace, beloved of Jesus, Jesus, thou art his table, his chair, his coffer. Most precious prize of the world, in glory dost thou bathe.

O holy city, o open door, o jewelled gate. Whoever here receives Jesus Christ may atone lightly for his sins, he is greeted with music and jubilation, and no longer suffers torment.

A firm plan was decreed. No wild grass was tolerated, the lines of streets were marked with strings, squares were staked out, fields delineated for each group, for each family, a work plan drawn up that took account of sun, heat, rain. What should be done today and tomorrow was clearly specified, a granary was built. The dark people learned what a week is, and during it you work and every day has a name, and on Sunday you rest and pray.

Had they not heard a hundred times that the natives are lazy? That the whole place could have been built by the grudging labour of sullen serfs? It swept on like the undammed waters of a stream, of its own volition. They tended manioc fields, dates, coconut and figs, potatoes and sweet potatoes grew in rows, flax, cotton. Men stepped out every morning, organised by their foreman, to work the fields, gardens, forest. They set off singing, a banner at their head with the image of the holy patron of their work, larger groups accompanied by drum and fife. Thus they went after Mass, tools shouldered, all dressed the same, cap, short tunic, trousers, no one higher, no one lower, they toiled to fulfill the words that were written: "Give us this day our daily bread," and wanted no possessions because "It is easier for a camel to go through the eye of a needle, than for a rich man to enter into the kingdom of God." Once at the place of work they set down their tools, said prayers in the open air, then toiled each according to his ability. They worked half the day, it was fertile untilled soil, yielded a hundredfold increase of every seed, the air was mild. Singing they returned: *Soul of Christ, sanctify me, body of Christ, deliver me, blood of Christ, ease my thirst, water from the side of Christ, cleanse me. Good Jesus, hear me. Let no one sunder me from thee. In my hour of death summon me. And let me then come unto thee, that I may praise thee eternally in the company of your saints. Amen.*

At home and in the open, in the rainy season in a great hall that served also for other gatherings, sat those bigger boys and girls of the town who were not busy with infants or tending the fire, they processed cotton brought in from the fields, wove. All the while they chatted, pictures of the Virgin hung on the walls, painted by natives in garish colours, she wore a huge crown, angels swarmed about her. Now and then all the women set up a pious song, and let their hands drop.

Progress was remarkable. Under the guidance of the White carpenter they built little houses, felled trees, dragged them over the ground, sawed them, dressed them, made beams and boards. The thoughts of the people mingled curiously with the material and spread like dye into the objects. So it was in the beginning, and so it continued. The architects affirmed with a laugh: "Nothing that you give them and they take into their hand stays as it was. They are magicians!" The dark people were interested in sawing and joinery and hammering, in the construction of a roof, the hanging of doors and in the greatest marvel: the hinges on a cabinet. But this was exactly the same interest they showed for pious instruction! It was on the same line, although a prayer to Mary had nothing to do with the planing of a beam. But they thought otherwise. It made a comical impression on the Whites: the beam, the plane and Mary all went into a scandalous, burlesque mix. There stood houses one, two and three, but were not houses one, two and three, rather fragments of a narrative, a pious Indian account overflowing with plants and animals. Hammer blows were associated with the punching of holes for a rosary, screws they drove squealed, called out, the board answered, not once but every time, and everybody noticed and attested to it. And it went even farther – to what Father Emanuel had feared and to which he had in the end capitulated. The flywheel spun, the work was taken out of the hands of the Fathers, they themselves were taken out of their own hands.

They had intended to play this game: here Christian clerics, Fathers of the Company of Jesus – there, dark heathen to be converted. For this they had travelled far across the sea, knew every move of the game, had mastered it thoroughly. In the forefront of their thoughts they kept the words of the catechism, of scripture, and of themselves as they were formed in college and sent over here to carry out the will of the Order.

But no longer were they, as they at first believed, on the Paraná river, several hundred miles from Sao Paolo and separated from it by broad grassy plains and rugged highlands, and even farther away the town of Tucuman. But although this was in fact the case and a governor sat in Asuncion and beside him the bishop, the Dominican, although they themselves were still just the Fathers Emanuel, Maceta, Cataldino, Faber, Arminio, they were – in the land of Canaan. Without knowing it, and without wishing it, they had arrived in Canaan!

And something happened which once they thought they knew all about, and now it came to them with fervour and delight.

And if you rubbed your eyes you still could not dismiss the image displayed solidly there before you, of the peaceful happy life of simple fisherfolk on the sea of Galilee, Simon and Andrew cast their nets, and Jesus spoke to them saying: "I shall make you fishers of men", and so they abandoned their nets and followed him. And there was James, son of Zebedee, and his brother John in their boat repairing their nets, and Simon and Andrew and the Saviour sat by the sea, a mass of people thronged to them, and he showed himself master of all the ancient laws, they clung to him, he climbed into a boat, the great crowd stood on the shore, and he spoke to them of the sower and the seed, how the seed fell on good soil, the seed grew and bore fruit, thirtyfold, sixtyfold, a hundredfold.

The natives, drolly mingling the holy and the quotidian, such children, were blithe, grateful, contented in their movements, you never heard a quarrel, no one was angry. Yes, here were enacted the teachings of Jesus. How good to have come here after so much European crime, cruelty and infamy. "Who are we?" the clerics asked, this new breed of men sent out by Europe, the first to stand still and gaze calmly about: "What has happened?"

≈≈≈

Their cowls were not cast off, they took no notion to daub themselves and dance like Mariana. But their cowls were no longer the habit of their Order, rather of apostles. So mightily were they seized by the Word. Truly: idle chatter had ceased. How earnest they became. Where was the cheerfulness of the first weeks as they hewed timber, reveled in manual labour. How changed it all was now, even more than they had envisaged from that official document.

Now they saw themselves like people who sit shivering in a room, at last they open the shutters to check if the air is warm – like those in Noah's Ark, who floated for forty days on the waters of the Deluge between nailed planks, in a coffin, and then they notice the waters are receding, we'll be able to leave the Ark, the downpour eases, we release birds, a raven, a dove, then it's time, the keel of the Ark bumps against something hard, we sink – onto land.

≈≈≈

What an astonishing country!

They knew tales of saints who immersed themselves in scripture, mortified themselves and were then blessed with visions of Heaven in their little cells. In Peru, some decades before, the hallowed Franciscan monk Solano had chastised his flesh, he lived on sips of water and a little maize, they told of how once in Lima he stirred up a crowd with his oratory, they would all be cast into perdition for their sins, the frightened people stayed awake the whole night, the Last Rites were administered, there weren't enough priests there to grant absolution, so they cried out their sins in the church, confessed and repented.

The Jesuit Fathers did not mortify themselves. Their flock did not torment themselves into agony. A wonderful game, a game full of grace, had begun.

You sat on the greensward, had five loaves and two fishes, but these yielded so much all could eat their fill and still there are twelve baskets full of crusts and fish – for five thousand.

All things come to an end, the priests dreamed, the lines run deep, abysmally deep, and at last are lost. It was only their monastic life that had run its course.

"All things come to an end," Emanuel said to Cataldino, "and…"

"What do you mean, and?"

"And earthly death and something else come into being. This, that we are now living. In this country there is no death."

Cataldino: "Perhaps it is the fruit of an earlier life."

"You think? We would be judged blessed indeed, to have deserved this."

Lay down your books!

Head, relinquish your learning.

Heart, rise up.

Swooning delight

LIKE MOST OF the others, Maladonata was small and strong. She had a trim feminine face. Her forehead was wide and smooth, the hair a straight fringe across it. Taut copper-coloured cheeks were stretched into a smile by broad zygomatic arches. Her wide expressive mouth always showed a gentle smile. The eyelids hooded her half-closed eyes. These eyes that had seen such horrors, and were capable of blazing hatred, now gazed in gentle ardour. Whoever saw her as she went about knew: this is Love.

Unlike Emanuel she was not chosen, but she was his equal in the worship of Jesus' name. This womanly face, concentrated in sweetness, received its glow from the devotional practices to which she gave herself every night, stretched on the cold floor of her hut, dreaming, praying in the words of her master: *Jesu, sweeter than honey is thy presence to me.* And daily she brought this womanly face into Emanuel's presence. Now not even silently did he dare to call her Red Cat. He felt: she is the power that drives all of us in Loreto.

≈≈≈

The place swarmed with people. Rumours spread of the great hope it offered.

Among those who had fled from the governor's mercenaries were the cacique Atyacaya and his clan. He sent people across the Paraná to invite clansmen to come over to Loreto. He advised the building of a second town to the northwest, about one and a half miles away, at the place where the little Yabebiry drops into the Paraná. There, for the salvation of the Indian tribes and to the glory of God, the Fathers founded the second 'reduction', or 'doctrine' as the Fathers called it: San Ignacio. For you had to honour the founder of the Order, who taught: quit the monastery, go among people, take it on yourselves.

In the burgeoning weeks when they were laying down San Ignacio on the Yabebiry, a remarkable guest appeared in the embryonic town and wandered over to Loreto, where he remained. Accompanying Father Barsena from Cuzco was a small tender man of dark olive hue: the last living male of the line of Huayna Capac and the Incas, who before the arrival of Pizarro had ruled the empire of Tahuanti-suya.

Father Barsena had approached the silent grieving man in his secluded dwelling in Cuzco, and spoken to him of the Christian religion. The resistance of the dusky prince was insuperable. Only when the priest began to talk of villages across the Paraná, where preachers toil only among native people, did he become attentive. Barsena, who had been tasked to make contact with the Fathers on the Paraná, exploited the interest shown by the expiring man and invited him to come to Loreto. The prince agreed.

Calm, acquiescent, guided by Father Barsena, the olive-dark scion of Huayna Capac, emperor of Peru, trekked through Paraguay. He crossed the Paraná and appeared in Loreto. He asked permission to stay a while, then went with cacique Atyacaya to San Ignacio. He wanted to be as busy as everyone else. After living happily, even blessedly, among people for several months he died, baptised. In the last days the Jesuits heard from the mouth of the ailing prince from Cuzco the words: "A position lost, but the Kingdom of Heaven gained," and further: "I no longer lament the loss of my country Tahuanti-suya. I no longer wish to dwell on the atrocities of the conquerors." The dying man kept to himself the hope given him by the sight of this place: that the blood of these people would one day produce the avengers awaited by his fathers and father's fathers and all those still living in the mountains.

Miracles happened. Wild beasts roamed the countryside in great numbers. Sturdy fences were erected against them. One evening, after a prolonged thunderstorm that softened the soil, a steer broke in by overturning the loosened fence, raced down the street amid piercing shrieks from the people, knocked several of them down – and then Emanuel emerged from the little church. He could have stepped back, alerted by the screams. But he stood there in his black robes, big, calm, in the round plaza with its flowerbeds. As the crowd cried out in horror, the steer ran straight at him, only to slow as it approached, uncertain which way to turn, and came to a halt behind Emanuel. The priest turned to face it and murmured something. Many people witnessed the incident. The beast, now ambling calmly around the little church, was freed into the wild.

To the north there flowed the little Yeribary river. The Paraná itself was a good step away. One day the little wells all dried up. The people were greatly concerned, even the priests were uneasy, many people were only just adapting to life in a fixed place. A few days later all thoughts were overwhelmed by one fear: shall we have water tomorrow, we can't move away, the church is here, this place Loreto. Only a group of women, led by Maladonata, remained calm. They organised a procession through the town fronted by an image of the Mother of God, a service of supplication was held in the church, then the band of women paraded the image through the town. Doves perched on the shoulders of the image. They went singing through the streets, out into the open country. There the birds flew up from the shoulders of the image of the Mother of God, accompanied by a general wailing. They observed where the birds landed, dug there, and found a spring of good water. They danced and sang around the spring the whole evening and on into the night.

The fate of cacique Atyacaya impressed everyone deeply. Along with many of his former clansmen he had moved across to San Ignacio and made a lively contribution to the building work. But the old wanderlust would not leave him. Sent out hunting he stayed away a long time, he was baptised but missed several Masses. You could see his thoughts were elsewhere. The Fathers admonished him, he begged forgiveness, the urge was stronger than him. To help recent converts and new arrivals to adjust more easily, and to guide them, the Fathers had instituted a covert supervision, which they entrusted to elders and the cleverer people. One day while the cacique was away hunting, they fetched from his house a little jug in which lay a small root of remarkable shape. The native supervisors recognised this kind of root, which people hid in a little jug and guarded carefully: it was a spirit. The cacique was a backslider.

When he fell into a rage at the confiscation of the root and would not hold back even in front of Father Montoya, he was threatened with excommunication. Atyacaya withdrew angrily into the little hut he had built for himself, his wife and her child were called away to Montoya, who kept them with him all day in order to give them into the keeping of others if Atyacaya did not come to his senses. Then at noon a fire broke out. Three huts went up in flames, no one knew the cause, but one was Atyacaya's. The charred body of the poor sinner was dragged from the ashes that evening. Loreto and San Ignacio took part in the funeral service for this man they had all known. They prayed that Atyacaya, victim of Satan's temptation, should find his way to Heaven, that Saint Ignatius, Jesus and Mary should help him, that his dreadful sin should be forgiven.

≈≈≈

Happy anticipation. They lived on in patient good cheer. Every day brought new successes. Every good deed, every disclosed sin was a rung on the golden ladder that they all climbed side by side. Priests and angels tallied the rungs.

One day in the spinning shed a woman danced, yarn hung from her skirt, she stepped outside: "My child is calling" – her child was dead – "he is in Heaven, he found his way there, I must help him take the last steps. I am coming, hold on to me, I shall carry you." She leapt, scattered spinning wheels.

The priests had to tend to converts who lay down in a field, cried out in rapture and babbled, foaming in pain, they were suffering the scourges of poor innocent Jesus. In these wonderful days all sobbed as they left the daily Mass. Daily the Mass renewed itself, the congregation never diminished. The priests, giving thanks for the blessing that God had sent down, could speak only cautiously of the Stations of the Cross. The entirety of the people that had gathered around them felt themselves to be Jesus, Mary Magdalene, Judas Iscariot.

The shadow of death

WHILE THE JESUIT Fathers, broken out from Europe to spread Christianity in accordance with the teachings of Ignatius de Loyola, lay in the province of Guayrá with their darkskinned flock, not far away Spaniards dwelled in towns and fortresses and grumbled because the Fathers protected the dark people and removed them from their grasp, and to the north and east the Mamelus, the Paolistas, roamed about.

The Mamelus practised a scoundrelly politics against the Jesuits. Now one year, now the next, they penetrated to the region of the Iguazú, but forbore to come down from the hills that tracked the Paraná at some remove. All they did was unsettle the native tribes, drive them into the Fathers' hands. Thus there was founded village after village, all known to the Mamelus.

The town of the Mamelus, Sao Paolo over towards the ocean, grew no less rapidly than the settlements of the Christian missionaries. The Paolistas increased through rapine and slave hunts, through prospecting for gold and precious stones. Though the Europe that had driven them out could build and plough just as well as rob and conquer, all they wanted was robbery and conquest. Their campaigns extended ever farther west into a country swarming with people, the Indians were dense schools of fish that they swept into their net. Now they grew strong enough to hire whole armies of mercenaries, natives of course; tributary tribes accrued to them, and since conquest and booty were to be had, other tribes followed along. And thus they ruined the country. The Mamelus, whose fearsome reputation spread far and wide, described a broad arc of destruction. No mountain or forest or river could hold them back. It was said they wanted to press on from the east coast straight across to the west coast, to Peru, take over the gold mines. Such plans were credible, for the Mamelus.

Already they had crossed the Sierras de Coritcha and del Espinazo to the north of the Pequiry river and the broad Iguazú where tribes of gentle Guaraní dwelled. Who could withstand them?

≈≈≈

The plan for a 'Christian republic' was often discussed by the Fathers, among whom Montoya (but Emanuel did not like him) proved the most energetic. Their Indian Canaan would be independent of all save the Spanish Crown and Rome. They hoped to make the thousands of dark people who had placed themselves under their protection, and whom they were guiding along the path of a Christian life, independent of the purview of ever-changing governors. To this end they took steps with the Crown, the Council of the Indies, and in Rome. The footloose Fathers Maceta and Cataldino set off one day to make contact in Asuncion with their old friend the governor, who was still the very noble Don Alvaro, and the bishop.

The bishop received them grumpily: "I expected you long before this. You sit there on the Paraná and no longer know me." They swore devotion, alluded to the tremendous burden of work piled on their shoulders. They read to him the petition that had occasioned their visit.

"If we are to convert the tribes, we must remove them from the influence of the Whites, their bad influence and their tyranny." The bishop laughed out loud, no longer ill-humoured: "We've become used to many of your ways, but this is the end! Where do you think you are living? In the moon? Does the Paraná flow in the moon, hmm? Have you descended from the moon? The simplest plan would be to remove the dear savages from the influence of the Whites by having us all ship ourselves back to Europe. Do you agree? Would that suffice?"

"No," the visitor replied amiably, "that would not accord with our intentions. The Whites, who possess the message of Jesus, must haul the savages out of their sad state of darkness."

The bishop continued to mock: "Your task, in all honour. But I simply cannot understand what you're up to. These are Indians, natives, who should at last do useful work for the country. What do you do with them? You shut them up where there's no wind. The savages are not flowers. We have no use in this country for such flowers."

The Fathers waited to see if he would come out openly with the traders' argument: you are taking away our labour force. But he checked himself. They showed themselves deeply moved by his utterances, took notes and begged him nevertheless to see to it that help would be given whenever danger threatened from Tupis or Paolistas. "Look here," the mollified bishop blustered, "you see how it is: the whole world wants to overrun you, and you bang your heads against the wall." But since they pleaded, he promised to do what he could with the governor.

To be on the safe side, they themselves waited on the governor. And indeed the bishop had not presented himself. The noble Don Alvaro, whose very marrow still felt the effects of the Holy Thursday adventure (he had been forced to dig deep in his pockets, not to mention the exchange of correspondence with the King) received them most genially and was already less sanguine than when he set out. He was fully up to date. He was most obliged to the Jesuits, as he quite openly declared, for taking in those thousands of refugees, who would not now be so quick to cause him trouble. He allowed them to relate details of their work and was bowled over with admiration. He had nothing but praise. He said: "The savages you're training there will one day be good workers for us." But when they read from their petition he became grave: "Gentlemen, gentlemen, what do you ask of me? Such clever men, and now whatever are you thinking? You can't isolate yourselves like that. It seems you are forming a state within a state."

They said they did not want to expel or exclude Whites once and for all, but asked only the right to keep at a distance people of bad character and notorious scoundrels, because these reductions are really a kind of school, and you don't let all and sundry into a school. "Now you make more sense. Quite right. It's just that your school is rather large. But it's not up to me. I hate to poke my finger into spiritual matters."

And when they broached the question of help against possible threats from Mamelus or Tupis, they received a blunt Yes. "That is squarely in my line. I look forward to the day of reckoning with the Tupis who allow themselves to be harnessed by the Portuguese, these Mamelus. Peace throughout the land, I say." He offered his hand. He seemed very tired.

The Jesuit Fathers stayed only a few days in Asuncion. People hoped they would preach in the church, so they could be booed. There was a thick unfathomable animus against them. Women shouted after them in the street: "Those savages who meant to slaughter us during the procession, you protect them? Call yourselves priests?" As Cataldino and Maceta stood outside the gate and once again took up their heavy walking sticks, they covered their ears.

Maceta: "Who has been slandering us so horribly?" He marched off in a fury. "They won't help us when danger comes."

"I think they will. You really think so? Tupis and Mamelus are their enemies too."

"They'll think: let us be massacred first."

As they rowed north they heard of unrest back in Guayrá, and made haste. As soon as they landed they obtained horses and rode on in great anxiety. Then they reached Loreto, and as they stood before Emanuel and Montoya they both lost their composure. Maceta, younger than Cataldino, lifted his thick beard and showed grey threads: "We rode like maniacs. We kept thinking we saw smoke from an attack."

Emanuel embraced them. "Was it so bad in the town? Still so bad?"

Cataldino made a fist: "We must be soldiers. We must arm ourselves. Even a beast has horns for defence. They want to slaughter us all. None will stand with us. They joke about it. They hate us. The bishop most of all."

Maceta: "And why? Cataldino nailed it: because they see we are right, and they're ashamed and must drown out the voice of their conscience."

Young stern Montoya: "As the Scripture says: He went into the temple, and began to cast out them that sold and bought in the temple, and overthrew the tables of the moneychangers, and the seats of them that sold doves; and would not suffer that any man should carry any vessel through the temple." For the first time Emanuel cast a friendly, even tender, look at small tight-lipped brother Montoya, the young man left with them by Torrez.

Emanuel had them relate everything at leisure, admonished them to stay calm and to trust: "Did the Paolistas not chase us from the coast over the mountains, and yet we still live? Did we not have grand plans and were we not driven from towns and even from the little Indian village? And are we succeeding here, by the grace of God? Who could have better reason than us to trust in God and leave our fate in His hands?"

He went with the priests among the people, sent Fathers out to neighbouring settlements, and himself visited those nearby. The priests spoke openly of the looming danger. Their darkskinned flock made clear to them how little they could depend on outside help. The Son of Man would come in his glory, and then all would pass according to His deeds.

"What would be the life of man," Emanuel lamented and rejoiced from the pitiful wooden pulpit in the little church of Loreto, "if there were no path to the Saviour. Yeah, it is written: Verily I say unto you, there be some standing here, which shall not taste of death, till they see the Son of Man coming in his kingdom."

A premonition of death coloured life in all the settlements. Such solemnity, brotherly and sisterly concern, day after day. They had arrows, bows, spears, but now the Fathers, so that no one would fall into temptation, made sure everything that might be used as a weapon was stored in magazines to which only they had access.

King Nicolaus Riubuni

THEN THE MAMELU wave drew near. The great scythe hissed.

The hellish glow of crime burst into flame. The primal Enemy came, along with everything evil, the desolate eerie forest, the green seething sea from which serpents, insects, jaguars, monkeys, birds, humans emerged, brown, white. The triumphant wave with its piping swaggering music surged. It was into just such a horrid maw that Mariana had disappeared.

The Mamelus did not travel alone. Simple cruel brutes though they were, they came this time in a garish parade. At their head they had placed a white adventurer, as unscrupulous as they, who was wanted in his Spanish homeland for the murder of a royal official and various acts of fraud. This scoundrel, once a Jesuit novice in Saragossa, treasurer only with intent to embezzle, discovered when he fled across the sea and arrived on the east coast of this new continent how much hatred the dark people – slaves and free tribes – nourished against the Whites. Although he himself had never felt this hatred, for he was quite comfortable with every kind of White vice and debauchery, and esteemed the life as long as it threw wine, luxury and women his way, he saw that here he could take revenge for the flight forced on him by the authorities, the abandonment of his main love in Saragossa, and the odious voyage.

This daredevil soon had a crowd of insurgent Indians with him near the new Portuguese fort of San Sacramento. How he enjoyed attacking and driving away the missionaries of the region, not excepting even a priest of his own former Order. A refugee stream preceded him towards Buenos Aires. Who would want to fall into his clutches. The Indian revolt was long expected, fear paralysed the Whites. In San Sacramento, where an armed crew of White adventurers joined him, the megalomaniac had medals struck with the inscription: *Vengeance is for God, and for the one He sends.* The reverse of the medal showed thundering Jove.

With his horde, soon numbering five thousand men, he turned northwest, impelled by Whites lusting after the supposed riches of the new settlements, towards the Uruguay river and the

Ibicuy. The slogan that he made sure to spread as they advanced promised "Freedom for the Indian from the White man's yoke." The Jesuit Fathers, he made known, were among the worst of slave-gatherers. This slogan worked to the Jesuit's detriment long after the criminal was in the ground.

Once through the mountains, Riubuni fell upon the outlying missions, stole such people and goods as he could lay hands on, and instituted a mighty bloodbath among the natives. There's no other way, he declared, they are traitors, they run from us and must be punished. Following these acts of heroism, and in possession of substantial booty, he returned to his robbers' nest of San Sacramento, welcomed with jubilation by the stay-at-homes and acclaimed by them as their king. He caused it to be trumpeted through the streets: all this he had achieved with the help of God Almighty. A swarm of men set out from Sao Paolo to serve under him. Wherever warpath and adventure could be found, the Mamelus were always there.

Then the rulers in Sao Paolo took note of San Sacramento, and it seemed to them that a dangerous rival was in the making. They sent enquiries to San Sacramento, might Riubuni be disposed to make common cause? They shared the same view of the Jesuits, whom they had come to know only too well in Sao Paolo, and planned to punish sooner rather than later. Moreover, Riubuni and Sao Paolo had common friends in the Tupi tribes. Riubuni did not reject the overtures. So the Paolistas, who had no doubt that they would be able at some point to be rid of him, sent a formal delegation to the great robber from Saragossa and invited him to join them at Piratininga. There he would find experienced people with extensive practical knowledge, who would all haul with him on the same rope.

And so this fellow, this great Riubuni, who had been the misfortune of his family in Aragonian Taratos and of many other people and who loved flattery especially, did not wait to be asked twice, failing to note the contradiction between slave-gathering and his slogan 'Freedom for the Indian from the White man's yoke.' For everyone knew about the Paolistas, those manhunters.

But the gentlemen of Sao Paolo made it easy for him by declaring, through the mouths of the formal delegation sent to invite him: they would all be subject to him.

He had ships built, and with six thousand men sailed up the east coast and appeared in Sao Paolo, welcomed by pealing bells. Such priests as remained there preached to the rascals. The Mamelus summarily named Riubuni their commander in chief, and he allowed his people to call him king: King Nicolaus. Only a few Paolistas did so, their rulers were too sensible to provoke a quarrel with the King of Portugal, whose officials here helped them to save face.

As the first two outlying reductions in the southeast towards the Uruguay went up in flames and crowds of refugees streamed towards the Paraná, some Fathers wanted to hasten to the aid of the victims. But they were held back. It was already too late for those settlements, and everyone could see they were needed here and now. They remained steadfast: no weapons, no resistance, only God and prayer, no timorous unease must be allowed to shake their faith. Yet envoys were despatched in secret to Asuncion and Villarica to inform the governor, the bishop and the residents of what was happening to the east and south.

≈≈≈

Over ten thousand men, among them Tupis from the hills and swamp country, emerged from the forested hills of the east down to the upper waters of the rivers Caracapa and Parnaymini that flow into the Paraná, at their head Nicolaus Riubuni, broad face, black hair, with the coals of his restless eyes and his drooping mustachios. He had himself carried (for now even savages succumbed to the yoke) in a litter. His bodyguard were native warriors from San Sacramento. They rode alongside, at their head a White with drawn sword. The Mamelus had distributed their own heavily armed mounted men among the others, they had experience of such columns and knew how to manage them. To meet any contingency, they kept a troop some hundreds strong together for themselves.

Down the broad valley through which flowed the sweet

waters of the Paraná they advanced, down the valley of orange groves, of sugarcane, manioc, and maize fields, of hymns and songs of peace. They crossed the surging grassy plains of the savannah, birds climbed in the warm air, now and then small ostriches ran past, you saw trees you never saw elsewhere, their foliage supported on branches like candelabras, these were araucaria, planted by the Jesuit Fathers and already spreading eastwards.

In Loreto, San Ignacio, San Miguel the Fathers allowed no change in routine. They merely instructed that no one should stray too far while at work. Everyone knew the danger that loomed. They implored the saints in services of rogation. No one fled the settlements.

Every day Maladonata sought out the Superior. Although the Fathers kept women at a distance, there was no strictness during these early days of the new settlements, they were Brother human and Sister human and all were blessed in their prayers and apprehensions. Maladonata, who wears the Superior's beard-clippings knotted at her breast (she never confesses this) once a day or several times presents her taut solemn face to him, the broad smooth forehead, the firm copper-coloured cheeks beneath the zygomatic arches always squeezing out a smile, and the eyes half closed, these eyes like open caskets into which something has crept and been accepted and is held fast.

"Why won't we let the men go out to the fields, Brother Emanuel? They find it strange."

"Find it strange?" – "Yes, they want to go out."

"One should not challenge God."

"I know the Mamelus, they burned my village over by Villarica. And you don't believe that God is with us, Brother Emanuel." She lifts the eyelids, her naked engulfing eyes are open, her gentle womanly smile, she covers the gleaming orbs again.

"I don't believe, Maladonata, that anything will happen to our people. But we should not challenge God." Woe, he thought, woe to me if she persists, if she drags from me permission to go to the fields. And why should God not be with us, whom should he be with, for whom did you give your life, sweet Jesus?

She goes and comes, she goes and comes. The Fathers are pleased to have such a one as she in Loreto. She is stronger than any Father.

When Emanuel heard that the Mamelus had come down with their mighty army from the northern hills and were moving into the valley, he sent to the northerly reductions to gather all their people in San Loreto. They must not tarry, and are to bring all their sick along. Tangled in Emanuel and the other Fathers were the will to defend themselves, horror at the thought of a bloodbath, and trust in Heaven. A troop of a hundred armed men arrived from Asuncion, the governor informed them that this troop will suffice to scare away the robbers, the main part of his forces unfortunately are in the Gran Chaco, he will call for reinforcements. But reinforcements were no longer needed.

King Nicolaus Riubuni camped south of the little Caracapa river. There at one of his forward posts a delegation of missionaries appeared, natives behind them. They wanted to negotiate with Riubuni. At first the troops were reluctant to lead them on, wanted only to take them prisoner. But the commander of the forward post, Mario, a White, formerly a Spanish sergeant, intervened and allowed Cataldino and Maceta to proceed to the camp. The mighty army had already heard that a Spanish force was on the march; defences were being reinforced. The Fathers were astonished at the preparations, ramparts, ditches, countless armed men, and all to attack them and their poor flock. They followed to a huge pennanted tent. First they had to wait a long time outside the tent. Gorgeously attired personages, White and native, went here and there, for a long while the Fathers in the grass by the tent were ignored, they thought they must have been forgotten. Then a White officer with drawn sword came up and led them into the tent, which was furnished ostentatiously with tables, chairs, cushions, banners.

There like a king in a scarlet cloak sat blackhaired broadfaced Riubuni, his face was paler than those of his people, he sat on gaudy cushions, big gold buttons glinted in his scarlet cloak, he wore a green belt from which hung chains of glass beads, on the table in front of him lay a drawn sword, his belt held a long dagger. As the Fathers, who had not yet been addressed, stood before him, three young native women with feathers in the hair and wearing a red cloth around the hips served him fruit and drinks in vessels of gold and silver.

When the drunkard had gloated long enough over the Fathers, he asked them, without interrupting his chewing, what the idea was in coming here. Before Cataldino came to the end of his courteous statement of greeting, the scarlet man spoke across him: "That's all superfluous. We don't need you. In this country, we impose order." He pinched one of the serving girls on the bottom and asked in the Indian tongue: "What do you think, would you like such a man? Tell me." The Fathers understood. Cataldino, glowering, continued speaking, his imperturbability reduced the man to silence. He called Riubuni "Leader of a free people", forced out some flattering remarks, referred to the sword of righteousness lying there in front of Riubuni. This made an impression on the man, even more so the appeal to their common fraternity in the Order of Jesuits. No more talk of embezzlement, that's water under the bridge. "Good," he nodded, "but what do you want?" And when they begged for peace he was gracious: "The reductions must offer no resistance," and lectured his black-robed brethren: "God will hand the country to whoever knows how to conquer and govern it."

The envoys withdrew in utter bewilderment, the scarlet man had demanded 'submission of the reductions', 'submission' was the megalomaniac's favourite word, surrender of all metal objects, surrender of cattle. That might constitute peace, but none dared vouch for it.

Without delay the Fathers in Loreto loaded up several hundred people with everything they had in the storehouses, amid wailing from the people opened up the stalls, and a huge train of cattle laden with implements was driven through the streets of the settlement. Cattle were not rare here, but people were attached to the beasts. When two days passed without the return of any of the delegation, anxiety grew in the Fathers, and when on the morning of the third day men came rushing back from the fields to report many horsemen, the Fathers knew: they must make ready.

The scythe sweeps

THE MANY THOUSANDS who heeded the Fathers and gathered in and around Loreto knelt from early morning in the streets, the church. They had banners and devotional images. The magazines where spears, bows and arrows were stored were finally nailed shut on Emanuel's orders. Pious singing arose everywhere, accompanied by flutes, voices of men, women and children. They waited for a miracle. The Fathers were with them. The Fathers sang with them of the kingdom of Heaven. *Jerusalem, you holy city! O holy city, o open door, o jewelled gate. Whoever here receives Jesus Christ may atone lightly for his sins, he is greeted with music and jubilation, and no longer suffers torment.*

The natives sang: *Jerusalem! O holy city, o open door.* With the Fathers, the mighty White priests, they implored God in Heaven. If they call out and the bells raise their voices, He will send a sign to those who have obeyed His word, and fall on the enemy with fire just as He fell on the huts of the apostate cacique. The priests in Loreto sat among the natives in the little church, on the grass and in the streets in rapturous prayer. A miracle could not be withheld. They administered the Last Rites to one another. Heaven, eternal bliss, so yearningly desired, was near. Prayers rose on a myriad wings.

Maladonata's moment had come. Emanuel was content to have her by him. It was clear Loreto was lost. A sacrifice is required of us. We forgot the Saviour's words: my kingdom is not of this world. I have committed many sins in my life, and after sloughing many off, pride still remains. I would not yield and would not yield. Truly, Mariana was my dearest friend, my reflection, a part of me, I learned nothing from the path he took. I regret that it is now happening with me as with him, I am rejected, condemned. I repent, Lord, I repent. I did not want to follow your path of suffering among men, I thought I must be clever and bring thousands with me. Woe is me, how can I bear it.

Woe is me, what kind of murderer am I.

Lord, in this hour of my repentance you punish me. Woe is me, woe is us, that thousands suffer along with us. Save them, Lord, do not demand too much, they are innocent, they were led astray, led astray by me, take me, be satisfied with me, Lord.

He walked among them, thinner than ever, his long beard grey, arms stretched high. Not many understood what he cried out, but they saw him. Men and women kissed his footsteps. "Take up no weapons! Do not move! There is a God! God lives! He will forgive us. He sent Jesus to save us." Oh, now and then he hoped for rescue. They waited, they knew they could wait, that was how he had waited for the rampaging steer, and tethered it.

His voice: "Jesus died. If God wills, we shall die for him. The kingdom of heaven, Lord, your glory. To you, Lord, to you!"

They sat in the grass and sang, their eyes to heaven. Emanuel flung himself to the ground among them. He writhed in pain. The battle began.

The governor's hundred men held the entrance to Loreto, half fought and were killed, the other half rode or ran back yelling: "Flee! Flee! Mamelus are upon us!" The victors' roars drowned their cries, they came no farther through the crush of people. Not till the murderous horde itself came riding from the fields, shooting, stabbing, hundreds and ever more hundreds, firearms cracking, was there flight, confusion, horror, sudden furious desperate resistance.

At the entrance to Loreto natives stood in a mass, unyielding, unwavering. They caused horses to tumble, boiling with hate they defended themselves with the daggers and swords of their fallen adversaries. But these were just episodes. Riubuni's army had an easy task.

Emanuel was sucked into the melee. He wanted to admonish them. Maladonata, who saw the danger, kept close to him, she did not know from which side to protect him. He was taller than the natives, his black robe stood out among their lighter garb. She heard how he called out. He calls, still calls! At the entrance to the village he calls out over the tangled mass, shots crack into it.

God is not helping, how have we transgressed. A musket ball hits Emanuel from behind under the shoulder. The great priest sinks, she drags him with the help of a crowd of men who clear the way into the nearest house. The men form a guard outside the door.

Now I am alone with you, now the red life runs out of you. Emanuel on the floor is fully conscious. He clutches the crucifix at his breast, repents his sins, prays God for mercy. She has torn away his robe at the shoulder, his upper body is bare, whimpering, sobbing, stammering his words after him she staunches the gaping wound with both fists. But blood spurts through the cloth and between her fingers. She kneels at his side as she presses the wound and breathes on his body, which grows cooler, her breath comes wilder, she lies with her mouth on his skin. She screams to Emanuel, grips his head with her bloody hands and shakes it, his eyes become unfocused: "Take me with you, Emanuel, me, oh, oh."

And now, close by him, she can no longer resist kissing his eyes, his throat, his beard, his still warm, unresisting, stiffening face. He has no more thoughts. He was Brother Emanuel.

When she sees that his eyes no longer move, the waxy hollow face smeared with blood, Death – she jumps up with a scream, beats on the door, cries, screams, they must let her out, outside she forces her way through, Death is at my back, I am damned, Hell is seizing me, Emanuel escaped, he must not escape me, do not escape me.

The savage blood-drenched face, arms soaked in blood, in his blood, where is the gentle smile, the eyes, she could never hood them enough with the shrouds of her lids, the eyes twitch, breath flies away. And when she clutches at a Mamelu who lunges for her, she obstructs his arms, is killed by a dagger thrust from behind.

They slew hundreds in this battle. Heavy-bodied Faber, young ambitious Daniel, both of them pupils of Salmeron, died. Of those they killed, none matched Maladonata in the degree to which her life belonged to the settlements, and yet remained so unfulfilled.

≈≈≈

Part Seven

NOAH'S ARK

~

Riubuni rules in Sao Paolo

WHEN THE PAOLISTAS had collected a king to lead them, and such a mighty army to which new troops still came from the Tupis with their skull-smasher clubs, they felt strong enough to attack even the Spanish. The flood swept south. Villarica, Ciudad Real, Xeres, Espiritu Santo were besieged, taken, looted, Xeres, Ontiveros on the Periquy were destroyed. No White troops were at the scene.

When the Mamelus and Tupis withdrew they took along an enormous booty, the full storehouses of a dozen settlements and towns. Their jubilation was beyond measure. Tupis and Mamelus parted happily. Riubuni, heeding a slight presentiment, invited a small number of Tupis to be his escort, to lend him a greater appearance of strength in Sao Paolo.

The royal Mamelus drove along with them fifteen thousand native pupils of the Jesuits. They sent runners to the town to make ready for their reception. There were now no priests there. The last had slipped away as soon as the army marched off, enquiries were made in all directions for a replacement, but none could be found at short notice. So one of the old people, who looked worthy enough and claimed to know Latin, a White shoemaker, was dressed in a monk's brown cowl and shaved in a tonsure. The victorious royal army came in through the gate of Sao Paolo amid tumultuous cheers, bells rang out, triumphal arches welcomed King Nicolaus and dubbed him the Sword of Righteousness. And when he was carried in his chair into the church and set down at the altar with his long-trained purple cloak, Nicolaus Riubuni observed without surprise an actual cleric fussing about up there and greeting him. Ever since his successes began to accumulate, Nicolaus affected a ferocious mien in public; outraged by his bulldog face the old shoemaker chanted and worked away, and feared a shot in the back whenever he turned to bow to the altar.

The Paolistas did not keep their King Nicolaus for long. They were too much the wild beast, too used to being their own master as they went about with musket and knife, to let one of their own dictate to them. All Nicolaus had to do to ignite the anger of the locals was settle himself in the big house opposite the municipal building, placed at his disposal by town strongman Rafael Pinto (the warrior and money-grubber Pinto was a descendant of that glum old 'governor' with the half-eaten face and the Indian arrowhead in his lung) and then, in his constant fear, to surround the house (there was plenty of space) with palisades and a ditch in good old Piratiningan fashion. Their town had not yet cohered properly, there were still bogs and meadows here and there within it, but this plaza was their market square and they weren't about to give up a third of it. He refused to discuss the matter, he needed the plaza for his court, for comings and goings, for his horses, his bodyguard, they only needed it for their slave auctions. But he would tolerate no auctions outside his residence: they brought dirt and din; and above all Nicolaus feared large gatherings that he could not control; and on top of that he was annoyed with the Mamelus for carrying on their slave trading under his very nose; did not his high-sounding slogan declare 'Freedom for the Indian'; they were compromising him. The Mamelus pressed Riubuni. He would not yield. He was unused to giving in – a method which had brought him much good fortune. But not with the Mamelus. Suddenly they had no more need of him. He bothered and annoyed them. They had only appointed him for raiding and plundering Jesuits. He should, as they made absolutely clear to his so-called ministers, heave off back to where he came from. The robustness of the Mamelus' approach came simply from the fact that they saw they were the stronger.

But they had not reckoned on Nicolaus Riubuni. Soon the mighty jaguars knew what manner of beast they supped with. For Riubuni was clever, crafty. He planned his game several moves ahead, in great stealth. As he prepared the ground he showed masterful indifference to the dreadful insults they inflicted on him, beginning with the slave market right under his nose, such an affront to his dignity, then their insolent public demand, as if he were just anybody, to heave off, go on his way. The great Manuel Pinto, slaveholder, wanted his house back and was jealous! You err, my good sirs, he wheezed, those times are gone, they're gone; and he never slept.

He was supported by Sergeant Mario, chief of his general staff, who had led the operation against the reductions and was loyal to him. Certain women, mulattos, were willing to walk through fire for him. Riubuni gave out that he was closing down his Sao Paolo business and heading back to his old base of Sacramento. This provided cover for endless comings and goings by his emissaries between the two places. Until the final week he kept his plan secret even from his bodyguard, and made them privy to his intentions only when they were already ensnared in irreparable quarrels with the Paolistas. Now he considered them ready and revealed his plan: on a day to be decided by him, they would take over the town's three armouries and set upon the Paolistas in retribution for their treason against him. They had committed crimes against free Indians.

"We were lured into a war against the reductions and Spanish towns on the premise that they were full of Indians who should be freed. That's what we fought for in Sacramento, and that's why we moved our headquarters here. We led the liberated Indians here. I kept the solemn promise I made in Sacramento, that all prisoners we take shall either be freed or made into an army against the Whites. You know what happened. Now mingle as you can among the prisoners, in the slave camps, and tell them to await my signal. Passwords confirmed."

Nothing of Riubuni's plan leaked out. On the day fixed for his departure, he headed in full pomp to the south gate of the town, followed by a crowd of Mamelus. Emissaries from Sacramento were waiting there to escort their king. But behind them, in the forest, huge numbers of armed men, compatriots and allies, had gathered. And when the gate was opened, a riot broke out in which the king in his chair was borne backwards. Then a proper battle started around the gate, the Mamelus were overwhelmed, the gate captured. And then street fighting. The king was lucky. His people were very swift. The Paolistas could not reach their armouries, and when they finally fought through the stores had already been emptied, weapons distributed to the alerted slaves in the holding camps. The situation appeared hopeless. Ever more dark masses surged into the town. Indian humanity at last seemed poised for revenge against the wickedest of their persecutors.

But the Whites from Sacramento and their native allies were opposed by men who had built this town, it was all in all to them, and never in their lives had they ever willingly conceded ground to anybody. After the first shock they set about them, as in all their innumerable previous battles, with tenacity, coolness, utter contempt for death. The opposition was better armed and more numerous but, as it turned out, crumbled easily. By the time the Tupis, freed slaves and the Sacramento contingent had gained two-thirds of the town including church, market, storehouses, Riubuni had disappeared. After the first onslaught he had abandoned his chair, and surrounded by his bodyguard fired on troops in the streets, the banner of Indian righteousness fluttering overhead. He was pulled into a house to save him from gunfire. And never emerged. For at that very moment a counterattack began, which gave the Mamelus possession of this winding lane. The bodyguard had to flee. Riubuni sat tight, and no one but his bodyguard knew he was there. But this brave band, determined to regain their king, fought with such savagery that they were annihilated to the last man.

The battle raged on. A rumour – Riubuni is lost – spread among his own people as well as the Paolistas. The fighting had several motives, but not all were apparent at any moment. If Riubuni was no longer around, the struggle seemed pointless. The conquest of Sao Paolo now being attempted could have led under Riubuni to the first great emancipation of the Indian peoples, whether he wanted it or not. Now he sat in the little house and hid, because for the moment his opponents held the lane and even his bodyguard had had to retreat. Meanwhile out there his power was evaporating.

Manuel Pinto, leader of the Mamelus, surveyed the situation. He knew Sergeant Mario, Riubuni's field-marshal, and while the Tupis fought furiously in the streets, advancing house by house, while the Sacramento people retreated in confusion to find word of their king and hasten to his rescue, but where was he, Pinto despatched a dozen Mamelus to make contact with Mario and give him a letter. This note, scribbled out ten times, of which three arrow-pierced exemplars reached Mario one after the other, read:

> *We should reach an understanding now Riubuni is defeated*
> *and his body is in possession of the Mamelus. What*
> *grounds for war now exist between Sao Paolo and Sacra-*
> *mento?*

This question made swashbuckler Mario's head spin, unused to thinking he was checkmated on the spot. There really were no grounds for war between Sao Paolo and Sacramento, Riubuni was insulted, but if he's dead now, so what? He fought on for a while, the dreadful street fighting was going nowhere, so Mario replied, still indecisive, by means of an arrow-letter:

> *We should meet in the church, which is in our hands, we*
> *shall secure access for you.*

Despite advice to the contrary, Manuel Pinto presented himself with a dozen armed men and persuaded Mario: child's play for forceful Manuel. They agreed on a peaceful parting of ways, the assembly and withdrawal of armies, release of half of all the Indians stolen from the Jesuit colonies, transfer of two-thirds of all booty to Sacramento, and finally preparations for an alliance between the two towns.

They had to join forces to bring the Tupis under control. The unruly natives already had a notion to settle down in town. The ice-cold and ever surefooted Pinto was able to win them over with large presents to their chiefs. That night, as fires were put out, the dead were collected and guns were kept at the ready, the question remained: where is Riubuni? Pinto was supposed to fulfill the contract by delivering the king next morning, but he didn't have him. He sent enquiries into the night to find who had news of him, and in particular how the rumour that he was dead had started. No reports. When morning came, the only course left to the resolute Mamelu leader was to collect a thoroughly battered White corpse off the street, place it in a coffin and display it in the church. The corpse was naked, that fitted, it had been robbed, only to be expected given Riubuni's fine clothes. Luckily they had found Riubuni's belt and sword on one of his bodyguards, he always had them borne behind him, so they were able to lay something like legitimacy upon the unknown warrior's charmingly decorated coffin. To the great satisfaction of anxious Pinto and those of his entourage who were in the know, the other side voiced not the slightest suspicion. Weeping and wailing filled the church that morning, during the funeral service and blessing at which the shoemaker officiated.

At noon the evacuation of the town began. Already that morning the Mamelus had regained full control, Mario had provide all the weapons needed to secure order, in particular to prevent a general absconding of slaves. And when the evening of that day came, the town gates closed behind the men of Sacramento. A huge crowd of natives, people from the colonies and Tupis, went sadly along with them. The Paolistas too were sad, and collected their dead. Their adventure with King Nicolaus, so cleverly contrived, had cost them dear.

≈≈≈

And where was the missing king? Still alive. When the bodyguards failed to return, he was in a sticky situation. The narrow lane was deserted, he was as afraid to leave the house as to stay in it. In the dark he made a move as far as the neighbouring house, which was also deserted. He hid there for the night behind logs in the attic. Shots still cracked outside; half-waking, half-lying he fell asleep behind the logpile. In the morning he heard movement outside, and after divesting himself of his outer clothing, after smearing mud on his white shirt, he slipped into the lane like a local, and nobody paid him any attention. As he did not know what was happening – this was the hour when everyone had assembled

in and around the church for the funeral of King Nicolaus – he
questioned passing Tupis. They took him for a townsman, for
one of those, one of those who had betrayed them, and instead
of an answer one of the warriors shoved him in the back, and the
next one caught him across the shoulders with his club as he ran
away, knocking him senseless to the ground. There Riubuni lay
till evening, when locals returning to their houses picked him up,
gave him food, and brought him up to date. They thought he was
a wounded Sacramento man.

Rage roused the ailing king, without betraying himself he
stayed the night. In the morning he set off on foot after the Sacramento army, his army. He would fall on them like a thunderbolt.
He would stop them, turn them around to hurl them on Sao Paolo,
town of traitors. He limped, his shoulder was swollen, he couldn't
lift his arm. If only he had a horse.

Two days later, in the company of mounted Indian raiders who
took pity on him, he caught up with the army – it was marching
very slowly – on the Ribera river. The unruly mass calling itself
an army was camped there, seething with anger at their misfortune
and the failure of the whole glorious campaign. Many wanted to
split off. Were fortune now to smile on Riubuni, this would be his
hour. And when he came into camp, his demeanour, his limp and
his stubble unrecognised by the Tupis, none of whom knew him,
it seemed to him: I've come just at the right time.

A number of Whites and mulattos from Sacramento had
banded together, and were considering felling trees in the coastal
forest to build small boats to carry them more swiftly than the army
along the coast to Sacramento. Mario, the field-marshal, had given
permission, but he also saw the danger, for he knew what these
men wanted: to exploit the bad news before he himself arrived,
say he had committed treason and handed Sao Paolo over, this was
already being thrown in his face quite openly. Amid the pressures
of the moment, negotiating with his captains and under-of-
ficers, feeling threatened, he was told of a wounded White man
who would not be put off and had news from Sao Paolo. Mario,
without a plan, accustomed to following orders, listened in painful

distraction, and sent men to bring him the wounded man.

It is Riubuni. He recognises him right away as he approaches, all bent and crippled. And already Riubuni's fist has made contact with his face. Mario staggers back. Riubuni is hoarse as a crow, it's a good thing the men outside can't understand him. Riubuni – it really is Riubuni – rages, Mario kicks the chair on which his sword lies away from him, to the wall. "What have you done?" asks the former king. Riubuni, the tatterdemalion, shakes Mario – the bigger, and armed – by the shoulders. Mario stammers: "We couldn't find you, they said you were dead."

"They said. And you believed it."

"They found your belt and sword, and a body."

"And you believed the scoundrels, and handed over a town that was already ours." This was the accusation Mario had feared. Mario himself is horrified by the monstrous turn of events: Riubuni has reappeared to hold him to account. He is pale as a corpse, and cold, stammers again and has no idea what to say, and knows only that someone is going to do something, either him or Riubuni.

Now Nicolaus stands by the fancy chair with the crown, on which he always sits during conferences, pats the arm in greeting and settles on it, dirty as he is, pulls himself upright, winces at the pain in his shoulder, pulls on his moustache with his left hand and looks straight through Mario as if he were thin air: "Summon my people."

Mario, big broad warrior, plumed hat on his head, moves, he has picked his sword up from the chair, high riding boots reach to his hips, he steps slowly, for this is the moment. And as he walks slowly to the exit of the gaudy tent, made to Riubuni's order, he sees the coming interrogation, the death sentence of which there can be no doubt. And anyway, Riubuni was already dead, and now this on top of all the other disasters, was he not already good and dead. And when he glances back for a moment and sees the haughty rascal sitting there brooding and undefended on his throne, still tugging at his moustache, and he's considering how to do me in, Mario knows: it's ridiculous, at least we can sort this out soon enough. And in an instant he turns around, draws his sword and runs the defenceless man through before he can even stand up. "You're dead," Mario whispers, making thrust after thrust, Riubuni lying at his feet, "now you're dead, d'you hear, so nothing's changed, you won't drive me mad, damn you."

And calls the tent guards in and slaps the first one in the face, then the other: "Who let this fellow in? Which one of you? He had a knife. See! Look at it! Those dogs in Sao Paolo sent him after us, and you let him through, with his knife!" Riubuni actually does have a knife on him, given him by the Tupis along the road. The guards are tongue-tied. Mario orders them to take the body away. The captains come along now, drawn by his shouts, they had wondered why he let the dubious fellow in. They ask questions and congratulate Mario.

The affair gives him courage, he no longer needs a forced march. The Sacramento people dare nothing against him. They had put on a splendid funeral in Sao Paolo, disloyal town, for their King Nicolaus fallen in the street fighting, for the mangled body they haul along in its coffin. Tears were even shed, tears of rage for the defeat. They said: once doesn't count.

Exodus from Guayrá

IN THE PROVINCE of Guayrá, the Fathers gathered the remnants of their darkskinned flock.

Thirteen blooming settlements had been theirs. Of a hundred thousand people, by the end of that terrible week the Fathers had located twelve thousand. Eighty five thousand had been abducted eastwards into slavery, or killed.

Young Montoya, Emanuel Nobrega's right hand, led the roundup and exodus. He showed himself a Superior before ever being named as such. After the burials he allowed no day of rest. His plan was: deeper into the country, put more forests, hills and rivers between us and the Whites and – arm ourselves.

On Montoya's orders, seven hundred wide rafts were constructed. The twelve thousand were to travel on these down the Paraná to a point far enough away and suited to their needs. The natives were given no time to reflect and come to terms with what had happened. When it became evident after the first dreadful days that none of the twelve thousand had absconded, Montoya's angry forceful zeal eased up. Then he embraced his friends and admitted: he had laboured under a nightmare, that all was lost, that the flock would scatter completely. And he granted himself an outbreak of weeping. Then for the first time he revealed the new Montoya, as he walked with them in the sad ruins of Loreto among the traces of inexpressible sorrow:

"I have not been here long. I wouldn't have stayed with you much longer. Another year and I'd have advised Torrez to set up an enquiry. Into you too. You tolerated what happened here, you are complicit." And he grasped each in turn by the hand. "Crimes were committed here. Yes! Did you see what happened when the Mamelus came? Here, in this street, people lay on the ground and hoped for a miracle. A miracle! Has anyone the right to importune God for a miracle? Is that Christian? And this is how they were all taught and what they became: enthusiasts. If you had not been there too, I would have called it heathendom."

Cataldino sighed: "I sometimes felt it was too much. Sometimes it seemed to me we would be off to Heaven in the morning."

Maceta: "Nothing ill of the dead. We've suffered a major calamity. I never wept in Europe, but I weep here. Day and night. I loved these gardens. They're all trampled."

Montoya: "A garden needs fences."

Maceta: "Should we become warriors?"

Montoya kept silent, then observed: "So deep does evil lie. That such questions are asked here. What do you want, really? I don't know what has happened to you all since you became missionaries, for you can't have thought this way in Spain. Holding such views, how could you gather tribes and expose them to destruction? You should lead people to live a Christian life. This is all that's asked of you. Whatever came into your head, Brother Maceta?"

"We had a vision of the holy city, Jerusalem."

Montoya: "Which is in Heaven."

"We wanted to live in its image. Oh, Brother Montoya, we had a dream and it's over."

Montoya: "Emanuel, an old soldier, at the head. Explain to me. Did this sorceress, this Maladonata, addle his wits?"

Maceta: "She died too."

"There must be an end to it."

Cataldino, softly: "You'll do a better job, Brother Montoya. May God be with you."

Maceta: "May God be with you."

Montoya clapped the grieving man on the back: "Go, and weep."

≈≈≈

Twelve thousand people, men, women and children, let themselves be carried on rafts by the Paraná's current.

Why did the twelve thousand follow the Fathers, when no miracle had occurred, they had not suddenly found themselves in Jerusalem, the heavenly city? The Fathers who were still with them said: "Be patient, meek and pious, then God will bestow his grace on you." They said no more. The Fathers wept. And we have no home to go to, Whites will keep hunting people, we shall stay with the good Fathers.

A journey rich in sorrows. At the rapids of Maracayu they had to halt, cut a path through the forest to haul the rafts past the rapids, they climbed back on below. After endless exertions – there was no complaining, patient as they were they kept calm, but they were growing feeble, the heat, the hardships of the journey, their gloomy thoughts caused many to wilt – after great sorrows the drum beat out one morning on the foremost raft, which bore Father Montoya. They halted, Fathers and some natives inspected the terrain, fishermen were consulted, people were sent out into the country. Three days later they made a decision, and stayed.

Gone, the days of youth

GONE, THE DAYS of youth, dreams, exuberance, rapture. Gone, the expectation of Heaven's coming. The distant mighty God was not so fast to show mercy to his people, however passionately they loved Him and His son and the Virgin Mary and all the saints, and built churches, decorated altars, prayed to them daily, morning and evening sang hymns to praise them, followed the commandments and confessed and repented all sins.

Montoya, cool decisive man, pupil of Torrez, had been alerted early on by Torrez to the unusually ecstatic spirit of the young colony. Torrez had said: "They're happy, it's as if they are among children, you could believe what they believe, that they are in Galilee among the poor fishermen and country folk our Lord spoke to. Maybe it's good, at the start; actually, everything we do here is an experiment, we should scorn no path that leads to our goal. But – we need to keep an eye on this, Montoya. When I talk with Brother Emanuel, it sometimes seems I am to be, ah, kept at arm's length. You too. They would keep all the rest of the world away. This does not please me."

There was hushed talk at the time of the case of Brother Mariana, who died a heathen heretic, the circumstances were strange, he seemed to have identified greatly with the savages: "They're a remarkable bunch, these brothers of ours from Sao Paolo. They were clever clear-sighted warriors of our company, simple and determined, as is only fitting. The climate seems to have affected them." It was as if he spoke Montoya's thoughts, for he too had found "a repellent atmosphere" in the settlements. Now they were floating down the Paraná. Montoya viewed what had happened as justified punishment. As they drifted day after day on the torrid river and so much misery played about them, at one point he accosted Maceta and spoke his thoughts: "Surely you don't think it arose from nothing? You became heathens, like Mariana!"

Maceta made no reply, said nothing at all, their lovely kingdom of Jerusalem was gone, it was no heathen kingdom, how hard, how poor life would become now. But it grew easier. And when, two years later at a requiem for the Guayrá dead, Maceta and Cataldino were reminded of that distant land where so many pious people lay in the earth, among them the great Superior

Emanuel and the astonishing indefatigable Maladonata – then even they now hardly understood that earlier time. The only ones who still understood were the natives from Guayrá. They prayed to Emanuel, erected memorial stones to him in the cemeteries of the new colony, which were never left untended, whole fables accrued to the person of Emanuel, who had come to them from the sea through dark forests, over mountains. Emanuel became in the memories of the people – the new Fathers had to concede it – a counter-image to the Pizarros, Quesadas and Alfingers, who came west to the New Indies to enslave and kill the natives. Emanuel came from the sunrise and gathered them in, after he had been persecuted by the Whites. At his side the image of Maladonata also grew large, the woman from their tribe, often she was placed above Emanuel, and they told stories of her mysterious love for the priest and how she died with him, many had seen it, and they understood this death very well, who knows where she now wanders with him, where she lives, what face she wears.

≈≈≈

Meanwhile the new hard life began. They set to work with zeal, but lacked the right kind of strength, lacked the spark of those days in Guayrá when Maceta and Cataldino and the artisans were swept along by the natives' enthusiasm. They still sang, and everything had its regular place, but they no longer sang *Jerusalem, oh holy city*. When anyone hummed the tune, people started crying. Too many lay dead in the north. They prepared themselves for the grave.

They preserved all that had grown up back there: the ordering of days, work in communal groups, fair distribution of tasks, selection of magistrates from the ranks of the natives. The Fathers were directors of the various settlements that sprang up quickly one after another, for the people had to be accommodated and, hard to believe, they had to tend to newcomers who began to stream in as soon as they appeared on the Uruguay. For the calamity they had suffered – news of it spread at lightning speed – could not obscure the other calamity that hung constantly over them: the Whites.

The Jesuits distributed themselves in pairs among the ramshackle, hastily improvised settlements, the emergency structures: one to look after worldly matters, the other to provide spiritual guidance and supervision. Everything took shape more quietly and quickly than at Guayrá, fear trembled for years in the settlements, where was the excitement now about tools the Fathers had brought, no screw now sang the song of the plank into which it was bored, they had hardly any screws, most had been left lying and were lost. Huts and little houses arose, too swiftly, with little inspection, slapped together by harried hands.

As Montoya, the new Superior, declared that now the struggle for security would begin, he spoke what the natives and most of the Fathers felt in their hearts. The Mamelus were still in the east, there was now a greater distance between them, but they could still be found here, that odious town San Sacramento lay to the southeast, a second Sao Paolo, and to the west Spanish towns were encroaching, perhaps they would not attack, but others were urging the destruction of the settlements. There was no security in this world.

Pope Urban's advice

AT THIS TIME a delegation of Fathers headed for Rome, to bring to the attention of the Holy Father the troubles afflicting the Christian mission in the New World, and request his help. Montoya himself was the leader, it was his idea, with him went two newly-arrived priests, Fathers Taño and Orighi.

In Rome the eighth Urban reigned, a sprightly man in his fifties, of the wealthy Barberini merchant family in Florence. Affairs in the countries of the Whites proceeded with astonishing logicality. In Spain, the throne of I the King was occupied now by this man, now by that, Indian gold flowed to him, now only a feeble trickle, it vanished in wars and courtly pomp, and the more wars were fought the more enemies appeared, who all wanted the same thing: to have more. Pope Urban was the custodian of Catholic Christendom, for now there were several Christendoms, all fighting each other. The Pope of the Catholic Christians ruled like a king over a country, he built fortresses at the borders and declared that arms must make his country feared. And so he heaped up weapons in his city of Rome, built an arsenal in Tivoli and made an armoury of his library. Let no one think Pope Urban was arming himself against the heathen; this had nothing to do with heathens. Or that he was arming against heretical Christians: they were a long way off. On the contrary, when the arch-heretic, the King of Sweden, at one point appeared on the mainland and swept Catholic armies before him, Pope Urban was not displeased. Because he wanted the German Catholic Emperor weakened. At that time all were each other's enemies, the powers among the Whites, Spain, Germany, Italy, France all fought one another, and Pope Urban wanted to be in the game.

When Father Montoya appeared in Rome, it took him some time to recover from his enormous surprise. What was this Rome? They came from the hot plains of the Paraná and Uruguay, from profound solitude and quiet. Things had happened down there that should move White humanity. But not a breath of it had reached here. Who here knew anything of a Christian republic in Guayrá, of the tormented heaven-dreaming life of Father Emanuel and his adherents (for so it now seemed); of the destruction of the colony, the journey of a whole people down the Paraná, the new settlements. Here no one knew anything, and here it was of no matter. They looked like savages, and people entertained themselves with tales of brigands.

The general of the Jesuit order was called Muzio Vitelleschi. It began with him. He lived in a splendid new mansion; – in the south they lived in straw-thatched huts of plaster, and wooden barracks, even their little church was thatched. Vitelleschi was ill, he let them come to his bedside, he was a mild old fellow, nicknamed the Angel of Peace. Thrilled, amazed, sometimes laughing out loud in satisfaction, he had Montoya tell him everything, it took a week. To Montoya's annoyance Vitelleschi heaped the highest praises on Father Emanuel, Montoya had to adjust his words on the hop, the general wanted most of all to hear great things about the dead Superior, the martyr, and his works.

It went no better with Urban the Eighth. This man, who sported the large beard and moustachios of a warrior, received them as he lifted weights. The Pope was an athlete and had no objection to being admired in his gymnasium, which had once formed another part of his library. The three of them, Montoya, Taño and Orighi, had to wait even longer than with the general, two whole weeks, before they could present their requests. There was also the fact that the Pope was used to hearing only his own voice. He was mistrustful of requests, and if after several audiences he warily allowed a visitor to express what exactly he wanted, the visitor could at best expect to be dismissed with a snarl; most often the Pope took exactly the opposite line to the one the visitor thought desirable.

The Fathers had opportunity during their week of audiences to listen to a whole series of papal monologues, each picking up from where the previous audience left off. They were made privy to the Pope's open hostility towards the German Emperor – and, alas, towards Spain. He was arming, the Pope said, only against these imperial chaps and their Spanish allies, and now they were treated to the Nuncio's reports and his glosses on them. The travellers from the tropics observed: it's difficult in Europe, difficult.

From the last of these introductory audiences, at which Urban once again gave free rein to his sentiments regarding Spain-Austria, and declaimed to them from his latest effort, a rendering of Scriptural quotations into Horatian verse, from these long tedious sessions which afforded pleasure only to the robust Pope, Montoya returned distraught together with Orighi. They sat in the fine chairs of the Order's college-house and avoided each other's gaze. Montoya spoke first, his body shivered:

"Dear Orighi, what will become of us? For Jesus' sake, what will become of us! We can go back and continue our work with the dark people – ever since we arrived I have loved them as a part of me – but what will become of us. We are a twig, a leaf on a tree, but what sort of tree." Orighi was no more cheerful: "He talks to us only of 'my brother the cardinal'. I don't even know if they're acquainted."

"Loyola created the Order to support the papacy. But what

does the Pope do? He hates Spain and Germany. If he's honest he'd be happy for the Swedes to win a conclusive victory, as long as they don't come calling at his door. Brother Orighi, it's appalling. How can we return with this." Orighi: "We must await a better hour."

And he was right. The hour soon came. It was the day when Pope Urban took them along to Castel Sant'Angelo. There he tried on a new breastplate. So Montoya asked him as one professional to another for advice on defensive possibilities in a region such as theirs on the Paraná. Now the Pope, powerful, talkative, in his white silk shirt and silken cap, in the midst of his engineers, allowed them to make their report, but only in regard to the strategic aspects. And then a debate – in which he of course was the only party – all the way back to his palace.

The next day he had the Fathers summoned in the afternoon; they knew he had already exhausted four delegations and their business. The Holy Father seemed to have concluded that the Jesuit Fathers had come over from the New Indies to seek his military advice. For the next few days he would not let them from his sight. They had to go with him to Castelfranco, on the border towards Bologna. It was of no concern to him that their nature and circumstances were quite different. Whatever interested Urban they should study, do exactly as he indicated, it was the only proper and sure thing.

At the farewell audience, convinced he was seeing off well-schooled pupils on whom he had bestowed a good deed, the Pope heaped true tenderness upon the Fathers. Their visit, as even his nephew told them, had put him in an extraordinarily good mood. All state business proceeded more smoothly with the Pope in good spirits. The Fathers received pictures and books from his hands.

All letters to the Spanish Nuncio and the bishops of Paraguay and Chile were composed exactly in accordance with the Fathers' wishes, no haggling.

Roman echo

ORIGHI WENT TO Madrid with Taño, to see the Spanish King. Montoya would not and could not tarry longer in Europe. He made a short side trip to Spain, introduced himself to the Council of the Indies, and set off for home.

He was deeply shaken. He left behind a mountain spewing fire. Had the New Indies changed him so greatly, or what was it? No, terrible things were happening in Europe. He dared not put them into words. He wanted to think only of the country to which he was returning. Now images welled in him again of the Whites in Sao Paolo and Sacramento, and those Spaniards in the towns who looked on, quietly gloating, as colonies were massacred. These were people of the same blood as those who dwelt in Europe. People of this kind had earlier come into the lovely new lands and shown the face of the white man for the first time, representing Christianity. The horror, the despair.

On the voyage Montoya began to do what he had never done even as a novice: he scourged himself. He imposed on himself a vow of silence for the whole voyage, prayed more than he'd ever done before. When he landed in Buenos Aires he was no longer the old Montoya, he was gentle and friendly, looked like someone who had suffered a blow of fate and was struggling to recover from it. Brothers Maceta and Cataldino found him thus, and embraced him.

≈≈≈

This earnest energetic Father Montoya, the pride of old Torrez, once the bane of enthusiasts, a man of iron whose fingers itched to sink themselves in the soft flesh of the reductions – now he had melted. His broad square head still sat low and tight on his neck. Something gasped within him, beseeched: I want to go back to the monastery, I must find clarity. The words of the Pope rang in his ears, he heard him talk of fortifications and only of fortifications, and gentle General Vitelleschi, the old man, lay in his bed and knew nothing and wanted to hear tales of the Indies. It was a torment, unbearable.

The young reductions would learn a lot more about this new Superior. In his first talk to the Fathers, with whom he gathered some weeks after his return from Rome in the new San Ignacio, he said, and they trembled: "It is a matter of life and death. We shall do what is in our power. We must do it all by ourselves and think it through only by ourselves. No one shall take anything from us. But there is not one among us who is weaker for this. I want to speak of Emanuel. Some of us saw how he died. He was certain he was right. When he died, it was a blessed death. I need to apologise to him for several matters. I was in Rome, and stand before you. What Whites, Christians, are capable of you know all too well. You fled from Sao Paolo to Guayrá, we had to flee from Guayrá to here, not from heathen, but from Whites and baptised people. We should not blame the Mamelus and those of San Sacramento too much. Things are grim everywhere. One should not complain of the branch when the tree is bad. Our holy Church is engaged in a terrible struggle. We've lost some settlements, but Europe... ."

He spoke very softly, with an uncanny intensity: "If Europe succumbs, what then are we?"

After a long pause he looked around at the brothers: "Do not think that we create a few settlements here to extend protection to persecuted Indians. That would not be very much. Our task is bigger. Grit your teeth and stand fast. Pray tirelessly that God may stand with us and lend us strength. And that something of our strength may flow across to where our faith is struggling so." His words left an oppressive mood, some Fathers had tears in their eyes, all mastered an inexpressible fear. It was necessary for them to go down on their knees and call to the one who decides what shall pass.

The building of Noah's Ark

THEY FOUND THEMSELVES on the middle reaches of the Paraná and Uruguay in even deeper poverty than at Guayrá. They built huts and little houses one just like the other along the designated street line, daubed them with straw plaster. There were no windows, no chimneys, no beds in the houses, these were

Indian dwellings. The bed was a hammock, the fireplace was in the middle of the room, smoke escaped through the door. For eating and housework they squatted on the ground, at the door and outside the house. The people had no wants. Later there were contacts with Whites, the Fathers often lent groups of people to help out the Whites, and there they saw European ways, European cleanliness and White wants, but they were not tempted, they borrowed none of it.

In the new San Ignacio, which greatly resembled its earlier abandoned namesake – even the country was very nearly the same – in shady valleys, near to streams and beneath palm trees, the multitude toiled, built and went about and gradually found peace. Montoya gazed on them. There they go, the dark people. Our lifebuoy, our anchor. How strange that God tolerates the White man, savage, ingenious, and has entrusted to him alone the message of salvation, while here people go around as gentle as these, whole tribes of children. Let us cling to them! From this point on we renew the message. It was the song of old Canaan.

And as women walked slowly by, singing, children at the hip, thoughts of Maladonata flashed into his mind: this is what the bridge looked like between themselves and the natives, back at Guayrá, that is how she served Emanuel. Perhaps even Emanuel had despaired.

Build an ark, a Noah's Ark. The deluge is upon us.

Montoya brooded, and felt better.

And this, unspoken – for they were afraid to meddle in affairs over there in Europe – was the great plan for the new settlements that grew up between the Paraná and the Uruguay: to build a Noah's Ark. It was no idle fancy. Dreamily remote, the new Jerusalem. Only salvation. Avoid destruction.

≈≈≈

They began in endless zeal. The Fathers of the Company of Jesus, brothers one beside the other, formed a circle into which they drew the natives. Incursions by Paolistas into the new region eased off at this time, but by all reports the great stroke against Guayrá had only sharpened their appetite. To the west, Asuncion and other Spanish towns whose populations viewed them with a jaundiced eye were now nearer than before. Defend the new reductions, make the Ark watertight, take as many natives as possible, shut the windows and doors at the proper time: these were the watchwords of their labour.

Everything happened as old Las Casas foresaw in his vision. Christianity, saving itself from its White adherents by fleeing to the natives. So far had things come with the Whites.

Isolation from the Whites was strictly enforced. Nothing was more congenial to the natives, who now felt secure.

≈≈≈

Fathers Orighi and Taño, who had taken themselves off to Spain from Rome, managed to obtain a document from the King and the Council of the Indies, the contents of which reflected the old burned document that the itinerant Fathers Maceta and Cataldino had brought to Emanuel. The settlements of the Jesuits were accorded the right of separation, on the explicit grounds that the Whites made the Christian religion hateful to the natives because of the way Whites treated them, even those who accepted Christ.

> "And whereas missions and pious men strive in the
> New World to demonstrate the holiness of Scripture
> to unbelievers, many believers in no respect follow
> its precepts but indulge in a life of vice. In order that
> the natives whose conversion is desired may be kept
> firm in the faith, it is necessary to distance them from
> such bad examples and tyranny."

In other communications that arrived from Europe, the Crown felt moved to draw the attention of all to the odium the Fathers attracted as they followed through on their principles, and would continue to attract, and what consequences their settlements, so rich in blessings, were exposed to, especially from immigrant Spaniards. The Crown admonished the governors, warned, threatened.

≈≈≈

I the King sat as usual at his writing desk and listened, read, wrote. Now he was called Philip, now Charles. His right elbow still nudged the box containing the 'consolations of his heart', where secret reports on those around him and news from South America piled up. The name of the king might change, but the Company of Jesus loved them all.

The kings, whether lustful or chaste, pacific or warlike, were all drenched in a feeling of sin and guilt. They were taught early and late to be sinners, to be guilty. And whoever occupied high office wore two heavy cloaks. One cloak was of purple and green, embroidered in gold with crowns, knights, nobles, jousts, happy animals, verdant gardens and prettily beckoning women, there were children, too, at their games, men raising goblets at table and having a good time. Over this cloak of royal honour and joy lay the cloak of sin and guilt. This depicted the same people on a black ground, they ate and drank, but among them sat a frightful figure that observed them with amiable scorn. Some saw this figure as they drained their cup, in fear they forgot to drink, it was Satan awaiting them. The women beckoned, bared their bosom, swam in water and stretched out arms in yearning, beneath their clothes a little pig's tail curled, their ivory legs ended in horses' hooves and cat's claws. And where jousting knights crossed lances with the happy crack of battle, and where strapping children played in sand and a mother suckled her youngest and sang to it with dreamy eyes, there to one side in the grass a peasant honed his sickle on a stone. But the peasant's cap sat on a gaping skull, the smock fell away in front and revealed white ribs, and in the shoes were white bones and inside were no heart, no lungs, no entrails.

The black cloak covered the purple and green. From early on the kings were taught to see to it that the black fully covered the purple. And if the purple was heavy, the priests took care that the black should be even heavier. So I the King would have been happy to enjoy his power, his court, his wars and victories, but he must be mindful always of his priests and his confessor. He bestowed more and more on the monasteries. And the Jesuit Fathers, they were a delight, they constantly needed help.

Taking up arms

THEY WROTE AND sent requests to Spain, they swarmed like bumblebees about the Council of the Indies and the Court. For their dark subjects they extracted from the King the title of 'most loyal vassals'. This was a triumph. The King exempted his most loyal vassals from the tribute that others had to pay. He decreed: from their eighteenth year they must pay per caput and per annum one peso. The tribute was regulated by the Viceroy of Peru, the Crown undertook to provide for the living of one missionary in each of the several settlements; the living of the other – for each of the new settlements was provided with two directors by the Order of Jesuits – was the responsibility of the respective Provincial of the Order.

≈≈≈

Montoya the Superior, now in San Ignacio, now in Corpus on the Paraná, now farther south in Santa Ana, pondered the mass of communications flowing to him from the royal chancellery. How fine it all looked from over there. But neither Mamelus nor Tupis were intimidated by scrolls of paper with dangling seals. When one day a roving gang of Mamelus was reported in the neighbourhood, Montoya was not displeased. Whether the Governor in Asuncion and his people liked it or not, he would have to accept that the Fathers were arming their people with what weapons they possessed, spears, arrows, slings, and drilling them. When Tupi tribes approached from the Sierra del Tape in the southeast, crossed the upper reaches of the rivers Ijuhy and Piratini and threatened the reductions of San Lorenzo, San Miguel, and San Juan, Montoya first of all pulled these reductions, which lay too far into the danger zone, back to the Uruguay. Then at San Cristoval and Maria Teresa, the Tupis, supported by Mamelus, out for loot in their old way, were opposed by well organised formations of native Christians led by militarily schooled Jesuits, Fathers Mola, Romero, Bernal. These Fathers were able to send back triumphant reports from the Uruguay and Paraná: the attackers have been thrown back, chased away, the insolent waves have broken.

Montoya absorbed this uncommon news without excitement.

He arranged a chain of watch posts along the Sierra del Tape, linked to the hinterland by couriers. At the consecration of a new reduction on the Uruguay, near to its confluence with the Ijuhy, Montoya spoke to the warrior Fathers Mola and Romero:

"God's servant is meek and a light to the heathen, so it is said. Are we meek? Can we be a light to the heathen? It is written: to open the blind eyes, to bring out the prisoners from the prison, and them that sit in darkness out of the prison house. Are we doing this? When we go armed, what thoughts do the heathen entertain of Christianity, before it can show its meekness? Those to whom light and truth are given, are given them so that they may carry them out into the world. Just as in the beginning the earth was without form and void and darkness was upon the deep and God said Let there be light, and there was light, so is the world of men even now without form and void, and there is a darkness upon the deep. Even now the spirit of God moves on the waters. Truth and light were brought by Jesus Christ. We were sent by the ordained followers of Christ to bring truth and light. God cannot will that his light be swallowed by the darkness, or he would not have spoken, not sent his son.

"Then should we be meek and destroy our weapons? Should we seal up our thoughts and act as if the Saviour had never appeared, as if there were no truth and no light, should we be meek because it is comfortable and flatters us, should we look on as darkness and heathendom triumph? Let no one dare to be godlier than God."

Later, as debate among the Fathers about future tactics simmered on, Montoya, never for a moment diffident, gave his opinion: "It is not our fault that we must gather the Indian tribes. It is not we who drive them together in one spot. What happened to the ancient people of God is happening to us: the kings and kingdoms of all heathendom are afoot and set up their camps all about us. We shall not rely on some Egyptian's reed staff. We know that it will go with us exactly as it says in the Scripture: if a man lean on the reed staff of Egypt it will go into his hand and pierce it. Generals and kings are all on the march, and summon their soldiers: to arms! What are they defending? Whom do they attack? And truth is supposed to go down without a murmur?

"At no time has truth been under such dreadful threat as now. We know what is entrusted to us. We defend the truth. If truth should disappear, the blame will not be ours."

≈≈≈

Two years later Fathers travelled to Rome and to Spain to complete the final step: licence to bear arms.

≈≈≈

While consultations in Spain continued and matters were weighed up from every side, while Whites in the neighbouring lands to north and east discussed the absurd and outrageous plan and unanimously rejected it, the Mamelus broke out, untroubled by all the pious and impassioned attention they attracted, and swept like a deluge from the coast westward, aiming to cross the whole continent and fall on Spanish Peru, its riches not yet exhausted, pick from this fallen giant's corpse whatever scraps the greedy Spaniards had left. They thrust aside reductions and Spanish forts erected against their coming; after enormous distances of wilderness, forest, swamp were behind them, after they had battled through the region of Cayapos, along the Rio Tiete on the upper reaches of the Paraná, they crossed the Sierra de Cayapo and penetrated into the Matto Grosso.

Europe shrank from these demons, in which it secretly recognised itself – well, Europe was already shaky. But even there, no measures would have been taken to protect the reductions, had not the shameless Mamelus laid hands on the gold mines of Cuyaba and Montegrosso. What the pleas of the Jesuits, their appeals to a common faith had failed to achieve now became possible. Patience was exhausted, a resort to arms was wanted. "Heaven is with us!" crowed Orighi in a letter to Montoya, "it has led the Mamelus to make a grab for the King's gold mines. These are the ways of God." Yes, the ways of God, thought Montoya, still numb, he was already past bitterness. But even he recognised something like an act of Providence: they have been struck blind, they shall be destroyed.

The Crown consented to everything the negotiators requested, after the most touching conversations about the cost of armaments and whether, if the worst came to the worst, the Fathers really could protect their pious pupils. Orighi reassured the Crown, from profoundest conviction. They were more certain of their flock than the King of his army. The Crown was astonished, and pleased. (The thought, emanating from Peruvian heads, that the Jesuit Fathers and their flock might themselves rebel one day never crossed anyone's mind.)

And so Montoya achieved what he wanted. Noah's Ark was made watertight. Let the deluge come. It surged about them. The ark would float and survive annihilation.

Thirty years of killing among the Whites

IN THE TWILIT countries of the colourless people, of whom thousands so far had broken away in savagery and emptiness, nations went into convulsions. All the riches they had gathered in the newly discovered continent came to them in vain. They were not comforted. Mad frenzy broke into the open. White horde faced White horde.

Everything was poisoned by the sense of sin and guilt. Ghostly figures, images of madness drifted about in broad daylight. It had come to wars between groups of Whites under the sign of the very religion that should have quietened them. They held scraps of this religion like daggers between their teeth, and ran at one another.

Decades of death fell on unhappy White humankind like rain and hailstones.

The war lasted thirty years, but smaller wars had presaged it for decades before.

It was as if the White people sensed what they lacked, and so hurled themselves at one another and dragged doom into their existence.

They lay broken as the storm receded. Whole countries, devastated. The numbers of those slaughtered was not less than the numbers they had slaughtered in the New Indies.

Peace upon the Christian republic

PEACE UPON THE Christian republic on the Paraná.

It was mild, fertile country, where people could spread and grow. Soon they had thirty colonies. On the right bank of the Paraná lay Trinidad, San Cosme, Itapua, Jesus, nearer to the Tebicuary the colonies of Santa Maria de Fe, Santa Rosa, Santiago, San Ignacio-Guazu, in the north of the province of Paraguay the reductions of San Joaquin, Belem, Estanislao, between Paraná and Uruguay numerous new and older colonies, Yapeyú, La Cruz, Santo Tome, Apostoles, Martires del Japon, San Ignacio-Mini, Loreto, Corpus, Santa Ana, San Borja.

They were a hundred and fifty thousand people. No gold or silver mines in their region. Sugarcane, indigo grew here, and cotton bushes in clumps. The bushes started out green and nondescript, at blossom time the pale buds were covered by a green calyx, then came the ripening, the buds opened, turned golden yellow on a dark ground, and seed capsules, the fruit, swelled out of the dark ground and their bursting loosed tufts of thick white filament, a tangle of hairs, and the plants released the seeds to sail freely through the air and find themselves a place. The date palm grew here, groves of coconut palm, the fig, oil palm, in the fields manioc grew, fine cassava flour was won from its clumpy roots, potatoes, sweet potatoes.

And whole groves were filled with the remarkable prized evergreen of yerba-maté. There are countries that have only the barest necessities, and their inhabitants must grow strong and cunning to coax the soil to feed them and their descendants. There are other countries that provide everything people need, but all of it coarse and scanty. Then there are rich countries. And then others that even cosset their people. They do this in many ways: with the wine grape, with opium, coca leaves. On the Paraná and Paraguay, the maté tree took this role. It grew dense in the eastern mountains, in Tupi country and the foothills, around the headwaters of the Ijuhy. Groves tracked the upper course of the Uruguay. And along the right bank of the Paraná, in the hills of the Mirangua river as far as Igatimi and farther westward where you come to the reductions of Conception and Belem, the precious groves extended all along the Paraguay river. The tree grew tall as the apple tree of northern lands. They called it *caa*, its ribbed leaves *caa-nazu*, the unribbed *caa-mine*. People went in groups into the woods to gather maté, dug trenches and put in sackfuls of leaves. They took cowhides from their carts and covered the trenches. The leaves were left in the ground to dry, then loaded onto carts and brought to people. From the leaves they made a tea with hot water. The tree's sap infused into the tea, the spirit of the maté was not lost. They sat, those White and dark people who wished to partake of the thin yellow brew, day after day, stuck a hollow reed between their lips and invited the spirit of the maté, who lived in the mountains of the Jerbales, to speak to them. He never spoke loudly. If they put many leaves in the water, the spirit would intoxicate them, if they used only a few, he made them cheerful, comforted them, even induced sleep.

On the broad plains of La Plata, horses and oxen brought by the first conquerors multiplied and became wild, as did hounds that ran off. Horses and cattle roamed the plains in herds. There were many kinds of bee. The one that gave the whitest wax they called opemus.

A kind of large falcon was called macagua. The snakes of this country, large and small, would annoy the falcon, it would square up to them for a big fight. Natives who lived in the forest explained: it deceives the snake by hiding its head under its wing and pretending to sleep. When the snake approaches, it lunges with its beak. The snake counters with a bite. Then, the natives say, the falcon flies down from the tree and eats a herb that protects against snakebite, it knows this. It flies up again, continues the fight, and every time it is bitten it goes back to the herb. But it keeps on at the snake until it has killed and eaten it.

≈≈≈

An enormous chain of mountains tracked the coast of this continent, its peaks were skittles and spearpoints, ice covered some of them, several spouted fire. Down from the peaks and flanks of the enormous mountain range waters tumbled, the

Marañon hurtled from its lake down into the abyss of the valley, and when it found its opening it broke through the mountains. And there lay its plain.

And like a monster with flowing mane the Amazon leapt from the mountains down into its plain. From left and right, rivers attached themselves to its might, its coming affected vast tracts, they followed entranced and sank into its waters. When the Amazon rose, it overflowed its banks for great distances, devastation encroached on the land, animals fled, waterfowl left their islands. Floodwaters surged in tumult. Often the waters forced their way in single-minded fury into loose earth, and then the river, the seething sea, carried away whole floating islands with trees, plants, birds, monkeys, even people. The trunks of giant palms were washed by a muddy tide. Dark people glided in boats over the crowns of sunken trees, settled in hollow trunks, monkeys leapt around them, ants left the ground and stuck nests together in branches. Trees bloomed in colourful profusion, a garden above the mud, farther than the eye could see. And then the river gave back hill after hill, sandbank after sandbank. And people were on the move again, turtles returned to the sandbanks, it was the season of the riverside, heat brooded over tree-corpses, gaudy plants rose out of them, pushed up mighty stems.

Belonging to this continent and growing on it were dark people, who entrusted themselves to the Jesuits. They followed the new magical teaching, of a ruler over animals, trees, over spirits and births, and of a Saviour. In them was not the slightest trace of the soul's suffering and torment that had engendered this alien doctrine.

The Fathers on the Paraná often wondered at the anxious care taken by new converts to follow rules precisely; but how could magic succeed otherwise?

Tirelessly, insatiably they decorated their streets, squares, chapels, altars, cemeteries. The Fathers never had to urge on, had only to dampen down zeal. Natives cut and carved fine big crucifixes at the ends of the dead-straight streets. They erected little wooden chapels outside the reduction, on feast days processions wended to them. They cared for every single tree in the avenues, and the settlements became orchards of palm and orange. They had not selected the place for the reduction, this the Fathers had done, and they had not decided the layout, but with the little houses, streets, churches and chapels they made these places their own, bringing in flowers and shrubs and trees, and in their midst a whole dense cloud of birds, monkeys, draught animals, cattle, horses, wild beasts from the plain.

At the churches they hedged the graveyards, nurtured rows of cypress, orange and lemon trees beneath which lay their people who had died and were waiting here for the trump of judgement in order to live again and be delivered forever from Death. They laid a great central avenue through the cemetery, placed crosses in the middle and at each end, sited little chapels by the boundary hedge, where they came every Monday to hear a requiem.

In the churches one side was for men, the other for women, in accord with the guidance of the great Carlo Borromeo. The two sides were separated by a barrier, children sat at the front, behind them their guardians with rods, then the young people and behind them the older people, their guardians.

As much as they could, they decorated with pretty pictures the big common areas used by women for weaving, spinning and basketry. The pictures showed, for those who could not read, the passion of the Saviour and the joy of Heaven.

The singing of hymns had attracted Indians from the time of Father Emanuel's exodus from Sao Paolo to Guayrá. Their children picked up by themselves the wonderful songs of praise, invocation and entreaty. Older natives formed orchestras. They constructed their own violins, cellos, pipes, trumpets, even little organs.

They developed a tremendous inclination to convert others, returned as often as they were allowed to their old villages, into the forest they had abandoned, and sought acquaintances and clansfolk. They invited them to their homes, treated them hospitably, showed them around, took them to lessons, to the chapels. Their patience was boundless, they went to all sorts of trouble and exposed themselves to ridicule and insults. But everyone in the settlement rejoiced whenever a friend was won over.

The Fathers told them about sin. Whatever they were told they held fast to, word for word. Since heaven or hell depended on their right conduct, they often fell into brooding. They were beset with doubts, pestered the Fathers, who had their work cut out to put everything straight. The natives' scruples and exactitude knew no bounds. They confessed at Christmas, Whitsun, Easter, on the year-day of the church's patron saint, and on holy days specified by the Pope.

≈≈≈

Life in the new settlements was at first gloomy and strict; gradually it lightened. The natives obeyed the Whites. They learned from them and developed great skills, learned to work stone for the building of houses and to make tiles in kilns, knotted carpets. And as their peaceful life continued they set up studios for painters, gilders, goldsmiths, for locksmiths, cabinet makers, carpenters, watchmakers, weavers, iron founders.

The goods they produced – ever more as they grew more secure in their lives – varied according to the terrain they inhabited. In regions nearer the tropics they promoted the cultivation of cotton, maize, gathered honey and wax, in other regions they planted cotton, hemp and wheat, maté and cattle were everywhere.

Huts and houses belonged to the community. Everything produced went to the public storehouses and was distributed equitably. Portions were set aside for widows, orphans, for emergencies, for the church, for the small elected administration of the settlement. Any excess was traded, and from this was taken a tax for the tribute, for any weapons needed, for bronze, for gold, silver to decorate the churches.

And so everything was shared fairly.

Since they had a good ear and a fine musical sense, their choirs amazed all visitors.

The Fathers did not teach them Spanish. They knew what they were doing. Rather they taught Latin. It took a long time for the Spanish Crown, chivvied by the hostility of neighbouring provinces, to hear of this and admonish the Fathers not to neglect Spanish.

The Jesuits, the directors, the elder for general governance, the younger for spiritual and external matters, were housed just like the natives, and enjoyed no privileges.

≈≈≈

So Noah's Ark, the construction of which was begun by Father Montoya and his brethren, proved quite sturdy.

The hostility of neighbours and the wider world washed around the new entity as it became ever more visible.

For Montoya and his people there were no longer forest, plain and river with their innumerable insects, birds, fish, jaguars. Nothing there instilled fear. Murky shadows, the enchanted confusion into which these had cast young Mariana: in the end he had to surrender, and died. How Maladonata, the Red Cat, rustled and clinked and sang all around Emanuel. And he understood it, the rolling wave of Tupis and King Riubuni, he saw the hellish light of their crimes, the green surging sea, the scythe sang, struck. Bedazzled, holding its breath, the forest full of trees, birds, animals, ants and snakes had received the Jesuit Fathers. They were a mysterious crowd of spirits such as the groves and fields had never seen. They scurried across ponds, dived into the river, they had the heavy bodies of men, hung all about in black.

That was over.

Hard, proud and cold, Montoya took possession of his castle alongside the Fathers. They slammed the gates, drew up the bridge. They took with them a plaintive swarm of dark people.

≈≈≈

The Fathers became more certain and determined, like the people they took under their wing. And with certainty came greater courage. And now they were not satisfied with tribes that flowed to them from the middle reaches of the Paraná, between Paraguay and Paraná. They sent emissaries to the province of Chile, to the Indians of the south. Father Mascardi wandered that way, and founded a mission on the island of Nahuel Huapi. Father Arce went to the Panoki, and San Rafael and San Francisco Xavier were founded. Fathers Zea and Hervas taught among the Chiquito.

And the more they spread out, the more they irritated the Whites. There were Indian revolts, which were attributed to their machinations.

State visit to Yapeyú

A SOLEMN DAY in Yapeyú on the Paraná.

The colonies were blooming.

It was reported from Tucuman that a royal Visitor, the counsellor Francesco Alvaro, was on his way from Cordoba and Asuncion. Yapeyú was the permanent residence of the Superior of this province. Montoya wanted to receive him in Yapeyú, below the confluence of the Ibicuy river. With Montoya came the Bishop of Asuncion, who was just then making a tour of the reductions.

Montoya was no longer the young man brought by Torrez to Father Emanuel. He was broad and stocky, beardless; the other Fathers too, who stayed put now and taught and directed, had done away with their wild vagrant beards. Montoya's hair was grey, white at the temples, his angular face was lean. A fanatical severity permeated his being. The eyes under the strong brow ridge gazed out suspicious and restless. He rode, escorted by a company of native cavalry, beside the new Bishop of Asuncion whom he had fetched, Felix, a lanky, dignified, handsome man of his own age.

Bishop Felix was of a different nature to his predecessor, Don Reginald de Lizarraga, who together with the very noble governor had so bewailed his sojourn in this country.

Felix, an Italian, sat on his horse like a knight and enjoyed the gentle landscape. He lifted himself in the saddle to gaze behind and to the side. They passed dense groves of bamboo that accompanied the river's course and concealed the low growth along the deep roadside ditches, in which water stood. His face, grave and calm, exuded benevolence, a dark brown beard framed the face, melancholy black eyes queried and greeted the landscape. Now he was riding along the bank of the Paraná. Rome, Florence, Ferrara were far away, he had given up his Classical studies in order to hear no longer the hideous din of European wars. He dreamed of the magic of a southern landscape, of a great peace.

He had a particular reason to seek out the remarkable and much discussed reductions of the pugnacious Jesuits. He was tracking down his nephew, young Gonzales da Santa Cruz, who had lodged with him in Asuncion and had disappeared in the direction of the settlements. What could have led my unruly secretive Gonzales, my prickly scion, to transplant himself here? It is already so long, two years, three, since he buried himself away. He could have been my vicar apostolic despite his youth, he could have stayed for good in Asuncion, where he was born. Of course, then I would never have come to ride through this remarkable, remarkable world. It is like another planet.

And when they were on the hilly grassland some miles distant from Yapeyú, they saw grass moving, feathered heads bobbed up and down in the grass, they were mounted Indians, a strong contingent. Felix turned in shock to silent Montoya, who had seen them already and nodded calmly: "We'll stop and wait for them. They want to welcome you."

Then the vanguard of the horsemen, a cavalry company from Yapeyú, was with them, ceremoniously welcoming the episcopal visitor. The whole troop caught up with them at an open place farther from the riverbank, strong riders armed with lances. They unfurled their flags, paraded with their mounts in tight formation this way and that. Then they halted, sprang from their horses and threw themselves to the ground before the bishop. Montoya whispered: "They await your blessing." Felix, absorbed in the astonishing scene, raised a hand and spoke some words. At once the bodies were back in the saddle, forming up around the guest and his escort, banners fluttered at their head, trumpets and drums sounded.

As they rode the bishop drew Montoya close, they had hardly spoken for the major part of the journey, the bishop, usually jolly and talkative, had no idea once initial courtesies were done how to approach this enigmatic man. To think of his fine brisk Gonzales among these sourpusses. Felix turned his handsome bearded face to Montoya: "Well, my dear Father, what is this? These are your people?"

"A company from Yapeyú."

"There are more of them?"

"They sent the one company on ahead. No doubt the second awaits you at the gate."

"My God, and they are all armed and have horses and are trained?"

"Of course."

"My dear Father, I had heard of it. I just never imagined it like this."

Montoya cast a casual glance at his companion. It worked away in Felix as they trotted slowly on. I'm being received by a military power, an actual state. How alarming. These lads of old Ignatius are an outrageously assertive bunch. Even have flags. What do they gain from it. It's quite incredible. Over there they have no idea, the eyes would start from their heads.

"Tell me, dear Father Montoya, do the other reductions have such horsemen, and armed?"

"Of course."

"But this is dangerous. I assure you, when I saw them approaching, my heart pounded."

"Dangerous for whom?"

"Why, for the towns of the Whites."

"They obey us. For the rest we never have to give them orders. We just tell them what is good for them. And they persuade themselves that it is so."

"But if they were to fall on our towns?"

"It never enters their heads."

"It just occurred to me."

"Our natives have no desire to acquaint themselves with the sinfulness of towns, and sensible townsfolk do not fear them. Anyway, why should lions and tigers fear the shepherd."

The bishop was shocked. "Who are the lions and tigers?"

"Not our people."

"Our townspeople? Are our townspeople so wicked?"

Montoya's face flickered, without looking at the bishop he said: "Not any more."

The second cavalry company fell in at the gate, through which, bearing insignia of their rank, came dark men, the corregidor, town officials of various grades. Father Vinzenze Griffi, priest of the settlement, approached the bishop's feet. And behind him, to Felix' great joy, was his good Gonzales; he came forward to kiss the hand of the bishop, who had dismounted. The bishop took him by the arm and gazed into his face: "Nothing changed. Exactly as you were." But he saw that he had changed. The bishop had little time to surrender to his thoughts.

The people of the settlement had taken great pains to welcome the bishop and prepare the town for the royal Visitor who was to come with him, or a little later. They brought flowers from the fields into the church, erected triumphal arches in the streets and wove garlands. And how they decorated the arches and garlands. They went fishing and hunting, caught the most splendid fish in the river, organised a drive for jaguar and deer, trapped fowl. They hung trophies from the river on fishhooks among the great palm fronds of the garlands, and these were the pride of the fishermen. They disembowelled the jaguars and deer, tied the great carcasses to the poles of the triumphal arches. Amid the green foliage they tethered colourful fowl, humming-birds and parrots on long cords. The garlands shimmered with whole flocks of such birds. They carried huge masses of foliage into town, spread a carpet all the way from the gate to the church. Flowers, fruit, fowl in front of every door.

And so, preceded by a vanguard of cavalry, amid blaring music, the bishop entered sun-drenched bell-loud merry Yapeyú. He was buffeted by cheers from the people lined up in dense crowds on both sides of the street, behind him rode Superior Montoya, Father Griffi, and his Gonzales. The Italian bishop had never dreamt of such a sight. He wondered, as he distributed blessings left and right, how this reception and his journey could be described, reported to Rome. Really you can only praise it, but it is surprising and a little bit illicit. Native infantry, and a troop with actual arquebuses, brought up the rear. The music fell silent, they were nearing the church, the cavalry moved aside for bishop, clergy and town officials. Organ sounds swelled towards them from the church. As they entered they were enveloped in the lovely clear tones of a children's choir. Women knelt in the church, flowers at their breast, you could hear them sobbing as the bishop prayed at the altar. The Te Deum rang out.

As the bishop left the church and was led to the house that would serve him for the visit – it was no different from the other houses, but they had spread soft fabrics and linens on a cot, placed skins on the floor, set up a table and some chairs – he became aware of large bowls and baskets outside many of the houses, filled with maize and other seed. On enquiring he was told: these are for sowing, they have been put out so they too can receive the blessings he bestows as he goes through the town. And then the little creatures gambolling about the posts of the garlands like small and middle-sized dogs, but on the other hand not like dogs in their catlike slinking, they jumped at him as he went into his house, and the bishop saw he was expected to smile and say a friendly word. He smiled obediently and asked Montoya what these creatures were called. Young jaguars, he learned.

≈≈≈

He had a day to recover from these impressions. The royal Visitor was delayed. That evening a meal was arranged for Felix in the spacious magistracy building. For an hour afterwards he sat with three Fathers of the Company of Jesus over a bowl of maté. Here he noticed how his Gonzales had changed. What kind of men they were, these Jesuit Fathers, and Gonzales had taken something of them on. Clever, practical men, serious, but they could laugh sometimes, were interested in everything, but all from one angle only: the saving of souls. Which is good, but it can be overdone and tires one. It is, found Bishop Felix, in the long term – and a few weeks are already too long – tedious and miserable and tries one's patience. He sat with these young people – for even his contemporary Montoya he considered young, belonging in the same class as Griffi and his scion Gonzales – really only for the purpose of observing them. They are a strict company, the Jesuits, he found, the Church can depend on them, but they are infuriating. They kiss my hand, but at bottom they deny and condemn me. Oh, they are merciless. They are just like those who stand behind the princes and kings of Europe, whom not even the Pope can fend off, who press for war against everything that is not Catholic. They know only decisiveness.

Finally Gonzales came to him next morning, and he was able to attempt a conversation with him alone. But to his bewilderment it was not Gonzales who spoke, but a young adherent of Ignatius de Loyola. That was what the Fathers had made of him.

Felix had with him the Odes of Horace, he told of the lovely new verses the Pope had crafted, translated from the Psalms of David in antique style. The young man was silent.

"Do you not play the flute still?" asked Felix, already sensing the pain a No would inflict.

"Yes," said Gonzales, "and I am grateful to you, uncle, for the lovely instrument you gave me. All the flutes they make here are modelled on it. I teach them."

"I'm pleased. And do you enjoy it?"

"How could I not, when I see how they learn, how they follow, how light arises in them."

"You are like Orpheus, who makes walls move with his fluting."

"But these are not stones."

Whatever can I say that he won't contradict. Felix praised the boundless labour of the Jesuit Fathers, and the pleasure it afforded him to see his young nephew active in this place, which was really still a wilderness, and that he had abandoned Asuncion, where a glittering career beckoned him, for this.

"What should we do," smiled the bishop half in earnest, rubbing his delicate fleshy beringed hands, "when our youth and our pride abandon us. We Whites are still around, after all, and we live in towns." Gonzales stared straight ahead, pursed his lips in the old way Felix loved so well, and lowered his head firmly and with determination between his shoulders, oh he takes this from Montoya, these Jesuits, how they have ruined him.

"What is there in these towns?" asked Gonzales, "I could

even say, what is there among the Whites, uncle? The Gospel does not mention Whites. It recognises only heathen and believers." And at once Gonzales began to denounce the towns, sparing not even Asuncion, the Asuncion where he himself had been born and where Felix wanted to make him vicar-general. He spoke of Asuncion and the towns of the Whites as if they were pits of depravity.

The unhappy bishop hid his hands, which were no use to him, under his belt and would have liked to hide himself entirely: "Gonzales, really our towns have much else to offer. I too deplore them in many respects, but still I would rather hold on to them."

But despite this mild riposte the young priest held firm in his condemnation, it was the others speaking, what sort of people are they, they're not people at all, people take a rest sometimes, but a Jesuit is a Jesuit morning, noon and night, at every hour he prods, whips, drives, what breed of men has risen up here, to whom has the Church committed herself – what actually does she seek to save through these men?

When Gonzales at last concluded his denunciations – they flew about like building blocks a boy has tired of playing with – the bishop leaned back calmly, closed his eyes, stroked his soft wavy beard and pulled himself together. You must overcome every trial, even this.

"I believe, my dear Gonzales, that your father would have done better to send you right away for a monk. Perhaps you still want that?"

Since Felix had closed his eyes in self preservation, he did not see the curt shake of Gonzales' head, but he heard the ejaculation: "To the monastery? Us? You'd like that, you lot!"

The bishop stood and clapped him gently on the shoulder. He had said *you*. So, it was true.

Differing opinions on various matters

THE FOLLOWING DAY the King's Visitor, the counsellor Alvaro, arrived. Maceta, grown so old and still footloose, had attached himself to him. The visit was not strictly necessary, since the decree he had to announce related to non-Jesuit settlements. But the Viceroy of Peru had advised him to call on the Jesuit Fathers as well, and take a look at their great work. In the simple, humble but spacious town hall, the only building with windows, the Visitor read out the royal decree, which had been included in a communication to the Viceroy of Peru. The bishop and the assembled Fathers listened.

"My cousin, state counsellor, noble lord, my Viceroy, Governor and Captain-general of Peru. To all those who find themselves charged with matters of governance. It will not have escaped your memory that, through diverse royal decrees promulgated by me and by Their Majesties my predecessors, it has been laid down that the Indians of this Province shall remain in the enjoyment of their liberties equally with the other vassals of my kingdoms. You know also that this is not consistent with personal service, which in diverse places is grafted onto the tribute which the Indians are to pay, and that on many occasions it has been expressly decreed that such personal service is to be suppressed and substituted by a due amount of tribute in the form of money or grain, maize, root crops, fowl, fish, cotton, grasses, honey, vegetables. Meanwhile I am informed that, despite repeated prohibitions, personal service persists to the great disadvantage of these peoples, whom the Spanish commandery regards and treats as slaves. Therefore I have decided as follows, to charge and to order you, by means of the present communication, as soon as you receive this, to delay not in dismantling completely and irrevocably this so-called relationship of personal service wherever and in whatever form it may occur in the Provinces."

The King had attached a letter to this missive, revealing his particular concern over the matter:

"You will be mindful, my cousin, state counsellor and noble lord, my Viceroy, Governor and Captain-general, that the slightest delay or aggravation in this matter will be perceived by me as a personal injury, and that in addition to the strict and thorough report which I request of you, your own conscience is burdened by the harms suffered by the Indians and which you must make good.

At Madrid.

By command of our lord the King:

Don Fernando de Contreras."

No conversation followed the reading. The gentlemen had various thoughts about the missive.

Then they rode, the bishop and the Visitor, accompanied by Father Maceta, Griffi and young Gonzales, out to the meadows and pastures.

Bishop Felix chatted about cattle drives he had witnessed near Asuncion:

"These natives have an inborn skill. And how they wrangle on horseback. When they creep past us in town you would not think them capable of anything. Now let me assure you I am well-disposed towards them, but I could never stand them in town with their indolence, their laggard wits. My God, how slow the poor creatures are to understand anything! Out on the plain they are transformed. They are still savages, of course. I was charmed every time. They sit on their mounts, every lad has an axe in his hand on a long cord that he winds about his arm. And then off they go and hurl the axe when they catch up with a herd that's running before them, they hurl it at the legs of a steer. The axe has a blade like a half-moon, and when it strikes it slices through a ligament, just one ligament, and the beast lies there."

"And what do they do with it then? It can't move."

"Certainly not. Where would they take it. We have not many cattlesheds here, nature is one gigantic cattleshed, a blessed country that relieves you of everything. When the beast lies there they cut it up as if in a slaughterhouse, and carry off the good meat and the hide. The rest they leave for vultures. Not so many vultures here, but whole flocks fly in our region."

Young Gonzales: "That, dear uncle, is because we chased all the vultures away to you. There's nothing for them here."

"Why is that? Do the people here carry everything back with them?"

"We don't hunt. We consider hunting un-Christian. We raise cattle."

Impudent didacticism. You open your mouth, and every time they know better. "This is really all new to me, my dear Gonzales. You put yourselves to a lot of trouble."

Old Maceta interrupted, to lighten the tone. "Of course we have just as many cattle in the fields as you have around Asuncion. But we like to keep the people close to hand, and we wanted to wean them from that detestable use of the axe, which we know well."

This is better, the tone at least.

The bishop thought how fine those young fellows must be on their steeds, hurling axes. He said: "I see how you attend to every detail. And how do you hunt horses? That too is a marvellously skilled task, the way our savages manage it. Because they are lazy. They used to stay in the saddle and organise a big hunt over the plain after the big herds, lasso overhead, and thrown. What do our lazybones do now! It made me laugh when I saw. They search out a spot in the plain where the horses are wont to pass. There they construct a kind of barricade or barrier, and conceal themselves nearby. And when the animals come along they have to slow down as they approach the barrier, and stop at the barrier and sooner or later turn around. At that moment our lazybones jump into action and lasso them as calm as you like."

Maceta: "We keep horses in the meadows, and in stables. Since we have so many in the meadows and in our stables, we have to concern ourselves only with breeding. We haven't hunted horse for a long time now."

Horrid people, thought the bishop, now this ancient fellow has to chip in.

And as they rode the heavens overtook them. A severe thunderstorm approached. At the first drops the bishop turned around. He was disgruntled but gave no sign. As they trotted along, Maceta reported to his deafened ears on the development of the ranching operation, here in Yapeyú it was only small-scale, he should check out the reductions farther north. The bishop made no reply, really he had no interest in ranching.

As the Visitor sat in the bishop's quarters that afternoon, Felix asked: "Will you stay here long? I shall leave tomorrow or the day after."

"A pity. I'd have liked to travel back with you. But I want to see more things along the Paraná, since I'm here. The Viceroy will be interested."

"Yes, do stay. It's of great interest to everyone, what these Jesuit Fathers are achieving. Nothing less than overwhelming. I was aware of some of it, but even I have been astonished."

"Such calm. Such order."

"True. It all runs like clockwork. One is quite ashamed when one thinks of our towns."

The counsellor laughed: "Of course not! And anyway, there are Whites in our towns. They wouldn't submit to such dictates."

"There's the nub: dictates. I say, you hit on just the right word. I'm so relieved. They dictate."

"For sure. They dictate everything. They leave nothing to the people. They specify how high the collar shall be on a man's clothing, and the garment is made accordingly, and everyone wears it, and there are no exceptions. The people are content with this."

The bishop: "They're content?"

"They're happy. I'll stay on to study the experiment more closely. But I see this already: I've lived a long while among natives, up there in the north; the Jesuit Fathers have found the magic formula for handling these people, making them good for something. They leave them in their packs, or clans as they say, protect them, and what's more, imbue them with religion."

"Why do you smile, counsellor?" The counsellor whispered: "The Christianity here is quite amusing. Have you not noticed, my lord bishop? One rejoices at the Fathers' tremendous cunning." The bishop's fingers played uneasily on his knees: "Then we others, monks and bishops, should be ashamed of ourselves."

"That's not what I meant, some do it like so, others so, there's only one Christianity but you can teach it in many different ways. They've hit the mark here wonderfully. But sometimes you just have to laugh. You ask as a White man: what does Christianity have to do with sandals? Father Maceta, that ancient fellow – he even knew Father Emanuel! – he told me that because the people here are full of scruples, you must provide them with a rule for everything. They denounce one another, not out of malice or to seek advantage. They force a sinner in their midst to confess, and such a one is himself not content until he has taken his penance in church or in the marketplace, a couple of harmless blows with a stick or such. I'd like to see that happen among our lot."

"You spoke of sandals."

"Yes, Father Maceta told me the people are so dependable and so strict with themselves that they take it for a sin to leave their sandals in the wrong place in the house. For there's a precise rule for the proper placement of sandals. Of course this is just for tidiness, but they take it quite differently, they're terribly serious. Anyway, I'd like to examine it all from an economic perspective. How they raise livestock, how they treat the cattle, this is an important chapter. They will overtop us if they go on like this."

"Counsellor, please! What is this? Tens of thousands, hundreds of thousands of cows and horses run around out there, jaguars eat them, and they multiply in the wild without any Jesuits or cattlesheds. So they create ranches and tend the cattle and raise calves. Dear God, I find it ridiculous."

The counsellor regarded the bishop gravely: "Do you have something against the Jesuits?"

"But for God's sake, what are you suggesting? We were speaking of husbandry."

"You wouldn't be the first, and not the first bishop of Asuncion, to refuse to have dealings with them. I can understand why, these gentlemen are quite brazen. But their method for handling the natives cannot be brushed aside so easily. So many have caused nothing but devastation among the Indians, and do so still. What are we supposed to do then with a country where all the gold has been shipped off and there are no labourers or only people who won't work. They spare the people, guide them to regular toil. – Don't look so glum. Have I hurt your feelings?"

Bishop Felix kept his eyes half closed, chin sunk to his breast, he spoke softly: "One should observe new phenomena carefully, over a long period. I cannot presume to judge. So please do not misunderstand me. Some other time, when my affairs afford me more leisure, I shall come here again. But there are still Whites as well, and we have our towns, and I must see to their interests. – You ask if I am hurt. Not for myself. But it has made me a little unhappy to see a man such as you, a good servant of the Crown, an experienced judge of character, allow himself to be charmed and forget what is important. The natives live here, lead a kind of Christian life with the Jesuits – as a cleric I rejoice, goes without saying, but I don't know if we can trust this calm. When one of these dark souls looks at me, it sometimes seems like the gaze of a deer, and when they utter our prayers, even today, after so long, I am speechless, and ask myself: how is this possible, and is it right that we – no, what I mean is whether we go to too much trouble to insert our opinions into their heads.

"But," he raised his eyes and looked at the counsellor, a dignified man conscious of his dignity, "in all these arrangements we see here, the marvellous orderliness, much more lies behind it than they admit. They talk of conversion, baptism, saving the natives, guiding them to work. But they want to tame more than the Indians and, it seems to me, they parade Christian Indians before us as a model. They mean to argue with us. Lecture us. Do you understand this handwaving: we shall see real Christians, because actually we don't know what such a thing is."

The counsellor nodded gravely.

"You see. And so I don't go along with it, how could I. One has one's self respect. They withdraw from us, flee, protest. Once they learned that appeals and open letters of the kind Las Casas indulged in have no effect, they take another tack, protest through deeds. And how! When I look around here I feel sad for our White people, for all of us living in towns and making honest efforts."

The counsellor pulled his stool closer. "Speak softer, lord

bishop, walls have ears. There's nothing to be done about the reductions, they exist, King and Church have given their approval."

"I know, I know. And I grieve, yes grieve, to think it is so. They nail us fast to our shame."

"There was no other way, lord bishop."

"Who can say. This reply, there was no other way, has been proclaimed in black and white, posted up as living churches, houses, cowsheds, whole villages. Mistakes were made, and that is now official. Who can make such an apodictic verdict and settle for all time what counts as a mistake? I speak quite freely. And when I'm back in Asuncion, I shall set out my views in writing. I consider this policy false and insulting. My verdict on what they parade before us here as Christianity I leave aside for the moment. Perhaps I may conclude it is no Christianity at all. But this policy, instead of pacifying the country, will antagonise it. Encapsulation is never a solution. To build a monastery as big as Spain and heap up prosperity within it while poverty and unrest are all around, this is no good thing."

The bishop stood, in agitation paced up and down the room, tugged at his beard, his gaze was unfocused, he forced himself to speak low, but sounded merely hoarse: "The whole thing is approved, but they'll regret it one day. They are all people, those in the settlements and those outside. They all strive honestly. Privilege is unjust. And there is no basis for privileging anyone. Outside they also do what they can. Life is hard, but that's how it is."

The bishop's agitation became so great that he took his seat without a word. Once he had calmed down he grasped the counsellor's hand and stroked it with a pleading expression.

The counsellor said: "A pity I can't come with you on the return journey. But with your permission I shall call on you in Asuncion."

"I shall be delighted. And now let's drink a cup of maté. For I concede without reservation: maté is the master drink. It is wonderful to drink it with them."

"Perhaps you could stay a day or two longer, lord bishop?"

Felix smiled slyly: "Affairs, counsellor. Since I am a White man, and must protect myself against Jesuits."

Indian Mass

AS THE BISHOP prepared to depart they went again to the church that stood broad and deep and very low on its wooden pillars. It had big windows, the walls were painted in childish style by native artists with scenes from Scripture, an inexhaustible feast for the eyes, a source of entertainment for the dark people. The bishop prayed at the altar and gave the blessing. He looked around and thought: what a strange world I'm in, it's almost too much to bear.

Jesus, son of the living God, have pity on us.

Glory of the Father, have pity on us.

Ray of eternal light, sun of righteousness, have pity on us.

God of peace, paragon of virtue, storehouse of tears, good shepherd,
joy of angels, crown of all saints, have pity on us.

The bishop knelt facing the altar. They have no Latin, but that's all right, neither do our people, but what are they setting up here with the ray of righteousness, paragon of virtue. Now they look at the big golden cross on my back and almost expect a miracle from me.

"I approach the altar of God. Judge over me and preserve me from the godless. Why hast thou rejected me? And why dost thou leave me in tears, oppressed by mine enemies?"

How can they understand our burbling. What do they know of our Heaven. They have souls, but these are rather the souls of deer, if not wolves. They listen astonished to our words and prayers and parrot them after us, because they do not understand. They should be sent into our towns for a few decades to be chased from pillar to post, perhaps then they would understand something.

They sang in antiphonal chorus: *Soul of Christ, sanctify me. Body of Christ, save me. Blood of Christ, inebriate me. Water from the side of Christ, wash me. Passion of Christ, strengthen me. O good Jesus, hear me. Within Thy wounds hide me. Permit me not to be separated from Thee. In the hour of my death, call me. And bid me come unto Thee that with Thy saints I may be praising Thee, forever and ever. Amen.*

Sobs and sighs filled the church.

They cry, they become anxious, they fear punishment. A remarkably lachrymose people. I don't understand them. My presence here is repugnant to me. I want to go home. I must be among people again.

≈≈≈

The bishop avoided a conversation with Montoya. He appeared happy as he departed, and deeply moved by all he had seen. He praised his nephew and expressed satisfaction that the lad was working here. The cavalry troop that had escorted him in went with him across country for a stretch. When they left him, and only his small escort from Asuncion remained, he breathed a sigh of relief. Now he did not feast his eyes on the wide river. They ferried across and spurred their horses.

Returning from the gate at Yapeyú, Montoya took Gonzales' arm. "Did your uncle upset you? His departure was so precipitate."

"Let him go, Montoya. He was quite shaken. We disturb him. He doesn't like that. But he won't harm us."

"You think so?"

"He never harms anyone. In fact he never does anything. He gazes about and equivocates. I've never seen any case where he actually took a stand. He has told me a lot about Rome and how it upset him, and so he came here with his books, Horace and Virgil of course."

They exchanged endless greetings along the street. Montoya's lips were pressed together: "Virgil. I know. It's the fashion in Rome."

Alfio

WHEN THE BISHOP entered his new stone house in Asuncion, his stiff lanky valet was standing in the hall holding a tray, and without a word Felix seized the glass and gulped the wine. He looked at Alfio, and Alfio returned the look, the bishop seemed to be toasting his valet. Then he thanked Alfio, put down the glass, spread his arms and let them drop slack at his side. He stepped slowly, head drooping, up the stairs.

Alfio came and led Felix, who was waiting quietly in the antechamber to his library, to the bathroom. This was a low little room with a massive wooden tub. The hot water was perfumed, jugs of hot and cold water stood by the door. Alfio removed one garment after another from his master, rolled up his sleeves and helped him into the tub. In the tub Felix began to sigh, and spoke: "Thank Heaven! Thank Heaven!"

"Was it so difficult?" asked Alfio, as he stirred the water, placed towels, brought in house clothes, "was it arduous?"

"You've no idea, Alfio. The journey started wonderfully. I had good weather. There were several sensible people with us, you know them of course."

"I selected them and gave them instructions."

"Their conduct was exemplary. They gave no cause for dissatisfaction."

"The food."

"It was all right, I know what travelling is like, they did their best. And the scenery, Alfio, the scenery along the river is glorious, they certainly know how to pick the right spot, I'll send you there next time, the best part of the province."

"So what is it, all so good and you so exhausted, my lord?"

"It can't be explained in a word. I'll just say: never again to the reductions."

"Noted."

"Never, I say."

"Was Gonzales disagreeable?"

"I've taken my leave of that youth, Alfio. He's uncouth. One tried one's best to reach an understanding. No use."

"As I thought. It's the age."

"It is not the age, Alfio. It's the Jesuits."

"Them too."

"Them most of all. Pour a little cold water over my shoulders, slowly, thank you. What I endured from these Jesuits I cannot begin to say. You can have no conception of what I saw. They let nobody in."

"Then there's a scandal brewing."

"For God's sake, what are you saying, scandal! Who would become so worked up about it?"

"Has young master Gonzales become a Jesuit?"

"He is a Jesuit. Our lovely good Gonzales."

"Well, why did my lord not wade in? As the bishop, after all."

"I wanted to. Don't imagine it's so easy. The things I saw. Cowsheds."

"Pooh, surely my lord did not walk through cowsheds."

"It was raining. I was spared that. Otherwise the weather was splendid the whole time. And the air did me a world of good. It's not so oppressive as here. We'll journey there one day, Alfio. Now, enough."

And he stood up. Alfio belaboured his outside with towels while Felix did arm gymnastics, lowered, raised and turned his head. He sat on a stool, Alfio placed a light colourful linen housecoat around him, slid slippers onto his feet, diligently combed and brushed beard and head. As he did so, Alfio asked: "Was his honour the Visitor Alvaro also in Yapeyú?"

"He arrived shortly after me, he stayed on. The fellow was enthused. I invited him to call when he comes back."

"He made no good impression. All the time he was here the people kept themselves in check, out of courtesy. Afterwards a storm broke. In one way, I regret my lord bishop wasn't here to see it, he'd have been pleased with the sensible views of the people, and their resoluteness."

"In one way. And the other?"

"It seemed to me better that my lord should not be drawn into the commotion."

"Correct, Alfio."

"They cursed the Jesuits who stand behind this royal edict the Visitor brought. They consult among themselves and want to undertake something."

"My dear Alfio, I completely understand, the people have my

sympathy. Anyway," the bishop put on a happy face, "what is our little Ada up to? I've brought nothing for her. Have you something I might give her as a present?"

Ada was the bishop's little daughter, given out to be Alfio's.

Alfio: "My supply of playthings is still adequate, my lord. It includes birdcages."

"She likes birds?"

"For a while now. We might give her a birdcage."

"Good. But no birds in it, they squawk."

"Of course. Anyway, she'd let them fly away after a while."

As Felix, followed by Alfio, entered his library – a bright big room full of books and antique statuary, with a writing stand and sofa and chairs, a lifesize standing Apollo in one corner – he gestured with both hands: "Salve, dear friends, here I am again. Greetings one and all. I shall eat some fruit now, Alfio, and then you can send little Minx in."

Alfio, amiable as ever, first brought two baskets with oranges and figs. Then the Minx entered with two fingerbowls. Alfio closed the door softly behind her.

Little Minx

THE MINX WAS Alfio's wife, but she belonged to my lord, who was now bishop, and he had married her to Alfio, his valet, purely to simplify his domestic arrangements. He had already done Alfio many favours, for example in taking him on. For in his youth Alfio had been the worst kind of pirate, of which the Mediterranean has many. The young man had the misfortune to be captured by Moors along with his ship, they were all carried off to prison, and because he was handsome and had manners he was there made a eunuch, and for several years served in the harem of a rich Mussulman. This sad predicament ended in escape. But back in Italy, rootless, lacking zest for life and with his bodily defect, he had no prospects. For a time he sang in the castrati choir in Rome, and then was employed by the choirmaster for messages and discreet commissions, and came thereby to affable Count Felix, who was preparing for a clerical career and found him pleasant.

Felix took him along to the various locations of his activity, and Alfio accepted the respectable position of valet to this gentleman. Felix included him in his Classical enthusiasms, Alfio developed into a middleman for the procurement of antique art and the support of artists. So it was only natural for Alfio to take on the role of husband to Clelia. Alfio had grown jealous of this person, and felt profound satisfaction when Felix, who knew his feelings, made the offer.

"My lord may depend on me," he declared, "I was for many years eunuch in a harem, if I had stayed I would be head eunuch by now, and that post outranks even a major domo."

Felix was content, now he had everything, his Alfio was pacified, Clelia would not be taken away, and their daughter even gained a father.

But it was not entirely certain that Felix was the father of Clelia's little daughter. And that was one of the reasons why he married Clelia to his valet and kept her in his household. At that time Felix would sing the praises of his clerical vocation to his friends, Roman nobility, although otherwise he showed little enthusiasm for it: "If I were of noble family like her, how would it go with me. I would pension her off. Would that guarantee against foolishness on her part? Bah. But I have no wish to deprive her of her liberty. I am no slave-owner. She shall have what she needs. But I must be able to keep it under control, at least. My Clelia needs watching."

My lord put his arms around Clelia in his chair in the library: "When, some time ago, Christopher Columbus discovered the New World, he disembarked and erected a flag on the shore bearing the insignia of his king. I come on behalf of no Spanish king, Minx. I hereby take thee in possession in the name of my crown, and if in my absence any other kingdom has raised a claim on thee, I hereby declare a feud."

"If it comes to knives, Felix?"

"No need for knives. Anyway, you seem to have grown slimmer."

"For longing, Guido."

"Really?"

She cried on his neck and made him damp: "Forgive me."

"Now now, Minx."

"I want to go home."

He was disappointed, he had thought the longing was for him. "You'll go home again. Have you news from over there?"

"No. It's so far away."

"But it's nice here, and interesting."

"Let me sit quietly with you for a while. Hold me. Ah, that's good."

He began to talk as she sat quietly in his lap, a big girl with black curly hair and round lips, little upturned nose, big ringlets hanging from concealed ears – wonderful, this the mother of my Ada, this is how mothers look, this is how we are men to them, this is how warmth flows from their breast and makes our life sweet, they bring us always to the world, was I actually alive yesterday riding across the countryside, oh source of my being, dear Minx, mother who bore me, how wonderful to be born, wonderful the world, wonderful its women, love, sweet flame in which I would burn forever, great God, just let me live so and expire, sinner that I am – "We saw things, little Minx, that you cannot imagine. It's a fantastical country, believe me."

"Alfio smacked his hands together and said you had to go into a cowshed."

"He didn't tell you everything. It began to rain, Heaven watched over me and spared me."

"And what did you do then."

"We rode back. And we saw savages, Clelia."

She sobbed gently a little more. "Forgive me. There's so much I miss."

"Is Alfio not good to you? I shall speak to him."

"No. But I don't want to stay here, Guido, I really don't, believe me."

"How often have you said, in Rome, Ferrara: I don't want, I want something else, the people here bore me?"

"Yes, they bored me, I wanted to follow you here where it's nice and different."

"It is nice here, and different. And so much still to see. You must not think Asuncion is the whole country. Merchants and slave dealers and cattle dealers have settled here and conduct their business, a wretched society which I tend to because I must, somebody has to, because they claim to be Christians and one should not prick their illusion. But out there it's better. Clelia, I swear to you it's better, heaven and earth and rivers and trees. And there, over towards the Paraná, there dwell the Jesuits."

"So what do they do there, what is Gonzales up to?"

"Gonzales?"

"Admit it, Guido, you only went on his account, and because you're fed up with me."

"It's true I wanted to see him, and you understand my love for him, you too were an admirer."

She smiled into his beard: "Too much perhaps. He ran away from me."

"You see. And I wanted to restore him to you."

Suddenly she flung her arms about his head and kissed him wildly. He struggled with her and did not let his distress show. "Stop strangling me. I wouldn't want to leave you a widow among the redskins. Anyway, I found Gonzales with the Jesuits, who are the most insolent, arrogant, provocative society in the world. He has apprenticed himself to them."

"That sounds like him."

"He badgered me dreadfully. Fortunately I've forgotten all about it."

"And how does he look? Bring him back here, Uncle Felix."

"Uncle Felix would gladly do so, he allowed him to utter the most appalling impudences, he thought of his little Minx and the fact that little Minx shares his tastes; in short, he looked wonderful, Gonzales."

"How does he wear his beard, Guido?"

"You see, you're interested only in him, you don't see me at all."

She dug her fingers in his throat so that he fell back. "You're a murderess," he wheezed once he had picked himself up, "you've adopted cannibal ways."

"You will tell me now what you know of Gonzales. I don't have him here any more, so the least you can do is tell me about him."

The handsome count sighed: "It's the same for you as for me, we've both lost him, but I have it rather better than you, for I have you. And now you must undergo a transformation, Clelia, you must become Gonzales too."

She jumped up from his lap, shocked, and stood there, hands at her forehead: "I – Gonzales?" And all at once, blushing bright red as if found out, she hurled herself at the calmly smiling count and pressed her face to his: "Oh you! The things you think of."

"A fine thought, no? I shall buy you scarlet hose, a brocade jacket, a walking cane. I already thought of it on the way here. I thought and thought what present I could bring you. Luckily Alfio was able to help me out with Ada."

She calmed down now: "A birdcage, but there aren't any birds."

"They'll come. It's more exciting when the cage is empty, then when it has birds it's a double present. But I really wanted to bring Gonzales back to you, and to me. And then I thought –." He paused, could not go on, turned his head aside, swallowed tears.

"Guido!"

He continued softly: "Such is life. You lose one thing after another, retreat into fantasy."

"I am not a fantasy."

"You are not."

"Oh Guido, how silly you are. You bring Gonzales back to me, it's heavenly of you. We shall both enjoy him. Alfio will laugh."

"He'll think us mad."

And after she had charmed him and he sat with her over wine, he told her what was on his mind, she wanted to talk about the household, about Ada and Alfio and the town, there was much news, but he would not let her begin, he begged: "Have pity on me, Minx, be merciful to me. Along the way they told me about ants. When the flood comes they leave the ground and carry all they are and have up into the trees and attach themselves to branches. That's how it is with me. I traipse around the world with my possessions, homeless, I have to attach to something, allow me this, Clelia."

"So you want me to become a mule!"

"Never a mule! But a horse, a fine grey?"

"Stop it, Guido."

"But you know what splendid horses they have here. Listen, I mean real horses, out on the plain. Now on that point I've something quite scandalous to tell you, and when I've attached it to you I must see how things stand with me. They do not hunt horses, Clelia, just imagine!"

"Who?"

"The Jesuits."

"So why should they hunt horses?"

"Well, are horses happy in a stable? Do they not enjoy it better out on the plain?"

"I don't know."

"They shut the horses in stables, feed them, bring them grass and hay, raise their young."

"That has nothing to do with me, Guido. You're boring me."

"You must have seen how they hunt, how they sit so upright on their horses, and then the lasso! Marvellous!"

"But you didn't want to tell me about the Jesuits hunting horses."

"The Indians. But they don't allow them to hunt any more. They forbid it as immoral. They must build stables or plant hedges, the horses live there and form families and make young. It's a ghastly simulacrum of our human society. Clelia, you know how little I esteem human society. But the Greeks and the Romans, oh it was different then. I came over here to be free of the whole wretched thing, the stupid squabbles, the bawling and carryings-on of mercenaries posing as warriors. And once I'm here and see warriors and hunters out there and now I ride out and think I've arrived in the innermost of the country – there sit the Jesuits and they have brought the whole detestable mess with them. They've even turned animals into a bad sort of people. They've taken away all the beauty and freedom, all the nobility of life."

"And the Indians?"

"I despair for them. Surely there are weaklings and superior people among them. They fill whole towns with these dark people, they sing and work. Clelia, when I think of it I feel ill." And Felix took an enormous swig, draining his glass, and poured himself another from which he sipped. "You know termites in the forest, they build hills."

"Horrid things."

"Yes. Drink, Clelia. It is horrid. Just like the Indians in these towns. That's what the Jesuits have made of them. They walk and run and carry, they come out of their houses, one house exactly like another, each wearing clothes exactly like the others."

"That's horrible."

"While I was there I was only astonished, and it wasn't clear why it was so repugnant to me, what it was that irked me so. Afterwards I became dizzy."

"And the Jesuits do this, and Gonzales has gone to them."

"Oh little Minx, they are doing a great deal. I believe our hair will stand on end one day at what they're doing."

He stood, walked slowly in his slippers along the bookshelves. A glorious Deposition from the Cross hung there. "Dear Saviour, what are these people up to. Everything has its measure, after all. Making people into monkeys, animals into dumb humans, this was never meant to be. They'll strip religion of all its meaning. A man who sits proud on a horse and looks beautiful and has the form God gave him is removed from his horse and stuck in a stable, where he feeds the horses! Driving them together into a prison they call a town, with ten thousand little smoky cells, and then letting them sing in church! I ask myself: what have we gained if these people are Christians. Which anyway they are not. And they're right. I oppose fakery."

He stood next to a statue of young David, recalled his last conversation with Gonzales: "And the desolation they wreak upon our youth. What a seething mass of barbarians is growing here. They know nothing of it in Europe, not the Pope or the cardinals. People think they want to serve the Church. Yes, the true Church that makes people good and pious, Clelia."

He stood beside her and played with her hand, she flinched for a moment, for his hand was cold. "We have our task, but it is not to destroy the work of God or play dear God ourselves. I give thanks for that dear God whom the Jesuits have cast off. If it grows over us, Clelia, then – it's all up with my library, they'll burn the books of the ancients, just as mad Savonarola did in Florence, and then let the Pope in Rome see how he sits. Today they swear eternal loyalty and boundless obedience to him. Boundless obedience! He's happy with that. But tomorrow, tomorrow! And I don't like their vow to surrender their own judgement. That is as inhuman as everything else they do."

She sat stunned, and watched her beloved walk up and down.

"Come back here, Guido, stop walking away from me! Sit here."

And when he sat by her, sunk in thought, anger still in his face, her hands ruffled his head. "You head, Guido's head, head of my count, listen to me, what have you done with my friend, I shall beat you, head, if you don't stop tormenting him. Take care, now –" and she tugged one ear – "and now," she tugged the other, and the anger left his lips and forehead, "and now," she stroked his cheeks, and a smile replaced the anger on his brow, and then, bringing her face slowly close to his, fixing him with her eyes, she put her lips to his, and then the clouds lifted which had made his eyes blind, and he saw again and rejoiced in her and took deep breaths. He sat back in his chair: "Forgive me, Clelia. Oh, grappling with darkness makes a man dark."

"But how could you, great Felix, my pride, my beloved. It's enough that we've lost Gonzales to those black robes."

"Quite right."

"Think of Horace, and what you read to me recently of Sophocles, I learned it by heart, but not in Greek." She stood up, the big girl – again it stirred in him: mother of my Ada, my life, a woman, there she stands, my joy, gentle flame where I warm myself, in which I would lose myself – she declaimed in front of his chair with little hand gestures:

> Here, stranger,
> here in the land where horses are a glory
> you have reached the noblest home on earth
> Colonus glistening, brilliant in the sun –
> where the nightingale sings on,
> her dying music rising clear,
> hovering always, never leaving,
> down the shadows deepening green she haunts the glades, the
> > wine-dark ivy,
> dense and dark and untrodden, sacred wood of god
> rich with laurel and olives never touched by the sun
> untouched by storms that blast from every quarter –
> where the Reveler Dionysus strides the earth forever
> where the wild nymphs are dancing round him, nymphs who
> > nursed his life.
> And here it blooms, fed by the dews of heaven,
> lovely, clustering morning-fresh forever,
> narcissus, crown of the Great Goddesses, Mother and
> > Daughter dying
> into life from the dawn of time,
> and the gold crocus bursts like break of day
> and the springs will never sleep, will never fail,
> the fountainhead of Cephisus
> flowing nomad quickening life forever, fresh each day –
> life rising up with the river's pure tide
> flowing over the plains, the swelling breast of earth –
> nor can the dancing Muses bear to leave this land
> or the Goddess Aphrodite, the charioteer with the golden reins of
> > love.

From the chair he took hold of her hands, and continued in Greek:

> And there is a marvel here, I have not heard its equal,
> nothing famed in the vast expanse of Asia, nothing
> like it in Pelops' broad Dorian island ever sprang to light –
> a creation, self-creating, never conquered,

a terror to our enemies and their spears,
it flourishes to greatness in our soil,
the gray-leafed olive, mother, nurse of children,
perennial generations growing in her arms —
neither young nor old can tear her from her roots,
the eternal eyes of Guardian Zeus look down upon her always,
great Athena too, her eyes gray-green and gleaming as the sea.

He stroked his beard slowly and with pride: "And although I speak thus and love you dearly, Clelia, which I should not, I consider myself a good Christian."

"And so you are, dear Guido."

He gave a little chuckle and was fully himself again. "And then it was not I, but a Father Torrez of the Company of Jesus in Lima, who was summoned before the Inquisition. They let him off, alas."

Earthly and heavenly love

TWO WEEKS LATER the royal Visitor Alvaro allowed Bishop Felix to show him around his library, and was amazed at the comforts of the house, the pictures and books.

"Don't you think, my dear counsellor, that a house such as this and these books and art treasures mean something for the country? I have a notion, without wishing to overrate myself, that these paltry and apparently merely lovely objects have a task to fulfil here. They show to those few who come to my house that there exist beauty, culture, antiquity, Greece and Rome."

"Rome, ancient and modern, of which you yourself are a representative, lord bishop."

"If you like. What a wondrous doctrine is Christianity! What a great doctrine! What indescribable beauties and truths does our faith ever reveal to us anew. I'm not the youngest of men, dear counsellor, and I know many regions of life and the spirit — nothing human is alien to me — but ever and again I am led by our religion to new discoveries. And especially now, dwelling quietly and out of the way, but amid ancient Greece and Rome. Christianity is a strong and glorious plant, it roots itself and blossoms in every land and every clime. But just try living with it amid these ancient works: you have the feeling Christianity has nowhere flourished in so genuine and unforced a way as here. It's at home here, this is the ground from which it first sprang. You ask what has our Saviour, the Man of Sorrows on the Cross, to do with the delightful youths here, spear-throwers, uprooters of thorns. True, there are malicious souls who seek to open an abyss between them and our faith. I sense no such abyss."

"I confess, lord bishop – being a layman – I do not understand what the Dying Gladiator has to do with Our Saviour on the Cross."

They sat. Alfio served fruit. Felix, head cocked on his shoulder, rested his gentle gaze on the little bronze statue. "You must not think to make a mischievous comparison between the sufferings of our Lord and this man. The gladiator is raising himself from the ground with his right arm, his left hand rests on his right leg, which he has drawn up under him, he has stretched out his other leg and his head is sunk low in agony over the wound in his breast. Soon he will stretch out the leg on which he sits, the body is already falling, he will topple like a flower severed at the stem. From here you see only a round head and slack shoulders, the downward pointing face is hidden, the earth awaits him, I know the face, the sombre brow is wrinkled, the eyebrows," Felix indicated his own, "stand bushily out, the mouth is open in pain. It is the face of a simple man who has tilled a field somewhere, or if not he, his parents. Now a sword has opened his right side, there the wide wound, it is blood that oozes out in rivulets. All that is left for the man is to give in, sink down, darkness is already around him."

Alvaro nodded: "Just so."

"You can see it, how the one who made this observed just such a man. How he stood by him and died with him."

"You are right."

"And next to it, the big plaster moulding. I have pushed it into the corner, you can't see it behind the angle of the bookcase. Go closer. Come."

"Really, I didn't notice."

"A womanly torso. She's crouching. Perhaps she wants to pick something up. The head is missing, the left arm, of the right arm only a stump remains, and there is other damage. Who is this female figure? She's called 'the kneeling Venus'. See how she's lowered herself, she sits directly on her right ankle, the ball of the foot bears her weight, the toes spread out, he has observed each of her toes, given them his love. He sees the lower leg push strongly forward, flat on the ground, thigh and calf are pressed together. The knee must make a firm hinge to hold them together. For balance she has placed her other foot wide on the ground. The knee, since the woman is crouching down, is raised, close to the body. They are two sisters, the left leg firmly on the ground, and the right preparing to press the knee onto the earth. One follows the other, they wait for each other, do the same thing. See how similar they are. They are little machines of the body, hoists, levers, but how charming, lively, how clever these toes. These feet with their toes and the placement of the legs remind me a little of fins. And now we come to the body. It is not jointed like a leg, but see the hollow below the ribs, above sit the breasts like wonderfully mobile wineskins, and down below the body opens, and everything it contains is carried now by the pelvis, and that is carried by the two supports, the legs, the sisters. I say sisters, and you think it perhaps a poetic cliché. But what a pity we can't see the arms and eyes and cheeks. Just read from this torso how the two sides, right leg and left, work together without repeating themselves. There on the belly, as she crouches down, the skin must be squeezed in folds, to the right where she is lower. No doubt she'll move her knee down at any moment, then she'll be able to stretch her arm out to the ground and hold steady. How tenderly the left breast is modelled, this is a strong woman, you don't think of a young girl when you see these shoulders. Well, counsellor Alvaro, who could surpass in meticulousness and devotion the person who made this. He loved people, this woman, he loved her in everything his eyes could encompass, he knew much and laid it out here. It speaks for itself, of what joy, what knowledge and sympathy does such stonework not speak.

How one's eyes and soul are opened. The Greeks did not leave us many words. But their stones are an eloquent substitute. To speak the true word, after all, was kept for us, the Christians."

Counsellor Alvarado was not an uneducated man, but these statues and the entire disquisition of the bishop and art lover were not at all to his taste – it was Roman talk. He reported on the reductions.

But as he spoke of the organisation of the Jesuit army, its exercises, the powder factory, Felix, veiled eyes, ears stopped, continued his inner conversation with Clelia. Truly I consider us Christians heirs of Greece, they dabbled in stone and words, they poured their love for humanity and every living thing into chorus and sculpture, we'd be bad Christians if we did not accept this Venus crouching here, and recognise in her a heavenly love for all creation. But our senses have been quite unlocked, scales have fallen from our eyes, and that's the work of our Saviour who brought love into the world. Thus we are Christians. We see the world's beauty and godliness most clearly in the human. He is the rainbow that stretches from Earth to Heaven. I'd be happy, Clelia, if you understood me. This thought makes me very happy. I greet you, my Clelia, my earthly mother, who enables me to anticipate Heaven.

Echoes of Yapeyú

ALVARO WAS ABLE to report on curious incidents he had noticed in the reductions: "With all due respect to the Jesuits' achievements, but the Indians are a difficult case. I saw a woman toiling in a maize field with her arm in a sling, and she limped. We rode by, I saw them. I asked the Father who was with me what was wrong with the woman. He said: it's nothing. I saw he didn't want to speak of it. He said: she has been ill and drags herself to work. I'd already forgotten about it when at noon, as we rode back, one of my interpreters I brought along, they mingle with the Indians – a great source of enlightenment, such people – when this chap tells me: the woman is watched very closely by the Fathers, they have put overseers – informers they send among the Indians – to keep an eye on her. The woman's husband had died a few weeks before. In accordance with the ancient custom of her tribe, which lives not far away and is still intact, secret enquiries were started by some people to find out who was to blame for his death. Remarkable, no? Ineradicable. The tribe blamed the woman. And just imagine, my lord bishop, the woman, although otherwise she confessed everything, dared not go to her confessor. They forced her to throw herself off a cliff. The spiritual director of the village noticed one morning that she was missing, and that the other women at work in the weaving hut took little notice of her absence. They asked around, searched, it was not until nightfall that they found the women with the help of dogs. Can you imagine that these people, who stick so closely together, allow one of their own to lie out there seriously injured and are not even worried she might be eaten by jaguars? Apparently there was a huge trial, the Fathers preached fire and brimstone upon the community, and then it still took a long time before they dared to release the woman, who had broken her arms and legs, from the sick bay back to her people. The Fathers had to take turns to watch over her and protect her."

"Protect?" asked Felix, "how ghastly."

"Well," smiled Alvaro, "in your lovely library it sounds more ghastly than it really is. Yes, they still wanted to hound her to death, these model Christians."

Felix crossed his arms on his chest and made himself smaller, but kept his benevolent serene expression: "Well then. That's very interesting to hear. They have a hard task, the Jesuit Fathers. What they do is good and extraordinarily useful. They've chosen a career of complete self-denial. It's just the same as in our town when the refuse from the alleyways is collected and taken away and so on. They are dealing with the elementary awkwardnesses of life."

"Indisputably. And the native are cannibals and have given it up, at least I hope so."

The bishop shook himself: "I must grant the Jesuits a great deal when I think of such beastliness. I wish them every success in their work. They can count on my support, insofar as they need it. Oh how the human soul is beset with jungles, serpents, wild beasts before it ever rises up to meet God."

"A woman," Alvaro remembered, "one of my interpreters told me, to stay with the same theme, after her husband was buried, hid herself in the graveyard at night. She lay down on the fresh grave, shovelled a great pile of earth aside, and then covered herself with it. By chance, a Father came through the graveyard on his way to Mass next morning, noticed her and hauled her out. What a hullabaloo ensued, so I heard. They storm about to get to the bottom of it, whether anyone forced her to it. But this time everyone else was innocent. And the explanation the woman gave was the right one: she hadn't covered herself in soil to kill herself, but to help her husband bear the weight of it."

The bishop had his hands over his ears: "Gruesome. But I am grateful, dear counsellor, that you have told me of these curiosities."

Revolts

IN THE DAYS that followed, Asuncion seethed. There were three times as many people as usual in town, and it looked somewhat like that perilous Holy Thursday when the new governor invited nearby tribes to view his magnificent procession, whereat the Indians' thoughts turned more to arrows and the bare shoulders of the Whites. The natives who now moved through the town were peaceable, led by Whites. They were sad *work detachments* performing the proscribed *personal service* mentioned in the royal edict, thousands of natives gathered from various regions, some from subjugated tribes round about the town who had been leased out en bloc for a consideration, others simply bought and paid for.

Notables of the town stood together in the marketplace, domineering and angry, in plumed hats, sword at the side, and hurled curses at the Visitor (who kept out of sight), at Bishop Felix, the Jesuits, let them dare come to town just once more, and the natives. The Whites wore heavy riding boots, leather jerkins. Their sturdy horses were held by natives a short way off. For all the

variety among the Whites in size and facial features, they all had
darting eyes, tight mouths and coarse fists, they were descendants
and heirs of the first conquerors and adventurers who had cried:
all mine, hey dear mother. But adventures and the hunt for gold
were over now. Every one of the Whites who stood outside the
governor's mansion bore scars from encounters with wild beasts
and Indian tribes. Many tribes, whose members now stood about
here as their slaves, they had known in the untrodden wilderness,
in war regalia with spears and arrows; countless of their fellows
had been struck down in the wilderness or been snatched away
by swamp fever and the dreadful glandular disease, which now
flourished merrily in Europe as the curse of Venus.

The rebellious gathering was not altogether disagreeable to
the governor. He lived in his handsome house on the market,
opposite the bishop's palace, and showed the shocked Visitor the
mob of Whites surrounded by savages. This energetic benevolent
man, whose province meant more to him than it had to many
of his predecessors, this jovial swashbuckler, dog-fancier, great
hunter wrinkled his brow as he presented the theatre below to his
guest: "Just look at that, my lord. Pray advise me. You hand me
the edict, and tomorrow you ride off."

"I am not the governor. You must see how you will deal with
it."

"How I'll deal with it! Same old story. They pen decrees and
bring decrees, and we shall see how we deal with it. At least you
can tell your Viceroy what you've seen."

"But why do the people just stand there? It seems someone
has gone mad. Why do they not drive them to work? You should
send some soldiers down."

"We'll see in due course, my dear counsellor, I am in no
haste."

And as they sat in the governor's little council chamber, the
Visitor troubled and uneasy, the burly governor smiling, imperturbable – a brown goatee rested on the snow-white ruff, his
powerful face with its wine-red nose seemed always on the point
of some mischief – five Whites entered. The governor flapped his

big hand in greeting and invited them to sit, at once they sensed a good wind, thanked him, and stayed clustered at the door.

The leader had a scroll in his hand, a copy of the decree, of course. As soon as the governor, who knew them all, had introduced them to the counsellor, he read out the whole text, paying no attention to the Visitor's headshakes and the governor's lively interjections. He responded calmly: "That's important," and his companions nodded energetically. Then he was finished, he smacked the scroll against his boot and announced: it goes no farther. With all due respect to officialdom, Spanish Crown, Viceroy and so forth, it goes no farther. And then he began sneeringly to pull the edict apart:

"'Through diverse royal decrees promulgated by me and by Their Majesties my predecessors, it has been laid down that the Indians of this Province shall remain in the enjoyment of their liberties equally with the other vassals of my kingdoms.' With all due respect, we say: You have your vassals, there they are down there, let them work. Please." Smacked the scroll once more against his boot, glanced at his friends, and then they waited.

When no answer came – the Visitor had no idea what to say, and the big governor, comfortable sat there in his brocade, had no thought to interfere, let the gentlemen express themselves and the Visitor can be left dangling a while longer – the leader of the colonists repeated: "Let them work, your vassals. You'll learn something." The people at the door burst out laughing. Behind them in the corridor appeared several natives, crowding up the stairs, these were their stewards, they carried sticks as token of their rank. Amid laughter and scorn there ensued a barbed lecture on the laziness, gluttony and wickedness of the Indians.

When the leader had finished imparting his wisdom, he yielded the floor, without objection from the two gentlemen, to an older, quieter man at his side, who appealed to the political acumen of the two high officials. His words showed some education:

"Here in this colony we have a great task for civilization. Here there's only jungle, grass, plain and swamp. With the support of the army we construct forts and towns. We are not many. If there were more of us we wouldn't need the Indians at all. But no more come, back in Spain they know how hard it is here. But in the end the savages need us too, to accustom them to a settled life. Rome wasn't built in a day. And that is what those on high don't understand. Our bishop is a clever man of the world. We met him yesterday, he granted us an audience. He'll tell the two gentlemen himself that in these parts it can't be done just with singing and going to church. The savages must be trained. They've no idea what work is. Sometimes we ask ourselves, however do they survive out there."

Someone called from behind: "The jungle throws everything into their mouths."

The educated speaker agreed: "Just so. They can do nothing and are as idle as sin. The previous speaker applied just the right words to this idleness and lack of culture. But in order to convince the gentlemen, we have brought along some stewards. These coloured people will speak from their own experience."

At this the Whites at the door drew back, and a good dozen dark people squeezed through into the room, with some help from behind. They held big bamboo staves, clustered together timidly and goggled at the governor and Visitor. The Whites prodded them forward. They looked at the ceiling, walls, floor, the table, chairs. Once they all bent down to look under the table, something had moved there, the governor's two big hounds, they pointed at them and whispered, these were the animals that hunted them.

The second speaker introduced them, using the Indian names by which they were called, some also had Christian names. As soon as one recognised his name, he raised his stave, pressed closer to the others, screwed up his eyes to focus better, and looked as if he were about to attack. "These men can confirm how lazy their compatriots are, how hard it is to secure any work from them, and what a bad character most of them have. Since we only speak Spanish here and the gentlemen probably do not know the dialect of the Indians, I shall question them."

And he turned to the Indians with incomprehensible words.

They answered softly and shyly. Eventually the sober fellow opened his arms wide and for the benefit of the two officials exclaimed: "Well then! If these people don't know all about it, who does?"

The blusterer who had read out the scroll had to remind him that a translation and explication were needed of what the people had actually said, but the other brushed him off: "They've confirmed what we have said. In any case the whole town knows it."

And everyone nodded sadly, sighed and raised their arms to indicate resignation. The Indians in their midst kept a sharp eye on the hounds.

Meanwhile the governor had been calmly observing the Indians. Now he growled jovially: "Are these people actually needed here? You see how frightened they are of my hounds."

The educated speaker: "We wouldn't want to do without them, or people might say we speak without evidence and are slaveholders, as people already so kindly call us."

At that moment a White broke away from the group, the biggest of them and clearly the oldest, he had a long grey beard and made room for himself among the natives. He was sunburnt, wrinkled like an old peasant, his eyes bloodshot, the lower lids downturned and flaming red. This gave him an alarming expression. He spoke in a growl and to the horror of the Indians strode towards the table where the two gentlemen sat – one of the hounds, huge, white with brown spots, its eyes red as the man's, stood and placed itself in his path, he pushed the sniffing head aside with his left hand: "Do I look like a slaveholder?" Since he and the other four expected an answer, the two disconcerted gentlemen had to shuffle off their sluggish role of onlooker and one after the other say: "No." With this victory achieved, the big man went back to his four friends.

Since they made no further argument, the governor, who was more and more offended by the smell of the Indians and their very presence, again raised the question, whether perhaps the many people down there in the marketplace shouldn't be cleared away, they would be better employed going about their work than idling there. The sturdy leader, bluntly: "No. We have appeared in Asuncion with our people to lay before the Crown that we are not slaveholders. We cannot allow this insult to stand. We are true subjects of the King and pay taxes. We want the stain of slaveholding removed from us. We insist on it. Our enemies are the Fathers of the Company of Jesuits. They instigated this edict against us. Must I now take the bull by the horns, must I?"

The man strode over to the table where the melancholy giant had made his complaint. The lanky Visitor stood up in alarm, the governor placed both hands on the table and settled himself more comfortably in his chair. The affair was shaping up splendidly. The leader of the delegation knocked with the knuckle of his index finger on the table, they saw in astonishment that the finger was a stump with only its first joint, but he could knock powerfully with it: "This is a competitive struggle! A mean, shabby struggle! We are proceeded against with legitimate, with legal measures, but the Jesuit Fathers are deceitful and we stand no chance against them. They won't allow us our people. They've already swindled a whole kingdom for themselves along the Paraná. The Spanish Crown will have bitter reason to regret it one day. They want all the Indians for themselves, to work for them. They want to break the neck of our province. If the Jesuits continue working here and spread disparaging rumours about the Whites and stir up the Indians, then one day a storm will break and we can't answer for what will happen."

All faces had become fierce and hard. The big red-eyed man with the grey beard, who always kept his head low and appeared to be asking for sympathy, had lowered his head even more between his shoulders, the sick beggar had become an enraged steer. The natives, who had retreated into the background, were abruptly ordered out by one of the Whites, and went silently down the stairs.

The grey-bearded man, growling in basso profundo, complained: "No one supports us. We live here with our families. If our own officials can't protect us, then we must protest in person." He broke off; said in a low voice: "We're glad that counsellor Alvarado has come here."

A fourth man, robustly built, with beetroot-red cheeks and a glowing red nose, an older man of apoplectic mien who wore his head unnaturally stiff on his fat neck as if in a cravat, scolded completely motionless, it was as if an automaton screamed from inside him: "The King has been hoodwinked. The Indians are being armed." He stammered, the apparatus wobbled: "We are good Christians, as good as any stinking Indian."

Now the governor felt impelled to rise. They were growing aggressive in his house. He requested the delegation, standing there like a wall, to calm down. The Visitor too stood up, paced back and forth behind the chairs, head down, hands at his back. The coarse leader spoke again: "The long and short of it, we will not obey the new decree. We shall close our farms and let our fields lie."

And without asking the frowning governor, whose ears had reddened, he went between the two hounds behind the table towards the Visitor, who stood bewildered, the man was coming directly at him. He flung open the window. The dull roar of a throng of people swept in. The man at the window said: "So, listen to that. Let them tell us if they are our children, or if they mean to wage war on us."

Again without asking he flung open the other window, invited the officials, who had no idea what was happening, to step closer, and leaned out: "Hollo there! Quiet! Hey!"

At which those below all started shouting. The two high officials had come to one window and saw the unruly dark mass. Directly beneath them on the square before the house was a small company of Spaniards, it did them good to see it. A thousand faces surged below, men and women, blackhaired heads, little creatures. Their frightened expressions were not apparent from up there. Only the three dozen stewards were agitated, twirling their stout staves tirelessly over their heads.

The voice shouted from the window: "What do you want? Do you want to stay with us? Be our children?" Confused shouts from below: "Children! Children!" It was endless. Just this one word. And the goading cries of the stewards.

The men upstairs maintained their hard expressions and scrutinised the faces of the officials. These turned back into the room. The Visitor was pale and shaken, he wiped his brow. The governor had a threatening look and slowly, without moving from the window, looked from one to the other. This look was not a comfort to them. The sturdy governor had hooked both thumbs into his belt and stuck out his elbows, enhancing the ominous impression.

The old man with red eyes felt compelled, the leader keeping silent, to stutter:

"They want to stay with us. They're our children."

The courteous refined voice of the Visitor, who was drying his palms with a handkerchief: "If the lord governor will permit, and if the gentlemen concur, this audience is at an end. As far as I am concerned I was sent here only as an inspector, and have no other powers. But before I depart I would like to be further informed."

His authoritative tone made an impression. It released the tension. The governor came away from the window. They were pleased to see that he had at least removed his left thumb from the belt and his arm was hanging down; his ears were still red. For a moment they stood undecided. Then the governor moved towards the big red-eyed man who was close to him, and clapped him on the leather collar: "Now, Thomas, send your people about their work. Otherwise they'll gain a false conception of us." Everyone was agreeable, and content.

The leavetaking was accompanied with serious and searching glances. Soon the din receded from the marketplace. The governor closed both windows. Before he sat down, slowly, reflectively, brow still furrowed, he asked Alvaro, whom he invited with a preoccupied wave of the hand to be seated, whether he might prefer the window open. Alvaro shook his head curtly. They sat silently side by side. The watch patrolled past with a rattle of drums. Peace restored below. Alvaro: "This incident will make a bad impression on the Viceroy. I'm not sure if it would be a good thing for me to report it."

The governor: "Why? You heard: there's no slavery here. So the decree has been effective."

Alvaro turned and looked directly at the governor, head thrust forward.

The governor: "You heard them. The natives accept it. That's the main thing. More than that, it's the only way to solve the problem."

Alvaro chewed his upper lip. "Don Diaz, you know that what we saw here was theatre, a wretched, despicable play, one which, I have to say, I would not have thought possible."

The governor shook his head: "Theatre, theatre. Alas there's a serious backdrop there. These people won't let themselves be ruined without further ado. Moreover, just so we keep no secrets, I've heard from a reliable source: they have established contact with the Portuguese in the east, with traders. I can't see through their game yet. But anyway, I wouldn't put anything past these gentlemen."

Alvaro, who had listened intently, whistled in surprise:

"Well well, is that so? They would draw Portugal in? That's bold. A pretty kettle of fish! But for Heaven's sake, how have we not heard of it?"

"Of what?" – the governor was once again seated comfortably in his chair, his ears no longer red, his eyes glinted slyly – "of the Portuguese? I'm telling you now. The business is not yet ripe. I'm keeping an eye on it."

"I shall have to whisper it to the Viceroy."

"That would help. With the edict too. You see we already have enough on our plate here."

The world lives from the middle

THE TOWN CALMED down. Suddenly a triumphal arch, almost like those in Yapeyú, appeared outside the Visitor's house. A small deputation of natives arrived with flowers and live birds and assured him how grateful they were that he had not disrupted them in their love for the Whites. They were two stewards with staves and eight others, all smiled happily, and were drunk. They stole from him a new bridle, a mosquito net and a hat.

≈≈≈

While out for a little ride in the outskirts of Asuncion, Alvaro and the bishop spoke together for the last time. The tall greybeard with the basso profundo voice accompanied them on an enormous nag. He rode ahead like a messenger of doom, his horse went through its paces. The impression Alvaro and the bishop had of this region, which was not new to them, was pleasant. Horse and cattle ranches, maize, sugarcane, manioc fields: in what respect did these places differ from those of the Jesuits? Admittedly, when they asked about the dwellings of the mobile labour detachments, the greybeard became hard of hearing, had his work cut out to control his unruly steed, later the question penetrated his ear and his long arms made violent windmill movements: so far away did the dwellings of the detachment lie, scattered all round about, you wouldn't reach them today.

"Well then, how do they themselves reach their workplace?"

"Oh, most of them ride, horses are cheap here."

As Alvaro and the bishop chewed on this indigestible reply, they came to a miserable steading, and two white men with arquebuses doffed hats in greeting. Children ran about, a multitude of dogs, of the kind that ran wild in packs out there. Alvaro mentioned the Indian deputation that had sought him out the previous day. The bishop, smiling: "You poor man, you let them into your room? Would you do that back home?"

"Not really, I dealt with them purely on an official basis, I have White servants. So that nothing should happen to me in the reductions."

"In the hothouse things grow differently. The objects weren't valuable?" – "Trifles."

They rested at a kind of ranch. Some Whites had settled far from town, dwelt here with a small number of Indians, and led a hazardous life with their Indian wives and the natives assigned to them as a labour detachment. They had to contend with animals, the careworn men explained as they received the unexpected visitors with some suspicion, but then, after some whispering aside with the tall greybeard, they served Spanish wine on a table that they carried onto the veranda of the long building, which served as stables, storeroom and dwelling for several families, as well as a magazine for guns and powder. Their half-Indian children hid, their wives were visible only fleetingly, in no way distinguishable from the other farmhands who wandered about attending to tasks or gawping. The two hosts told their guests about the savage Guaycuru, a tribe from the Chaco to the north, which had raided as far down as here. A troop of these had laid siege to the place not long before, they were just about done for, the house burnt, they'd hidden themselves in the bush, in holes in the ground, and had to be sparing of ammunition, they were starving and thirsty – when the savages withdrew suddenly. Cavalry had been mobilised against them in Asuncion. "They look like wild beasts," they said, "wear skins, and it's thanks to our wine that we're still alive, it had only just arrived. The savages couldn't handle it, and when the cavalry came they were drunk. They wear two coils of hair and a little topknot, they make a hole in their lips, the lower lip, and keep a spike in it, the mata." And they fetched a good dozen of these stone spikes from the house.

The bishop asked: "Did they give you these?"

The hosts exchanged grins: "We pulled them out. They didn't resist. A memento."

And they invited the gentlemen to look up at the opening to the veranda. There on a clothesline colourful feathers, Indian adornments, twists of red cotton, and bundles of these matas hung in an arc. The bishop commented: "Next you'll be hanging up skulls."

Since the bishop was so amiable they laughed: "You have to scare them off." And the elder of the two, who placed a broad hat improvised from palm leaves on his head as his horse was brought to him, fixed the gentlemen with a sharp eye as he held the great unsaddled beast by the bridle, and said: "They won't be rid of us so soon. Even if we have no help from the town."

The man jumped onto the horse, it kicked and turned. Felix: "What's happening?"

Two Whites and a dozen natives on horseback had galloped up, surrounded the rancher. "Ask them. We have to chase. Fifty have run away from this lot. Didn't you see there's no one in our fields?" The posse raced away, natives with spears, the two Whites with arquebuses.

During the subsequent brief conversations between the remaining White and the many natives who came up at intervals to seek and receive instructions, it was evident that good relations existed between them. When Alvaro acknowledged this to the placid man, he shrugged: "They're friendly to us only as far as they fear us. If my brother, the one who just rode off, didn't go about with his gun and thrash without mercy anyone he catches running away, we'd sit here alone and would already be massacred." And he lowered his head sadly: "But we'd dearly love to live in peace with them, we need them as we need our daily bread, we keep at their heels, we'd like to grant them everything, but there's no two ways about it, the work has to be done."

When their tall grey companion was called away some distance from the veranda, the two at the table became thoughtful, and felt at ease. "Remarkable," said Alvaro, "when I think of our visit to the Jesuits in Yapeyú. No doubt it was magnificent, and the longer I am away the more I am struck by what they are achieving. But what we see here is also not to be despised. So sad, the inequality between here and the Jesuit Fathers."

Felix hummed and nodded: "If only we knew how to find stronger people for them. I have heard of Moors, Negroes from Guinea, even old Las Casas spoke of them. Perhaps that would be a way." – "Perhaps."

Felix: "I feel the same way as you. The longer I'm back from the Paraná, the more profound my impression of the work they're doing there. Here they are not so pious. They are rough. We should be careful. Everything has somewhat of an incli-nation to descend into a state of war. The Jesuits – make it easy for themselves. Only two in each settlement, and five thousand

Indians. But if you recall: those are really enormous schools, or barracks. The natives are regulated down to their slippers, as you mentioned. To a certain degree, it's an army of peace that the Jesuits have created for themselves. You can see how they've never left off their soldiering since the days of their captain Saint Ignatius. If they can't stretch a straight line, straight streets, straight as a die, one house exactly the same distance from another, if they can't work with a compass and reckon and give orders, they feel unsettled. A remarkable type of human, of cleric. We have never had anything like it in the Church. Actual architects, engineers. Very well. I shall be the last to say anything against them."

"Nevertheless," Alvarado chuckled, "as I heard to my regret in Asuncion, they robbed you of your nephew Gonzales, whom you thought to make your vicar-general."

"Robbed! A strong expression. The things they say in Asuncion. Of course I was reluctant to see him go. But youth must follow its imperatives. The Jesuits exercise such an attraction. They're a whirlwind. I can't compete. – Of course if you ask me whether I'm happy about this development, I can't provide you with an unreserved assurance. And in the end are you yourself, a man of officialdom, are you content with what you've seen?"

"The Jesuits bring an enormous renewal into the world. You're right, they're a whirlwind, full of vim and vigour. These people head straight for their goal, know what they want and won't be played with."

"God knows," laughed Felix.

Alvaro: "And this is attractive to youth. All in all, lord bishop, the trip has been uncommonly informative. All I was commissioned to do was deliver the edict, but I shall report to his Excellency the Viceroy on all I've seen and heard. We must not be driven to commit injustices. The Jesuits are doing splendid work, eyes will pop out of heads in Europe when they find out exactly what they're doing. The rather coarser work we find out here also deserves our undivided respect. No doubt we shall be able to introduce minor remedies."

"Well, I'm glad to hear it. I have nothing to add. Now, these

Jesuit Fathers – I cannot deny that they dealt me a blow by taking away my vicar. As an elderly, learned cleric one is to some extent pushed to the side, one has failed to keep up with the history of the world, only the Jesuits read the signs of the times. Yes, the Jesuits. They do what they want. They're obsessed, and pursue their obsession to the end with yardstick and compass. But just because they do something well, does it mean others are doing badly? Amazing what they're achieving, you recall all those scenes from Yapeyú. They occupy an entire province, hold all the power there, admit no Whites, no priests of other orders, I'm surprised they let in an official of the Crown. Even the civil officials in the reductions, who ought to be appointed by the government, are installed by them. It's a parallel Church state, trodden out of the earth. It suits what they are and what they do everywhere. They stir up the whole world. They have a seat at every court. Their schools and lectures are full to bursting. They'll turn the whole world Jesuit."

Alvaro looked startled: "You think so, my lord bishop? We already have enough problems."

"They're energetic, young, and extreme. The youth follow them. If I must be honest, and you won't repeat this to anyone, I believe it but hope it will not be so. What they are building here is a fool's paradise. That is what I accuse them of. To them it doesn't matter if this wonderful country should fail. But this is false to human nature and to Christianity itself, it provokes. They know no measure, no happy middle. They despise it. But –" With his proud calm expression he stretched an arm across the table: "The world lives from the middle. All excess can be traced back to this measure."

Mendoza and Tayuba

THE CHRISTIAN REPUBLIC expanded.

Father Mendoza of the Jesuits was not dealt a lucky hand. But even his misfortune worked to the Fathers' advantage.

He had gathered two thousand Indian families about him in the reduction of Jesus Maria. The work prospered, as everywhere in the Jesuit republic. Some days' ride from the reduction there lived free tribes as yet unreached by the gospel of salvation. Then Spanish traders appeared, bringing European goods, and reduced the people to debt servitude. And when the Indians could not deliver enough and their debts for arrowheads, axes, cloth grew over their heads, and were as usual encouraged by the traders to work for them at particular places in field or forest, and after the ensuing refusal laid a legal claim with officials in the town, a militia was despatched to force the debtors to work.

From a legal point of view the business was irreproachable. The natives fled. The traders cursed them for thieves and scoundrels. The priest followed them up into the mountains of the northwest. Their cacique was called Tayuba, like all his people he was filled with the most savage hatred of Whites. And when he heard that this priest, one of those in charge of the reductions, was on the way, his hatred grew, for he and many other free tribes could not forgive the Jesuits for offering a refuge to their people and thereby weakening their ability to resist. At that time tribes often attacked reductions simply to reclaim their own fugitives and punish them. But relations between cacique Tayuba and Mendoza were rather unusual. He and Mendoza, the Jesuit Father, knew each other from an incident which lingered unpleasantly in the memories of both. It happened like this.

When Father Mendoza was still teaching in the reduction of San Miguel, Tayuba had pretended to seek conversion, but was unmasked by the Jesuits' informers for his incendiary speeches, warnings against baptism and advice that the people, instead of hiding away and following the White god, who would not help them, should steal horses and guns and burn the place down. The converts had overpowered Tayuba and locked him in the mission house pending Mendoza's arrival. Mendoza was an energetic man. When he arrived he heard the report and questioned the cacique, who at first denied everything, then made a sham confession and begged forgiveness. He pretended to weep, Mendoza threatened that if he should ever again be tempted to such rabble-rousing, he would be expelled from the reduction and, worse, driven out of the Christian community. He then released the man, who promptly vanished into the night. The natives in San Miguel all said he should never have been released, he would attack the place sooner or later. He did not. Nothing was heard of him. He was afraid of the power of the Jesuit Fathers. He bore them a grudge for having chained him up in the mission house at San Miguel.

So now as Mendoza came riding up the valley with a small escort of natives and drew near the mountains where some of the fugitive tribes were hiding, the vengeful man exulted. He was at first unsure how to act. His feelings towards Mendoza were a mix of vengefulness and fear. Mendoza was a great sorcerer with a tremendous reputation. So he gave Mendoza a friendly reception, entertained him in their caves, and fed him. Mendoza expressed regret that the tribe, once so peaceable and happy, had had to withdraw to the chilly mountains. He condemned the cruelty of the Spanish traders, he would lodge a complaint with the Spanish governor, seek release from their debts. Mendoza was prudent enough to refrain from asking why they hadn't sought protection with the Jesuits. Tayuba kept his counsel; he provided skin cloaks to the priest and his escort and led them deeper into the mountains. He thought the tribes would take the matter off his hands by making short work of Mendoza.

But some weeks later his spies brought further reports: the Jesuit was returning safe and sound with an increased following. Tayuba was enraged. He wanted to punish the stupid treacherous people who had attached themselves to Mendoza, as well as the White corruptors.

Rainy weather had set in. Mendoza, unsuspecting, was happy to be put up in the caves with Tayuba's tribe. But he had no desire to prolong the hospitality. There were reasons for Mendoza to be uneasy among these people. His followers, people who wanted to go with him to Jesus Maria, told him Tayuba was up to mischief. Mendoza disingenuously told Tayuba what he had heard, and spent long hours attempting to convert the cacique. They laughed as they recalled earlier times, when they had already attempted the same thing and failed. The cacique promised as they parted that he would stay in touch with Mendoza in order to complete his conversion, and hypocritically and with some urgency reminded the guest of his promise to intervene with the governor in the matter of debts.

Mendoza's train, mostly on horseback, set off in pouring rain wrapped in shapeless skins of ox and calf. The cacique himself with three others accompanied them for some distance. The path led over a low ridge and then dropped into a wide valley of conifers and scrub through which a little river flowed. The harmless stream was swollen by the rains, Mendoza's native escort went ahead to seek a fording place. It was not yet noon.

Then those waiting behind heard calls and confused cries from up ahead. Soon some came rushing up shouting that they'd been attacked, masses of Indians were concealed all over the place, they sprang out of the undergrowth. The people cried that these were Tayuba's men. Tayuba, riding at Mendoza's side in a great feathered headdress, acted shocked, gave his horse its head and raced off. Mendoza spoke soothingly to the people surrounding and pressing in on him. Turn around? No. If they were afraid, they should flee. He considered Tayuba no traitor, and in no event would he abandon his companions up ahead. Then he trotted calmly along the river, alone. As the thought arose in Mendoza that this Tayuba, with whom he had already had such bad experiences, might perhaps be treacherous, he became angry. He'd make the scoundrel answer for it. His people raced after him, threw themselves in front of Mendoza's horse, held on to it, begged him to ride no farther. Fighting could be heard close by. The crowd of natives led by Mendoza out of the mountains had joined battle with Tayuba's warriors. Their warcries shrilled, the struggle was hopeless, Tayuba had the greater forces. "Flee," Mendoza signalled to his people when he saw how things lay, "save yourselves." He left them standing there. At first they were irresolute, then fear lent wings to their feet.

At the ford, more and more Indians emerged from the bush. As Mendoza approached they formed up and directed warcries at him. The priest saw bodies of his people lying on the bank, he was filled with pain and rage. He shrugged off the heavy ox-skin that Tayuba had placed on his shoulders against the rain, let them see the black robe and the cross that he took in his hand. They should see that he did not fear them. He shouted: "Where's Tayuba? Tayuba! Where's Tayuba hiding?" Tayuba emerged from the throng, stood on the riverbank within hearing distance. "So there you are, Tayuba. Why don't you come nearer, you bad man? What have my people done to you that you kill them?"

Tayuba: "You call me bad man, you whiteface, you insolent face. You chase us from our grazing grounds, force us into mountains and swamps. We killed these because they are with you. We shall kill all who stay with you."

"Now you show the real Tayuba. Do you feel no shame in deceiving me? Did I not promise to secure your release from debt servitude? Come to us in Jesus Maria, we shall protect you."

Tayuba rode nearer and flourished his spear: "Call on your god to help you, whiteface, and cease your babbling."

As Tayuba approached across the ford, Mendoza tried instinctively to pull the heavy oxskin that lay across his mount's hindquarters back over his shoulders. But the horse reared at the sight of onrushing Tayuba, Mendoza lurched, and as he grabbed the horse's neck, even before Tayuba reached him, arrows zipped and caught him in breast and temple. He flung out his arms and fell to the ground. The horse pulled itself up and galloped along the riverbank, still carrying the ox-skin.

Now Tayuba jumped down, the whole throng behind him, there lay the great sorcerer of the Whites. Tayuba remounted and let them get on with it.

They stripped the priest, cut off one of his ears, spat on his crucifix. Then they rolled him onto his face and left him there. The rain poured down. But Mendoza, naked on the riverbank amid the bodies of his people, was not dead. In the afternoon he regained consciousness. It took a long time before he could sit up, he was wracked with terrible pain. Arrows had broken in his body. He felt: this is the end. Through the tumult of his suffering he found thoughts of God. The eternal, all-knowing, all-seeing in Heaven. He felt in the wet around him for his crucifix. Couldn't find it. Then he crawled on all fours in unspeakable pain through the mud searching for it. And when he didn't find it he crawled away from the river. He wanted a cross in his hand, wanted to die with a cross. He reached bushes. Cold water dripped on his naked body, he looked around, pines had cast off branches, small brittle fragments lay about, he scrabbled and grabbed a couple of sturdier pieces, his fingers stuck them together, it was a cross, it was good, calm flowed through his torment. And God was there, and words that carried him to Him, and some that bound him to the far-off brothers in the reductions.

A hard night came. And when the black endless night was over, Tayuba's Indians, following his trail from the river, found him at the edge of the bush. His white skin made him visible. He heard their voices. Stiff with cold, and weak, he could not raise his head, they stood around him and saw without shock that his eyes were open and he was still alive. They were all drunk, Tayuba was among them, they had indulged in a kind of victory feast. Tayuba mocked, his people laughed: "There you lie in the bushes, we saw you, your god did not see you. You serve a blind god. He cannot find you."

"Wicked man!" Mendoza gurgled, he tried to move his legs and lift his head to see if the cross was still in his right hand, for the arm had no feeling.

Then Tayuba sank his spear straight down into his mouth. The others swung their axes and butchered him like an ox. They tore out his heart and ran with it from the trees out into bright day. They pierced it with arrows as it floated on the water, they wanted to see how his spirit would find its way to Heaven.

Mendoza's fleeing followers spread the dreadful news. What happened now would have been unthinkable in the time of Father Emanuel: the converted Indians of the reductions Jesus Maria and San Miguel came together to avenge their priest. At that time San Miguel was ruled over by Father Mola; he tried to dissuade the people but seeing they were unhappy with his decision gave them a free hand. Montoya's only response was to show a balled fist.

Cacique Tayuba met an end he had not expected. In his

childish way he thought, as he drew near the reduction of San Miguel following the massacre, that the Indians there would rise and fall upon the Whites with him. For he had defeated the great White sorcerer. Instead he found himself confronted by a heavily armed cavalry battalion, fourteen hundred men thirsting for vengeance, which scattered his people like a flock of hens. They spared no one.

The native cacique of San Miguel had Tayuba tied to a horse, and led him to the place in the mountains where Mendoza had died. When they came to the valley, Tayuba had to point out where the priest was to have been led across the river, where the ford was where they had first wounded him, where he fell from his horse, and where they had murdered him next day. There at the edge of the bush, at the exact spot, the cacique of San Miguel threw Tayuba to the ground, grabbed him by the hair, and beheaded him with his axe.

The foundation of a new reduction, and the return and conversion of many fugitives from the mountains, brought to a conclusion the story of Mendoza's martyrdom.

Difficulties for Bishop Felix

BUT WHEN SHORTLY afterwards some priests came down from those mountains where Father Mendoza had made his glorious sacrifice, they were attacked by young colonists from Asuncion. They took the natives from the Fathers, claimed they were fugitives from town. They made a ceremonial entrance into Asuncion with their two hundred prisoners. Among the prisoners there happened to be a young Jesuit, a novice. They staged a veritable victory celebration, a victory over the Jesuits and royal decrees. It was not far from rebellion.

≈≈≈

The bishop was horrified to hear of the procession entering the town. As the marketplace filled to the sound of pipes and drums to celebrate the triumph of righteousness, he sent his vicar down. But then, when no one would listen to the man, he had to go down himself to the veranda of his house and negotiate with some

Whites, who made way for him, to at least let the young cleric go. Felix was profoundly distressed. It was thanks only to the fact that he vigorously suppressed his feelings and spoke amiably to the Whites that they handed the novice over. They had in any case no idea what to do with him.

Then Felix sat in his living room with the young man, had food and drink served, showed him to a room, bade him have no fear. The prisoner was a friendly youth, he wept in front of Felix because he'd been so unlucky, people would blame him for his ineptitude; but he had no experience of this country. He had not known the Whites here were so ill disposed to Jesuits.

That night Felix awoke, roused Alfio, went with him through the house to see if anyone had broken in to attack the young guest. He and Alfio barricaded the front door from within. Alfio regarded his master with concern. He at once informed Clelia, who was asleep in his room with her child. Next morning she wanted to go to Felix, to take breakfast with him as usual, but he was already there with the young priest and she dared not enter. Later she came across Felix in the library. He gave a start when she entered, he hadn't expected her. But how did he look! Limp, wilting. She took his hand and sat beside him. She felt no connection between them, she could not make one. Only when she sat angrily on his knee, grasped and shook his stupid head and pulled his beard did he smile, raise his arm and draw her to him. He sighed, and his face at once regained its familiar contours. He pressed her close and whispered: "That such a thing could happen, Clelia. I come directly from the underworld."

"Don't speak, Guido."

"Directly, I assure you. I tremble."

"You frighten me."

"It was the underworld. I can tell you nothing about it; we must look in Homer for a description. I couldn't find my soul. It was wandering somewhere. Let's see."

She stood up, sensing that he wanted to rise from his chair. He did so, the Newly Returned, and strode across the library. He moved vigorously and looked around at the room and at Clelia, still standing by the chair. He declaimed from across the room: "The ghost of stricken Patroclus drifted up... He was like the man to the life, every feature, the same tall build and the fine eyes, and spoke: Sleeping, Achilles? You've forgotten me, my friend."

Felix broke off, his face lightened: "Here it is, Odysseus on his way home, he speaks having reached the city and country of the Cimmerians at the end of the ocean, and poured libations for all the dead: 'And up out of Erebus they came, flocking toward me now, the ghosts of the dead and gone... Brides and unwed youths and old men who had suffered much, and girls with tender hearts.' Oh, Clelia, see now, so many dwell there, and you left me to wander alone."

"You didn't call me, Guido."

"Would you have come?" She stood by the chair, arms bare, feet in sandals, in a red Roman gown, let her curly head droop, rested her left arm on the arm of the chair, her face clouded in sorrow. Then she flew across the room to him, pressed her head to his breast. He hugged her: "So you would have come. But when Odysseus saw Achilles himself, his shade, and said to him: 'And grieve no more at dying, great Achilles,' Achilles replied: 'No winning words about death to *me*, shining Odysseus! By god, I'd rather slave on earth for another man — some dirt-poor tenant farmer who scrapes to keep alive — than rule down here over all the breathless dead.' And I shall have this by heart and think to live a long life."

Clelia looked up: "But not here, Guido."

He laughed and walked with her across the room.

But suddenly, as they reached the middle of the room, he was seized with anger, he dropped Clelia's arm, flung wide his arms as if casting off fetters: "Run, Clelia, tell Alfio I will ride, ride, now, this minute. If you like — no, you stay here. Alfio shall come with me."

Then came a headlong dash, an hour's ride out into the plain. Whenever Alfio's horse drew level, he saw the bishop shout and threaten as he clung to the beast's neck. When they came home they had the old Bishop Felix back again. His expansive mood charmed the young cleric who joined them at table.

≈≈≈

What the bishop at his bath that evening confided to Alfio met with Alfio's complete approval. The steam stuck his soft hair to his head, loose strands of his beard clung together, his face emerged from it strong and stern, the lips did not smile: "What are these cattlemen and horse dealers thinking? They want to force my hand! Force me! They want to draw me into their business. They'll come here very soon, Alfio, and offer you a sweetener to make me more compliant and amenable. Perhaps they've done so already?"

"They should know better, sir."

"I shouldn't have taken the young man from them. They should have seen what they could do with him. I'll show him the door. I will not be burdened with it. I'm not a jailer."

"We'll have him out of the house, sir. We'll help him go back. He is so timid. He should continue his studies."

"You think so too. He won't be shifted on that point. When do you think we should bring him away?"

"Early afternoon. We'll take him to the nearest village. He'll have a place to stay for the night. I'll go to the Governor and ask for an escort of two men. Really there's no need for the Count to involve himself."

That afternoon they rode away from the episcopal residence six strong, three armed soldiers, the bishop himself and Alfio. In their midst the nervous young cleric, enveloped, for his protection and to render him unrecognisable, in a heavy leather cloak.

≈≈≈

The stealing away of the prisoner, their hostage, first came to the notice of the Spaniards on the day when they gained admittance to the governor, expecting from him an exemplary punishment of all the prisoners. As they waited in the antechamber to the governor's office and the amiable lofty bishop walked past, the colonists exulted, certain of their case. And when they entered the governor's room and the bishop was sitting at his side, they presented their complaint and added that now at last there was a chance to show the Jesuits which way the wind blows, and they wouldn't let their prisoners go until those over there showed themselves ready for an accommodation.

The bishop explained that he no longer had the novice. Blood throbbed in their necks. The bishop reiterated: he himself had accompanied the novice part of the way; one could not expose oneself to blame in the case of such a young man, so ignorant of politics. At first they were speechless. Then they screamed across one another: "Traitor!" The governor had to stand and end the meeting. There was a risk of an assault on Felix.

"You should have handed the young man over to me, my lord bishop," said the unhappy governor, standing, while the men waited outside.

Felix was calm: "Why? I wanted to spare you trouble. It would have plagued you no end."

The genial governor nodded and regarded the bishop attentively: "Of course, and I'm obliged to you. But you've landed yourself in hot water."

Stones were thrown through the bishop's windows, Alfio was seized in the street and beaten, the governor had to set guards at the bishop's house. That morning the town was in uproar, at church Felix was whistled down.

And when these men appeared menacingly in the marketplace next day and there was danger of an assault on the bishop's palace, the governor had them summoned to him surrounded by captains of the garrison. Thereupon they contented themselves with a few impertinences against the bishop, and a demand that those they had seized should be punished in the public marketplace as a warning. After some hemming and hawing the governor acceded.

The punishment then took place, before a large crowd of natives rounded up to watch. The supposed ringleaders were tied to a wooden frame and beaten savagely until blood flowed.

Gonzales is grateful

THAT EVENING a knocking sounded through the darkness at the firmly bolted door of the bishop's house. Two soldiers stood there with their mounts. They knocked and knocked. Finally Alfio was roused, he left his bed bringing his arquebus with him.

511

A heated conversation ensued between the two men outside and Alfio. Fearing attack, Alfio peeped through a crack in the door and refused to admit them. Clelia, also alarmed, came and listened from a distance. Suddenly she ran up, peeped through the crack, and her face brightened. It was Gonzales with an older priest.

Clelia roused the bishop, who was still reading in the library. He considered it impossible. She herself led them both up the stairs, Alfio following, she ignored Alfio's attempts to shoo her away. How bold, how handsome Gonzales looked beside the stocky bearded older priest, in his soldier's hat, high boots, his belt and sword. While Alfio stabled the horses and prepared rooms for the two, Clelia eavesdropped at the half-open library door.

In the library there was a separate little alcove by a window, provided for the reception of clerics and other sensitive visitors. Uncertain candlelight flickered on the table, Felix stretched out his arms in the heartiest of greetings to his unexpected guests, regarded Gonzales with unconcealed joy, and tried to entice a smile from the young face. But to the bishop's chagrin they both retained that odious fanatical gravity. They tried to overwhelm him at once with a letter, but this did not go down at all well. He had Clelia, to her joy, bring them bread and fruit, and a jug of their maté drink. Then he indicated he was tired, and Alfio had to lead them to their room. He and Clelia then talked at length about the situation, both were excited and happy, would not be parted.

Next day, to his chagrin, Felix had to accept the letter. The emissaries wanted to head back, a longer stay in this house was impossible. Montoya urged the bishop, whose decisiveness he praised, to exert his full influence in Asuncion to keep the colonists in check. How hard it was to keep the agitated Indians of the reductions in a state of peace, when their brethren outside were being maltreated, beaten, enslaved. But both men shared a common purpose: to persevere in the conversion of the New Indies and so adhere to royal guidance. He hoped Bishop Felix would accept his most sincere greetings.

Annoyed, mouth pressed tight, Felix read the letter: what did this request mean, they seem to think I want to be of service to them. When the elder priest withdrew to converse with the bishop's vicar, Felix at last had an opportunity to speak alone with his young friend. He strode with Gonzales into the spacious library.

But they were not given long to walk among the bookshelves and statues, for from below, from the market, came lamentable sounds of groaning. A crowd of prisoners was being led in for punishment. Dark men were bound to stakes, they had to squat there fasting from morn till night. Wooden frames were hauled in, dark men had to lie on them, whips cracked.

Gonzales stepped to the window. Felix knew: they had arranged these terrible punishments in the marketplace so he would feel their fists. And there knelt his young Gonzales, in the shadows by the window, head bent, rosary pressed to his lips, praying. And after Felix had stood for a while and given in to his rage, he too, as whips cracked again, had to sink to his knees in his lovely, joyous, light-filled library, in this hall of antiquities which had never witnessed Felix on his knees. And it was not to pray that Felix knelt, but impotence and bitterness forced him down, and for this reason he stayed on the floor even after Gonzales stood up. I have done what I could, I could not prevent it. They are right, the Jesuits, I leave the country to the Jesuit Fathers.

He said as he stood: "Let us go from the library." But he was unable to move, sat in his chair. He motioned Gonzales to the chair beside him, but he stayed standing. At last Gonzales, observing his uncle closely, found words. He spoke very softly, seemed in sympathy with his uncle: "They are shameful. What they are doing is outrageous. You could not have prevented it, uncle." Felix shook his head. Gonzales went to him, how strange that his strong uncle, sitting there now so collapsed, should challenge him to disagree: "You always thought things would go well, uncle."

"And now that they go badly?"

"However it goes is nothing to them." (He has an answer for everything, as clear as one times one) "I've known them since I was a child. Come, uncle," and he gave his shoulder a little shake, "take your rosary, and let us pray together."

But Felix made no move. He heard the words, but also the screams from below, the pain and shame they sought to inflict on him. He waited and looked inwards to see if the underworld would appear again. But it failed to announce itself. Instead a mighty heat swept over him, disgust, a glowing joyful cloud of anger that set him going. What, they thought to crush him between them, those down there with their whips on bare flesh and these Jesuits, these clueless fellows, these beginners, these simpletons, these enemies of the world?

"Come," he said to Gonzales, would not take the rosary the other held out but squeezed Gonzales' hand in his, rosary and all. "Come!" And he strode ahead with vigorous steps as if a great weight had gone from his shoulders, into the refectory, a small simple room. The noise from the marketplace did not penetrate here.

The bishop flung himself into his chair, Gonzales had often sat in this room, he took up position, tall, lanky and proud as he was, the figure of a youth quite without sweetness, behind the chair which once was his. "Uncle, why don't you go down and simply have them released?"

"Leave it!" roared Felix, "I need no advice from you. I am bishop and know what I must do."

Gonzales stood still, lowered his head, then stepped to the table, pushed the chair back. He sat down slowly, laid his head in his arms on the table.

"What is it, Gonzales?"

The young man raised his head: "They've stopped."

They said nothing for a long while, Felix staring straight ahead with a black fixed gaze. Felix said coldly: "Was there something else you wanted?"

"To thank you, uncle, for freeing the novice. I've some apologies to make, I'm glad to do so."

"Well then, Gonzales. Do you feel uneasy?"

Gonzales kept his head down and looked at the rosary in his left hand. A joy, he had not suspected it, leapt in Felix: "And what is unsettling you?"

Gonzales looked thoughtful: "You were with us, uncle, you know Yapeyú. I've been there three years now. When the novice came and told me all that had happened, I – literally felt drawn to you. I felt an intense love for you, uncle. And at once I knew what torment you were in here. I saw that my uncle is not what I had thought. He knows what's true. And he doesn't shy from confrontation. And so I wanted –"

Felix stretched out comfortably in his chair, he thought how nice if Clelia were to be summoned, she should hear what the young man says to me, she gave me a piece of her mind yesterday when stones came through the window and nearly hit the child. Felix shrouded himself in a cloud of contentment as protection against various possibilities he could foresee. He laughed brightly and finished Gonzales' sentence: "'And so I wanted to nag at you a little.'"

"Why not. One should strike while the iron is hot. I know my uncle Felix."

"You know him."

"We follow in the footsteps of the Apostles to the heathen, to proclaim the word of God as it is written. With Loyola comes the victory that will subdue the world. Help us, uncle, you are leaning that way already, now step firmly over to our side."

Felix held a hand to his forehead. They seem to address me as if I were not their own bishop of Paraguay, but any old monk not quite sure of himself. They think I'm not all there. Their insolence knows no bounds. And the more he felt this, the deeper his anger burrowed into him, and he seemed to listen calmly as Gonzales talked on, but he could not listen, and after some time heard himself say: "You people want me by the throat." And then the thought came, as he leaned back and his gaze crossed that of the youngster: you scoundrel, you scoundrel, in your pocket is a judgment of heresy against me, why come to me again, why must you flush me out again, why start so prettily and now the conversation has turned bad, for I shall defend myself to my very blood, granted I'm no longer young, I'm old enough to do without, I can do without you, I've already done without you, I, and Clelia too, whom you despise because she attracts you, but she is a person and more than all your sinister ideas, which I despise. She is a joy to my heart and gives me the greatest delight and sweetness of my life. Scoundrel, you scoundrel, whatever ailment lies in wait for me, heart or liver or small of the back: you will bear a load of guilt for returning here and unsettling me.

The bishop paced up and down, Gonzales stood, gripped his chair tight with both hands. The bishop was his old self again as he paced. "Don't lend your voice to those out there, your brothers! I'm not just anyone, you know that. The Church lived before you, and will live on after you. I love these people," he felt his words weren't the whole truth, but couldn't say otherwise, he raged that Gonzales should drive him so far; "they let themselves be carried away sometimes, but they must plough, plant, fight, struggle through with their families. We must stay by them every step of the way. Sometimes we're glad they don't forget us entirely."

And he stood in front of his nephew, overtopping him by half a head, he was bigger and heavier than the young warrior: "This isn't enough for you. Your lot should not demand too much of us. Under no circumstances should one shout advice from the shore to a ship struggling in a storm. Take a look at your history, how Fathers Emanuel and Montoya had to retreat step by step. They failed, but we cannot fail. If you were to try again here, for just half a year, you'd soon be on your wanderings again, but what condition would our people be in."

Felix paced about the room and spoke quite loftily: "These Indians, they are weak, they're certainly not hardworking, why should they work, on the other hand the Whites are newcomers, how does it come together, a problem."

Gonzales stood with downcast eyes, made no reply, I completely misread him, I thought him willing to draw near to us again, but he's still the old cynic, playing with his ideas.

Felix had regained his chair, his unease always left him when he came to his chair and let himself down into it, now he could stretch his legs, and even though his head was still tucked low between his shoulders he was in complete control of himself, and his left hand sought his beard. Now his voice was friendly: "Of course you have no answer to this, and I don't require one, dear boy. A thousand people in the Church and out there break their heads over it, in vain. It's all a botch. Anyway, old Las Casas spoke of Negroes. That's a thought. People from the east coast were here, and told us about it, things were going well with them. I have discussed the matter forwards and backwards with the governor, and with the town elders. Anyway, Negroes won't come here of their own free will."

Contemplative and satisfied with the difficulty of the question, he stretched and spoke quite over Gonzales' head. Finally he gave a deep sigh: "But of course this doesn't interest you. These are the cares of old, mouldering practical men. Ah, who could have it as good as you lot." He lumbered to his feet: "And now you will send the priest downstairs to me, dear boy, I shall give him a letter for Montoya."

They left the room. On the landing their path crossed with Clelia's. Gonzales passed her without raising his eyes from the floor, Clelia had not yet managed a single word with him. The bishop accorded her a majestic nod.

Later, as Felix sat in his library, she appeared from behind the kneeling Venus: "What have you done with him?"

"My love, I believe I have persuaded him."

"Why doesn't he speak, why won't he come out of his room?"

"Clelia, the priest is with him."

"You frightened him, he was happy when he arrived, now he has a black look, what happened between you?"

"I was supposed to help them."

"So help him at least."

"They want to take charge of everything here. I cannot accede. I cannot give them what I do not have. In any case you would not agree to it."

"I have nothing to do with it."

"You'd bother your pretty head mightily, Minx."

"You spoke with him all evening and today and not a syllable to me. And," she wept, "just now he passed me without a glance."

"A Jesuit. They've ruined him. Do you really want their sort in charge here?"

She wept without speaking.

Next afternoon the two guests took their leave. After they were gone the bishop remained a long time at the window.

Now the decision's made. A chapter of my life is over, completed. They wrested it from me.

An exodus from Paraguay

ANYONE WHO CAME across the ocean into this wide country, with its huge basin shaped by the primal stream that binds together heaven and earth, Amazonas, Mother of Seas, might for a little while turn to the right and give play to his smile and his old appetites, and might turn to the left and continue as if he noticed nothing. It made no difference at all if the feet he set on this soil were protected by stout shoes, at his back was a Somebody who kept an eye on him and noted everything about him, his moods, his wishes, his colour, his gait, and who followed him through the years. It was a Being that took the most intimate interest in him, and carried a balance in its hand, held it over his head and observed its movements. A downy feather lay in one tray. The balance quivered at every breath the newcomer took.

This Being made a sinister sound as it followed close behind, which came neither from its footsteps, for it was barefoot, nor from its clothing, for it was naked, but was a kind of soliloquy, carried on in such a steady murmur that you thought it the wind, or distant rain. Only gradually, if you stayed longer in the country, did you hear more clearly the soliloquy and the dovishly cooing siren calls into which it sometimes swelled. The sound had something of the draught that forces its way through a gap, and of the distant gleam that lets itself trickle into a cave. Inconspicuous as it was, it had the power to make the person it was following lose equilibrium, so he no longer knew who he was yesterday, the day before, his youth, his parents, his books, his statues, the clothes fell away from him, the old I melted away. It was consumed in silence and hollowed out, as if by white ants.

In this hot country with its rainy seasons and dry seasons, in countless discussions with laity and clergy and officials, in fights and evasions, Felix had slowly ripened; and now – he felt this obscurely and noticed it in his movements – he had reached a boundary. How lovely and plump, actually a little fat, had his big girl Clelia grown, he had no desire to leave her, and her child, their link, was his never-ending delight: so life renewed itself, his and Clelia's together – should one not graze insatiably on the miracle?

But something slithered in behind his thoughts and whispered: it is enough. He was not yet old, no grey streaks in his beard, but his eyes no longer saw well close to, and those around him noticed his hearing had grown less acute. These thoughts came easily to the handsome bishop they'd named Felix, happy man. He had every reason to feel settled and secure, how his birth had smoothed the path, how wealth had come to him early – he never demanded the impossible, self-denial came easily to him; he despised those who grasped beyond their reach and despaired. As the air in Europe filled with demons and war raged through Italy, Germany, Moravia, Bohemia, Austria all the way to Denmark, he left Italy behind like a dark room and made his way to the New Indies. He was not ready to give up one iota of his freedom.

When rumours of his union with Clelia reached him through his vicar, who begged him to counter them, when the Inquisition in Lima was said to be concerned about certain utterances and also his way of life – but he shouldn't worry, the local government, the Viceroy of Peru, indeed the whole province stands behind him, sees through the manoeuvre – he was again seized with astonishment at the energy of the Jesuit Fathers. To the governor, who thought he should offer reassurance, for it was within his power to detain Felix, he said: "The Jesuits are trying it on. I imagine it won't be easy to defend myself, Excellency. People underestimate them. Setting up their Christian republic on the Paraná was no mean feat. I don't know if they will bring me down. But this huge monastery on the Paraná, a hundred thousand native monks all wanting to fly to Heaven with their wives and children! It never ceases to amaze me."

"Why be amazed," said the grey governor, who was used to the presence of the moody old sceptic, "we politicians shrug our shoulders."

"Shrug away, governor, they'll create enough difficulties for you. These people have nerves of iron, they'll bring it to the point where many heretics will have to be burned. They don't love our kind."

"Fortunately they have some grounds for that. As for your nephew, this shadow of Montoya, you know the youth of today do not follow that path. The wind is turning. Some of our young noblemen went down to study in the Paraná republic, the ideas they came back with are not Jesuitical. They marvelled at the practical arrangements, the obedience. The economy and the social order impressed them. But only so far. I heard sceptical remarks. They are radical these days, but in a different way from the Jesuits. Some considered the whole system outmoded, unfit for the times, others said it was good but only for Indians, only a few came back infected with a fatal enthusiasm; they said we should despatch the Duke of Alba and others of our grand seigneurs over here, to learn how to work."

Felix: "Take care, Excellency. Some things should not be called by name."

"Except yours, my lord bishop. And that applies not just to any bishop, but to our very own Bishop Felix."

But there was no holding him. A darker, domestic problem beset him: the dreadful reaction of Alfio, his major domo, to the rumours. The eunuch paraded around Asuncion so proudly with his wife and child, Clelia had grown so used to him, she was devoted to him in a certain sense, at first she was ashamed when Felix bound her to this eunuch and overseer, and then came to enjoy his affection and the pleasant strolls in between the two men. But Alfio had no doubt that Gonzales and no one else was the source of the despicable rumours. His theory ran thus: Gonzales once loved Clelia, was jealous of Felix, and that's why he left Asuncion and went to the Jesuits, and now takes his revenge. When Clelia could not be calmed of her fears regarding violent plots against Gonzales by Alfio, the former pirate, and the bishop's attempts at reassurance fell flat, Felix had had enough. It would have been difficult for him to retreat without arousing attention and conjuring a sense of triumph among his enemies, to the detriment of his flock. But, as if summoned, scarlet fever entered the country, and he too was stricken by the disease which raged worst in the Indian reductions. For several months the fever kept him at death's door. It snatched away his child, his little Ada.

Any who saw Felix on his feet all pale and bent understood: he's no longer fit for work. The rumours persisted. The Church swiftly relieved him of his post. He could swim free once again.

Alfio

CLELIA AND ALFIO wanted to travel by a later ship, along with the baggage. It was merely a pretext by Alfio. Clelia suspected something, and only half agreed that the bishop should return alone.

Alfio tried every way he could to gain access to the reductions, as a trader, an agent, he could not come past the sentries at Yapeyú. He hired a dissolute White of the town whom he befriended, gave him money and promised more if he could deal with Gonzales by whatever means. This fellow had no better luck.

Then chance led Gonzales himself to Asuncion. A new church was to be consecrated, permission had been given to establish a new Jesuit college in the town, it all smacked of peace and reconciliation. Gonzales was one of the five Jesuit emissaries. The episcopal palace was of course deserted, but the vicar-general still had his offices there. A house removal was in progress, chests filled with the bishop's books and artworks filled the hallway. Here Alfio lay in wait for Gonzales the first time. But he stumbled with his dagger over a loose board, ducked down, Gonzales looked around, went upstairs unawares.

Clelio implored Alfio to keep the peace, but a murky stew churned in his brain: the child's death, grief, fury at his exposure, torment over his old misery, and all blended into one figure, Gonzales, and only one relief for everything: Gonzales. It was all his fault, the bishop's sickness, his hasty departure, and that they must all go back, for Alfio had grown comfortable here, and now Rome lay in wait with all its temptations for Clelia, and Clelia had become very close to him, here where they were alone; the poor eunuch had never hoped he might yet attain a wife.

After the failure of Alfio's attempt in the house, he tailed Gonzales, who would not stay many days in Asuncion, through the streets. In the end, although Gonzales was always accompanied by a crowd of his native pupils, Alfio had to make a move. In order to avoid Clelia and her nagging, Alfio spent the whole of one night with friends in the town. They drank. Together with those he had brought in on the plot, and who were not averse to a run-in with the Jesuits, he set off in the dark to deal with the impugner of his honour. But Fate would not be played with. It had already sent a signal to the former pirate by unmanning him. After that his angry violence had calmed down and retreated; Alfio lived a peaceful life, and was able to enjoy Clelia's company. Now the burned man screamed again, rage and delirium blinded him, he had been jolted by a new blow.

As the little bell sounded through the darkness for early Mass and the Fathers came out of their lodgings and made their way to church, they were set upon by several people at a corner in the confusion of little alleys. Other people, attracted by the cries, came out, the Jesuits' black robes were not loved, from the cries it seemed that accounts were being settled. The Fathers' native companions ran up. Before anyone knew it there was a riot, a street fracas. The participation of the Fathers' native companions lent the affair an ominous character. Knives and clubs came into play.

Alfio's eyes searched the throng for his Gonzales. He'd better be quick, for the town watch would soon be sorting them out. But he couldn't find Gonzales. Bodies lay on the ground, trampled in the melee. Maybe Gonzales was one of them. He searched furiously, dawn was breaking. Life and death meant nothing at that moment.

He was opposed by a sinister force, and could feel it. As the drums of the watch rattled and troops approached at a run, the mob dispersed and hid in houses. Alfio too took refuge in a house, he hadn't found Gonzales, it was morning now. He felt low and tired. He slipped out to the palace by the back way. It was quiet there, the child was no longer alive, the bishop was aboard his ship, he might already be in Europe. Where was Clelia? He searched for her, called out in the empty rooms. The vicar made no appearance, his servant too was missing. She must still be at church. I shall wait.

Then noises came from the market. A slow heavy tread on the steps. Then a loud knock.

And when he ran to open the door, they carried in – Clelia. They placed the bier among the packing cases in the hallway. She'd gone into the throng and been trampled, the men said. She'd been looking for Alfio, maybe wanted to restrain him, but he hadn't seen her, maybe she wanted to protect Gonzales.

The bearers tipped Alfio off that the watch were looking for him. But he didn't run away. He stayed with her an hour, before they came to take him.

Felix in Rome

THE HARBOUR AT Livorno. Cargoes came from the New Indies, ships were loaded, sailors gathered in sheds along the shore, there were entire barracks.

Through this happy bustle moved Bishop Felix, with the friends from Rome who had come to welcome him. "Escaped from the jaws of Cerberus," is how they received him. He cocked his head a little, as if listening for a distant sound: "What Cerberus? And who said, escaped? I don't have my luggage yet." And as soon as he reached the hostelry where his Roman friends had arranged a room for him, he began to tell them about over there, day after day, on into the night, they were happy to listen, there was no need to prod him, he himself, they noticed in wonderment, was remembering, fixing the memories, spinning the threads like a silkworm forming its cocoon. The Roman friends arranged it so they could be with him for two months, and help him bear his loneliness.

They knew he was waiting for Alfio and Clelia, from whom he was inseparable.

A ship arrived, and to his astonishment it brought no Alfio, nor Clelia, nor his chests. So he sent a letter to the governor by the next ship. But before he received a reply, another ship came – agonizing, the jubilation in the harbour – and he was notified of his baggage, but, how puzzling, Alfio and Clelia failed to appear. The bishop was seized with gloomy foreboding, what had happened, they'd sent his luggage on, was Alfio a deceiver, and his Clelia, unthinkable, had she conspired behind his back to stay there with him? The Roman friends said as much. The blackguards.

But a terrible vision, dream or whatever, came now suddenly into Felix's mind, from the voyage over. He was sitting awake, half awake, Clelia, his big girl, on his lap among the sails facing the great big sea, she had her arms around him as so often in Rome and in Asuncion, in his library. And when she grew too heavy, she was slowly growing unspeakably heavy, he tried to free his knees gently with a little joke, but she refused to budge, wouldn't loosen her arms, her arms clung to him, she squeezed harder, harder, her face pressed to his, her face on his grew cold, colder, icy. Looking sideways he saw her damaged eye. Then he groaned and sat up straight– he was on the deck of a ship, air, he felt unwell, he scuttled on hands and knees, burst into the messroom below deck and calmed himself with wine, he quickly forgot all about it. Now here it was again, horrible.

And already a messenger from the ship was in the courtyard of his inn, bearing a letter from the governor in Asuncion. The bishop was so pale that the friends took the letter, and at a nod from him opened it. "What are you afraid of? Why shouldn't the Governor write to you, he's your friend after all!" He couldn't look at them as they began to read. They whispered among themselves, came up to him, he sighed, they said there had been an accident, and shed tears. Then he clutched his chest and learned what had happened.

≈≈≈

That was Bishop Felix, who lived on for years and years in Rome, without office.

It was the age of the lively and tender Pope Innocent the Tenth.

The great war was over. Victors and defeated lay in the earth. It had been demonstrated that the Church no longer ruled the world. In Rome the pope consorted with Italian princes, himself an Italian prince. His capital was ruled by several families, and mainly by two women, one of them his sister in law Donna Olympia, the other, her daughter in law, also called Olympia, of the Aldobrandini family. The pope incurred debts, the two Olympias quarrelled, the elder one was rich, energetic, held the reins, foreign emissaries had to go through her, cardinals hung her portrait in their palaces.

Among the great families of Rome lived Bishop Felix, former spiritual shepherd of Paraguay, who never forgot his distant southern land. How the families – Orsini, Borghese, Ludovisi, Barberini – formed alliances, how the game between the two Olympias was going, whether they greeted one another at Carnival, these were earth-shattering questions. Must the carriage of a lower-ranking noble halt for a higher-ranking noble, which families had precedence at Vatican receptions, for which families must one open both wings of the door, for which only one. Here no Inquisition could be seen. Felix had peace. He lived in his villa, an elderly man of the world, took part in the life of the Eternal City, and was honestly upset when on one occasion he read a letter from a cardinal to the pope, alerting him to delays in judgments by the court, bribery and even worse: "These sufferings are worse, Holy Father, than all the sufferings of the Hebrews in Egypt. Gentiles who through presents have secured access to the Roman court are treated more inhumanely than slaves in Syria or Africa. Who can see this without tears." Felix was saddened by this because he knew it was true. He dwelt among his artworks, old and many newly acquired.

In his view (his worldly friends agreed with him, men of the Church contested it, his gaze was focused on the New Indies where more than one little decade of his life lay buried): "The Church, the old guardian of peace, has been strongly overtaken by appeasement. Do not be deceived. Today's peace is no peace. Soon the Church will have only one hope left, the last: the Jesuits.

And then we shall be a sect." This caused a fuss. "Well, we haven't reached the end yet, we sit here comfortably in Rome, keep our doors locked, but life goes on outside the city, the Jesuits are there as our heavy and light artillery, and facing them is barbarism, of Whites and dark people. We others can no longer keep barbarism in check, the war proved that. They stretch their talons out for us, we're not yet weak enough for them. I've always been reluctant to acknowledge it, but the world must decide between the most advanced and decisive forces, between Jesuits and barbarians. Those of us caught in the middle are out of the game."

"A Jesuit Pope!"

"They don't want that. I think them most foolish. But perhaps one day they will deviate from this principle, for if they don't control all the levers of power, it will go badly for them one day. They saw this already on the Paraná, and as a result they armed themselves; they should not hold back here either."

"And then?"

"Our lovely statues, our Aphrodites, Hermes, Apollos will lie buried in the earth again. Have no doubt. You must choose. Really, we should bury them with our own hands. They've proved to be lovely illusions, wonderful enchantments, leading us into the abyss."

≈≈≈

You love him, but don't let him unsettle you. These were his aphorisms. He lives among the old statues, the evil wonderful spirits, and you'd break his heart to take them off him.

The cheerful daily prattle of the two Olympias, the cooler air of the mountains, his friends and ancient artworks kept him alive a long time, although the terrible agony he had suffered in Asuncion, where they still sang his praises, had rapidly made him older, gloomier and more timid. "Piety begins with the trembles," his friends mocked.

Part Eight

TURNING POINT
~

The new call

THIS WAS THE turning point. The former bishop of Paraguay had foreseen it rightly when Father Montoya, on leaving Rome, armed his Christian Indians and organised his Noah's Ark.

It all took a long time.

Something mysteriously ominous, which even those who feared it did not merely fear, closed in on the Whites. They sensed it in many ways, had many ways of alluding to it, it came sooner over one people than another. The books and lovely statues kept by Bishop Felix were harbingers of the great convulsion.

≈≈≈

You can make a house as solid as you like, build it of stone blocks, wall up windows and doors and bury it in bedrock, one day the stones will burst asunder, even without cannon. Air, light, water will pour in, you do not dwell alone in this world, it tolerates nothing that sets itself apart and says "I, I", all is heaped on that great table where you dine and where the game of life and death is played out.

Boundless arrogance of the White men! Desperation of the White men! They felt themselves untethered from the wonderful fecund earth, they were strong, and in their gloomy devastated lands they fought beasts, forests, elements; many died, many survived. Sicknesses came upon them – how to save yourself! Such monstrous solitude. Then, as saviours in their darkness, there appeared those who said that amid the terror of existence there is a blessing over the world. Monstrous the torments of this life, but eternal bliss in Heaven. Oh, the ebb and flow of joy and misery, ever more torments and despair. Many were led by their disgust and yearning to immure themselves in a monastery cell, mortify the flesh that lured them into such misery.

Into the fecund dissolving earth, a thousand years before, had sunk temples, columns, capitals and sacrificial altars, images of deities, youths, heroes, the lovely women of free southern peoples. Above them strutted the dreary victorious Church, which rejected this world and hoped for salvation in the hereafter. For a thousand years the laughing joyous bodies of stone rested beneath the victor's feet, the earth guarded them as its secret.

But they were made of marble and granite. And when people began grubbing in the earth and the stone bodies came to light again, you clutched your breast in shock and delight. Only a few suspected what it was that emerged from the soil.

From rows of columns your gaze flitted to people and things. As irresistible as magicians and pipers, these statues stepped out before the living, their lovers, and began to lead them on. And as soon as you hymned praises of this newly discovered beauty, its siren song never left you, penetrated ever deeper into you, and when you looked around, you were in a new country. Where are we, you asked. The statues answered: On Earth. You held ancient parchments, read wonderful stories, so luminous and plangent. You asked: Where are we? The parchments answered: On Earth.

Now you gazed around and looked at that old great Heaven. You were turned inside out. You filled the heavens with exuberant, drunken, fervent, surging figures from within yourself.

Others came. And now it grew clearer what had happened. They dared to gaze with more courage. Always the same answer: this is the Earth.

They looked up at the stars. One raised a telescope and gazed often and long into the heavens, reverently, praising God. He spent decades of his life at this. Up there in the darkness of space hung heavenly grapes, the stars. And see! They turn and move. And the Earth too, the Earth with them. It turns with the others. It revolves around the sun. The sun, that great hot star, stands still. For a long time he refused to believe. It was shocking. He wrote it down, perplexed and prayerful. He dedicated his book to the pope. As he lay on his deathbed, he was pleased when someone brought him the first copy of his book. His name was Nicholas Copernicus, a Pole. He died aged seventy.

Heaven was the central point of all their secrets. They were prisoners lying in chains, and when they cast off the chains they slipped through the gate, looked around at the environs of the house in which they had languished, and only then slipped back in and looked around the house itself.

After Copernicus came one who saw planets up there, they were just planets, the fixed stars merely fixed stars, a star gathered satellites about itself, Saturn had a ring, the Venus star showed itself in phases. The man had no doubt they all moved by themselves, no external force, no extraneous will had set them in motion, he was able to describe their movements and their paths in numbers. This man was called Galileo Galilei. He was not as fortunate as Copernicus. In Rome he was forced to admit that he only suspected it was so. In the end they held him under supervision in a villa near Florence, to enforce his silence.

A drunken visionary appeared, and what the other two had kept concealed he gushed forth in a fountain of words. He was burned at the Campo de' Fiori in Rome, he would not look at the crucifix they held up to him as he died. This visionary had been apprenticed to the Dominicans in his youth. He accepted what the Pole Copernicus said, to him it was truer than the words of saints and Church Fathers, all his life he had to wander, to Geneva, Paris, the Church pursued him, to England, but even those who turned away from the Roman Church had no desire to hear of this new thinking. He was persecuted by the pious of the old religion, and by those of the new, the Protestants. And when he came to Venice he was approached by a friendly young man, Mocenigo, apparently loyal, but he was an agent of the Inquisition and gave him up to them. When his clerical judges pronounced the death sentence, he said: "You who pronounce this sentence on me have a greater fear than I who receive it."

He had spent his whole life poised over flames: there was no place in the world for a distant being, Eternal Being plays itself out in *this* world. The world rolls magisterially, majestically on. That was the song of Giordano Bruno.

Unruly men came into the world, who had no understanding of themselves or of the path they were taking. Girolamo Cardano, a doctor born in Pavia, thought it the most astonishing coincidence that he should have been born in the very century that learned of the orbiting Earth. He could sense this force now shaking the Earth more powerfully than any earthquake. He carried his head atop a long scrawny neck, his voice was loud and scolding, one hand, the left, was good, the right was withered. For many years he served his father, an advocate, who treated him with contempt. His heart was cold, his head was hot. When he married a beautiful woman she brought him three children, the daughter remained barren, the elder son was beheaded for a murder by poisoning, the younger was thrown into prison as a criminal.

Cardano wrestled with a myriad things: he puzzled over equations of the third degree, tried to weigh air, studied universal joints. He performed blood transfusions, sought thereby to change people, influence their character, for the mixture of elements in a body determines qualities. Then he said: "Changes in Nature obey the law of numbers, to which God has delegated His work. All beings have a soul, even plants can love and hate." At that time there was no one who could understand him, unless perhaps in the New Indies, among natives. "Man is not an animal, but all animals, the highest stage of all animate life, and Nature frequently creates new forms which then disappear when they cannot endure." The man was led by a demon, the Inquisition seized him when he was seventy, he was released from prison but not allowed to teach. He bowed to this, for what was there in the world for him to cling to.

How tenderly Visalius in Padua approached the human body, how humbly he peeled muscle back from muscle, laid bare the entrails. With what cautious joy did the Spaniard Servet respond as the secret of the circulation of the blood gradually dawned on him; they chased him from country to country until in Geneva a tyrant locked him up, one of that baleful old Church stock who declared himself a reformer: "To defend the world against contagion and cut off a diseased limb, we condemn you to be led in chains to Champel and there, bound to a stake, to be burned alive together with your book. So will your life be ended, as a warning to others who conduct themselves as you have done."

Montoya's sinister end

MONTOYA'S LAST YEARS on the Paraná at the reduction of Yapeyú were filled with great fervor. The older Fathers who saw him at that time remarked how he resembled Emanuel. He strove to embed religious observances ever more deeply. White-haired, bony, he went like an apostle among the natives, who feared him as a god. The stern organizer who had achieved the arming of the Indians rejoiced in the fraternity that took the holy name of Jesus, whose adherents came over from Peru, clutched rosaries in order to awaken the fifteen mysteries, five of joy, five of sorrow, five of glory, and sang with them and their dark and white friends:

> *Jesus our saviour, our love, our desire, God the Maker, Man at the end of time, how has meekness prevailed in you, that for us you bear all our sins. O dreadful the death you suffered, to preserve us from death. You descend to the pits of Hell and tear the prisoners therefrom and seat them at the right hand of God. O may you be moved by pity to prevail over our misery, may we be comforted by the sight of you, glory be to you, Lord. Jesu nostra redemptio, amor et desiderium.*

≈≈≈

They sent envoys to Spain and Italy, gathered news, made enquiries. The question of Indian marriage was broached. Father Juan de Lugo, who lectured at the College in Rome, was dispatched by the general of the Order to obtain a clear decision from the Pope. Juan de Lugo, a steely plain-speaking man, presented the case before the Pope who, outwardly grave, listened attentively. As protection against Juan de Lugo, who belonged to that pitiless and omniscient tribe, the Pope had brought in two younger cardinals, whose state of knowledge was irrelevant; the Pope chose them for that reason.

The question concerned the Guarani Indians, these Guarani in the New Indies had marital problems when they entered the reductions and became Christians. With no trace of a smile, to the disdainful bemusement of the worldly Pope, Professor Lugo reported that the Guarani were unaccustomed to be satisfied with just one wife, the Fathers on the Paraná told them they must decide on one, and this should be the one they had married first.

"One imagines this would be a simple matter, but it is not. For difficulties arise at this very point. The fact is that the Indians regard their wives as servants, slaves even, and when they no longer want them they send them away. They keep several, in some deplorable cases they take a mother and daughter to wife at the same time. And the shamelessness of these people is also evidenced by the way they make use of their wives. They offer them to friends, or to guests, or even, if they are chiefs, lend them out to vassals."

The Pope glanced at his resplendent young cardinals: "And these are the Indians that the Fathers of the Company of Jesus keep in their reductions?"

The professor could not understand why the pontifex spoke so complacently. He declared in bitter earnest: "The women they lend out or send away may under certain circumstances be taken by them again as wives, to live with them once more. They take them along on wanderings, warpaths, or leave them behind in one place or another, as suits their fancy."

"How curious," said the Pope, "and the women make no protest? One would like to know what kind of women these are."

The professor did not answer, his piercing glance travelled from the Pope to the two cardinals, who timidly avoided his unnerving gaze, it was of no matter whether the women were content with their lot, the question was whether this was a marriage.

The Pope twined his heavy soft hands together: "So what are the questions posed to us by the pious Fathers of the Company of Jesus in their reductions?"

Professor Lugo handed a document to the Pope's secretary and said as he gestured to it: "The Fathers request the Holy See to issue a definitive ruling as to how the difficulties described should be handled, which wife should be considered the first, and therefore entitled to the status of true wife. It should be taken into account that this first wife may also be the first wife of another,

"The Pope trusts us," Gonzales pointed out.

"Yes, he trusts us, Gonzales," and Montoya, distraught and weeping, turned his pale thin face away, "but I – do not trust us." Gonzales dared not respond. The old man continued: "They leave us to own devices. I know it."

Gonzales dared to touch his sleeve: "The Church lives! There is still the Church!" Montoya grasped his hand: "Yes, this is good, young man. The Church lives."

He faced a dark present, a dark future loomed.

Montoya grew frailer, he was excused work. For a time he lived quite speechless, he was deaf now.

Then he died. He had become a nightmare to those around him.

Splendour of the Christian republic

NOAH'S ARK! HOW did it float? How did the waters swell? How high was the Ark borne?

It came to a decisive moment between the Jesuits of the Ark and the barbarians. The Ark was no longer an Ark, the barbarians no longer barbarians. Driven out of Sao Paolo, the Fathers with Emanuel at their head had plunged into the forest, a flock of spirits. Into Sukuruja's southern forests they plunged, these fluttering spirits cloaked in the black of death. They were transformed. The rapture of a new existence surged even in them. They had not caulked their Ark against this. The new Fathers opened their eyes and saw what they had. They ruled. And ruling suited them well.

The reductions thrived wonderfully. With the surplus the Fathers bought gold, copper, bronze, silver, paid the King's tribute. Yerba-maté remained their most precious medium of exchange, the north brought honey, wax, maize, cotton, the south gave wool, hemp, wheat, forests, fish, meadows for the cattle, and horses everywhere. The Fathers in the reductions shut themselves up in their college houses. They appeared only on big occasions. They ruled with the help of a lay magistracy, corregidor, alcalde, assessors, all of them dark men. They appeared in church surrounded by a gorgeously attired boy choir. They never visited houses or huts, the sick were brought to a building in the college. When the Fathers showed themselves, they did so in a great procession, with pomp and majesty.

The founders of the reductions had from the first stressed the value of lovely churches. Now they became extravagant. Architects and painters were fetched from Europe, churches began to glitter with objects of gold. These absorbed the greater part of the wealth that flowed to the reductions from diligent systematic work. You must, they explained, attract, enthuse, dazzle the Indians, these children. All through the reductions there was music from morn till night, drums and pipes were never silent.

Women were not allowed to dance, but the Fathers organized tournaments for the men. They set off fireworks from Europe, nothing amazed the dark people more than this.

And as grass grows up between the marble slabs of a palace and leads its old life, and as the wind wafts and surges, now through the trees of a primal forest, now down magnificent manmade streets, so Indians squatted on their heels in church as they always had, hands folded, gazing at pictures of saints. With grave insistence they laid their concerns before the saints. They were artless in their dealings with God. Those who were long baptized and converted were peaceable and meek. Others were cruder and spoke in threatening tones. For all of them it was a trade. They brought gifts, and the gifts had to match the value of the requested boon, the calculation was meticulous. There were set amounts for one's own healing, the healing of this or that family member, for a domestic animal, an ox, a horse. Mostly they brought a jug or half a jug or a basket with fruit. For serious cases they indulged in a hare, or even a pig. They would explain to the saint or the Virgin Mary in long exhaustive commentaries with frequent emphases exactly what the offering was for. They paid the relevant price. Then they expected equivalent value in return. They were not to be played with, and the reputation of any saint who failed to deliver was ruined, they talked about it among themselves and no one brought that saint anything ever again. It caused considerable attrition among the saints, and the Fathers had to struggle to find new ones. But there were still some saints who retained adherents despite the occasional failure, they had their fixed clientele who praised and flattered them in order not to lose their favour, and to spur them on.

The clerics were their good Fathers. They still remembered the fanaticism of the earliest, Emanuel, Montoya, they were spoken of as saints, tales of their miracles ran wild. But they themselves were of another kind. They tended their flock, ruled with pride. The natives remained children, the spiritual torment of the White people remained alien to them. The Jesuits failed to make them wicked. Hatred of oneself, sin, failed to penetrate. The same old air, the trees, the animals, the same people were with them.

They clung to Sukuruja's neck, Sukuruja did not let them go.

≈≈≈

Friends – religious and lay – came to the Paraná. The fame of the Christian Republic had spread far and wide, people spoke nervously, enthusiastically of the communism established by the Jesuits in the New Indies; this was mixed with inflammatory talk, the Spanish Crown grew uneasy. Then, just as in the time of Bishop Felix, a Jesuit Father stepped out of his house, strolled with a guest – lay or religious – through the neat town with its dead-straight streets, palm trees, you looked at the lovely church, storehouses filled with the products of toil. You encountered friendly industrious people, heard laughter and singing, everyone wore the same cotton clothing, women a long skirt, belt, little jacket, the men a shirt and hose, all faces looked alike, even men and women looked alike, but the men had their hair cut short, officials and overseers wore clothes of a different colour. Then you mounted a horse, were joined by a dashing troop of cavalry which saluted you and led you out into a landscape of Paradise.

The lay visitor's eyes popped at the good order, the prosperity evident everywhere, the complacency. The priest replied: "We are vulnerable to certain accusations. People often say we exploit the Indians, hoard the wealth, that we want an independent republic, aim to cast off the Spanish Crown. What don't they say! We're happy that we are what we are and the Spanish Crown relieves us of politics. You see the Spanish King's portrait in all our reductions."

"And the exploitation?"

The priest laughed: "That's where our opponents betray themselves. Look around you, do you see any overseers with whips? Show me a scowling or reluctant man. For sure we keep them at their work, they are simple children of nature, and we take care they should not become spoiled, they are inclined to laziness, but we overcome it through our example. We shame them, single them out, they are sensitive to this. For the rest, everything with us is planning, reason, organization – nothing more. Others must make do with exploitation, because they are not reasonable. We achieve through play a prosperity that eludes others, with all their slavery and slaughter. Everything we have rests on the Christian religion. Nothing could be simpler. It's there for the whole world to use."

The lay visitor is astonished, the priest laps it up. "So the key to understanding our reductions is Christianity. You, sir, come from Europe. You know the quarrels, religious, political. Our good old Christianity has been torn apart like a rotten cloth, and everyone wants to steal a scrap of it. What a mess of incendiary ideas. And all aimed at achieving happiness. But why? We shan't throw away a thing that has proved its value. Don't be deceived. We would be the last to indulge in modern folderol, in communism. That accusation rings hollow. We have taken up lodgings in the sturdy house built for us by the old Church."

In the time of the great Superior la Roca, there appeared in Yapeyú another royal Visitor, on a tour of the province. The splendid Luis de la Roca asked him with a certain hauteur about the condition of the free Indian settlements out there, how many labour battalions, completely free Yanaconas, and occasional Mitayos were still found in the region. The significance of the display of drilling troops that the Superior arranged for the Visitor was quite explicit. The people out there, with their savage envy of the thriving reductions, should see that we have teeth. This important official, accompanied by the Master of Horse and the

Sergeant-major, was taken to the armoury. Hundreds of horses were kept always in reserve, there were huge numbers of lances, clubs, iron spikes, good bows, stones for sling and hand-throw, firearms and the paraphernalia of powder. The Visitor became anxious at times, recalling wicked rumours. They even took him to a military display by children!

Majestic la Roca said: "You may see from this what experience we have gained since the time of the Mamelus, and how we preserve it. Perhaps we have made our lovely region," la Roca's voice was scornful, he balled his fist, "a little too conspicuous to those out there. For a long time we were utterly naïve and trusting. It was not at all our fault if people failed to meet us with love. We were in love with a whole continent. But they didn't want us. We weren't even granted enough space to live. Now we no longer trust anyone! We stay put! We are quite open. These days our dear neighbours have no need of friendly approaches to us. We have grown up. We have hair on our teeth. Anyone who wants to try it on with us may do so. I assure you, and you have convinced yourself: the time when Mamelus and Tupis could march in here and sit at our well-stocked table are over." He laughed, and told of doughty warrior Fathers, of Mateo, Sanchez, Alfare. The Visitor listened to it all in dismay.

They showed the Visitor the famous cattle ranches each with its chapels, fruit trees, orange groves. Such prosperity! Such strength! He saw the lovely oratories in their elevated positions. He was truly amazed as he passed through the reductions and farms of Tambuineta, San Agustin, along the Ibera lagoon to San Borgita, San Gonzalo. In the forest they explained proudly how yerba-maté was cultivated and the harvested leaves treated, none in the country could emulate their process. The final event was an open-air wrestling contest in the hour after Vespers. La Roca beamed as the Visitor congratulated him during a call at his low dark house. He enjoyed with casual condescension the recognition bestowed on him by the royal official. They ate and drank, la Roca was a hearty eater, Indian servants ran in and out, the royal Visitor sat small beside him and found that the Superior had a Roman air. The Visitor asked about Europe, he himself was Peru-born. What was it like over there. The Superior laughed: "Different from here. But don't feel homesick for it. You can achieve something anywhere. The only foundation you need if you want to govern is an understanding of human nature and a healthy dose of common sense. You remember Bishop Felix, who went back to Rome after being in charge here once, I knew his family. Of such timber are capable men made. It's just that things did not go well for him here."

"Private matters, so they say."

"Of course. Dear God. I had to shake my head when I heard. Everyone was so nervous at that time, even among us. These were teething troubles, let's be honest. We could have used a capable, clearheaded man like Felix for longer. He and I could have worked well together! Common sense and human friendship, my dear sir, are ever the basis for one's encounters with others."

The royal Visitor, a small, provincial man, sat awed and subdued at the table of imperial la Roca. He offered small flatteries. He asked: "Does the Society of Jesus still forbid a member to become bishop or cardinal, should he be called upon? From my mother I am a great friend of the Society. We believe that a Jesuit as bishop, or even higher, would be a gain for the Church."

La Roca wiped his mouth complacently: "Of course. We could fill such a post as well as anyone. But what are fame and glory? We have poverty and obedience. We go wherever we are sent. The holy Apostles did the same. And they are our shining example!"

The Visitor, who had already eaten his fill, folded his hands and looked piously at the ceiling. The native servants cleared the table and laid out maté bowls. La Roca pushed himself upright in his chair and watched them until they left the room. He winked at his guest: "And what do you think of them? The natives? Our dear savages?"

The Visitor was startled, he himself had native blood on his grandfather's side, and feared allusions. But la Roca whispered: "How do you deal with them out there? I can tell you, I was sent here and, really, it suits me down to the ground, you see for yourself. But you, how exactly to you manage it?"

"They are docile, and fearful too."

"That is the decisive point. Fear. You've nailed it. And they have no clue, none of our children are as childish as they. The stories I could tell. But you grew up over here, so you know all about it." And he beamed: "You see, it was a stroke of genius on the part of our first Fathers to apply our Jesuit principles, merely our own principles, to these people. So there's no great thinking and questioning, no individual judgment, for in the end who is capable of that even in Europe, and with these little pigeon-brains all we need is teaching, simple friendly teaching, and they obey."

"And oh, how obedient they are!" acknowledged the Visitor.

"They are indeed, the best of all people," emphasized la Roca, "but please, take some of their tea, it is made by Indian hands according to our principles. They follow one as closely as a breath. God gave them this gift, having withheld other gifts from them."

"They are as trainable as dogs," said the Visitor, glad that la Roca had not found him out.

"Trained poodles, just what I always say," said la Roca. "It's good for them that we treat them so and do not demand more of them. That was the mistake, now and again, in the old days. Now they behave themselves. They go to church, work, dear God, what a blessing that is for people who once lived in caves and ate each other." With an arch smile he leaned towards his guest, the charmed recipient of such benevolence: "What's more, here they can guzzle all they want, even if we don't serve human meat. They'd like nothing more than to stuff themselves from morn till night, just like a cow. And why not! It gives them pleasure."

"And fireworks!"

"True," they laughed, "and shooting and riding. Wonderful riders."

≈≈≈

The Visitor was given a ceremonial send-off when he departed with his little escort of Whites and natives. An old Indian from

Tucuman was his manservant, the Visitor was deeply attached to the man, who had served in his father's house. As they rode across the plain, in that paradisiacal landscape of cattle ranches and reductions, past fields of maize and manioc – such relentless order imposed on Nature – the official felt impelled to reveal to his native friend in veiled form something of his conversations with la Roca. The Indian had been subdued ever since they left the reductions.

"Would you like to live there?" asked the Visitor.

"If you come here, master, I shall live here with you."

"And for yourself?"

"Master, when I see dark people gathered together, in the past I always wept. That comes from the stories we used to hear from our parents. And I have seen many things myself. Then I came to your parents and grew accustomed to it. In Yapeyú I wept again!"

"Why, Lucas?"

"Forgive me, I am old."

"But why did you weep, Lucas?"

"Lucas always weeps when he recalls earlier days. I was glad to see them living together. The reverend Superior la Roca graciously deigned to address me, so I kissed his feet because he protects dark people so they can live together in peace. It is not the same as living in their old places, because they no longer have their chiefs. But the Fathers are good Fathers, master."

Later, the Visitor upset Lucas by repeating what he had heard in Yapeyú: the dark people are descended from savages who may have had human form but were only ever occupied in stilling their boundless hunger. The old man shook his head: "Boundless hunger? I don't think so. They were like all of us. We eat less than the Whites. Have you ever seen a fat man or a fat woman among us? We are more puny than the Whites."

"What they meant, Lucas, is that they had something of the animals about them."

The old man nodded: "That is well said. They were birds or lizards or jaguars."

"You keep telling the old fables, Lucas. You really should not."

"Forgive me, master."

"You found it good, with the Fathers, Lucas?"

"Better than my people in the towns. Our people are always happy when they can live together and fish together and hunt together. We'd be even happier if we were quite free."

"Then they would not have the dear Fathers and the villages and a church of their own."

"But the forest, master, the plains." Always the same song. They were still in the region of the reductions when they encountered Father Joseph de Arce, a lively greybearded missionary who came riding along with a large troop of natives. He had taught among the Chiquitos and boasted of his successes:

"There was a tribe whose chief declared: your Christian god is supposed to know everything. You say nothing is hidden from him, that he is on all the paths. But we don't want a god with such sharp eyes. – Wonderful, no? –We want to live in our forests without a judge there over our heads all the time, watching!" The missionary, a giant, stretched out his arms: "He wanted to seek out his own god! Our choice was not to his taste."

And the told how a tribe of Chiquitos had let themselves be converted. The cacique called his people together for discussion, they came to the place at night, danced to flutes and drank, and in the morning the cacique laid the matter before them. They debated a few hours, and then started drinking again. By now it was noon, and they all went to bathe. Afterwards they decked themselves in pretty feathers and painted their bodies. Then they had a sumptuous meal. Then there was a unanimous decision to adopt Christianity. The missionary's laughter boomed out: "These are good people. We had to give them lots of presents to ensure this result. We had to promise to protect them, make sure they never came into a labour battalion, and so on. But even then they would accept Christianity only on two conditions: first, that those who wouldn't convert should not be driven from the area, and then that their children, even if they are Christian, shouldn't be used for altar service." He raised his arms heavenwards.

"Tricky," the Visitor agreed. "We could have proceeded quite differently with these people. We pull them a little by the ears as it is. But in the end we're Christians and must wear kid gloves." And with this the huge missionary, who looked like a knight in disguise or a prince off to the wars, extended a hand to the Visitor from his mount. A drumbeat, a bugle call, and the baggage train with its goods and people and animals set off once more across the verdant plain.

A few years later de Arce was murdered by Papaguas.

Trees and bushes

THE WORLD IS soft, and though it has thrust up cliffs, rocks and entire mountain ranges, it tends towards decay. It loves decay – but not in order to wither. Nothing is ever enough for it, the last word is never spoken.

All the deeds of Fathers and kings were cast into doubt.

When those ancient statues emerged from the soil and the Earth began to sing its song, it did not stop with the voices of Copernicus, Galileo, Bruno, the joyful visionaries and enthusiasts, or with the deeds of courageous men going out across the world.

Across the water, between harbours in Spain, Portugal, Italy, Holland and those in the New World, more and more ships passed from one coastal port to another, different ships from those earlier ones that transported ravening generals and soldiers and zealous priests. And new forces advanced across the South American continent. They were called coffee, sugarcane, cotton, tobacco, cocoa, maize, timber. New people established themselves on the continent, Whites, natives, mixed.

Sugarcane was a species of grass. It grew in the distant Indies, its stalks swayed above scrub, it was flexible and bent over, its hollow interior contained a fleshy pulp which sucked up juices from the soil to nourish it and enable it to grow. The sweet juice of this grass had long been known to mankind, they squeezed it out and condensed it – for humans were not set loose on the Earth as an alien species that must struggle for existence, the Earth was made with them in mind. Sugar grows in tall grasses, they can discover these grasses and sustain themselves. The cane was taken from the islands of Asia to Syria, the Crusaders wanted many things, they found other things, brought sugarcane to Spain. Now it advanced to the hot Americas, and bloomed around Sao Paolo and Rio de Janeiro.

And now, from Sao Paolo and Rio de Janeiro up to Pernambuco to where the plant had crept, people could multiply, they found sustenance, plantation after plantation was developed. To win the sugar, factories were built, they needed people, these were hard to find, landowners learned to improve their tools. And when they found so much sugar that they could not consume it all themselves, they took it to seaports, loaded ships with it for the coast and for Portugal. It was another cargo the ships carried back than that vainglorious gold which fuelled the wars of bygone kings. More and more ships crowded seaports here, there and everywhere, harbours grew, and towns around them.

Over hills and hot plains marched coffee bushes; from their Ethiopian homeland they had spread across Arabia. They were brought to Guyana by Dutch sailors, turned up in the Amazon valley and moved on into Brazil. The New Indies had many poisons, their plants produced many kinds of intoxicant, the arc between death and life is narrower in the land of Sukuruja, the tiniest nudge can lead from one to the other. But the fruit of the coffee bush contained two beans in one pod, their liquor gripped the heart, made it throb, limbs became light. People in every country craved the liquor prepared for them by the hot southern soil. It packed two beans in a pod, people drank the liquor.

The cocoa tree grows wild on the Amazon, in the flood plain, along banks, on the hot damp seacoast. It soars six meters above ground, it feels good up there, its dainty trunk is covered in a brownish tender bark, it dangles its fruit like melons from the lower branches, embedded in the pulp are little almonds with a brown kernel, the seed with which, when the time comes, it will propagate itself. But like all things in the world the cocoa tree is not alone, and just as it seeks to leach the soil to serve its own needs, so do others seek something else from it. This is the law of life. So the cocoa tree embeds its seeds in a pulp, many creatures are nourished by the pulp, people learned to grind the seeds and drink them.

And with sugarcane, coffee, cocoa trees come cotton, tobacco, the fine hard timber of trees.

The Amazon, that flowing sea, those old, young, measureless rolling waters! How it pours down from the rocky wall of the Andes, quitting the icy horror of peaks and plateaus down into its plain and eastward. Earth-shatterer, Earth-builder, it carries sediments in such quantity that they are borne along all the way to the ocean, there it lays down sandbanks, plugs the coastal waters between Caviana and Cabo Norte so full that they silt up entirely, and to the south, where it debouches, banks form along the coast, islands grow, the sea assaults them, the sea into whose jaws the river tirelessly pours its white water, sand, mud, floating grass, ubussi palms complete with fruit. And the sea shakes its fist, sends its tidal bore, the pororoca, up the valley, the sea builds itself into a wall, thunders onward, fills the rivermouths and rolls on upriver. But finally it must collapse and become stranded on the banks. All around the primal force of this river flowing over Earth's ancient rocks, a forest has planted itself. The river does not leave untouched the land it has borne along. It penetrates it with a thousand rivers, rivulets, creeks, channels, lakes, soaks into the ground like placental veins in the body of a pregnant woman, there where the fruit grows. The river rolls for a while steady and assured in its deep bed, sends out mists as reminders to everything above that thinks itself secure. And then when the time of its swelling arrives, it invades the land that it has carried along. Fire has receded from the Earth, now the distant Sun must warm it. But the giant river, Amazonas, is not terrible and shrivelling like the hot Sun, through its mouth the Sun speaks to ancient Earth, it is the Sun's proconsul. From the Sun it receives the snowmelt of the mountains, and enters intoxicated into its land and proclaims the power of the Sun, its king. This is the time of floods. The river worries away at its banks. It turns the land into a floating garden, scoops languid lakes into itself again, even forces back the rivers that contribute water to it, and colours their dark currents milky.

It is no simple forest that springs out of the ground after the Son of the Sun has touched it. A swamp forest accompanies him, delineates him with the buttresses of giant trees, and primal forest smothers the land, no lovely flowers can be seen, and here are forests that sink slowly back into boggy ground and die. Rubber trees live in this damp primal land. They come into leaf, grow slim and smooth, and there are long tubes in their bodies, wide hoses with bitter milk that helps the slender tree-being to heal its wounds. White sap leaks where a leaf breaks, people noticed, in glades on the Amazon, on the Madeira, Purus, Acre, Uako, Javary, Jurua. Some natives, Guaripa, call the tree *syringa*, the Mainna *caucho*; from its juice, which they dry and blacken with smoke, they make bowls, jugs. And other people who now come to settle here learn how to put rubber to use.

And as plantations spread, farms grow, new villages and towns and roads develop, a new kind of humanity arrives on the scene. Into Sukuruja's continent, driven from the bellies of giant ships, stumbling, woeful, starving, oh terrible their suffering, there step a thousand, ten thousand, a hundred thousand black people! They are linked by chains and ropes. They have crinkly hair, their blood-red lips protrude. Around them prowl the same bloodhounds that brought down frightened people in Peru and Cundinamarca. Whites found them along the Congo and the Niger, in Angola and Liberia. They set about them in the same way they had set about the tribes and peoples who dwelled along the Amazon, Orinoco, Magdalena. They found not much gold over there. So they carried away black slaves to toil here in the fields, tend plants that had spread all across the New Indies.

And these Negroes were stronger and more resilient than the Indians, they thrived in this continent as hot as their own, multiplied, and began to mix with the original inhabitants.

I the King and San Sacramento

IT HAD BEEN a single face: I the King, whose knee hurt from long sitting at his writing desk, and who nudged with his right elbow the box containing surveillance reports on his family and news of the Jesuits in distant Paraguay – his Catalonia emptied of people, his Aragon hardly built up, his Castile almost a desert, a thousand cloisters of monks and nuns, a hundred thousand monks and supplicants who through bequests and donations owned half the kingdom; hidalgos looking for fame and knighthood and making pilgrimages across the land, weighed down by guilt, mercenaries, knaves, gamblers, criminals who were willingly recruited to an expedition to fall upon the new colonies for pillage and slaughter. These together with I the King composed a single huge face, as ravaged as that of a chronic drunk, stupidity and despair lodged in its folds. Recently a new trait had engraved itself into this face: the Fathers of the Society of Jesus, of the Indian country on the Paraná where they struggled for heavenly bliss on Earth.

That face had crumbled to dust.

Thrones, palaces, wells, and many houses from the old times still stood, but many new ones had sprung up, and the people were different. Many bewailed the earthquake that left Lisbon, the capital of Portugal, in ruins and at a stroke killed an uncountable number of strong White people. Working away more slowly, powerfully was that secret force, felt by all, which had led Bishop Felix to enthuse over his statues, had led Galileo to his thoughts, had put fear into the old Church, caused the old power holders to tremble.

If you looked at the Iberian peninsula now, down south along the coast you saw big flourishing seaports, these ports and towns home to merchants engaged in overseas trade, heirs to the energy of explorers and adventurers. One day the king of this country received long, nay interminable, petitions from shipowners and merchants in Cadiz, Seville, Malaga, complaining that to the detriment of the Spanish Crown and domestic trade, an outrageous contraband is being conducted between South American ports. Opposite the town of Buenos Aires, across the River Plate, lies the colony of Sacramento. This is the disturber of the peace.

We know this river. La Plata is the name of the enormous estuary formed by the confluence of Paraná and Uruguay, those mighty rivers along whose broad fertile banks the Jesuits had settled with their pious Indian republic. The inhabitants of Sacramento, over whom King Nicolaus Riubuni once ruled, were, if truth be told, anything but pious and peaceful. They were the same robust stock as the people of Sao Paolo, and did whatever brought a quick return. They were happy that Buenos Aires, a Spanish town, sat there across the water, the Sacramenters, Portuguese, did well for themselves in its shadow.

For the trade of Buenos Aires had its dark side. The residents were allowed to dispatch their goods to Europe only twice a year, and they themselves were not permitted to import anything directly from Europe. Whatever they needed must be ordered from Peru or via Peru. There was good reason for this: Peru was still a prosperous country, rich in gold and other minerals, and the ravenous Spanish Crown had to offer something in return for these riches, the mine owners of Peru expected payment. But the people of Buenos Aires and its enormous hinterland suffered under this policy, they produced only foodstuffs, these were the new forces, new powers that spread across the continent and nourished a hundred thousand people, new generations. The continent produced a surplus of whatever it grew, but it was stuck.

As the people of Buenos Aires despaired —mountains of goods piled up, not much was sent to Peru, Peru really had no need of it, Peru tried to hold it down, and how much spoiled on the journey from Buenos Aires to Spain via Peru — as South America waged a paper war on Madrid, our good Sacramenters, in remembrance of that glorious though not faultless King Nicolaus Riubuni, stealthily built a port in the shadow of Buenos Aires. They bought up all the ships that plied the east coast and loaded them with goods that desired direct passage to Spain or Portugal or Italy. For the sea is free, ships can be bought, and Portuguese subjects need obey only Portuguese law.

And so wicked contradictions appeared in the order of the world. The Sacramenters travelled hither and yon, the sea raised no protest, the coffee, sugar, tobacco raised no protest. That left — Buenos Aires.

As Sacramento praised the Spanish Crown for bestowing such good laws to the benefit of the Portuguese nation, the inhabitants of Buenos Aires filled the air with desperate cries. But support came there none. What they failed to achieve for so long with all the letter writing and complaining fell into their laps one day through the hubris of hateful Sacramento. By and by that town became too successful. And once their trade with Europe reached a scale that could not be ignored, it became a thorn in the flesh of the shipowners and merchants of Cadiz, Seville and Malaga. They'd lost the entrepot trade. So, the gentlemen said, there's injustice here. And they thought about it, and suddenly discovered how dear Buenos Aires was to their hearts. They read petitions and complaints from there and suddenly found them justified. They felt enormous vexation and sympathy. A dark suspicion began to be expressed secretly among them, which led to a conclusion: some Spanish merchants, even people from Buenos Aires itself, are taking part in the contraband, these (incredibly) even own Portuguese ships, the profits from which (incomprehensibly) they share with Sacramento! Hence an evasion of the law, and literally high treason. All from the basest of profit motives. They choked on these secret suspicions, and united around the war cry: punitive expedition against Sacramento.

And reports from over there showed: something must be done, ands fast. For ever more ships called at the parasitical harbour to carry cargo back to Portugal and Italy avoiding Spanish ports. The people of Buenos Aires watched in horror as their destruction was wrought in broad daylight. Normally, of course, such an outcome would not stir a hair. Let them go down, man and mouse, nothing in the world will weep for them, why should it. They'd reaped and reaped, and the wind sows, you must reckon on a storm. But that Spaniards should hand the South America trade to Portugal, it was a new perspective, you could be sure of that.

Suddenly there was alarm in Madrid among the ministers surrounding I the King, who was still in place and ruling. The brutish merchants and shipowners of Cadiz, Seville and Malaga came along in person. They stormed and laid siege to the halls of government. They were not at all genteel. The nobles of Madrid observed with distaste what a common breed was springing up now, down on the coast. It was colonization in reverse, Spanish riffraff puffed up into moneybags, failed hidalgos forced to work for a living, wheeler-dealers, exporters, all daring to make inroads on the home country that had spat them out. Of this oafish but strangely forceful windblown race, some, but only a few, appeared in the capital wearing a nobleman's sword. Most strutted oafishly around in port, office and warehouse, acted as if all merit rested on them alone. They came to town to present themselves to ministers and the Council of the Indies without even a coach of their own. How did these semi-criminals, this galley-fodder tread the halls of palaces built by the King for his ministers and guarded with drawn sword, swaying plumes, boots and spurs by soldiers pacing up and down outside, the flag of the Crown fluttering overhead? The creature barged in like a vegetable hawker, huffing like a water-carrier, never a glance at the sentry saluting the visitor, rushed up the steps and almost before it was in the antechamber pulled out a fat pocket watch and demanded to see the minister and, if he was not in, shouted: "What!", gazed around without a word and rushed back down the steps, so that someone had to be sent after it, the minister, apologies, already on his way, he'll be back in a little quarter of an hour, your King, of course, I the King, His Majesty, has been informed. And when the minister arrived, a stranger would be hard put to say which here was minister and which tradesman, merchant, supplicant.

Generals, courtiers, officials, all grew small in the presence of the intruders, the most senior ministers urged sensitivity, all now revolved around money, and if they didn't make any then who would. And the indolent dukes, counts and marquises understood this. It horrified them. And they changed their faces; their medals, sashes, coaches and forefathers suddenly had nothing sensible to say, the great names no longer resounded, people came along who counted for something but had never heard of the noble names from great battles and the defence of the faith. These people came with coffee, sugar and tea. How to respond.

When the disreputable rabble failed to dissipate, kept shouting and threatening, their proposals came under consideration. They demanded war against Portugal, it was long overdue. But ministers were not so sure. They were not of a belligerent mind. The traders ranted, causing all the kings and dukes, cardinals and heroes of religion along the walls to turn pale: Well then, they'll fit out ships themselves and take control of the Portuguese harbours. Their most noble excellencies turn to one another, speechless. These gallows-birds are capable of taking war into their own hands, and exposing the King to the censure of the whole world. They found themselves one day in the appalling situation of having to discipline the son of a ministerial official, a young marquis who had served as secretary at one of these discussions, because, scandalised by the behaviour of these people, he confronted some in the street with his sword, challenged them to a duel, they screamed for the police, whereupon the marquis and some of his friends gave them a thrashing in front of some ministry. One of the victims recognized the young marquis, and the barbarian had to receive satisfaction, even though everyone took the side of the assailants.

To be rid of the traders, those millstones, the aggrieved power brokers both temporal and spiritual first turned to Christianity for help. They dispatched two respected priests to Lisbon to ascertain its interest in the South American dispute. These pious fellows, upon arrival in Lisbon, moved every heart. The Portuguese yielded to no Spaniard in terms of piety. They initiated joint prayer services in churches, which were all half destroyed from the earthquake, and lit huge candles so that those scoundrels in Sacramento would give up their smuggling. They prayed in Latin, Spanish and Portuguese for the South American trade to be rectified.

When they had done all this they raised the matter formally. It turned out that God had not softened Portuguese hearts. They listened at length and with concern to the presentations of the pious Spanish delegation, joined them in deploring the sad state of the world, desired to gather more information, bade the pious gentlemen for Heaven's sake not to think ill of them and the Portuguese Crown, and raced back for more joint prayers.

When the clerical delegation returned to Madrid with this result, the dignitaries of Spain trembled. You knew of no device more powerful than Christian morality. You sat old and hard of hearing at the table with your sashes and tall wigs, and fidgeted with your medals. You hit upon bribes as a solution. A new delegation was dispatched and, to the great relief of the Spanish court, important functionaries in Lisbon accepted the money. And that was all.

So Spanish anxieties grew. Lisbon really had left Madrid in the lurch. And now you began to understand those barbarous traders in the antechambers. You summoned them, they proposed war, and said: the only language Portugal understands is the dagger. This seemed the bitter truth. But you are so weak, so old, so poor. Oh, Spain, Spain! Spain of earlier days! You bring generals, proven strategists and knowledgeable financial consultants into the council chamber. Inspectors of the royal arsenals in Ferrol, Cartagena and Cadiz step in, they look splendid, their reports on the state of the arsenals throw everything into despair.

So you turn to the King.

Ferdinand the Somnolent

AS THE TURNING point became outlined more clearly, and instead of conquerors, murderers, robbers, rapists attended by mumbling priests, it was now trees and useful plants that spread across the southern continent, as Copernicus, Galileo and Giordano Bruno arose among European humanity and uttered their words – at this same time the custodians of the old European world began to shrivel. The violence they had wrought now began to cause all kinds of unpleasantness.

An array of remarkable figures occupied the throne of I the King, one after the other. One became mad. One proved incapable of behaving sensibly, a tyrannical wife had to conduct the government for him, they lay upon the land for twenty years and squeezed huge sums from the half-dead empire so the idiot and his wife Luisa could be happy and have their Versailles.

This was the palace of Granja de San Ildefonse. At the time of which we speak it housed a son, a dull unhappy lad, he was sorely tormented, suffered attacks of moroseness and spasms. For his wife they had given him a Braganza, a small person of devastating ugliness, with small eyes, bulging lips, sagging jowls, but she carried herself charmingly. For company, the couple had brought to the late idiot's resplendent palace two men from whom they were inseparable, neither was a real man, one was a cleric, Rabago, a Jesuit, her confessor, the other Farinelli, a castrato from Naples, whose singing provided diversion.

Rumours penetrated to Granja de San Ildefonse of difficulties in the New Indies and the fact that ministers were at a complete loss. And Barbara of Braganza, the Queen, smelled with her little nose that this concerned money, something she never joked about. Recently the whole country had come to revolve around money, the situation was already desperate. She had her confessor tell her all about it, and when she heard about the merchants from the ports whose representatives could be found in Madrid, she expressed a wish to hear them. The whole world was shocked. But Barbara insisted, and now everyone was happy that at last somebody insisted on something, this was a ray of hope.

So raders were dispatched to San Ildefonse, an undertaking accepted with some irritation on account of all the ceremonial they had to submit to, but in the end, because of the sums in question, they let themselves be persuaded. They weren't dazzled by all the palace glitter, they expressed themselves in insulting terms back in Madrid regarding the shameless and quite unjustifiable pomp and excess indulged in there. The arrogant demeanour of the two elder emissaries shocked the Queen's entourage, several breaches of ceremonial etiquette were noted and discussed.

The Queen was most indignant. She complained to her first minister, who had accompanied the coffee-sacks, a certain Marquis de Ensenada (alas, she was unaware that this gentleman, who shared her opinion of the barbarous ship owners, was himself a dubious upstart in the ranks of the gentry, albeit from many generations back). This magnificent bewigged giant of a gentleman with a protruding belly managed by whispers, laughter, complaints and pleas to calm the royal bird-scarer down. They agreed: we are dealing with a mob of colonials, a concept alien both to those of royal degree and to feminine charms. Since Madame Braganza had no response to this, she began to cry. And she sent away the purported gentleman, and wept before the King.

His Majesty, when she sat beside him, happened to be afflicted with one of his frequent spells of melancholy, which at that time one could suffer without being ill, even at the head of a kingdom. Their protégé Farinelli was sent in to them. His warbling and trilling alerted the whole palace to the royal couple's dejection.

On the third day the King asked his Queen why she'd been crying. She told him. So he had maps of Spain and the New Indies brought in and spread before them on a table. They looked together at the maps, and saw that if money from the Indies stayed away they must starve, perhaps even leave the palace of Ildefonse and move to a smaller place, less well furnished.

So she began to cry again. And this time the major-domo became uneasy and alerted Rabago, the black-robed man, confessor to their Highnesses now sunk in apathetic stupor. First he asked Farinelli what he had been singing. Then he went to the Mistress of the Robes and asked what she knew of la Braganza. Then he went to Braganza and asked after the King. Then he requested an audience with the royal couple.

He found them sitting alone and forlorn in a corner of the huge state room, like two sick parrots in a giant cage. All along the walls were mirrors, and when you entered you saw a dozen sick parrots side by side, a whole gallery of parrots with red noses and drooping heads.

The black man asked them both how they felt. They replied, hesitant and shamefaced, that they would die of hunger, would have to leave the palace of Ildefonse which the King's father had built with contributions from the whole of Spain, and move to a smaller place not so nicely furnished. – How so? – The New Indies, the New Indies are lost. – How so?

Then Barbara de Braganza wept, screwing her face into

such fearsome grimaces that even the seasoned Father Confessor couldn't stop himself from clapping his hands over his eyes.

"They sent merchants here from Cadiz and Malaga, they told us how the Portuguese are taking over our territories." King Ferdinand nodded in despair and stretched out his skinny arms, lovingly they regarded his dirty hands and long black nails, it was royal blood, he had it from his father.

"And then," she couldn't go on for grief, "these men only bowed twice, once when they came in and once when they left."

"Disgraceful," said Rabago.

Barbara emitted a long wail, and fluids streamed from nose, mouth and eyes. Such wailing, not otherwise bothersome, was well known to the priest. When the King sat like that and the Queen wailed like that, you'd best leave them to it for the whole day. All you had to do was pull their chairs into a corner, draw the curtains, bring food and drink, and then put them to bed – nothing would happen, you should just leave them undisturbed. Rabago went to the windows, closed all the curtains, checked to see that chairs were suitably placed, that candles were well lit. Then he withdrew from the chamber of sorrows, executing the prescribed number of bows.

Two days later, when the King and Queen raised timid voices and called for their Farinelli, you knew they were ready to rejoin the world. And behind Farinelli appeared Rabago the Jesuit. The Queen at once asked what had been happening meanwhile in the New Indies. Rabago reassured her, the lands are still there, enjoying the protection of the Spanish Crown. – And Sacramento. – Also still there. And in addition, we have our navy. – Our navy is too small, wailed the Queen. The King, who was not quite there yet, jerked upright and spread out his arms in despair. – Then we must work on the Portuguese court, apply spiritual pressure, use bribery, said Rabago. – That's all been tried, cried Barbara behind her handkerchief. Rabago knew this. The King collapsed again, wearily laid his head back down, a certain quantity of grief played on his face as he relapsed into a doze. – Then we must try something completely different, declared Rabago

"Well, what then? What?" This was the expected riposte. He pointed a finger at the map of the New Indies, still spread out on the table before their sorrowing majesties – as if it were the portrait of a relative overseas who had failed, and you keep him in your thoughts: "We drive the Sacramenters inland, away from their harbour. In exchange for that pernicious little town, we offer the Portuguese a strip of land in the interior, as big as they like." And with a generous flourish his hand described a great arc across the map.

The King (the Indies are lost) was already snoring. Barbara, taken aback by the proposal, wavered between two feelings: should she start sobbing again, or stand up? Considering it possible that King Ferdinand the Sixth would wake up if she stopped sobbing, the left hand in her lap made little signals to the priest to stay, while above it she sobbed on for half an hour.

Then she stood up carefully, tear-streaked, left her damp handkerchief lying , her face was red and swollen, the priest cast a furtive hasty glance and was pleasantly surprised to see that it wasn't as bad as it had been recently, the crying had evened out the swellings so that individual bulges had disappeared.

"Where is Sacramento?" Barbara asked the man in black at the big table. He pointed. "Oh, there?" she sighed, "Ferdinand and I were searching in quite another place."

"It's easy to be confused," said Rabago, "King Ferdinand's realm is very large."

She breathed: "Don't say his name, he'll wake up." And she began to sob cautiously for a while, watching the King, this time she had no need of a handkerchief, there were no tears. After several minutes tensely observing the sleeper, she turned again to Rabago: "And where is Buenos Aires?" He showed her. She was puzzled: "But they lie together."

"That's precisely the problem," declared Rabago. "What can we do, for God's sake, we can't simply tear them one from the other."

She didn't understand. So he started from the beginning, pointing to the whole enormous adjoining region, still unexplored, the hinterland, Brazil, which could be offered, in part of course, to the Sacramenters in compensation. That way you don't need money. The Queen felt herself wavering again. Should she, as was proper, sit back down on her chair, her perch of sorrows, at the King's side, and cry, or should she rejoice, for this really seemed like a way out. She looked at the priest. He understood. He whispered, wanting to harvest his victory: "His Majesty is resting. It would be best not to disturb him." She quickly escorted him to the door, turned around and said, perhaps to the sleeping King: "I'll be back in half an hour."

≈≈≈

The priest chased from the antechamber all the idlers and lickspittles gathered there, after first presenting his beaming face and his prize, Barbara de Braganza and her handkerchief. Then they walked up and down on the soft carpet for a good half hour, the priest was happy, it seemed to him he had solved the quarrel between the two countries, and South America could live in peace; the Queen was delighted, for they would give the Sacramenters some land and they would no longer steal. She advised: "But no land with gold mines."

He: "Certainly not."

She: "And if gold should be found there later, it belongs to us."

"But of course."

She: "For it would be an unjust trade, if we were to give them gold for their harbour."

"Without a doubt."

She gazed tenderly into the priest's eyes, squeezed his hand and slipped away.

In the doorway she stopped and practised a sob. And Barbara crossed the threshold sobbing and whispered to the priest, before she went to her perch: "Have handkerchiefs brought to me, the big new ones." She had ordered the making of some, extra large.

Delphic advice

AT THE PORT of Lisbon, people from San Sacramento in South America came ashore. They were prospering, and wanted to pay fewer taxes. The whole world was astonished to find that this jewel in their crown was Coloured, as bad as, as what exactly? As a mixture of Whites, Negroes, Indians, perhaps other races too with which one was not familiar. They were such a horrible, bewildering sport of nature that the people of Lisbon felt ashamed for them, the poor creatures were clearly the victims of a terrible muddle. They were neither White nor Black nor Red, had protruding lips, wore earrings like Negroes, one had smooth black hair like an Indian, another had Indian cheekbones but a really pale skin, and what is more, they none of them had the slightest idea what they looked like, and showed no embarrassment. The nobility of Madrid had experienced something similar, but in a weaker form, with their shipowners.

Just as ministers were sitting down with them for a chat, news came from Madrid that a happy solution had been found, inspired by Ferdinand the Somnolent himself. He offered a strip of Spanish territory in exchange for the harbour of Sacramento. The ministers were sitting there with those sports of nature from Sacramento. The sports of nature of course could not read. The proposal was read out to them several times, they grasped the idea, scratched their heads, behind their ears, their backs, rolled their eyes, looked at one another, then asked for something to drink and a map. Wine and spirits and a map were brought, and they were left alone.

Half a day later the ministers crowded back into the meeting room. The delegation lay drunkenly on the carpet, but had an answer ready. Although they could only laugh and babble, it was a devilishly realistic answer. These southerners were more cunning under the influence of strong liquor than a sober European. In their drink the Sacramento delegation had located the hinterland they wanted. They pointed to the map. And the Portuguese ministers shuddered to see: these fellows want a piece of the Jesuit republic! Their hearts grew heavy.

They hummed and hawed, implored the motley crew to think it over. The exotics scratched themselves again, even more immodestly, and again demanded the map and more drink. And when they came together again they were again drunk, singing so loud you could hear it through the whole Ministry, and the dignitaries were ashamed. The doorkeepers said the gentlemen had been discussing in this condition for some time already. The progress was meagre: they demanded the same as before, and some extra besides.

What to do? You hoped not to ruin things with these brutes, they already wanted relief from taxes. A most cordial letter was sent to Madrid. You wished to live in peace with your sister country. In consequence, with a view to settling the vexatious South American situation, you agreed with the proposal of His Majesty King Ferdinand the Wise. As painful as it may be for the people of Sacramento to abandon the harbour with which they feel so intimately linked, they will do so for the common good. How the ministers in Madrid sighed with relief when this reply arrived. What insight, what nobility of feeling, one felt quite humbled. And ministers, generals, directors, inspectors laughed: "If those Portuguese want it, give it them. Be quick, before they change their minds."

But that so-called gentleman the Marquis of Ensenada read the communication from Lisbon attentively in his palace in Madrid, splendid man in jewel-encrusted robes, and remarked to his assistant, one Don Jose de Caron: "They've chosen a piece of the Jesuit Republic. This is good. We can swat two flies with one blow: we neutralize that robbers' nest Sacramento, and rid ourselves of a bunch of Jesuits."

And this was something of which the Jesuit Fathers who headed out to the New Indies under Father Emanuel and received favours from the Spanish Crown had never dreamed: that one day people would deal with them this way. How, not all that long ago, had a silent King in that same Madrid expressed his pleasure at their settlements; every peaceful year over there brought him blessings and relief from cares. And now his place is taken by some jewel-encrusted marquis: "How much income do they bring us? A kicking won't hurt them."

≈≈≈

The two birds of sorrow in Ildefonse uttered terrible cries when they learned in passing from the mouth of the Marquis of Ensenada, who sympathized totally with their distress, that the only choice lay between a ruinously reduced income, and the surrender of a pious colony. Ferdinand the Sixth shuddered. But he recovered quickly from the blow. He was wise. This was because he was having a more lucid moment.

Following the minister's shattering revelation, he walked with his wife, little Barbara, in the park. Father Rabago was on his travels just then. This did not displease the King. The long-legged serious chap marched at such a pace along the avenues, leaning on his walking-cane, that his wife could hardly keep up. They breathed the sweet spring air. The husband spoke now and again, she caught fragments. "Barbara, don't worry about Father Rabago, he'll understand."

"Oh, Ferdinand, why did he have to be away just at this moment?"

"It's an act of providence, Barbara. I shall make haste to sign before he returns."

"You're right, it would be terrible if we had to leave the palace. Now those horrid men of Cadiz will be content, and keep paying. It's a pity about the Jesuits. I shall ask our marquis to apply a little pressure on you to sign at once."

"Do so, Barbara. Ensenada will explain everything to the priest. No, the marquis should sign it. I am still not entirely myself again."

"You're right, Ferdinand, it's vexing you. How clever you are! They already call you the Wise!" Ferdinand made angry grimaces: "Let them not think me stupid. If I were in good health they would not be permitted call me the Wise."

Along another avenue he said: "The priest will surely be grateful. By doing this I relieve him of a conflict of conscience."

"How tender your feelings are, Ferdinand. Anyway, they say

they have gold mines and silver mines, the Jesuits."

"We'll be able to ascertain that, too, at last."

They were both very sensible. The minister applied his pressure, Ferdinand sat on his perch and declared himself incapable of ruling. The marquis was requested to sign urgent documents himself. And when the priest returned from his inspection trip, it was all sewn up.

Good Rabago wandered in a daze. What had become of the Ildefonse palace! Farinelli no longer sang, the royal couple were all smiles as they strolled about the park together watching the peacocks. What had happened? He questioned the royal couple, they heaped signs of affection on him, well, they'd been ill. So Rabago knew it was all the fault of the wicked marquis who had sent him on a school inspection trip at exactly this time. What should he do? He couldn't cast the royal couple back into the watery depths of sorrow. And he didn't want to make his own life difficult. So Rabago put a good face on a bad situation and granted absolution to Barbara and Ferdinand the Wise.

But he was infiltrated by a slight mistrust of these two birds who wept so readily to his face.

Those on the Paraná are also human

WHILE THEY DEBATED back and forth in Spain and Portugal, and at last decided to slice a couple of strips off the hide of the Jesuit republic, they had no idea that down on the Paraná there were people like themselves.

The stern fervent architect Montoya was succeeded by administrators, splendid men. Directors reigned strictly over their hundred thousand Indians, allowed them to sing, pray, celebrate. Their land had prospered more and more. The shepherds of the enormous flock knew they were surrounded by wolves, and kept weapons and warriors at the ready.

Now strange rumours emerged in distant Peru, that rich country where the Spanish viceroy had his seat and there was jealousy of the Jesuit republic. The Jesuits, it was said, would have to give up a good number of reductions to the Portuguese, including San Borja, Luis, Lorenzo, Nicolas, Juan, Angel, Miguel, each place with five thousand people, so a total of thirty thousand, a tidy haul. It seemed that a massive plundering was about to begin.

When the treaty became known, letters of protest rained down from ministers, bishops, governors across the whole continent, not out of sympathy for the pious republic, but because Portugal had been invited onto the Paraná. Peruvians recognized the disaster sooner than the people of Buenos Aires, who were still pealing victory bells because they were now rid of Sacramento. For it was true the Sacramenters had lost a harbour, but now, instead of a single leak, the whole Spanish flank had been handed to them. And incredible but true, as soon as they migrated from Sacramento to the interior, they began smuggling again, but on what a basis, with what shameless new geographical possibilities!

Inconceivable events occurred, and within a few months it was clear that things could not continue so. While the displaced Sacramenters persisted in their old trade on the banks of the Paraná – now they did not simply smuggle goods from Buenos Aires, they intercepted them before they reached that town; it was as if a wounded man had begged someone to staunch the blood spurting from his arm, and instead of binding the arm they take him by the throat – while all the world talked of this interesting turn, how they'd pulled a fast one on Madrid, the Spanish authorities on the ground were obliged to help them at it! According to the treaty they had to assist the Portuguese to install themselves in the region assigned to them between the Sierra de Herval, Uruguay and Ibicuy. The Spanish authorities embarked on this unworthy, suicidal work seething with rage, the butt of a whole continent's scorn.

≈≈≈

But whether separately or allied, in love or in hate, both sides, Portuguese and Spanish, had to march against the Jesuits and remove the Christian republic, the flower of a defunct human yearning, from the face of the earth.

For Noah's Ark was no more. A ghost ship drifted through the real world. Whether as foes or allies, the Spaniards and Portuguese had to pave the way for lush fruitful plants, sugarcane, coffee, cocoa, and replace pale obsolete Beauty with this new heavenly-earthly primal power.

For it was not merely words and bookish wisdom that Copernicus and Galileo had uttered, it was not out of obstinacy that Giordano Bruno stepped into the fire, it was not out of wickedness and arrogance that his opponents burned him and continued to hunt down his friends. Something was trying to establish itself on the earth which challenged the very existence of the old powers. White men tried to grasp a new means to heal themselves. Once again you approached – yourself. It was a good omen that the young plants and trees you followed out here were those that yielded life's pleasures, that at the feet of ancient statues you celebrated earthly riches.

≈≈≈

The treaty signed for the Spanish Crown by Don Carvajal and for the Portuguese by Don Tomas Teles da Silva – and which in Spain was suddenly repudiated by everyone, Council of the Indies, Admiralty, Foreign Ministry, and which even the alarmed Marquis de Ensenada wished to back away from, and the traders from the ports who had been so jubilant now sat there all of a dither – the treaty in its sixteen articles made provision for everything to the benefit of that place on the east coast of Uruguay which was to be relinquished by His Catholic Majesty. It instructed the missionaries to depart with all their effects and movable possessions, to take the Indians with them and settle in some other part of Spanish territory. The Indians were permitted to take along their goods, furnishings and semi-mobile property, troops their weapons, their powder. The places were then to be handed over to the Portuguese Crown along with houses, huts, buildings, livestock sheds.

But the massive population of Indians, having dwelt and borne arms for a century on this land, had no desire to fly to Heaven like those of Emanuel's day, and nor did they want to give up their ground. Any more than Spaniards or Portuguese or Sacramenters would.

For here stood their churches and houses, here their cemeteries, they celebrated their festivals, conducted their trade, lived an orderly peaceful life. Although they were a Christian republic, when you saw their churches and black-robed priests, heard their names and songs, they had in other respects remained – this became ever more clear – Indians who wished to know nothing of Whites, and who had a thoroughly Indian conception of their Christianity.

And the black-robed black-hatted Fathers were, to be sure, learned and honourable priests, but they found the position of ruler agreeable and in the churches and ceremonial processions, at least, elaborated the same gaudy pomp as those monarchs across the sea; also, for them, trade had long ceased to be a mere sideline. These were said to be the realities. Two centuries before, even one century, something else had been called reality.

And when the Spanish-Portuguese commissions appeared in the region of Los Patos lagoon, to survey the sources of the Ibicuy and fix the new borders, a cacique from the reduction of San Miguel by the name of Jose Tiraya, called Sepe, showed up at Fort Santa Tecla. He was accompanied by a large crowd of mounted and armed Indians, Christians from San Miguel, their numbers grew as they waited and mustered. Cacique Tiraya, at the head of his armed band, rode along the forested boundary where the commissioners were at work with their little team, approached them with a courteous greeting, jumped from his horse and introduced himself as a cacique from San Miguel. The Guarani at his back were a cavalry battalion from that settlement, and he asked what the commissioners were up to here.

The officials, who had been dispatched from Buenos Aires, were astonished at this show of force, and had a bad feeling. The Spanish commissioner explained that they were engaged in a survey to ascertain the new border. Tiraya, surrounded by his people who had ridden up close and seen the short beribboned stakes that had been hammered into the soil, said: No one is allowed to plant sticks in the earth without permission, they cannot allow it, their cattle pastures lie not far off. The Spaniard, flanked by his own assistants and those of the Portuguese, who were eager to follow the conversation, requested Tiraya not to impede their work, they had to complete a certain number of miles before noon, and would the cacique please apply to the Jesuits in his reduction for any clarifications he desired. The cacique and his cavalry had decorated their hair and their lances with feathers, their appearance and demeanour annoyed the Spaniards, they were even more irritated by these martial adornments, these people were only Indians. After a short discussion between Tiraya and his people in a language the Whites did not understand – so, the natives have preserved their tribal vernacular – several jumped from their horses, without further ado pulled the stakes and ribbons out of the ground and piled them up with their strings attached at the Spaniard's feet. The commissioner's assistants stood there, not moving.

While this was going on, Tiraya calmly held the commissioner back with a hand to his chest: "God and Saint Michael gave this region to the Indians. No one can give it away."

The Portuguese, a former soldier, who was enjoying this confrontation, had no doubt the Indians would defend themselves. He intervened, planted himself in front of the twitchy Spaniard, and chided the chieftain: "Cacique, how dare you disobey the orders of your king?"

By his accent Tiraya recognized him as Portuguese, and replied: "My king is not your king. He does not need you to defend him."

At these respectful words, the Spanish commissioner stepped around the Portuguese and said reproachfully: "Tiraya, how can you oppose the orders of this king?"

Tiraya was dumbstruck for a moment, then gestured to his people to mount up and shrugged his shoulders: "I recognize the orders only of my Superior and our Directors." Whereupon he made a bow, climbed back on his horse and rode away with his people. He left a dozen riders behind to keep watch. The commissioners packed up their maps and surveying gear and moved on. Then Indian riders carefully smoothed over the ground.

The cacique and his battalion were greeted with jubilation in San Miguel. A service of thanksgiving was arranged next day in the church and on the open ground before it, in which the entire civil and military population took part. The priest called on God and Saint Michael, the guard was strengthened, the garrison remained on the alert. The two Directors were nervous, even aghast at Tiraya's proud answers, but it would not do to annoy the people.

When the commissioners returned to base, the Portuguese wanted to attack at once, but because the Spaniards had reservations they first sent a high-ranking special commissioner, the Marquis de Lirios, to whom they attached the Jesuit priest Altamirano, who had come from Rome tasked with bringing the rebellious Fathers to heel. But what happened to de Lirios and the good priest Altamirano, a man of proven ability? Altamirano went by himself to San Tome, exhorted the Fathers to obey and remain peaceful. The Fathers became meek, there was no doubting their submissiveness. Then a resolute Father Balba turned up from San Miguel, which at that time lived up to its bellicose name. Balba had not come to receive instructions from the reverend delegates of the general of the Order, but merely to check on the state of defensive measures. When he was taken to the delegates, he folded his arms in amazement, let the old man say his piece, and said in a wondering tone:

"You come from the moon, brother. If you have any sense, you will refrain from undertakings here that you don't understand. The whole world is in uproar over the chicanery of the Portuguese, and here we have a Jesuit Father, no less, prepared to defend them. We weren't born yesterday, dearest child of Jesus. And you think we wait here just so you can come and incite us to commit follies?"

The ancient priest looked left and right, he had never heard such a tone, he was lost for an answer. Then he fired off his biggest gun: "It's an order from the general."

Balba countered with a hefty swing of the arm diagonally through the air that almost overturned the old man: "We don't accept it. The general has been wrongly informed. Go home and make enquiries."

Altamirano turned to the German priest Father Thaddeus at his side, who remained suspiciously silent, staring at the ground: "Dear Thaddeus, you've read my written instructions."

"From the moon," Balba interposed calmly. "You're playing a nasty game with us over there. You no longer care about missions to the heathen, and have given us up. We aren't needed any more. And you think nothing of the natives we converted, you throw them into the jaws of the Portuguese. But two can play at this game. The Portuguese have been our enemy ever since we set foot in this country. Ever since that time they have dogged our heels, hoping to best us. So far they have failed. Now they hide behind you. Brother Altamirano, you have lost nothing here. Go home."

Since no one made a response, Balba clapped brother Thaddeus on the shoulder: "Now, what do you say, Thaddeus, what are your thoughts?" Thaddeus sighed. Balba. "Sigh away, friend. Nothing but sighs."

As it happened, even Father Thaddeus Henes did not sigh for long after Altamirano stalked angrily away. For brother Balba from San Miguel thoroughly convinced him of Rome's treachery and the looming event of which sparrows on every rooftop in Europe trilled: in Rome and around the world preparations are in train to take the Jesuits by the throat, and not even the pope will stand by them, for he and the rest are all so weak it would make a dog howl. "And so they'll set on us and throw us overboard like ballast and believe this will pacify the Portuguese. What a business. The Portuguese, peaceful! What are our weapons for? Our trained battalions? Should we shame ourselves before our own people? What? Are you not ashamed even now, brother Thaddeus?"

"We're breaking our oath."

"After others have broken their oath, to our detriment. Now no one on Earth can plead innocent, and none can pass judgment. We defer to higher authority. I accept responsibility." And he stood with arms akimbo and cried out: "I shall do this. I am no beast to be sold off."

Young Thaddeus then started to tell what he had heard of the latest Portuguese measures, military preparations, which led to a discussion of practical matters. This was what Balba had come for. He gave advice. People embraced him. Without bringing himself any more to the attention of the ancient delegate, Balba dashed away that evening.

Next day Altamirano tried to swing the mulishly silent community of San Tome to his side with a sermon. He sought to persuade them to obey the orders of the king, and prepare to move out. He preached to thin air. No one stirred a finger. On the contrary, as he went through the settlement he noticed that no one went to their work, they lounged about, magazines were open, weapons were being distributed, young warriors were mounting up.

None heeded his remonstrances. When he finally bearded one of the two Directors, he received the gloomy reply that there was no holding the people back. Incensed, he exclaimed: "Then they are right, those who say the Indians should never have been armed."

They were rescued from pointless arguing over how it could have been avoided and who was to blame for it all by the arrival of shocking news: a great armed band of Indians had set off from San Miguel, cavalry and infantry, and was on its way to San Tome to raise the alarm.

"Scandalous!" cried the old man. He could think of nothing else to say. He stayed on in San Tome, and so was not spared the feverish excitement, the jubilation and war-dances in the settlement performed by the troops as they prepared to march. And the terrible scene that caused his mouth to hang agape: as the whole army marched out from the festively decorated town to the sound of blaring music, at the fore, beside the cacique in his full feathered glory, sat his dear reverend Father Thaddeus on a heavy nag, for he was a heavy fellow, wearing a leather caplet like the other riders and merrily brandishing a sword.

"It has come to this," wailed good Altamirano at the window to his companions. He too mounted a horse once the battalions had left. He was afraid. He fled.

Battle in the plain

MATTERS HAD PROGRESSED much farther than he suspected.

He could wail like that only because he had no idea what was happening. How he would have cried bloody murder if he knew what it was irrupting here.

In the guise of the Portuguese and Spanish, there now appeared that great new power whose prophets had been hunted down and murdered by the Church, whose name it had sought in vain to obliterate. This great new power did not speak the names of Copernicus, Galileo and Bruno, it had no knowledge of its provenance, it did not say and did not know that it would take revenge for those and all their children, but it did so, and was already doing so, as it broke the will of their enemy and their enemy too lost all memory of itself, so that it appeared empty and ragged despite all the sumptuous churches, despite the wonderful order it had created, despite its gilded festivals. The hurricane roared, lifted sand and stones, yea whole beams, roofs, houses, villages up into the air.

≈≈≈

What followed cacique Tiraya's march out of San Tome was a war like any other, and Indians fought under the Fathers for their territory. On the island of Martin Garcia, commissioners decided on their plan of operations. But they were too weak to put it into effect. Indians under the command of Tiraya and two Jesuits attacked the Portuguese at Rio Pardo, the Portuguese had cannon, they were able to fend off the attack, but the settlement of Jesus Maria could not be held, the Portuguese had to withdraw.

There came two years when the Indians and their Fathers could sing songs of triumph and build up their strength. What did these Fathers look like? They looked like those popes who rode fully armed to inspect the fortifications around Rome. But those popes, not without reason, were long since dead.

Near San Juan the Guarani constructed a fortress for the Jesuits. It was equipped with powder and ammunition and heavy guns. The Indian corregidor of Concepcion, Nicolas Languiru by name, was put in command. The priests Balba and Thaddeus went recruiting. They had some success, but noticed that they frightened many of their flock. For the Guarani were a gentle friendly people, peaceable, and this was why they had placed themselves, for protection against savage Spaniards and Portuguese, under the care of the Jesuits. Only a small number of people came, like those in San Tome, from harder tribes.

Balba fired himself up in the image of old saints and martyrs. In the marketplace of San Tome he cried out after Vespers: "We are God-fearing placid people, we till our fields, gather fruit, tend our cattle. We have never caused injury to our King of Spain. Now they want to drive us from our villages. They want to take all we have. They want to make themselves richer. So they have sold us off." But he felt he had upset the people; instead of protesting they wept. You could not say such things too often, it undermined priestly authority. The two ringleaders, Balba and Thaddeus, morosely discussed the situation. Balba was at his wits' end.

But Thaddeus fought bravely at his side. He was with him at every skirmish. They couldn't bring the people to a general uprising, and didn't want to lead them to a sacrificial death. So it was up to the battalions under Corregidor Nicolas, who was dug in near San Juan. He sat there with the Indian elite, five thousand battle-ready people. An army of a thousand Portuguese and fifteen hundred Spaniards was progressing towards them, they passed near several reductions, no one stood in their way. The battle for San Juan lasted a week. When the fort had been reduced to rubble and was called on to surrender, the defenders refused. They made a decisive breakout. This was now the final battle.

The battle, fought in open country on the plain, revealed horribly what it was that clashed here. With their embroidered and brightly painted pious flags, with huge wooden crucifixes, the Indian troops, cavalry and infantry, starving as they were, poured out from the fort. They knelt before the onslaught and sang hymns, terrible to the ears of the Whites. Saints' names were their warcries. White officers, Spanish and Portuguese, had drums and trumpets sound as loudly as they could. They feared their men would falter. They feared especially that the Indians would fling themselves down and let themselves be slaughtered. But the dark cavalry galloped forth, and the infantry swarmed out. Terrible losses on both sides. They fought with passion, embittered. They did not face each other as Christians. Whites and natives murdered one another. Nicolas fell with twelve hundred Indians.

The remnants of his forces fled into the forest. They were still two thousand strong, mostly disarmed, and with no heavy weapons at all. But they made cannon from logs wrapped in animal skins. They made firearms from bamboo tubes wrapped in leather. And with these they attacked the White expeditionary force and stole weapons and food. A few Fathers took part in these skirmishes. Then they withdrew. Even Balba did not stay. They were uneasy at the Indians' rage, their mobilising of heathen tribes in the forest as allies. The old hostility to Whites flowered again. The allied hordes knew no bounds. They even attacked reductions to take food, powder and weapons. The local priests hastily evacuated the settlements. And so fearful were they that in some places they put themselves under the protection of their enemies, the allied Spanish and Portuguese. But after all that had happened, the heavy losses of the Whites at San Juan, the Jesuits could count on no mercy. Jesuit churches were set on fire behind them. Directors were hunted down. Balba and Thaddeus were captured near San Lorenzo. Thaddeus was martyred in jail. Balba escaped.

It was war. The bands left behind by Corregidor Nicolas, allied with heathen tribes, did not surrender, killed patrols in the plain, stole cattle, sometimes occupied entire settlements only to vanish once the plundering was complete. They no longer carried with them flags and images of saints. From the affected reductions, unrest infected the whole Christian republic. Travel overland was dangerous. The Superior and the priests in the main colonies that were left unaffected by the treaty and the war had only one wish: that the war would end. An ominous dread settled over the Christian republic.

Spain does some spring cleaning

PEOPLE HAD REBELLED against Portugal and Spain.

At that time the throne of I the King was occupied by a certain Carlos. He had lived a long time outside Spain and knew which way the wind was blowing. No writing desk wore out the seat of his hose, his knees were not ruined from too much prayer. He lived like a gentleman of his time, and his passion was the hunt. He had thirteen children by his wife, and a crowd of friends, of whom many were not Spaniards.

When this man became King at the age of forty-three and took a look around the kingdom he was to rule, he had a shock. Other states out there were a mess, but Spain was worse! The holy Church and the hidalgos had run it so thoroughly into the ground that not even the discovery of the Americas, the conquest of Peru, Cundinamarca, Mexico, Brazil and all the rivers of gold had been of any help.

Charles's friends had a dangerous newness about them. Together with others, worldly landowners and worldly writers, they formed a circle that called itself the Lawyers and the Golillos – from the ruffs they wore. During a hunt in the Pyrenees, Carlos conversed with them at length. Campomanes, leader of the Golillos, a young scholar, said: "At last we can breathe. We waited such a long time for Your Majesty to appear. Heaven only knows if it is not already too late. Whatever you do, Your Majesty, Spain will not like it. Spain is rotting, and will rot further. Whatever the circumstances, Spain will behave like a weaning infant, it will scream and thrash about and stamp its feet."

"That is no problem for me, I know my way about the nursery."

"Your Majesty was abroad for many years. You see how things are here. But if you only knew how it came to be like this."

The Genoan Grimaldi, Carlos's friend, gripped his sword: "There we are out in the world, everywhere trying to cook the Church's goose."

"Hush," the stocky, solid King signaled, shocked, as he stepped along. They were all in hunting green and thigh boots, only the King had plumes in his hat, their horses were being led behind them, riders were ahead and at the rear.

Pale Campomanes, a sharp fanatical face, suggested quietly: "How good to hear such words at the Court of Spain."

Carlos: "Softly, please. Always speak softly. One should only act loudly."

"We have plundered the whole world dry, we've been chased out across the whole world, until now we see it: they wanted to stop us from looking around at our own house. We were no Don Quixotes, we were fools and knaves. The first book I would place on the Index is *Don Quixote*, because it tells every fool and knave in Spain that he can make something of himself."

Carlos: "Campomanes, we will not bring in censorship."

Campomanes: "And then we had the fifth Philip, after the other four. My father knew him, attended as a doctor at his last illness. Philip was mad. He died in utter squalor, shaggy hair everywhere, he let his nails grow long like a wild beast, he never spoke, no one could persuade him to change his underwear. That was the last Philip to be bestowed on us."

Carlos: "I know. His wife did all she could to hold things together."

The young leader of the Golillas: "She wanted to secure realms for her children."

Carlos: "I see that you won't forgive her."

Campomanes: "No, not for anything."

Carlos: "How will I fare here with you, Campomanes?"

"I think that King Carlos will undertake a house-cleaning."

"Exactly so, my friend."

"For something is afoot in the world, and some people look to settle accounts. They say that those whom the gods would destroy they first make blind. After the madman we had a melancholic. I have no doubt he really was sick, even if his madness was only sporadic."

"I know. Go on."

"Everyone who ruled for this king knows it. His confessor, Rabago, still lives somewhere about. Harmlessly, I hope."

"Why?"

"As long as that creature has lived, he has caused harm."

"That goes for two. Continue."

"We have compiled a list concerning the efficacy of the Inquisition over the past thirty years, it will be presented to Your Majesty. Forty thousand have been condemned in Spain, a thousand people have gone to the stake."

The King stood still, fiddled nervously with the plumes dangling from his hat. "Is this true?"

"I shall bring you the list myself, so that it does not become stalled somewhere."

The King laughed and walked on: "Who would keep submissions from me?"

"Influences might be brought to bear."

"Show me them. I shall lay into them."

"Whoever lays into the Church and the Jesuits stabs at thin air, Majesty."

"I don't know, I don't know."

Such were their stimulating conversations. This Carlos, propelled onto mad Philip's throne, made no great use of the gaudy pleasure palaces. He feasted his eyes on the three thousand monasteries still in the country, on the almost one hundred thousand monks and nuns, the almost sixty thousand priests, the almost twenty-five thousand sacristans, a veritable army to hold up a collapsing Heaven. With his dashing Golillas he drew near to this clerical swarm, and went on the offensive. Twenty thousand disappeared from the ranks of the clergy. Onerous cash taxes were imposed on the Church, which still held a fifth of all Spanish soil. Criminals could no longer claim asylum in a church.

≈≈≈

Then he turned his attention to the Jesuits, who smelled a rat. The Jesuits showed themselves opponents of the King, the sacrifice laid itself on the altar. They saw that the new Carlos was no god, his minister Squillace a foreigner, Squillace's wife was a charming person, there was a mutual attraction between her and the King, and rumours could not be quashed that, at the same regular intervals as had his late queen, Squillace's pretty young consort, little brown Pastora, brought the King's children into the world. And then disturbances arose in several towns, partly because the King was who he was, partly because of the missing twenty thousand clerics, partly because begging had been outlawed, partly because the towns were being cleansed under the eyes of the police. Word spread that worse was in prospect for the wretched Spaniards. And one Palm Sunday it was actually brought to the point where masses of people gathered in Madrid and started advancing on the palace with the cry: "Long live Spain! Down with Squillace!" The mob was led by a monk and a transported convict. But the Walloon guard held the palace, dispersed the crowd and dragged the loudest from it.

I the King was a taciturn man. In the palace he consulted only Squillace and Campomanes. And with no notice or warning, on that very day he closed down every Jesuit house in Spain.

He made it known that the Jesuits were behind the mob. They wanted to overthrow the King and set his brother on the throne.

≈≈≈

The Pope in Rome admonished the Spanish King. "What a fuss over a few Jesuits," the King said to Campomanes, who held the Pope's letter out to him, "as if our lovely wretched country were nothing." And he responded soothingly that the Jesuits had become insufficiently spiritual, they were involved in trade, and what is more had tried to drive him from his throne. Furthermore, he was not obliged to account to any Roman authority for his acts of state.

Who could the old pale Roman Pope complain to now? To the Austrian empress, who was called Maria Theresia? She commiserated with him. Later she read the note which her ministers submitted to her, and wrote on it dismissively: "The banishment of the Jesuits is a matter of state, not of religion." Even this pious sovereign used such modern phrases.

≈≈≈

Then it reached the New Indies.

The governor of Buenos Aires, Bucareli, undertook to

implement the royal decree. He was an erect, strongly-built man, who detested the Jesuits and their republic and in this was at one with all good merchants, traders and soldiers. For the state on the Paraná was nothing but a power centre in the hands of the Jesuits, the resistance of the last few years proved it. Apart from that it was clear as daylight that the Indians must be liberated from the Jesuits. They were wretched slaves, forced to toil for the splendour and wealth of Jesuits.

They were cleared from all the reductions. The assembled Directors were taken on a stroll out of their college and administration centre in Cordoba, and a century and a half after they had come into this country with nothing, had suffered martyrdom, sacrificed themselves, built up a whole country and protected millions of dark people, they were led away – with nothing. They were taken by coach to Buenos Aires and set aboard ship. On the voyage they were again just ordinary clerics, standing under heavy suspicion.

≈≈≈

Certainly they suffered injustice, if injustice is what befalls an individual. But the King's edict of dissolution, the arrests, the violent removals, had nothing to do with individuals.

Their empire on the Paraná was burdened with hatred. They had settled themselves in the country like a bad conscience, then began to grow strong and spoil business for others, they were cunning and shrewd, no one was their equal, decades and centuries passed.

Now people took their revenge. Hoi-polloi gathered at the harbour of Buenos Aires, the Fathers had to run the gauntlet. The column of priests shoved its way through to the ship like worms pulled from a fruit, like lurking vermin unwilling to see daylight. There were whistles and yells: "Jesuits." It had become a swearword.

The populace threw stones.

≈≈≈

The ships bearing their woebegone cargo sailed away from the southern continent. Into the dark ocean the mouths of the

Amazon poured its milky water. They were leaving behind palms, jaguars, heat and rain, forests, plains, rivers, and the millions of dark people. They looked back. They shivered. It filled them with horror.

≈≈≈

It was not like the time of that Francisco Orellana, who travelled from Peru down the giant stream and fought with the Amazons; when he reached the sea the forest closed behind him just as savannah grass closes behind fleeing game, the sea wind swept away all trace of his boat, it was nothing, the river pursued them and cried out across the sea: you were never here!

On and on still the giant stream rolled down from the mountains, slithered across the land like a tongue-flicking serpent and darted into the sea. Not even this gigantic serpent, the country's guardian, had managed to scare away the White people. The soldiers, adventurers, murderers, assassins and gamblers that Europe flung here, dross from the European volcano, had now become farmers, ranchers, tradesmen. Rapacious Paolistas, gold diggers, seekers of precious stones, slave hunters had become colonists, pioneers, founders of towns.

And they prospered. They yielded to the land. They mingled with the natives, followed the new heavenly-earthly call that swept over them, sugarcane, coffee, tobacco, horses, cattle, and they multiplied.

On their big sailing ships the former leaders, the persecuted priests, had to face the storm. Soon everyone will leave the giant monastery they had built on the Paraná. Cells and chapels will go up in flames. Noah's Ark will sink.

They gazed at the foaming endless water. The flying fish. The Cape Verde islands. Clouds enveloped the peak of Tenerife. Still there were palms everywhere, the last palms.

Theocracy, the magnificent, the only humane approach, initiated by Father Emanuel had failed.

How the mighty ocean surrounded them, how the greedy waters circled their ship, how the soughing wind surged in the canvas of the sails as it sought to press the ship down. It will devour us.

Tears, day and night. Wailing and prayers, desperation.

Until they reached port. And no country was willing to take them in.

Many went to Russia.

The end of the Christian republic

WHILE THE JESUIT Fathers were still aboard ship, Indians from the reduction of San Luis wrote to Marquis Bucareli in Buenos Aires:

> Corregidor Peredo and Pantaleo Coyuari wrote to us concerning certain birds that they desire in order to send them to the King of Spain. We regret we are unable to provide these. For they live in the forest as God intended, and they flee from us so we cannot catch them. But we are nonetheless devoted subjects of the King.
>
> And now we pray that the loveliest of all birds, the Holy Ghost, may descend upon His Majesty.
>
> Filled with confidence in Your Excellency, we come with deepest humility and in tears to pray that the children of Saint Ignatius, the Fathers of the Company of Jesus, be permitted to remain with us. Our whole town, men, women and children, direct this prayer to you with tears in their eyes. We do not want the monks and priests that are sent to us in their stead. Saint Thomas himself, so we have learned, preached to our ancestors in this country, our forefathers were taught by the Jesuit Fathers and saved through baptism. But under no circumstances do we desire these monks and priests. The Jesuit Fathers were very patient with us, we were happy under their direction. If Your Excellency will lend us a gracious ear, we shall deliver a large tribute of yerba-maté. We are not slaves. If our people who now toil in the fields and the forests return to find the Fathers gone, they will flee into the forest and do bad things. The people of San Joaquin, Estanislao and Fernando are already lost. So, good Governor, please help us. May God preserve and protect you.
>
> *Signed* by all members of the Cabildo of San Luis."

Marquis Bucareli read this letter as a declaration of insurrection, and moved against the town with a thousand armed men and artillery. And when he appeared outside the town, all were going peaceably about their work, all the town officials, when they learned of his approach, came out to greet him, and he had to endure a ceremonial welcome with hastily prepared triumphal arches, garlands and music. The Indians were diffident, and felt deeply honoured that the King should send so many people to them in response to their letter. They felt sad that their petition could not be accepted, and Bucareli himself was ashamed when he saw their resignation. But he was able to report to his King Carlos in Madrid that his orders had been executed and had met with no significant resistance.

The Indian reductions held on for some decades yet. They crumbled slowly. People coexisted, but without the Fathers there was no permanence. They crumbled, just as had the old Indian empires at the approach of the Whites. And once again the southern continent experienced the occupation of Indian realms.

When Franciscans came to replace the Jesuits, the last reductions accepted them in silence. These were not so worthy of reverence as the old Fathers. The new priests did what they could, no one knew how to engage with them. In place of the old Directors came administrators, Spanish civil officials, with strict injunctions to develop trade. They were ruthless, and things became bad. Their decrees conflicted with the needs of the Indian community. Quarrels were inevitable. Inevitably the new administrators encroached on the rights of the Indian councils, the cabildos, consisting of a corregidor, a vice-corregidor, alcaldes, directors, all elected. The administrators wanted other corregidors, and had no time for the unwieldy cabildos.

Soon the worst happened: at the prompting of the governor, Spanish officials reverted to the terrible system of earlier times, work details, labour battalions. The newly arrived administrators crowed when they found that the old method was still the most rational. Now many ran away. Workers were fed bad food. Money was no longer available for community needs, streets, plazas, schools. Nor for churches. Valuable religious objects were taken from altars to be melted down. Churches began to fall into decay. Festivals could no longer be celebrated. No one felt like celebrating.

A new governor-general was dispatched, he was to reorganise the old Indian communities. But how, on what basis, with monks, with administrators? He did his best. Nothing changed.

Portuguese plundered the eastern missions. Not much blood was spilled. San Miguel, San Juan, Angel, Borja, Luis, those lovely places full of wonderful refinements and memories, were occupied without effort. Much went up in flames. Indians fled in droves. Cattle were stolen. Disorder mounted. In the end few people sheltered in the ruins.

In the west this work was organised by Colonel Rivera. He undertook a massive raid into peaceful terrain, and carried everything off that fell into his hands. He split families up and sent them to Brazil. Any strong men were inducted into his army.

When the old empires fell, hundreds of thousands fled into the mountains, trekked through forests. In the pampas, along the Marañon, remnants tried to save themselves, squatted at the edge of the broad plain that was permeated by the breath of the great river.

The Guarani of the Christian republic sank into the most wretched state of Indian defencelessness. Many became slaves in the towns of the Whites, in plantations of rubber trees. Many became savages again.

Pombal

BUT THE OCCIDENT turned its back on those teachers who had tried to build the Kingdom of God on the Paraná. No one remembered the peace they had brought to the native tribes, the conversions, and the numerous martyrs.

Shattering blows rained down on them. The worst were inflicted by a Portuguese, Pombal.

The Whites now wanted utterly to spurn that holy Church which once they could not embrace tightly enough. The seed planted by Galileo, Copernicus, Bruno had sprouted. Men in England and France uttered inflammatory words, their ranks were always filled. It was clear that they replenished themselves at a source no less deep and holy than that of the Church.

A lazy, weak voluptuary occupied the throne of Portugal at this time. His mother thought he needed a strong man at his side to protect the throne. She planned to rule herself through this man. She summoned Pombal. And then it was all up with her. He was a handsome cruel man, former ambassador to Vienna and London. He had married, for the second time, the young niece of Marshall de Aun. He was fifty-one years old when the queen mother recalled him to Lisbon. He remained in his post for decades.

He swiftly pushed the King aside. He let him build pleasure palaces on the Tagus, as many as he wanted. He himself constructed prisons next to them, above and below ground. He dispatched the queen mother, who had expected so much of him, to her widow's quarters, where she could grieve and quarrel with her priests and atone whenever she wanted. Whatever Pombal did he did in the name of the State, which was why he had been summoned. He had found, he explained, a considerable neglect. It was high time something was done. He threw out part of the government. Adventurers and amenable clerics became his creatures. His son became president of the Senate and Treasurer, his brother, the patriarch of Lisbon. His other son he made Grand Inquisitor – for although he held no brief for the Inquisition he could still bend it to his purposes. He was a grotesque counterpoint to the Spaniard Carlos, who surrounded himself in Madrid with the younger men of science and the new spirit, and made reforms. Pombal was harder. He accumulated money and wealth. He drove justice from the land with prisons, secret police, truncheons and exile.

But whether he would or no, he had to place himself at the service of the tasks that fell to him, and carry them out. He caressed the infant Trade. He allowed great freedom to the companies on the Para, in Brazil, Pernambuco. It amused him, this philosopher and cynic, to play off finery, silks, linen cloth against Masses and prayers. The Portuguese, he opined, would be better occupied exercising their lungs in glassworks instead of breathing stale incense in churches. Weaving, he said, was better for the eyes than reading in prayer books. He wanted to destroy the over-mighty nobility. This he did systematically. He secured his power from their noble lordships by hiring mercenaries and creating an army of twenty-four infantry regiments, twelve of cavalry and four of artillery. At its head he placed a foreigner, the Duke of Schaumberg-Lippe. Then he waited for his chance. It soon came.

≈≈≈

The lecherous King had once again imposed himself on a girl of good family. Her relations were not inclined to stand idly by. And since in Pombal's Portugal you were not allowed to complain, they took counsel with their muskets and presented the King, during a stroll around the streets of Lisbon, with a petition of complaint in the form of lead shot. The merry young man was hit by two bullets, but not seriously. He was preserved for a long reign, and his country would savour the Marquis de Pombal to the full, so that it might understand that even the strongest holders of power count for nothing, if strong is all they are.

The assassins were caught soon after the failed attempt. And when Pombal had these proud avengers of family honour in his grasp, he said: "We shall make much more of your failure than just this attempted assassination." In league with General von Schaumberg-Lippe and his Minister of Police, he twisted the attempt into a monstrous plot. He implicated all the mightiest nobles of the land who displeased him, and a number of others too. He pestered the judiciary until they knew not if they were coming or going. And after a long trial that suffocated in a swamp of lies, the great men were thrown in jail and the Tavoras, the family of the latest royal mistress, were executed, along with Duke Aveiro and Count Atuguia.

And who else might be bagged? Such an assassination does not fall into one's lap every day. Pretty Miss Tavora had already been discarded by the King, the ruler was now more interested in her cousins and sisters in law, the attack had revived his zest for life, you knew where you stood with the King. Pombal stumbled on the Jesuits. The Sacramento Portuguese had been barred from their reductions. This was not forgotten. The Spanish King had already given them a taste of the Stare's fist. Now they lounged abput here seeking refuge from the global storm brewing overhead. They had property, hid themselves behind King and queen mother.

Now Pombal ordered the printing of ten thousand copies of a pamphlet, wherein he proved what harm the Jesuits inflicted on the State. The Jesuits kept silent. Chance placed another card in his hand.

A very old priest of the Company of Jesus, Gabriel Malagrida, still lived in the country. This good man had spent twenty-six years as a missionary in the New Indies, on the Para, on the left bank of the Itapecuru river, in Tocantins. When he grew old and could no longer bear the burdens of a missionary life, he made his way to the court in Lisbon and sat around with the sulking queen mother, whom Pombal had so sorely disappointed. She had Malagrida tell her comforting stories from South America, and bequeathed the Jesuits a large sum in her will. Mighty Pombal, originally Jose de Carvalho and later Duke of Oeiras, impervious to fear, had long despised this old toothless dodderer, who following the terrible earthquake had written a simple book containing pious thoughts at which one could only laugh, but it bore the title *Verdict on the True Causes of the Earthquake that Struck the City of Lisbon*, and of course it was the sins of the world that were to blame, and the government was not mentioned, at least openly. But it gave Pombal an excuse to kick him out of the court and confine him to the village of Setuval, outside the city.

This Father Gabriel had gone a bit native in the Indies. He spoke little, his thoughts were not logical, he mixed things up and had intuitions. He suffered from swamp fever. And after he had left the court to dwell quietly among fishermen in the village of Setuval and everything he had seen lately in Lisbon whirled around in his aged head – oh, this Europe, these barbarous White people, why did I not die in Tocantins to be buried beside my little straw-thatched church – there came again the heated thoughts that had led him to write his little book on the causes of the earthquake:

this world cannot endure, it is ruled by men of violence and freethinkers, the Blue Jaguar they talk of in the south, that evil beast, instrument of destruction, has come down from Heaven and is tearing the world to pieces, the terrible great earthquake was a first sign, others will come, and he thought of the King who failed to perform his office, the young man will be toppled, he'd better take care, God likes to make use of wicked worldly wretches, someone will kill the King. And he set out, this white-haired philanthropist, to warn the young wastrel, and wrote a letter to the queen mother's elderly governess, whom he knew well. The governess received the letter from her old friend, and was shocked to read about threats against the King, who should be careful and conduct his life in such a way that God would protect him. She dared not pass this letter on, for weeks it lay there in her prayer-book, finally she returned it to the priest in Setuval, with a greeting.

So now when the merry young King, faint with terror, bleeding and dirty – in his fright the gallant fellow had flung himself into the filth of the street – was carried into the palace following the assassination attempt, and the queen ran around screaming wildly, the governess remembered the letter, she could not suppress a dread that she had failed to pass on the pious man's warning, perhaps worse was to come, she had to speak out. And as soon as the queen mother, after the turmoil of the first arrests, which included some court personnel, sat alone in her chamber, she ran to her, threw herself at her feet and, unable to speak at first, confessed that old Father Gabriel, our good Malagrida whom Pombal dismissed from the court, had predicted it all, had prophesied the assassination, he wrote from Setuval, she had kept the letter to herself because it frightened her, it concerned the King, and it said, what did it say, it said the King, our poor King, was under threat, his life was in danger, he should be warned.

Beside herself with agitation and furious with the governess, the queen kicked the old woman aside and sent for Pombal. He was not otherwise her friend, but now she needed someone with a strong arm. Pombal came at once, the plump phlegmatic man.

When he arrived she made the contrite governess, who again prostrated herself, tell it all again. Only when she directed her gaze to the great potentate leaning there on his cane calm and attentive, nodding invitingly to the old governess, did she realize that nothing he would do now would be of help to herself or her poor son, nor would he punish the negligent woman as she deserved, but he would think only of his power, and she had handed him a weapon to use against his enemies, perhaps even against herself and her son. I've done myself no favours with this complaint, ran through her head, but already it was too late. She saw how contentedly he swallowed the morsel offered him, his eyes lit up, you could almost see the morsel passing through him. Courteously and with compassion he asked the governess for the letter, or a copy. The old person confessed with a howl that she had sent the letter back without even showing it to anybody. Pombal shook his head, vexed. Oh lord, now she's caught up in the case. But his thoughts were elsewhere.

He sent his police to Setuval. Old Gabriel had been gone half the day fishing out to sea with his landlord. When the boat reached shore and the men were wading barelegged through the surf, the policemen tied him up where he stood, threw him onto a cart and transported him to the capital. A second cart carried the priest's entire movable possessions: his desk, bed, chairs, books, papers. A quite superfluous guard was placed over the fisherman's house, from which the occupants were removed. They were locked up in the little village jail.

In Lisbon, the missionary caused them but little trouble. He at once admitted to the letter mentioned by the governess. They also found the original among his papers, along with the accompanying note from the governess. During those days Pombal nurtured a plan to enlist the aid of the old governess in compromising and neutralizing the queen mother, it would be a simple matter, but he decided to leave her dangling. Good Father Gabriel was thrown into jail as leader of a plot against the life of the King. The whole world must concede, on the basis of the letter and the confession, that the Jesuits had a hand in the attempted assassination. They were monstrous criminals, of a kind never before known to history. Over there in America, using pious donations and under the protection of Catholic monarchs, they had inveigled a whole empire for themselves, out of motives that were still unclear, but little by little it emerged that it had been constructed on communist principles. There they had amassed riches, stripped gold mines whose very existence they had kept concealed; cunning as they were, on the excuse that Whites were ruining the customs of the natives, they had even prevented any inspections, those foxes, those wolves in sheep's clothing. They had manufactured gunpowder in quantities sufficient to blow up every European capital. On the pretext of protecting poor Indians, they had enabled these cannibals and savages to acquire modern weapons. Furthermore, they had recently shown their teeth in the Sacramento affair, when they conducted open warfare against Spain and Portugal. And now, impatient, they have revealed their hand by taking aim at the sainted person of the King. To them, any means is justified if it leads to the goal, treachery, perjury, even regicide.

The perpetrator Gabriel could expect no mercy. But he was oblivious to it all. He was in his late seventies. And simple and amiable as he was in his Indian and doddery ways, under the tortures to which he was subjected to extract names of accomplices he became even simpler. If he failed to confess something, it was because he understood nothing. He screamed and sang alternately under the torture. He knew it was a martyrdom. Baffled, Pombal's creatures finally left him alone. They let the small sallow man lie in his cell, where he recuperated and chattered away all the time in Indian to something not there. Apparently he was arranging conversions across the sea.

They had to report their meagre results to mighty Pombal. The minister had expected this, it made no impression on him. At that time, whatever news reaching him from some dungeon was all the same to him. He had no intention of relying on chance, his plans were cut and dried and his measures decided on. He would, as he explained to his General von Schaumberg-Lippe and the

Minister of Police, be no minister of a civilized state, and deserve no confidence of his King, if he did not proceed cold-bloodedly against the most artful and brutal criminals and adopt all and any methods to enable Justice and Civilization to triumph. He would not be diverted from any use of force to which others drove him. In the struggle against even these criminals he would adhere to the rules of justice and respect formal procedures, although the situation was almost a national emergency. And he put together a court. The judges all knew their own heads were on the line.

And since nothing could be proven from the babblings of old Father Gabriel and no more confessions could be wrested from him, they left him a while longer in his dungeon. And as the wizened prisoner sat there in his cell and they allowed him pen and ink and even provided him with a writing desk, he began to sketch the life of Saint Ann, and then embarked on a tract about the Realm of the Antichrist. The guards treated him more gently, now and then brought him fruit and better bread. He felt himself into the life of St Ann, his own life flowed peacefully on, and he wrote strange and highly phantastical things, which to him were as clear as daylight. There were three Antichrists, the Father, the Son and the Nephew. People now were living in the age of the second. The last would be born in Madrid, in a thousand years, to a monk and a nun, and would marry Proserpina, one of the Furies. Of course, as soon as he finished scribbling they took the papers away. He himself offered them to the guards, so that people outside could learn something to their advantage.

Pombal cast an eye over them and found what he was looking for and had long predicted: the writings and the person of the priest would be of interest to the Inquisition. For it was his intention to bring the matter to a climax, which would not only throw light on the abominable nature of the intrigues of nobles and Jesuits against the State, but also dispel any doubts about his determination to be done with them. And after the priest had lain two years and four months in the prison at Belem, he was transferred to the prison of the Inquisition in Lisbon, the Dominican monastery. The head of the Inquisition, Pombal's brother, saw at once that the man in Jesuit robes, this amiable white-haired gentleman, hard of hearing, who smiled at him, was a thoroughly insignificant being, a childlike ancient from the infirmary. Puzzled, he wondered what he was supposed to do with him; his brother, the powerful minister, did indeed set him hard tasks. But they must all be dealt with.

The Tribunal of the Holy Inquisition was comprised of two courts, a Lower and an Upper Board. The man had to be sentenced. So the Grand Inquisitor deemed it appropriate in the case of the Jesuit priest Malagrida to convene both Boards jointly, not least to forestall the lower chamber from taking too great an interest in the alas all too evident spiritual condition of the accused. It should of course not be assumed, even if one of them were to suspect something, that he would make damaging use of that suspicion. Why, indeed, show the slightest weakness. And so the amiable priest, eager to express himself after the long silence of the prison cell, was without delay interrogated by the joint tribunal of the Inquisition convened in his honour, against which no appeal was possible. And willingly and abundantly he laid himself bare to this pious and august audience, related to them his mysterious prophecies, spoke of his voices and warned, babbled about the earthquake.

The Grand Inquisitor was hard put to interrupt the flood of words from the old man. Gabriel seemed to forget most of the time what all this was about, he requested that they pass him his manuscripts, and made additions to them. Carvalho, Pombal's brother, forced himself to take these absurdities in deadly earnest. He took care that everything should be recorded, allowed no suspicion to arise that this nonsense wearied him. And when, after a hearing that lasted hours, they withdrew to consider their verdict, gathered around the massive table with its huge silver crucifix in the centre, no one dared say a word. They avoided each other's eyes, tried not to show that they had been listening to a lovable old chatterbox. They prayed together. Carvalho, like his brother a powerfully built man, raised his mournful bass voice and entreated God to cleanse their souls of all the horrid ordure that had poured over them this day. A unanimous verdict was reached:

another of Pombal's creatures, a cleric who had played prosecutor, was appointed to excommunicate the heretic and sentence him to a period of imprisonment. "To this end we command that, in accordance with the provisions of canon law, he shall be deconsecrated from his holy estate and handed over with the bit, the cap and the mark of an arch-heretic to the secular authorities, who are devoutly implored to treat him with kindness and sympathy and not to proceed against him with capital punishment, nor any spilling of blood."

The little white-haired man heard this in the courtroom from the mouth of Carvalho. Father Gabriel, as he watched the judges come back in, was cheerful, tender and full of hope. He believed they would take his pronouncements to heart. But when they made no reference to these, but spoke only of him and sentenced him as a heretic and committed such a dire injustice, for who could revere God and the Trinity and the saints more fervently than he, then he knew that all his thoughts were confirmed and he grew sad and clapped hands over his face, weeping. Whereupon Carvalho thundered: he should show them that he understood everything, and let the mask now finally fall.

The supreme temporal court in Lisbon to which the Inquisition's verdict was referred, after a formal hearing at which the old man spoke not a word, sentenced him to death: "Having seen the verdicts of the Inquisition, the Chancery and the Deputies of the Holy Office, and having thus arrived at our finding, it is our sentence that he be led by the hangman's assistant on a rope through the public streets of the city to the Plaza do Rocio, where he shall be strangled and, once dead, be burned to ashes, so no trace remains of him or his burial place."

≈≈≈

And so it happened. On the day of the auto da fé Pombal ordered five thousand troops onto the streets, each armed with eight sharp-nosed bullets, they occupied every alleyway from the gate of the Dominican monastery, where they had kept the old man for the purposes of the Inquisition, to the Plaza do Rocio. On the square itself stood a double line of soldiers. The King hid in his pleasure palace; ever since the sentence and the announcement of the day of the auto da fé he had tried to feign illness. But his stalwart guardian Pombal drove out to see him, assailed him with scornful words, humiliated him: the only sickness was his dissolute lifestyle, with which he compromised the Throne and made the task of government harder. Josef promised to appear at the auto da fé. And so there he sat on the rostrum, behind curtains, under a purple baldachin with crowns, the quivering young man whom Pombal had accused of endangering the security of the nation, he, the King. He thought about fleeing, to England or Brazil, he wanted to rouse his people up against tyranny, but who were his people, he knew nobody, they never let anyone come to him. What's more, he was slightly drunk there at the auto da fé, and had a silly vacant grin, a mask he adopted to put Pombal off the scent.

And now, down below along the sundrenched street, hands bound, a gag in his mouth, a tall heretic's cap on his head, came the little white-haired missionary, led by two Benedictine monks. They brought him to a halt in front of the stage. Pombal, in a heavy powdered wig that fell to his shoulders, laid a plump arm on the balustrade, gazed sternly at the little man, and invited him, through one of the monks, to ask the King's forgiveness for his crimes. Josef, who had painted over his pallor with makeup, was nauseated by the spectacle. He found it horrible to sit enthroned here in honour of his minister and watch this poor old man suffer an injustice, as his mother said. He nodded, without arousing himself from his torpor, and continued grinning into the air. For what could he do, he asked himself. If he kicked against the traces, he might find himself cast down by morning.

They removed the gag from the old man's mouth, he spat blood to one side. A Benedictine shouted Pombal's invitation into his ear. The sun shone in the priest's face, he shaded his eyes and recognized his King squinting down at him. They were acquainted, at their last meeting the old man had admonished the King in the chambers of the queen mother, he hadn't seen him for four years, he gazed up in wonder at the painted quivering face, looked to the right where Pombal sat, to the left where the bishops sat, O King, are you forsaken, and said in a clear voice: "I am not aware I have offended His Majesty, the one true King, in the slightest. But if nevertheless I have ever offended him or anyone else, then I humbly beg pardon."

The King gulped, suddenly he felt sick. Without a word he jumped up, hand at his mouth, and retched. They made way for him, shocked, as he plunged through the gaggle of courtiers and officers. At the back of the rostrum, decked in lovely blue carpets, he vomited, clung tight to the railing. His major-domo came running and removed his hat, stood in front to shield him from sight, and as soon as the heaving ceased pushed a chair under him. In full view of the splendid cavalry regiment stationed here, sabres drawn, the King vomited again. Then he straightened the chair himself, and rested his head on the carpeted balustrade.

Meanwhile events were proceeding. Pombal, in a rage, was unable to rise. He sent one of his sons backstage. The King would not come, said he was ill, would they leave him alone. Pombal pounded the floor with his heavy bamboo cane.

Down below in the dazzling light, the little missionary, mouth gagged again, ambled after the two monks. He tripped across the empty sundrenched plaza, encircled by soldiers and mob, towards the pyre. The old man went with a cheerful light step. The Duke of Cadaval and the Count of Villanova had attached themselves to him as companions, they led him between them, he knew them for pious men and was glad of their company. He had no fear of death. Who would have thought they'd make such a to-do over an old man like him. A familiar of the Holy Office came running behind with a bowl in his hand. They glanced around and stopped.

The man asked the aged prisoner whether he would comply with the commands of the holy tribunal. Astonished, the old man answered: "Yes."

At which the familiar: "You must partake of these sweet-meats." The priest obediently took some, for he was pious, it was not necessary to put his obedience to the test. But when he was already standing by the pyre they sent again to ask if he would obey. A great restiveness came over the mob, which grew when the priest, who had answered yes, was led at the familiar's command together with the two companions back to the royal dais, beside which, in a kind of black-draped booth, sat members of the Inquisition. At once there flew through the throng: He's going to confess. Pombal's people in the crowd spread word that the minister himself had arranged it. The holy tribunal had indeed ordered the priest to request the so-called tablet, that is, to be brought forward to confess, but when he stood before them all he did was bow and smile happily, as simpleminded as during the trial. In order to preserve appearances they had to direct a couple of inconsequential questions at him, then they allowed him to be led away again, across the wide deathly-quiet plaza, to his pyre. There he settled himself calmly against the stake, for the last time they removed the gag from his mouth. He prayed in a loud voice. One of the executioners lowered the rope over the stake behind him. At the Amen he pushed the rope down around his throat and turned the peg, the shoulders lifted, the legs kicked and bent, the head went back and then fell forward onto the breast. It was done.

Really there was no need for three people to toss the little corpse with a single swing onto the pile of faggots, so that the sentence of the court should be carried out: that once dead, he should be burned to ashes so that no memory would remain of him or his burial place.

The last Jesuits

THREE HOURS FROM Lisbon, at the mouth of the Tagus, the fortress of St Julian sits on a clifftop. To St Julian they brought the one hundred and twenty four Jesuits they had managed to catch in the country. Most remained there for eighteen years. A few were released after ten years, around thirty died.

The prison lay to either side of an underground passage, the dungeons were ventilated by a hole above, light came through the door. Proximity to the sea made it damp. Everything they had rotted. The commandant reported to Lisbon: "All rots, apart from the pious Fathers." They were denied the Sacrament and

Mass, once a year they received a shirt. Little manikins bent with sorrow, they sat in their stinking holes by lantern light, and knitted socks.

This was not yet enough. There was expectation that a pope might be persuaded to condemn the Jesuits, his most loyal followers, and disband them once and for all. One pope died in the course of this, he fell into a seizure during a hearing, the affair passed to another pope, an innocent Franciscan, elected by the cardinals in Rome because they were desperate, caught between the devil and the deep blue sea; he became pious out of fear. To the meek man who called himself Clement the Fourteenth, it seemed good to yield and have done with what could not be stopped, and there was so terribly much that could not be stopped.

A spiritual commission of enquiry came to his aid, they handed him a list of transgressions of his most obedient warriors: involvement in temporal affairs (but who could avoid such, unless they lived in a monastery, it would mean leaving the world to the Devil), toleration of heathen practices in the missions (ah, my predecessors often busied themselves with this question, one can only proceed by small steps, and instead of looking to the Paraná they would do better to eliminate the heathendom they themselves are so devoted to, here and now), accumulation of considerable wealth through trading activities (I see their game, the Fathers did not keep all the wealth for themselves, much of it flowed to us, it is us they target, they want to bring us down by forcing us to a verdict, a false verdict).

And the verdict came from the mouth of this man, who was harmony incarnate (O Lord, help me pronounce these words, forgive me, don't hold it too much against me, it's not suicide, not at all, if now I spurn our dear children and helpers; what is dead can be made to live again), and he spoke with courage, mindful of the malevolence of the powers that forced him, and in the certainty that one day it would be possible to triumph over them:

> Inspired by the divine Spirit in which we trust, impelled by
> the duty to restore harmony to the Church, convinced that
> the Society of Jesus can no longer provide the useful service

for which it was founded, and swayed by other reasons of prudence and statecraft which we retain within our own hearts, we rescind *(Lord, forgive me)* and abolish *(do not listen to these words, oh God of righteousness, punish those who force me to utter them)* the Society of Jesus, its offices, houses and appurtenances."

≈≈≈

When the courier came from Madrid – for Pombal wished to bring the news to his frogs and toads on the swampy coast without the least delay – the prisoners of St Julian were brought out of their dungeons into the central passage, and the commandant read to them the dreadful papal decree. Three of the prisoners were already mad, they whimpered day and night. And when the commandant was done, the Fathers, white-bearded, grey-bearded, unkempt as they were, looked at one another speechless. One started crying, then they all wept, the horrible male sobbing of a hundred old, sick men filled the damp stone passage they had known for so many years, which with its lanterns and guards and soldiers was all that remained of their world. So they were to be buried alive. Even the pope had abandoned them.

The lunatics screamed and jumped out of the line in which they had been drawn up, shouted the hymns that had been driving the others to martyrdom day and night, they were led away. The commandant had to utter soothing words when it came to the lamentable act he had been ordered to perform: to remove from the prisoners their black clerical robes. The robes were dirty, worn out and rotten, but as they divested themselves one after the other and handed the robes to the guards, who tallied them aloud: thirty, thirty-one, thirty-two, it seemed to them they were falling into a void. They stood in socks and underhose, they had nothing more. There was no sense of shame. They cried and embraced one another. Shirts and gowns were handed out. They cried for weeks, until their stupor swallowed even this.

≈≈≈

A sentence of death hangs also over the body of the King. The cowed wastrel Josef used himself up and was thrown, a nearly weightless bag of bones decked with not much flesh and a bit of skin and hair, onto a bier, and after some music and speeches and ceremonies was given to the earth, which disposed of him even more quickly than he had disposed of himself.

And now it was all up with Pombal. He fled. He was over eighty years old. He could not have grown much older anyway. And so he was the victor. Behind his back they spoke of him as of a criminal, and the exemplary punishments he deserved. But he had money, and lived a good while yet beyond his eighty years.

Then the last Jesuits were released from the dungeons of St Julian.

Not many were left.

END OF VOLUME TWO

VOLUME 3

THE NEW JUNGLE

Part Nine

THE NEW JUNGLE

~

THEY NO LONGER allowed themselves to gather at seaports and be set aboard ship, to proceed with axe and machete against primeval jungle in some far-off land.

Now they could find everything at home. The Earth was thoroughly discovered and conquered from one end to the next. Any part that did not belong to the White people was as good as White, they had spread their ways to yellow, brown, red, black people, and these had adopted their weapons and methods.

No longer was there any magic. They could calculate everything, from the heavens above to the earth below; they had even thrown their ghostly god onto the scrapheap. Something terrible had happened: they had ventured out to lose themselves and their kind in the earth, to transform and renew themselves like birds of passage that fly year after year back to their old hot homeland, to the lovely wide rivers, plateaus, swamps, and return only when they have recouped their strength. The New World had been good to them, but had also increased their strength, their arrogance and brutality, and brought them even more misfortune.

Now they had no need to board ships. No strange lands lay across the ocean, promising freedom and fortune. They proliferated, and made inroads into the jungles.

For this was Europe.

Thorns came, beetles, worms, scorpions, heat, cold, wet, hunger, thirst. Trees grew horribly close-packed. They straggled from forest to swamp, from swamp to thickets, thorny scrub. They were driven from valleys up into high mountains, from steaming heat to frost.

Sweat ran down their faces, salt in the mouth. When the sun came up it set them to work. When it went down and the starry host appeared, exuberant with fiddles and flutes and shawms, that was the signal to sink back and sleep and regain strength for the new day.

But the forest had no end. It walked with them, closed in again behind

599

them. They fell by the thousands.

Now and then a voice rang out: "Abandon ship, we're doomed."
Another: "Onward, don't give up, don't give up!"

Pan Twardowski

CRACOW, ST MARY'S church.

It's snowing. White guardstones around the church, in long rows. At the main door a young blind man with hollow eye-sockets, two raggedy-skirted old women with wrinkled ruddy faces, they stand immobile, right hand outstretched.

The ancient pile of the church sits grey over the marketplace, huge windows open it to the light but the windows are filled with pictures. The floor inside is thick with people, kneeling black bodies, an organ sounds, a small voice pipes far off, candles flicker on the columns at each side.

Night. The church is shut, the wide marketplace, arcades, silent towers, the ancient silent city walls lie under a white quilt of snow.

Someone is groaning in the church.

Groans come from out of the darkness, from the nave. Now away from the altar along the side chapels, now back to the nave, accompanied by a whispering voice.

The snow's whiteness casts a wan light through the tall windows. In the gloom two people in mediaeval dress walk past a row of hassocks, both are bareheaded, long curly hair falls to the shoulders, they clutch their swirling robes high under the chin. One is two heads taller than the other, his boots are spurred, he walks ahead, the other follows, hesitant, looks up, aside, covers his face with his cloak.

The groaning comes from the tall man with the spurs.

He is Pan Twardowski, who centuries ago grappled with the Devil. He kneels in a pew, and the sword drops from his belt and clatters on the boards by his knees.

The other waits behind him, and when the tall man stops groaning says: "Let me go now."

Twardowski: "Go, if you wish. But say something."

The other is silent.

Twardowski: "You've nothing to say. You go. And what you started bothers you not at all. You lie in your coffin. You sleep. How long will you sleep, and know nothing of what's happening?"

"Let me go."

"You and your kind lie there and sleep. How cosy. You stomp around for forty, sixty years, stir up monstrosities, turn everything upside down, preach, threaten, there's no escape from you, and when everything is in train, all nicely meshed together, unstoppable and the time has come for you to vouch for your deeds, just at that point – you all disappear."

"Let me go, Twardowski."

"And I should let them go. Hey, Copernicus, you splendid fellow, Nikolaus, I showed you what there is to see here. I even heeded your whining and last night showed you the Wawel, the royal castle. The moon floated over the Wawel, towers lay below like shadows, you could see everything without and within. I took you to the Jagellonian Library, so you could view your statue in the courtyard. They've not forgotten you, old friend, they even carved the title of your book into the plinth."

"On the plinth it says I died four hundred years ago."

"They should never have let you get away. The pleasures of death should be denied such as you. Whoever says A and says B should be forced to recite the whole alphabet. You must pay what you owe."

"You won't release me?"

The tall man said nothing. Copernicus sank to the cold stone floor and wept silently.

Twardowski in his pew growled: "At last."

Copernicus: "I am not at fault, I remained pious to the last."

"People knew you only after your death. You are the root of all evil."

"What should I have done? I described what I saw. I observed with care, over a long period. I grew ever more certain. And beyond doubt: the Earth circles the sun, the sun does not move."

"Just so. It seemed like nothing. Even you did not see what it was you said. Otherwise you would not have dedicated your book to the pope. They knew it afterwards. You are the root of all evil. Concede: the Earth stands still, is the centre of the universe, sun, moon and stars all move around the Earth. That's how God created the world."

"This I cannot concede."

"Because you're the root of all evil. Concede it now, at least."

"I saw it differently."

"Then you should have plucked out your eyes."

"I calculated it, Twardowski."

"You should have thrown away your brain."

"God in Heaven, I implore Thee. Jesus, Mary, help me."

"Implore whom, you old fraud? God in Heaven? I think you know heaven, you saw it and calculated it."

"Do not mock."

"Where in heaven?"

"God preserve me. Make me free."

"Of Pan Twardowski! To sleep again! No, my friend. No one alive in Cracow, in St Mary's church, or in Heaven heeds the name of God. This church was built around the time when you were living. At least you couldn't burn this church down."

"My God, my God."

"He's not listening. And he won't trouble me, and I can summon you because I am Righteousness and shall deny sleep to all of you, all such wretches."

The man on the floor shuffled, creaked upright. Twardowski turned to him. Copernicus stood frank and calm, tidied the long white hair at his neck, his grave attentive old man's face regarded Twardowski: "Certainly you were able to summon me from my tomb. I give you no more credence than that. I don't believe you can do anything more with me."

For some time he heard only Twardowski's groans as they faded down the gloomy nave. The old man crept into a side chapel and laid himself down on a marble plinth.

≈≈≈

Another night. Snow still lying.

In the nave of the church, near the altar, three men in mediaeval dress creep past the columns down the stone aisle. Tall Twardowski sweeps the other two along behind him. He sinks wearily into a pew, his companions remain in the aisle, heads bared, broad hats held in front of them. Twardowski wears a tall fur cap, he sits muffled in his cloak up to his ears. Another figure steps from a side aisle into the nave, vanishes from gloom into darkness, then stands with the others. They hear Twardowski's low groaning.

The one beside little whitehaired Copernicus speaks, an old man with a huge bald skull and thick white beard. "Doff your cap, Twardowski, you're in church." He repeats this. Twardowski snatches off the cap, puts it beside him. The old whitebeard: "You fetched us from our graves by sorcery. It would be a good idea for you to kneel and pray. We'd like to help you."

Twardowski, a still youthful man, drops his cloak, he has a small dark beard, a lean strong face, his little restless eyes gleam: "Don't worry about me. Say what you have to say."

The whitebeard, who is as tall as Twardowski: "If you were not a sorcerer and lacking in humility, you would not suffer so."

"You need not be concerned for me. That's not why I summoned you." And he stood and cried out: "Have you not seen, you three? Was it not enough, do you need to see more?" And he roared and kicked his tall cap away: "Everything a failure. All in vain. Wrong, wrong. Galileo, old man, you see, this is the world you introduced. Here you are, Giordano Bruno, this is what they burnt you for, so that mankind might drudge for princes and rich men, never know itself, war and murder everywhere, a thousand times more hate than before, a desolate world. You demolished it down to the ground."

Copernicus, placid spirit: "A man like you cannot make us answer for this."

The third, the last to arrive, opened his cloak. At once they were suffused in a pale ruddy glow. This man burned and gleamed, his body was not consumed by the flames, even the hands projecting from the sleeves glowed. Twardowski flinched, the other two looked amiably on. The newcomer, arms wide, bowed to the two in the aisle: "I have just heard who you are, Copernicus, Galileo. Allow me to greet you."

Galileo: "What are you called?"

"I come from Nola in Italy, Giordano Bruno. Because I believed what you said, they hounded me through many cities, I came to Geneva, Lyon, Toulouse, Paris, Oxford and Wittenberg; I was never allowed to settle, at last they threw me into the piombi in Venice, they could not shake my thoughts, all that I owed to you. They packed me off to Rome, to the cellars of the Inquisition. In Rome the only thing left them was to burn me." He spread his cloak wide and laughed: "See how I burn, endlessly, incurably. My mouth still speaks."

Galileo shook his head: "You could have recanted. It's no sin to recant. What did you teach?"

"Always the same, what you and Copernicus discovered, and what is true and wonderful. My judges had power, and nothing more. To give in to them would be as if a savage with a spear leapt at me demanding that I share his meal of human flesh, and I do so."

Copernicus clapped his hands: "You speak of the Holy Church."

"And I spoke of the great Unity, of the Infinite, and the numberless worlds. Space has no end, and is filled with worlds that shine by their own fire, and all worlds have a soul. The relationship to a supreme intelligence sustains them. That is what I said. Is it any less holy than what the Church says?"

Copernicus regarded him gravely, after some time said: "And where did this come from?"

"From you. And from me."

"I don't know you. I know myself. I would never dare speak so. What the Church says is revealed, God himself conveyed it. He sent his Son, our Saviour. Thus the doctrines of the Church stand above all other doctrines and are not amenable to refutation."

Bruno asked the man with the huge skull: "What is your opinion?"

Galileo: "I recanted. In the end I kept silent."

"That is not enough. You should have recanted publicly and condemned your views. Why did you keep working and thinking afterwards, as you surely did?"

Galileo, softly: "Yes. I was wrong. I see now. This Twardowski may be a sorcerer, a reckless man. But I'm glad he summoned me here to take stock of everything. I see that I committed serious, terrible wrongs. I regret it. I should have plucked out my eyes, thrown away my brain."

Then he sank to his knees; Copernicus joined him, they whispered prayers and shuffled towards the altar. Twardowski, watching the two old men on their knees, dashed his sword on the flagstones in a rage. He grabbed his cap, shoved it on his head, and snarled: "This, this! How anxious they are to begone from here. Hey you, you snails, what are you thinking? Perhaps you think regrets are enough. You, the root of all evil, think one little prayer can absolve you of everything. To whom do you pray, you lunatics? You stupid snails. Murderers. They beg forgiveness of their victims." He came up behind them.

Bruno watched them fade into the gloom of the nave: "I worshipped them. They try to take it all back. I, I remain true, I shall never recant. The night is over."

At a word from Twardowski the two old men halted, they should stand, the Devil-raiser railed, shook his fist, berated them as cowards. Then he howled in agony and groaned horribly: "Oh traitors, criminals! Such errors! And the instigators flee. They care nothing for what's happening. They want forgiveness, the scoundrels. Forgive this! We didn't mean it, please excuse us! Murderers."

Giordano's fiery arm prodded him in the back: "Twardowski, why do you groan?"

"You saw. I summoned you to see and speak and help, for you three caused it all." Giordano reached out a fiery hand and placed it over the man's mouth, Twardowski groaned again. Giordano: "This is better than shouting. Those two old men weep and would like to be four hundred years younger and take it all back. What it is you want, I do not see."

"Then you have seen nothing, fiery man. You haven't seen the horror that unfolds here, the misery – in houses, in the street, aboard ship, in trains, in factories, offices where people sit alone, and where they live with families. You think: so much is happening. No, in this world nothing happens. It just rolls on."

"You want the old God back! Why curse these two old men? Come now, crawl after them."

"I groan because it all started so well, I was there and believed it. Wars were waged, countries laid waste, we were there. See how they flee. They know. They saw the horror."

"Horror?"

"Yes. They accept no responsibility for it."

Giordano stood still before him. He and Twardowski took no more notice of the two old men prostrate at the altar; they could hear them chanting. The gaunt sorcerer calmed down as he stood in the fiery man's glow. Only now did Twardowski hear, emanating from Giordano, a constant faint hiss like the soughing of a breeze: it was the flames. And when Giordano opened his cloak, Twardowski, eyes adapted now to the gloom, saw the fiery man stand transparent before him: the beating heart, how it pumped blood into the vessels, how the lungs lifted, swelled and deflated, the tongue playing in the mouth, intestines coiling like a nest of snakes, it was frightening, ghastly.

But Giordano's face was pleasant and grave, and he let his voice speak: "I thank you, Twardowski, for bringing me here. And I shall show my gratitude. Leave me here a while. Let me live and see, and see. I should like to stay a while here and see a great deal."

"How can you say this, Giordano?"

Giordano laughed, turned around, flung his arms like a flame about him: "I am possessed, I am drunk. What I have seen possesses me. The towns, the towns! Machines, I have seen a thousand machines! You haven't seen them."

"I have seen them."

"You haven't seen them. What has happened to this Mankind? What have they achieved. How did they preserve themselves. And who were the instigators."

"You gloat."

"We raised animals, hens, doves, cows, calves, goats, for meat, milk, hides. But they have created giants of iron and steel, imprisoned them in their halls to toil for them, machines, machines. They are called machines, seem to be made of iron, steel, copper, just as we seem to be skin, hair and bones, but are really Spirit and Life. Man the Creator, that is what we instigated, man not merely a servant and worshipper. We unchained those powers that were bound up in Man, the powers of creation. They have made iron mountains that they set in their halls to stamp and spit and hum, and they sprout more than the grass and clover that wither in autumn and dry in the sun. People lead cables into this mountain, they feed oil into it, and then it begins to move, eyeless, earless, and must perform and function with the power of humans and what they have imparted to it. Oh Twardowski, such humans, such machines! Twardowski, night used to fall on towns because the sun vanished from the sky and the Earth turned away from it. Then someone in the halls lifted a finger and darkness was banished, streets, squares, theatres, houses all lit up. Have you seen this?"

"Yes."

"Those huge galleries, empty of people, big as a town square, filled with wonderful machines, machines more beautiful, more complex than a flower, the machines hummed softly and sometimes clanged, it was lovely music, they wove without human help, my tongue cannot describe these wonders. People ran about the halls and sat, they watched the machines and took care that they worked properly, they played gently along."

"Did you see these people, Giordano?"

"The lords of the giants that must serve them."

"Yes, Giordano. If you had seen them, and others outside, you would have noticed that not all is well with them. They look more like slaves than lords."

"Twardowski! Don't let appearances deceive you. They are not happy, I can believe this, it must be hard and terrible in this society. I believe this. They are too stupendous to be happy."

"They toil dreadfully, Giordano."

"Let them struggle, how could it be otherwise. We have made them lords of the world. Yes, I accept the guilt! We showed them their power. They grow used to it. A new mankind will arise. Let me stay here, let me, Twardowski, I'll silence your groans. I want to show you once more. For this is my realm! O eternal change! Such power! O multiplicity of worlds."

Twardowski snarled. He sniffed: "I am to keep you here. You seem an enthusiast. You have seen nothing yet. At least the two old men weep."

"Think what you like, Twardowski. But let me stay here."

"I think you must be blind, Giordano, the way you burn there."

"Don't send me back, I want to see all this, I must." He flung himself at Twardowski's feet: "I implore you, let me stay."

Twardowski played with his sword and growled: "I'd like you to see how everything went wrong. You should pay."

"Let me pay! If I am still blind, then let me open my eyes to it all. Send me to the stake ten times over."

"You are possessed! Criminal!"

"Come with me, Twardowski."

Dawn crept over Cracow. Twardowski stood, flourished his sword a couple of times in the air, fur cap low on his forehead, muttered. The two old men at the altar felt their thoughts vanish, their outlines became vague, swirled and evaporated in the grey light of dawn.

Twardowski and Bruno pulled their cloaks over their heads. They floated, long dark ovals among the shadows creeping behind the columns, and slowly rose with the dawning light up to the blue glinting roof.

≈≈≈

There were houses, tramlines stretched into the distance, buildings with soaring towers, long buildings, cables slung between poles across streets, below them wagons moved without horses, stopped, darted on again.

Cables strung on tall stalks stretched away from the city across fields, endless, towards other cities. There again were houses, row after row, more buildings with towers. And steam-spouting thundering machines rolled on rails pulling wagons behind them, over fields into towns and out again.

Towns seethed with people, amid buildings of stone and concrete, on pavements of chipped granite, asphalt poured and pressed. People were the same species as before. But they had no Heaven, no animals, no plants, no spirits. These had all been conquered by flint and cannon, and struck down as they ran. Earth, sun and all the stars moved, hurtled on, fled towards a distant, distant, awful goal.

The sun shone, and it really seemed that flowers, faces, had some colour. But this was deceptive: it was merely vibrations. And the sounds you heard also came from invisible vibrations. All this living and striving amid invisibilities, sending rays out this way and that.

But air and wind wafted as they always had through towns and streets. Rivers and streams meandered as always through their valleys. Fly high as you like above mountains and lakes, dig tunnels through mountains, still they stand as they always have since time immemorial. Now as ever there was water, rain, the placid brook that washes and wears away at mountains, eternal heat and eternal cold enmeshing them, affecting them.

And people still went about as before, sought to know each other, experienced youth, the prime, drifted towards their end.

Twardowski shouted: "Behold, Giordano. Look on them."

The Extra

A YOUNG THING stood at the mirror and considered itself.

It was naked to the waist and absorbed in its reflection.

I'm not pretty, it thought, my body's giving up, my legs, I'm too thin. But the neck, the mouth.

The longer she looked, the sadder she became. She wanted to console the reflection, came up against glass. We can't make contact, but let's still be good friends.

She had no money. She wanted something from life. There

was no money to be had on the streets. People kept their purses closed. There were shops, you were supposed to buy things. I must sell something, she thought. She joined a theatre as an Extra. She could pretend, nothing much came of it, hardly enough for stockings and shoes.

Behind the theatre, at the stage entrance, an unattractive old man was smoking a cigar. He eyed the actors and actresses. The girl thought, he's choosing one. No one paid him any attention. He wore a bowler, had a bristly brown moustache, sagging trousers. When she saw him at the door again, holding his brolly up even though the rain had stopped, she allowed herself to be drawn under the brolly.

In a tavern he let her eat what she wanted, he tucked in vigorously. It seemed to her he must have lots of money. He's an old man, no girl fancies him, a perfect mark. Then they sat for a while on their stools with their beers, hand in hand. She went home pleased with herself.

Later he picked her up a few streets away, she didn't want anyone to see her with the shabby old man, and no one was going to take him from her.

By Easter he wanted more than just supper together, he invited her on a short holiday, three days. As always she had no money. He'll bring a little suitcase, they can choose her spring hat together. That was all. She calculated the trip, needed new dresses, shoes and underwear if she was to move among more elegant people. She jollied her two-legged enterprise along to the station, stowed him carefully in an empty compartment and showered him with affection.

On the journey the dull boring fellow began to reciprocate her affections, he sighed, pawed her the whole time. Whyever did she choose an empty compartment. Then, just as they were leaving the train, she was vexed when a nice man climbing aboard caught her eye. And as they sauntered slowly arm in arm through the little town, people looked at her. Loving couples attract glances, everyone wants to know what they're up to, even fine gentlemen look at you.

The weather was lovely, they strolled in a wood, surrounded

by families. He didn't throw his money around, only for food, drink and transport.

That evening on the boat he kept sighing, and she grew nervous and weepy: was he Mr Right. Leaning over the rail she cast one lie after another into the water, about things she'd done, bad things. Her great enterprise, the repulsive fellow, grew tender, she was ashamed when he put his arm around her on the boat. Then as they stood embracing shortly before they arrived and she looked past his shoulder, she saw a young lady under a big feathered hat, her head and throat over her man's shoulder. The girl in the feathered hat peeped smiling, untroubled, mischievous, cheeky, devil may care, their eyes met. Tenderly, vigorously the feather girl rubbed her cheek against her man's cheek, nuzzled it, she twinkled at the glitzy Extra who felt she was looking into a mirror, she took her hands from her man's back, the girl in the feathered hat stretched past her lover's arms, they brushed fingertips and interlocked the little fingers. The theatre girl pressed hard against her man so he wouldn't notice, but the other rested her chin on her man's shoulder as if it was a windowsill, tolerated his embrace below while she kept lookout above.

Harsh lights glared from the landing stage, they unlocked hands. You stand separated and have to disembark. They bumped into each other again on the little gangway, how quickly they'd lost contact. But at the hotel the theatre girl was glad they had taken the boat.

Next morning they drank coffee monosyllabically on the verandah. The man sat there and kept his money out of sight. When the waiter came with the bill she wanted to see his wallet, he let her take a look, there was one big note and several smaller. He said gravely: "We'll make do." Then it occurred to her she had to be home this evening because she had an audition tomorrow at noon. And she strolled moodily with him in the lovely sunshine and tormented him, he was meek as a lamb, he told her how beer drinking suited him now. Ever since he'd forced himself to enjoy it by drinking a few pints regularly every day, he had become a sociable chap and never annoyed anyone; she should try it.

And in the park he lay on the chilly grass and uttered intimacies that usually, he explained, he could achieve only after a few beers. She wanted to talk about his wallet, but he was lying on it, she was sitting upright beside him. He expounded to her on the beauties of nature, maybugs would soon be about, you shouldn't torment them or keep them in cigar boxes, birds would return, that was his biggest joy in summer, to lie on his back in the woods and snooze.

"I imagine that must be rather uncomfortable for your back," she said. She was formal with him again.

"No," he said, "but it creases my jacket and I have to press it again afterwards."

She plucked grass and stuffed it in his ears. He indulged her. When she stuck some up his nose he asked her to leave one nostril free. "Young ladies always have such fancies," he opined. "Last Whitsun one ran off with a boot of mine and I had to hop along the street in my sock."

"Do you come on trips like this often?"

"Since my wife died. If I could find a nice girl I'd marry her. But they're all just out for fun."

The theatre girl: "But it's a good deal, right? You have variety, and it doesn't cost much."

"Don't say that, child. When you add it all up, hat, suitcase, fares, everything for two people, hotel, food, drink, it's a pretty penny. When you're married it's not half so much, you take everything with you and the wife pays her own share."

"The girls never do that?"

"No. But they're welcome to those few days."

This was her big enterprise. Suddenly she threw herself onto him and rubbed the grass she was holding into his face. He pushed her roughly away: "Now you're just like all the others." And he tidied himself, sat up and pulled her gently to him. "At your age girls only like to fool around. You're not suited to be a regular housewife."

"But I have no intention of marrying you."

"I know, child."

That evening, on the way to the train, they met the couple from the boat again. The feather woman did not at first recognise the theatre girl. When the Extra made a little motion of her head towards her cavalier, the girl with the feathers gave a mocking smile and extended clawlike fingers. They walked hand in hand to the station.

"You look so cross," whispered feather-hat. "Headache," whispered the Extra.

"I understand," feather-hat nodded. The two men looked gravely ahead, preparing for the journey. On the train they separated.

The young lady rose in the esteem of her female colleagues, partly because of the little trip and partly from the new hat and handbag he had given her. Men kept a respectful distance, believing she was about to marry. She continued for a while to drink beer with the man, so as not to dispel this impression.

But after Whitsun he dropped her. She spied on him, saw him at the back door of another theatre in his stiff black bowler, sagging trousers. I wonder, she thought angrily, if anyone will bite. And it wasn't long before a girl turned towards him and he moved off. She followed for a few streets, she knew the way, they were going to his local. Maybe he'll take her on a long holiday, he never spends anything on a girl. So she tells the theatre people that she's broken off with the man, he wanted to marry her, a Christmas wedding would be best, he's too old.

Soon she found something else, because she was clever and wouldn't give up. She was always afraid of contracting an infection or becoming pregnant. It was the same with the other girls, they spoke about it and gave each other advice, some never overcame their anxiety, some showed bravado but all were afraid. The men were no different, they wanted rid of a girl as quickly as possible before they became hooked and had to support a child.

And so it happened that an elegant man, a foreigner, was drawn to the girl, and for two short weeks of eternity never let her out of his sight. More transpired than she expected. He had money, he wasn't stingy, during those weeks she couldn't be at the theatre and so lost her position. With this Polish man she had love, joy, bliss.

Then he vanished, leaving her a handful of money. And then the baby. Her youth was over.

She became an usherette in a cinema, married a waiter. He had other girls. And like the man from the tavern he stood at the back door of theatres, lurking.

When she followed him one day, there was the old man with the sagging trousers smoking a cigar. No one gave him a glance. When her husband had gone off she approached the old man. He didn't recognise her, he looked the same as before. They went through the gate, he led her down the street she knew so well, to the same tavern. She wasn't sure if she should go in with him. But why upset him. Inside he said the same old things. Alcohol sustained him. Only now he was more free with his money. He pushed a banknote across to her after the first beer and said: "Best give it away while you still have it, when you get old there's no point saving. They don't put it in the grave with you. Anyway, inflation's taking its toll."

She looked at the banknote and tucked it away. If he'd given me money back then I would have a fine cavalier. Her thoughts reached this point, then she remembered her great love, the Pole, the joy, the bliss, she had found him in just the same way, then the baby came, and her husband. She sat on her stool for an hour, then the old man had had enough, he'd wait at the same place tomorrow, she pretended to agree. Then she went home.

Her husband was not back yet. The baby was asleep. She rummaged in the wardrobe for the little box where she kept mementos of the Pole, no letters, no handwriting, but his gold watch wrapped along with its chain in one of his fine handker-chiefs, an armband, two ties he had worn and left behind at her place, and a coat button that had come loose on the last day and she had meant to sew back on. She wrapped the banknote in a sheet of paper, repacked the box and put it away in the wardrobe under her smalls. Then she sat by the lamp, knitting. For some reason she didn't feel sleepy. She imagined she was at the cinema, endless scenes scrolled past. But she couldn't make any of them out.

When the waiter crept into the flat in his socks he was surprised to find her still up. She hemmed and hawed, said this and that, put away her things. He pushed in behind her under the blanket.

She lay there for hours. Always pictures, memories churning, fireworks, she didn't know what was happening to her. In the middle of the night, all at once it stopped. It burned itself out. She slept.

When she washed her face in the morning and saw herself in the mirror – the waiter was still asleep – she didn't recognise herself. She looked tense and pale. A stranger in the mirror. The face moved with hers. On the boat she had looked at a young woman in a feathered hat, stretched hands out to her. The face in the mirror was still tense. She shivered, turned away.

The man in the tavern was right, people grow old.

She threw on some clothes, picked the baby out of the cot, carried it around the flat. It cried. Her husband wanted quiet. A long time passed before she was herself again.

The Pole

THE POLE WAS rich and elegant. He was young and good for nothing. He threw money out the window and thought nothing of it. He had many liaisons, girls included. His face seemed chiselled from stone, extremely regular, austere as marble, dark. This gentleman was always hoarse, and wore a big scarf around his neck. He never said much, though he was always contemplative. He seemed to pay close attention to long conversations, and some visitors thought to engage him in verbal sparring, but he never took the bait.

Women threw themselves at him. Once in Berlin, where he was supposed to be studying, in the north of the city he saw a young, chic and rather discontented person on the arm of a complete oaf. He felt outraged, and followed them. They went into a cinema, the young person was miserable and didn't notice him. He devoted his whole evening to the business and failed to reach his goal, for the couple did not separate, finally they went into a dingy building, they must be married. He persisted. A detective identified the Extra. She was completely taken aback one morning, just as she was getting up, when the detective stood in her room and said he was not there on his own account, but for a friend who was interested in her. She liked the brisk detective.

And then the Pole. She thought: it can't be possible. That noble, austere face, the brown curly hair, the wonderful little mouth, and the huge mournful eyes. He feasted on her incredulity. For half a day she suspected the foreigner had evil designs, maybe he'd kidnap her to America or China, to that sort of house. Then she visited him at his hotel. He behaved like one possessed, because of her, because of her. He knew elegant ladies, wonderful dew-fresh girls were his to command, they sent him notes, phoned the hotel.

He dressed the Extra from head to toe. He still had enough sense not to move her in with him. He told the grave older man who accompanied him and played his secretary, Lukazinski, to threaten him with the revolver or tie him up if ever he took a notion to marry the girl. "Really, I'd like to, Lukazinski." And he shook himself: "For heaven's sake keep me from that."

It lasted two weeks, from a Thursday to the next but one. During this time, to avoid attention, he moved to another hotel. Every morning he repeated to the secretary his desire to marry the girl, but only to elicit his objection, and when the other remained firm and warned him off he was satisfied, gathered his bouquet and went to see her. Finally, on a Tuesday, he took her on a motor tour. That lasted till the Thursday. He came back tired. When the secretary found him on Friday morning lying on the sofa still fully dressed, he asked if he felt unwell. The man turned his head and whispered: "No, quite well. Just my throat, I can't speak."

He really had lost his voice. That very morning they went to a doctor already acquainted with the Pole, who examined him with speculum and swab. After that he sat quietly with Lukazinski in the hotel, looked through the mail that had piled up in the last few days, and was interested in all manner of trivia from the past week.

That afternoon they left town. The young Pole stood in fur coat and hat, his companion beside him, at the washbasin in the room which was already being cleaned, and put a perfume bottle in his pocket: "You no doubt consider me a complete cad. Leaving like this with no goodbye."

"Have you quarrelled?"

"Absolutely not. Only I'm single again. It's just the two of us, Lukazinski."

"Don't strain your voice."

"So you don't think me a complete cad."

"Come come."

"I think I am. But I can't change anything." And with a savage gesture at the last suitcase: So, off we go.

In the train they remained thoughtful the whole afternoon. The secretary opined, when Jagna started up again: "I imagine you'd had enough of her, after two weeks."

"It was like an abyss. I'm still poised on the brink. But I can't."

"She really wanted to marry you, I could see."

"Marry, nonsense. What would the damage be. Worse." But he didn't say what, and Lukazinski didn't ask.

The train sped on, the gentleman turned again towards the older man, smiled a somewhat pathetic and forced smile: "What a feeling, beaten up and escaping with just a black eye. About to be hung, and the pardon arrives."

The train belted out its iron song, rampaged under bridges, now and then raced through a tunnel emitting fearsome shrieks, they listened, it dragged them along, held them in its mouth like a wild beast escaping the hunter. Jagna played with his rings, straightened his trousers above the knee: "Anyway, you understand what we're doing now?"

"First priority is your throat. We'll stop for a couple of weeks in some sizable town. I'm looking now."

"Why sizable? Why not just somewhere south?"

"If you like. But you'll need entertainment."

"True."

In the taxi after they had alighted in Munich, Jagna broke

his hours-long silence: "No mail from her. And you don't send money. Or anything."

The secretary nodded. An adventure. It was over.

≈≈≈

But they did not travel on from Munich to winter sports. For in the hotel lobby the gentleman bumped into a clerical dignitary from his homeland, who at once took him by the arm and, brooking no resistance, took him along to a lecture by a Dominican monk, who was just starting a course on the Human Soul in the studio of a painter. The prelate wanted to say hello to the famous monk.

The young Pole was delighted with this company of men and women that gathered once or twice a week. The studio was in a loft, itself forming a little house with stairs and balconies. A massive electric candelabrum hung from a rafter, the lights were shaded above so the ceiling lay in darkness, light blazed down from black night. Little rooms furnished like dolls' houses opened off the balconies, visitors wandered around, rugs hung from the balconies, below were wooden statues from the Americas and Malaya, and a porcelain figure of Madonna and child. The artist had tidied his things away to one side behind a green curtain. The room was wide and warm, and had a slightly raffish air. Some fifty more or less elegantly attired ladies and gentlemen milled about, and after a while gathered around a lectern in one corner, which the Dominican mounted. Then the huge overhead lights went out, darkness enshrouded the people, the lectern light illuminated the monk's strong healthy face, the round skullcap on the back of his head, the front of his habit. There was whispering from the balcony.

Here is what the Dominican told the assembly, the gentlemen in evening dress who had shaved for the occasion, the lawyers and doctors who had completed their day's appointments and now gazed expectantly at the man dressed as a monk, tired teachers from an academy of painting, some jovial bankers and their ladies, several art dealers, young men from a ministry and a handful of artists and journalists, and all their wives and girlfriends:

"People concern themselves ever and again with two things:

with God, and their own soul. As with the theory of God, so with the theory of the Soul: the leading light is Thomas Aquinas. And whatever the theory of the Soul may touch, or the theory of Man, it serves in the last resort as a reference point for life in which God is the centre, God all in all."

Young Jagna, spick and span as usual, dinner jacket, lacquered shoes, monocle, felt quite at ease in this remarkable room, among these strangers. He listened to the monk's sonorous voice. It never occurred to him he might have some connection to these words. It was amusing how concerned everyone was for themselves, how they swaddled themselves in a huge serious entity, for example in the monk and all these people left and right. There was something fantastically conspiratorial about the company that Jagna found particularly congenial, and so he took part with pleasure. Later the theme of the first lecture proper was announced: "Life is self-motion. It lives in organic and spiritual substances. Motion is action, activity, transition from one state to another."

Several guests left after this, barely half stayed for tea. Mr Jagna was introduced to some, normally people were too much for him, these he listened to gladly, they uttered banalities but it bothered him not at all. He made the acquaintance of several ladies, they commented on the lecture, the ladies praised the monk and were eager for the next gathering. Would Jagna be there. The prelate who had brought him took his leave with the utmost cordiality, hoped he'd led him to a good place.

Jagna knew that in every situation there was a reason either to leave quickly or to stay a while. He missed not a single lecture, even enthused Lukazinski into coming – who put a brave face on it, though bored to death. But if his master wanted him along, something must be in play. You did not always know what, at first.

Around the handsome Pole there began the usual female dance. They said: "How handsome and rich he is. What a lucky man." The monk lectured from behind his lamp, preaching force-fully: "There are three kinds of life and three kinds of soul, the plant soul, the animal soul, and the spiritual soul of the human being. The pure spirit lives a spiritual life, the infinite spirit an infinite life."

Ladies sat around the handsome man. Without realising it, he had become a budding branch hung with a swarm of bees. They listened to the monk, but only enough to gather crumbs to serve as conversational openers with Jagna. Lukazinski, Jagna's gatekeeper, basked a little in the reflected glow, this was nothing new, but in this city it took a particular turn. The crush, the enthusiasm of the ladies, their fervour even, was enormous. The little adventure with the Extra had added a certain something to Jagna's fascination, he had become even more stony and remote. That such stone-cold chiselled features could belong to someone living. His face had a kind of nacreous sheen. Lukazinski was no match for the people who thronged around Jagna. He, the gate to this enchanting creature, this seductive sport of nature, the gate turned out to be human. They hung on him, imploring. What wouldn't they give for access, and since access was difficult, several contented themselves with the starter course. Lukazinski revelled in it. Not bad playing Leporello, even if his master was no Don Juan.

And Jagna. To this swarm of bumble bees he appeared no less fantastical than the human soul depicted by the monk, with one crucial difference: he did not stand at the lectern in habit and skullcap, but showed from an armchair his disturbingly, heart-throbbingly lovely face and eyes, mouth, expressive hands. How glad they were at first, having climbed up five storeys, instead of unrelieved erudition to have come face to face with Jagna. Then they grew annoyed with the monk for the effect he had on this man. The ladies, received with all propriety in the sitting room of his apartment, or at a restaurant for dinner, had to engage with him in conversations that – touched on the deepest questions. Jagna could not shake free from the trains of thought elaborated by the Dominican. The ladies kept urging him to talk to the Dominican, he was his best pupil, he should take up with him this topic they'd just broached and alas been unable to drop, the monk would be delighted. But Jagna had no wish to do so, he wanted to discuss it with them, their suggestion irritated him. He avoided the monk.

But all the more passionate were his conversations with the ladies in their lovely dresses, the ripe flesh and blood that attended him perfumed and draped in bright silks. Conversations with the wonderful unapproachable man became a nightmare for the ladies, enough to bring bitter tears to their eyes. You hang onto him like a hooked fish while he dangles on the theoretical profundities of saintly Thomas. You sit by orchids, on thick carpets, music tinkles, you drink sweet wine and relish the enchanting sight of a man you might have been very happy with. But if sometimes you forget yourself and touch that hand, the response is a look of profound suspicion. You let go, chilled, aghast. My God, what was that?

In the enchanted darkened studio the monk addressed his congregation, whose numbers did not diminish, on the Values of Life. Man is the High Priest of creation. He bears a great responsibility. Everything strives towards the Spiritual. For although Man shares vegetative activity with plants, and sensory activity with animals, he has no real sensory soul of his own. Its role has been taken over by a Spirit-Soul. When he uttered the word 'spirit-soul', out of the darkness where the congregation sat came a lone, deeply affirming "Yes". The monk, pleasantly surprised, looked up from his papers, people turned in their chairs, it was young Mr Jagna, chin resting on the seatback in front of him. You smile at one another, you know his passionate interest in these expositions. The monk emphasised that in man's threefold life the streams do not run parallel alongside each other, but constantly intermingle in such a way that the lower life makes a foundation for the higher, and the higher refines the lower. Where, accordingly, everything is inclined to subject itself to the Spiritual, it is exceedingly perverse of modern man to turn things upside down by placing the Spiritual at the service of the Sensory.

Now you are in a very rarefied sphere. Refined and gratified, you stand and shake yourself for the transition back to the sadly inevitable mundane world.

Gradually the figures of Jagna and Lukazinski became disagreeable to the monk. This arose from stories in which the young skirt-chaser persisted in quite transparent aims, thereby unexpectedly illustrating the meaning of his lectures. Here in the attic studio Satan dared to show himself in this lovely mask, what's more had been led here by a Church dignitary. At the next meeting the monk angrily read out the scheduled chapter on the Provenance of Mankind. The human soul is not derived from matter, or from parents, but comes into existence only through the creative power of God. The same is true of the soul of the first man. As for the theory of man's descent from monkeys, it is utterly false. And now the monk launched into a vigorous and uncharacteristic rant. He admonished against laughing at monkeys. You can only weep for them. They are the mirror image of wicked and corrupt humanity. They are greedy, mischievous, vain, they imitate true people in such a way that one can speak bluntly of deception by evil spirits. Their cunning is repugnant. In fact the whole animal kingdom is replete with mocking images of humanity. Oh, if only those who have been blessed with the Holy Scriptures would also read the terrible book of Nature, where their shame is pilloried.

Following this tirade the monk invited young Jagna to meet with him in the host's private quarters. But the monk's intention misfired. For he had never seen anyone so full of fear and trembling. Instead of launching into Jagna he had to speak kindly to him, release him with soothing words, and appoint a further meeting next day in the nearby home of the priest with whom he lodged.

And with that, Jagna was finished with the philosophico-religious course. Distraught he left the monk's room, skirted the studio and called Lukazinski to him in the cloakroom, where the shocked gatekeeper took him in charge. "Put on your coat," Jagna spat. Outside as they drove through a snow shower to their hotel, Jagna cursed and in his room replayed the conversation for Lukazinski, who found it incomprehensible.

"For God's sake, Mr Jagna, there must be more to it than that. Else how could you wind yourself up into such a state?"

Jagna, who had taken time only to fling his fur coat and cane onto a chair in the large comfortable room, paced seething, pale, trembling, eyes big and deepset, between mirror and sofa, from window to door, from one corner to the other.

"It's enough. It's quite enough. Who is he to drag me to a reckoning? To whom do I owe a reckoning? What for? Who is this person? This monk?"

"But he said nothing."

"He made me shout out."

Lukazinski recalled his own sins, maybe some of the ladies had mentioned something in confession, an awkward situation, the monk had targeted the wrong man. "Mr Jagna, please allow me to seek out the clerical gentleman tomorrow on your behalf."

"You're crazy. You plan to betray me, deliver me up to this fellow."

For God's sake, what's happening here? "Well, if you don't want me to, of course I shan't go. I just thought I might be able to help."

Jagna, who had completely lost his voice, whispered: "Going to that, to that..." And he lowered himself onto the sofa, eyes wide, inwardly agitated: "We should extend not so much as a finger to them. Why did I have to go there? To learn something. Now he uses his position against me. He wants me. The Church is determined to have me."

"Is that what he said?"

"They're trying to snare me. Why else did he summon me?" Jagna pounded the table with both fists: "Speaking to me as if I were a child."

"You didn't have to go."

"He took me by surprise. I wasn't prepared. He thought I'd surrender. He was going to shanghai me. He knew I'd had a pious upbringing, so he hoped to snare me." He paced up and down: "I need no Church over me. Just wait! Before you know it they'll restore the Inquisition."

Lukazinski's suggestion next morning – they should simply move on – fell on stony ground. He wanted revenge. At noon Lukazinski, who sought out the monk without telling his master, learned nothing useful. The monk was most cordial, had been delighted with Jagna's visit, it had made an extraordinarily positive impression on him. Another surprise for Lukazinski, that Jagna had made a good impression on the monk. "He is a shy, profoundly sensitive person," the Dominican said. "God granted him beauty and thereby set him apart. This imposes a heavy burden on the young man, which obviously he feels. We want to help him bear it."

Jagna remained in a belligerent indecisive mood during the following weeks. The lecture course was over for him. Lukazinski maintained contact with ladies from the course, and saw how they mourned his absence: even the monk looks round for you every evening and asks what the problem is, of course some have been gossiping, but that's not enough to put off a man like Jagna. Letters and flowers arrived at the hotel, Lukazinski displayed them in the sitting room, he knew Jagna liked that. Strange, he stood for ages stroking and sniffing the bouquets in their vases. If only he'd treat one of the donors so tenderly. He'd managed it with the Extra, two whole weeks.

A lady said to Lukazinski: "He'll not delight us any more. I'm not unhappy. Others nurse their wounds. But I can tell you why, Lukas. That man is the vainest, most arrogant, most prideful creature ever to tread God's earth. He has immeasurable wealth, and his beauty is a sin. He knows it, and they all adore him. The man is an old-time despot, a sultan living up there in his palace. You can't even kiss his feet. Emperors in old Byzantium must have looked like that. And yet he is no Byzantine emperor. We – don't laugh – we did come onto him a little too strongly, the gentleman showed himself ungracious, but the monk took a gamble. And he can't tolerate that. Now his Polish Highness is in a sulk..."

Lukazinski considered, shook his head: "I've been with him three years. I'm never allowed to come too close. If he won't talk, I can't ask. I'm a simple man, I don't understand him."

"Princes relish an excessive solitude."

"You're joking. We get on well, because he knows I don't understand him. He values that. He keeps his cards close to his chest."

"And is he unhappy? A lost love?"

"It's nonsense to talk of love where he's concerned. I've been with him three years."

Jagna determined to enjoy his stay in Munich. He settled in. He became easier to engage with. The gatekeeper was no longer needed. He was a pushover for women, but in a strange way that did not please all. He took them not as ladies, girls, but as things, animals. Like a trainer he made them jump like a poodle, hup! through the hoop, done. It was horrible, debasing. But he could do nothing else. Several relished it nonetheless, and clung to him.

Some ladies from the course came. Lukazinski asked him to keep his hands off, in case of scandal. "Why not scandal? When were we ever scared, Lukazinski?" Lukazinski sighed, Jagna's mother had written, the Church dignitary had given good reports of her son, she hoped he was keeping to the path, the prelate said Jagna looked like a feather from an angel's wing.

Then this happened. A scientific conference took place in the city, attracting worthies from the region. Jagna wound the big scarf around his throat and mouth, left the hotel and strolled along the streets. In a passage beside an umbrella shop he spied a not quite young person, a neat woman, lady perhaps, middle class, looking in the window. She attracted him from behind and, when she turned aside, from the front as well. Her face was broad, healthy and stolid, with a fresh healthy complexion. She's an honest housewife, has a husband and two brats – why is it, the question darted through his brain, that I feel a connection with this woman that I never feel with one of my fine ladies, why can't the fine ladies give me this, why must I always go to these? Then he stood beside her at the display window. She will surely move away. And she did. He followed her, determined to pursue the matter. The prey was run to earth in a dark alley with no one about. She only wanted to be unobserved. She acted shocked, uncertain. And then went with him. Since she kept stopping, it seemed she had a mind to flee but did not know when or how.

In the company of women who meant nothing to him, Jagna was calculating, capable of anything. The woman's banal face, simple manner, the coarse cut of her clothes, made her wonderfully appealing. He'll soon find out who she is. It's like peeling an onion. Perhaps she's come out looking for adventure, he's trapped her as a snake traps a bird, and she doesn't know which way to turn. She wanted to buy an umbrella, she'd been visiting someone, meant to go home for supper, lay the table, those hungry sparrows her husband and two children would already be standing around the table drooling. And here he was, strolling with her.

She could not pull away from this proud figure with its ivory features and inexhaustible, impudent, inconsequential chatter. Truly, my child, you need feel no embarrassment walking beside me in your cheap winter coat, finer and more experienced creatures than you have clung to me.

And he didn't beat about the bush. She was outraged when he pushed her into a cheap hotel in a side street they happened to be passing, their conversation had not gone very far, she knew nothing about him, nor he of her. But she was unable to pull away from this man who had stood beside her at the umbrella shop. She wept in the street outside the old grey hotel, yet dared not run away. And before she had thought it through he rang the bell, a maid with a candle opened up, and three minutes later they were in a narrow shabby room, a single bed along one wall, along the other a table with a green water pitcher and two glasses with no tray, a metal stand by the door with washbasin, ewer and hand towels. Whitewashed walls bare of pictures, a gas lamp on the ceiling. Everything declared without pretence: "This will do."

There was no lengthy love talk.

Two hours later, when she wanted to go, he would not let her. She implored. He was merciless. She must stay. And she stayed. They slept till morning. Then he phoned his hotel and spoke to Lukazinski, who brought cash. Jagna did not know when he would return to their hotel. He had a wonderful time all that day. The respectable woman, who refused to reveal her name, was desperate to go, he wouldn't let her leave the hotel, they ate there, he wanted to be with her one more day and night. She begged him at least to let her send a message to her husband – they'll be looking for me, I'm ruined – but he prevailed, and she knew this would be the only occasion, never again, and threw herself into his arms and it was like a veritable abyss.

The thought twitched in him during those hours: I'm in my grave again, nothing in the world makes me happier, I'd like to stay here, stay here forever, for the rest of my life. Oh, if only I'd been born here, if only my whole existence had taken this course. Cursed the parents who bore me, they let me go bad and become the blackguard I am.

And he clasped her tight, this blissful woman. How long before I send you on your way and you will be nothing and I shall be nothing.

≈≈≈

His desire to play with her, frighten her, oh this desire grew and was great and enormously authentic, he loved her for it, and she was in ecstasy when his kisses made this plain.

In the afternoon at coffee in the hotel's lounge – they never left the little hotel – she told him something of herself. Little housekeeping worries. She had come on a week's visit with her husband to a scientific conference, her husband was a professor, a poorly paid science teacher, she had to make it stretch, they needed this and that for themselves and the children – she really did have two children, which pleased Jagna, he gave her a hug across the table – she explained that everything was terribly difficult and every month when payday came it involved more juggling.

Then Jagna asked if he might make her a little present, and pushed a banknote across, he had no intention of insulting her, she went red, stared, clutched his hand imploringly, he insisted on stuffing the note into her handbag, she passed a hand over her eyes, but he put his arm around her again as they sat there, she felt blissful at his side, and as they sat cheek to cheek she thought: I'm glad my husband brought me along to the conference, I'll make him feel better, bring him something, his cigars, oh if only I could take this man home with me, he could live in the same street and bring me presents now and then, I could be an even better housekeeper.

She consented to remain his prisoner for one more night in the hotel, he had the chambermaid buy necessaries, underwear, comb.

But while he was trying to decide what should happen, that

night brought it to an unexpected, wonderful conclusion. The police turned up. The hotel was notorious. At first, when she heard the knocking and the command: "Open up! Police!" the woman wanted to leap up and throw herself from the window. As Jagna put on some clothes and opened the door, she hid under the bedclothes. A detective showed his badge, allowed Jagna to provide proof of identity at the door. Then a whole gaggle came along. Meanwhile Jagna finished dressing. It was a jolly adventure, a tremendous conclusion, he thought only of the woman, relished her as she dressed, jabbering in confusion, tried to reach the window, was held back.

She had no papers. They would not let her off, she had to go with the police. And as he stood there in fur coat and hat, booted and spurred, the scene brought him one more big pleasure. The officer asked how he had met this woman. The answer was easy. They were talking in the little gaslit corridor, the door to the room stood half open, the chambermaid was helping the woman dress, they must hurry. So Jagna replied: "I spoke to her outside a shop, she let me take her along, I paid her."

From inside the room the woman screamed, the officer angrily shut the door, it was night, they should be quiet. Jagna looked at him and shrugged:

"I paid her. She can't deny it. She explained her circumstances to me. There's a little contribution there on the table."

Jagna can leave. He turned slowly away listening in delight and love to the woman's screams. He turned back: "Perhaps I can help calm her."

He stepped past the detective, opened the door himself, she was sitting bolt upright, hat on her head, she hit him in the face, the chambermaid shouted: "Go away, sir!" He went, it was fine, even though his lip was split.

And then, fur collar upturned, he strolled slowly along the deathly silent dark streets to his hotel, and Lukazinski was astonished to be woken up to spend an hour sitting on his bed chatting, with his bleeding lip and a glass of cognac, in an excellent mood.

≈≈≈

The road to crime was paved with such pleasures. When Jagna concluded the tale, Lukazinski declared bluntly that he found his behaviour abhorrent. His cold smug master did not lose composure, stressed that he was not about to argue morality when not even clerics could make progress in that direction. "The woman came with me, the professor's wife, and she even stayed. Then she ran out of breath. I was stronger than her. She wasn't up to it. Pah, it should be a matter of indifference to us if once in a while we're asked to pay."

After the adventure with the professor's wife, things really did take a turn. Jagna was unstoppable. Lukazinski urged him to return to his parents' estate, even travelled there himself to report to Jagna's mother how things stood with her son, but not too explicitly in case he himself might attract blame. They concluded that his allowance was too high, she reduced the remittances. It made no impression on Jagna. When Lukazinski reported that his parents' income was dropping, he really should find a proper profession, maybe take an interest in the estate in the not too distant future, Jagna laughed him off: "Whatever for?"

"They're letting it fall into ruin, Mr Jagna. The managers are useless."

"So, that's life, why shouldn't they go under, no one can stop them. At the worst we shall have no income. The world will go on. Perhaps even without us."

The conversation had reached a critical point. Lukazinski did not press it further. Jagna himself reverted to it a few days later, his face drawn and sallow: "Your talk of my income has done me good. I've seen people here who have a regular income. I've no wish to be like them."

He pulled petals from flowers and blew them across the table. Suddenly he ground his teeth, swung his fists, his voice was almost restored to its usual rasp: "Would you like to see my heart?" Jagna suddenly brandished a balled fist: "It's like this, small, hard, fat, a fat fellow, an old fellow, sitting idle beside the hearth, warms himself, drinks, and won't be spoken to. A peasant, a ruffian, a donkey. When you come to him he sleeps and eats and drinks and is unavailable for consultation. The world might be ending, and he's not available. If you throw me in the water, the body rots away around it, but this thing in my breast wriggles out, rolls in the sand, and there it lies and beats and goes on living. If I could just grab it with my hands and rip it out to see what it's made of. Lukazinski, I dream sometimes, ergo I'm alive, ergo I exist. Occasionally I recall something by the light of day. I assure you I am speechless to think that I can dream."

"What's wrong, Mr Jagna?"

"I don't know." Jagna has turned his face away with a sob: "I believe it would be best to go off to war, to battle. I was born at the wrong time. That's the problem."

Lukazinski was astonished at this unwonted flow of words, it was not a good sign. Jagna's whole demeanour was wild and uncertain. "Yes, into battle! You fling yourself into the struggle, bullets, explosions, wounds, death, and an end to the whole mess."

Lukazinski grasped him by the shoulders: "Such dreams, in broad daylight."

Jagna, by the wall, frowned, preoccupied by something: "Wait. So they want to keep me on a tighter rein. Good. I shall join the army."

"We talked about that."

"It's a thought." But it came not to departure and a trip to the recruitment office, but to a conventional affair, albeit with a gruesome twist.

≈≈≈

In a bar Jagna made the acquaintance of two young Germans. They went together to gambling clubs. The two young Germans were, like him, sons of rich parents and had passions that helped them while away their lives: gambling, sports, alcohol. They were farther down that road than Jagna. They were utterly reckless. They owned motors that they took on wild road trips. From them Jagna learned, among other things, the joys of speed and an amusing trick for picking up passers-by and deriving some sort of entertainment from them. These were mostly women. Since they raced on, never alighting, soon they were everywhere and nowhere, and on the way all laws were suspended.

Once Jagna was returning with Lukazinski from a trip to the mountains. Traffic into the city was slow. Driving close to the footpath, by the light of a street lamp he saw a solitary lady turn slowly into a dark side alley. He made Lukazinski climb out and set off in pursuit. Success! The pretty lady with the stylish face behind a veil – little hat perched like a shell on the back of her wavy black hair, long mohair coat, violet dress, she was wearing high shiny overshoes – pointed the way into the city under the light of the corner lamp. And when she smiled because he stood there trying to think up another question, he smiled too, and after a few questions about the suburb they happened to find themselves in, he invited her to ride into the city with them. They had dinner that night, he brought her back. She allowed herself to be picked up next afternoon for an excursion, he had no idea who he was dealing with. Now he managed a good look at her.

She was almost as tall as him. She wore the mohair coat open, revealing a shiny black dress with no belt, a silver guitar hung at her breast under the wide décolletage. Her full face radiated vitality, her lips were generous, thick, rising in the middle and falling in a curious way at the corners, so she always seemed to be sulking. Her hair was parted in the middle, to fall in a dense bun at her neck. At the moment when she took her seat beside him in the car and tucked the coat away behind her, Jagna was enchanted with the way she put her left hand up to the bun and ruffled it while she was talking. She rolled her r's.

As they drove she confided her misfortunes to him. Her husband had left her a week ago, she was looking for someone she could speak frankly with. Then he had an irrepressible feeling: he did not know how this would unfold. He hung in lecherous excitement on every word she said, he had her on a line, must reel her in. She said she was sure her husband would come back, he'd done this before, it was hard for her to put such things behind her but she loved him, he had given her life meaning, so she was grateful to him, he was a famous orchestral conductor in the city, a composer too, and his best work still lay ahead of him.

As evening came after this friendly calm day and they stopped outside her suburban house, it was already inevitable she would invite him – maybe he'll decline – to spend half an hour with her. They drank tea. And then – initiated nervously by her, he held back – a love scene played out. She offered herself, he lost all restraint.

What happened to her, how he demeaned and shamed her and left her lying there, belongs in the same chapter that began with the professor's wife. This time it ended just before a death. He said: I am in an abyss, one day it will end like this.

She waited for him next day and the three days following. Letters came from her husband. In her disgraced condition she had no way to respond. She wanted an apology from Jagna, some sign of humanity. Nothing came. She had fallen into the hands of a scoundrel.

And just at this time it happened that a minister's train was attacked in central Germany, the track was destroyed, several witnesses saw a suspicious man with a motor car at the site of the incident. They gave a thorough description, and when this woman who was also seeking a missing man saw the description on the wanted posters, the thought came to her in icy horror: it's the man who was with me, it's him! She was absolutely sure of it for a day and a night. Next morning the post brought another letter from her husband announcing his return, and imploring her to forgive him this time too. She dressed, walked past the concierge, and in a wood threw herself under a suburban train.

Jagna's name did not emerge in this affair, she left not a trace of it in the intimate suicide note to her husband, in which she asked forgiveness. But Jagna was brought into the case through the crude treachery of his two young German friends. He had told these cronies about his adventure, and they thought little of it. But now, with the suicide in the papers attracting attention because of the husband's name, they discovered scope for mischief. Let's do an experiment, see how the proud Pole reacts. Through one of their ladies they provided information to a reporter from an afternoon scandal sheet, he wrote up a report that in its essentials was not far from the truth. The police called the Pole in. He declined to respond to the story in that rag, did not deny knowing the lady. Anyway it was a private matter, surely they don't accuse him of pushing her under the train. They let him go. But a week after the funeral the husband barged into the hotel, and Jagna let Lukazinski show him in.

A lamentable sight. Tall Jagna, wrapped in a green silk dressing gown, stood up from his armchair to face a young man in black, as tall as he, with a brown goatee, twisting a black slouch hat in his hands. As Lukazinski closed the door behind him and he had his first glimpse of Jagna – this is the room, this the man – his legs gave way and he sank to his knees on the carpet by the door, hands outstretched, and groaned and groaned. Jagna came to his aid. He had let him in to find out what else the two Germans might have revealed. The man allowed himself to be lifted up, and staggered to an armchair on the other side of the table. Jagna pushed the blue vase aside to see him.

"You must excuse me for troubling you with matters that strictly speaking only concern my family. You have become involved in a most shocking manner. I never suspected, I never envisaged this, it's all my fault." And he bent groaning over his hat, which he clutched to his knees in both hands.

Jagna regarded him.

"Marianne left me a letter giving no details. Then I read this in the paper. You refused to explain. I understand. But I can't see clearly. It's like being hit by lightning. She told me nothing. What happened?"

Jagna: "Did someone send you here?"

"No no. She's my wife. When I left her she was in blooming health. My unhappy fate drove me away, my damnable frivolity, I depended on Marianne. If I could be sure of anyone, anything in the world, it was Marianne. What happened? Tell me. I shall be struggling with this for the rest of my life."

"You read all about it in the paper."

"Why do you say that? I never believed it for a second."

"Did you believe your wife could kill herself, before this?"

The man shifted and looked across the table: "No."

"Well then."

"The paper said you'd never seen my wife before, and didn't see her in the days before her death." – "It's true."

"No one believes it. You were having an affair with her. It's my fault. She destroyed your letters." – "No."

"And when I left she threw herself at you and then she made an end of it."

"Apparently she received a last letter from you."

"She couldn't trust me any more. She regretted her affair with you."

"If you like."

"Please, don't say such things: if you like. Consider, Mr Jagna, every word you say here – for this will be our only conversation – will be branded on my brain until I die. I shall forever hear: if you like. I do not like. I must settle accounts between her and me. I have placed her hat, her little veil on the table in our house, her mohair coat on a chair, just as if she's about to go out and I ask her where to. And the umbrella with the bird's head, no doubt you remember it."

"I don't remember it."

"You do. She'd carried it for half a year. Perhaps you gave it her."

"I gave her no presents."

"You keep to your story because you refuse to grant me the truth. But that is only because you don't know how relations were between Marianne and me."

"Sir, please, I do not ask for details of your family circumstances."

The man rested an arm on the table, hesitated: "But you knew my wife." – "Yes."

"Do you hate me?" – "No." Jagna clenched his teeth.

"Then you'll understand why I'm here begging for help. Oh Mr Jagna, if you only knew everything that's happened, I'm broken, her mother knows of the tragedy and hovers between life and death. Nothing can help us, only truth. Tell me the truth, unadorned, keep nothing back, don't think to spare me, I've no desire for games at a time like this. And for Marianne's sake, who surely meant something to you and whose husband I remained to the last, in spite of everything." Now he was sobbing: "I was faithful to her, I never meant it seriously, I swear, I raise my voice to God, he shall judge if I'm telling the truth, she must have told you otherwise. I was good to her, I loved her, she was everything to me, everything, my life."

"Then why did you abandon her?"

"She should have trusted me during those months, I could have explained to her."

"What months?"

"When you were seeing her."

"I told you, I knew her for just two days."

The man sat upright in the armchair, rested his head on one hand. He searched Jagna's face, Jagna did not flinch.

"So it is true?"

Jagna said nothing.

"Then I don't understand."

Jagna made as if to rise and looked irritably around the room, to the door, the meeting was coming to an end. The man understood. He stood, gazed into his hat but made no move.

"This conversation cannot end like this, Mr Jagna. You insist you knew her for just two days. I'm not the kind of man who as a husband demands an accounting in such a situation. But an explanation, dear Heaven, after I've told you everything, after you see what a terrible riddle this death is for us all, you who experienced the last days, at least the last days, with her, you must surely help with an explanation."

"I spent two days with her. Experienced is too strong a word. Those were not the last days before her death."

"And what happened in those two days, grant me this at least."

"No."

"Why not?"

"Because – I have no connection with you. This conversation

is now really at an end."

But the man just stood there looking at Jagna, the handsome stony fellow in the green dressing gown which he now drew tighter around him.

And suddenly the man, as he stood there looking at Jagna, seemed seized by emotion. He saw Jagna – with Marianne's eyes. He stood before him – like Marianne, who had been his wife, and this is a fine elegant man, a seducer according to the newspapers, and he did not deny it, a man who exploited her forlorn state and then threw her away.

And without conscious thought he drew a revolver from his coat pocket, and fired.

Jagna, who had been expecting this ever since the man arrived, fell to one side and fired from below simultaneously with the man's second shot, just as Lukazinski came rushing in.

Jagna was hit behind the ear. The man lay motionless.

The man died next day in hospital, liver wound, internal bleeding. They extracted the bullet from Jagna. A week later he was transferred to a prison hospital. Public opinion would not allow Jagna, who had murdered the husband after the wife, to go free. They needed to pin something on him, and under pressure of public concern a wide-ranging investigation of the circumstances was launched.

But the Pole, lying in the prison hospital, was like a horse that shied and ran away with the cart, crashed the cart and now stands trembling and foam-flecked. Other prisoners pushed newspapers at him with gossip about his case. He would not read them. Lukazinski sat on his bed, he felt it was partly his fault, wavered between concern for his employer and anxiety about his own position. Jagna consoled him from under thick bandages. Once he expressed a view of his situation: "Why all the fuss? It's all as it should be. The woman wanted a bit of fun with me, and she had some. I took my fun. I can't offer endless entertainment. Then that musician. An idiot. I spared him a lifetime of arguing with his wife. Now he's caught up with her after only a week's delay. They can both slander me up there, and sort out all their issues."

The vigorous Dominican from the lecture course visited. He thought the invalid, caught up in some bloodcurdling affair, needed talking to. Jagna was obdurate. He told the monk: "Why come to me in particular. Talk to anyone else but me. Talk to yourself."

The monk couldn't believe his ears, he controlled himself: "I believe we're all sinners. But I believe in God and the salvation he brings."

Jagna shrugged, indifferent. The monk became angry, he bent over the invalid: "Are you baptised? Are you a Christian?"

"Baptised but no Christian. It's all right for an evening's conversation, but it leads nowhere."

"Unhappy wretch. You don't believe in God?"

"No, certainly not."

When the monk had gone, the patients in the neighbouring beds started applauding Jagna. He heard, blanket pulled over his head.

He was collected by Lukazinski. The investigation was closed. He allowed himself to be led back to his country like a bull on a rope. But he did not go on to his home, to his mother. He stayed in Cracow, where he wandered aimlessly. He sat silent for hours in St Mary's church. At first Lukazinski feared he would revert to his bad old ways. He wrote to Jagna's mother: "He seems to be growing pious. He started down this road already in Munich. Now he seems set on it. It gives me pleasure to report this."

But one day Jagna ran away. The letter he left behind read: "You will have to do without me for a few weeks. I do not see why I need a guardian. You will recall our discussion after you heard from my parents that my allowance was to be curtailed. I was supposed to learn a sensible trade. My dear man, I have known for a long time all the sensible things a man can learn. On that occasion I made desperate and stupid remarks about my heart. My heart is clever enough. But you are all too modest. There is nothing to restrain us. People forge ahead. I could forge even farther ahead. You know how far I went along that road. I do not enjoy it any more. I shudder in the face of the next stage, but know nothing other than the next stage. Then again, I fail to see why a man has a head. You assume that the purpose of a man's head is to persuade him to go along with the general enterprise. I think otherwise, but have not yet reached the end.

"You will see me again in a few weeks, provided you do not alert the police or come hunting for me yourself."

Despite this, Lukazinski sought out several detectives through his social contacts. Jagna must have spotted them, because he disappeared from various small mountain resorts in the Carpathians as soon as the detectives confirmed his presence. The cash he had taken with him would be exhausted within two months. He made no contact.

Now the police were alerted. After a few months they closed the case. Jagna was nowhere to be found within the country. He might have gone abroad.

He remained missing.

The two young Germans

THE TWO YOUNG Germans first met at school. Their fathers were already acquainted, their origins were in the North Sea fishing industry, together they had established a fish smoking and preserving business. Little by little they built up a small fleet, and grew rich. The father of one was long since dead. The father of the other had still lived until a few years before, grey-haired and cheerful, in a decaying villa near Berlin.

While still at school the two young men understood very well that if you want to get on you must study hard and work hard. This attitude was shared by the rest of their class, a few numskulls excepted. At home their fathers lectured them:

"You can't rely on people... People are worse than ravening beasts... One hand washes the other... There's no such thing as free... If you've nothing to offer, people will show no mercy... Keep your chin up...

"As soon as we're dead people will pester you, try to trip

you, you'll be left without a penny. Read about the Rockefellers, Vanderbilts, all the railroad and oil kings. Then you'll know how it goes. Not all beggars in the street were born beggars, some were fleeced alive. But the Rockefellers and Vanderbilts are on top, they control politics, and if they want they build churches, schools, and no one interferes with them. If you flirt with the workers, in the fashion of today, you may think yourselves sophisticated, but we want nothing to do with sons like that, we'll disinherit you."

The young men had no thought of such folly. From the heart they took life seriously. They were the cleverest in their talented class. By the time they left school they played sports, their first love affairs were behind them. They threw themselves into university studies in various faculties, Science, Law, History, Philosophy. It seemed a little Faustian, but was rather something else: they aimed to peep behind the curtain of these disciplines so that, later on, philosophers and learned men could not pull the wool over their eyes. But even without this, the lay of the land was already clear to them.

They were a different breed of youth than those earlier legions of poets and dreamers who stood around, lay around, smoked, composed verses, played music, debated far into the night. Erwin Posten and Heinrich Klinkert studied in order to cope with their times, and when they cast an eye over history they could find no time that suited them better than the twenties of the twentieth century. The so-called World War had just ended, Germany was in the throes of powerful changes. You had to know the score if you wanted to seize the day, and anything with any strength was drawn to seize the day because all was in flux, state, society, church, laity, industry, trade.

Erwin Posten was the stronger of the two. Of medium height, broad, everything about him was broad, he was sculpted in right angles, his nose was broad and so his eyes, set deep in their sockets, lay far apart in the expanse of his face, and a thick fold of skin ran like a train on a mountain track from eyebrow to eyebrow across the top of his nose, lending him a strangely glowering air even when he was cheerful. Football and rowing had developed his shoulders and legs. Clearly this muscular chap was not to be trifled with. From early on he was drawn to marriage and family; the young stalwart soon gave up the usual nonsense with females. This too set him apart from the young men of earlier days. He avoided love affairs because they led nowhere, and he found the emotional wear and tear abhorrent. Airy youths with higher interests and a mincing walk made him nauseous, and the same went for his friend Klinkert.

Both considered their country, Germany, horribly obsolete from top to bottom, everywhere you saw signs of a disintegrating moribund age. There were student lodges where old songs were sung and useless sabres were worn; what good were romantic castles and knights, they were all idlers, ruining themselves with drink. The female students were better, they understood the times and crammed diligently for exams. They tried to out-compete the men, otherwise picked up whatever lay in their path. But the stupid thing was, they thought they should excel in manliness, the sad stale masculinity of the day. This came from their status as slaves yearning for freedom; now they made love in every way, a phenomenon straight from the middle of the previous century. In the main, the students at the university were as pathetic as you might expect. A dull crowd from common stock, not bad, hoping for a foot in the professions, but what a tepid and scatterbrained crowd, sleepwalking its way to the cultivation of its so-called mind, a vegetable patch good only for a dog to lift its leg.

Posten's friend and contemporary Klinkert had the same practical and sober outlook, but was less tough and thuggish than Posten, who really was a ruffian. Klinkert's childhood home harboured an educated mother, who died not long after the imperious father. From her he had acquired a certain sense of "ideology", to Posten's annoyance. But Klinkert overcame his atavistic mood changes and directed them into music; he was an excellent pianist, Schumann and Brahms his favourite composers.

The experience of the two youths during those few years at universities in Berlin and elsewhere differed from the boisterous fraternities of an earlier and the vegetable passivity of a later period. *"That I may detect the inmost force Which binds the world, and guides its course; Its germs, productive powers explore, And rummage in empty words no more!"* as the learned sorcerer Faust declared. These two certainly had no desire to rummage in words. What holds the world together, at heart, is the Deed. The only question was: what deed?

≈≈≈

Klinkert took a young lady with him to Heidelberg on the Neckar, an elegant thing who played housewife in his apartment – "She's an orphan, an officer's daughter," he excused himself to Posten, "I'm giving her a helping hand for a year or two, and she's nice to have around" – for Klinkert must have his comforts. He was taller and thinner than Posten, had a severe, clean-shaven face, grey penetrating eyes. He provided his little group (a few young people swiftly gravitated to them) with essential food for thought.

They had no time for the state they lived in, this "Weimar abortion". It was a blessing to have such a state, for it was weak; the previous one had been no less rotten, but robust. "Our strength lies in technology and industry. We have left behind a soft sleazy age. We live in the age of steel. We tolerate no debate about the utility or inutility of money, possessions, poverty, about 'the new order' and so on. Anyone waiting for justice, humanity and the Bible has already lost. Phrases about 'Mammonism' and 'the equality of man' are just as contrived and empty as their opposites. We must understand that there is no time left. Every superfluous thought is as damaging as grit in the gears.

"Our conception of morality derives neither from the Gospels nor from Kant, not from Nietzsche, nor from ourselves. We proceed logically, according to current circumstances. Our intelligence kicks in when the situation demands it. Immorality is whatever does not fit the situation. Immorality is refusing to let the situation decide. On what grounds can you refuse the situation its rights? On grounds of inadequate precision, attachment to superannuated ideas. – It all depends on what we want: reality, or merely the dregs of thought. Conserving the past is a task for museums. We are not even free to leave things as they are. Things simply don't stay as they are. And power relations change even if you leave them to themselves.

"You must put to the test the endowment you carry within you of spirit, feelings, will – what you usually think of as your Self. We are surrounded and filled by ghosts! We are ghosts! This is not to impugn our parents and grandparents. Thousands and thousands of people spend their whole life wrapping their flesh around dead wishes. Meanwhile, reality becomes stunted. Primitive tribes practice a cult of the dead, nothing but prayers and sacrifice. We sacrifice ourselves to the dead. Could anything be more stupid, was there ever a greedier Moloch than the one we sacrifice ourselves to?"

Then thoughts were set in train that harked back to the teachings of the late Klinkert and Posten *pères*. "Don't think it's all right to be lazy just because you have thoughts, education, material comforts. Others will overtake you. You can't hide yourself away like Harpagon with his coins and his thoughts and bury them in the garden. For even if *you* don't know what's going on, others do."

Klinkert sat upright on his backless stool. It was the only one of its kind in this low room. A big light-grey sofa along the wall filled one corner, a big carpet with a red and black pattern, a small bookstand with about fifty books in two rows, under the wide window a metal desk with attachments, half a dozen light grey metal chairs. Klinkert's place was on the stool at the window; you couldn't imagine him lounging back.

Klinkert explained: "The big, clear, simple examplar is not the noble hero-figure of olden times. The momentous times of great men lie behind us. Our symbol is the Machine. Some say that God created mankind. If so – let's assume – then we are now in an age when the Created has overtaken the Creator as the order of the day. We have brought forth machines, and they are the masters to our apprentices, and seem destined to overtake us."

From his waistcoat pocket he pulled out a small pair of scissors on a chain: "Christians used to carry a cross around with them, a remarkable custom, very widespread, people fought wars over it, fortunately we no longer understand this. There's nothing useless about these nickel scissors, two loops for the fingers, you squeeze, it cuts. That's our style: clear, relevant, correct. If you read an old book and find yourself puzzling over cockeyed notions, and then look at these scissors, you have to thank them, they restore your balance. The scissors are the better philosopher. They stand above all those ancient heroes. My scissors remind me of Socrates, who went among the fatal Sophists and with a few simple questions shook them out of their received ideas. The masses didn't like this, being lazy, abstract, a dead object. What do the masses like? Schnapps. Give them schnapps and you're their god. If it was all up to the masses, we'd still be sitting in the jungle."

His girlfriend was the ash-blonde Marie Schön, a Catholic, who worshipped him. She asked her stereotypical questions, he listened patiently, for despite his unbending nature Klinkert was always extremely courteous and patient.

"Well yes, it's all totally true, so totally right what you say, Heinrich. I think we all feel it. But would you I wonder explain to us now how we should conduct ourselves and what you propose. I quoted Hamlet to you a little while ago: 'The world is out of joint – O cursèd spite, That ever I was born to set it right!' You don't like that quote, but I don't understand why not."

Klinkert nodded, thoughtful and obliging, his expression unchanged: "The world is not out of joint, Marie. Nor are we out of joint. The world is on the brink of going rotten through our own cowardice and lack of clarity."

She sighed: "Your answers are all like that, Heinrich. I'm sure we'd like to hear more. You see, Nietzsche said the same thing about the masses. Perhaps you have the same idea as him."

He raised a hand and snapped his fingers: "*Pas du tout.* I grant him the Superman and Dionysus. Hymns are remote from me."

He picked up a leaflet lying nearby: "Someone writes here: 'The modern world, in the fullness of its power, in possession of a tremendous technical capital, thoroughly infused with purely objective methods, has failed to create alongside this a politics, an ethics, an ideal, a civil or criminal legal system, capable of harmonising with the forms of life it has brought forth, or even with the forms of thought that have imposed themselves gradually on everyone as a result of the general spread and expansion of a specifically scientific spirit.' That's the Frenchman Paul Valéry. I make no enquiries as to politics, ethics, ideals. I dispute that the modern world is suffused with objective methods. The exact opposite is true. It is suffused with mythology, with convictions, beliefs, the dross of earlier centuries. These pass themselves off as reality in the midst of our present reality. It's as if at carnival time all the beggars and tramps pour into town, and are allowed to sit at table with everyone else. So they eat everything up. No forms of thought are imposed on the people of today. What we need to do, in fact, is create forms of thought suited to the age. In reality, technology and industry have pushed themselves to the fore and conjured up chaos. We face this chaos. We must push back."

"So you want to tidy things up, Heinrich?"

He gave her a friendly smile: "You always like things tidy. I talk about what is appropriate for us to do, and what is dross. Our moral concepts, our political concepts are all strongly implicated in the chaos. Not to speak of art. Please, look at the scissors. They open, and cut. Our thought-tools must achieve the same simplicity and purity.

"We must not shy from applying them to all our institutions: justice, education, training, family, and to relations between enterprises and workers, even the state itself. The state should retreat before the demands of strictly technical thinking. The state will find itself the target of our sharpest attacks."

Everyone stopped breathing. After a pause someone asked: "And what role does money play in this?"

Klinkert: "The terror of the workers, capitalism. You should trouble yourself as little about the feelings of workers as of rentiers. Poverty is not justified and cannot be justified, and money is inherited or accumulated power. Not when it's kept in a box. Only when put to use. What creates a use for money? Technology, and its application to industry." He hesitated and looked at his hands, the slender pianist's fingers: "You shouldn't allow any questions of workers or proletariat to arise. They're a sign of polluted thinking, of spoilage through outmoded morality, of incapacity to become possible. You don't leave flammable materials lying about the house."

The young men in the room were silent and thoughtful. It was the energy and hardness with which he spoke that fired them. Even Marie — known here as Margarethe to Heinrich's Faust — became thoughtful, was elated, and had no idea what to say. There was a tension about Klinkert.

Klinkert sat stiffly on his stool, hard and tense, a man of violence heralding his violent Deed. What was happening here was idol-worship, Klinkert celebrating a Mass. Along the walls of the silent room sat a handful of people, descendants and heirs of those who had fought all the wars of past centuries. They were the descendants and reincarnations of those people who had grown up in a cold land under stars that hung far back in the sky. They had faded away, as they must, like ghosts, but had defended themselves against Death, had grown strong, savage, overweening. Emerging from the struggle against Death, they had stomped aggressively around their countries in order to annihilate or lose or renew themselves, like birds of passage that head south in autumn, fly cloud-high back to their old hot homelands, to the lovely wide fecund rivers, the plateaus and swamps, and only return when they have recouped their strength.

Such wars and exterminations had their ancestors brought to hot southern lands, such a wretched, raving, self-lacerating tribe of humans had sought an exit there. And here sat the heirs of this hardness and petrifaction. In a quiet room in a house in the German city of Heidelberg, a handful of young men, young women. And if some king or captain were now to give the signal, they would all rush off again to war and adventure, rapine and murder, and jump aboard ship to annihilate and be annihilated.

Erect and unyielding, Klinkert sat on the stool facing them, throttled by his thoughts. In his hand was the hammer with which Commandant Quesada, first Viceroy of Cundinamarca, broke the skull of the cacique who failed to deliver the correct quantity of gold. How do they sound, in the ears of the one who swings the club, who sits in an aeroplane and by pulling a lever drops the death-dealing bombs – how do they sound, the words *murder, annihilation, ruin, suffering, deluge?* Airy, lyrical. To these people, who had come from the street to him in this quiet room and who would have resisted any orders, Klinkert proffered ideas that throttled and oppressed them. They prostrated themselves, let him trample them so they could become ever more cramped and numb. Waiting, those who believed themselves free, for the creaking war-wagon, the clanking iron footfall of their idol. The ghostly God of Power was not dead, he sat among them, they were proud to have him among them.

Klinkert spoke softly, but his eyes and the pallor of his face screamed out loud. All perceived the scream and were enraptured by the thrill that accompanies annihilation:

"I give you the truth, you know I do, truth for you is like bread for a hungry man or light for the eye, no one could find a different truth for any of you. You sense that I impel you to cast a thousand new cannon to bring you dominion and power, what more do you want? Let one of you stand up and say: I want more! I want something else! You know that whatever questions and difficulties arise, they are solved. Hey dear mother, you bore me and I grew to a rogue and left you. Hey dear father, you sired me, I cursed and despised you, hey dear sister, dear bride. You already know what will come, it has come to pass a thousand times, forest, thorns, insects, worms, scorpions, heat – you will go hungry, many will die – the others – many will go blind – the others – they will be tied onto horses, the forest weeps and roars, it is speechless – but afterwards we shall babble, for there (I cannot speak the words) lies an enormous empire, power, violence, boundless dominion."

≈≈≈

While Posten pursued technical studies relevant to the business he was to take over, Klinkert was drawn into a sinister conflict. He had taken Marie in not only, as he claimed, as a comfort he could not do without. He sought to safeguard something in himself, and persisted in the face of Posten's sarcasm. Klinkert thought that cosy Marie could redeem him from the many kinds of darkness he sensed in himself. So he tolerated her questions, her housewifely homebaked fussing over him.

But during a long evening concert, Marie came to know a woman who lived not far away.

Therese was older than Marie, graceful, very pale, with natural curls at the forehead and over the ears. Her untidy chestnut hair suited the pale childlike face, which was enlivened by a truly sweet charm. Only gradually did you realize what it was that lent her face its appeal when she smiled and spoke and relaxed: the left corner of her mouth hung slack, the whole left side of her face moved sluggishly, while the right side was vibrant. Judge Partenay was her second husband, she never spoke of the first. She was not on good terms with the young judge. Marie learned that Klinkert's circle knew of this, and thought badly of Therese.

Now and then Therese brought back to her house some young man she had met somewhere or other, much as she had met Marie. She left it to the judge to quarrel with him. Generally the young man, reluctant to follow her home but unable to tear himself away from the charming creature, noticed while he was at the house that the woman actually loved her husband. The judge was polite, friendly, tolerant. To camouflage her dubious behavior Therese would invite another woman along, so that mostly there were four people present. The conflict with her husband, his fear that she would leave him, made her feel good and fonder of him than ever, and so he always acquiesced.

She mothered her lovers like a big girl her dolls, spoke tenderly to them in a childish silly voice. But she never gave herself entirely, would slap away naughty hands and forbid herself improprieties, but then become heavenly again and beg forgiveness and once again be the young man's utter joy, which he knew at once would fill the dreams of later years. Theresa's love always fell on them unexpectedly, without preamble. She took her time preparing the ground, and then it lasted no great while. It always followed a cycle. Slowly, inexorably she overcame her husband's distress and opposition, he had to become ever gentler, and then – she lost all interest in her lover. She did not grow hard, just cried a little to his face that she had to lose her dear big man-doll, surrendered herself a couple of times more wildly and tenderly than ever with an authentic dash of despair, and then it was over, she lived quietly at home, sat with her husband, organised the files he brought back, discussed his cases. For a while the house continued to enjoy the presence of the female decoy from the last affair, the judge had no idea how to relate to her, but Therese found all kinds of excuses to cultivate the acquaintance. The unspoken understanding: she'll be useful next time around.

≈≈≈

When, following the concert, Klinkert's girlfriend and house-keeper Marie had gone for a stroll a few times with this woman, Therese discovered in herself a new person. She realized there was more to her than just men. Seeing a gold cross at Marie's throat, peeping through the tight-fitting black silk blouse, Therese confessed to a particular fondness for old Church songs and Latin texts. Marie said she was a Catholic, Therese felt compelled to add that she was too, and Marie gave her hand an intimate little squeeze, they nattered on about all sorts of things, a great cordi-ality infused everything they touched, and finally they agreed to meet for Mass next morning. Therese came, knelt beside Marie, she had never been pious in her life. She felt it had been withheld from her, and she flung herself into it on Marie's arm. Months passed in this way, an upheaval in Therese's life, her existence had a new zest and an unfamiliar delight.

During those months Marie, who enjoyed her company, tried to invite Therese to her home. But Therese had no desire to become acquainted with the household of rich young Klinkert, nor to introduce him to her husband. Having enjoyed her fill of sensuality, Therese settled herself quietly in a rocking chair on the open verandah at the rear of the house, overlooking the green flower-specked hill, and even on hot days sunned herself with her knees covered in rugs. Her husband saw that, ever since she had started going with Marie, whom he bumped into with her several times in the street, she had become paler and less hectic, more circumspect, friendly but distant, she favoured black clothes. He asked in jest: "Who's died, Therese, who have you buried?"

She answered with a smile: "A certain Therese."

"I certainly hope not."

"You should hope so, my love, for you and for me."

It made no sense. In his heart he was not dissatisfied with the change, but mistrusted it. When she sat on the hot veranda under her rugs and blinked at him, a thought flew past that he could not grasp: what lay there rocking and tucked itself in under rugs and snored and sunned itself had something of the nature of a swamp creature, a lizard, trapped in a human body. So alien was she. But still Therese.

Until one day the change came over Therese that her husband had been expecting. Once again there was the questing vibration of the nostrils, the sharp glance. Therese was on the hunt. Since Marie came just at that moment and invited her to visit, she agreed, she wanted action. Marie was happy that Therese wanted to come, she said to her: "At bottom Klinkert is not without faith, he just refuses to believe. His friend Posten is the ruin of him, he feels ashamed in front of him, you'll see."

And Marie blithely led her ally and companion-in-arms to Klinkert.

Klinkert was standing at the window – it was late morning – looking down into the street. The door opened behind him, Marie's voice floated in: "Back again! I hope you didn't miss me."

He murmured. The remarkable dreamlike play of sun and shadow on the silent street occupied his attention, he thought: how it lies so peacefully on the carriageway, and just then a small car drove past and on, light and shade continued their play, the car had no effect, they touched the car's roof and doors for a moment, the car did not carry them away. Then something stung him on the throat above the collar, he rubbed at it, turned his head, there beside blithely smiling Marie stood a stranger, a lady, looking at him, no, observing him, as if annoyed.

"You look quite flustered," said Marie, "we must have taken you by surprise."

He said: "Forgive me." Marie made introductions: "This is my friend Therese I told you about, we meet up every day for Mass."

Nervously he said: "Alas, I can't compete with such piety."

Therese held out a feather-light little hand. And then they sat down, and Klinkert had lost face. As they chatted he went back to the window remembering how it had been earlier, were the sunbeams still playing with the shadows of the lime trees, yes they were. And he turned again, recalled that something had stung him on the throat, sat back down, and there she was, sitting next to his Marie.

Therese walked across the room, he watched her from the side, from behind, she acted as if unobserved, stood at his desk, looked at the calendar: "It's still yesterday's date," and turned the page. She stood with her back to him at the little bookcase, he sighed softly, she'd better move away from there, and when he gasped again as if in a nightmare and the two women turned and made surprised faces he managed to stand up and joke with them, and really it was all forgotten in an instant, and he was glad that Marie was showing him this interesting person, and his room was again his room, and it was almost as if nothing had happened.

≈≈≈

Therese was not one to beat about the bush. She was back again that evening, and saw Posten and several regular guests and heard Klinkert speak and argue. That voice and those tense features made an impression. She had already felt: she would invite him to her place, show him to her husband, Marie will be pleased, she won't suspect a thing. Now she felt: Klinkert will be a special project, and she gave Marie's hand, resting there beside her, a heartfelt squeeze, she's brought me two things now, first faith and now Klinkert, will I have to fight her for him, should we fight for him together, that could be nice, perhaps it's nice for two to possess a man, I'd like to try it with her.

And then she went home. Over coffee next morning her husband interrogated her because she was unusually laconic, she said a few words about Marie and Klinkert, the husband had no idea what his role in this was supposed to be. Moreover, he had sometimes thought of developing a crush or even a love affair on his own account, he knew he was capable and Therese would make no obstacles, but he would always see her eyes at his back mocking him, and his position would be no better, so he dropped the idea.

≈≈≈

Klinkert had believed his liaison with Marie a sufficient sacrifice to the gods of the underworld, he had "paid off" the underworld, as he explained to Posten. He had no defence against the storm unleashed on him by Therese. She wanted more than just a Marie, she wanted Klinkert, who sat there so rigid on his stool talking of 'instrumental thinking' and carried nickel scissors in his waistcoat pocket like an amulet. In his case, no nasty little domestic imp would have infected him to crawl out and offer itself to her, she'd had enough of the kind of man who uses a woman as an emergency exit.

The way Therese proceeded fascinated Marie. Without jealousy, indeed with a tender wicked glee, she saw that Klinkert had eyes for Therese. Excellent, she had hit the bullseye: horned Siegfried had a vulnerable spot. At no time did Klinkert see Therese without Marie present. Then he noticed that he both desired and feared to see her alone, sensing fear he pulled himself together, his heart often started pounding when he saw her. Whenever he stood at the window he recalled his initial trepidation.

≈≈≈

Autumn came. The circle around Klinkert held together. But some people came along who challenged him, and he was faced with serious opposition. The young men who stepped out to challenge him were every bit as caustic as he. A certain Hassler, who belonged to a violent organisation, was a good speaker, and depicted the current situation in the country in a way that some agreed with. He spoke of artists who were thoroughly rotten, concocting refined coffeehouse music or operas with an eye to their bank account; the worst no better than those who foist bad beer on the masses. Diplomats, scholars, poets, writers form a single huge market in vanity. Inauthentic, cunning people, turning their talent into a business. Puny fellows with a big name, who rhapsodize for their own comfort, sinister egoists jealous of their own reputation, at their back a crowd of paid-for admirers like a Caesar with his Praetorian guard. This plague claims to represent the public. The consequence is there's no violence capable of kicking them into the corner. And yet! The nation lives. And now he brought out his big gun (he did not point it at Klinkert just yet, said it was entirely up to Klinkert whether it would be aimed at him): "The nation is the greatest of all realities. It must turn against the masses of today. Rule by the best will be tomorrow's reality, and will dissolve the dictatorship of the subhuman."

Since you had no animals, no plants, no Heaven and no stars near at hand, you were alone, and each one of you was glad to find a club with which to lash out at everything around.

There was also a young playwright, a likable stammering man given to blushing. He volunteered that the Battle of Langemarck, where many young Germans had gone to their deaths, was the only true stuff of drama today. He spoke of the Front Generation and its successors. Experience of war will transform the Volk. He was a shy quivering person with a sick mother at home and no girlfriend, because he was timid. To blow off steam he once expressed himself menacingly with the words: "We'll soon see how the true soldier of war will put an end to peace. The time for heroic decisions is near." And then he quivered and waited to be squashed. No longer, as once in earlier centuries, could one break out of the twilight lands to find annihilation.

One by one they offered up their fetishes. Klinkert accepted their challenge. He never interrupted.

"Nation was ever a popular item in Germany, now it's a runaway bestseller. A smart chap can surely make something of it. This is a time of disappointments and dissatisfactions, and so everyone complains. You chew, cough, you think: I need a cough sweet. Nation! If all you mean is the same way of living, customs, language, you needn't worry about it; you certainly don't need dominion over it. But what you propose is something else. You want to conserve an attitude from the time of our grandfathers, and add one more narcotic to the mix. Nation was the business of kings, now we are the kings. Our business is technology and industry, nothing else, and these are turning the world upside down. The goal is to overthrow the barricades erected by workers, moneybags and sentimentalists against the whirlwind of technology.

"I'm accused of passivity. It reminds me of the accusation the old metaphysicians flung at Kant, because he left no more room for windbaggery; they liked their windbaggery. – Whoever believes that what he carries within himself is good and provides a guideline, with such a one there is no negotiating. You do not become lord over others before you are lord over yourself."

The timid playwright snapped at air: "This is intolerable. I have to disagree. Precisely the unconscious, the irrational, makes us strong."

"What is the irrational?"

The playwright shrugged despairingly: "But you know what it is."

"Inexpressible feelings that cannot become thoughts and evade our control. Mouldy stuff passing itself off as the Ego. It's one of the worst things there is, because it never shows its face and places an internal block on our actions. To say the unconscious makes us strong is to stand things on their head."

"What is your object, your goal?" This was the caustic nationalist student.

"For example, to expose and demolish outmoded ideas such as Nation."

"Then you are an internationalist and should go to the Communists."

"I shall go to no one other than you, sir. And if you do not wish to listen, I shall speak to myself. Truth does not need a public."

Now, clearly, he was alone.

≈≈≈

Of course several deserted him, the "poetical" movements swallowed them up. Posten, who often came over from Karlsruhe where he was studying his technical course, and where he observed the same things as Klinkert, scoffed: "True poetry between the covers of a book is no longer produced in Germany. That's because people now put it into practice. Politics has swallowed everything. Our politics have sunk to the level of poetry. A frightfully pious people, the Germans. The Kingdom of Heaven can't get away from them."

He was busier than usual with modern food conservation methods, he was off to Holland and England where he could find fresh air and laugh out loud to his heart's content. Just before he left he found Klinkert quieter than usual, and thought solitude was to blame:

"Come to England with me." Klinkert nodded: "Perhaps."

They spoke of mutual acquaintances: "All feeble, unclean. Many spoiled by Nietzsche. This neo-religious rehash; they always have to consume religion in some form. Nietzsche, the pastor's son, once said God was not yet dead; but he himself helped greatly to bring it about."

Klinkert told his friend of an incident that had shocked him, though Posten just shrugged: "An elderly man recently said to me, quite seriously: 'We knew God in the barrage of the guns, we must awaken this god again.' That's the kind of drunkard we have to deal with."

Posten grabbed his shoulder and pointed to the window: "Fly, out with you, out into the wide world!"

Now Therese set to work on Klinkert. She took part in several discussions, even her husband, the judge, turned up now and then, but took no interest in the debates then raging throughout the land, and Therese's interest in Klinkert seemed to him not too great, since it had gone on like this quite a while already.

He was wrong. She was still observing Klinkert, testing, weighing the tastiest way to prepare him, he must not be allowed to spoil like the others. After the ecstasy of religion she was no longer planning a standard lunch.

Klinkert, unsettled by this female busying herself indecisively around him, made several trips with Posten, who delayed his visit to England on his friend's account, partly for diversion and partly to hear what was going on around the country. They spent some time in Bavaria. It was in Munich that they encountered Jagna, the handsome blasé Pole. Even Klinkert was taken with this listless, enchanting phenomenon of a person, who never stirred and did not know what to do with himself; he reminded him vaguely of Therese, for some weeks he stayed close to him. Posten mocked the handsome Pole. Jagna enjoyed Posten's company more than Klinkert's, Posten's swashbuckling thuggishness, his cold nature, impressed him. In the company of foolhardy Posten, the three ended up one evening at a nightclub where they were offered cocaine. Posten was the instigator, he teased the Pole, he could keep himself under control, he put Klinkert to the test, it pleased him to watch Klinkert struggle indignantly with the narcotic. At that time Posten's coarseness was in full bloom. Klinkert returned from the trip shattered. Back in his apartment with the old crowd around him, he realized: none of these are still with me! Mystical 'national' ideas were the order of the day. Klinkert confessed to Marie his adventure with narcotics: "You'll scold me. I scold myself. When I see how they all intoxicate themselves, I feel doubly ashamed. No need for you to bring me to heel."

Now Therese began her advance. She held her first conversation alone with Klinkert, who was tired and thought of going away for good: "Your mistake is that you sharpen knives and then leave them lying in a drawer. Others, when they want something, don't give a fig how sharp the knife is. They hack and saw away at their piece of flesh and swallow it down."

"What do you mean, Madam Therese?"

"You see the consequence: you are alone."

"I never saw myself as a shepherd."

"But you must act – or suffer."

He smiled: "Be the hammer, or the anvil," but then remembered that he was speaking with Therese, he looked at her, yes, she was sitting across from him by the wall, on a metal chair, the huge sofa that was usually crammed with guests was quite empty, she the last remaining fragment, she the last voice of a vanished choir.

"You often spoke, quite rightly, about mastery over oneself.

You said, if I remember correctly, Herr Klinkert, that this is the first essential task. You rejected mystical feelings, considered them a relic from the time of our forefathers."

"Yes."

"Well then, do something with yourself."

"What do you mean?"

Her delightfully childish expression remained unchanged, she regarded him gravely and almost pleaded: "Make use of yourself. What are you for, otherwise?" She said this innocently.

He drew himself up to his usual rigid posture: "That – is not what I meant."

"Then what? And why not? If one is master and possesses something, one does not hide it under a footstool. One does not stint oneself like a clerk with his paltry salary."

"Yes, if that were the case one might as well throw oneself away, and that would give property the victory."

At this she looked for a while pensively down at her knees: "Throw away, no. But you're right about morality. We preserve relics from earlier times without knowing it, grandfathers and grandmothers. Maybe you do too. With your masterfulness."

Calmly she smoothed the dress over her knees, as if to conclude the matter: "It was just a thought. It just happened to pop into my head, seeing you sit there so pompous and severe."

This conversation affected him profoundly. She had aimed true. A few days later when they met by chance in the street, something that had never happened before, to his own astonishment he confided in her about the trials of strength he had indulged in, alongside Posten of course, during his youth. Not in this conversation but the next, he told her about the elegant Pole and his experiments with narcotics, and confessed that he was no match for Posten in this regard. She thought: Posten, do I like him, no.

"To think you let yourself be pushed around by your friend Posten, Herr Klinkert! I like what Herr Posten does and the way he does it. But what does the Pole get up to?"

Klinkert told her what he knew, how handsome he was, not to speak of his wealth, he travels around with a guardian foisted on him by his mother in Poland, but to little effect.

"And he experiments on himself, as well?"

Klinkert was startled by her choice of words, spoken so calmly and amiably as they walked through the lonely snow-covered Neckar valley while cars and market trucks sped past. Nonplussed he said: "I know nothing about that."

"You may be sure he does."

And she laughed and shook her head so that her curls flew, laid a hand on his arm to pull him back again: "You're puzzled because I said 'as well'? No, you don't experiment on yourself, Herr Klinkert. You truly are Herr Klinkert, master of his own Klinkert. But do you enjoy it?"

"I don't understand your question."

"Who actually gave you the task of being master of your own Klinkert? For somebody must have done so, and now you're serving time for him? It seems that way to me. For without such a task and with no one to benefit from it, simply being master of oneself is surely quite boring."

He walked along beside her, agitated. She was pleased that he made no reply. The harpoon had struck, he couldn't pull it out.

Therese would have liked, or so she claimed at least, to bring Marie along to their meetings, but Klinkert objected: let's not complicate matters. Therese explained that she liked to go on excursions during fine snowy weather while her husband was busy at court, Marie and Klinkert were welcome to join her. Of course Marie said yes, and Klinkert sensed: Therese is up to something with me. A sleigh was hired, Klinkert sat in the back with Marie, Therese in front with the coachman. She turned her head often to smile at them. And when Therese suggested on the homeward journey that they swap seats, it turned out that she – wanted to sit in the back with Marie. Not to torment Klinkert, it was just that she had no idea how to set about him. She often thought she should simply come quickly to the point, take him as he was (which would not be difficult) and present him to her husband and start the old game again. But that lacked appeal.

One day she confessed to Marie, as they sat alone in Klinkert's apartment, that she was worried about Klinkert, he couldn't see his path clearly. And as Marie gushed tears and castigated Posten, Therese begged Marie not to be cross with her, but she too was very attached to Klinkert, he was such a wonderful man.

"You can help me," said Marie happily, "you'll help me. Both of them, Klinkert and Posten, have such a horrible streak, they respect nothing, everyone says so. They trample on corpses."

"Actually they don't (alas), Klinkert at least only talks that way, you mustn't take him seriously, I can already see through him. You won't be cross, Marie, if I worry about him for his own sake. Are you jealous?"

And Marie told the truth as she gave her friend a hug: "No, no! If you don't help me, how long before he throws me over too."

"He won't. And don't say anything to my husband."

Marie gave her friend a heartfelt kiss, made her damp with tears and kisses. Marie was truly happy and relieved: they shared a secret, and they would not lose Klinkert.

But Therese's behaviour during the next sleigh-ride caused Marie a stab of anxiety. This time on the homeward ride Therese sat in the back with Klinkert, and when Marie turned her head in response to a tap on the shoulder from Therese and her question: "Do you mind if I stroke him?" and she nodded, Therese wagged a mock-threatening finger at Klinkert, took off his fur hat, placed it on his knees, and then stroked his forehead. Marie looked on tittering, then Therese pulled the bemused man to her and pressed her face to his. Marie clapped her hands encouragingly, and when they climbed down a little later Klinkert, cap in hand and hair disheveled, asked: "Am I the victim of a conspiracy?" Marie, who had been waiting for the moment of alighting, gave Therese a hug and laughed: "Yes, you are," and delighted asked: "Are you afraid, Klinkert? Two of us against one?"

He was uneasy, and mumbled in embarrassment: "Better wait and see." And on they went through soft deep snow, along the utterly silent paths. The trees, black trunks and crippled branches, which in spring were covered with blossom and then layered over with a green cloud, stood each for itself, naked, the snow had thrown a thin white shirt over them.

Marie asked: "Who'll go in the middle?" She changed places, and Therese, a little reluctant, came between her and Klinkert, but only for a short stretch, then Klinkert came in the middle and this was right, he was the biggest, the two women swung on his arms as if on a railing.

Back home Klinkert asked: "What's your idea, Marie? What's all this with Madam Therese?"

"Don't you like her?"

"That was not my question."

"But answer that first."

"There's no reason, Marie, why I should answer any random question." Klinkert regarded his girlfriend: "You've formed an alliance against me with Madam Therese. She invited you to do so. Please, don't indulge in childish games."

"Have we upset you?"

"Anything can become irksome. And besides, who organised that thing in the sleigh with my cap and so on?"

"How strange you are, Klinkert. It just happened. And it was wonderful. Say it was."

"You didn't plan it?" –"No."

Then it became clear to him what Therese wanted, and he became even more uneasy. Marie hugged him, sitting there so quiet, and cuddled him, which he enjoyed. He held her tight: "Is she plotting something with you?"

"What gave you that idea? You seem to think she's a werewolf."

"Say nothing to her about this. I can't figure her out. And you're such an innocent lamb."

Dear God, he said to himself when he sat alone, what's wrong with me. This has been such a wonderful day. If Posten came and I were to tell him all about it – which I won't – it's the most ridiculous thing that could happen to a man. Perhaps my whole situation is bad. Otherwise such a thing could never have occurred. What a rotten ménage, we're landing in a tricky business, woman trouble. Two women attached to one man. A problem for me, and no mistake! And as he paced up and down past the empty sofa and the empty chairs: no one here, quite alone, all fled, everyone seeks a place to stay, a refuge for the night. I must do something with myself. They want to break my spirit.

≈≈≈

Now Klinkert gave himself a kicking. To work, to Posten. But despite himself he had to go once more to Therese, only, as he pretended, to thank her for her recent words: that one should be one's own master, and do something with oneself.

"You shouldn't visit me alone, Klinkert."

"I leave at noon."

"For long?"

"I think so."

"A pity. So, farewell then." They were in her living room, he bowed, left. At the door he had to look back, she was sitting at the table in the same attitude, supporting her chin, with a pleasant, thoughtful expression. She nodded: "Do well, Klinkert. I'll keep my fingers crossed."

Then he went.

Summer was beginning when he came back. In the meantime there had occurred all kinds of excess, including the cat and mouse game with the young Pole following the suicide of his lover for a day, which he had tried to depict as a romantic adventure; they baited him and then his behaviour improved and he shot the man avenging his honour. Klinkert appeared again to Marie, still with a whiff of the affair about him. Posten had already gone back to his work, sitting in a factory and whistling his Radetzky March of politics and ideas. He had advised Klinkert to do the same: "Because if it's right what you say, all that stuff about instrumental thought, you ought to use your head as a practical tool, that's all anyone's good for. And as for those other people you tried to impress with your clever insights, there's only one thing for them: either they do exactly the same as me, or there's no hope for them. Anyone who needs convincing is already lost. And as for you, Klinkert, you'll be lost too if you keep up your song too long, Mister Pied Piper of Hamelin."

Back in Heidelberg Klinkert at once sought a meeting with Therese. For he could not help himself. They had exchanged no letters. He had to bring Marie along to her, she'd been ill for weeks. Marie implored him to delay the visit, or first wait to see what Therese would say. Klinkert's haste unnerved her: "You can't just barge in." But she yielded. And after she had sat a few minutes with Therese, who lay on a chaise longue, he entered the room. Her face was pleasant, just as at the time of their parting, no hint of surprise, she motioned to him to sit. Then she sat up and turned to face Klinkert. Marie's presence vanished. After they had chatted for ten minutes, Therese became fatigued, turned back to Marie: "Would you, Marie, allow Klinkert and me to meet alone now and then?"

Marie: "Yes, yes of course," but then without thinking drew closer to Klinkert. They passed the whole of that day in silence. Marie sat paralysed in her room, not knowing if Klinkert was in, he didn't come to see her.

And when evening came she slipped away to Therese, wept before her (the judge would return at any moment): "He only came back because of you. It's all over for me."

"How you suffer," said Therese, her arms around Marie, "how you suffer over a man and weep and give everything up for lost. I never learned to do this. Weeping over a man. How helpless you are. What a child. You let him treat you like one. Now he's back. You waited for him so long, and he doesn't even look at you."

"Wasn't he here this afternoon?"

"Yes, a long visit, more than an hour." Marie erupted in a storm of tears, and tried to free herself from Therese's arms. "No, stay here, Marie. Am I to blame that he came to me?"

"He doesn't love me any more."

"It would be just like him, go from one woman to another and doff his hat and say: I don't love you any more. But I don't love him either."

"Did you tell him that?" – "Yes."

"So that's why he didn't come home all day. Or he's already gone away again."

"Calm down, Marie. He's still around, he'll come back. He knows I don't want him. And anyway, I'm still married. This whole conversation is a joke. We're talking like two silly girls."

"Did you really tell him, and is it true you don't like him? It's not true, Therese." Marie searched Therese's face, she received a kiss.

"It's true. I'm no robber. Anyway," she fell back, "I'm ill, I'm done for. You need have no worries on my account."

That evening Klinkert went to Marie's room, she came to meet him, and as she embraced him and sought the mouth so long denied her, those lips met hers, submissive, and Marie took them and cried out and wept. Silently, seemingly intent on kissing the face, the radiant tear-streaked cheeks, the eyes closed in bliss and supporting the near-fainting woman, Klinkert observed Marie. He obeyed. He ordered himself to love Marie, who was never in his thoughts, who belonged to a time when he had treated himself as a plaything, stomped around like a warhorse and was merely a frisky poodle. "I can love her as well, I can love when I tell myself to." And he could still hear Therese's words from an hour before:

"I don't do love affairs. I'm married. And anyway, you can see I'm ill. If your – let us say – inclination to me is so great, you could have shown it long before now. We didn't just meet today. Perhaps you're laying on such a siege because – either you have a bet on, perhaps with Herr Posten or some new acquaintance, perhaps with a lady, or because you've been left in the lurch. There's Madam Therese, she'll open her arms, look, so so wide. Leave me in peace."

And later she sat in his lap: "I like, I really like what you told me, Heinrich. You have developed. Your Pole is a fine figure. You've learned something from him. And you look better, not so wet behind the ears – you've taken off. You know, Heinrich, the world extends in two directions, one above, that one we hear about constantly, and one down below. How does one reach down? You stare at me? Yes, how does one reach down. This is much more interesting to me than your eternally stupid: how does one reach up? Now you are a man. You dare to do it. I – have already done so for a long time."

"You, the pious Catholic."

"Yes, Heinrich, how could I measure how far down it goes if I were not pious? Maybe someone will come and save me, and it will go even deeper." She sank onto the divan. A flicker played over the tender childish face: "Kiss my foot." She clenched her teeth, kicked off her slipper, he bent down, kissed the foot. She dismissed him with the order to return to Marie. He wandered aimlessly for half the day, had a drink, and finally gave a kick to the beast in him, which was rebelling. Therese's formula was right: "You must be master of yourself before you can do anything with yourself." He wanted to start something, sound his depths. Now he embraced Marie and made her happy.

Next morning she gazed lovingly on him, as if they had met only yesterday: "What do you look like, Heinrich, so haggard. Posten is bad for you. What have you men been up to. You're ruining my Klinkert. I'll have to feed you up."

"Yes, please do," murmured Klinkert, "really, I don't feel well."

She bit her finger at this, alarmed, Klinkert had never said such a thing before: "I'll fetch the doctor. What's wrong?"

"Weakness, indescribable weakness. Stay here with me." She helped him to the sofa and he lay curled up, then stretched out: "It started while I was away. As if I'd been poisoned. No feeling in the limbs. Just don't feel right."

At noon Marie clapped her hands, he was still lying on the sofa: "Now I have two patients, you and Therese. I must run back and forth from one to the other." Then he felt better, took a glass of port and huddled, his head empty.

≈≈≈

Therese's presence in the world, Therese's image. As if a deep-toned tocsin is ringing out within him. A wonderful sustaining music. Something that fills all of consciousness. It allows me to forget that I am. But I live within it. I have never lived. Incomprehensible: that some woman, one of thousands, a judge's wife, a person from some family or other, fool of a father, silly mother, no doubt

some stupid siblings – she sends me off with Posten on adventures
that disgust me so my insides cramp until I can neither live nor die,
and I have to take my seat in a train, panting like a thirsty dog, and
come back here: to her, her, her! And here I am. And she can do
with me what she will. She can do anything, anything with me.
Marie is with her now. Just one street away. I wonder what they're
talking about. What Therese is saying. The letters T.H.E.R.E.S.E.
(he spoke these aloud.) Therese. There she stands, in the air. She's
here with me. What are you up to, how did it go? Marie was with
you. – She's still with me. – Doesn't she get on your nerves? – I
forbid you to speak so, Heinrich. I want her with me and you must
be good to her, if I must be a traitor that doesn't mean I want to be
bad, she deserves to be treated well. – I am good to her. – So much
the better. I'll ask her for all the details. – I do what you want. –
You troubadour. Saying such things.

The judge asked Therese: "I hear Klinkert is back. Why don't
you invite him over?" He had no understanding of Therese.

"You can see I'm not well. I may invite him. He's only just
back."

"I know you think a lot of him, Therese. He was in your
thoughts even while he was away. Are you happy now?"

She lay on her chaise longue, after a long pause said: "These
matters don't concern you."

He was shocked. She let him leave the room quietly.

≈≈≈

Klinkert was now greatly changed. He sensed it when, on his
'rounds', he visited a blond youth who was all for him, heart and
soul. The shock-headed youth had studied Theology. "There's
absolutely nothing worth studying in Christianity, it's not a book,
just speeches with advice on sensible or remarkable things, as you
will. No need to drive people crazy. Baffling, the way people have
fought over it."

"And what about Jesus?"

"Jesus wanted at the same time to have both God, whom he
believed to be his father, and Caesar, who really was one." The
young man laughed brightly. "And of course the experiment failed.

And on top of that he wanted to consummate the law, I mean the Jewish law of course, he wanted to consummate Jewishness. He was just a man, with his contradictions."

Klinkert prodded him to say more on the topic, and so heard some fine things that lit a few lamps. But the youth floundered: "No, no more theorizing. You're trying to trap me. All human life begins by killing theoreticians. If you start digging beneath the foundations on which human societies rest, you stumble on a thousand unsolved problems, on the corpses that first made society possible." He laughed: "A man doesn't ask questions. He answers them. He acts." And he regarded Klinkert: "But of course you know this already."

Oh, Klinkert knew: here was one of his instrument-natures. He grew anxious, dizzy, glum.

≈≈≈

Marie came to him, delighted with the change since his travels. To be sure he was suffering, but he was much less severe than she'd known him before, than she'd ever hoped to expect from her Klinkert. Yes, he loved having her beside him. He began, at Therese's urging, once again to study her face, this soft calm rapt face, to study her eyebrows (Marie squealed in delight), and everything that had already been his for so long.

At first he sighed, turned away: why this, what for, Therese is such a timid creature, does not want to lose her husband, wants to stay married, has no trust in what I do, I must prove myself. What I'm doing here is hard, fatuous, unworthy, I'm making a fool of myself, what must little plump Marie think, the sweet dumpling I tote around. I abase myself before her, maybe that's what Therese wants, oh she's a sly creature, she laughs, enjoys tormenting me.

And then again, Marie's face before him: But Therese shouldn't think I'll be driven by some emotion to run away. She thinks I'll feel disgust when I kiss this silly imploring creature, she's been in her company for so long checking her out, feeling how little there is in her. But I can do that too. I shall pull myself out of even this swamp. They shall see that I am what I am.

And as he read this script inscribed in flesh, and the beguiling curly head, this heavenly doll's face looked up at his, he thought: Now I leaf through her face as it tries to close itself to me, but I open its lips, open and close the eyelids (my God, what a stupid task, so perverse), but it has been ordered, and I order myself to do it, this is what unites me with Therese, and I am with her now, and shall bring her everything. Good little Marie, poor girl, my sweet, you have no idea how I betray you, and I never knew how good you are. But up there is someone who, just like me down here, holds my life in her hands. I serve her. The Bible tells of Jacob, he came to Laban who had two daughters, the older was Leah, the younger Rachel, Jacob loved Rachel, who was lovely and beautiful, and served seven years for her, and he was first given Leah, she was stupid, but he did not thrust her from him, he served longer for Rachel, another seven years. So do I serve, and accept you and will not let you go.

But Marie's face was not stupid, her eyes, lips and she herself were quite eloquent.

Heinrich dreamed: I'm an actor in a strange play, I've been given a part and I have ordered myself to play it. Then – Marie took wing.

People are like meals placed on a great table, there's a huge metal bowl, in it a tureen with a tight lid, and the porcelain tureen is filled with hot water, and above it, enveloped in steam from the hot water, you finally come to the pastries laid out there. Could Marie, good and eager as she was, ever have measured up to herself after her hard, miserable childhood, her temporary jobs as help and governess? She came along because she spotted someone heading into danger. Heinrich had never noticed this Marie, his housekeeper, he felt no shame until she revealed herself, dared to reveal herself. For this was not the shop he wanted to enter to buy something.

Marie groaned out everything she had kept inside her: "I'm in bliss, I am yours, I am Marie, I am your Marie, I am your servant, I worship you, I want to be a part of your body, I would be happy just to be like your collar and your shirt, lying against your body. I feel alive only when you're with me. I've only come alive since you appeared. You laugh, Heinrich. I'm glad you're here. What have you made of me."

And Heinrich was astonished at her behaviour, how she bloomed, danced, a different being, a butterfly emerged from a pupa, what a few words, a few tender gestures can achieve, he regarded his work with curiosity: "Love, love is a magical force."

Marie said: "You're more cheerful now, you look on the world more kindly. You look at me now. Believe me, Heinrich, I sometimes thought you always spoke from your head and I was actually frightened for you because you were so terribly blind although you know everything and can never understand what somebody says to you and what is happening to you, and at some point disaster will strike you. That's what I always thought. A terrible disaster will strike you because you're blind. And that's another reason why I didn't want to lose you."

"And your eyes are open, Marie, and you see everything and know me, even me?"

"Yes, better than you know yourself."

Klinkert thought: what a crazy adventure Therese has pushed me into. What am I hearing, what am I seeing. And I've been living with this woman under the same roof for months, I've possessed her – what is it of hers that I possess. It seems Marie might be a little bit right, that she knows me better than I know myself, the little Cinderella.

And the play-acting turned serious. And it came about that Klinkert, urged by Posten to come to his factory, take up some work, was unable to tear himself away, and asked himself through gritted teeth: they have me tied down here, how should I reply? He was on the point of confessing to Marie that he'd been toying with her. But then he knew it was no longer true. It was not true. He was unnerved. Oh, I flee to her from Therese, and how she felt ashamed and yet surrendered, and how every gesture of his made her happy, and all in harmony. It was no game, he crept into her, and when he went to Therese and came back again it seemed to him, now it seemed to him, that he was coming home. He crafted secret plans to escape from Heidelberg with Marie and never return. Then he remembered the first long absence, and did not know what to do with himself.

Therese knew what was going on with him. Marie, happy, grateful, told her much, and Therese observed him from behind this curtain, she was able to check on him and savour the situation. It gained in savour the more she believed he had to take it all on himself, so profound was his self-abasement. This made him a truly tasty morsel for her. And at a gathering, once Therese felt quite better again, Klinkert had to appear together with Marie, Therese relished this. And then she saw them together in a nook, he embraced her from behind and kissed her. The curtain was torn aside. This was purest intimacy. Therese was barely able to see the evening through to its end. Then next morning, when Heinrich presented himself, she sent him away, told him to marry Marie, was formal with him, and when he became importunate she summoned the housemaid.

On the days that followed he was not admitted, "the fool, the puffed-up Philistine", he loves his girl, he's a domestic creature like all the others, nothing but a swindler and a common clerk. Perplexed, he returned again, his conscience undermined, there must be some misunderstanding, had Marie said something wrong, what, he was turned away. He wrote, the letters went unanswered.

Marie grew alarmed at his distress, all at once he no longer treated her kindly. And now it all fell apart, all the happiness. He raged against Therese, against Marie. Marie tried her best to restore the breach between Klinkert and Therese. She couldn't understand why Klinkert was so upset, now and then a suspicion arose, but only for minutes, fading moments, things from before, no, Therese had simply annoyed Klinkert somehow. It seemed Therese wanted to break with her as well, she couldn't say a word about him, Therese was in such a mood.

A terrible back-and-forth started up between her and Heinrich, profound rancour, then the old and always surprising tenderness again.

And Heinrich cursing himself, tearing his hair out, what had happened, surely he wasn't defeated, she couldn't have dismissed him. He was consumed by it, and hated and loved Therese, and wished himself dead.

The notion came into his head that Therese, this wonderful, dreadful being that was tearing him asunder, was a person who had set her hopes on him. True, she hated him now because she couldn't forgive him for disappointing her. She had thought he would be harder and stronger than her and would trample her down and at last drag her out of her misery.

For this cold slithering creature was a rock, a lump of lava flung from a volcano, but the memory of fire still lingered. And so she went among people, was drawn to where flames could be found, sought distraction from her life, and would have mouldered and died like thousands beside her, but then strong Klinkert appeared. He turned out to be a commonplace cad. And so, even more passionately than before, she went on the hunt again.

She told her doctor something of herself, and went on to reveal everything she knew: "But there's nothing wrong with me, nothing wrong at all, I just want to talk, I need to see myself in a mirror, it's not a pretty sight, tell me it is so, doctor, but please don't mock." She related everything without shame, she forgot only to mention her latest pain and helplessness and disappointment. The image occurred to the doctor of a dog being sick at his feet and snuffling in the vomit. He let her talk, her ears then became closed, she had spoken, she wanted nothing more, she left feeling cross.

Her hatred for Klinkert infected the judge. He spoke with friends about these rich good-for-nothings and the mischief they caused. They knew much more about his wife than he had suspected, they recommended he let the Klinkert business lie since it seemed over; he was unhappy with this advice. When he tried to start a conversation with Therese about Klinkert, she became speechless with rage. She stood there pale, seething and deeply insulted. He retreated, groaned to himself at his desk.

The hunt for young men did not satisfy her. Through Marie, who was delighted to hear from her, she told Klinkert she wanted to see him, with or without Marie. In the meantime Posten had visited, and nagged him. As he watched Posten take a canter around all the things they used to say, Klinkert thought how many decades had flowed by since those days.

Posten described what was happening in the country: "Those people of yours who sat here so often are peddling a monstrous propaganda; just look around, you know who they are, you'll be thoroughly cured when you see. It's a complete farce: young people marching in the oldest, most motheaten costumes, and you shouldn't think they're stupid; no, the costumes are a draw. No Paris fashions can stand against these bearskins from a museum. The primal forest is the fashion now, Heinrich. We've been defeated all along the line. You have to look. The believers, the mystics! It's a joy to be alive."

Heinrich: "I do keep an eye on it."

"From your corner here. You really must see how they interpret your handiwork! Enthusiasm is today's hot stock. The masses want nothing else today. We might as well pickle ourselves along with our herrings. Heinrich, I'm in deadly earnest: it would be no bad thing for you to pull yourself together and join in. Within a few weeks you'd be on top. They only have a couple of serious figures. The mass taken as a whole is of course serious, in the same way as a lover or a habitual drunk."

"I don't want to."

"Then come back to the office, to the factory."

"Sure. I just have to finish something here."

"Heinrich, if you're tangled up in some crazy situation, heed my advice. I'm your good conscience. It's all well and good, this fooling around. But I'm finished with it too. That thing with the Pole we left in the lurch shook me to the core. I hear the fellow has reformed, wants to become a monk, they say he's vanished from the face of the earth."

"I'm not fooling around. I have some personal business to settle, it won't take long."

"My dear chap. Personal. I don't like the sound of that. Nothing personal, please."

Heinrich sat on his stool in his old rigid posture, leaning

forward towards the sofa, elbows projecting from his knees. Posten regarded him: "You look as if you're under assault, Klinkert. Surely you don't mean to become a scholar in this dump? Has your Marie turned your head?"

"I told you, I'll come along soon. In a few weeks."

"If you take me seriously, then not in a few weeks. It's splendid out there in the world and will become more splendid. They need people like us. The world's full of drunkards."

"You Siren!"

"When then? Four weeks?" – "Done."

"Last respite, Klinkert. If anything reaches my ears that displeases me, I'll come and fetch you myself."

At last word came from Therese: he can consider it over. So he thought. Then he lay before her again, in distress. The way she raged. The way she treated him. He felt he would never ever be free of her. Just as Posten had foreseen.

He shut himself up in his room and groaned. I shan't take it upon myself, I can't bear it, I can't, take your hand off me, your hand from my throat, I'm in someone else's power, my life is torn apart, I am free, or am I not? The face with its curls, the little white hand with the silver bracelet, these tell me there is a devil in the world. Cursed, cursed face. Miserable wretch that I am, sitting at her feet, and when I glance at her I have to go down on my knees, all my words change, I become a buffoon, a monkey. Ah, is this the heritage I carry within me? So she has me. Me the loudmouth. What can I do, oh God what should I do to escape the shame.

She too had no idea what to do with him. But because he was bad and not, as it turned out, what she had once taken him for, he could not be allowed to run around and enjoy himself. He should at least stay nearby until she was quite finished with him. "And what's more, my husband hates you. He's on your trail. Maybe he'll come to your room one day and shoot you.

"It's possible. Why not."

"And?"

Klinkert sat stiffly in the chair, as if he were at his place. He looks good, this is what a traitor looks like: "Do you love me, Heinrich?"

Now say it: "What are you talking about? What's the point?"

"Whether you love me."

She's trying to humiliate me, that's why she lays out these stupid words, I know it, if only I can resist, Klinkert, Klinkert, Heinrich, rouse yourself, to arms!

"So you don't love me. Then why did you come? Look at me. For whom have you thrown away those long months with me?"

"Not thrown away."

She took a deep breath: "Is it true?" – "Yes."

"You just ran away?" – "Yes."

"And Marie?" – "You gave the order."

"That was all?" – "No."

"What then."

"Running from you." He clenched his fists, closed his eyes. She looked at him in disbelief:

"Is it true? Heinrich?" She pulled him to her: "I'm glad."

≈≈≈

When he left her, he was broken. He wandered the streets, stood at shop windows, the fatal words always on his lips: "Exit Klinkert, exit Klinkert." On the way back he passed close to her house and thought, as of a stranger: "This thing between Heinrich and Therese will end badly."

At last, towards midday, he strolled more calmly back home and seemed to have emerged from a dream when Marie opened the door and at once put her arms around him. They were good arms. You can breathe easily here. Let yourself be held. And when Klinkert spent a day and one more day with Marie, and Therese let no word fall, he could pretend he'd been living a nightmare, a black cloud descended on me, everything is as it was, I'm no fool like the Pole, since when did I indulge my senses, and as for love, if it really be love, I have all I need entirely from my Marie.

How happy was Marie when out of his distraction he said: we'll strike camp here soon, and set to work.

≈≈≈

There was no saving him from Therese's image. Every night he told himself: "Love is passion. Love is madness, I've read it a thousand times. I've seen it in others. I have been smitten. This is not love, it's madness, possession. I understand what they mean when they talk of sorcery. If this were the Middle Ages I'd go to the Inquisition and accuse Therese of witchcraft. But that's nonsense. I'm as much to blame as she is, the sorcery is in me as well and I should be burned alongside her. – Who can help me?"

And again he watched himself wandering the streets: "Exit Klinkert, exit Klinkert, there's a bad end coming."

And then morning refused to come, the clock was never out of his hand, the sun delayed its appearance, and then came coffee and the sight of Marie was unwelcome and nothing could be said and he was all bitterness and glowering. And then – go to her, and the bliss, annihilation, disintegration, delight. No pride. Just go. Dissolve. Exit Klinkert, exit Klinkert, may he never arise again, the miserable defenceless wretch. He no longer wants to live, no longer wants to return to the day, to his house, to his table.

Then Klinkert slunk home once more, and without removing his hat pulled Marie, as she opened the door, into the living room and sobbing, accompanied by her sobs, confessed all, that he could not let Therese dismiss him, he knew it and it would kill him: "Satan is within us, Marie, what I said was wrong, there's no hope for us."

And Marie, pale around the mouth, stammered: "What will happen, who can I ask." When after a while she said she'd ask Posten to come, she'd write to him straightaway, he was so far gone as to nod and say yes several times. She stayed in Klinkert's room, never left him alone the whole day, he seemed happy with this.

Next morning he decided: "You can send the letter to Posten. Posten will meet us. We shall leave. Today." She threw herself to her knees, gold cross in her hands, there in the middle of the room, and thanked the Mother of God, she had prayed for help to the Virgin during the night, and leaving this place was her dearest wish.

Around her were the big empty sofa, the bookcase, Klinkert's desk, the metal chairs, and there the window and the street where Therese's house stood, and in just a few hours all this would be behind her, the horror would be behind her, thanks be to the heavenly Virgin.

By noon the cases were packed, Klinkert in his travelling clothes went from room to room. He stood in the doorway to his room and gazed on the disorder. And after long, silent reflection he moved into the hall, picked up his travelling hat: "I'll say goodbye to her," opened the front door and pulled it shut behind him before Marie, who was still packing, realized what was happening. Unhappy, fearful, she sat for half an hour on a trunk, oh if only they were gone already, if only it was all behind them, this horrible house, horrible town, if only we'd never come here, what a strong man Klinkert was, a real man, when he first came here and sat and lectured, and it was all so certain and good, and now the desolation, she herself brought Therese, yes, she was Satan, she'd already destroyed so many young men, she never made anything of any of them, and now Klinkert, strong Klinkert, is running off to see her.

The door opened softly, she started at the sound, there was movement in the hall. Klinkert stood in the doorway, smiling, happy, and Therese was behind him.

In her shock Marie couldn't rise from the trunk. Therese wore a black mackintosh, another light coat over her arm, umbrella and walking stick hung from her wrist, she wore no hat, she had an unfamiliar, severe expression. Without ado she walked past Klinkert and up to Marie, who let her arms fall: "I've decided to travel with you, Marie. I hope you don't mind."

Marie's movements were slow, she glanced at Klinkert, who smiled at her, he was so happy, he had such an expectant look. At last Marie said: "Naturally I'm surprised."

"You thought he could tear himself away from me, leave with you. You see it is not so."

"What is happening?"

"I'm coming too."

"And I?"

"We'll travel together."

"I don't understand. Is it an excursion? We're all packed."

Klinkert came in: "Everything is as we agreed, Marie. We shall hand back the key shortly. Let me take care of it. I'll have the furniture sent on."

"I don't understand, Heinrich."

He laid his hand on her arm and implored: "Come, Marie."

She stood there a few minutes more and said: "Yes." As if Therese had been waiting for just this moment, she dropped coat, umbrella and walking stick onto the carpet beside her and twined, squeezed, pressed herself around Marie. Marie had no idea what to think. She cried when Therese eventually released her: "What are you doing to us?"

Looking up and from the side, Therese turned her flushed face with its fierce severe expression to Marie's, her breath came fast: "You think of yourself. It doesn't occur to you that I'm here too." Marie had never seen her like this, she had taken Therese for a friend and then for a thief. Marie wiped her eyes. Then she had to go into the next room and weep stormy tears on her bed until the door opened and Therese came in. She spoke curtly and decisively: "Clearly you misunderstand the situation. I shall not be deterred from this journey by anyone, not by you and not by my husband. You must come too. Klinkert wishes it. So do I. It is my doing that you will come along. This is my precondition for the trip. If you now declare that you won't join us, then I wash my hands of the whole thing."

Marie sat on the bed with a handkerchief to her eyes: "You know, Therese, that Klinkert has confessed everything to me. So why should you want me along?"

"He wants it. Go to him, let him explain. And I – I want it too. I'm not married to Klinkert."

"So hard, Therese."

"Decide, Marie."

"I've already decided. I shall come." And she stood up, walked past Therese into Klinkert's room, he was standing there. She gave his hand a silent squeeze.

Then they busied themselves with luggage. And that afternoon they set off, sat in the speeding train as it roared north, the unthinkable had happened, and the unthinkable was visible: they had not left Heidelberg behind, the empty house stood there like a cave, sent its breath after them. And what had emerged from Klinkert could not be scrubbed from the world and was visible, the inclination that kept him at Marie's side, and the pride and savagery and all that Therese had set down beside him – and it was visible too that Therese had found this man and clung fast to him in order to suffer her fate – and that Marie sat beside the friend of her heart who had fallen into error and whom – she felt this more and more strongly as the hours went by, and was glad they had persuaded her to come along – and whom she wanted to help. "I could have wished for no better situation."

≈≈≈

Klinkert lived with Marie in Berlin. This was decided by a single gesture of Therese's: at the station she gave her bags to another porter and chose another hotel. And when it was all over, the departure from Heidelberg, the journey, arrival, separation from Therese, and when all the luggage was in the hotel room and no more people knocked and entered, Marie sat in the room at Klinkert's side and took his head in her hands: "And what have you let yourself in for now? Do you know, Heinrich? You're here now and have what you want. Do you know what you've let yourself in for?"

"When I look back at the time in Heidelberg, I have no thoughts left. But slowly, here, in this hotel room, I start to understand something, Marie. And I tell you this because I love you – there, I've said it – you know I never say empty words – because I see that you are good to me and do not desert me and because you stay by me, even now. I am very grateful to you, Marie. Matters are coming to a head around me. That's my answer. All my life until now has been prologue. It's true: I've been sharpening my knife and never using it."

"Your scissors, Heinrich."

He felt in his waistcoat pocket, there it was, still on its little chain: "The symbol. You see, Marie, now the doctor himself is sick, and looks at the instrument he extolled to others."

"You won't cut anything with it, Heinrich." – "What do you mean?"

She stroked his hands: "You won't use your scissors. You can put it away nicely."

He stood up: "But I want to. I will. I will. What do you think of me?"

"You never even expected Therese."

≈≈≈

For two days he did not see Therese. He saw Posten, comfortable contented Posten, who rejoiced to see him. Then Therese's voice complained from the telephone.

The quiet hotel she was staying in was seven stories high, with several hundred rooms. The ground floor was taken up with reception rooms, big lounges, a restaurant, café, there was the reception desk, the porter, telephone booth, and above these the rooms, single, double, whole apartments, bathrooms, laundry rooms, carpets everywhere, staff walking or lurking, and it was a typical hotel in a big European city where itinerant people could alight on their path of flight. But Therese had not come here to hide away in a cell in some hotel, and it was not to assure her of the love of the man Klinkert that Klinkert rode up in the lift to see her.

Nothing was left of his intended actions.

And as he stood in her room, Heinrich Klinkert with his severe clean-shaven face, a twitch at the corner of the mouth, grey eyes open no wider than usual, at that moment – her sun shone upon him and the flower unfolded and he spoke words he had never known before. And feelings flowed through him that had not grown up between stones.

Once upon a time an emperor gave a signal, the emperor thought to accomplish evil deeds, at the signal people mustered in seaports and made themselves ready for a voyage to destruction. But the emperor's word had also lifted a stone from a well within them, they could hear water gurgling, they drank, and washed.

Therese in a light white dress, puffed sleeves with wide cuffs, a blue sash around her slender waist, no bracelets, no rings, curls dangling, Heinrich had never seen this Therese. And it was the summons of another, invisible emperor.

Her voice, at first she had complained by telephone, and now she complained some more. Once she was a ravening serpent. Now she gazed at him trembling, her fingers cold, her big pale blue eyes were full of tears. She drew the man in from the doorway to which he had climbed from the stony canyon of buildings and struggled his way to her through the labyrinth. One yearning human being gushed tears onto the face of another, to whom once she had said in cold calculation: "You must be more than what you are, you must take yourself completely in hand and make something of yourself, that is what life means, you can't be human any other way." And now the well overflowed.

Between them was no more rapine, wrecking, annihilation, debasement. The blooming earth spread before them, they delighted in it, reveled in their joy.

He called her jailer, guard, unexpected help, salvation, breeze speeding him over the deep. "I know, Therese, where I went wrong. I wanted and spoke to a thousand people. I wanted to dominate. I no longer want to dominate anything, not even myself. No, and not you either. It's just covetousness, greed. What did I become. I bring you the corpse of Heinrich."

"You mustn't remind me of my shame. There was something horrible about us, Heinrich. All the things I did. I've been crying over it these past two days, because I've ruined so much and am ashamed before you. I'm filled with regret, Heinrich. Oh, if only regrets could help."

Then he searched into her eyes, and smiles and laughter were restored to them. He read in the book of the woman who was called Therese – and who remembered from afar, and did not remember, a life in a little southern town, with a man who was a judge, with whom she had played a murky game, and then there were lots of men, Heinrich appeared – and as if they were waiting for this moment words came easily from his tongue and he recognised everything about her, the teeth she used for biting, the lips that covered them, the tongue playing in the cavity of her mouth. On her hands ten fingers, each a ray targeting him. In her breast a heart was beating, he could feel it, it was an animal in there, it had concealed itself, it's your heart, and here's mine. You're a tree and I'm a tree, when we embrace our branches become entangled.

"Can you feel our flesh like a wall between you and me, Heinrich? I don't like what separates us, I don't want to return to myself. Oh Heinrich, what will become of us?"

Hours passed. Finally: "Are you still mine, Heinrich?"

"Yes."

≈≈≈

When he closed her door behind him and walked down the corridor and the bright-lit lift descended with him and at the bottom he was greeted by the jumpy rhythm of a dance tune from the banqueting hall, he was still not just one person, someone went with him invisibly whom he clutched to his breast, set down, a light airy figure, they kept pace with one another. All the while Klinkert's body moved mechanically, found its way out of the hotel, set its hat straight in the street, pulled gloves on. And as he walked – but still they sang together – the trams on the Damm rattled and screeched on their rails, buses pounded, cars darted, the roaring and thundering grew ever louder. The frail airy figure drew away from Klinkert. Traffic policemen stood in place on corners and controlled the crossings. This was Potsdamer Platz with its control plinth in the middle. Klinkert looked around and saw that he had wandered down the long wide street in a dream – such throngs of people, lines of traffic lurching forward, a bright warm sun was shining, this was Berlin. Ah, they'd left Heidelberg, that hill-girt leafy wooded little town with its pealing bells. They had come from there in a train, and travelling with them on black bat wings was – the little empty house, the judge's house, beside him in the train sat Therese, Marie – Marie, Therese – Therese, Marie. I left Berlin with so little baggage, he thought, Marie came along, she weighed almost nothing, now I'm back again loaded down by the hundredweight, Klinkert, Heinrich Klinkert. And he sat down in a café because his knees had become weak and shaky.

But those two, Therese and Heinrich, had not ascended as strangers to the cell in the stone hotel, it was already their cell, they lived there. They were friends with the stones, the asphalt, pipes, telephone wires, buses of this city, and every row of houses knew them again. Around Klinkert and Therese lay the city made all of stone, iron, glass, with streets of stone, tar and asphalt, penetrated by water mains, electric cables, gas pipes, occupied by houses, office blocks, factories, warehouses, marketplaces. Like mountains on the shoulders of giants of old, soaring to the heavens, so this dead weight lay upon people in their millions and buried them, but it was their handiwork, they were not suffocated by it. From faults in the mountainside, wafting and groaning out of its fissures came the hot breath, endless, sporadic, sometimes tempestuous, of the people who lay beneath, and it curled menacing around the houses.

When Klinkert left the café he went to see Posten, who kept an office in the city. He spent all day with him, in the office, on calls. Klinkert breathed the air of the city, regained his old, steady, confident gait. That evening Posten took him to a workers' meeting, noisy from the start. The air was filled with hate, adherents of different factions exchanged blows. Outside Posten said: "There, you see, the seeds are ready to sprout. There's no need to intervene. They've been struck blind, like it says in the Bible. They'll be no trouble when the time comes."

He extolled the arrangements which, after the War, had brought labour leaders to the pinnacle of state power, they had behaved like a bull in a china shop, there's every good reason to eject them, they're ruined and exposed, and stupid, stupid! Posten sat with Klinkert deep into the night, they ended up in Posten's shabby, even squalid, bachelor apartment. As Klinkert walked down the dark empty streets he knew so well, he smoked and was content. He thought about what Posten had shown and said to him. His steps guided him as if by themselves back to Marie. She woke up, was glad to see him. He was happy to be there.

Next morning, Marie still asleep, he sat up in bed sunk in thought. He had woken with a sense that much of what Posten said yesterday was alien to him, no longer close to his concerns, and slowly his thoughts drifted to Theres lying far away in the centre of the city in a huge heavy stone hotel near the station. She came, she's here, what a wonderful, miracle-filled morning yesterday. A soft fragrant bud had opened, and he himself. He bent over, covered his eyes: what has been laid upon me. I'm no longer who I was, Posten's ideas are cockeyed, everything I used to think is cockeyed, I no longer know how to regain my balance.

Then Marie seemed to stir, he lay back, pretended to sleep, and did in fact doze off, and when he awoke there was Marie with her fresh rosy face, she smiled at him, she had already been to early Mass, it was quite close by. Afterwards they had coffee together, Klinkert, pensive, told her about yesterday, about Posten, Therese.

"I wanted to take her to Mass," said Marie, "but everything is so dreadfully far apart here, and perhaps she doesn't even want to."

"Why shouldn't she want to? Don't be afraid of her. You said yourself how good I look this morning. She's just the same."

"I'd like to think so," sighed Marie, "oh, I'm such a poor wretch."

"Don't, Marie," he rubbed his forehead, recalled his thoughts while sitting up earlier that morning, "I don't like it," and squeezed Marie's hand.

"Heinrich, what do you want from me, what are your plans for me? Oh, it was such a weary day yesterday. But if I could just be with her more and be with her always and talk to her about you."

Heinrich thought he would let things take their course. All his stars had changed position, he wanted to find his way slowly back to an inward balance, wanted to bathe endlessly in the light that fell on him from Therese. Why try to hurry things. He had no friends. He would not let Posten peer into his soul. "I can't reveal to anyone what is going on in me. They'd laugh: woman trouble, an especially stupid affair, two women. To whom can I explain that it's not the women I'm troubled by. They could just as well be two men, there needn't be anyone external, it's all within me, and not just me, the things of our age are summoned to account for themselves, want me to interrogate them." And he felt blessed and strong enough to keep hold of both the women to whom he owed his life.

And all the while Therese dwelt in her cell in the stone palace, hummed like a bee, then the bee grew weaker and weaker and collapsed. And the same struggle set up in her that Heinrich had grappled with when he closed her door behind him, descended in the lift and wandered the streets of this city to which he belonged and which had been built up piece by piece just as he had, a mountain bearing down on millions of people, groaning breaths wafting from its fissures. She groped for the thoughts she had just had, she called to Heinrich, no answer came, she thought, tossed and turned, paced up and down along the walls of her cell, opened the door, this is where he went out, finally she became cold and wrapped herself in rugs brought from home, pale, her mind empty, now and then a magical memory ran through her of blissful days when a young ardent lover, a hot young blood, sat beside her and let himself be taken, and revenge on Heinrich. But she kept herself calm, it ebbed and flowed, she let it fight itself out all day long until – still he didn't come, and it reached a point where she couldn't bear it, she yearned, yearned for him, she had to admit it, but he didn't come, what is he up to, he's sitting with his Marie, should I go back, he only wants to humiliate me, oh how I yearn for him, oh the scoundrel, and she had to prowl around the telephone until her fingers wouldn't relax their grip, and lift the receiver, call him and lament. And when he came it was all buried once more. "Why must you leave again, Heinrich? You can't leave me here alone."

But he was impelled to leave, had to pry her hands from his shoulders, her damp face from his, he could not endure this for long, he wanted it, did not want it, was afraid of himself.

"Why do you want to leave, Heinrich? Look in the mirror, see the joy in your face."

He smiled, closed the door, she fell back and did not weep, she gnawed her finger and was ashamed and lamented, and then came long days, nights, she laid herself down on the glowing gridiron of waiting. He had opted for Marie, who could doubt it, he was a liar. She recalled those dreadful days back home when Heinrich had left her, they were still back home then, how she had surprised him in his own house standing there happily with Marie. He's up to his old tricks again. Oh how wretched I am. I must ruin them both.

≈≈≈

Heinrich was not granted the long months he needed to draw a line between himself and the past and settle accounts with Posten and others. More and more his ears were assailed by the terrible groaning of the human masses out of the fissures of the city-mountain in which he lived. Sorrow, pain, fear and anger grew in him.

Therese had deployed herself in his rear. She pursued Heinrich, she glided from her cell and appeared in Heinrich's lodgings and sat with Marie. Weeks passed, her husband came, the young judge, in a broken voice he said to Heinrich: "You have taken Therese from me. If you want to marry her, I'll set her free. Make her happy. I couldn't."

Heinrich – they were sitting in Therese's hotel room – passed a hand over his eyes. But before he could answer, Therese's voice sounded from behind his chair: "I have never thought of marriage." Her eyes had a strange sharp glint, her lovely face was rigid, her husband knew the cold severe expression, Therese always looked like this looming over her prey. The judge stayed a few more days in Berlin, his heart was lighter, there was hope. He left thinking: this time my Therese is heading for a major coup, I'll see her again soon, with or without the man.

Amid the comings and goings, the ups and downs, Therese was at her wits' end. She awoke every morning feeling she had not a trace of love for Heinrich, she hated him and wanted him and Marie dead. And when he came to her still in her dark mood, profoundly numb, full of rancour against him for casting her down into this numbness, she kept to herself, waited, was unable to decide, she felt something lurking in the background, and then it emerged, her arms relaxed, her features softened and became animated, and all at once she was back in the world with Heinrich and love and Marie.

Proud Therese sat small and timid beside him. "I really

should curse you and shall curse you, because you hold the key to my innermost being. I've no idea how you managed it. But it's unbearable to have someone around me locking and unlocking as he pleases, making me powerless. Oh, it's the height of tyranny. I'll have to start a war of liberation against you, Heinrich." Here she gave a little smile. She implored: "If black and white really want to mix together, tell them please that they should stay as they are. White here, black over there. I want to be only one of them. Tell them not to mix themselves up, Heinrich."

≈≈≈

They fluttered through the streets like butterflies, into the open air, she gazed radiantly at Heinrich, how changed he looked, she was happy to have made him so; it was all so long ago that he sat stiffly on his stool, lecturing; now he paid attention to things and people, he was sad; tomorrow you'll be happy.

Then she looked at him and the thought rose in her: how you slip away from me, I cling to you, oh why must I cling to you? How tragic, that I am nothing without him.

For a whole week she kept him, though he struggled, close by her in a suburb, he must stay closeted with her, she wrote this prescription for herself. Love gave way to annihilation, subjugation, and back to love. Therese was proud, she wanted to save herself from him, she forced him into the role of her earlier lovers. He had to acquiesce. Heinrich felt she was floating in a current he already knew. He wanted to help her, tried to entice her back, but there was no stopping it. She had begun to take him on trips out of the city, and when they returned, and to her surprise she wanted to return and insisted on it – "it was wonderful, Heinrich but we mustn't leave Marie alone for so long" – she drew Marie to her and began to go with her to Mass. She chivied Marie. Marie must help her. She wouldn't leave Marie alone, they went to prayers twice a day, Heinrich looked on uneasy and anxious, their immoderation made him unhappy, he and Marie never spoke of Therese.

But it was the intimacy in which Heinrich and Marie wrapped themselves that drove Therese to her final despair. She recalled, seemed to remember: I was a placid creature in Heidelberg, I had husband, friends, then Heinrich came and tore me away – why hasn't he left Marie, I'd have been a different person – now I gulp and gulp and still can't swallow him – what should I do with him, what to do about Marie? Once she demanded that Heinrich kill Marie. After tormenting him with this for an hour, she wept and called herself a criminal, and she didn't deserve to have him stay with her and have Marie worried about her, they should both flee, she cursed herself, and yet – she pressed her face to his, her eyes had a mad gleam, "and yet, Heinrich, it's all your fault!"

≈≈≈

July came. Therese, delicate, pale, stepped one morning after a good night onto the balcony of her hotel room, in her morning gown. The streets were very quiet, Heinrich was coming to take her on an excursion. He had a blue car. She saw it roll up the street. It was her lover, her beloved. He climbed out, saw her, waved, she waved back. He waited at the car, her beloved.

She felt the lovely young wonderful day and all the joy that awaited, the brightness and lustre and sweetness around Heinrich and Marie and how it would decay and she must annihilate it.

And no more reflection, a firm hand grasped her and led her back into the dimness of the room. Therese unlocked the door, she was in the corridor, her thoughts clear, the passage, where is the door, here are the bathrooms, the firm hand guided her.

She opened the frosted glass window overlooking the forecourt. Nothing forced her, it was her own will, she pulled herself up onto the windowsill, knelt on the parapet, and stretching her arms out to the lovely severe face of her man, dust motes dancing in the sunlight, let herself fall into the shadows.

≈≈≈

After the funeral, which took place in Heidelberg, Klinkert wandered about the country and returned no more to Berlin. Marie suggested that they separate. Something uncanny radiated from the disaster, forbade happiness.

Klinkert was in the Ruhr region, along the Rhine, town after town, like tunnels through which a train rushes. Every day brought letters from Posten, enticing him to come and work together, set to work at last, the times were developing exactly as they'd desired. Military and business standing shoulder to shoulder, a single bloc, there'd be a massive cleanup of the state, the national loudmouths would unfortunately find a place, but we can use them, where we Germans are concerned nothing ever happens without noise and bad tempers. But Klinkert did not surrender what he had gained. As he passed through town after town, he remained in a stupefied bewilderment. When he spoke his voice shook. When he touched on his experience, even from afar, he fell into a lamentable weeping.

Hellish, satanic world! Such scorn for allg that we are and might be. Therese lying on her face, smashed limb from limb. No mercy, no one intervenes, we're defenceless and abandoned.

In the morning sunshine people thronged a marketplace. Cries, laughter, swearing, the smell of fruit, dust, half-potatoes, trodden bananas. Who will save us. It flows to us from the fields, we stuff ourselves, it helps us live. They bring it to the city on trucks, for bellies large and small, we're hungry, now we're sated and burn on. You evaporate. You sprinkle more water on top and stoke more fire below and heat your oven. It's a carnival bear dancing on a hot grid. Meat stalls, big baskets of vegetables, pigeons and hens alive in their cages.

The terrible weeping welled up in his throat.

And this should be the last word?

Giordano Bruno

"I HAVE GIVEN you ample time," said Twardowski, one arm dangling over a prayer stool, to Giordano Bruno, "you stand there and give no answer." Bruno stood by the columns of the nave, head bowed, cloak gathered tight and covering his eyes. Only a faint glow from his flames showed through. The vast benighted church was silent.

Since Bruno gave no answer, Twardowski lowered himself onto the end of a pew, laid the sword across his knees, waited. He sat with his back to the other. After a while the ruddy glow drew closer. Twardowski stood and cleared his throat: "So, Giordano, you deign to appear."

"Why do you force me a second time to a church, when you wish to speak with me?"

"A courtesy to you. You must see that they still do not have the measure of you."

"I make no demands on them."

"You must justify yourself, even to them. Just as there is an eternal Conscience, just as there is the prick of repentance, so you must stay here and answer for yourself. You can't escape me. Confess −."

"Confess! Accursed word. Repent, accursed word. They kept me in a dungeon seven years, for seven years I was chained up, rats and vermin crawled over me, no fresh air to breathe − no sun, no trees, no flowers. No human laughter, no crying, only the men of the Inquisition with their litany: confess, repent. Twardowski, in those seven years they did to me all they could possibly do. They took me from the dungeon only to throw me into another cellar, where they bound my limbs and stretched them until they broke. They set my feet in blocks and beat them with wet rods. They took glowing lumps of metal and held them against my skin. Always someone asked: Do you confess, Giordano? Do you repent, Giordano? Then they tied my arms behind my back and raised me high and dropped me onto a sharp-edged beam. And when they could do no more and still I would not yield, their eyes started from their heads, they knew their helplessness and took themselves off to the court. And the court came to their aid. And they were so villainous, so shabby and so pitiful as to burn me at the stake, the mighty powerful Church, me, a lone wretch who brought only words against them, me whom they lured into a trap and delivered against all common law to the pope's Inquisition."

Giordano approached closer to Twardowski: "And now what do you want from me? Do you want to help them? Never, say I, not here and not anywhere, never shall you grant them their triumph by hearing me utter the words: I confess, I repent."

"Calm down, Giordano. The reason I summoned you is

precisely because you have won. I expect you to adhere just as strictly to the truth today as you did then."

"What do you want. Reveal yourself at last."

"We followed a poor little woman, a pretty young thing, we found her charmingly sweet. Not beautiful, she had no money, no prospects, just wanted her little bit of human happiness. That was in the city. You saw the dull fellow she hitched up with. I heard you groan, Giordano. Then you said: 'This is nothing special, it's fate, it can happen to anyone, rich or poor, pretty or ugly.' I forbade you to utter such churchy twaddle. If that's how it is and always shall be, why do we need you and the others. And before your time and without your help I believe it all went somewhat more gently. Then my compatriot Jagna went to the pretty young thing. You were horrified when he turned up. But why. As if you would not grant her five minutes of joy. Of course it turned out badly, he dropped her. She sank into despair, blackness, went to an oafish man, a dead marriage, an arduous life, work, some pleasure in her child – just breathing in, breathing out, worries, sleep and worries. And it is for this, my dear Giordano, that the Earth circles the sun. It is done, the Church had to concede in the end, but you were burnt. And it is for this that we have the infinity of worlds you never tired of praising."

Giordano was silent. A long pause.

Twardowski resumed from his seat: "We left the little creature, the poor drowning woman. You said you wanted to see what the Pole was up to. For he had plenty of money, good looks, and these are the powers that rule the world now. No others stand a chance."

"He was weak, this Jagna, he had no idea what to do with his gifts. He was a ball, a cork on the water."

"Things turned out badly for him. You saw. It hasn't gone any better for weak people since the Earth acquired the power to revolve around the sun and everyone conceded that power. Not even money and beauty can help, yet these are the powers that supposedly replaced the dear God of old. But since this weak man Jagna rebuffed you so swiftly, we had to turn to Doctor Faust.

That was the two young German gentlemen. One was called Heinrich. He at least was strong and decisive. You seemed to take to him."

Giordano nodded: "At first."

"And you also took to the serpent Therese. You saw well that these were people after your own image, people of your creation, you dear God of nowadays, dear God number two, and I gave you the opportunity to know your Adam-and-Eve couple, so you could have your seventh day and bless them."

Giordano groaned: "I suffer, I suffer. Yet it's good, Twardowski, that you summon me here."

"It seems you are not interested in blessings."

"What I saw was horrible. I cannot grasp it. I cannot resign myself to what my eyes have seen, I must know it more deeply. I and the others never wanted this. These times do indeed contain more horrors and are more terrible than the times when I was alive. And if you want a confession from me, then there you have it. But this – is not my world."

"It's the one you started, you, Copernicus and Galileo."

"Oh please listen to me. Do not break the rod over my back so soon. Did you come to me as a judge, are you one of my murderers, do you really mean to contrive a posthumous triumph for them?"

"I am listening, and waiting."

"I thank you, I do, for summoning me. My soul was already in another existence, and is glad to see all this again. Wonderful world! Wonderful world! Whatever I did to you, I did not kill God. I removed from the divine the petty human face, and set it in its eternal, mysterious, everywhere radiant place. I did not turn beasts into gods. You forests and streams that I have now seen again, you clouds and stars, surging seas, flowing airs of the sky, sun, this one of the many great worlds, all of you, you words of the Eternal, I greet you. Accept me again into your circle. Receive me once more. There are none who praise you more devoutly than I. Show me freely your cruelties, your guns and cudgels, your miseries, your dead, I remain steadfast, I know the world does not smile like a little girl. It is so vast, without beginning or end, plunging into eternity. You primal Being, power of powers, you live and rule here and everywhere. My arms seek to embrace your knees, my voice seeks to reach your ears, you veer away into eons, swirl in the stars, planets, comets. You glow in fire, you breathe the cold, hurl yourself as water on our fields, in wind and hurricane you scud across mountains, billow as smoke from volcanoes, you lift up the mountains, you scoop out the valleys, you draw the compass needle to the pole, the boulder falls, who lets it fall if not you. Who lets rivers fill and empty, rise and fall, and Man arise, animals grow, plants bloom. From whom do we come if not from your hand. We shoot like sparks from your primal flame. We are all of us sparks of your primal light. Oh, are you not divine, primal and eternal, like a serpent winding quick as lightning through the temporal, sloughing off world after world. Wonderful, more than wonderful, that once again I can praise you, having been cast down. Now I see you again in your profusion, you the uncreated, immortal, most deep, most high, brightest and darkest, you everything in us: the ladder and the climber. I have but one complaint: that I cannot worship you sufficiently, you who enter through the portals of my senses and leave through the portals of my senses. As sunlight falls on empty husks, as breezes waft through reeds and make them sing, reeds and wafting breeze, so do you suffuse my being. Oh power and glory, dominion and true life, power and deed and wisdom and love, all-encompassing sustaining love, endless Centre."

This was Giordano's softly sung hymn, his rapturous sigh. It faded. Giordano stood motionless as he sang. His head was lowered, cloak drawn around him. The church was huge. But although Giordano's voice was feeble, it resonated around the columns, statues, pictures, overlaid the high gloomy vaults of the roof like wax on a young fruit. And as he fell silent, he was answered by whispers, murmurs, susurrations from above and from the sides.

Pan Twardowski stroked his little goatee. After a while he cleared his throat. "All this does not answer my question. It was not for this I summoned you. You always spoke in such fashion.

There was no need to traipse through cities just for this. You will sing this song regardless of the times, and the world can be destroyed by fire and a Deluge can come upon us. What trouble does it put you to, praising Glory and Eternity. Who are these lies aimed at? Take them to that poor girl, the Extra, whose life is wasting, ask the Pole, ask unhappy Therese lying there on her face."

As if Twardowski had not spoken, Giordano again started chanting.

"Love, oh Love! You make manifest the deepest foundations of truth. You uncover the darkness, and where there are clouds you shine through them. You alone have this power. You are the eye of reason. You shatter the iron gates of error. What Heaven, Earth and Hell hold fast and guard, you make manifest and all can see it. Oh doltish people, do you want to see the Truth? Open your stupid eyes. If Love has not entered into you, you shall seek in vain."

The whispering around the columns, in the nave, from the sides grew louder. Already it was a soft harmonious song, billowing towards Giordano. It kept sounding long after Giordano had finished. Twardowski had pounded his sword on the floor, now he cried in fury: "You will stop now! I think it is enough. I had assumed that one who went to the stake for his beliefs was a somebody. But you are a nothing. You're a windbag, an orator, beguiler. You're a scandal, after all that you have seen. So shameless: to mock those who lie dead, who carry hideous death in their hearts, and squirm! That's nothing, you say to them in consolation, for God is wonderful and sits on his throne. No! That god is dead. He is dead! And never again shall he dare to come alive in the world and show his face. Misery is in the world, wickedness, arrant perfidy, and no reason at all, no wisdom at all, and no love!"

The church was deathly quiet. The whispering had stopped. Giordano shrank into his cloak. No glow came from him, unbroken darkness filled the church.

A long time passed before a word came from the black figure at the feet of Twardowski, who was drawn up to his full height. It was a breath: "I know, I know."

"Well then," growled the other.

The black figure groaned, and sobbed: "I saw more than just the three I was sent to see. I sat in lecture halls and heard what they teach. I walked through libraries and browsed in books. I stood beside workers in factories, men and women in these wonderful factories. Pardon my tears. I have spent many hours doing nothing but weep. It is a debased humanity. All we did was in vain. They sit deeper in shame than in our day. We gave them everything we saw and felt. And this is what they have made of it, this is what has become of it: the possibility of acknowledging no laws, of glorifying all that they do in their wickedness, of hardening themselves against all feeling. Where is the villainy they would shrink from, what lies will they not fling in humanity's face. Yes, it happens, and I saw it and heard it. In the lecture halls I learned how they justify themselves: there are only numbers and weights and motion, all else is illusion and deception, now they can unlock their chains. This is not me, Twardowski, it is not me. Hear how I curse them.

"We meant to lead them to the Earth, to the glory of the Earth, to its inexhaustible riches, its inexhaustible spirit in which the human has a share. They were to see who they are, find themselves again. Why prate of a Paradise that existed somewhere, sometime? We wanted to open their eyes so they would see what lies right beside them, created by the primal Eternal and laid out before them.

"It failed. What we offered was torn from our hands by evil spirits. The powers, the wicked who rule on Earth, took control of our gifts and now, I tell you, they are ripe for the flaming sword of retribution. It shall come to pass. Oh, they think they can know everything, they think that every secret, every mystery was chased from the world along with their distant god. But it only buried itself deeper. The wicked, the degenerate, the depraved, how they have hollowed out the world, how they have poisoned, impoverished, and stultified all of humanity. And they call on us, on me, to be their witness. If they could, they would make me their saint. I gave them a noble songbird, they plucked its feathers to stuff their stupid beds. And it was not Copernicus, and not Galileo, and not I. We wanted to make humanity more divine in a divine world, they drove it into a swamp, turned it into a ravening toad. No love, no reason, no wisdom – only violence, murder, loneliness, and fear! This is what I saw."

"Now I have heard the case for the prosecution, Giordano Bruno. How do you answer it?"

"Destroy the world! Destroy it! Destroy it! The Eternal, the primal Eternal, lives on! Truth destroys those who shackle it! Humanity is sinking into a depravity of new lies and delusions. This is not the will of God, this is not what we died for." Giordano's glow flickered here and there in the space between two columns, his voice, not loud, had taken on a piercing hiss: "Bring a mirror! New singers, new poets! New warriors! New martyrs! The human species has foundered. The wicked are among you, they have dominion over you. Grieve, oh grieve! See it and grieve! Grieve more, still more. From the soul of grief comes a helping hand, consciousness, the avenging arm. The time is ripe. Save humanity from its downfall! Oh defiled world, oh wonderful Earth!" He was surrounded by the murmuring of a thousand voices. He flew wildly up into the heights of the nave.

Twardowski tracked him: "Where to, Giordano?"

The voice rang out: "For five hundred years we strove to draw the eyes of men back down to Earth. I need five hundred years more."

"And then there'll be Paradise? That's what they said after Jesus Christ. Five hundred years more, let's make a Church that encompasses all humanity, then everything will be all right."

"The world is in flux. There is always a need for new churches. Look at the grief, it shows that truth lives. Say again, Twardowski, who are you? How were you able to summon me?"

"I am the conscience of your age. I have been granted the power to summon you and hold you to account."

"Twardowski, you summoned me too soon. Another five hundred years."

Giordano stood in flames before him, the entire nave and star-spangled ceiling were lit by the glow. His fiery eyes glared at Twardowski, who stood, both hands on the pommel of his sword. How the heart beat behind the ribs in Giordano's fiery transparent breast, how it pulsed, rose and fell. How his lungs expanded and sagged. How the tongue played in his mouth. How intently, hands outstretched, challenging, did he await Twardowski's response.

Twardowski threw back his bony head. He raised the sword high, closed his eyes.

All at once Twardowski's sword swung through the air. Dense black multitudes rustled all around him. Giordano, screaming, whirled, flung himself about. Twardowski, huddled in his cloak, groaned, wept as he had at the beginning: "I say no. I won't do it."

"You must."

"I won't do it. I will not be lied to. You can lie your way like this through ten centuries, twenty centuries and still complain and still cry out for yet another five hundred years. You will not succeed. You brought misfortune on mankind. And you must pay."

"I brought them the truth, and you shall not touch me."

"Because you believe this and still have some hope for these dregs of the Earth, this humanity, I shall put an end to you. Humanity is cursed. They shall be cursed. And you with them. You shall be dead, a nothing."

"You shall do nothing to me."

Giordano, spinning like a pillar of fire, was surrounded by a cloud of whispering voices. Twardowski swung his sword at the cloud. It parted, receded from him, flowed around him like a swarm of bees, enveloped him. From one side of the nave, from the statues and pictures, bright streaks emerged shouting, merged with the cloud that hovered there. Twardowski swung about him, roared. But already the bright mass was veering away through the air. A window high in the vaulted ceiling cracked open.

The bright cloud flew out, Twardowski screamed in pursuit. Over the silent marketplace, high above the houses beneath the clouds Giordano flowed, flung himself, whooped, swirled.

Twardowski in his black cloak pursued like a dark rag. In vain he snatched at the bright tumultuous figure ahead. He gave up. He sank into himself, floated with the other clouds.

The stone church stood there in the night.

≈≈≈

Part Ten

SWANSONG

The Man who Disappeared

AT FIRST KLINKERT, a man of his time, no different from most of those around him, settled for a few short weeks on the hill road above Frankfurt am Main. It was a lurch towards Heidelberg, Therese's home town. Along the way he lay low in Frankfurt, then pushed on farther, and then one day he wrote letters and received replies and was despatched far away by Posten and the business his father had founded, across the national border (it was another border he wanted to cross): to Paris.

Paris. Work, visits, tasks, impressions. At first he seemed lost in empty space, and in quiet moments it grew unbearable, then unfamiliar impressions seeped in, and inward questionings and conflicts faded. To forget, cast it all away: this was hard to achieve. After a visit from Posten, who boosted his morale and for the first time made him laugh again, he planned, since it all seemed to be working out, to rent an office in the city for their firm. And so he sits one morning at a table in the hotel's breakfast room. Few guests, waiters chatting at the buffet. Klinkert has opened two business letters, laid them aside, holds a third in his left hand, which has dropped to his lap. The letter bears a Polish stamp, the handwriting is unfamiliar, perhaps a woman. The mother of Jagna, the handsome Pole. She had obtained his address from Posten, her son has been missing for ages, they have tried in vain to find him, apparently he is in France. If Klinkert could perhaps find some trace of him ...

Jagna the roué. That was then. Unconsciously, Klinkert sits stiff and upright as in the old days, his face tense, his gaze seemingly aimed at the pattern in the carpet. But he doesn't see these tulips that merge into lilies and hyacinths. He stares into the distance, because behind his eyes an imperious voice is speaking in his head.

Our dear Jagna, rogue, gambler, skirt-chaser, debates with a monk, we tested his mettle, the husband visited, he shot him. *How gracefully, O man, with thy palm-bough, Upon the waning century standest thou, In proud and noble manhood's prime.* And as if from a pulpit a voice speaks to him: You knew nothing of it. And what in fact did you know. I shall open the door to your past, your dead past. You gulped down wisdom from Socrates to Nietzsche and strove to add your own little bit. You had to busy yourself with everything except what concerns you. Let a wolf eat what it may, it stay s a wolf. For what battlefield, for what desolate struggles have you spent yourself, not your battles, your soil is patient, covers itself deep in debris. All those decades gone, years of your life. You grew up like this with Posten, oh, where did you grow up. Look at you sitting in this fine hotel. Far from the shooting, that's your motto.

You did not join in the game. You were never in the game. Your game never got started. You came in only at the end, and now you run away. You lacked all awareness. Evil times! Now you sit stiff and upright as before. But you stayed a long time down there.

The pale young waiter in his black apron gravely pours coffee from the big pot, retreats without a word. After a while Klinkert stands up. The boy at the door hands him hat and gloves. He is a man of medium build in his thirties, but looks much older. Face grey and bony.

He starts the search for Jagna without delay. He hires detectives.

Just look at the city. Hellish, satanic world. Dancing bear on a hot grid.

Sometimes along the street you sink onto a chair at a café, stir your coffee, look through the window, out there people walking happily, calmly along in a crowd. It looks like chaos, but it all flows smoothly. Even the hearses here are smart motor cars that sail over the asphalt with their dead and the bright wreaths people have piled onto them. And for the living and for the dead it's all like a peaceful garden, you smile, walk by one another, exchange greetings.

Klinkert has to find Jagna, it's his task. After weeks of hunting he tracks him down, in Paris. Jagna works in a suburb, in a cork factory. Klinkert waits for him one evening in the street. The Pole is stunned to see him, then angry. Then Jagna walks beside him in his blue shirt, hands deep in the pockets of his baggy dungarees, he puffs his pipe, on his head is a peaked cap. He's much thinner than before, his chin is sharp, he has a little black moustache. Klinkert recognises him by the big black eyes, now mournful, now icily immobile.

How did you find me, he asks Klinkert. It's a dusty autumn evening, they sit outside a little café. When Jagna hears of the letter from his mother, he is silent. He shakes his head: "That woman won't give up. As if I were her son."

Klinkert is astonished: "She's not your mother?"

"In the sense people mean. She can do nothing for me."

"I never knew she meant you ill, Jagna. Her letters are friendly enough."

"We were never on bad terms. It was the usual theatre. Forget all that nonsense. What are you doing here?"

"I'm in business."

"With Posten?"

"You remember him?"

"Oho, you villains, you landed me in hot water. Fine brothers you are. Now you regret it, want to drag me back to my mother, is that it? Or what are you after? Earn money off me?"

Klinkert had nothing to say to this ironic tone. As they parted, Jagna tested him: "A noble youth, as ever. Probably think you're the cat's whiskers, finding me at last. Are you going to play a new game with me? Where's Posten?" He spun on his heel, was Posten nearby, then nodded disdainfully to Klinkert: "When you see him, say hello from me. And my mother. I guess that's all you can take back, yes?" He held out a languid hand, took the pipe from his mouth with his left hand, now his face wore an expression of disgust.

Klinkert ran after him to the Metro entrance, asked if he could see him again. Jagna stood on the landing, drew slowly on his pipe not looking at Klinkert, then raised his head, frowned and said yes.

A few evenings later they were to meet at the same place. Jagna turned up an hour late, puffed smoke for ages before saying a word. When he had gulped his glass of wine he said Klinkert was lucky: he's going away next morning.

"Where to, Jagna?" – "Since when was it your business?"

Now it was time to put cards on the table. "I want to go too."

"Just as I thought." – "You did?"

"Of course. You didn't hunt me down on behalf of an old woman in Poland you've never met. You want to know how I managed to hide myself away."

"Jagna, I want to go too. Tell me, where are you going?"

"So you can betray me. I'll never trust your sort again as long as I live. You fine scum."

"You're right, Jagna. We know it all too well. What are your plans?"

Jagna laughed: "Detectives these days, they want their prey to confess on the spot." All of a sudden he stared directly at Klinkert: "What's up with you?"

Klinkert: "It concerns others, not just you."

"They're following you? Want to collar you?"

"One day you realise what a stinking mess you're in. And you want out, for God's sake."

Jagna drank from his glass, wiped his little moustache and gave Klinkert a long hard look. He started to fill his pipe, muttered "So so" several times. Then he punched Klinkert on the arm and smiled craftily: "Has the money run out?"

"No, it's – gone."

Jagna understood. "Good." He reached a hand to Klinkert across the table, a firm grip.

Now Jagna filled his pipe, he had a grave determined look, said reflectively as he took the first puff: "Yes, I'm going away. You can know that much. You can write to my mother and tell her. She needn't worry her head any more about the one she calls her son, and who is her son if she wants." Jagna's lips twitched, you could see it working away inside him, he coughed, and without looking up said: "Meanwhile, something's happened that draws a line under my account." He looked up at Klinkert: "Have you heard of Houteville?" – "No."

"Robbery with murder."

My God, where is this going.

"I got to know him well, here in Paris. And his girlfriend. She was a streetwalker. He didn't like it. They were very much in love. She fawned over him like a schoolgirl. At first I thought her a bit common, but later –. Maybe you'll see her, she's coming to collect me. Then she fell ill, and the two of them couldn't get by without cocaine. He was no ordinary fellow, his parents threw him out over some foolishness, he told me about it, they never gave him a penny, he was meant to eat humble pie. Then he was desperate, they went hungry, and then cocaine. So he took a taxi, meaning to go over to his parents' place and make them see reason. Then the taxi had to go past a jeweller's. It's evening, a little quiet street, the jeweller's arranging his shop window. So the taxi drives on a bit and then Houteville tells it to stop. He has an idea, goes back. He was a fine big lad, how the woman clung to him, such love, and he for her. What he did, he did only for her. And she knew it. He'd take a handful of pearls and some watches, it all went well in the shop, he'd already stashed some things in his pocket. Only the man had to notice, he demands it back, grabs the lad, begins to shout, the loser. You can picture the scene. Can't you, Klinkert?"

Klinkert nods slowly.

"So you're just like him. But the prosecutor saw it differently. He said: you throttled and shot the jeweller. That's why you had a revolver with you. Of course he had a revolver with him. It was premeditated murder. Says the prosecutor. So they sentenced him. Penal colony, for life. I'm going with him. To Cayenne. Can't be as bad as here."

"How many years did he get?"

"I told you, life. It was all for a scalp. When they haven't a clue they always demand a scalp. Their machine never errs, but if anyone comes along to point it out, they foam at the mouth."

"He did it for his girl, and no extenuating circumstances?"

"It was the extenuating circumstances that put him in the penal colony. And for that I won't grant them any extenuating circumstances."

"What will you do in Guiana?"

"Turn my back on them, Klinkert. There's only two options: tear it all down here, or leave."

"Jagna, think it over. I was in despair once, but I didn't give up."

Jagna laughed in his face: "Klinkert in despair! I know despair. No doubt you wrote something in your diary or felt bad for an hour, poor little rabbit. But I went to the Dominican as well, you remember, back in Munich."

Before Klinkert could reply, Jagna put the money for his coffee on the table, took a deep breath, stood and clapped Klinkert on the shoulder in farewell. For a common-looking woman was standing on the pavement a few paces away, hatless, holding a shopping bag, a broad gaunt face, deepset dark-circled eyes, thick scarf around throat and shoulders, big earrings, she seemed to have no teeth, her mouth was clamped like an old woman's, a colourless line. She watched them both without expression. Klinkert went with them. They walked to a Metro station. The woman said: "Perhaps the gentleman has something to spare. We could use it."

Klinkert came again early next morning to bring the woman money for the convict. She was wearing a cap and a dark green overcoat, dragging a suitcase. She had no objection to Klinkert going with her to the train station. On the way he gave her the money, she nodded, tucked it away, barely said thanks. She said goodbye outside the station.

A few days after this, Klinkert looked for Jagna in his lodgings, not far from the café. The landlady was suspicious, there had been a lot of visits by detectives on account of the murder.

"He's going to Guiana. You're his friend? Why couldn't you talk him out of it? To listen to him he's a terrible tearaway, but he's the most peaceable fellow in the world."

She announced that he'd waited until the prison transport

sailed with his friend, then bought his ticket. His suitcase is no longer here.

You learn to live more slowly

KLINKERT LIVED through savage days.

He gnawed his fingers in impotence and despair. I don't know what's meant to happen. Blessed those who have a faith. Should I stay alive, should I try again, should I follow you, Therese?

Because he had no one around him, because the news from home was dreadful, he went back to Germany. The great coup had succeeded. The parties that had fought each other were defeated by the most robust, which then, amid the general confusion and cheered on by many people in Klinkert's circle, proclaimed itself the State.

As it was dangerous to talk, Klinkert kept his views to himself. It stabbed him to the heart to see how many radiant faces greeted him and in a way congratulated him: the victors were behaving as he had always advocated, steely, instrumental. Broad robust Posten, smug savage daredevil, was intoxicated with the methods and their impact. He was delighted that Klinkert, whose spiritual strength (now Posten speaks of spiritual strength!) could be put to good use, had returned to take part in the reconstruction. Klinkert had no regrets about returning. It pulled him out of his confusion. People seemed reborn, they went about in a kind of holiday mood. But he could see what was also going on, like the muddy trickles after a thunderstorm – how petty vindictiveness reared its head, how friends and acquaintances sniffed around each other and dared not speak, how mistrust loomed like a monster over everyone, how mindless hordes of careerists, a wretched downtrodden tribe, hurled themselves into public positions and offices and kicked others in the face.

"How now, wise owl," cried faithful Posten, "you see: home is best." And Posten confided that he had excellent connections, they'd be working full steam. "It really is a revolution!"

"Whose property has been confiscated," Klinkert wanted to know.

"Why?"

"Because you all act as if you've come into a massive inheritance, or it's your birthday."

"The uncle from America," said Posten, "is us, ourselves. That's what's new, dear boy. The strength of the people is our bank, and it's available to all."

"Free of charge?"

"Workers and trades unions are all in it with us. There's never been a revolution like it." He said this without winking.

And young people Klinkert came across in the street, whom he had known in Heidelberg, said the same. They besieged him, remarked excitedly on the turnaround, the deliverance. It should have come ten years ago. They sounded Klinkert out. Then one after another they stole quietly by themselves to Klinkert in his lodgings and wanted to know how he stood. They were unsure, uneasy, a few were frightened. Klinkert did not reveal himself, he trusted no one. One who came presented a shocking picture. He had become a journalist, and swiftly joined the new movement. He was a shining success. Before, he was thoughtful and restrained. Now he acted as if he had found himself, railed against the old epoch that had suppressed him, spat fire and flames against perfidy and corruption and painted himself as a flag-bearer for the new age. Klinkert let the words flow over him. They all seemed happy to have their elbows free, so they could lash out as the fancy took them.

In a tête à tête with his friend, Posten delivered his views: "Now you see what it was we lacked. In the Middle Ages the proper gentry, the knights, sat in their castles and ran a true regime. Then the emperors came and mashed it all up. They suppressed the knights and tried to rule all by themselves. There was only serfdom. Now we're free. We shall reach an understanding with the people. The regime will be strict, but that's as it should be."

In the evenings industrialists and engineers, friends of Posten, came to visit. They smoked. An engineer, pale and greasy, clever smooth face, blew smoke into the air meditatively: "Bah. Talk of dictatorship, despotism. We should be glad there are people willing to take it on, such positions are dangerous. Instead of thanking

God that someone's prepared to play the dictator, people slander him."

"You're right," said Posten.

"I'd never want to be dictator under any circumstances. But what we need is a pack mule, ready to take on everything they hang about its neck."

Posten twinkled at Klinkert: "Even liberty?"

"Even liberty. And astronomy. And tar from coal. It's all the same to me. Plunder, plunder, I say. Plunder, I say for the third time. What should a man do? Fritter away his life. That's all there is. Or is there something more, Posten, Klinkert? Then tell me the secret. Since you won't, I assume you too know nothing. Fritter it away, fall in love, annoy people."

The same rotund young engineer, only a couple of strands of blonde hair on his bald head, repeated during a pause in the card game: "My principle: steer life towards the gentle not-life. Keep spinning along. And then I think: a war now and then, as a freshener. What do you say?"

≈≈≈

After a few weeks it was clear to Klinkert that he had to leave, come what may. There were two phenomena: whispers, and shouting. Menacing shouts filled the foreground, keeping quiet had become dangerous. They tipped Klinkert off: he's being watched. And he noticed it himself. They tried to challenge him with remarks about bloodless heads and brain-creatures whose time was past. They valued the Deed, and mocked him: "The Deed arises not from knowledge, but from instinct, from our demonic desire, from belief in our mission."

Klinkert gritted his teeth, was defenceless. People who had never opened a book crowed about "cowardly intellectual courtesans crawling ever deeper into their mouseholes". In the beer gardens they spoke loudly about the patriarchy that had created states, they wanted to reintroduce the ancestral tablet, but were scared of their wives and superiors; and instead of honouring or even idolising their dead parents they nursed a rage against them, preferred not to think of them, and none could be stirred to visit the cemetery more than once a year.

≈≈≈

Klinkert was Posten's guest. He had no plan yet. He shut himself away a great deal in Posten's little library, tried to come to terms with himself and put himself back on his feet.

In the street, near the Zoo station one misty day, as Klinkert was turning into the zoo, a slight, elderly, very plainly dressed man looked at him attentively as he passed. Klinkert felt uneasy, he turned round, followed the man, looked sidelong at him, recognised him: Professor Krug, his Latin teacher from school. They spoke. The teacher had been pensioned off long ago. As they stood there he asked, after a pause and a long strangely penetrating look, for Klinkert's address. Barely a week later he turned up at the door.

"Do you sit in here often?" he asked Klinkert in Posten's library. "Do you read?"

"Of course," Klinkert nodded. Again that probing look from the old man. He moved closer, said softly: "You don't approve?"

"What do you mean?" The visitor repeated: "You don't approve?"

Klinkert understood, a chill went through him, he was hesitant even before this old man who was surely not capable of betrayal. The man whispered: "You see, that's how it is. You too have no courage. We're all the same. They should have told you that a year ago. You're afraid of me. You're afraid of the whole world." And the frail professor with the trim snow-white hair sat upright, his hard blue eyes fixed Klinkert, and now Klinkert knew who it was facing him, his stern teacher, incorruptible, relentless.

"No," said Klinkert, returning his gaze, "I do not approve."

"So what will you do?" – "I don't know."

"I'm a pensioned civil servant. My father fell in 1870. I'm Prussian, remain Prussian and won't allow myself to be made Asiatic or African. I will not betray my father, my teachers and my books. My colleagues in service do that. Shame on them. Tell me, what is happening?"

"I don't know."

"You don't know. But you know these people. This is your generation."

"I really don't know, Professor. And really I have no desire to understand it."

"Well. This is what our education leads to. Some betray, and the others shrug it off."

"Our hands are tied, professor, now that things have gone so far."

"What is your opinion of Christianity?"

"Why?"

"They're courting it. You think of everything when you're in a tight spot. In my family we followed only a lukewarm Christianity, unsurprising, we were all scholars of ancient languages. I've thought hard about it. Even Christianity is no use. Christianity is despair. It affects only the ego. We are lost, betrayed and sold left and right: that is Christianity's starting point. You can only depend on yourself and your faith: that, frankly, means despair."

He looked expectantly at Klinkert. Klinkert: "I've had little to do with Christianity. Though I haven't broken with it. It wasn't worth the effort. If you ask me," he thought for a moment, "in times like these you still need Christianity precisely because people are lost, left and right. You have only yourself to fall back on."

"That takes us no farther. What do people hope for from a doctrine that says: abandon your father and mother and follow me? It nullifies us from the start. And what do people do? They hide behind prayers, they assert a particular character called God – with what methods, with what possibility, let's be frank, with what recklessness, even if they do actually mean anything when they use that word. Someone said: a world that dares to do without God will be its own ruin. And vice versa: whoever dares to engage with such a God is ruined."

Klinkert listened, attentive and deeply moved: "Could be. Could be." After a pause: "And what then should a God be?"

The eyes of the old Latin teacher flashed, he laughed: "What should light be? What should lightning be? I don't know. That's what he should be. He should show himself. How, that's up to him. And if he doesn't reveal himself – especially now – and you see that nothing at all depends on his solemn approval, then we should stop playing the fool, cast off the whole spell."

Klinkert nodded again: "I see, I see. Perhaps you really mean it, perhaps you're just posing the question to yourself."

"And you?"

Klinkert considered: "Many new necessities confront us. The way is not yet clear. You're right, of course: the ego, the ego."

The old man shook his head: "I never said that. But what then? A king? Education?" He bit his lower lip, which was trembling: "All that is gone too."

"Were we ever guided by education?" asked Klinkert. The professor looked at him with a frightened expression: "How do you answer?"

"The question just occurred to me. It's easy to answer 'no'. But I just see the question." He rested his arms on his knees, sank into himself and said softly to the floor: "The ego. It must be the ego. Maybe not our ego, as we conceive of it. Maybe another, stronger, mightier ego that contains something, wants this, does not want that – that knows what it wants."

The professor shook his head in frustration: "Leave it. It doesn't help. Brooding is no help."

"There's no help, today or tomorrow," said the man who had lost Therese.

≈≈≈

After the professor left, Klinkert sat a long while at the desk in the library, head in his hands. Who had said: "It's wonderful being good, it does you good to be good – what wellsprings we tap when we can be good, what torments fall silent!" Who said that? Therese.

At last he raised his eyes. There on the shelves stood the theologian Angelus Silesius, leather-bound Goethe, on a high shelf Nietzsche, Hölderlin, Novalis; Posten had raised them to the dusty heights. *Come, you rarest vial, you precious potion, that I now fetch down in deep devotion.*

Klinkert sprawled in the leather armchair.

I'm being punished. My enemies go about triumphant. They

deny me air. Your enemies, why your enemies? – Because they set themselves up as my masters, but I have not granted them that status. And I refuse to accept it. – But you see how they go about and hope. Stand up and hope along with them. Or don't you need to? It's a fact you gave up on Latin. – I'd like to hope. It shouldn't upset me to go along with them, with their hundreds of thousands, and millions. I can't imagine anything finer. That's what I've learned, I know it, I was blighted without it. But this. – Why not this? Why not? Just do it. – Don't tempt me. They don't go together. It's a pretence. Rapture is not enough for me, I want transformation. This is not it. They don't act. They are led, herded, driven into a garlanded trap.

He leafed through Goethe's poems. Suddenly he shook convulsively. He felt that if he could cry, this would be the time. He read: *A violet stood upon the lea, Hunched o'er in anonymity.* He whispered: "Hunched o'er in anonymity." He lighted on the Sorcerer's Apprentice, long-lost friend: *Good! That old sorcerer has vanished, And for once has gone away! Spirits called by him, now banished, My commands shall soon obey!*

There, see the *Roman Elegies*, here you are:

Speak, ye stones, I entreat! Oh speak, ye palaces lofty!
Utter a word, oh ye streets! Wilt thou not, Genius, awake?
All that thy sacred walls, eternal Rome, hold within them
Teemeth with life; but to me, all is still silent and dead.
Oh, who will whisper unto me,--when shall I see at the casement
That one beauteous form, which, while it scorcheth, revives?
Can I as yet not discern the road, on which I for ever
To her and from her shall go, heeding not time as it flies?

He closed the book on his knees. Eternal Rome, silent for so long. Long-lost world. I knew it once. You creep up on it like a criminal. Unmasked as a criminal. But what can I do. I couldn't avert what's happening out there, I was wicked to help it along, now it's on my shoulders. Eat, bird, or die.

Silently he glowered into the room, clutched the book tightly. Locked up like a criminal, here in this room. They'll burst open the door and come to me to loosen my tongue. Cursed logic of existence: first Therese, that was a hint to me, now I'm in the firing line.

His hands kneaded the book, he whispered, swore at the carpet. Fetters, they'll try to seize me, they'll dare, they'll presume, my young men, and if I do what I must and speak what I must, it'll be all over for me.

A newspaper lay on the little table beside him. Posten had marked something in red: "Theoderich the Great was the vehicle and executor of an inevitable historical catastrophe. Teutonicism confronted Christianity and the classical world. The fulcrum of history lies between the Mediterranean and the north." Klinkert stood up in anger, carefully put the Goethe volume down on the table. Teutons! Teutons! They're Germans. They scream it daily. They do nothing but scream. I've never made head or tail of that claptrap. Let them support what they want. But I too am a German. I am a German. Yes, I am. I am just as good a German as those with their foam-flecked mouths. This is my country. Mine too. I shall defend myself. I am not Jagna, I shall not leave.

Just then a piano began playing overhead, a female voice sang Schubert's "Trout". My homeland, they have the power, but they shan't drive me out, these grotesques, these grubs.

He ground his teeth.

They were marching in the streets, these neo-Sbirri. Their singing and the stamp of their marching boots sounded through the window. He groaned, buried his face in his hands. Oh, stop looking in the mirror! Stop looking every day at the corpse you are.

≈≈≈

He stayed, unable to tear himself away. He wanted to see it through. It was hard.

It's the law of the strong, I myself swore by it.

Little by little it grew easier, and different. He performed his work on the coast, in the factory, in the office in the city. Posten mocked: "We bungled it, Mr World Improver. Now it's back to the herrings."

He noticed, a thousand times more clearly than before, how

like millions of others he kept silent about the life around him, how it retreated, concealed itself, disguised itself even, in order to cope in its own way. It was a strange, uncanny world, no one opened up for others to know, but you sensed yourself, feared and loved yourself, even esteemed yourself. Once he came upon an employee eating at his desk in the office, the elderly man calmly put away his sandwich and apologized: "One must eat, alas, Dr Klinkert, there's no government that can cure my sick stomach."

This dumb struggle that adapted itself to objects. It was like the sea, washing around mighty cliffs thrusting jagged out of it. Posten tried to hear his friend out: "Now, old man, isn't it better for you, following in your father's footsteps, free from the plague of politics. When we could do nothing but speechify?" Klinkert kept silent. He felt: yes, we leave it to them, it has its bright side: at last we're able to see ourselves. Perhaps violence and tyranny must first become monstrous, perhaps you must become desperate, before things will become better.

Despair was a long time coming. It gathered in all sorts of ways, washed ashore, the violence was sometimes hard and brutal, sometimes it let up, but always it lapped around the mass of people. Day by day, night by night, the deeper and fuller life was absorbed into it. People went around clad in shame, countless faces were closed in against the disgrace that had to be endured, but a thousand things that power desired were effortlessly transformed.

It became difficult and utterly serious. And it became harsh, harsher and utterly harsh – towards the gentle, gentler, utterly gentle.

At that time the adversaries were not identified by their colour, White or dark. They all had White skins, the lords and enforcers were distinguished by grimaces and clothing from those who offered resistance. The harsh shouts of command, shrill rabble-rousing cries you heard came from the throats of the conquerors. What once bloodhounds and firearms had done against naked natives with bows and arrows was done now by speeches, newspapers, radio, police, prison. People's thoughts were upended until ideas no longer had a secure foundation, then people were tame lunatics in cages. Thus had methods changed since the days of the weary emperor Charles, and I the King of Spain.

It was the misfortune of the masters and enforcers that tribes could not be killed and annihilated as in earlier times, and moreover did not commit collective suicide.

Patience, patience was the big word. Time, stronger than bloodhounds and weapons, became a force that could not be seized from the people.

You learned to live more slowly.

Voyage to the penal colony

THE TRANSPORT SHIP *La Martinière* anchored off the Ile de Ré. In the jail on the island were assembled convicts from the whole country, some sentenced to life, some to twenty years, some to ten. They were escorted from the jail by small troops of armed guards, chained and unchained, led down to the dockside, jostled aboard the little steam launch that took them to the prison ship.

It was a last echo from the time of the old kings and lords.

The great ocean lay at play. Calm and smooth, it lay there giving away nothing. It lapped on the shore with a sweet soporific sound, swirled around the landing stages. It emitted a gentle, steady breathing. The grey surface sparkled under the sun's rays.

The little ferry came steaming back. On the shore more troops marched down in step. They looked around, sniffed the keen air, their lungs expanded, they waited.

They were those the land was not yet finished with.

The young broad-shouldered man who had gone for a soldier stood with a mean gloomy look. In his younger days he had served time in reform school. He grew up cunning. Among soldiers he made it to sergeant. He liked a drink. And then he lost his temper in a tavern, the fight spilled into the street, a lieutenant came by, Fate had led the unlucky man there just for this moment, but the bell tolled for the sergeant too. The lieutenant confronted him, told him to move on quietly. There was a rabble of soldiers, all excited and drunk. Then the sergeant, in a blind fury from his time in reform school, drew his revolver and shot the lieutenant. When he came to his senses it was all over for him. They gave him a hard time, kept careful watch over him, maybe his spirit was weak. Drunkenness was no excuse. He's for the penal colony. He sat in the courtroom with the learned judge and sworn laymen. They observed the man, heard him and the witnesses, had to make up their minds. They knew the country and his kind. Before the judge were piles of books old and new, specifying what crimes there were and how they should be punished. They searched through them to see what the crime was in this case. Then they read out the sentence. They knew: this is a man just like us. They knew what a difficult childhood and reform school meant. But they were not allowed to follow those thoughts. So they judged it murder, sat solemnly in their chairs and went home, uneasy.

Beside him as they wait for the launch stands a fat pale man. He is young, hollow-eyed, has the face of a fanatic. Long dark hair falls over his temples, his shoulders droop, an untidy moustache sits on the thick slack upper lip. He looks neither right nor left. He too has come to the end of the road. What did they say, men in these countries of White men? You have to make something of yourself, do great deeds, become famous maybe. This hollow-eyed man had thought of nothing else from the start. But everyone on every side wanted to be something. As trees in the forest stretch towards the light and try to overtop each other, so too you must strive. He didn't grow very tall, never amounted to much. So he made his way with violence. His wife nagged him. He took refuge in a delusion. What everyone dreamed about became a compulsion with him. So he exists alongside the wife, quiet and distant, invests in a silver-fox farm, and one day, when the wife asks all innocently about his work, he is provoked, starts on her, cuts her down, and later attests that he had no regrets, still has no regrets. In fact he is filled with manic joy, he blesses the corpse with holy water, he feels the envious eyes of his environment on him. He did this; he has shown who he is. They expel him, this ugly face of their passions. How long will he survive over there.

And what happens when he dies. They are appalled when they read about him. But they devour it. They suspect something. Out, they say. But it has taken root in them.

He murdered from jealousy. Out, they say. Out of our sight. But it has taken root in them.

They stand four abreast. The launch approaches. Now it ties up at the landing stage. They start moving. Tramp over the gangplank. The boarding gate closes, the engine throbs.

Hey dear Mother, you bore me and I grew to a rogue and ran away, hey, dear Mother, it's all up with me now.

Hey dear Father, you sired me, let me grow to robber, murderer, rogue, you'll not beat me again, your task is done. Huzza huzza. It's over.

Adieu dear homeland, dear homeland adieu. What a thoroughly loathsome land. Wait till I see you again. I'll burn down your houses, you judges, jurors, witnesses, sitting so calm in your houses, you think you're done with us, we'll show you.

You pack of curs, you pigs, you band of robbers, you hypocrites. We're off to the penal colony, and one day we'll come home again.

On the back of the giant monster called Ocean, they glided to the transport steamer.

Waves marvelled at the mighty ship. What strong ribs you have, ship. How did people know to shape your breast and make it hard, so you can float on the sea with heavy loads and not sink. They built thudding engines. They put them in your belly. They give you the power to swim along. People are not fish, but they made you stronger and hardier than any fish. Oh how powerful people are.

On the transport ship they chorused: "You jurors with your fat wives, you stuff your gobs, then sit on your green bench and pronounce judgment on us condemned men. On your table you have jam, butter, wine, white bread. To us they give watery coffee, tinned food and tough vegetables."

The herring is a joy we're given. Every day he leaves his tun and shows himself unto the sun, and stinks to highest heaven. He'll never rot, we slurp him down, we ought to turn his life around, we of course can rot away, over that, no lords hold sway.

The sea snuggled tenderly against the ship's belly. There's nothing to compare with White people. Whoever could think like them. They look as if they could never walk. They can't last long in water, but they've transformed themselves into a giant fish. They lay cables over your bed, they call each other up and say how are you, over many miles. They often praise our waves. But they have no idea how wonderful they themselves are. They're like gods, creating everything. We mourn every human who drowns. We'd like to hear what he knows. But he's silent then. You can toss him around, he won't reveal a thing.

The New Indies

ON THE SOUTHERN continent a mountain range extends along the west coast, hundreds of miles wide, a rampart for the land. The land with its primal masses rises from the white-haired mumbling sea that knows day and night, heat and cold, moonlight, stars and the sun that glides up and sinks back down. The sea responds to it all with soughing and thunder, flood and ebb, thunder and retreat. It rasps for words like a deaf and dumb man, gropes for the land like a blind man, and falls back to its lair.

The land piles up its towering peaks, spreads out its plains, leaves the sea to its roaring and looks to the stars, moon and sun. Proudly lines up peak after peak. From the frigid zone of Tierra del Fuego they advance to the Equator's furnace. Snow-clad unattainable crowns, volcanoes: high plains and coasts tremble below. And onto land and mountains there must pour the water that rasps and rages out there at sea. In yearning it sends its emissaries across the mountains, they fall, become brooks, rivers that trickle and splash across the earth.

The lands where Alfinger, Quesada, Belalcazar, Federmann rampaged with their small bands of adventurers were divided now among Venezuela, Colombia, Guiana. The mountainous coast belonged to Peru, Chile, Ecuador. Orellana ventured down the Amazon between the walls of its gallery forests, and fought with the Women People. That wide country was now Brazil, a colony of the Portuguese Crown and later a free state. Where the Jesuit Fathers built their Christian republic was today called Paraguay, Uruguay. Argentina sprawled away into the distance, and touched Bolivia.

Now it was all about imports and exports, trade, industry, finance.

In Brazil they had a rubber zone, a sugarcane region, a coffee region, cotton region, a region for grain and large-scale livestock rearing. They bothered their heads with questions of wage labour, latifundia, small businesses, banks, democracy. Everywhere the question was how to loot the natural treasures of the country, discover new processes for the task, dismantle the old methods, inject money. On the east coast, in Minas Gerais, not far from that old robbers' nest Sao Paolo, now a modern city, they found seams of copper, mercury, lead, and in Rio Grande do Sul, wolfram and sulphur. In Ipanema blast furnaces smoked, near Ouro Preto an iron smelter.

Coalbeds in the state of Rio Grande do Sul, coalbeds on the banks of the Uruguay river.

From the trees of the primeval forest they extracted a thousand kinds of timber, the hardest wood on earth, of many colours and scents. There were such quantities of timber and felled trees that in many regions people heated their ovens with cedar and laurel. They cut ipé wood for railway sleepers and shipbuilding, rosewood for furniture and fine cabinetry. There was even a veritable ironwood; on the Paranà gopherwood, then teak, cedar, peroba, barouna, jacaranda, massaranduba. These gave work for railways, sawmills, ships.

On the surging, rolling, flooding Amazon, in riverside clearings, winding channels, swamps, in this hot steamy world, rubber was the thing. Forests tracked the waters of the Madeira, Purus, Acre, Vaco, Javary, Juruà. They were Hevea, the rubber tree, a leafy tree thirty meters tall, the tapura that men sought, attacked with hand axes, tapped its thick white sap.

In great factories in the cities they produced linen goods,

silks, blankets, ropes, hats of straw and felt, hammocks, paper goods, leather, cigars, cigarettes, beer, matches, biscuits, vinegar, oil, ceramics, soap, candles, vehicles, acids, salts, resins, chalk, umbrellas, tinware, perfumes, artificial flowers, woollens, cotton fabrics, socks, knitwear, glassware.

Small businesses manufactured fats, jams, banana flour, fishmeal, inks, lacquer, coloured coatings, saddles, bridles, brushes, brooms, mattresses, clocks, spoons, nails, clogs, silverware, travel rugs, barrels, billiard balls, buttons, meat extract, gloves, lamps, combs, shoe polish. Much of this was exported to North America and Europe.

Escape into the Jungle

GUIANA, IN THE southern hills.

The people lay in grass. They stared down through brush. There was a gully, this was hill country. Stags called and played in the gully. When the dance was over, the people withdrew. They walked through many gullies. On the way home they said nothing, so as to remember the leaping and calling. The mountains were the Tumuc-Humac, the highest peak was called Timotakem. In a valley with a river flowing through it lay their village Pirai-fish. The people called themselves Pirai. Some walked south through the scrub to the village of Ash-crane, some stayed the night with the Crane People and next morning went on to Hocco. Each of them in their own village practiced the dance they had observed and heard. Their king was sick. These were the Oyampi people.

After several days people went to Pirai, where the king lay. They carried him from his hut and danced the stag-dance, shook the horned masks and clapped maracas. All the while the villagers hid away.

That evening the king died. The people gathered anxiously together. They burned his hut. They dug a deep hole behind and placed him in it. They gave him an oar, his staff, bow and arrows, eating utensils, all his feather ornaments, metal pendants. They drummed the news to the neighbourhood. There was a great feast in Pirai. The spirit of this tribe was a stag. They drank cashiri for a day and a night, and danced. They had often had to punish the king for his harshness and the failure of several harvests. He was also blamed for an attack of termites in a distant village, the creatures had vanished by now.

After the king died the village waited a long time before choosing a new king. First they wanted to see how the dead king behaved. Food was plentiful, no illness appeared, the Tupi tribe between the Maroni and Plabo held back, as did the Emerillon on the Maroni. So they decided to live without a chief, let the dead king go on ruling. The piache, the sorcerer who performed the correct dances in the villages and brought gifts to the king, uttered loud cries.

From the sea where the Salvation Islands – Devil's Island, St Joseph's Island, Royal Island – lay, bush, savannah, swamp and primeval forest stretched southward from the coast of Cayenne. There were river valleys and hills all the way to the massif of Tumuc-Humac, source of the Maroni and Oyapock. The savannah was boundless, in winter it was covered in pale green grass, in summer it became red and yellow, the swampy plains were transformed into a continuous sea of vegetation. Mauritia palms with their fans followed streams and rivers, and palms also stood in clumps. Then the dark silent forest climbed away, it was already the forest of that great stream the Amazon, which had its being farther south.

The convicts had escaped from the penal colony and were hacking their way through bush and savannah. One had tried some years before to escape to sea, but was caught and brought back. On his advice they were making their way south through the bush. They knew they were risking their lives. They were three Whites, two Blacks, an Annamite, and came from the colony of Saint-Laurent on the Maroni. The Annamite was blind in one eye, coarse panacoco grass grows in the savannah, he had rubbed one eye blind with it, the other eye was milky. He had spent five years on St Joseph, after his escape was chained up as punishment. When they brought him to Saint Laurent on the Maroni to work, he found the panacoco grass and rubbed his eye so he would not have to work.

They called him Ahmed.

The two Blacks were Largi and Mustafa. They took turns toting the gun and ammunition box they had stolen from a bush Negro. They were burly men. In the middle of his chest Largi had a tattoo of a blue heart, under it the words 'Death to Traitors'. Mustafa, the smaller man, had tattooed himself as an officer, he wore a medal, a big red ribbon across his whole torso, a long white dagger on his right leg, each arm depicted a rifle with bayonet.

A defrocked cleric, the White they called Chaplain, wore a red kerchief around his neck. His blue shirt was sleeveless. On one arm were the words: 'Fear not the judgment seat', on the other: 'Sorry Cecilia, amen'. Under it a snake. He limped, and his right leg was wrapped like a parcel, palm leaves tied with liana cords.

The other two were Perros and Vivien, both White.

They trudged through the bush. Now they dared to follow watercourses, where they risked coming across settlements. There was a reward of five dollars on each convict's head. In the first weeks, colonists had posed a mortal danger. They were nine when they slipped away from Saint Laurent, their real leader, a Negro, was already dead.

The bush forest was often like a cave, heavy rain washed away the soil around big trees, roots stood exposed, you walked in half-dark through man-high roots, long branches with leaves and hanging ropes dangled down into the root-caves.

At the start they had good days on the way south from Saint Laurent, they had three rifles and ammo, acquired by Vivien, who wasn't a prisoner (once he was called Jagna, he was a Pole) but wanted to help a friend (already dead) to escape. He had collected choppers, knives, hammocks, even salt and sugar for snakebite. Most was lost in ambushes and the organized roundups that pursued them. They loaded the Annamite with provisions they came across on the way and couldn't consume at once, lizards, plums from the carambola tree, wild cacao. Sometimes they shot a bird. In the swampy zone on the Maroni they even tried to bag a deer.

Long weeks passed. The hills rose. "We're coming to hill

country. Once we're over the hills, Guiana will be behind us, we'll be in Brazil." They made a fire night after night, camped, ate and slept. They started to spend whole days not marching.

Emerillon Indians latched onto them, three men also making their way through the bush, they ran away and then came back. It turned out lucky they'd brought the Annamite along, he'd met Indians on his first escape and could communicate with them. The three Emerillon said they were engaged on a vendetta, had to stay away from the tribe for a while. An old man, a relative, had died suddenly, the chief of a distant village was to blame, they had to kill this chief and his clan, but he was protected by his village and their own village wouldn't let them back until they'd taken revenge and pacified the dead man.

The Chaplain wanted to know why they were in the bush and their people wouldn't let them back, had they perhaps killed someone in their own village. They denied it, were puzzled that their situation wasn't obvious; of course they couldn't live with their tribe until the dead man had been avenged. They were armed with spear, bow and arrows, and also carried axes. They tried to exchange all they had for the convicts' guns. That was why they'd returned to the convicts. They were refused, at night were kept away from the fire, they were rabid, complete savages, it was a matter of life and death for them, you could see it wouldn't be long – three men against a village – before they paid for the revenge with their lives. But they had no choice. Now they eyed the rifles and tried it on with the two Negroes on guard. When the three avengers saw the treasure so well guarded and the men in any case hostile to them, they gave up. For three days more they slunk around the group like cats. The Negro Largi, with the words 'Death to Traitors' on his chest, was hit in the thigh by one of their arrows, luckily it wasn't poisoned, they fired a shot in their direction and then were free of the sinister stalkers.

Largi's wound slowed the march even more, finding food became difficult. Largi had been the best climber and had the luckiest hand. They made only a few hours progress each day. In the evening the temperature dropped sharply and they were chilled, dew fell overnight. When the sun sank in a fiery glow, the moon rose over the hills and shone into the abyss of forest where they lay. Bats flitted like ghosts around them, possums scurried by. And in the mornings, when the moon disappeared and the stars paled – bejeweled hordes of the heavenly host parading in the face of their misery – then a mist loosened from the ground, it rose in swathes, parrots set up their cacophony, a many-voiced birdsong arose. The men, transported convicts, got up and walked wordlessly on. They were exhausted, drank swamp water when they found any. Spiders bit them, at night leeches clung to their legs and fed. It was harsh along the Maroni, the banks reflected a terrible heat, but there were manioc, maize, cattle and turtles, the fugitives could break in and steal vegetables.

Now one of the Whites, Perros, became waxy pale. He was once a sergeant, that broad-shouldered young man from reform school who shot his lieutenant in the street while drunk. They'd been reluctant to take him along, he was already sick at Saint Laurent, but he was in on their secret and would not be put off. One of the two Whites who had died mistreated him at the start of their trek as a dead weight, the Negroes took him under their wing, the White, the attacker, died sooner than Perros. This whole forest and the swamps and savannah were full of creatures, not many big ones but countless small ones, and in Perros' skin and guts there were swarms of little worms that multiplied and destroyed his blood. He had acquired them in the ponds at Saint Laurent as he worked, they came from the guts of cattle he herded.

Young Perros, waxy pale, dragged himself on with super-human strength. They watched anxiously for who might die next, for each death increased the risk that the others would die. Ever since Largi's wounding the Negro and the Annamite had drawn closer, and the Whites feared a rift. They had three hammocks, Largi had always slept on the ground unafraid of insects, after he was wounded they had to let him use a hammock, and for several days until they wove a new one from palm leaves, raffia and lianas three of them had to take turns sleeping and keeping watch, which slowed the march even more. It was the dry season, they'd planned for that, and it was good, but now there were forest fires and they had to make detours, and there was always the danger of finding themselves too far from a water source when the last of their drinking water was gone.

In the evenings, tall strong Largi sat on the ground until late and let Perros use the hammock. Night after night Largi narrated and hummed new verses about young Sambi, who had to flee from his wicked uncle. They even talked about Sambi during their daytime marches. The farther they moved from the Maroni, the more the dark men spoke of their homeland, and grew quieter and more serious. Now the crazy Chaplain had to stop his profanity and cursing, he was warned by the Negroes, they thought his words dangerous.

"He went away, Sambi, son of Galadieyi, he had to flee from his uncle who took away his father's property. He went away, Sambi, head bowed but with fire in his eyes. He left his land, his family, his troops, his prisoners. With fire in his eyes he carried vengeance with him."

The Negro ballad told of the tests that poor young Sambi had to undergo on his travels in faraway lands. At first only the dark men listened, then the Whites too. The Chaplain, his beard now long and white – the other two Whites as well looked like men of the forest, Vivien in his European hotel five years ago could never have imagined this – laughed and hissed:

"Listen! It's all up with Christianity! A new heathen age is dawning! Leave the Christians behind! They cling to a spar, they're drowning! Every man for himself! Pooh! Christianity has betrayed and sold us. Life is holy, whose life is holy, no one's life is holy, there's only hunger and thirst and murder and killing."

This was his old prison song. No one listened now to the crazy Chaplain, he babbled to himself. He was the first to go to Largi and clean maggots and flies from his oozing wound; the leaf dressing they used to cover it soon tore loose in the bush.

A little later Perros and Vivien joined in and hummed about Sambi, there was no more gossip of prison, cheating, stabbings. Sambi's tale was better for hacking through the forest. His aged mother who wept for her husband, his sister, his younger brother all followed on unsteady legs. But his spear had an iron tip that could penetrate a shield and bring down an eagle. His trusty squire walks by his side. His wife too walks beside him, arm across his shoulder, speaks more sweetly than the nightingale. He hasn't yet reached the borders of his land, and his prisoners – he's watched them grow to adulthood –guard him as a mother guards her child, and his dog, whose teeth can maul a jackal, looks up at him.

Swarms of flies surrounded the six fugitives. They'd been on the run so long, were so exhausted, that sometimes their conversation turned to staying here in the hills, felling trees along a watercourse, planting manioc and sugarcane like the others, keeping hens in a coop and then some larger livestock. But passing Negroes and Indians told them they were still in Guiana. So Largi again shouldered the rifle. Despite all precautions their ammo was now a soggy mess, but strong cheerful Largi kept this to himself, every morning he looked into the metal box and announced with a grin: "All dry." But they daren't fire the guns now.

A time came when they had to carry sickly Perros. The young soldier said: "Throw me away, the ants will eat me soon enough." But he was light enough for two to carry on branches. In open country even the Annamite helped.

Largi limped cheerfully along singing his endless song of Sambi; the tests imposed on Sambi before he could return and strike down his wicked uncle were legion. When Largi's deep voice rang out each morning they stood up – as if they hadn't shivered half the chilly night and weren't sluggish as death – and walked, carried, endured. Niab was a lion, two hundred years old, a fearsome beast big as an elephant. His roar made mountains tremble. When he walked through the forest, trees tumbled like maize stalks, his eyes streamed fire into the night. Sambi had to overcome the lion Niab. Sambi rose without fear, thought of his mother, his wife, his children. The night was black, the moon hid her face, the stars had gone to sleep in the vault of heaven. Then Sambi goes into battle, his servant at his side, his trusty dog following. They wander through the forest, and after they've wandered for an hour a bird croaks, and suddenly everything is filled with a harsh light, the trees seem to be on fire, a terrible roar rends the air. It's Niab, the old lion. Sambi's spear has an iron tip, it's smooth as a flint that a child picks from a streambed, it's made of bentinie wood. Oh my eyes, you must be deceiving me! Oh my eyes, what are you showing me! See there the dead lion, the terrible beast, two hundred years old, big as an elephant, mountains tremble at his roar. He's dead. A spear stands there thrust into the ground, a living dog is tied to it, see the sandals beside it. And Sambi stands before the king, the king asks: "Why do you come without sandals?" And the king asks: "Why do you go without a spear?" And then the king asks: "Where is your dog?"

Largi's endless tale of courage is their newspaper, sermon, roll-call. They need think of nothing else. Their thoughts are confused. The six of them are nothing but a heap of debris. They're in a more open and much hillier region. They don't know if these are the mountains they're aiming for. Now Vivien, who still drags around the body of Jagna and the shame of his past, comes out of the forest with a new sorrow. His face is swollen, his head aches, he falls down. This is on top of his swamp fever.

The Oyampi

AS THEY LINGER a long while near a plantation that they assume belongs to bush Negroes, they are observed by Indians. They had come already to the Tumuc-Humac hills, the high peak they could see was Timotaken. The Oyampi want first of all to know what kind of people these are, and if others are following. So for several days they allow Largi to gather maize from a field without interfering. But when the convicts started pulling themselves together for a march into the hills, where the village of Hocco lay, the Pirai people sent word to the people of Hocco. Largi's loud singing seemed threatening. People from Hocco blocked the forest path up into the hills, people from Pirai surrounded the climbers. Poor Largi tried to shoot, he took aim, his precious rifle must do its job now, the others flourished their bows and arrows that were good only for shooting fish and birds. But the powder was damp. Largi was hit by a spear, lay there, blood streaming from his mouth. Since he couldn't speak he encouraged them by hand movements to defend themselves, shook an angry fist at the assailants, and died.

The other five were taken to Pirai: the mad Chaplain who walked bent like an old man and talked to the ground; the blind Annamite, hands tied behind his back – now the strongest of them, he'd defended himself; the stocky Negro Mustafa who wept and whimpered, not for himself but because his friend Largi had been left behind, he was towed by a rope around his waist because he kept trying to pull away; the two White men, Vivien with his swollen brow and nose, seeming blind, and the young soldier Perros, shrivelled to a skeleton, stumbling at Vivien's back, clinging tight around his neck. All five wore ragged breechcloths, the Chaplain still had a torn shirt, howling Mustafa still displayed the blue-red officer's tattoos on his scrawny black body, scratched and bleeding. On one arm the mad Chaplain had 'Fear not the judgment seat' and on the other, 'Sorry Cecilia, amen' with a snake underneath.

The path leads down for a stretch. They go very slowly, Vivien and Perros often have to lie down, the warriors daren't grab at them. At last they're in the valley, a little shining stream meanders through it. They cross tilled fields, the convicts look about, they're among people.

They weren't taken into the village. The sorcerer appeared at the old shacks beyond the village, looked at them, a chief and several warriors kept their distance. Mustafa and the blind Annamite sat bound in one shack, the three Whites in another. They were given manioc mash, bananas, a great deal of thin beer. The young soldier died the first night. Dark men came in the morning, drawn by the Chaplain's loud prayers and singing, peered into the shack. Soon others came, dug a hole behind the shacks, laid the dead young soldier in and filled it. Vivien and the Chaplain sat through the afternoon in shade near the grave, the Chaplain grew calmer.

That night, when the light of the fire between the shacks and the village died down, Mustafa and the Annamite broke free. They didn't go far. They were confronted on Tacapatere hill by one of the Cussari tribes. Although both were unarmed and the Cussari were merely checking them out, they barricaded themselves in a thicket. When the Indians signaled to them to come out they refused. Mustafa fell after the Annamite.

≈≈≈

In the first days the Chaplain grew very quiet and lucid. When not sitting silently by Perros' grave, he occupied himself with Vivien, who squatted moaning in the rear of the shack. Both sported wild beards. The dark people had sent out into neighbouring villages to find someone who knew the language of the Whites. Every two days the sorcerer grabbed Vivien by the hand and pulled him out of the shack, clappered around him and blew smoke. It was no use. Vivien pointed to his head. His face was now so swollen he couldn't open his eyes.

Then several people appeared with the witch doctor, and the Chaplain grew fearful when he saw their preparations. Vivien lay quite passive. When all the procedures were completed, the sorcerer lit the kindling piled outside the shacks, kicked aside a few embers and threw down a handful of leaves from a sack carried by a child. Then he made a sign, forced Vivien to lie on a plank placed over the embers. He was reluctant. And the Chaplain said he shouldn't. Finally the sorcerer, a strong man, seized him, flung him down on the plank and held him there. Jagna had to breathe acrid smoke. He lost consciousness, but he didn't die.

He awoke with a terrible cough. He was still stretched over the fire, the dark man's fist pressing on his neck. Fly larvae swarmed out of his nose. He spat more out. His head rang. He could see better. He turned his head to the side. When the sorcerer felt the movement he let go, helped him sit up. He pointed to the larvae. The dark people went away. Vivien stumbled by himself into the shack. The Chaplain sat outside, face hidden in his hands.

By evening Vivien felt better. He ate and drank. The Indians didn't bother them again.

Cast out

THE PIRAI PEOPLE debated what to do with the two Whites, they weren't guests, couldn't be sent back to their own people, no one knew who they were. In the end they decided to lead them back into the forest and show them a path. So one morning Vivien, still weak, and the little Chaplain, now almost mute, were fetched from the shack. They were each handed a leaf basket of provisions, they had no idea what they were meant to do. The little band of dark people hemmed them in. When they were barely half an hour into the forest, the leader of the dark people signalled with his spear, the path forked, the dark man asked which direction they wanted to go in. Now they understood: they were being cast out. They exchanged glances, looked in the baskets they'd been given, so this was for them. But before they could answer, the dark people had vanished. The last one turned round, broke off a branch, and glaring at the Whites laid it across the path, for a moment held his spear over it: don't dare to come back.

They didn't stray many paces from the path. For two days and three nights they lay low. During that time no one came by in either direction. Vivien was still not steady on his feet, his head was again growing thick. He felt it was starting again, he touched his forehead, nose, they were swollen. He was tempted to run back, but he could only crawl and couldn't make it through the scrub. The little Chaplain, completely mute, hugged him and tried to hold him back. He went around, gathered dry leaves in a heap and did his best to keep Vivien at the campsite. They still had bananas, they hadn't touched the manioc mash, it smelled sour now and seethed with worms. They were thirsty. Kiskale birds screamed all day long from trees, sometimes monkeys appeared, small and medium sized, came down from the trees in curiosity. During the second night there was a crashing in the bush nearby, they saw a big creature with phosphorescent eyes in a darkness lit by stars and white clouds. They sat up, clutched one another, the Chaplain held a hand over Vivien's mouth. They sat immobile for a long while, then the jaguar took a step closer, turned around, and slowly ambled off.

Early next morning the Chaplain went in search of water and fruit. Vivien slept on his bed of leaves. A crab spider crawled out of the leaves. It was big, black and hairy. Each leg, thick as a grub, had a yellow claw, two small backwards-pointing horns projected from its head. It crawled over Vivien's body and bit him in the navel. He woke up and screamed. The spider scuttled off. The bite burned. Vivien sat up. His eyelids were swollen shut, he could see only dimly. His hands supported him on the ground. "I shall die soon, the Chaplain's gone off. They've left me here." He spoke out loud. His head was swimming. He said aloud in a monotone: "They've left me here, left me here, left me. Jagna will die, Jagna will die today, today Jagna will die, yes he will, he will."

As he lay prostrate a deer came out of the scrub, stepped close on slender knobby legs and eyed the big white body on the ground. It looked at Jagna's feet, didn't know they were feet. It stepped closer, and as the feet revealed nothing, explored further up the lanky body. It turned its lissome brown head. The narrow slit of the man's eyes looked into its eyes. Jagna's dry lips did not move. His eyes said, and the deer understood: I'm dying, deer, I'm dying, I have to die. The deer had never seen a white man or a dying man, it made a couple of sudden jumps and came back with its mother the hind. The eyes down there looked as before. I'm dying, you deer, I have to die. You have it good, wish I could be you.

The hind: Come. What a funny shape you are, are you a tree? – No.

Someone has bewitched you, come with us. – I can't. I'm dying.

You're bewitched. You're not speaking right. I'll fetch my husband. Stay here, little deer.

She crashed through scrub. When she found the stag browsing among the trees they hurried back. On the way the stag made signs. Men were following. The stag wanted to go back but the hind forced him on towards her child, the stag ran with her, arrows whistled past, they found the little deer by the pale body, the deer was hit by an arrow, it ran after its parents, the men were able to catch it with their hands. And so they found Vivien. He was still alive.

These were Crane people, come with one of their men who was familiar with Whites. They were on their way to Pirai, for Whites were being held prisoner there and had to be questioned.

The five of them stood around Vivien and nudged him. He moved his lips and shivered. His eyes asked: Where's the deer?

They had gourds, gave him water to drink. His swollen bluish face shocked them. They took him for one of the runaway prisoners. They debated whether they should go to Pirai and bring news. But because the little deer had stood over him and they had been led here by the stag and the hind, they dared not leave him lying here. They gathered bamboo staves and laid Vivien on them. They tugged the little deer along behind.

Uproar in the village when the strangers appeared. They took Vivien to the old shack, and sent for the witch doctor. Then they were worried about the Chaplain, and sent out a search party. They failed to find him that day. Next day they went out with dogs. He had located a spring, and lay there. The little bearded man looked terrible, scorpions clung to him, their pincers had bitten deep into his skin, he seemed not to notice. The dark people brushed the creatures off, there was no blood. He went with them quietly. He mumbled at the ground.

Mutushi and Loveherb

THE VILLAGE GAVE an awed welcome to the Whites. They spent the evening of unconscious Vivien's arrival discussing the case. The spirits of the forest, who usually kill, had spared him. So Vivien was carried from the shack to the guesthouse next to the chief's house. The wounded deer was handed over to the sorcerer's care. A debate ensued about what should happen now. Next day they dug up the body of young Sergeant Perros from behind the shacks, held a mourning ceremony to appease his spirit, burned and buried the remains. Then they concerned themselves with the two Whites, observed their demeanour.

Vivien regained consciousness, expelled a lot more fly larvae, and felt better. They had trekked a long way from Saint Laurent on the Maroni, from the start of the dry season to the start of the big rains. Now clouds hurtled down from the heavens and burst. Trees were overturned, leaves strewn over the ground. It went on for days, then it poured for hours, the sun brooded in between. The two Whites froze in the wet hot air, fever was setting in. Dark forests stretched away north and west of the hill, to the east the savannah began. And when the haze lifted and the sun shone over it, the fresh green grass down below bent to the breeze. The wind sighed and howled over hill and plain, swaying grasses and vegetation all the way to the distant green horizon. Men sat and fished at the lake in the valley, which before was just a pond. They sang from morning till night.

The interpreter, a Crane man, sat in the guesthouse with the Whites, an elderly, clever man. He knew his task. The Whites thought they were dreaming when they heard the dark man utter words they understood. They squeezed his hand, were glad, then afraid. Vivien asked him to thank the chief and the tribe for their hospitality, the witch doctor too. The interpreter asked who they were, what they wanted. Vivien said they were heading from the coast in the north to Brazil, to a sugar plantation, at first they were a whole gang, the others died. The interpreter studied the tattoos on the Chaplain's arms; he explained they were charms, prayers. The interpreter wondered if others were coming through the forest and the savannah. They didn't know.

They wore the raffia skirts they were given. They asked the interpreter to bring sharp wood or grass, then sat behind the guest-house and hacked away at their beards, people warned them to bury the shavings. Seeing their feet torn to shreds, people made raffia soles for them, tied at the ankle. The chief sent word he would receive them. Following the silent formal reception, where they squatted a long time on mats facing each other, ate mash and drank, the clever man visited them several times. He promised to provide guides to take them as far as possible south to the great river basin. He invited them to be his guests. They both sighed with relief and hugged each other. The Chaplain was now a serious man, his madness had left him.

They were taken fishing and hunting, shot waterfowl that thronged the marshes. There were hours when the sky was cloudless, and a sweet gentle air drifted across the land. They travelled along a winding watercourse in canoes, in the shade of overhanging branches. Vivien forgot his dull aching head. The Chaplain spoke calmly. Vivien had never heard him like this. Fishermen from other villages came in canoes to meet them, happy laughter sounded from boat to boat.

Then rain crashed down again, storming from the heavens out of nowhere like a raging trampling beast. It tore the ground, and Vivien and the Chaplain recalled terrible days in the forest when they lived in root-caves, that forest lay far back, the young White lad Vivien had tried to free now rested there and was no more, Largi, the strong Black they all loved, was gone too, how lustily he sang of the king's son Sambi, the lion Niab was two hundred years old, Sambi set out from his camp without fear, thought of his mother, his children, his wife, why have you come without sandals, Sambi, why do you go without your spear, where is your dog?

≈≈≈

The interpreter stayed. The Pirai wanted to learn a lot from them. It was the chief's job to win their trust. For his sallow face and long dark hair they gave the little shrunken Chaplain the name Mutushi, after the cork tree whose bark is streaked yellow and brown. Vivien, once Jagna, they called Cungerecu after a plant that infuses love, for even here Vivien-Jagna delighted the girls.

The Blue Jaguar

MUTUSHI THE CHAPLAIN, head hunched between his shoulders and little eyes screwed up as if he were gazing into the distance, sat during those long days of rain beside Vivien the Loveherb while they talked with the chief.

Mutushi was surprised that so many men sat quietly with the chief, and asked: "Why do so few go hunting, fishing or to the fields?"

"What could they do," they answered.

"The fields are waiting for them."

"It is the rain time. Everything is wet, later the sun will come, everything will grow quickly."

The people were happy, they ate and drank, wove, slept in their hammocks, whittled, painted masks. "Oh you have it good," Mutushi said to the chief, whom they called Mira.

"We work a lot," laughed Mira. "Farther south are tribes that have no fields, they have the issara palm, coconuts hang from it, they have the palmito, they eat its buds and leaves, the women knock down trees, they have the inga, it provides sweet shoots, they have a tree that bears green beans. When the dry season comes they move to another place. What trees grow in the land of the Whites?"

"Not many. We must till many fields to win food from the earth. It doesn't yield willingly."

"A difficult land."

"Winters are hard and cold. Nothing grows. We go hungry. And there are many more of us than here in your villages. We must always gather stores of provisions, and make our way to others to obtain more provisions. We Whites are never free from toil."

"Then your paths must be wide, and you must do much walking and carrying."

Mutushi thought, but did not say aloud: calamity has already befallen us. We have many paths to walk, few places to sit. We are always pushed to work and accumulate and cannot leave it alone. We don't even know why we accumulate. We can leave nothing undisturbed, cannot wait for anything.

Mutushi said: "If I sat like this so quietly at home, I would be ashamed."

Mira wore a woven ribbon with feathers, he pointed to it: "Can you weave and dye?"

"Your women and girls wear ribbons of raffia as ornaments on arms and ankles. In our country they wear chains and rings of fine gold and silver. They add shiny cut stones to them. They wear plaited and woven hats and caps, they have many clothes that they change. Cloths have many colours and patterns."

"Oh lovely ornaments." The dark people were very attentive.

But Mutushi the little Chaplain sighed: "To have ornaments we must work hard." And made pensive by memories of the crimes he had committed, he looked across at his poor companion Vivien: "If we can't achieve what we set out to do, we do terrible things. Bad deeds come about. An evil spirit drives us to it."

Vivien stared at him: "You're right." The interpreter was puzzled, frowned. Mutushi soothed him: "I was talking to my friend."

Vivien: "You're right. We are scum. I'm glad to be clear of Europe."

"Hush," whispered Mutushi, "they're watching us." Mutushi cast an enquiring glance at the witchdoctor, who came out with a question that had long lain in his heart:

"Who wished evil on the Loveherb, or what is he guilty of, that flies crawled into his head? Flies don't go into everyone's head."

Vivien-Cungerecu spoke. Though still young he had a long joyless life behind him. And now he wanted to know – strange for Jagna to be so curious, but he'd come through the forest with fugitives from the penal colony, seen the crab spider crawl on his body, the deer held an enigmatic conversation with him which he would never forget – Cungerecu wanted to know: "Do the flies listen if you tell them to do something?"

"The words must be strong. Their king will listen."

Following these words the white man Cungerecu had a dream. Nothing of his misery, nothing of hotels, revolver shots. He felt the eyes of the deer on him. They conducted an enigmatic conversation. He lay on leaves. No one was with him.

≈≈≈

Next day, despite Vivien's warnings, the Chaplain made the mistake of talking about home. But he was brooding on a particular topic, it just came to his tongue. He said: he'd had to flee his homeland where life was so hard. He'd made mistakes. But everyone in Europe, good or bad, makes mistakes. His people were not without guilt and had made even more mistakes.

The dark people were disturbed. They had taken the Whites for fugitives, but thought nothing of them beyond that, they were under the protection of forest creatures. Now they seemed abominable. Mutushi, oblivious, added: an evil spirit rules over the White people.

For a week after this conversation, which ended in an ominous silence, they were avoided. Momentous action appeared to be in preparation against them. At last the chief summoned them. They went. The interpreter was there. Mutushi sat down nervously, Vivien was docile. Mira the chief scowled as he repeated the abominable words of the cork-tree man:

"Your tribe made more mistakes than you. What mistakes did your tribe make?"

The Chaplain turned aside. Vivien, who was more sensitive than he, had warned him again not to speak of the past ("And for our own sakes too, Chaplain, leave it alone"), but he felt so compelled to speak, and exactly on this topic, in order to know themselves, purify themselves. In this silence, in this other world, he had begun to see everything differently. When the dark people saw that Mira's question put Corktree in some difficulty, they were content, it seemed he recognized his error. But the chief persisted: "How can your tribe make mistakes? How can Corktree know this? Who was Corktree in his tribe?"

Then Mutushi pulled himself together and began to speak of the Great War that not long ago had raged for four years in the countries of the Whites. There was no good reason for the war. More people died than were found in all the tribes here. Afterwards the countries fell into even worse disorder, which continued still.

The dark people recalled confused rumours of disorder and violence among the Whites; and when they appeared among the dark people, they brought only disorder and violence. The chief asked the little Chaplain to tell more about his tribe, perhaps these two Whites were sacrifices, like so many of the dark people. Mutushi said: "We don't have tribes. We live together as great nations. We speak different languages."

"Who is your ancestor?" – "I know of no ancestor."

"You are a people. So you have ancestors."

"We know of no ancestors. None have been named to us. We know people who rule our nations, and some who have subjugated other peoples, we learn their names but they're not our ancestors."

"Who created your people?"

Corktree glanced at Vivien and smiled: "We believe that humans are descended from animals, from monkeys. People laugh about it."

"Monkeys are not the ancestors of all humans, only of some tribes."

"Before, everyone believed (and many believe it still) that the creator of all humans, our great ancestor, lives in Heaven. He is called God. But many laugh at this."

"Do you bring him presents?"

"Some speak softly and sing together in big houses that they have built for him. They call this praying. Many laugh at it."

There was a long pause. The dark people exchanged comments. In response to Mutushi's query the interpreter said: "They discuss the fact that people in your country laugh so much. They are puzzled that you can be so merry when disorder and violence prevail in your country."

"We are not merry, we do not laugh out of joy."

The unease among the dark people persisted, no meeting of minds had occurred between the Whites and their hosts. A few days later they visited the Whites, there had been many discussions among themselves, they filled the whole space in the guesthouse beside the Whites, several elders came along, brought mats. The witch doctor, who was more amiable than the chief – Mutushi's words about the guilt of the tribe had infuriated the chief, and like most of the others he couldn't let the topic go – turned to Mutushi, the little Chaplain, and after a few pleasantries with Vivien, his patient, began his cross-examination:

"Where are your dead?" – "We bury them in the earth."

"Who takes care of them? Who honours them?"

"People don't think about them much. Most are happy to forget them. Their lives were no different than ours."

Again the people sat in deepest astonishment. But the witch doctor, not allowing this to affect him, played his trump card: "But you have children. Where do your children come from?"

At this remarkable question all eyes turned to the Chaplain. It seemed they saw this question as conclusive. Their smiles were eager. When Mutushi hesitated, the witch doctor posed a supplementary question: "You give names to your children. What are these names?"

"We give them whatever name we like."

"According to what rules? Who determines the name? Under what conditions are they determined?"

"The parents choose them, as they like."

"Who initiates the enquiries?" – "What enquiries?"

"About the child, about its name, who the child is."

Mutushi understood, he nodded: "Ah, who the spirit of the child is, the spirit of the newborn. We believe it comes from the parents."

"The parents? How can the parents obtain a spirit for them? Where are they supposed to fetch it from, how do they induce it to come? It is very hard to control a spirit. Or do you magic a spirit into the newborn once it is born?"

"No."

Now they all looked on smiling, Mutushi was refuted, a spirit must come from somewhere, after all the two Whites were sitting there, alive and able to talk. The chief waded in and said sternly: "We can see you. You are alive."

Corktree shrugged his shoulders unhappily: "We think so."

The dark people were unclear whether the two White men were trying to mislead them, or if such muddled conditions really did prevail among the Whites. There was much whispering. It was not just an interrogation: they really wanted to know who it was they were dealing with. The chief, Mira, though stern and not well-disposed, remained patient, and took pains to show them their error: "You are great nations. You have no ancestors. How do you live together?"

"We live in one place, it's where we were born, our parents and grandparents too. We till the soil, keep cattle and other animals. We gather provisions and exchange them with others."

"Who assigns tasks and rewards?"

"All look for employment where they can. Whoever doesn't find it has a hard time. There are rich and poor, most are poor. Nothing trickles down to them. There are many crimes."

Now loud cries erupted. It was what they'd expected. But Mutushi confounded their acclaim by adding: ""Many crimes arise from poverty, and because everyone wants to be rich. If poverty could be abolished, we believe, the disorder among us would cease. Many people struggle for this."

The people laughed uproariously when this was translated. It was the height of foolishness. The elders laughed until tears flowed down their cheeks. The chief asked: "Do the rich want to rid themselves of the poor, and kill them so that only the rich remain?"

"No, the poor want to rid themselves of the rich and take away their wealth."

The chief calmed the new outburst of hilarity, said: "But that's impossible. From where do the poor get the idea they should take away the wealth of the rich and order will then prevail?"

"It is justice."

Now they sat up. Such madness was beyond comprehension. In utter disgust the chief Mira contradicted Mutishi: "No, it is not justice. The rich should kill the poor who want to rob them, for they disturb the peace and have no authority."

"Among us it is believed you need no authority to assert your rights. And everyone knows what justice is."

"We have heard this already. Your ignorance is appalling. You give your children any old name, you do not care for your dead, you have no ancestors. Then you claim to know what justice is."

He turned courteously to the witchdoctor at his side: "Among us not even the oldest and most experienced know at once and in every case what justice is. We have to come together and enquire and observe. We must observe in many places, and what we see must be pondered. Not everyone has the power to receive answers. The sorcerer, the elders and the chief must fast and prepare themselves, so that they have the power to ascertain the truth and speak what is right. It is very hard to find the truth and convey what is just."

Now the dark people sat without talking and weighed up what they had heard. The two Whites had not lied, but they and everything they said aroused profound misgivings. Some elders were frightened. As the interpreter chatted to the Chaplain – Vivien listened intently, but said not a word – the people muttered among themselves.

And then an elder who was hard of hearing had someone repeat Mutushi's words to him. The elder looked at the two Whites and nodded: "They spoke the truth," and said: "We know who the Whites are. They come from their countries where disorder reigns and bring destruction. It has been reported: in Heaven, under the bed of the great Father, lies the Blue Jaguar. When the Earth grows bad, the great Father becomes angry, sends the Blue Jaguar down to Earth to destroy it."

≈≈≈

They dispersed. Unrest among the dark people was growing out of control.

There was an informal private visit from the doctor, who wanted to know: "In your country, who throws the knucklebones in a trial? Who prepares the poison when judgments are made? What plants do they use? How do you secure the perpetrator?"

Mutushi: "In our country the court sets up an investigation. Clever people follow the trail."

"What sort of people?" The witchdoctor smiled, anticipating the answer.

"Normal people, but especially cunning."

"They can identify the perpetrator? Uncover crimes? Mutushi, you must admit, when your friend Loveherb is sick, it is not just some normal cunning man who can find the cause. He doesn't know the sickness, cannot reveal the true cause. And the guilty one is not yet revealed."

Now Loveherb was alert. Mutushi saw that he wanted to speak, hesitated, then in great excitement, his face tense, Jagna said: "You're right. They are bad at revealing the truth, in our country. They don't know. They can't know. That's why we left it all behind. We don't know how to change it."

≈≈≈

During the night Vivien woke the Chaplain:

"What shall we do when they send us away? They will, soon." – "I don't know."

"But Chaplain, you know your Bible." – "Leave me in peace, Vivien."

They lay side by side in their hammocks, the darkness was profound, a gentle drizzle rustled in the roof. Vivien's voice:

"I just thought. I don't know much about it, idol worship, Tower of Babel. Lots of things. It's the truth, Chaplain."

"Could be."

"It is. So we don't know anything and can't change anything and stay the way we are."

"Let me sleep."

"It's the price we have to pay."

"Do shut up."

≈≈≈

In the morning Mutushi found Jagna on the mat, face buried in his hands. Jagna spoke through his hands as Mutushi sat beside him: "You know our situation. But who will come to our rescue? It's just how we are. And even if we're cast out and rejected, still we are –."

≈≈≈

The dark people talked of the terrible things these Whites had reported. The Blue Jaguar has come down to Earth and is doing his work of destruction in the lands of the Whites. They were afraid of their guests.

Young people sang to each other from the palm trees as they tapped sap for wine. They were preparing a feast. Canoes went out into the neighbourhood. A girl in the Pirai village was called Nimoa. She painted a circle on each cheek, then two lines across, she drew two continuous lines from the corners of her mouth, circles between her breasts, snakes down her arms, black dots on her chin. She rubbed in a red paste from the sap of the urucu tree. She stuck flowers from the forest in her hair. When the young people were out strolling together, she went to Vivien, led him into the forest and laughed with him.

When Vivien came back to the hut the Chaplain was alarmed. His eyes were big and rapt and lay deep in their sockets. Vivien had flowers in his hair and belt. He sank onto the mat, laughed like a madman, stroked the mat.

"What is it, Vivien?" – "I'll tell you later."

That evening he said: "We men are guilty. Guilty of everything. Men only know how to kill. All life comes from the woman."

After the feast people said: the interpreter wants to go back to his own place. The witchdoctor came, leading the young deer on a string. The interpreter told the Whites: the deer has recovered, we can't keep it. Vivien had not stood up, he sat with the creature for a while, arms around its neck, stroked it, gazed into its dark brown lovely eyes. The witchdoctor said people would guide them wherever they wanted to go.

In the night the Chaplain asked: "Vivien, what should we do?"

Vivien was sound asleep, hard to waken. He mumbled "South," and went back to sleep.

In the morning he lay in his hammock and did not rise. The doctor came with the interpreter.

Vivien whispered: "To the south." His gaze was vacant. The witchdoctor seemed worried. He observed him carefully and bent down to him: "You can go wherever you like."

Vivien was delirious: "Not back, not back."

The chief came, saw his condition, asked after the deer. It was in the forest. The chief said: "It's the deer."

In the hammock Vivien's limbs flailed, he clenched his teeth, lips pressed together, his eyes deep in their sockets rolled white, wide open. His breath rasped. He was cold. The witchdoctor stayed with him. He danced in a stag mask, prepared a potion for Vivien, blew smoke on him.

Vivien-Jagna died that afternoon.

They discussed what to do with him. That evening they carried him from the village, buried him in the forest at the spot where the deer had found him.

Mutushi, the little yellow Chaplain, sat all night at the grave of the last of the fugitives from the penal colony. They saw him there next morning. Madness lay on him again. Then they saw him no more.

On the Amazon

AMAZON ROLLED IN its broad bed across the plain, called to the spirits of the dead, the fallen. Many spirits gathered around. They came from the savannah of Venezuela, the grassy plains and swamps of the south, the bogs and jungles of Guiana. They dropped by the wayside as they fled the penal colony, fell during military campaigns, died in the bush, their lives were not over yet, and whose life could be over.

Swarms of spirits who had died when scarcely born. Some who had a long life behind them, whom fulfillment evaded like a pixie on a rolling ball. Some who seemed mighty, and cried out the usual "All in vain, all for nothing" and wouldn't give up, who collapsed, died, rose again and gathered with the multitudes lying dead at their feet and the thousands torn away by fever and flood.

They thronged to the gigantic tableau of the Amazon.

The wide stream surged. Green-yellow fans of the cobya palm swayed over the llanos. Cloud shadows drifted over dreary monotonous grassy plains. Hot air wafted, bringing distant lagoons close to seeking eyes. Scissor-birds with long quill feathers whirred over swamps. Narrow channels were lined with pretty trees, lotus flowers with green leaves like frying pans covered still waters. The electric eel buried itself in mud.

Surging sweetwater sea. Teeming fish. Nightly procession of

turtles. The loro sweeps in swarms of hundreds through the warm steam rising from the water, where enormous columns of insects dance. From trees, from bushes, the shrilling of cicadas.

The Amazon relinquishes a maze of islands, lakes, channels, absorbs them, draws them in again, like the clouds that it exhales.

A youth sat by the water. The sun went down. He was fishing, the nets were cast. Vines dangled behind him. He watched the forest fringe. He sang:

A maiden, there was a lovely maiden. At her breast she wore a string of pearls, she had a lovely string of pearls. The young man saw her and, oha, he loved her.

Once he looked up at the night sky. Stars sparkling, and one was especially lovely. Then the young man's eyes grew moist: 'You are so far away, in two hours you will go, oh, if only you could stay by me, most beautiful one.'

And as he lay in his hammock, a girl with bright eyes came to him. He took her for a spirit and said: 'Get thee gone from me.' Then she said: 'I am the star', and stayed by him. And in the morning he put her in his flask.

At night she came out of the flask. He loved her in his hammock. By day he took her into the forest.

His brothers saw the flask hanging. They said: 'We want to open the flask.' It fell from their hands and broke in two. They screamed: 'There's a creature in the flask, with eyes like a woman.' They ran away.

The young man came, she ran with him into the forest. They came to a bucuba palm, the maiden wanted to eat fruit. And as he climbed, she called up to him: 'Hold tight!' She jumped into the tree, the tree grew taller, the tree grew taller. The young man cried: 'I shall fall.' She held him tight in her arms and didn't let him fall.

They settled there in the sky. There were drums and blaring trumpets. She brought him food and drink. He looked at her and looked down at the earth. He wept. Even in Heaven there was no bliss.

And when the young man's song was done and he turned around, Sukuruja the river spirit came out of the forest.

She ran at him like an enemy warrior, she had ostrich feathers in her belt, gay parrot plumes in her dark hair. She leaped with her heavy club, he ducked, screamed for his friends.

She leaped in the water from treetrunk to treetrunk, the sun had gone down. She swam.

"Hui," she calls, throws water with both hands. She draws the spirits to her. The spirits dance with her. She splashes, stirs up dust, she stands in clouds of spray, the spirits snap at it.

They gather around Sukuruja. The throng grows as the night goes on. Sukuruja sprays and calls. They gather like birds around a peasant girl strewing maize kernels. Sukuruja lets the rivers carry her, laughs, chases the greedy spirits. They fall into the water, swallow some. They are fish and worms and insects. The ground takes them in. They fly as birds, a new skin.

Forgotten, the thousand lives that everyone has lived, the cares, the daily troubles and vexations, the growing frail and tired, the sorrow, the love, the crimes. The water that Sukuruja sprays flows through them.

Forgotten, the thousand lives.

Great Father and Blue Jaguar

AND AGAIN, AGAIN, people climb down from the highlands to seek the Land without Death.

They leave the heights of the Mato Grosso, the Sierra Hieronymo, the Sierra of Araras. They are the Apapocuva, Tanygua, Oguauiva. They want out of these highlands, out of this life, into the blessed land where none die and nothing bad exists. The blessed land is called Iwi Marag. The great evil under which they suffer is Mebu Megua.

In the Father's house there hangs the big bat. The Father's house is surrounded by darkness. The Great Father wants to destroy the Earth. Under the Great Father's bed lies the Blue Jaguar. The big snake guards the door. The Blue Jaguar has received the Father's order to carry fire to the Earth. He's already out there. The Blue Jaguar roams, he tears people to pieces.

The Apapocuva, Tanygua, Oguauiva know: the Earth has

eaten too many corpses. It is full. Fish in the water and birds in the trees all complain: Make an end of it, Father!

They pour down from the mountains to the plain of the Paranà. They are filled with great joy as they enter the plain. Vegetation opens before them. Sweet water wells up to meet them. They find fruit and honey. They dance down into the plain with their sorcerers: "No more shall we have to work, no longer shall we go into the fields. A land is coming where the harvest grows unaided. Grains and shoots and fruit come into houses unaided. Spades overturn the soil by themselves. Arrows beseech their master: let us fly, we shall go hunting for you."

Palms, ferns, herbs and grasses close around them as they wander. The dense forests that wail and roar will not stand still, the winds that whistle and swirl aloft, their cries of pain, their tittering and whining, the brooks of melted mountain snow, they trickle and beg: take us with you, padding jaguar, leaping hart, birds that swoop high and low.

Trees groaned, branches cracked, rainwater sapped their strength, and dripped. The speechless world babbled and gazed after the people. It moved along behind them like a gigantic comet tail. They prayed: Take us with you to the Father.

Men sat on horseback and sang.

Farewell, old friends, for I leave you now, oh friends, ai.
Farewell, oh brothers, for I am leaving you, my brothers.
Oh friends, take it not too much to heart that I leave you, oh
*   friends.*
Oh brothers, take it not too much to heart that I leave you, oh
*   brothers, ai, ai.*
It has been told to me, by one who cares for me, that I shall not be
*   long away, that I shall return to you, oh friends.*
I believe, oh friends, you should not worry greatly when I leave
*   you, oh friends.*

≈≈≈

The Apapocuva, Tanygua, Oguauiva climbed down from the hills of Mbaracayù, Hieronymo, Araras, into the plain of the Paranà where horses and cattle roamed. Their medicine man and chief was

Nanderikini, an old man. His nose was flat, with wide nostrils. Heavy folds lined his low forehead. His mouth was wide and thin. Little white hairs stuck out from his chin. He had sad long eyes with bags beneath. Once he was strong and sturdy. Now his back was bent.

They trekked with women and children, carried provisions and gathered more. When evening came they made a halt, lit fires. After the meal they moved away from the fire. A medicine man sang and shook his rattle, women beat the dancing pole on the ground. Facing east they sang of the blessed land. The sorcerer, urucu-daubed, danced until his spirit roamed.

And when his spirit came back it reported of the path they would take, of the owl that sits on the path, it does not let everyone pass, you must ask, plead, many must come and then it utters its cry and then people appear who have come this way before, they exchange greetings and go on. The children of this land live on honey water.

At this, the song of jubilation rises:

We come to the sea. We traverse the scrubland of Yaboticaba, we approach the house of our great ancestors, we find the familiar gardens and the banana grove.

We stride through. We step into the forest, our mouth is dry, who gives us honey.

We stride through the forest. We come to the sea. We turn towards the house of the Great Father.

O Great Father, we are here. As we approach, the arara-bird flies to us: 'What would my children eat?' – 'We would eat bread made of green maize.'

We meet the thrush Sabia: 'What would my children eat?' – 'We would eat kaui-nuts.'

And as we come, the Great Father weeps: 'You shall die, all of you, on the Earth. Never go back. Stay.'

The Apapocuva were in the van, the Tanygua followed, in the rear the Oguauiva. They suffered on the way. Hordes of Indian from the plantations came to join them. Many groups were left where they lay, the joy and expectation never let up.

Many groups were snatched away by measles. White priests came, implored them to stop, turn back. The migrants laughed, invited the White priests to follow them: come, it'll do you good.

Some crossed the river Paranapanema. The rainy season began. The approached the sea.

Rain poured down the whole night. The fire went out. They lay on the shore with no shelter. The sun rose magnificent out of the sea. They stood in silence.

They became sad. Seagulls swooped over the waves. Foam sprayed.

The old chief had a dance-hut built. They began the dance, first in the house, then around the house, then along the beach. They wanted to dance across the sea to the blessed land.

"The sea is dry," some called, and they danced into the sea. They never came back.

A young medicine man danced a whole night and a whole day on the shore. Two birds came and showed him the way over the sea. He never came back.

As the numbers on the shore grew, Nanderikini sent word to the others that they should wait. Let us be the first to go into the sky. They sat on the sand, hundreds, thousands. The sorcerer spun and leaped with his clapper, men and women beat the ground. Several jumped up and began to dance with him.

The sorcerer whispered. Evil spirits clung to him, tried to slow him down. He stretched out on the ground, screamed: "Ga – ga – ga." Three times he screamed "fedas", three times "annes", three times "hade", twice "condei". The people howled: "houk, houk".

Men and women held children in their arms as they danced. They wanted to take them along when they flew up. They had adorned themselves in the finest feathers. They laboured terribly hard, the flight to heaven must succeed.

For a day and a night the medicine man and chief Nanderikini danced. I am old, I must work harder than all of them. They helped him with the dance. He leaped high. He succeeded. He no longer felt his body. They called to him, he didn't hear their words. His body was weightless. He gave himself a push. He looked back.

The dance-hut swayed around him, the roof bent and opened, the posts loosened from the sand. He had to tread and tread and stamp and stamp and spin and fling himself and leap, for if he did not tread and did not stamp his feet he would plunge back into the depths. But Nanderikini the old man was already flying, he rose with the dance-hut into the air, he hovered and flew. The Earth lay beneath him, the sea rose. He crossed the threshold of Heaven and stopped by the hut of Nandecy the Great Mother. It was the Land without Death and without sorrow, the Heaven of eternal bliss and abundance, where maize and manioc grow by themselves and honey drips from the trees.

≈≈≈

They reached the sea at two places. Those in the north chose Nimbiarapony to succeed the old man. And when they retreated a little way inland to regain strength, and were in the region of Botas, a sickness came upon them and most died. Nimbiarapony led the rest back to the Mbaracaya hills, to the river Iguatemi from where they had set out. He wanted to gather new people. Youngsters trekked with him through the wide lands of the Paranà. Forests, grasslands, bush and rivers exulted. The chief died on the Ivahy river. They searched through the forest, wailed, called out to him who was supposed to lead them. They scattered. None came back.

In the north the chiefs Necguei and Avavucu went with the Tanygua people. They stood on the shore. And when they despaired and turned back they came to the forest of the Caingang.

The Caingang women gathered genipa berries and pineapple. The Caingang men went naked, wore wooden plugs in their lips, had shaven skulls, a big mat lay across the left shoulder. And when the strangers came through their forest they put on warpaint, set jaku feathers on the head, stuck feathers on the body, around the neck they hung bird bones, deer's hooves, monkey teeth. They attacked the migrants. They were tree climbers, hunted snakes, they carried axes to break up rotten trees and look for larvae and fat beetles. They took aim with their axes at the weary bands lost in the forest.

On their bodies the Caingang had painted jaguar skin, new moon, fish scales and bird footprints.

Two hundred Tanygua remained alive. They danced and sang and were happy. They crossed the Itariry river. There they saw railway sleepers laid across the graves of their ancestors. They cursed the Whites and went to the shore and danced on. Soon not a single foot trod the ground of this Earth.

≈≈≈

The storm blew Sukuruja's head feathers back, her long black hair fluttered, she gazed into the land.

She heard people calling, their laments without end, their rejoicing without end, their songs, their prayers. She saw the dance of the migrating tribes. Her proud face lit up. She went down, hid in a bush, spied on the sorcerer's dance on the shore. She saw old Nanderikini. We come to the sea, we traverse the scrubland of Yaboticaba, we approach the house of the great ancestors. What would my children eat? O Great Father, make an end of it.

Sukuruja swung her club. She whooped at the forest edge. Deer, tapirs and herons came. They followed her, they stepped along with her. They tried to dance as the people had danced when they called to the Great Father. There is a land where no one dies and there is no evil. Spades turn the soil by themselves. Fruit comes by itself into houses. Spirits came rustling, rustled in hordes around them.

On the riverbank, Sukuruja swished as a snake. She jumped into the water. Thousands after her, into the eddy.

END OF VOLUME 3